THE CITY OF MARBLE AND BLOOD

The Chronicles of Hanuvar 2

BAEN BOOKS
by HOWARD ANDREW JONES

THE CHRONICLES OF HANUVAR
Lord of a Shattered Land
The City of Marble and Blood
Shadow of the Smoking Mountain (forthcoming)

To purchase these titles in e-book form, please go to
www.baen.com.

THE CITY OF MARBLE AND BLOOD

The Chronicles of Hanuvar 2

Howard Andrew Jones

THE CITY OF MARBLE AND BLOOD

A Baen Books Original

Baen Publishing Enterprises
P.O. Box 1403
Riverdale, NY 10471
www.baen.com

ISBN: 978-1-9821-9294-5

Cover art by Dave Seeley
Map by Darian Jones

First printing, October 2023

Distributed by Simon & Schuster
1230 Avenue of the Americas
New York, NY 10020

Library of Congress Cataloging-in-Publication Data

Names: Jones, Howard A., author.
Title: The city of marble and blood / Howard Andrew Jones.
Description: Riverdale, NY : Baen Publishing Enterprises, 2023. | Series:
  The Chronicles of Hanuvar ; 2
Identifiers: LCCN 2023026704 (print) | LCCN 2023026705 (ebook) | ISBN
  9781982192945 (hardcover) | ISBN 9781625799340 (ebook)
Subjects: LCGFT: Fantasy fiction. | Novels.
Classification: LCC PS3610.O62535 C58 2023 (print) | LCC PS3610.O62535
  (ebook) | DDC 813/.6—dc23/eng/20230622
LC record available at https://lccn.loc.gov/2023026704
LC ebook record available at https://lccn.loc.gov/2023026705

Printed in the United States of America

10 9 8 7 6 5 4 3 2 1

Dedication
For Hannibal of Carthage, for innumerable reasons.

Contents

Book 2

Freely Adapted from
The Hanuvid of Antires Sosilos (the Elder),
with the commentary of Silenus

ANDRONIKOS SOSILOS (THE YOUNGER)

Preamble

Against the might of a vast empire Hanuvar had only a dwindling supply of funds, an aging sword arm, and me. It was precious little to take into the land of his enemies, especially when compared to the train of elephants and tens of thousands of soldiers he'd led against them years before. Had the Dervans understood the paucity of his resources, they might have reacted to rumors of his return very differently.

They assumed him bent on vengeance. After all, they had reduced his city to rubble and led the pitiful remnant of his people to slave blocks and thence their dismal futures. With that in mind, they were certain he schemed to drown the empire in blood.

Yes, they rightly feared him. The Dervans knew first hand that Hanuvar possessed characteristics held by few and fully matched by none. His was the finest military mind in the world, a searing, flexible intellect paired with an astonishing determination, bolstered by a lifetime of wisdom and experience.

Those were not his only gifts. He was endowed with an unparalleled clarity of vision, a confident surety that was never conceit. Trial and tragedy had burned off the dross of vanity and pride that weight the lives of normal men; his experiences had not transformed him so much as provided fuel for the forge he had used to shape himself into a tool to achieve aims the Dervans had misunderstood from the start. Hanuvar's war had never been one of conquest. He had first marched to stop the Dervan dream of empire through force of arms, thinking their defeat would preserve the liberty of his people. He'd advanced achingly close to victory and the Dervans never forgave him for it.

Now, upon his return, his goal remained essentially the same, and he labored ceaselessly toward it. No matter where they'd been sent, from

3

the sprawling capital to the furthest outpost of the Dervan Empire, Hanuvar meant to find his people. Every last one of them. And he would set them free.

—Antires Sosilos, Book Seven

Chapter 1:
A Theft of Years

The Tyvolian Autumn had not yet lost its battle to winter, but was hard beset. The browning oak leaves held a fiery red edge, and the leaves of poplar trees glowed a vibrant orange. Those already loosed from the branches decorated the trail ahead in patches like little carpets of flame. The air was rich with their musky sweetness, and the sharp, clean scent of pine needles.

Hanuvar and Antires worked to avoid the swish and crunch of the leaves they passed, even though they were deep enough into the woods they were unlikely to be overheard by humans. They were trespassers on this land.

The old knee wound was stiff in the chill, an intermittent, angry bite in Hanuvar's stride. He'd thrown an ebon cloak over his dark, long-sleeved tunic, pulled on leggings, and switched to boots, but his hood was down. His slate-colored eyes narrowed in concentration. His gray-threaded, black hair was worn short, cut straight across his forehead, and his face was clean shaven, accommodations to modern Dervan styles to better conceal his identity. If a little darker than the average Dervan citizen, his skin-tone was hardly uncommon, even among the ruling class, who spent far more time indoors than their social inferiors.

His companion continually fiddled with his own hood, indecisive about whether he wished to be shielded from the breeze, or to see along his periphery. Antires lowered it once more and scratched the side of his face. Hanuvar knew he was unused to the feel of the fringe beard and thin mustache he'd grown. Like the thick hair that topped Antires' head, his facial hair was dark and tightly coiled. He was younger than Hanuvar by nearly a quarter century, with fine features and smooth brown skin.

Antires addressed his friend quietly. "What's your backup plan if we can't get this land? Do you want to try for a different site?"

Hanuvar shook his head, no, and answered softly. "This little cove is ideal. Deep water. Well forested, which permits privacy as well as building materials, and it's just beyond the village's existing harbor." That would make the transportation of any additional supplies that much simpler, not to mention the movement of future passengers for the ships they would be launching.

"I thought you'd say that. But how are you going to get the old woman to sell?"

"First, we'll see the shrine. Then we'll see what we can do. It's not the owner who's the real problem. It's the priest." Alma herself had sounded amenable to selling the coastal portion of her land, but the priest, Eloren, had dissuaded her with an admonition that the gods would better bless the shrine if all the land around it was left inviolate.

The path beaten through the forest detritus by Alma's litter bearers extended in a mostly straight line from her villa and was impeded only by intervening oak and pine. It ended in a tiny clearing. A small stack of firewood had been piled beside a blackened cookfire. Leaves to the other side were flattened as if some large rectangular object had rested there—her conveyance, almost certainly. A fallen tree bole nearby had been carved repeatedly with a knife, providing a canvas for crude, silly faces with staring eyes and broken noses. "One of Alma's slaves has a lot of idle time," Hanuvar said.

"And he's a latent master, judging by this portraiture." Antires' attention wandered with him as he stopped at a set of stone stairs vanishing through a dark square beneath the earth. A fresh coating of leaves dusted them in red and yellow, but they were curiously clean of dirt and sticks and weeds. "Looks like the old woman's had her slaves clean this place. Can you imagine being ordered to see to the maintenance of some haunted stairs in a dark forest?"

"I can imagine a lot of things." Hanuvar moved off, scanning the ground around the stairs. Antires followed.

"It's hard to believe she'd want to come here every week."

"Three times a week, lately," Hanuvar corrected.

"Do you think there's any chance she really is speaking to her dead son here?"

Antires smirked at Hanuvar's skeptical return look. The Herrene opened his hands, in an admission of his own uncertainty. His inflection, though, suggested he wasn't ready to outright dismiss the story. "I've seen some of the things you have."

"It took an immense expenditure of resources for my brothers to be reached from the dead lands," Hanuvar reminded him. "Once. And they barely spoke."

"That's not to say it couldn't happen."

"Anything's possible. But some things are more possible than others."

Having a poet's soul, Antires was always credulous about the fantastic, though he strove to adopt Hanuvar's more measured outlook, at least in his friend's presence. He watched as Hanuvar finished walking the area, then voiced his conclusion. "You suspect that the priest is up to something."

"That goes without saying."

"But Alma contacted him."

"The priest might have set up a situation then conveniently made himself available. It wouldn't be difficult for someone clever to get a sense of what Alma's son looked like, since his image is all over her villa. And if Eloren and his associates have designs on the lady's property, they might be poisoning her. Some poisons will tire a person out, and routine exposure will make them look older than they really are as they're dying."

Antires' eyebrows climbed his forehead. "You think Eloren would poison an old woman?"

"I don't know that he would, but some people are capable of such a deed."

"I suppose you're right," Antires said, with a young man's subdued outrage over the callousness of humanity. "So what are you waiting for? Don't you want to take a look down these stairs?"

"In a moment." Hanuvar preferred to get a good sense of the

ground before he advanced. He was shifting his attention back to the stairs when he heard someone treading across the leaves along the path from the villa.

He'd been informed the widowed landowner was scheduled to visit hours from now, so the intrusion was unexpected. He motioned his friend to retreat, then lay beside him, his belly against the cool forest floor. They watched from under a juniper across the clearing from the carved tree trunk.

Those nearing the shrine made no attempt at stealth. There were two, crushing dried foliage underfoot as they advanced. Calleo, the aging house slave who'd conducted Hanuvar into his fruitless meeting with the Lady Alma Dolorosa, bore an unlit lantern, and a second young slave shouldered a pack and carried a lantern of his own, as well as a pair of brooms.

Once they arrived at the stairs, the younger one dropped the brooms and set down his pack. He pulled his patchy cloak tight. He was a slim youth with close-set eyes.

"We'd best be quick about it." Calleo adjusted his own cloak on his shoulders. "The mistress will be here soon."

"I am being quick about it." The younger man's voice twisted into a complaining whine. "Why did she want to come early?"

"The mistress is growing more and more . . . changeable as she ages."

"Changeable, or snippy?" the younger slave asked.

"Watch your tone."

The two men lit their lanterns, then descended the stairs. The younger one emerged very soon after, his hands empty and a warm glow of lantern light rising from the space below. He busied himself sweeping leaves from the upper stairs, then retreated. Calleo climbed into sight a little while after, his wrinkled face twisted into a frown.

"I needed help lighting the candles."

"You don't want to be down there any more than I do," the younger slave said stubbornly. "You just don't want to admit it."

More people were crunching up the path. Hanuvar shifted his attention from the bickering slaves to the priest Eloren, who arrived wrapped in an ankle-length blue cloak. The slope-shouldered dedicant to Lutar, lord of the dead, kept his hands in his sleeves and stepped to one side, a measure of pride in his manner that suggested a proprietary interest in his surroundings. He looked like an aristocrat walking the grounds he'd purchased for the construction of a new tenement. After Eloren came a similarly garbed younger priest bearing a basket of tinder. His face was smooth and rounded, his nose upturned at its tip. Two muscular blond Ceori slaves brought up the rear, supporting a small, curtained litter between them.

The younger priest knelt near the logs close to where Hanuvar and Antires lay, seemed to ponder adding some to the half-burned fuel in the dead camp fire, then arranged his tinder and pulled a stone from a pouch at his waist.

The litter slaves gently sat their burden down, and Eloren bent forward to open the litter's low door and offer his arm.

A veiny hand reached out to clasp it, and then Alma Dolorosa leveraged herself into sight, a small, pale, silver-haired woman in a black stola, wearing a black scarf under her black cloak. Her eyes, too, were black, as had been her expression when Hanuvar had met her this morning. Now, though, her face was bright with yearning. Locals claimed she was only in her fifth decade, though she looked and moved like an octogenarian.

Alma adjusted the heavy cloak on her spindly frame, and then the priest spoke with her in a low voice. They headed for the stairs, Alma walking swiftly, head thrust forward, face fixed in expectation. Together they descended into the earth.

The litter bearers stretched, greeted the two slaves who had tidied the place ahead of their arrival, then stepped over to the tree near the carvings. Hanuvar was momentarily puzzled by all their sideways and sometimes even backward movement until he realized that none wished to put their back to the stairs. They spoke in low voices, agreeing that Alma was looking worse. Her death was on their minds. One of the Ceori wondered aloud whether they would be manumitted in her will.

Closer by, the young priest sat on his knees, laboring a long while with his flint before he produced a spark to light his tinder. He'd just succeeded when Eloren returned from the shrine. The slaves barely glanced over. Apparently, they were accustomed to their mistress being left alone.

The younger priest made room for the older and showed his

palms to the flames as the fire spread. After a moment, he spoke quietly. "Did you suggest she spend less time there?"

Eloren's reply dripped scorn. "She's an old woman, Moneta. There's no changing her mind."

"Not if you don't try there isn't."

Eloren sniffed then spoke dismissively. "The gods set her on this path. And they've shown me what to do. If they wanted something different, they'd have spoken to you."

"So that's your decision?"

"You'll stay quiet," Eloren said.

The younger man pressed his lips together in disapproval.

Eloren pulled a wineskin from his belt and drank slowly, looking into the fire and ignoring his companion. Hanuvar wished Moneta would object further, so that more might be learned, but the younger man remained silent.

A quarter hour later the old woman called to Eloren, her voice weak and raspy. He capped his wineskin then walked for the stairs and down them. He returned with Alma on his arm.

She looked utterly drained, although she smiled dazedly. Before long she was loaded into her litter and was being carried back to the villa, the priests following. Calleo and his assistant put out the fire, then descended once more, returning with lanterns and brooms and pack. The younger was complaining again. "I hate this place. I feel like those faces are watching me the entire time."

"Nothing's gotten you yet," his older companion responded. As they walked away, the younger could be heard grumbling about the underground chamber until his voice faded with distance.

Antires was ready to rise soon after, but Hanuvar held a hand for silence, then waited another long while before finally climbing to his feet.

Antires swore about being cold, then asked Hanuvar what he thought of what they'd heard.

"The young priest thinks the visits are bad for the old woman."

"That's it?" Antires sounded scandalized that Hanuvar had deduced nothing more.

And so he shared a few more observations. "The young one's a weak point that may give us leverage. Eloren is unmotivated to help her, likely because he's gotten her to leave this land to his order, or to himself personally, after her death. And we need to see what's down there."

"I didn't see that last part coming at all," Antires said, rolling his eyes.

Hanuvar rummaged his shoulder pack and withdrew a small brass lantern. He discovered the Herrene eying him in admiration.

"How did you know we'd need a lantern?"

"It was a lucky guess."

"You don't guess, you plan," Antires said, which wasn't entirely accurate.

"I'd walked a lot of the land east of her home. I had seen no above-ground shrines or temples. The woods are thick enough that there might just have been one hiding here, but—"

"—but the odds were that it was below ground."

"Yes. But then even the inside of a temple would be dark."

"So, you're not quite as clever as I'd assumed."

"Or maybe I'm the one who packed the lantern." Hanuvar pointed back toward the villa. "Keep an eye out."

"Wait. You're going in alone?"

"Yes. Signal me if you hear anything. Can you mimic bird calls?"

"Oh, yes. Many confuse my dulcet tones with those of the heron, or an owl."

"Neither of which would be helpful."

"Neither of which I can actually imitate."

Hanuvar lit the lantern, shielding it with his body as he carried it in his left hand, and walked for the stairs. "Some time you'll have to remind me why I bring you along. Watch as well as listen. And not just for sounds—"

"—but the sudden lack of them. I know the routine. I'll just sit over there on the log and contemplate the local talent."

"No one likes a critic." Hanuvar started down. He took each step slowly, watching the edge of the lantern light as it fell upon each stair ahead. His gaze shifted to the ceiling, rounded above him. He saw then that he was advancing into a natural cave to which these steps had been added.

About halfway down he experienced the sensation that he was being observed. His skin prickled as hairs stood upright on his arms. He had anticipated the place would be disquieting from what Alma's younger slave said, but this was far more than that; the chamber toward which he descended radiated menace, and every one of his senses urged him to run.

He kept on.

A wide oval room lay at the bottom of the nine steps. The ceiling curved gently above to a high point of about three spear lengths. The chamber extended some sixty paces from side to side, and its ceiling dipped lower on the right edge before dropping raggedly to the floor, which was level apart from a rise on the left. Dirt and leaves had been swept into a neat pile to the right of the stairs.

The most interesting features faced the entryway. Just beyond a chest-high, square stone altar, a flat wall stretched the entire cave length, decorated by paintings of curiously unemotive faces with unnerving, pupilless eyes. He did not care to contemplate any of them at length; perhaps it was imagination, but it was from them that the spiritual malaise seemed to radiate.

The writing incised everywhere about the pictures was of a much more precise character, like that of an architect or professional scribe, though it too was curious, composed of a mix of Hadiran and Turian symbols.

He understood very little of the complex classical Hadiran language, with its bird-headed men and hundreds of symbols, but he had learned some Turian, and considered what the messages left here might mean. He then gave his attention to the life-sized image painted in the dead center of the wall just beyond the large stone altar, that of a sad-eyed, beardless youth in a sleeveless summer tunic, one hand offered to the viewer. The other held a bouquet of wildflowers and thyme. By those plants, Hanuvar recognized the image for the god Kovos, whom the Turians believed guided the dead to their final resting place. His depiction would not have been out of place in some cave in the southern hills, or in adjacent lands, for the Turians had been a power in the peninsula before Derva waxed large. They had survived long enough for some of their aristocracy to marry into that of the city-state before Derva expanded across the peninsula. But here, in the uttermost north of Tyvol, just south of the Ardenines, a Turian shrine to the opener of the ways had little precedence.

He turned his scrutiny upon the altar standing before the image.

Once it had been copiously plastered in red, but much of that plaster had crumbled, exposing plain stones of the same sort composing the cave walls, shaped and fit closely together. Dripped yellow wax stained the altar's center, where some red plaster remained, along with the golden outline of a hand.

Hanuvar heard steps behind him and turned to find Antires descending with a pretense of stealth.

"This place is worse than a tomb," the playwright said.

"I told you to stay above."

"And I did. And now I'm here. Gods. This place is terrible. How can you stand it?"

Hanuvar started to chide him, but decided it might not be a terrible idea to have the younger man posted closer, especially because Hanuvar wasn't sure what might happen when he exposed himself to the sorcery.

"Stay on the stairs. Try to listen for activity above as well as here."

"The art's a better cut here, but hardly monument worthy. The god in the center has striking eyes, though."

Hanuvar set the lantern on the altar and fixed his attention on the unfamiliar symbols, trying to jar any additional information free of his memory.

"Can you read any of that?" Antires asked.

"A little."

"Prayers?" the Herrene suggested.

"I'm neither a magical scholar nor a Turian one, but I don't think these are prayers. There's a lack of formality and the emphasis isn't upon the god, or glory." Hanuvar pointed to one lengthy stretch of text. "Kovos isn't even mentioned at all."

"Kovos?"

"The Turian lord of the dead." Hanuvar contemplated the golden handprint and knew he would have to place his palm there.

Assuming that there was any possible chance that this worked, which of the countless he had known and lost might best advise him? His brothers? His father? His brother-in-law? His even longer lost elder sister?

He had loved and respected them all, and each might have guided him in different ways, but as he continued to study the Turian writing he realized there was only one whom he should try to reach.

Still he hesitated. He had never wished for a moment like this. Not with her. What might he say to Ravella now, except that he missed her? Would they resume their final argument, or were the dead beyond such troubles?

He reminded himself that Ravella was unlikely to appear before him. Probably this old shrine was simply the basis for an elaborate deception played by the priests.

He put his hand upon the imprint and whispered a prayer to the opener of the ways.

His expectations had been low, so when the eyes of Kovos took up an amber sheen Hanuvar's own eyes widened in astonishment. A moment later a humanoid shape formed of light drifted from the god.

Antires murmured in awe. Hanuvar's breath caught in his throat and his heart quickened. The shape drifted toward the altar, and him, blurry and uncertain at first, then broadening at the hips and narrowing at the waist. Long curling dark hair drifted down and past a graceful neck. Long black eyelashes blinked and full red lips opened before him even as the transparent figure floated but a sword's length out. She didn't wear the stola she'd been buried in, but the light green dress that had suited her so well.

"You have thought of me, and I have come." Ravella's voice was a whisper, with her remembered accent. They had spoken sometimes in Dervan and sometimes in Herrene and often, once they had become lovers, in her native Turian. Today she spoke in Dervan.

"Is that your wife?" Antires asked, breathless in wonder.

Hanuvar answered without looking at him. "No. Is this truly you?" he asked her.

"It is me, beloved." As Ravella spoke, her image sharpened. He saw the individual hairs upon her eyebrows, and the pupils of her dark eyes.

Feelings he'd thought long resolved constricted his throat. Sometimes she'd scolded him for avoiding the difficult in their talks, as he did now, shifting immediately to the present. The past was too painful. "I need your help. Do you understand the words on the wall behind you?"

She turned her head and shifted her body, drifting the while in an invisible wind, so that her dress and hair streamed languidly behind her.

"I can see so little of the living world." She turned back to him. "Only you are in clear focus."

He burned to ask if she had deliberately taken the poison, or if it had been the accident he'd told her brother. He thought he knew the answer to that, though, just as he understood why she hadn't wanted to leave her homeland, and why she could not have lived in Utria after his retreat. The Dervans would have taken their vengeance upon her.

"What do you wish to speak of?" Her smile was open and warm. He found himself hoping that any resentment she'd harbored had faded with her death, and that all that was left between them was the love they'd shared.

She sounded like Ravella, and she looked like her . . . But he had long ago been taught to see what was truly before him, not what he wished, and not what he hoped. After a moment of consideration, he decided how he might best test the veracity of what he was experiencing. "I want you to sing," he said. "That Turian folk song about the winding road. I can no longer recall the words, just snatches of the melody." And even that, now, had faded from his memory.

She blinked her long lashes and her voice rose in song. She began strongly, singing in her native tongue of a shepherd boy readying for his trip, but then she faltered. The melody died, and the words trailed away.

And sadly, then, he knew he witnessed a lie. "You're not real." He'd thought himself sad when he said it, but his lips twitched into a snarl.

"I am real, beloved." Her eyes rounded in sorrow. "You see me before you."

"You know only what I know of you. And nothing more. What are you, really?"

"I am your love, for now, and always."

He shook his head. "You lie. What are you?"

She extended her arms to him.

He lifted his hand from the altar. The moment he broke contact his breath left him; he felt as though he'd run miles in full armor. Ravella smiled sadly, then her image blurred, though she hung in the air for a while longer, like the afterimage of a snuffed candleflame. Finally she was gone.

Antires swore softly. "Who was that?"

"No one I know." Hanuvar labored to catch his breath.

"Are you well?"

"I'm fine." Oddly, the chamber itself no longer troubled him. He sensed the eyes upon his back as he turned to Antires, but their regard now was welcoming. The change in his perspective disturbed him more than the previous dread.

He shook his head, striving to shake off the lure of illusory serenity. He paced the area, lantern light pointed against the wall. On closer inspection, it looked entirely too flat to be natural.

"Who was that?" Antires asked. "I mean, who was it supposed to be? You never mentioned another woman."

"Her name was Ravella."

"She called you beloved. Did you have a mistress?"

"You sound shocked." Hanuvar ran his hands along the wall, over a pair of wide-eyed faces, feeling for an opening or seam.

"Well . . . I suppose I shouldn't be. I just thought . . ."

"I was in Tyvol for more than a dozen years. Did you think I'd be celibate that entire time?"

"I never gave it much thought," Antires admitted. "Couldn't you have sent for Imilce?"

Hanuvar stepped to the left edge, running his hand along the juncture where the two cave walls met. "We exchanged letters on the subject, but there was much to do in Volanus in support of the war, and Imilce didn't want to leave Narisia with relatives. And I'd vowed not to raise my child in an armed camp like I had been." He discovered a crack, but it appeared to be completely normal.

"What are you looking for?"

"Some kind of entrance. You could help. Feel along the right edge there."

"An entrance to what?"

"There's obviously something very strange about this shrine. I think there's more to it."

Hanuvar retreated from the wall. Antires ran his fingers along the right edge. "Did you love her?"

"You're getting rather personal, aren't you?"

Antires glanced back, then bent to rub fingertips along the floor seam. "I'm supposed to be your chronicler. I should know these things. Did you love her?"

"Imilce, or Ravella?"

"Both. Were there others?"

"Yes."

"Yes to the others?"

"Yes, I loved them both."

Antires sighed in frustration. "You're being deliberately obscure."

"My love life isn't germane at the moment." Maybe the wall had no more secrets. Hanuvar turned his attention to the altar.

"How could you love both? At once?"

With extreme care he inspected the altar's front with his hands, mulling the notion to tell the young man to be quiet. But then he remembered his own vow to be open with Antires, who had again and again proven his loyalty, and answered. "Imilce and I were young. She, younger than me. Not long after our marriage I had to assume control of the army, and only a few years after that, I was marching across the Ardenines. I expected to return to her, or be able to send for her, but the war dragged on."

"And you sought a mistress when you got lonely."

"Sought?" He'd been too busy to seek a paramour. "No. Ravella and I stumbled into one another. She was a widow and witty and irreverent and..." Thinking of her opened up a tide of memories he was in no mood to examine at present, or to share with Antires. He shifted his search to the altar's narrower left side and sought a swift way to explain. "It was a relationship of older people. A deeper one than I'd formed with Imilce. Not because I loved my wife less, but because I wasn't mature enough to love her more when I was with her. Does that make sense?"

"Yes. There's no opening in this wall." Antires joined him at the altar. "Any luck here?"

"Not so far."

The playwright watched his efforts. "What happened when you met Imilce again?"

"A long time had passed. Imilce and I were almost strangers. Our relationship was difficult for a while, because I was used to one woman and she was used to someone else as well."

"She had a lover?"

"Yes."

"And you weren't bothered by that?"

"Each of us consented to the arrangements. She was as human as I."

Antires tried to digest that information, then shook his head. "You Volani are strange."

"Eventually we grew close again, but it was . . . tricky for both of us." Hanuvar was starting to doubt there was anything to be found, but he slid his fingers along the altar's right side.

"How did Ravella die?"

"She was poisoned."

"Gods. That's terrible. Did the Dervans kill her?"

"I suppose you could say she was out of good choices. Wait a moment. There are large seams in the floor here."

Antires bent to examine what Hanuvar had discovered. A fingernail's breadth of space lay between the altar and an irregularly shaped slab roughly two hand spans wide, cleverly worked into the floor beneath where he had stood before the altar. He tugged and found it unyielding.

"What do you think it is?" Antires had at last found something else to absorb his attention.

Hanuvar searched for leverage, finally finding a divot opposite the altar. He pulled harder and lifted the covering piece away. Green light splashed up from inside the dark space. Hanuvar set the stone slab against the altar's side. He motioned for Antires to bring the lantern.

His friend focused the beam, revealing a cavity a gladius length deep and nearly as long. And it was plastered smooth and painted over with small, precise Turian characters of red and black. They ran in straight lines upon the space's walls, then circled the glittering emerald that lay in its center in a precisely carved hollow. Part of the gem's glow owed to the lantern's reflected light. But something deep inside changed slowly, now lighter, now darker, like the pulse of an ancient heart.

"That stone—how does it glow like that?"

There was much about sorcery Hanuvar didn't understand, but he could answer that question. "It's a focusing stone. Only the most powerful spell users can employ them to store magics." He looked up at Antires. "I saw one once before, when we overtook a cadre of magicians the Dervans were trying to use against us in the war." He gestured to some flakes of paper lying near the emerald. "I think our priest must have found this cache. Some papyrus was stored here and removed. And there should have been built up debris or dirt hiding in the gap between the panel and the altar. He's opened it."

"Did he put the stone in here?"

"I think it's been in here for a long, long while. As long as this writing."

"What does the writing say?"

This was old style Turian, and some of the letters were slightly different from the ones Hanuvar had learned. Paired with Hanuvar's rusty and incomplete knowledge of the language and the odd angle he was forced to read at, it took him a while to understand enough to answer his friend's question.

"I think it's a spell, summoning some kind of spirit, or entity called a 'gatherer'—meant to protect the 'treasures' here. That might mean the vanished scrolls."

"Might it mean something else?"

It could at that. Hanuvar had already noted that there was another seam between the altar and the floor. He ran his fingers slowly along the lowest row of altar stones.

Antires had thought of another question. "If it's a guardian, why is it practically inviting interaction? Wouldn't a guardian try to scare people away?"

"The place is frightening," Hanuvar agreed. "Until you offer yourself. And then it becomes alluring. I no longer feel troubled here. I think it may be a honeyed trap. It drained some of my own life force when I tried to use it."

Antires swore in wonder. "You think if you were to keep coming here, you'd age like Alma?"

"Yes. And I'd wager the more I used it, the more I'd want to come. I just don't know what the purpose is." Hanuvar was about to abandon his search when the stone under his fingers yielded to pressure. The sound of stone grating on stone startled him; the altar side shifted ever so slightly toward him.

He ran his fingers over the face of the altar's side nearest the god. It had never been plastered and on close examination some of the grooves suggesting separate stones had been carved to convey that appearance. A sturdy push sent a whole piece wider than his shoulders scraping inward as its upper third tilted out. It proved only a finger's length thick. With Antires' help he eased the heavy slab to the ground.

The altar itself was hollow and opened into a narrow shaft of darkness.

"Well, that looks inviting." Antires shined the lantern into the cavity, revealing a decrepit wooden ladder covered in webs and dust. "Eloren might have found the first scrolls, but he hasn't found this. Or didn't want to drop into a spider infested hole. Yet you're going to want to look, aren't you?"

"I think I'll have to."

"You sound just as excited as I feel."

"You need to stay up there, on the stairs."

"You're going in there alone?" Antires' voice rose in consternation.

"Right now we're in a hole with only one exit. Pretty soon I'll be in a deeper hole. We're incredibly vulnerable. Anyone could sneak up on us."

Antires, who had just complained about venturing into the web-choked darkness, now sulked that he wouldn't be permitted to accompany him. Hanuvar walked him to the shrine's entry stairs, pausing on the threshold to listen but hearing only the natural noises of the woods. He exited to retrieve a sturdy branch, patted his friend on the shoulder, and returned to the altar.

He employed the stick against the webbing, then held the lantern further into the space. A rough floor lay only eight feet below. A passage opened to the ladder's rear.

Hanuvar tested the ladder's first rung, found that it held, dropped in the stick for further web-cleaning, and started down, lantern in hand.

When he reached the floor, he found himself in a rough stone fissure just wide enough to accommodate a single traveler. Lantern light shining before him, he advanced through the twisting tunnel and then the passage sloped gently up, opening finally into a wide natural chamber.

He stopped halfway into the area. The yellow light he bore spilled upon human teeth stretched in a mirthless grin. Two black eye sockets peered into eternity above. The man-high shelf-unit before him was crowded with human skulls, browned with age, each painted with Hadiran picture writing and cramped Turian letters. Hanuvar looked past the sightless decorations, seeing that another cavern opening lay beyond the wall their shelf rested against, then swung the light through the rest of the chamber.

More shelves stood in that cheerless place, crowded with sagging, spider-webbed scrolls. A great deal of the floor was inset with yet more pictograms and Turian writing, arranged in lines radiating from the blank wall that was the back of the surface Ravella's image had materialized from. Playing the light further, Hanuvar discovered another shelf holding different sized vials.

He advanced at last from his vantage point, keeping well clear of the lines and their writing, stopping in the threshold to the second cavern chamber.

Someone had labored to make this area more homey. It held a sagging bed, a table, three old wooden chests, and a shelf supporting various amphora. Some of them likely contained lamp oil, for old-fashioned lanthorns stood upon both the table and the desk. He caught a flash of movement on his right and whirled, only to see a figure with a lantern, half obscured in a web covered doorway.

Hanuvar dropped hand to sword hilt and the man he faced did the same. Hanuvar relaxed; so did the figure.

He had found no adversary, only himself in a fine body-length bronze mirror fastened to the cave wall and caked with grime. Apparently the sorcerer who had kept his quarters liked to model his appearance. Judging from the dust and disrepair, however, it was easy to guess no one had walked this space for long years, possibly centuries.

"Relnus!"

That was the name Hanuvar had adopted for this province of Tyvol, and it echoed faintly to him. Antires was calling, and there was no missing the insistent quality of his voice. Hanuvar responded on the instant, hurrying to the main room and down the sloping rock and into the narrow passage.

"Someone's coming," Antires called, shouting in the hushed way of actors when they meant to suggest they were actually whispering.

Hanuvar reached the ladder and started up, only to have the first step break under his foot, slamming his heel against the floor. He started up again, keeping his foot to the part of the rung closest to the rails.

Antires loomed above him, waggling his fingers to urge speed. Now he did whisper. "There's a bunch of them, really close now!"

Hanuvar handed up the lantern and threw himself over the side, scrambling clear. Antires started for the entryway, his eyes large as he looked back. Hanuvar motioned him to help in lifting the concealing slab back in place.

That was a mistake. By the time Hanuvar stooped to replace the covering to the gem cavity he heard footsteps on the stairs, and a familiar voice. "I know you're in there," Eloren called.

Hanuvar left the void as it was and advanced to the bottom of the steps.

Three burly dock-side ruffians were ranged along the middle and upper stairs, with Eloren just behind them. He carried a lantern; two of the others bore nail studded cudgels and the other carried an axe.

"You two!" the priest said. "I should have known. You're not really land buyers, are you? You're magicians…" That thought trailed off, and then Eloren's voice grew more excited. "You found the gem!"

He had observed the glow from the altar's foot. Eloren reached up to touch his collar, raising a smaller emerald dangling here. "Little good it will do you without this."

Hanuvar wasn't sure what that meant, but he agreed. "You have me there."

"How did you know we were down here?" Antires asked.

"I've mastered this shrine's secrets," Eloren boasted. "I know when its energy levels rise and flow."

"You're more well informed than I would have guessed," Hanuvar said.

"Who sent you?" Eloren demanded.

Hanuvar turned up an empty hand. "This really doesn't seem like the way two practitioners ought to discuss such a matter, does it?" He indicated the hired muscle with a tilt of his chin. "There's no need for them. We can share secrets. I've just found a large one that might interest you."

"You're bluffing."

"Am I?"

Eloren studied him. "You're an old man with only an effete functionary at your back. Outnumbered. And we have the high ground."

Apparently the priest suffered the common delusion about high ground being a superior offensive position in singular combat. The rabble grinned at Hanuvar, by which he saw that they possessed the identical misconception.

He lifted his lantern while shrugging, fiddling with the shutter that spilled light against the wall to his left, as if nervous. "I admit, we'd heard of the emerald. But I hadn't fully assessed its powers before my associate called to me about your approach. I can show you where the hidden information is, and you can tell me more about its nature."

For a moment he thought Eloren would relent. Then the priest's full lips pursed. "No. I think not. If a bumbler like yourself could find it without even knowing what it is you're seeking, then I can surely locate it."

"So it's death you're after, then?" Hanuvar asked.

"For me, it's life. I'm through with them, boys," he said. "Take them."

"You heard him," the axe man said. "Take them down!"

Roaring, all three charged.

When the first reached the second stair from bottom, his cudgel lifted overhead, Hanuvar beamed lantern light into his face. The fur-draped attacker turned his head, squinting against the glare. At the same moment Hanuvar drew and sliced the thug's protruding abdomen. Blood sprayed. The thug screamed and Hanuvar shoved him to the right, tripping the cudgel bearer rushing for Antires. Off balance, that man stumbled down the final stairs.

That was all the advantage Hanuvar could give his friend, for the third and final attacker, a hirsute blond, leapt at him with his axe raised. While still in mid-air the attacker discovered Hanuvar's lantern flying at his face. He warded himself with one arm and managed a fair landing, but his axe was out of line, with his arms exposed. Hanuvar's sword blow sheared straight through one forearm and halfway into the other. The axe dropped with the severed hand and the ruffian shrieked in agony.

A glowing, faceless humanoid shape streamed past Hanuvar and pressed to the axeman. Hanuvar's skin chilled even as the flow of blood from the terrible wound he'd delivered slackened and stilled.

Eloren called out in heavily accented Turian. "Attack him—the older one! Him!"

The faceless thing abandoned the pale axeman, who toppled limp and bloodless, then, swift as the winter wind, it swept forward. Not to Hanuvar, but to the man with the bloody belly wound, whose cries of pain rose to gasps of terror as it sank upon him.

That was apparently too much for Antires' club-wielding assailant, who gave up chasing the Herrene to dash for the stairs. His face was twisted in panic. He must have seen Hanuvar as an obstacle, for he came in with a wild swing. Hanuvar ducked and skewered him. He pulled out his blade as his opponent doubled over, then sliced again and kicked him clear. The attacker dropped, writhing in his death throes.

Hanuvar pulled his throwing knife.

"Not that one," Eloren was shouting. "Him. Him!" He pointed at Hanuvar. But the green spirit did not depart the man who moaned more and more feebly beneath its attentions.

Hanuvar took a single long stride and hurled his knife.

The cast was true, but the priest shifted, and the blade sank not into Eloren's throat, but his upper chest. He put hands to the blade, groaning in Turian: "Come back to me! Share the life—give me the life!" As Hanuvar charged, Eloren called out another phrase that sounded Hadiran.

The priest collapsed against the stair well, gasping as he yanked the knife free. He raised his emerald pendant like a shield. Hanuvar closed, grabbed the pendant, and yanked it forward. The heavy chain didn't snap as he'd expected, but it did pull the priest toward him, so that Eloren seemed to dive onto the sword Hanuvar thrust through his midsection.

And then the glowing, man-sized entity was upon them. It spilled its emerald radiance, delivering warmth at the same moment, as though it were the personification of a gentle summer day.

Muscles throughout Hanuvar's body twitched, so that he could no longer finely control his actions. He retained hold of his sword but was unable to drive it on to Eloren's heart. His grip likewise froze upon the necklace. His quivering calves could not hold him upright, and he sank to his knees, fighting for balance with one leg resting on a higher step than the other.

And yet despite his anxiety over his inability to control his movements, the intensely tingling sensation passing over him was not unpleasant. He just managed to turn his head to observe the man-thing at his shoulder, seeing only the suggestion of hollows where eyes could be. It was otherwise featureless. The green light streaming forth blended with the being's extended digits.

Of a sudden, the creature's form diminished, its outlines fading until nothing was left but a glowing central core, which retained its full brightness for a moment longer until only the hands were left, shedding light.

And then that radiance too vanished and the thing was gone, its physical presence expended with its spell.

Hanuvar's muscles ceased their shaking. He released his hold on the necklace, discovering that the stone it had framed was cracked and blackened. He flexed his free hand and looked back to Eloren.

The priest's lantern sat beside Hanuvar's reddened knife and a shrunken body slumped in blood-soaked robes. It was only when Hanuvar leaned closer that he saw a pale boy with a young version of Eloren's features lying in the midst of the blood-soaked cloth. Fearful eyes in that smooth-skinned face looked up at him, and Eloren spoke with a voice pitched higher than before. "Don't kill me."

"I already have killed you," Hanuvar said. "But I can make your final moments less painful."

Boy Eloren coughed blood as he pressed his small white hands near the weeping wound in his stomach and the sword blade sticking upright from it, flaring golden in the lantern light.

Hanuvar looked down at the hilt of his sword and paused, seeing that the wrinkles around his knuckles had vanished; the skin was tighter across the back of his hand. A long scar on his lower arm had entirely disappeared. His graying wrist hairs had been restored to black. Only then did he fully realize that the creature's strange magic had impacted him as well. His breath caught in his throat. "What has the spirit done?"

"What do you mean?" The scorn was strange from such a young voice. "Why do you play act?"

Hanuvar's voice was cool but it sounded somehow different to him. Less haggard. "I do not pretend. I don't know."

The boy's look was searching. "But you grasped the pendant so you would receive the energies!"

"I grasped the pendant so you could not ensorcell me."

The changed priest laughed fitfully, then coughed. Blood trickled from his mouth. He shook his head in disgust. "I've been undone by a fool. A lucky fool. You're young now. You stole my gift! My family has been searching for this shrine for generations, and you just stumbled into it."

Hanuvar was still wondering exactly how much of a transformation had been worked upon him. Antires stood at the base of the stairs, staring mutely. Certain that Eloren had little time, Hanuvar pressed for information.

"And what was the purpose of this shrine? To steal life force?"

"Mostly. There's supposed to be a hidden library as well—is that what you found?"

"I did. Rotted."

"And you really didn't know. Gods. Yes, the shrine was supposed to make casual visitors uneasy, and then steal the life force of those who insisted upon investigating. The life was to power the magics, meant to repeatedly restore the wizard. But he died nonetheless; from what cause I do not know." The boy's voice grew weaker. He coughed again. "My ancestor . . . apprentice. Got the pendant. But it was no use without the shrine." He looked up at Hanuvar. "It would have healed me of the knife wound. But you . . . stabbed right as it filled me with life."

Having experienced the energy's debilitating effects himself, Hanuvar knew how impossible it would have been for Eloren to have worked some other spell, even if he hadn't been distracted by a mortal injury.

The priest struggled to level his weakening voice. "If you're not a mage, and you weren't after the shrine, why did you want this land so badly?"

"I'm just a man trying to help some people."

Eloren didn't look as though he believed him. "It doesn't matter now. You said you'd ease my crossing."

"I can. How long will this effect last on me?"

"How long?" the boy/man laughed. "As long as you live, you bastard!"

Hanuvar tore out his sword and brought it down across the little boy with the older man's eyes.

He was wiping his blade on a clean spot of the dead priest's tunic when Antires climbed the stairs and stared, speaking with shocking reverence. "By all the gods of earth and sky."

Hanuvar gulped as he stood, fearing what he might hear. He knew he was not a boy, for he still had a man's size. "How young do I look?"

"Twenty at best." Antires' voice shook with disbelief. "More like seventeen."

Seventeen. He sheathed his sword and looked down at his hands. At seventeen, his father had still lived, and he had wished nothing more than to be a worthy officer for him, and his valiant brother-in-law. At seventeen his older sister was only recently dead, and he had still been placing flowers at her memory stone each month. Melgar, his youngest brother, had barely been nine.

He looked at his hands, turning them over and finding them almost unfamiliar.

Antires searched through his cloak and pulled out a little bronze mirror, offering it. Hanuvar took it gingerly, remembering the full-length mirror hung in the wizard's chamber and understanding now why it rested there.

He stepped into the autumn sunlight, scanning the surrounding trees. But Eloren had no hidden reinforcements, and Alma's villa was too distant for anyone there to have heard the battle.

He lifted the mirror, and his fingers tightened over it when he saw the face looking back at him.

He was so young.

His face was unlined, and soft to touch, and there were no circles beneath his eyes. His nose was smaller and even had a less pronounced hook. Gone were the lines upon his brow and at the outer edges of his eyes. His hair was darker and smoother.

Antires reached his side and watched with something like religious awe. "Finally, the fates themselves have been kind to you."

Hanuvar lowered the mirror and handed it over. "You think this was kind?" How could his friend not understand his alarm?

Antires laughed in disbelief. "Don't you see? You can go anywhere now, without disguise. You could walk through the forum of Derva itself and no one would recognize you!"

While Hanuvar had already anticipated that last point himself, it had done nothing to cheer his perception of the event. He had been profoundly altered, but Antires was so excited he seemed completely oblivious about the complications and untroubled by the mechanism of the transformation.

"And your aches and pains are over! Oh, I know you've had them, even if you never talk about them." He pointed at Hanuvar's right leg. "Like that limp you sometimes have when you first wake up. Does your leg hurt now?"

"No. Nothing hurts." Hanuvar breathed deep. He rolled up his sleeve and confirmed that the old sword slash along his forearm had completely vanished. Probably any other scars that marked him were gone as well. He shook his head numbly at a fresh wave of loss. "Understand, Antires. This is dark sorcery. There's no telling what further effects this magic might have. It was shaped to lure men and women and drain them of their lives. I'm young in part because Alma is old. Do you see?"

Antires looked unconvinced by his concern. "I hear what you're saying. But however it is you came by it, isn't this an advantage you can use to your benefit?"

"It seems I have no choice." He did not explain that his changed appearance would also be a hindrance as he sought out former allies. And while Antires was right that it was unlikely Dervans would be suspicious of a youth, it was also true that no one would take him seriously. To achieve his aims, he'd sometimes adopted other identities, but how could he now imitate a centurion, or a senator's aid, or a revenant? He looked barely old enough to have earned the right to wear a toga.

Slowly uncurling his fists, he turned from Antires and started down the stairs, pausing only to take Eloren's lantern.

His friend followed him down. "You move with the confidence of an older man. You're going to have to practice moving like a younger one."

Probably there would be all manner of unforeseen new difficulties that he'd have to address. Antires still sounded intrigued by this staggering alteration, as though it were all just a breezy adventure. But then he actually was young, even if he was older than Hanuvar now appeared.

Hearteningly, Antires was also capable of thinking strategically. "What are we going to do about these bodies? We can't just leave them here, can we?"

Hanuvar had already decided that "We'll hide Eloren in the wizard's chambers."

"The library? Shouldn't we take the scrolls?"

"What was back there was rotted and forgotten, like him. The ruffians we'll leave where they fell. I'll have to give one of them a blade to explain away the obvious sword wounds."

The emerald's glow had vanished, but Hanuvar wasn't certain the shrine was done for until he peered inside the cavity where the gem had rested. The emerald had blackened and cracked into a dozen pieces.

He bent beside it. "The magic's spent. I wonder how many lives it stole." He looked to Antires, picking his way around the bodies to join him. "In a fairer world, we could have given some of these years back to Alma."

"You, of all people, should know the world's not fair. Gods, man. Be happy, for once. You've a gift most men dream of."

This "gift" had been forced upon him without preparation or consent. Hanuvar pressed the panel over the opening and moved it around until he felt it lock in place. He stood, noting dourly that there wasn't the slightest twinge in his knee. His ligaments didn't even creak. Though he took some small satisfaction from this, he thought of the woman who'd imagined herself speaking with her lost child. "Alma already lost her son once. She'll think that she's lost him again. It will be a hard blow."

"I expect it will. She'll probably blame it on the blood spilled by these ruffians. But without Eloren, she'll be far more likely to sell." Antires clapped him on the shoulder. "Cheer up! This will all work out." The playwright stared at him, then shook his head once more. "I don't know how I'm going to get used to you looking like this."

"Me either."

"Come on. We need to hide Eloren's body."

Hanuvar nodded his agreement. "There are a few chests in the wizard's chamber we should open. They're probably full of dried up sorcery goods and rotted cloth, but maybe there's some Turian gold."

"Do you think?"

"Who knows? You seem to feel I've been lucky today. Let's see if fortune's smiled any wider."

※ ※ ※

As it happened, two of the chests were, indeed, full of rotting cloth. The third seemed to be so as well, but that cloth had been two large sacks of old Turian coinage, which was a minor fortune. Hanuvar was, indeed, lucky that day. As I have probably made clear, we had a supply of gemstones he had carried with him from his family tomb, but they were not so numerous as they once had been, and we had a host of expenses before us. There was not just the land Hanuvar meant to buy, there was an entire harbor expansion, including homes and docks and a small shipyard, and, eventually, ships. And beyond that, of course, were the Volani he meant to free who would be building many of these things.

Even with this infusion of resources these goals were well beyond our capabilities, and I had tried to convince Hanuvar we should buy rather than build ships, or use some existing harbor. But Hanuvar had chosen this remote location precisely because here he would have to deal with fewer Dervan eyes. He meant to build his own ships, the better to safeguard the passage of his people. For in the Inner Sea, the ships mostly hugged coastlines and fled to shelter in heavy winds and steep waves. They were not built to endure the deeper oceans, as were Volani vessels.

And in any event, the people of his new city needed more transport of their own—they were a seafaring culture who built their prosperity on trade. Any ships he constructed would serve further purposes in the future. Such were his plans, and had anyone else proposed them, I would have thought him mad.

As for Alma, I learned that she was confused by Eloren's disappearance, horrified by the bloody bodies desecrating her shrine, and emotionally shattered by the utter disappearance of her long dead son. Once the bodies had been cleared and the priest of the small local temple to Arepon had sobered himself up enough to ritually purify the place, she spent long days praying in the shrine.

Her son's false spirit never returned, of course, and she eventually retreated to her villa. It was only then that I contacted her once more about purchasing her land. I never actually saw her again. She agreed through her head slave, settled for a chunk of our Turian gold, then left for warmer climes, never to return. She ordered the shrine filled in sometime before and within a season it was impossible to detect it had ever existed.

As for Eloren's fate, the speculation in Selanto's two small taverns held that the dead men had murdered him when he wouldn't tell them where any hidden treasure was—whether there was or wasn't any hidden treasure in the shrine varied depending upon who told the tale. Regardless, gossip had it that the bandits had then gotten into a fight about the treasure themselves. It seemed as likely an explanation as any.

But this is a tale of Hanuvar, and it is time I returned to him. I confess that every time I thought myself used to his transformation I had but to see him again, in the flower of his youth, and be stunned once more. I worked with him for almost a week, trying to remind him of a young man's nervousness and eagerness to ingratiate, and how thin skinned and reckless he should pretend to be. I encouraged him to spend time among the village youths. This he did, though he applied himself more like a scholar than someone with any real love for the subject.

Hanuvar left shortly after the land purchase was confirmed. By that point we had noticed an additional odd consequence of his change. As I have probably made clear, when he was not in disguise, Hanuvar practiced martial drills every day. Owing to this and a lifetime of additional experiences, his hands had been calloused for the length of our acquaintance. But those callouses were vanished, and no matter the nature of his exercise, they did not return.

He remarked that unforeseen results were always the consequence of magic. I laughed the discovery off, not realizing that this was the first warning of a dire fate that lay before him.

Resigned to his condition, Hanuvar journeyed south. One week's travel would see him to a little resort town where the Dervan general Ciprion, once his most effective enemy and now his friend, had pledged to leave whatever information he'd been able to uncover about the whereabouts of the Volani slaves.

To safely reach the town, Hanuvar hired on as a caravan guard, a simple enough way to reach the destination without spending any more of our dwindling funds. Keep in mind that despite our recent windfall, I lacked full capital to further his plans in Selanto, and he hadn't even a tenth of the money he would need to pay for all his people.

The guard captain was immensely skeptical of Hanuvar's soft hands and would have refused him on the spot if Hanuvar had not promptly demonstrated martial acumen entirely remarkable for a man his apparent age. He was then able to explain away his hands by saying he'd been sick over the summer.

But I was not to learn that tale, nor much else that befell him, for long weeks. I cannot tell you how much I wished to be riding with him. I was flattered to have become crucial to Hanuvar's plans, but not so star struck that I failed to perceive there was no one else he had to rely upon.

And so, as I settled into my most unexpected role yet, that of a man constructing a shipping business, Hanuvar ventured south, where he was shortly to meet a trio of people crucial to his future.

—Sosilos, Book Seven

Chapter 2:
The People of the Marsh

I

Hanuvar had closed his eyes, still wondering about the woman, when the whistling began. It was a plaintive, lonely sound somewhere between the forlorn wind of the icy mountain heights and a drowning man's gurgle. Most of the campfire chatter had already died when the merchants and their families and slaves bedded down for the evening. Now it silenced completely and the camp strained its collective senses toward the unearthly sound emanating from somewhere to the northeast of their fragile refuge.

The horses, picketed nearby, neighed fearfully to one another, but no other creature, even the normally incessant droning insects, made a sound.

After a long while the whistling passed on to the north, fading gradually with distance, and despite the frightened, low-voiced talk about bog folk Hanuvar weighed the likelihood that the cry originated with some native owl or nocturnal mammal. Then long instilled habits took over with the return of normal night noises, and he fell quickly to sleep.

He roused the instant Tullus woke him with a touch to the shoulder, and the grizzled Dervan veteran sat back in surprise.

"Jovren's blaze," Tullus said under his breath. "You're quick to get that blade up!"

Hanuvar had risen with knife in hand. He grinned sheepishly, as though he were an embarrassed youth, and Tullus eventually chuckled. "Skittish, are you, Flavius?"

Hanuvar had adopted the name of a centurion he'd respected for this leg of the journey. He could barely make the guard captain out in the gloom, for the moon was down and the flicker of perimeter torches spoiled greater accommodation to the starlight, but from the shape it was the same thick-set fellow with heavy brow and graying hair he'd signed on with a few days previous. And judging by Tullus' relative calm, Hanuvar was being wakened for nothing more than the middle shift of the night watch.

"You don't need to worry," Tullus said. "The bog folk don't ever wander to the heights. They're mostly after foolish berry pickers who come into the marshes."

"Berries?"

"You really are new around here, aren't you. Come on, get your ass moving."

Hanuvar threw off the covers and sat up, astonished at how simple it was. Remembering how much more forgiving a younger man's frame was to changes in position proved very different from experiencing that flexibility first hand. He looked up at Tullus. "If the bog folk don't come up here, why do we light all the torches?"

"Mostly to make us feel better. It makes you feel better, doesn't it?"

"I guess," Hanuvar said, pulling on his sandals.

"Right. Now what you do is keep an eye on things to the east side of camp. Quintus has the west side. Most bandits would wet themselves if they went this deep in the Coreven Marshes, but you never know. Keep moving so you don't get sleepy, or I'll have your head. Is that clear?"

"Yes, sir." Hanuvar climbed to his feet, buckling on his sword belt.

"And keep your hands off the women, right?"

Hanuvar emitted an embarrassed gasp he was sure Antires would have approved. "Of course, sir."

Tullus sighed. "You keep those torches lit. You get nervous, you say something to Quintus before you bother me or anyone else. Got that? You rouse me and it turns out an owl made you jump I won't be happy."

"Yes, sir."

Tullus frowned at him, then stomped away to his own bedroll.

Hanuvar headed for the perimeter, intent on the land beyond, though his eyes occasionally strayed for Izivar's covered wagon. He'd heard her voice, but he'd yet to see her, for her wagon had pulled in to the caravan shortly before departure, and she'd never poked her head outside of it, at least not when he'd been watching. She'd surely climbed down to freshen up and eat with her maid and wagon driver, but as the most recent recruit, he'd been on the far side of camp, caring for the horses, for most of the meal hour.

He had little idea why Izivar Lenereva would be on this road, apart from it being one of the primary routes through northern Tyvol. Most wealthy folk would already have headed south before winter roared down from the Ardenines.

It was best not to speculate.

A half hour into his shift one of the torches began to sputter. Hanuvar pretended anxiety as he consulted Quintus, a surly red-haired guard who looked half Ceori. Quintus spoke to him exactly as he would if Hanuvar were a young man asking questions with obvious answers, then added more oil and resumed his duties.

While it was warmer here than it had been just south of the Ardenines, the night was cool. The full moon peered out through a break in the clouds and mist roiled at ankle level on the ground below the ridge. Sometimes it thinned enough to reveal the old black road threading through the highest parts of the land. Owls hooted and frogs croaked and crickets chirruped until the terrible whistling resumed. Once again, all natural sounds stopped on the instant.

This time the noise rose from the trees just beyond the road, and it was more plaintive, as though generated by something painfully alone and eager for company. Hanuvar's neck hairs stood at attention and his pulse rose.

He strode to the ridge's edge, away from the torch so his night vision would improve, and peered toward the source. This brought him closer to Izivar's wagon.

He heard the creak of the base as she shifted, the frightened whisper of her female attendant, and a calmer answer, and then the curtain parted behind him.

Izivar Lenereva spoke Dervan, betraying her Volani origins in the way she stretched the vowels and hung on hard consonants. Had he wished it, he could have spoken with the same accent, although he felt a far stronger pull to address her in their shared tongue. What would it be like to feel the words of his own people in his mouth and hear them from another being in response? Once, he had taken such simple pleasures for granted.

"Warrior, is that sound really made by someone dead?" she asked. Her voice was a pleasant alto. "I have heard tales, but thought them exaggerations. What is the truth?"

He ignored the impulse to answer her question with one of his own: how did it feel to have survived the massacre of your people by siding with the enemy? But then she herself was unlikely to have directed that course, for it was her father Tannis who led their family, and their shipping empire, relocated to Dervan lands. That hardly exonerated her, though, for as an adult, under Volani law and custom she had the right and the responsibility to choose her own course.

So long did Hanuvar delay the answer to Izivar's question that she called again to him. "Warrior?" She was only a vague shape, her face a slightly lighter oval than the hair that framed her, and the darkness of the wagon that surrounded her.

A figure shifted on his sleeping roll beneath a nearby open wagon and answered in a low voice. "He don't answer because he hasn't heard it before, milady. And yes, it's the bog folk. And yes they've been dead a long, long time."

"I do not understand," Izivar said.

"My father used to pass this way when he was trading," the man continued. "He harkened to stories about them, but only heard them himself a few times. Back then they'd only turn up when the water was very high and the moon was at its brightest."

"What do they want?"

The merchant's voice dropped lower still. "They want company, milady. In the old days, if you tried to cross a ford at high water, they'd turn up and drag you in, and the next night, you'd be out there, drowned and hooting your own self."

A woman gasped; Hanuvar guessed from the sound it was Izivar's maid.

"Why are they out now?" Hanuvar asked. "The moon's not yet full."

It wasn't the merchant who answered, but Quintus, walking quietly up from the left. He gave Hanuvar a hard stare, then spat into the weeds. "The bog folk can't do anything to us so long as we stay out of the lowlands."

"Can you kill them with a sword?" Hanuvar asked, partly because he expected the person he pretended to be would ask it, and partly because he wanted to prepare for any eventualities.

"Can you kill what's already dead?" Quintus shook his head. "I've no mind to find out. They can keep their soggy land. Now the rest of you'd best get back to sleep and let me and Flavius keep watch. The bog folk won't come up here." He curiously repeated the last bit as if he could make it true through repetition.

Izivar closed the curtain to her wagon and Hanuvar moved away. The thing keened beyond the camp for another hour then fell silent shortly before Hanuvar was relieved by the third shift and retreated to his bedroll. He fell immediately to sleep and did not rouse until dawn's light struck his eyelids.

Shortly after breakfast the caravan was back on the old dark road. Sometimes the black stones stretched straight on through the marsh and sometimes the wetlands receded and the terrain was dry and ordinary, flat enough to farm. At one point they appeared to have left the marshes entirely, but by mid-morning the road was passing through the thick of them again.

Hanuvar had been positioned at the rear of the column and was near enough to hear occasional snatches of conversation in Volani from within Izivar's covered wagon. The maid complained about the bumpiness of the roadway. Izivar replied that they could thank her brother when they finally saw him.

So far as Hanuvar knew, Izivar had only one brother, and Hanuvar had last seen him within the tomb of the Cabera family, one living Volani among so many dead ones. Almost certainly Indar had been among the first sources of rumors about Hanuvar's return, and Hanuvar had long wondered about the wisdom of sparing him.

That decision, though, had been made.

Eventually the maid asked for and received permission to ride the sturdy brown mare tied to the back of the Lenereva wagon. She was tall and fair and only a little older than Hanuvar appeared. She wore her auburn hair in a loose woven braid hanging down her back, as had been popular in Volanus when traveling or engaging in sport, but was otherwise dressed like a Dervan woman, with an off-white stola and simple sandals. She eyed Hanuvar dismissively and then enlisted the help of Quintus to secure the saddle. She mounted with the ease of an experienced horsewoman, then trotted joyfully up to the front of the column to chat with a pair of youths accompanying their father in the foremost wagon.

While he had chosen this route in part to examine its security, Hanuvar's most important objective had been to reach Adrumentum, where his former adversary Ciprion pledged to leave the sales records of Volani slaves for him. With that lure ahead, he chafed more at delays than the merchants eager to reach their markets. Hanuvar hoped come evening to finally possess the vital information, and then, at long last, launch the next phase of his plans.

But he had no way of knowing if Ciprion had succeeded. While the Dervan general was a man of integrity and intelligence, his research into the fate of Volani might well have been for naught, or worse, noted by men with different designs. Some agent of the revenants might be lying in wait even now to see who turned up in Adrumentum to retrieve the information.

There was no use worrying about the possibilities. If his plans required adjustments, Hanuvar would make them. He had no better alternatives.

By late morning the road was lower in the marshes once more. The vine-wrapped bushes and trees loomed heavily over the barely raised track, deepening the shadows in which they travelled, and water frequently lay to either side. They passed occasional clearings that might have been inviting were the sun shining, for weedy flowers bloomed there in profusion. In one field they glimpsed bushes heavy with small blood red berries. A couple in the wagon ahead exclaimed in surprise; the woman driver halted and the man climbed down from his wagon, then held back as Tullus cantered up, cursing. He threatened the man with a whip.

Startled, the merchant retreated to his wagon, casting a dark look after the head guard.

"No one leaves the road!" Tullus snarled. "You keep moving! All of you!"

Tullus waited on his horse at the verge of the field until the single riders and six caravan wagons and all the baggage animals filed past. He swung in beside Hanuvar, who was bringing up the rear.

"What's that all about?" Hanuvar asked.

"They were after the bog berries," Tullus said sourly. "The bog folk grow them to lure folks in."

"Really?" If he were not playing a role, Hanuvar would have asked a similar question.

"If you leave the road, it's hard to find your way back. It's easy to get turned around when you're calf deep in water among long grasses. And there's things back there apart from the bog folk. Things that might want to eat you."

"Why does anyone want those red berries, anyway?"

"They're supposed to taste like the nectar of the gods and give you visions. Folk pay well for them." He eyed Hanuvar. "And you may think, oh, I'll just nip back there and get some of those berries, but I've seen better men than you head out for a harvest. Big parties of seasoned men with all sort of clever plans on how to keep track of where they're going. Most of them don't come back. The bog people can kill or cripple with a touch."

"Why don't the legions do something about this road, if it's so dangerous?"

"Most of the legions are out on the borders right now, what with some of the Herrenes in revolt and the Cerdians threatening war and the damned Hadirans rioting about who's their rightful queen."

"Someone should do something." Hanuvar thought he struck just the right note of youthful determination. "About the roads, I mean."

"Then someone important needs to die up here. A senator, or a senator's wife, or a rich man. Or maybe the emperor's nephew. He's here, you know."

Hanuvar hadn't known that at all. Once, his intelligence network had been the envy of Derva and he had been well appraised as to the whereabouts, political leanings, dispositions and personalities of the empire's key military and political leaders. Now something as simple as the location of their likely heir was news to him.

"Here in the swamps?"

"No, dummy, in Adrumentum. Taking the spas. But he's really here for the berries, and a lot of people are saying that's what's got the bog folk stirred up."

"You said taking the berries was dangerous."

Tullus began his answer before Hanuvar had finished. "Which is why he has a platoon of slaves under guard harvesting them. The people of Adrumentum are in love with all the money he's brought to the village, but they're also frightened to death of what might be the result."

"And I guess asking him to stop is out of the question?"

Tullus snorted. "How many rich people have you known? He'll do what he wants. Sooner or later berry season will be through, but who knows? It might be that the bog folk are going to be a lot more active from now on. They get angry whenever a few berries get eaten, and he and his cronies have collected thousands."

Hanuvar didn't like that news at all. His challenge wasn't simply to free his people from their current owners, it was to arrange transport for them to his shipyard and thence to New Volanus. Only a few good roads traversed northern Tyvol, and he couldn't afford to have one of them too hazardous to use.

A quarter mile beyond the berry field the clouds opened with streamers of rainy mist. Were the weather warmer, the experience might have been a pleasure. But the soft cold rain deepened the chill, like a spectral hand that leached through garments and skin and numbed to the bones.

Tullus ordered Hanuvar forward with him. The captain liked to vary the placement of his guards so they wouldn't get complacent or chatty with the people they rode near. Hanuvar couldn't help noticing Tullus peering intently forward. Before, he'd swept his gaze from right to left at regular intervals.

"Are you expecting a problem?" Hanuvar asked.

He shot Hanuvar an irritated look, but explained anyway. "Part of the road's too low. It can get muddy but it usually isn't much deeper than a boot, and no more than twelve paces wide."

Hanuvar had heard the other guards talking about the spot as a landmark that morning. "And after that, we're out of the marshes?"

"Once we're past that, we have maybe a half hour of steady riding."

What he didn't say was that the low area would make an excellent ambush point, but Hanuvar understood. "Are the bog folk intelligent?"

Tullus searched his face, looking for signs of a keener intellect than Hanuvar had previously demonstrated. Hanuvar kept his expression guileless.

The guard captain didn't answer his question. "Eyes sharp. We're nearly there."

Only a short time later the ridge and its road dipped into a stream, and the rotted remains of an old bridge lay washed up against the trees to the south. The rain pattered drearily down from charcoal skies while frogs croaked.

The guard captain ordered Hanuvar forward to assist, then splashed to the head on his gray. The water climbed over the horse's fetlocks and finally just below the steady animal's belly for a few strides, but then the depth reversed itself and Tullus was on the far bank of the stream, scanning the foliage to either side. He waved the wagons forward.

Hanuvar waited on the near side, scanning with eyes and ears. The low spot was an even finer ambush spot than he had imagined. The crossing provided both distraction and obstacle, while a thick screen of vegetation concealed potential attackers to north and south. The entire line of march was hemmed in by trees.

Five of the six wagons, all of the walkers and all but three of the riders were across when the frogs abruptly stilled. The two merchants on horseback seemed oblivious to the change, but Izivar's maid scanned the brush to either side and then looked back at Izivar's wagon just before she crossed into the deepest water.

It was then the sinister keening of the bog people filled the air.

A pair of figures shambled forth from trees beside the stream, man-shaped things dark as cured meat, their flat stringy hair plastered to the tops of their heads and the sides of their faces. They had no eyes, only sunken pits of darkness. Hanuvar had no chance to observe greater detail, for even his well-trained horse whinnied in fright and tried to bolt. He fought it, struggling against his own instinctive fear.

The two mounted merchants shouted in alarm and one was dumped by his rearing horse into the water. He came up flailing and splashed forward at a diagonal, away from the terrible bog folk.

Quintus forced his horse back toward the water, spear ready, but then his mount refused to advance further, and the veteran's curses filled the air.

The driver of Izivar's wagon wrestled for control over the pair of frightened horses pulling him forward. In their alarm they veered right and the cartwheels slewed into a submerged rock. The sudden shock tilted the wagon seat and threw the driver into the reaching arms of one of the bog people. The thing immediately bent with him into the water, and his scream evolved into gurgles.

The other thing grasped the wagon's rear rail. Izivar's maid servant rode on, clinging desperately to the reins and shouting Izivar's name as the horse bolted up the bank out of her control.

Hanuvar had finally mastered his horse and kicked it close to the wagon opposite the moving dead man. "Izivar!" he shouted.

A woman in a light blue stola with curling black hair scrambled out from the wagon's front, across the driver's seat, eyes huge with fear. The bog man had crawled through the wagon and up onto the seat after her as she reached for Hanuvar.

His horse splashed its forelegs anxiously, but he forced it still and leaned for the woman as she fell against his side, feet hanging into the water. She clutched at his shirt and grasped his shoulder.

He urged the horse forward, steadying her against him.

The bog thing that had drowned the driver rose from the water before them, whistling and waving its emaciated arms. While Hanuvar had worked long with his animal, it still wasn't a true war mount, which he could have commanded to rear and strike. The gelding dodged left. Izivar gasped and her clutching fingers slid. Hanuvar grabbed over his shoulder and more by chance than design snagged her wrist.

Her weight almost pulled him out of the saddle. The mount whipsawed left and right then splashed out of the stream. Hanuvar pulled hard and Izivar somehow righted herself, found a seat behind him, and wrapped her arms about him.

The other bank was chaos, with two wagons driving ahead and another on its side. A merchant and his pair of slaves had abandoned it and were sprinting for their lives in the wake of four other riders, and Quintus was cutting their horses free. Tullus shouted at Hanuvar to hurry.

Hanuvar thought that a sensible order and joined the guards and the bolting horses in the general retreat. The horses pulling Izivar's ruined wagon managed to haul it devoid of all but one wheel onto the bank far to their right and looked unwilling to stop for the soggy unhorsed merchant in their path.

Hanuvar didn't look back until the attack site lay fifty paces to their rear, where the road rose and the marsh receded. The only trees along the west were stately oaks.

Behind them, the bog folk and their victim had vanished. One wagon lay abandoned on its side, its barrels and boxes strewn across the roadway. Izivar's horses had been cut loose by another guard now attempting to calm them, for they still danced frantically in their traces.

The rest of the caravan waited a quarter mile on. As Hanuvar and his companions reined in, the drizzle finally stopped. Ahead of them the clouds opened. A sunbeam illuminated a pine on a distant hill.

The flustered caravan master was pretending calm and insisting those newly on foot be given space in the wagons. Izivar's maid threw herself off her mount, her face tear streaked, arms stretched up for her mistress. Hanuvar eased Izivar gently down into the other woman's care.

Izivar was older than her maid, likely in her late thirties, with dark brows and a slim hooked nose and full lips. Her age showed in lines about her eyes and mouth. He could not help admiring her thick, curling dark hair, shoulder length and loose.

He loved hearing the flow of Volani words between the two women as they consoled one another. Izivar addressed the maid not like a stern Dervan slaveholder, but as a companion, and the maid was mortified she'd been unable to control her horse and help her. Izivar reassured her that she understood, and that even the brave warrior who'd saved her had barely mastered his horse. She turned and faced him. She spoke to him kindly in her accented Dervan. "What is your name?"

"I am called Flavius, milady," he answered.

She bowed her head respectfully. "I am grateful to you, Flavius. You were very brave."

"So were you."

She favored him with an amused smile then looked at the other survivors. The wagon folk had realized their relative safety now, and it had made them bold enough to complain about the caravan's terrible protection. The owner of the fallen cart was pointing back down the road and arguing that his goods should be recovered.

The maid looked up at Hanuvar, brazenly, and spoke in their

native tongue to Izivar: "He is rather handsome and not at all awkward for a boy his age."

"He could almost be Volani," Izivar mused, and she studied Hanuvar's eyes. He returned her gaze as if in idle curiosity. For a moment Hanuvar wondered if he'd given away that he understood them.

"You look familiar to me, Flavius," Izivar said in Dervan. "Is it possible that we've met? Or that I might know your family?"

"It might be possible, milady."

She smiled. "You called me Izivar, earlier."

"Yes, milady. I just wanted to make sure I got your attention."

"You're very quick thinking."

"Thank you. Was your driver also from Volanus? It was terrible, how he died."

"No, he was a Dervan man my father hired. He was very conscientious."

"Is it true that your father..." He hesitated as though he were deciding how to phrase the question. "...left Volanus because he liked Derva better?"

His question drolly amused her. "My father could not convince the government of Volanus to change their course to save the city, but he did what he could to help those under his protection—ship builders, craftsmen, and their families."

"You give your father credit?" the maid asked of her mistress, speaking Volani once more.

Izivar shot her a look to quiet her. "It is not his business," she replied sharply in the same language. The maid looked down, and Izivar addressed Hanuvar in Dervan, her anger ebbing. "I mean no insult, but these are private matters. I hope you will understand."

"Of course. I apologize if I was forward."

"It is of no consequence. I am in your debt, Flavius. Once we reach Adrumentum I'll see that you're properly rewarded."

"That's not necessary, milady."

"Nonsense. A young man like yourself might do well with a sponsor, and I could introduce you to a powerful one."

"That's really not necessary."

Izivar glanced down at a rip in her blouse near her waistline and probed it with her fingers.

"Perhaps," the maid said slyly in Volani, "I could give him a reward." Even if Hanuvar hadn't understood Volani he saw the inviting look in her eyes, though he looked only blankly back.

"You're incorrigible." Izivar's hands probed the rent in her garment more surely. She shifted unsteadily.

"Milady?" The maid sounded concerned.

Izivar had turned from Hanuvar so that she would not reveal any of her flesh and pried the rent apart so that she could peer at the skin. "It's just a scratch," she said, but her legs seemed to have trouble holding her upright.

"One of the creatures struck you?" Hanuvar demanded, his voice sharp.

"Hold still, milady," the maid was saying in Volani. "It's not deep."

"Tullus," Hanuvar shouted. Then, when he saw Tullus still in the midst of a debate with two of the merchants, he called to him more forcefully. "The lady's been wounded!"

Tullus broke away from the conversation and trotted over, tripping over a raised black road brick, then came to a halt, his expression grave. "From the bog folk? Let me see."

Izivar looked as though she meant to brush off his concern, but the arm she raised to object flopped loosely.

"It's here," the maid said.

Hanuvar guided his animal closer and observed a slim gash along Izivar's side, no worse than a kitten scratch. But Tullus' expression looked grave.

"What can we do?" Hanuvar asked.

"There's a healer only about forty minutes south, just past the gate. I hear she's saved some people poisoned by the bog folk."

"Forty minutes walking?" Hanuvar asked.

"Yes."

"Then I'll get her there faster. Milady?"

She seemed to have trouble focusing, but stretched her hands to him. Tullus hesitated only a moment, then boosted her up.

Hanuvar wrapped his arms around her before him and told her to stay awake. She sleepily vowed to do so.

The maid shouted that she wouldn't be left behind and hurried to her horse.

Tullus spoke quickly to Hanuvar. "There's a legion gate. Tell them I sent you and tell them it's Sullius' caravan."

"Yes, sir." Hanuvar pulled Izivar tight with one arm, grasped the reins with his right hand, and kicked the mount into a canter. The maid had managed to clamber onto her own horse and raced after.

"You'll be alright," she called in Volani, partially, it seemed, to reassure herself.

Izivar remained upright but she did not reply. Hanuvar thought she was trying to speak several times during the ride, but over the clatter of the horse's progress on the paving bricks he couldn't make out what she was saying. After a time, she began to slump.

"Stay awake," he urged her, more than once. "Just hold on and stay awake." Each time she roused.

They passed other dirt tracks. Three were smaller walking paths and cart trails to outlying residences, and two were full-fledged roads. Just as Hanuvar's horse was starting to foam he spotted a gate stretched across the road, so new that the wood was bright, as it was yet to be weathered. Unhelmed legionaries, alerted by his approach, lifted spears and shields and lined up behind it.

Hanuvar slowed. He heard the maid, whose own animal had fallen behind, still in pursuit.

He trotted forward even as a helmeted man behind the gate urged him to halt and identify himself.

"I'm Flavius, with Sullius' caravan. This woman's wounded and needs medical help!"

A surly solder with pock marked cheeks pushed to the front of the men. "What does that matter to me?" he asked. The leather pteruges dangling from his armored shoulders were white, the rank marking of an optio. "Have you got your papers?"

"Tullus told me to tell you to let me through," Hanuvar insisted. "There's a chance we can save her if we get her to the healer immediately!"

Most of the soldiers looked to their sour leader, as if silently urging him to unbend.

While the homely young officer frowned, the maid arrived on her wheezing horse. She spoke, breathing nearly as heavily as her animal. "What are you men waiting for? Let milady through! She's a friend to Enarius!"

Mention of the emperor's nephew decided the matter for the optio at last, and at his signal the men quickly shoved the gate to one side. A freckled soldier pointed to a small wood building no more than fifty feet beyond the gate, on the outskirts of a sprawling unwalled village. He said the healer was there.

Hanuvar held the swaying Izivar tight to him as he urged the horse forward. The freckled soldier, seeing his difficulty, trotted after. He helped further by receiving Izivar as Hanuvar eased her from the horse. Hanuvar thanked him, lifted her into his arms, and hurried up the short flight of steps.

The wide porch displayed a variety of wide-brimmed hats and sandals and walking sticks, their prices chalked on a nearby board. Inside the building proved a combination trade post and tavern. One wall shelved cloaks and wineskins and belts and other gear. Thrust out from the other was a counter behind which a woman poured drinks for a band of middle-aged men. At a nearby table sat a plump centurion in the ivory white armor and tunic of the Praetorian Guard, drinking beside a sullenly handsome young praetorian optio, his own uniform pteruges golden. Both looked up as Hanuvar made for a second counter at the store's rear.

Hanuvar drew to a stop before the older woman stationed there. "I'm looking for a healer. This woman's been wounded by one of the bog folk."

The wrinkles about the woman's mouth deepened as she frowned. Her voice was high and soft. "I'm not sure there's anything I can do for her, if it was really bog folk."

"Is that Izivar Lenereva?" a male voice asked of Hanuvar's back. He turned his head to find that the centurion and his optio had stumped up behind him. He didn't have time to answer, but Izivar's maid, bustling past them, replied breathlessly in the affirmative.

"Please," the maid said pressing herself to the counter. "Help her."

"I don't know," the woman behind the counter said, glaring at Hanuvar. "It's you Dervans who have the bog folk on the hunt, anyway."

In Hanuvar's experience, those living beyond the borders of the empire thought the Dervans a great, faceless mass with one vision and one purpose, sweeping forth like an ant horde to carry goods back to their nest. But within the Tyvolian peninsula itself many regions remained proud of their heritage and also thought themselves distinct, even if some young men from their lands marched under the empire's eagles. To Hanuvar's eyes the woman before him was almost indistinguishable from the people in Derva proper to the south, but he understood she did not consider herself so. To her, this community and probably those in the region surrounding were a distinct people, with different traditions and customs, and the Dervans were foreign interlopers. So had he known before his invasion of Tyvol and had thus found many allies among the Dervan territories, although not so many as he had hoped.

"She is not Dervan," Hanuvar said. "She is Volani."

"Please, help," the maid added in her accented Dervan. "Hundreds of people depend upon her. They truly need her."

The centurion now blustered that the healer would help if she knew what was good for her, but she didn't acknowledge him. The pair of praetorians must have been invested in Izivar's welfare because they were aware of her purported connection to Enarius.

"Bring her through and we'll see what can be done." The woman stepped to the break in the counter and motioned Hanuvar forward. Both the maid and the centurion followed, the latter demanding of the maid what had happened and how bad the wound was.

A small, orderly apartment lay beyond a curtained doorway, redolent with candlewax, cooking oils, and unfamiliar herbs. A dining area held two couches and the woman motioned Hanuvar to lay Izivar upon the closest while she hurried through another curtain. The instant he had placed her, the maid pushed past and knelt, clutching her mistress's hands.

The praetorian centurion considered Hanuvar coldly, as though he personally blamed Hanuvar for any inconvenience Izivar's injury might bring him. He was Hanuvar's height, with a long straight nose and bright blue eyes. He radiated the sense of superiority typical of the almost wealthy, and Hanuvar noted his citizen's ring held an amber stone. His flesh sagged on his powerful frame, like an athlete gone to seed.

He shouted into Hanuvar's face. "The woman should have been brought to the villa and presented to Enarius' healer. I'll have you up on charges."

"This healer was closer," Hanuvar countered calmly. "And is supposed to know about the bog poisons. Does your healer?"

Those points momentarily froze the centurion. He scowled, then turned to the young optio, waiting in the apartment doorway. "Metellus, go get the medic. Run! And bring back troops with you."

Metellus saluted and departed swiftly.

The centurion sneered at Hanuvar. "What's your name, boy?"

The maid turned her head. "His name is Flavius." She wiped one tear-streaked cheek. "And he already saved her life once. Don't you be mean to him. He's only been trying to help."

The centurion fumed but before he found a retort, the healer returned with a basket of herbs and oils. She lifted her face toward Hanuvar and the praetorian. "You two get out."

"Is she going to live?" Hanuvar asked.

"She might. Now clear out. There's nothing you can do and I have to cut more of her clothing. I don't need you in the way gawking."

"But you do think she'll live?" the centurion asked.

"Her chances are fair, if the boy brought her to me within the hour."

"I have."

"Good. Now both of you go."

Seeing that there was nothing more he could do, Hanuvar departed. The centurion grumbled at him as they left the back room, demanding more specifics. When he found out the caravan had been attacked, he declared he'd lead some men out to escort it the rest of the way in. Had the officer been under Hanuvar's command he would have told him that was a waste of time, but he was glad to see the centurion's wide back.

He retreated to his horse and walked the weary mount to a stable down a side street. Normally he'd have rubbed him down himself, but he paid a stable boy to pamper the animal and headed deeper into the resort village, saddlebag draped over his shoulder.

He pretended to be a wide-eyed youth goggling at the inns and gambling halls and brothels and, naturally, the famed bathhouses and spas. In actuality he was alert for hidden troops or the presence of revenants. He thought to see them only if Ciprion's aims had been discovered and the Dervans had learned Hanuvar planned to visit the settlement. But seeing none failed to reassure him.

While off-duty soldiers lounged in the bars and a few strolled the streets, he discovered from a fellow tavern goer that the legion presence here was relatively small. A century of praetorians was posted nearby, thanks to the presence of Enarius, the emperor's favorite nephew, but no one had seen any revenants, even though they naturally suspected spies or informants for the notorious group in the settlement.

In the midst of inquiring about the presence of troops over a meal, the subject of Hanuvar unexpectedly came up at a nearby table. Some thought the notion that Hanuvar lived was absurd while others believed just the opposite, though they laughed at the idea Hanuvar could be stopped by a few soldiers at a wooden gate. A short man of middle age expertly posited Hanuvar would obviously sneak through the wilds at night if he were alone, and if he was returning with an army, that gate was woefully undermanned. Opinion differed as to whether his army would be composed of Ceori and Ruminians and Herrenes or simply ghosts.

Hanuvar turned to listen with a slack jaw, as if overwhelmed by the wonder of it all. He privately agreed all three viewpoints held merit, including the absurdity of Hanuvar's survival in the first place.

After his late lunch he walked toward the most prosperous inn in the city, one displaying a brightly painted image of a smiling man with closed eyes reclining on a bed. Once past the gaudy, faux-gold leaf doorway he approached the well-groomed clerk at the desk and asked if there were any messages for Anex of Cylene.

The clerk said he wasn't sure but that he would check, which was to be expected, regardless if he were speaking truth or if he was running off to alert some soldiers. While Hanuvar didn't detect anything in the clerk's demeanor that suggested nervousness, he watched the exits and the curtained doorway through which the man disappeared.

During that short, tense wait, boisterous laughter rang from the common room through a nearby doorway, a sobering reminder of his own insignificance. No matter how vital he thought his actions, they were as meaningless to the greater swell of humanity as foam upon the tide. The daily and nightly activities of this tavern would continue as they had for generations, whether he were to walk free, or die in bloody ambush.

He did not have long to stand in somber rumination, for the clerk returned bearing a sealed scroll tube. His eyes were searching. "There's one here. But I really can't hand this over unless you know the code word—"

"Etulius."

The clerk's eyebrows rose minutely. "Very well." He placed the scroll tube upon the counter, and Hanuvar slid over a single small coin for the man's trouble, glancing at the scroll tube as if it were only of minor interest to him. He left the inn without a backward glance.

Within the tube might well be the future of his remaining people, but he handled the object nonchalantly, heading to the cheaper inn across the street and a cubicle on the upper floor he rented for himself, absent of all furnishing apart from a low bed. He peered once more through the window and down onto the street, alert for spies. No one appeared to have paid him the slightest notice.

He slid the lock bar on the door, then, at last, broke the seal on the scroll tube. He shook out a bundle of tightly rolled parchment paper and sat down on the bed.

The parchment itself was also sealed with wax, but Ciprion wisely hadn't applied his own seal to the contents, choosing an elephant instead, which raised a brief, wry smile. Hanuvar then broke the yellow wax and took the top paper in both hands so it would not curl in upon itself.

Ciprion had written him in Herrenic, hardly a fool-proof means of keeping communication secret, but one that entailed an extra hurdle for casual snoopers.

My Dear Friend,

I hope this information reaches you in a timely fashion, and that your own travels were without incident.

He hoped in vain, Hanuvar thought, and continued reading.

Our mutual acquaintance has been having a difficult time of it, as you may have learned, and I believe he will wisely keep from such overt steps against that family in the near future.

Here Ciprion must be referring to Aminius, who had plotted to kill Ciprion and whose agent had poisoned Ciprion's grandson. Hanuvar wished Ciprion could somehow have been more forthcoming with his plans on that front, as he worried for him, but Ciprion immediately shifted subjects, maintaining a slightly indefinite focus out of necessity.

The papers enclosed are a record of all of the slaves matching your qualifications that were sold to Dervan masters. You will find the name of the slave, the slave's age, and profession, if known, the amount paid, and the purchaser. Most were acquired by landowners, and I've provided information about them, their business representatives, and their dwelling places, in the hope that this will save you time.

Indeed it would. He wondered what challenges Ciprion had overcome to obtain the information, remembering how he'd said Hanuvar wasn't the only one who could work miracles.

Some were purchased directly by the government, and information on their whereabouts has been more challenging to obtain. Several dozen were sold to foreigners, and that specific information is stored separately under layers of bureaucracy that has proved difficult to penetrate. I haven't given up yet.

Hanuvar doubted that he would; persistence was one of their shared attributes.

I have confirmed that the woman you asked about survived with minor injuries.

He took a deep breath and breathed out slowly. His daughter Narisia lived. Here was the written proof, in his hands.

She and three friends managed to break free, although one died during the escape. She and her remaining companions disappeared into the Turian hills, and a rainstorm came on their heels, rendering tracking impossible. As you doubtless know, everyone's superstitious about travelling the Turian hills by night.

And some said that was with good reason. But he guessed that three armed Eltyr would probably manage well enough in most environments. The province of Turia was just south of Derva itself. From there she might have fled further to Utria or some of the former Herrenic colonies. But while they had once played host to the Volani forces, they were now firmly under Dervan control. Where might she have ended up?

The escape is a closely kept secret. Those few who are aware of it have been assured the haunts of the Turian hills found them. Another group continues to hunt them.

Revenants, this meant.

You know how to have your agents find me. I will continue to seek the rest of the information you're after.

Ciprion hadn't affixed his signature, naturally. Hanuvar let that page roll in upon itself and held it in his fist, a tight grip that did not crush it. Soon, he would burn it, but he took a moment to appreciate the great risks that had been taken upon his behalf, and to be thankful so honorable a man was his friend.

The rest of the papers consisted of Ciprion's promised information, cramped lists of tiny writing that he did not yet scrutinize in detail. For to do so would be not only to learn the names of those who lived, but by extrapolation the names of many more who had died. It was an irrational thought, but he could not help feeling that to read the parchment beside him was to seal the dooms of tens of thousands.

A philosopher would tell him he erred in making himself central to his understanding of the world. Hanuvar would have responded that he was aware of that, but that this was one of those rare moments where both knowing and not were painful. While some absent from these papers might yet live under the control of the government or in foreign hands, the odds were staggeringly high that any not contained herein were almost certainly dead.

Against his own wishes, both hands tightened, crushing Ciprion's letter. His pulse was a drum at his temples. Enemies and allies alike had called him calm, but he could feel rage, and it swept unchecked through him. His hands shook, his teeth bared. His neck muscles stood in relief as he silently screamed for the dead strewn beyond the borders of the papers beside him.

Silently he had screamed, and silently he wept. Had he been granted divine powers at that moment he would have crumbled the walls of Derva, thrown lightning against its temples, and sent fire coursing down its streets. Women, children, the elderly, slaves, servants, foreigners . . . he would not have cared, not at that moment. He would have jeered to see flames engulf the city.

Even the best of men know pain, and hate, and perhaps no other man had greater cause to dream such things, however briefly.[1]

He gave himself that moment of grief, then put Ciprion's letter aside, gently smoothing his hand across it as if in apology. After a moment to gather himself, he spread out the parchment papers he had crossed a continent to obtain.

---

[1] Those readers unfamiliar with the original edition of my ancestor's work will not recognize this passage, for he excised it in the multiple editions that followed. One wonders if this is because he invented the scene, because it is difficult to believe Hanuvar would share so personal a reaction with him, although it is not beyond the bounds of credulity. Certainly Hanuvar must have experienced something profound at this moment.

I have retained the scene both because I thought that the emotions seemed like something the man himself might have felt, and because of a fundamental truth it explores. While Hanuvar was not a deity, given all of the miracles he managed to accomplish through sheer willpower, fortitude, and his intellect, it is not at all impossible to imagine the kind of vengeance he might have delivered against Derva and its empire, had he wished to do so. The Dervans do not seem to realize how grateful they should be that he focused his energy upon the welfare of his people and not the terrible blood price the Dervans themselves assumed he planned to collect from them. That he did not act as they anticipated speaks to a strength of character that I cannot begin to pretend some other man might emulate. —Andronikos Sosilos

There they were, the names, slightly more than a thousand. Knowing that only one in two hundred people survived did not diminish his joy in discovering this because he had once been told less than a thousand had been dragged away in chains. Now he learned a few hundred more were alive, at least as of a half year ago.

If he had not already reflected upon the pain and indignities those people had suffered, he might have needed to pause for further reflection. But he squandered no more time and set to studying the list. As he had assumed, most of the survivors had not been soldiers, and almost all were old or young, but here they were. Many had been sold in lots, which ought to make their reacquisition simpler.

Most surprising was just how many names he recognized. Here was a man who had tended the gardens at the Assembly Hall. There was a stablemaster he'd interacted with. He'd eaten the excellent cakes of a woman known as a champion baker.

Fourteen of those listed as ship builders had been sold to Lenereva T. Tannis. Scattered here and there were dozens more purchased by a Lenereva, I. Indar or Izivar?

Hanuvar had met both and could guess what must have happened. The ever-cautious Tannis Lenereva had purchased a few men who might be of service to his interests, thinking he could explain away any suspicion that the emperor or his cronies might have of a Volani buying others of his kind.

And Izivar had spent her own money buying more. One was listed as Serliva, occupation hand maid. Likely these others were related to people already working with the Lenereva family, or related to the slaves Tannis had bought; anyone whom Izivar could possibly justify purchasing. And judging from the maid's reaction when Izivar had spoken in defense of her father, Hanuvar deduced her own actions had drawn Tannis' ire. Otherwise Serliva would not have been so incensed that Izivar had given him credit for their freedom.

Hanuvar rolled the list of names tightly together and placed them once more in the waterproof cylinder. This he then slipped into his saddlebag, into which were sewn the gems that would be the first step toward buying the freedom of those names. He was far shy of the capital to do so for all.

That one of the carefully politic Lenereva had dared to buy up Volani surprised him upon multiple levels. Tannis and his father and uncle before him had stymied the efforts of Himli Cabera in the first war and Hanuvar himself in the second, always concerned the Cabera family meant to leverage its power as the Lenereva would have. Thus had they ensured few reinforcements ever reached Hanuvar, and that funds were sent to other fronts in the war. Only when all hope was lost at the conclusion of the second war had they cried out that the time had come to fight, under better management. Lenereva management.

Such an absurd declaration had won them near universal condemnation, but they had clawed their way back into popular regard, arguing always that Volanus should work harder to appease the Dervan Empire. And then Tannis and his faction had accused Hanuvar of conspiring with the enemies of Derva. Their actions, and their traitorous alliance with Catius and his political faction, had led to Hanuvar's own flight from Volanus.

What then to make of Izivar? He remembered her from previous years as a polite background figure at a handful of state functions. She had been married to a loud-mouthed demagogue at the time, one who'd eventually died after a prolonged illness. Hanuvar's brother Melgar had opined that the fellow had choked to death on his own bile.

Hanuvar's impression of her today had been more positive. She had been forthright, grateful, and intelligent. She had wished to keep her family issues private. Then there had been her egalitarian interactions with her maid, and the telling quality that Serliva seemed not only to like Izivar, but to wish to make clear to others she was different from her father.

Why was Izivar even here? Assuming she lived, how safe might it be to approach her? Just because she had demonstrated empathy to her own people did not mean she would dare greater risks, or side with a man her father had planned to turn over to the Dervans.

But if the Lenereva could be persuaded to assist, Hanuvar would gain immediate access to a small fleet of ships useful for moving his people north. Some of those vessels might even be ocean worthy. The Lenereva would have access to workmen, wealth, contacts, and uncounted other benefits.

He nodded slowly to himself. For the sake of their people, he would seek her again, and this time, he would risk speaking a portion of the truth.

II

Metellus didn't at all mind being separated from the centurion. He'd been instructed to run, but he instead requisitioned a horse from an irate merchant. Before long he'd pulled the praetorian physician from his wine imbibing and returned to the street outside the general store where the healer lived, accompanied by the doctor and a half dozen praetorian soldiers.

By then Adrumentum was in an uproar because the caravan had arrived and rumors flew about attacks of the bog folk.

Metellus found the entire situation amusing. He extracted Centurion Corvus from the middle of the street, where he was heatedly questioning the caravan master, and then Corvus lifted his heavy chin, told the doc and the soldiers to follow, and marched straight into the store.

Corvus immediately threw his weight around, as Metellus could have predicted. The Volani woman was alive and apparently going to survive, though it didn't win the healer any favors, for she and the physician immediately fell into a war over treatment methods.

In the end Izivar Lenereva was carried away upon a cot borne by four ordinary legionaries. Corvus wasn't about to sully the Praetorian Guard with any unnecessary manual labor.

Given that Enarius thought so highly of the woman, Metellus had been disappointed to find her rather ordinary looking, and older than he had assumed.

He was tasked with overseeing her return to the villa. For some reason, Corvus insisted he was still working to get the truth about what had really happened out in the marsh, and said he'd be along when he had it. Metellus was happy to remain apart from him.

Back at the villa Metellus let the phyician take care of the woman and report anything important to Enarius, because he really didn't care. He would have headed straight for the bath, except that the century's wiry adjutant was waiting for him and came to attention the moment Metellus wearily noted him "Am I about to hear bad news?" he asked.

"Sorry sir," the adjutant said.

"What's happened this time? Enarius fall down a well? The cook leave a toenail in the stew?"

"Senator Aminius is here. He wants a briefing from you or the centurion."

Metellus stared in surprise.

"He seems quite agitated, sir. He says he finds the security situation here appalling."

"Does he. Where may our illustrious senator be found?"

"He's waiting in the centurion's office."

Any other aristocrat would just be chumming with Enarius, but the emperor's heir and Aminius weren't especially close, the more so because Aminius thought Enarius a rival. Enarius was too stupid to notice.

"Naturally he would be," Metellus said. "Well, carry on. I'll go handle it."

"Yes, sir."

Metellus knew what Aminius really wanted, although his arrival astounded him on several levels. Someone as clever as Aminius thought himself should have stayed well clear of both assassins and their quarry. As the adjutant started away, Metellus asked a final question. "Did he happen to say why he was here in the first place? Surely he didn't ride all the way north from Derva to pester me about security issues."

The adjutant halted and faced him. "He said nothing to me, sir, but I've heard he was up here speculating on some property."

Aminius was well known to have sunk a vast amount of his personal fortune into real estate. The properties continued to reap benefits for him, but in Metellus' limited association with the senator it seemed clear none of the wealth brought him happiness. And that was strange, because if Metellus possessed a tenth the money Aminius was reputed to have locked away, he could make himself very happy indeed.

He found Aminius tilted in Corvus' low-backed office chair, feet on the desk. The senator held a scroll so the window light in the little room fell directly on the text. Judging from the label on the scroll case on the table beside him, it was one of the silly Herrenic adventure novels Enarius carried around with him.

Aminius glanced at him as Metellus closed the door, then

returned his attention to the scroll. The senator was a portly, light-skinned man of middle age with thick, curly hair. Gossip had it he was fanatical about wrestling, and his heavy upper arms and pectoral muscles suggested he had once been in fighting trim. Probably he thought he remained so.

"Enjoying the book?" Metellus asked.

"I keep waiting for the Hadiran girl to lose her dress. The stupid writer keeps implying something will happen. It never does." Aminius tossed the scroll on the desk.

"Is that a veiled reference to some other topic?"

"It's not veiled at all." Aminius returned the front legs of the chair to the ground. "Where's your centurion, Metellus?"

"Out learning about an ambush on a caravan."

"Is that really his lookout?"

Metellus snorted and took a chair across from the senator. "You could argue that any nearby security threat was reason to obtain information, except that you know he shouldn't really care. I think Corvus just likes to feel needed."

"And you?"

"I just like to feel money."

"It's funny you should mention that. I like to feel I'm getting results for my money. And I'm not. I hear you and Corvus have spent each afternoon for the last three days waiting for the Volani woman."

"Not my idea," Metellus said, more gruffly than he intended. That he had been dispatched to await Izivar's arrival for the last three days had rankled him as well, until he realized he could relax in the comfortable interior of the general store while doing so. He strove to sound more at ease. "Considering Enarius' ongoing fascination, I expected her to be a raving beauty."

"Either she's aged poorly or you're too young to appreciate her."

Metellus shrugged; he was uninterested in a discussion about beauty standards and wished Aminius would get to his obvious point.

He did so immediately. "I can't help noticing his illustriousness is still alive and sucking down berry juices with his slack-jawed friends."

"You asked us to be discreet."

"Yes, I did. I might also wait for old age to take him, which is incredibly discreet and decidedly less expensive. What are you waiting for?"

"Corvus believes that if our future careers are to be more secure, we need to cover our steps."

"Corvus believes. What do you believe about his steps?"

"I would have preferred a more direct approach, to be sure. Not this elaborate plan he's cooked up."

"Oh?"

Metellus did not permit the smile he felt building. "You sound as though you wish to hear it. At our previous meeting you made clear you did not."

"That was before I began to wonder whether I'd spent my money wisely."

"I wonder if timing might be an issue as well. Rumor has it the emperor may soon formally adopt Enarius as his very own son. I seem to recall some rumors a few years ago that he was going to do the same with you."

The senator's face slid easily into hard lines. "I'm not sure why you're trying to pull my chain, boy. When this dog comes out of the kennel, he's ready to kill."

"You misunderstand me, Senator. I just mean to say that when things need to be done more quickly, you should come to me."

"I'll keep that in mind. Are you offering to do things more quickly now? For a higher fee, say?"

He ignored the senator's obvious attempt to test him. "No, I think we should let Corvus' plan play out. It should take place tonight, during Enarius' berry feast. The events early today will actually make his sudden death that much more plausible."

"Now you absolutely must tell me what's planned."

Metellus shrugged, as if the matter was of little consequence. "According to the sages, the best time to pick the bog berries is under the full moon, and if you mean to drink their juices, the best time is within an hour or two of when they're gathered."

"They only grow in the bogs, though. Even I know that much."

"Which is why Enarius' slaves have located a nice raised campsite about half hour's walk into the marshes beyond the villa. They're erecting tents as we speak, for an overnight stay. There will be lanterns and guards—praetorians, mind you—to keep out the terrible bog folk."

"Who apparently attacked Izivar Lenereva."

"Yes. One did. What will happen tonight is about a dozen of them will erupt out of the dark, right after Enarius and his friends have drunk deep. They'll actually be some of our men, dressed to look like the bog people. The slaves will scatter in fear, a few praetorians who've always been useless troublemakers will get killed in the defense . . ." He decided not to say what Enarius' final fate would be, but to imply it. ". . . and your problem will get solved."

"I suppose that could work," Aminius said grudgingly. "It is complicated. And you had to pay these men to let them into the plan."

Metellus conceded that by turning up his hand. "It's not my plan."

"I'm beginning to think Corvus isn't entirely clever."

"I would have assumed you'd noticed that before now."

"Well, one works with what one has. If I'd known you better to start with, I might not even have bothered with him in the first place."

That was nice to hear, but wasn't worth responding to.

"So here's a proposition," the senator said. "How would you like a bonus?"

"Go on."

"In the midst of things, make sure Corvus dies in the defense of the emperor's nephew. It will make his widow proud. Probably the emperor will give her some compensation."

"It's so courteous of you to keep her in your thoughts," Metellus said with feigned sympathy.

"Do we have a deal?"

"You haven't mentioned amounts." Metellus had planned on ensuring Corvus' death in any case.

"Five hundred sesterces."

Not an astronomical figure, but hardly a small one. Metellus decided against haggling. "Consider it done."

"The primary goal is achieving the first matter."

"Believe me, I understand. I'm even looking forward to it."

III

Izivar wasn't sure where she was when she woke, but she heard the chirrup of crickets and smelled incense. As she blinked she discovered she lay in a brown canvas tent lit by a bright lantern with glazed glass, so that the golden light was warm rather than glaring. She had no idea of the time, but something in the atmosphere suggested late evening.

As she groggily propped herself up on her left arm, her brother Indar said her name and then knelt at her side, his face uncharacteristically open in relief. A hint of boyish charm still touched his features, but his eyes were tired and careworn, as though five or ten years had passed rather than one since she'd been in his presence. Even his hair was poorly tended and a little wild, though he had not abandoned his sense of style, for he wore an exquisitely cut amber shaded tunic, and his hand glittered with rings.

Serliva drew up behind him with a cup.

"Where am I?" Izivar asked. Her voice was husky with fatigue.

"You don't remember?" Indar sounded concerned.

If she'd remembered she wouldn't have asked. She shook her head, no.

"You were conscious a few hours ago and we talked. Don't you recall?"

"I don't remember anything after . . . my goodness." She looked down at her injured side, but was unable to view it because she wore a long white under tunic. Serliva instructed her not to sit up but she ignored her and did so, fighting a wave of dizziness, then hiked up the side of the shift to inspect her injury. The thin scratch was faded to a dull brown and covered with a sticky yellow substance that bore a faint citrus scent when she brought it to her nose.

Serliva swiftly filled her in, telling her how Flavius had galloped so swiftly she hadn't been able to keep up, how there'd nearly been a fight at the gate when the Dervans hadn't wanted Flavius to come past, and how she and Flavius had to demand help from the healer at the trading post. After that, Izivar had been given a poultice and a drink and then the healer had argued with a praetorian physician about how to treat her condition. Serliva would have breathlessly continued to supply details in this manner if Izivar hadn't raised a hand to stop her.

"It seems I owe you and the healer my thanks, as well as quick-acting young Flavius. Where is he?"

Indar answered. "I sent a messenger to him, once we were certain you would be alright, and Enarius himself wants to thank him. Flavius sent word that he had to collect his pay from the caravan, but that he might come this evening. The messenger said he didn't look very excited about the prospect. Seemed to think he's embarrassed. Serliva said he didn't seem very prosperous, so I sent a slave to him with some money for a bath and clothing."

"Indar!" Izivar exclaimed. "That probably just embarrassed him further."

"It's the Dervan thing to do," Indar countered, as though Dervan conduct was the standard to emulate. He lifted a red glazed goblet to his lips and sipped delicately.

"What time is it, and where am I?"

"It's nearly sundown," he answered. "And you're in a camp outside Enarius' villa."

"A camp? Where?"

"We're out in the marshes."

"In the marshes? Don't you know I was just attacked by one of the bog people?"

Indar waved her concern away. "We're surrounded by an army of praetorians and slaves. You'll be safe."

There was rarely any way to get through to her brother, but such blind dismissal infuriated her. She couldn't help checking with Serliva. Out of sight behind Indar, she rolled her eyes.

Izivar stretched out a hand for him and he took it. She squeezed his fingers and spoke softly, determined to forge a connection with him. "Indar, what are you doing here? Father needs you to come home."

"Father wants to tell me how much I need to pay attention to him, and now you want me to do the same."

She sought his eyes. "He's getting old and needs to get his affairs in order."

"His affairs are in order, if he hands them off to you." He released her fingers and drank.

"He may not have much longer."

"He's been pretending that for at least ten years. I'll believe it when he's buried."

"Indar, I think it's true this time. I've been north to consult the Molitan oracle, and his time draws close. The family needs to come together."

Indar looked down into his shiny red goblet as if he expected to find answers there. Apparently he wanted to share them. "Here." He extended it toward her.

She started to say that she wasn't thirsty, but a heavenly sweet scent reached her.

"It will strengthen you," Indar promised. "Enarius' healer puts great stock in it. And it's better than Fadurian wine."

She licked her dry lips and took it, wondering why Serliva was shooting her brother a dark look. "Is it watered?"

He laughed. "It's juice, not wine."

She sipped, and it was delicious, sweet with a hint of blueberry tartness but possessing a delicious full-bodied flavor. It seemed to cut right to her core and set her glowing, as though she imbibed the purest moonlight. She drank deeply.

Indar chuckled good-naturedly. "Careful, sister." He gently eased the goblet from her grasp. "You don't want to down too much of the bog berry juice all at once."

"Nelgart and Tasarte!" She swore by the names of both gods to call attention to his folly. "You handed me the bog berry juice?"

Either the criticism in her tone swept right past him, or he was too well practiced at ignoring it. "Now do you see why we're here? Isn't the taste amazing? It's best at exactly this time of year, when the moon's high, at night, and consumed shortly after picking. You probably shouldn't have drunk so much though," he added.

Serliva could no longer contain herself. "You should have warned her," she said caustically, then, while he gaped at her daring, she turned to Izivar. "Or I should have stopped him. Are you alright, milady? I thought you knew what he was doing."

She hadn't been thinking as clearly as she thought, or she'd have been more suspicious. She glared at her brother, her outrage confused by a dizzying ebullience that swept out from her belly to crown and sole. "I feel . . . strange," she murmured.

"Are you seeing the city yet?" Indar asked excitedly. "The city with the golden walkways?"

She wanted to shout at him, but couldn't find her voice. It was so typical of him to slyly trick her into something she'd not normally have done. She tried to look at him so she could speak her mind, but he and the tent were a mere shadow across a high walled city of gleaming white stone, its sidewalks ornamented with shining golden pavers. Slim conical buildings swathed in spiraling glyphs towered above a circular forum. A smiling crowd of tanned men and women with blond hair were gathered, dressed in bright garments thin as gauze that did less to cover them than the decorative baubles hung about their necks and waists. Most held red clay cups. Others queued up to receive them from red robed priests and priestesses.

One of the young women smiled at her, took her hands, and led her into a dance. She laughed with joy even as she fought her growing fear.

She waved her hands and the city shifted places with the tent, so that it was the superimposed image. The change dizzied her, and she grasped the side of the cot to keep from plunging from it.

Her brother was oblivious to her distress. "It's fantastic, isn't it?" His smile was briefly less clear than that of a pretty young woman whose face was painted with small jagged triangles. "The joy you feel?"

He was almost right, but as usual, Indar failed to look with any depth. Even though the crowd was jubilant, fear lurked in their eyes. It was as though they hoped to blind themselves with the cups of sloshing juice being handed out. A robed man presented himself to her, pushing the drink into her hands. "We shall join with the earth," he promised.

"Get away," she said, speaking both to Indar and the stranger.

"They won't hurt you," Indar assured her. "They're not real. Not anymore. But their memories are, and their last memory is of that grand festival. They were going to be invaded or something, and instead of fighting they went out in one last extravaganza!"[2]

She strained to see him clearly. "I mean you!" Still clutching the mattress with one hand she shoved at him with the other. "Get out! Get away!"

Serliva steadied her and lay a hand to one shoulder. With that close contact the strange people and their city faded to a faint haze.

---

[2] Antires does not name the culture, but they are referred to by the locals as Danari, a nation of small city-states that flourished in the centuries immediately prior to the foundation of Derva itself. Their ruined fortresses are still to be seen in north and central Tyvol. Local tradition claims that their fascination with otherworldly matters brought their doom, although the Isubre tribe of the Ceori boast that work was theirs. —*Silenus, Commentaries*

Her idiot brother goggled at her. She pointed to the tent entrance, through which light spilled where the canvas gapped. "Out!"

The shout required nearly all the energy she had left, and she gasped.

Indar retreated, sulking. "You're always like this," he said. "You never want to try anything new. No wonder you look so old and dried up." With that he turned and pushed from the tent.

She sat trembling, furious and emotionally spent. The men and women danced all about her.

"You don't look old and dried up." Serliva squeezed her shoulder. "Just tired. He's terrible."

That close contact again reduced the images to phantoms superimposed across the real world.

Izivar worried that she did look rather aged, no matter Serliva's reassuring words. She nodded late agreement that Indar was capable of being terrible. Though grown, he remained a petulant child, spoiled by a mother doting on her only son.

"You should lie down," Serliva suggested, but Izivar shook her head, no. If she lay down again, she'd see nothing but that imaginary city and its frightened people.

"Food," she said.

There happened to be food in abundance, though she noted no details beyond them being pastries and hardboiled eggs and various fish dishes. All her attention was centered on chewing and anchoring herself in the here and now. She hoped that the food would soak up the berry juice the way it absorbed wine. She insisted on drinking only water, despite Serliva questioning her choice three times. The last thing she wanted was to have the wine distorting her perceptions as well.

The younger woman tended her, apologizing again and again for not interceding, then drifting into grievances about Indar, and how he didn't deserve Izivar's attention. It had been a long detour here after their visit with the oracle in the northwest. Serliva asked why Izivar hadn't told Indar more specifically what the oracle had said about their father's health.

"Because he wasn't listening, and it wouldn't have mattered," Izivar replied weakly.

Finally, after what seemed like an entire pitcher full of water, the visions ebbed until they were less than mist across her eyes. The noise they made was the buzz of a fly in a distant room. She thought she might still see them if she closed her eyes, or if the tent got dark, so she resolved to remain awake and in well-lit places.

It was then that Enarius entered.

Well-groomed, his slim body was draped in an ankle-length off-white tunic with curling red edging. She hadn't seen him in almost a year, but he remained essentially unchanged; boyishly handsome, with wavy hair that always ended up slightly mussed, even after attention from his slaves. His eyes were a bright blue, and his smile, though full lipped, was open and friendly. Her father had described it as a winning smile, and while Tannis Lenereva was given to hyperbole, it was an apt assessment.

Seeing him, she couldn't help smiling in turn, for she was genuinely fond of the young man. Then she remembered she wore only a light shift. She saw him note that and keep his eyes solely upon her face, emulating the conduct of a gentleman.

Izivar pushed her hair back from her face and drew up the blanket to cover herself. She expected she looked haggard, which might be a good thing in this instance, for it would emphasize the fifteen years between them.

Enarius bade her welcome and nodded politely to Serliva as well. He was famously pleasant to slave, freedman, and senator alike.

"Indar told me you were awake and annoyed with him," Enarius said as he came forward. "Then he told me he had you drink some of the juices. I nearly threw him into the bogs. Are you alright?"

"I'm tired. And please don't throw him in. I may push him myself later, though," she added.

Enarius chuckled. "And you've recovered from the infection?"

"I have. Enarius, the bogs are dangerous. Why are we here?"

He lifted his hands in a helpless gesture, as though he, one of the most powerful men in the world, were powerless to affect change in their circumstance. "I've been promising your brother and our friends this for weeks. I couldn't very well let them down. Not when tonight's the night of the full moon, when the berries are at their sweetest. After this, we can leave."

"And you couldn't tell them no? All this for that drink?"

Serliva had looked flustered at first, apparently waiting for a signal from her mistress to send Enarius away, and finally decided she would simply make Izivar's guest comfortable. She vacated the stool she'd been occupying and presented it to him, though she shifted it two feet further out.

Enarius thanked her with a nod and took it before answering Izivar. "It seemed like a fine idea at first. Do you know, I arranged the whole expedition for your brother? He hasn't been himself since he came back from the Isles of the Dead."

"He hasn't been himself since the war."

"I know that was a challenging time for your entire family. More challenging, I'm sure, than I can possibly imagine."

That was an understatement, but like so much of what Enarius said, she listened to his meaning rather than any unintended implications. He was young. "We will forever be grateful to you for your help in shielding us."

His smile was warm. "You have been such fine friends to me that it was the least I could do. Especially since your family has never tried to use me for their own ends."

This statement was so outrageous she couldn't keep from laughing.

"Oh, I know your father's transparent. I mean you and your brother. Indar couldn't really care who I was, just that I like boxing as much as he does. And you—you were downright cool to me for the longest while."

"I didn't know how kind you truly were."

"Uncle says I'm too kind, and it makes me weak. And maybe he's right."

Izivar wasn't about to tell him she agreed with the emperor. It seemed to her a little kindness in the emperor's likely successor was just what the Dervan empire needed.

He continued: "One thing led to another, and suddenly I find myself out here under the moonlight watching my friends get drunk on the memories of a forgotten people."

"Who were they?" she asked. "And how does drinking the berries gives us their memories?"

"One of the locals—claims he's not a druid, of course,—says that in ancient days there was a city here, and that some Ceori were sweeping through nearby settlements and putting them to the torch. The people of the city decided that rather than fighting they would join their lives with that of the wilds around them and live on forever. It didn't quite work how they intended."

"Is that why the bog people are here?" Izivar asked.

"Apparently. But then the people around here also tell you to stay clear of the berries, and that's where the most potent memories are stored."

He said the last with such undisguised relish it surprised her. "Why aren't you drinking?"

"It didn't feel right. Not when I couldn't be sure about you."

She was touched by his regard. "It didn't bother my brother."

"Your brother isn't himself."

"Or maybe he's more himself than ever. He wants to lose his identity. Just like the people who drank the berries." It wasn't until she said this that she felt the essential truth of her words.

"He wasn't always like this," Enarius said, sadly. "Ever since he met Hanuvar, or Hanuvar's ghost, he's been frightened of his own shadow."

"He's been frightened of Father's shadow long before that," she reminded him. "He's been trying to live up to him, or running from what he thought our father wanted, for most of his life."

"Those are harsh words. You're always direct, but I've never heard you so blunt."

"I nearly died on the way to see my brother. And then he drugged me."

"In his defense, I think he was trying to help, since it's what he uses to dull his own pain."

"You're right," she admitted. "But then I'm right too."

Enarius' sorrow touched his eyes, now. "That may be so."

"Why do you want to drink, Enarius? You're stronger than that. You don't need to lose yourself."

"You always see more strength in me than I really have."

"The strength is real," she assured him, hoping she was right.

As if suddenly growing aware of her company, Enarius glanced at Serliva. "Would you excuse us a moment, my dear?"

Serliva bowed her head formally, but her look was searching. "Shouldn't you let milady get fully dressed, your highness? You could continue this conversation after."

Enarius' brow furrowed, but then he looked to Izivar, hidden under a blanket, and his cheeks flushed. He bowed his head to Serliva. "You're quite right." He turned back to Izivar. "I'm sorry, Izivar. This was terribly rude of me."

"No, no." She raised a calming hand. "Nursing me to health and keeping me in luxurious surroundings? That's not at all rude. You're the soul of kindness, Enarius."

"There's that word again."

"You should embrace it. A ruler can be kind, can't he?"

He sighed in pretend annoyance, then promised to have a slave arrive with more refreshments, thanking Serliva again on the way out for reminding him of his manners.

He called for a slave the moment after the tent flap fell behind him.

Serliva advanced, speaking softly in Volani. "I honestly don't see why you don't let him court you. He's obviously in love with you."

"Because of so many reasons, as you should know."

"Do you mean your age? You can hold onto your beauty if you take certain measures. Stay out of the sun, exercise well and watch your diet."

"I will not change my life for him," she said with quiet resolve. "More importantly, romance between us would jeopardize our fragile relationship with the Dervans." She pushed herself to her feet, delighted to be steady upon them. "Is there anything for me to wear?"

"I've a selection of stolas," Serliva said, though from where they had come Izivar could not guess. Probably Enarius had planned to gift them to her.

Serliva opened a chest near the refreshment table and lifted one in each hand. "I think you're wrong. If you marry him, then our people will be secure."

She wasn't thinking clearly. "No, the emperor will see us as a threat. There's no political advantage to the empire for an alliance with the family of a . . . defeated city state." She forced the thought of Volanus from her mind. "The blue one, I think. I need to clean up first, however."

Shortly, Izivar had washed up and a slave arrived with main courses that smelled delicious, though Izivar's appetite had ebbed. Serliva fitted her into the stola and was combing through her hair, still talking, unable to see how dangerous the emperor would be if he discovered even a hint of a relationship between his nephew and Izivar.

"There's also the matter of Enarius growing tired of me," Izivar said.

"Tired of you? He hangs upon your every word."

"I would be like his mother. Constantly objecting to the things he wants to do. He uses me as his conscience, knowing I am right but ignoring me a good deal of the time. He means well, but he still has bad ideas. Like this one of taking people into the marshes to be drunk on these juices. He will mature eventually, but it could take years."

"You can guide him."

"I've done that once already and frankly I don't feel like doing it again."

Serliva sighed in frustration.

From outside the tent came a clear, confident voice. "Milady Izivar, the master says to inform you that your guest has arrived."

Weary and startled out of the line of conversation, Izivar was momentarily confused. Then she realized who the herald must mean. "Do you mean Flavius?"

"Yes," the herald answered. "That is the young man's name. Master Enarius wonders if you wish to greet him in the main tent with the others, but says that if you are feeling weak you might wish to greet him in your own tent instead, assuming that you are properly prepared to receive him."

"The main tent," Serliva whispered to Izivar in Volani. "Your hair is almost finished and you look lovely."

"Please have him brought here," Izivar said, and received another of Serliva's exasperated eye rolls.

The herald said that he would and departed. Izivar then asked for her sandals and discovered some clever slave had not only cleaned them but repaired the heel of the left one. She sat on the couch edge while Serliva fussed with Izivar's hair, pushing it upright, and then the herald's voice resumed: "Lady Izivar, I have arrived with the young man. Are you prepared to receive him?"

"I am," she answered, suddenly conscious she wasn't at all sure what she meant to say, except her thanks.

Even as the tent flap lifted Serliva continued to arrange her hair, only stepping to one side and concealing the brush behind her when Flavius ducked his head to pass through.

He looked different than Izivar recalled. In her mind he had been older. He was so pink cheeked and young he made Enarius look like a veteran, which obscurely disappointed her. He was more muscular than typical for his age, as though he had filled out early, without being weighed down with a layer of fat like a professional boxer or gladiator. He'd had a fresh trim of hair and was clean shaven with a sharp razor. He wore a white tunic so new it practically gleamed. He looked every inch the Dervan citizen so that any illusion he was some lost Volani seemed to have faded with the sinking sun. Izivar realized that must have been some strange wishful thinking on her part—although, to be honest, there was still something of Melgar Cabera in the hooked nose and jawline.

"Milady." Flavius bowed his head, then inclined it to Serliva as well. "Thank you for having me. I . . . should have come sooner, I guess. I just . . . I'm not used to being around such fine people." He had trouble meeting her eyes.

"Clothes do not make the man," Izivar reassured him. "I've met many a rich man who would not have dared what you did for me twice this day. I am in your debt."

"Clothes might well make the lady," Serliva said quietly in Volani.

Izivar ignored her. "Anything in my power to grant, I will. I can promise you a position on my brother Indar's staff, or my own, or even in the household of Enarius himself, I should think. You've saved my life, and I mean to help you with yours."

He shifted nervously.

Izivar gestured to the stool formerly occupied by Enarius. "Please, Flavius. Have a seat."

He did so, still looking utterly ill at ease as he placed his hands awkwardly on his knees. "I couldn't leave a lady to die," he explained.

There was nothing studied in his nature. He was honest and bold and forthright and she found herself wishing she'd known a man like him when she was younger.

"Would you care for some refreshments? Enarius had some brought for me but I'm afraid my appetite hasn't fully recovered."

"Not after you gorged yourself," Serliva said quietly in Volani.

Izivar shot her a warning look.

Flavius ignored their interplay. "You are most gracious, milady. As to that boon, I wonder if I might have a few moments for a private word."

Serliva tensed. Flavius addressed her. "I hope you know I can mean no harm to her ladyship. But this is a private matter, and I'd really prefer no one else to hear."

Under any other circumstance, with any other stranger, Izivar would not have entertained the request. But Flavius had saved her life twice, and he was in the midst of an armed camp where a single shout from her would bring armed guards running.

"It's fine, Serliva," she said. "You may go."

"Milady?" Serliva asked.

"I'll call for you if I need you." She then said, in Volani, "Give the man some space, if he feels it's that important."

"You really don't want me to listen in?" she asked, also in Volani.

"We owe him that, don't we? I think we can trust him with my life."

"What will Enarius say?"

"I don't know. Please, give us a few moments. I'll call you when I need you."

Serliva frowned. Earlier she had half-seriously joked about Flavius as a romantic partner, but being worthy of unguarded time with Serliva's mistress apparently merited a more careful accounting. Izivar was both amused and touched by her friend's devotion. Serliva gave Flavius a warning look, then departed.

He watched the tent flap swing to, then listened for the sound of Serliva's retreating footsteps. When they had subsided and all they could hear was the muted sound of drunken singing, he gave Izivar his full attention.

"How can I help you, Flavius?" she asked.

Any hint of his anxiety had vanished utterly, supplanted by a startling intensity in manner. "I need to know how serious you are about helping the Volani people."

"I'm not sure what you mean," she demurred. She watched closely, cautious of the change in him and suddenly alarmed at the thought this young man might be a revenant spy.

"You're about to hold my life in your hands. A word of what I'm going to say will doom not only me, but a thousand Volani."

"I have no idea what you might be referring to."

He shifted so smoothly into fluent, accentless Volani that for a moment she didn't fully register his words. "I have traveled a long way to help our people and did not think I would find an ally when I arrived. And yet you've devoted a good sum of your personal fortune to rescuing them yourself."

"Who are you?" she asked softly. "How do you know that, and what are you really doing here?"

"Who I am doesn't matter. I've already told you why I'm here. I need aid to help the rest of our people."

"You are one of the Caberas, aren't you? You look a little like Melgar. But I didn't think there were any young men in his immediate family... are you a cousin?"

The question seemed to exasperate him. "That's not what I'd like to focus on at the moment," he repeated.

The presence of an unknown Volani was strangely invigorating. "But how did you get away? Were you already out of the city? Are you an escaped slave?"

"I was there when it fell." The young man spoke with such grim sobriety there was no questioning the truth of the statement. "As for how I got away, you would not believe me, and that too is beside the point. Can I rely upon you to help what little remains of Volanus?"

"Yes. But how? We can do nothing overt. My father was furious I had dared to purchase so many."

"Because he feared it would anger the Dervans, who are already suspicious of us."

She nodded, then thought of those same suspicions. "Please tell me you mean nothing rash. That you aren't going to try to raise a rebellion or something crazy like that."

He shook his head, no.

"Who sent you? One of the Caberas survived, didn't they? What are you planning to do?"

"Now isn't the time or place for specifics. But I would like to call upon you later. Where are you based?"

"All over, really," she said, then realized how foolish that sounded. "You can find me in Ostra hence forth." Particularly since it seemed more and more certain she would have to manage the Lenereva holdings without her brother's aid as her father sickened. She scanned him more closely. "Did you know Indar and I would be here? Was this all some elaborate ploy to meet me?"

"No, milady, that was a stroke of luck. I was merely travelling south. After so many bad turns, it seems as though I've had a small run of good ones."

His manner was that of a much more mature man.

"How old are you?"

"Nineteen."

She found that even more startling than his seriousness. "You look a few years older."

"Do I?" He looked genuinely surprised.

"I wish you would tell me more about what you're planning. No one's listening."

He permitted a brief, sad smile. "And I wish that I could say more. But my being here is already a terrible risk."

She realized then that it was. Surely the citizen's ring upon his hand was a counterfeit, and that alone was punishable by death. And if he were some lost member of the Cabera family, any Dervan military leader would be thrilled to capture him for a spy and parade him through the streets. She understood just how much this young man had trusted her, and why he remained so cautious.

"I will always aid Volanus," she vowed, "but not if I must risk the safety of the people I have already freed in sake of some foolish plan. And," she added, "you may find this strange, but I am beholden to Enarius for safety. I will not countenance harm coming to him. Or his family," she added, hating herself for saying it, for the emperor had permitted the virtual elimination of her people.

"What we plan will not be heedless," the young man said. "And will not deliberately target any Dervans. I have friends among them myself. But in the end, there may be risks for all of us."

"I will have to hear more."

"I will share more, when we talk again."

"What shall I call you?"

"Flavius."

Almost, she asked him what his Volani name was, but knew if he'd wished to share it, he would have done so. "I will call you Flavius, then. And someday you can share your true name."

Flavius looked oddly reluctant about that idea. "Perhaps."

IV

Metellus would never have proposed the plan, but now, as the pieces were in play and he was fortuitously set to profit doubly from his part, he was pleased enough to be humming as he walked into the night toward the sentries.

The moon hung high and full, a pale mottled disc shadowed in dark blue. Hazy clouds drifted across its face, just as the fog rolled across the moors. If he were a bog man, he supposed he would have thought it a fine day for seeking vengeance, or whatever it was the bog folk were said to do when people came after their forbidden fruit.

So far Enarius hadn't yet surrendered himself to the berries, though the patrician's main guests had done so. Metellus supposed that was the important thing. If any of them happened to survive they would tell everyone about the bog people. Metellus had decided he'd have to save some of them or he'd end up looking completely ineffective and so had made careful note of which were wealthiest.

He advanced along the camp's western perimeter and came to the first pair of sentries, posted at the edge of the upland. He sent them on their way, claiming that he'd heard something to the north and wanted them on hand if anything should break through. He headed further south on the camp's west border, sharing the same alert as he ordered another pair of guards away, and finally reached a lantern burning on a pole at the corner of the south and west perimeter. He expected to find two more men posted there and was startled to discover three. One was Corvus, who would have been distinctive in the spread of his shoulders even without the centurion's transverse horsehair crest on his helmet. The officer turned, and Metellus came to attention. The other two praetorians smote their breastplates in salute. He answered with his own at the same time as Corvus. The centurion stood spear-straight, left hand behind his back.

"Ah, Metellus," Corvus said, as though he hadn't expected him to be on rounds. The centurion apparently was set on continuing the charade even though they were well beyond the tents, slaves, and aristocrats. "I was just pointing these men over to the north, where I thought I'd seen something questionable and wanted them to look."

"Yes," Metellus said, agreeing with exaggerated concern. "I had noticed the same thing. You two run along – the centurian and I will keep an eye out here."

The men gave them a funny look, then trudged off.

Corvus slipped both hands behind his back once more and planted his feet steadily. "Things seem to be going nicely. The men are playing along."

"Yes," Metellus agreed. He hated pointless conversations. "I thought I was to handle things along this perimeter and you were going to handle the pair of men to the south."

"Oh, I did. I just thought we should talk before things got messy."

Corvus certainly liked to talk. That was fine; having him out here alone would make the delivery of his final moment much simpler.

"The lads should be here soon," Corvus continued, and glanced off to the left, then stared. "What is that?" He even pointed.

Metellus automatically looked. He saw nothing but the mist below the hill, drifting just under the height of the broad-leafed bushes heavy with berries. Wondering what Corvus was on about, he turned back to him.

The centurion revealed his left hand at last, stuffed into a metal clawed glove swinging at Metellus' head.

Though he moved fast, Metellus couldn't entirely avoid the strike. The impact left a trail of searing pain along the side of his face. He cried out, one hand rising instinctively to the wound. Off balance from the blow, he misplaced his foot and sprawled backward.

Corvus came after, glove lifted. Metellus saw his own blood gleaming on three blades.

The centurion's meaty face was bared in a grimace. "Aminius promised a bonus," he said.

Metellus scrambled backward, thought it too hard to pull his sword at this angle, and fumbled with his knife.

Corvus stalked after, still talking. He always talked too much. "A sword would have been cleaner, but we've got to have you look like you were taken out by one of the creatures. Hold still, and I'll finish this fast."

As Corvus drew his hand back for another swipe, Metellus threw himself forward and buried his knife in the centurion's calf.

The heavier man squealed, then rocked back in pain. Metellus pushed to his feet, bloody knife ready. And then he spotted a figure behind Corvus. More than that, he *felt* it, for the thing exuded a clammy chill that lifted every hair along his arms and neck. His heart was already pounding from exertion and fear of death, but the presence of the being set it leaping faster still.

Corvus sensed it too and looked over his shoulder even as leathery hands closed around his throat. The centurion was hardly a small man, but he was dragged down with stunning ease. The gaunt man in rotting garments with empty black holes for eyes rode him to the earth, choking the life from him.

Another stalked up from the left, and a third limped out from the right, a long dead woman with scraggly gray hair. Her withered hands, time or sun or silt browned, twitched hungrily. He spotted a dim red glow in the back of her eye sockets.

He wished to see nothing more of her. Metellus whirled and fled back toward the tents. The bog things lurched after with inexorable determination, their emaciated hands thrust out before them. More climbed from the very region from which he had pulled sentries. Dozens and dozens of them. Skin damp and leathered. Eyes burning with dim red fire.

His face still flamed in agony, but his fear gave him speed. He shouted a call to stations and raced for the main tent of Enarius. Aminius had betrayed him? Well, he would betray Aminius, and see Enarius to safety. The little fool would be grateful. He tossed his knife away and pulled his sword.

A signalman had heard his shouts and sounded a horn; closer at hand a woman screamed, and he worried it was from the large tent. Slaves gazed in blank-eyed confusion at him as he ran up with his sword, hand pressed to his face, teeth gritted against the pain. From somewhere nearby horses whinnied.

A praetorian who should have stood sentry before Enarius' tent lay face down in a pool of his own blood. Metellus pushed through the entrance to find three sword wielding figures advancing on what was left of the aristocrats. Lantern light revealed the bloody figures lying motionless upon the couches and carpeted floor.

One of the figures turned. Having seen the actual bog folk this imitation one was laughable—a muscular man in grubby clothes, his face painted darkly. Metellus didn't recognize the disguised praetorian, though he'd probably seen him in passing. He ran him through before hurrying to aid Enarius, backing from another assailant, knife out, shielded by a vacant-eyed Indar, crouched with his own knife. Metellus was honestly surprised to see the Volani putting up any resistance. He was nearly always drunk.

Indar's attacker drove his sword through his chest and raised the bladed glove on his other hand, probably to better disguise the attack, then turned as Metellus launched into him with a savage blow that hacked deep into his chest. Blood sprayed into Metellus' eyes as he swung the blade half through the man's face. The dying assassin spasmed as he fell sideways.

A third faux bog man looked up from where he was finishing one of the two brothers whose humor Enarius so valued; Metellus swung with such savagery he nearly took his head from his body. The assassin's grisly body slipped across the corpse of the man he'd just slain.

Only then did Metellus turn back to the emperor's nephew, kneeling at the Volani's side.

"Enarius," Metellus said, "we have to go." It hurt to speak.

Tears streaked Enarius' face. He fruitlessly strove to staunch Indar's wound with the Volani's bunched up tunic. The dying man still breathed and his eyes blinked, but he lay white and pale and stinking.

"He's done for," Metellus said. "And we've got to get you out."

Indar said much the same thing, but so quietly it was hard for Metellus to understand. The Volani whispered something about his sister.

"I'll make sure she's safe," Enarius pledged, adding, "You may depend upon it."

Enarius clutched the dying fool's hand, even as Metellus grabbed his shoulder. "Come! Hurry!"

"He's dead," Enarius said softly, and slowly lay the hand aside.

"So will we be. Hurry, man!"

Only then did the emperor's nephew take a closer look at Metellus. His eyes widened in horror and Metellus wondered just how bad his wound really was.

"What happened to you?"

What he wanted to say was that Aminius was behind it all, but extricating himself from the entire story would be complicated, so he kept it simpler. "Corvus was a traitor. He tried to kill me. And it's worse. It's not just assassins. It's real bog folk, too. We've got to get out of here."

More screams filled the air, both of men and women, and he pushed Enarius forward even as the idiot demanded details. There was no time. It might be too late already. But Enarius was adamant on one thing—they had to see to Indar's sister. Her tent happened to be up one lane and a little to the left. They stopped in, only to find it empty, apart from another dead assassin lying on his side. Looking right, Metellus spotted a trio of figures lurching stiffly at the end of another lane of tents, and he pulled the emperor's nephew toward the whinny of frightened horses.

V

When the cries began Hanuvar stepped immediately to the tent exit, just in time to intercept a man painted in brown mud, wearing rags. The disguise would have been amusing save that his bared short sword was sheathed in blood. He came in with blade leading, a glove with clawlike blades pressed tight to his side. Hanuvar slammed the sword aside with a pitcher, then repeatedly plunged his knife into the man's torso. The attacker folded at the knees and dropped sideways, and Hanuvar stepped close, waiting only a moment to ensure the man was dead before taking possession of his sword. He switched his knife to his off hand.

He called Izivar to him and she came, swiftly. He liked that she didn't ask stupid questions, and he liked better that she knelt to take the attacker's knife from his belt.

The canvas was thrust violently open and Hanuvar looked up, sword ready. But it was Serliva, eyes wide and white. "Izivar!" she cried. Her eyes flicked uncertainly to him.

"He stopped the assassin," Izivar explained.

"Assassin?" the maid repeated, then looked down at the body. "There are bog people out here! A lot of them!"

At the same moment a male scream of pain and fear rang through the night.

"We've got to help my brother," Izivar said. "He's with Enarius."

"Then he's with the biggest target," Hanuvar said. "And must stand or fall with the praetorians."

"He's my brother," she repeated.

"I understand. But he would want you safe and clear."

Her voice rose sharply. "And what about what I want?"

"Do you want to throw your life away?"

Scowling, she pushed past him and started the wrong direction.

Serliva, looking both confused and alarmed, went after. Cursing silently, Hanuvar followed, only to hear screams, male and female, and even some from horses. A trumpeter sounded a call to arms. In the shadows to their right a thing plodded on dark legs, its hands stretched out and fingers writhing, as though they longed to wrap about a throat. From deep in its eye sockets a red fire glowed. It turned their direction. Another pair of the things shuffled along from the left.

"The bog folk are here," Hanuvar said.

Serliva grabbed Izivar's arm, pleading. "We've got to go!"

He saw the anguish on Izivar's features and felt a tinge of regret. It was not so hard to imagine what it was like to fear for a sibling's life. After a moment's hesitation she relented and came with them.

They mingled with a band of fleeing slaves, then diverted toward the horse pen, where they discovered most of the mounts remained, milling in agitation. The slaves didn't stop, hurrying along the long, torchlit path stretching through the mist and on for the villa. There were gaps along that way, as though someone or something had toppled them.

Rather than forming up, a quartet of the praetorians were riding horses toward safety. Further downhill a band of the bog folk dragged screaming, helmetless soldiers into the mists.

A praetorian with wild eyes was even now leading Hanuvar's horse from the pen.

Hanuvar followed. "That's my horse."

The man turned, whipping his sword free. "Get back, boy!"

Hanuvar whistled. The horse reared and the soldier spun to pull it down. Hanuvar didn't have time to argue; he drove his sword deep beneath the Dervan's armpit. Beside him, Serliva screamed. The soldier sank to the ground, eyes glazing. Hanuvar took possession of his animal, making soothing sounds while the praetorian bled out. More slaves hurried past.

And then Enarius himself rounded a tent corner, a praetorian officer at his side. At first Hanuvar didn't recognize the optio, for the man's left cheek was a red and pink mess and his eyes were wild. The praetorian caught sight of Hanuvar, Izivar, Serliva, and the horse, and stalked forward. The bared sword in his hand dripped blood. "The animal is ours," he said hoarsely.

"It's for the women," Hanuvar countered.

Enarius cried out Izivar's name, gladly, then shouted at the optio. "Metellus! Stand down! There are more horses."

The praetorian growled, but halted. He glared at Hanuvar, then stalked toward the horse pen. Out in the marshes someone's plea for help ended in a gurgle.

"Where's Indar?" Izivar demanded.

At Enarius' look her expression fell. Enarius said only: "He died protecting me. A better friend I never had."

Izivar choked back a sob.

Hanuvar wiped his bloody knife in the grass, dropped the sword, and lifted Izivar bodily onto the horse even as Metellus hurried forward with two white mounts, bridled but saddleless. Enarius helped Serliva onto one of them as Hanuvar snatched an abandoned javelin and climbed up behind Izivar. The optio's horse snorted, catching scents it didn't care for, and it shifted restlessly. Hanuvar's own roan whinnied in answer, eyes rolling, ears shifting.

Two dozen bog folk came limping from between the staggered line of tents.

Enarius struggled into the saddle behind the maid, and Metellus shouted at him. "Hurry, you fool!" Teeth gritted, he assisted Enarius to a better seat on his nervous mount. Serliva maintained a tight grip on the reins as their horse pivoted to point away from approaching danger.

"What about you?" Enarius asked the praetorian.

But Metellus wasn't about to be left behind. He leapt onto the remaining animal, and soon all three horses were racing forward.

Hanuvar's gelding was better trained and more certain on the hill; he passed Metellus and the emperor's nephew.

When they reached the bog, the mist rolled along at his horse's knees. The trail of lanterns stretched ahead, a feeble ward against the darkness. Scattered groups of slaves and praetorians dashed along it for their lives. A thousand paces on one of the bog folk pulled a running slave into the water. Hanuvar tightened his grip on the javelin, the reins in his off hand, guiding mostly with his knees, and noted Izivar clasping the saddle's pommel with white hands. "Don't let go for anything," he said.

She sounded tired and resolute. "I won't." She looked back toward Enarius and her maid.

Hanuvar cantered the faithful animal forward, not wishing to push too fast over ground he couldn't see.

As with his journey to the camp, the footing was mostly firm, but there was no knowing if he might be urging the horse into a hole or some other hazard. It flagged, tired still from its strained run earlier in the day.

At the sound of muddy hoofbeats he turned to find Enarius and Serliva riding to his left, Metellus on his right. A lone bog man stood just beyond a lantern's light, twenty paces on, the dead thing's shadows thrown onto the mist rolling before it. Hanuvar scanned right and saw a trio moving through the darkness.

"They're trying to scare us off the path," he said. "Stay in the light!" And he bore forward, the javelin ready. Izivar clung to the saddle.

The bog man raised its leathery hands and let out a croaking cry. Hanuvar's mount shifted beneath him and he swore at it in Dervan, hand tight on the reins. He understood its balking, for he revolted at the thought of coming anywhere close to the dead thing. But he had trained the animal to trust him, and he had to hope it would as he kicked it to gallop. He readied his javelin and pressed Izivar, who obligingly bent close to the gelding's neck. As the dead man lurched into his path, he drove the point through one glowing eye and tore through its face and skull with a squelching sound, as though he'd punched through a rotten gourd. The impact knocked it spinning. The horse snorted in something that might have been relief, and then they were past. Serliva with Enarius and the optio followed close on his heels.

A band of slaves had advanced halfway down slope from the villa, lanterns in hand, helping their fellows up. A dozen wide-eyed praetorians brandished spears nearby. They moved toward Hanuvar and Izivar as if they meant to help, but he kicked his mount further up slope and stopped just at the villa doors. He cast down the javelin, then slid off and helped Izivar down.

"I've got to be moving," he said. He kept to Dervan, though longed to return to Volani.

"I should go with you." Izivar mimicked his language switch.

At that he shook his head. "I've drawn too much attention to myself already." He looked back to the edge of the hill. The others had dismounted. Serliva was looking uncertainly toward them, but remained beside Enarius, kneeling and shouting for a healer. The slumped form beside him must be the optio.

Izivar's dark eyes searched his own. "Who really sent you, Flavius?"

"Now's not the time. I'm sorry about your brother. We've lost so many already. If I could, I would bear you far from this land of horrors, but you must play your part, and I must play mine, and I will speak with you again in the coming months."

She seemed to understand. She nodded deeply, then offered her hand formally. "Thank you," she said.

He clasped her arm, felt the touch of her cool fingertips against his flesh, then nodded once to her and released his grasp. He climbed onto his horse and hurried away before Enarius thought to favor him in some way.

No one stopped him as he rode around the side of the building or out into the causeway or down the long lane back to the inn.

There he changed into one of the clean tunics he'd purchased, retrieved his saddlebag from the clerk, then walked his horse into the night. If he remained even to daybreak he might be found and honored, and he dared not chance that. He had taken too many risks already.

But he had found an ally, and his people had another benefactor with greater means to set his plans in motion. Most importantly of all, he knew where many of his people had been sent.

Soon, very soon, he would acquire their freedom.

※ ※ ※

So much would have been different if Metellus had perished of his wounds. But, thinking the praetorian was a loyal retainer who had risked his life to protect him, Enarius instructed his healers to work their every miracle. The praetorian recovered soon enough and was left forever after with three long scars. He was also promoted to centurion and received a posting as young Enarius' personal bodyguard.

It is said women swooned at the sight of him, seeing those wounds as a badge of honor, and Metellus himself put out the word that his men called him Bravescar, which is how he was known among the admiring aristocrats. The soldiers under his command were less impressed, and called him Clawface, though they were careful never to do so while he was there. By any name, he was a viper, and would rise to become a great threat to Hanuvar and everything he held dear.

But that lay in the future. During those days we had no more inkling of his danger than Enarius himself.

I labored in the north, overseeing the renovation and construction of warehouses, docks, workshops and even modest new homes on the land just south of the village we had purchased. Hanuvar, meanwhile, rode south and further south, though that first night he led his poor, tired horse only a few miles before taking shelter at a small road-side inn. Something Izivar had said continued to trouble him, for it had aligned with minor observations he himself had made. After personally seeing to the care of his horse, Hanuvar paid for a private bath, then studied both his reflection in the water, and in the long bronze mirror.

He carried a small mirror that he used for shaving, but it is difficult to gather an entire picture of a situation when you can perceive only a small portion of it, as demonstrated by that famous fable of the three blind men trying to describe an elephant.

What Hanuvar discovered was that Izivar was right. He did look like a young man in his early twenties. Only a few weeks before, he had resembled someone in his late teens. His shaving mirror had suggested a slight change, but Hanuvar had wondered if he were simply haggard from the road.

The magic, then, was less than the priest had believed. The youthful spell appeared to be fading.

When I saw Hanuvar again, the change was even more obvious. I asked him what he had been thinking at this moment, when he first realized his gift would not last. He had disliked his changed appearance from the start, so he was not so much disappointed as irritated about an additional complication. There was nothing he could do to alter his situation, of course, so he spent no time in lamentation. His only option was to move forward with his plans and hope that the aging would not accelerate too quickly.

After another week of travel, he arrived at last at the city of marble and blood, there to seek another ally.

—Sosilos, Book Seven

Chapter 3:
The Muse in Bronze

I

When Hanuvar arrived at the famed Laminian arch that morning in late autumn, it was not at the head of a triumphant column of troops, but alone on a horse, one among countless fellow travelers. Pilgrims walked along his left, their sandals, calves, and cloak edges stained with road dust. Behind him three horse-drawn wagons laden with grain sacks had stopped before a bored band of inspectors. Ahead of him eight slaves paused with the curtained litter they bore on massive shoulders while the aristocrat inside leaned out to speak with a centurion monitoring the traffic with his troops.

The legionaries waved Hanuvar under the arch and into Derva itself with barely a second glance. Middle-aged jewelry merchants on the horses behind him were eyed more warily, probably because the soldiers remained alert for a gray-haired bearded man of late middle years burning with the desire to conquer Derva, or perhaps just trample it a bit with some elephants.

Hanuvar no longer resembled that person, although he hadn't looked much older than he did now when he'd assumed command of the Volani army, long ago. He'd been bearded during those years, and now he was clean shaven. His dark hair, cut in conservative Dervan style, ran straight and partless across his forehead, rimmed his ears, and did not extend further than the nape of his neck.

His kit looked fully Dervan as well, from his simple ankle boots to his belted off-white tunic and brown winter cloak. He seemed the son of some middle-class merchant comfortable enough to afford a decent mount. A bundle of spear, helmet, and old corselet was tied across the horse's rump, between his weather-beaten saddlebags, but that was to be expected. Only a fool traveled the countryside without some protection, and many sturdy young men took occasional jobs as caravan guards or rich man's sentinels, for not everyone could afford to hire former gladiators and legionaries.

Blinking against a shaft of sunlight, he crossed at last beneath the arch and into a wide square with a central fountain surrounded by two- and three-story buildings casting long shadows. Taverns and bakeries and butchers occupied their first floors. He rode past them, taking in the sights like the tourist he appeared to be. Decades before he had looked upon the city from afar and studied its maps. To travel it in person, though, was another thing.

Cross streets intersected the avenue further down its crowded length. Three of the city's famed five hills rose in the distance, the largest of which was crowned by a massive red-shingled building with columns, shining in sunlight. Hanuvar knew it for the temple of Jovren the lightning bearer.

After Hanuvar had retreated from the Tyvolian peninsula, the poet Orvenal had written that the general's greatest lust had been to tear down the arch of Laminius, cart the great Jovren statue away to decorate the harbor of Volanus, and raze the city. The Dervans had not produced a great poet since the previous generation, though few of them had noticed, blind as they were to propaganda masked as literature and barren as they were of compassion for those born beyond their borders. The same people who wept when presented with ornate rhymes describing the miseries of bereft Dervan war widows and orphans could exult without any sense of hypocrisy in the death, devastation, and destitution of those the empire conquered.

He moved through the streets with Dervans and could feign their manner, but he would never fully understand them, especially when it came to how such a fundamentally decent people could be capable of the cruelties of gladiatorial entertainment, much less slavery and genocide. While he lacked the time or inclination to luxuriate in bitterness, sometimes he could not help but brush it in passing, especially that autumn morning. Derva was vibrant, alive with sound and scent and people in motion. He wondered if any of those he passed gave thought to the blackened, empty streets of Volanus, or Orinth, or Ekamaya. He did not expect so.

Volanus, too, had been old, but its founders had laid the city out in long straight lines from the start, so it was not this warren of narrow twisting lanes. Derva had grown organically and with little guidance, although it did not lack all planning, for it possessed a famously efficient system of aqueducts, which rivaled those of lost Volanus. Its sewer system was said to be comparable as well, at least in principle, although upper-level apartments lacked access to it. The dumping of chamber pots from high windows was both a well-known hazard and the most prominent source of the city's underlying reek. That odor blended with the smell of horse and the stench of humanity, despite the folk of Derva making regular use of public baths. More pleasant scents of baking breads, sizzling sausages, and fragrant perfumes and sharp spices threaded themselves into the overlying fetor so that the worst factors rarely overwhelmed.

The great city presented an unceasing variety for the ears as well, Hanuvar found, and not just the clop of hooves on brick roadways or the chattering of men and women, gossiping at restaurant counters or bickering at merchant stalls. Derva was apparently a city in constant need of repair. In the span of six blocks Hanuvar passed three separate buildings under construction, the last occupied by a small army of carpenters hammering upon all three levels of its skeletal wooden frame.

Most buildings were fronted with shops and rose two or three floors. Further in, the city tenements climbed as high as five or six stories, and their windows stared at him from the flanks of two of Derva's hills. Villas with gardens sprawled higher upon those hills, crowned by pillared temples and stately buildings of the imperial bureaucracy.

As he traveled the winding avenue deeper into the city, he left behind tourists to blend with local men and women on their daily chores. He passed a line of off-duty soldiers, in the red tunics of the legionaries but wearing no obvious weapons in the city, by ancient law, and then came to a row of seated beggars.[3] One of the weather-beaten old men looked grimly up at him as he neared, shaking his stub of a left arm. He bore a placard identifying him as a soldier from the Sixth Legion. If that were true, he'd probably lost the limb fighting Hanuvar's troops over a dozen years ago.

The coins Hanuvar carried were quite literally intended for the preservation of lives, but he tossed one to the old soldier, wondering why a nation so given to conquest could not better care for the maimed who had marched to enact its decrees. In Volanus, a man like this without a family to care for him could have lived out the rest of his life in one of the complexes set aside for veterans, along the city's south shore.

He left the central road and meandered through side streets. He purchased pork skewers from a vendor on one avenue and eyed gaudy bracelets on another, as though he thought about gifts for a lady friend, and generally behaved as though he were in no hurry and had no particular place to be. He even pretended to flirt with a trio of pretty singing girls at a small market while they performed for coins.

Finally, as if by chance, he wandered down a side street only a few blocks beyond the forum. There he looked over several taverns before advancing a block further and stopping at a complex that offered both a tavern and a stable. Each building in the row bore a placard with a blue spoked wheel beside an additional implement, indicative of each shop's particular function—a bed, a wine jug, a table with steaming ribs, a horse.

Until he had seen those blue wheels he hadn't been certain he would

---

[3] Once the Dervans had thrown out their kings, the Republic's founders had decreed that armed hosts were not to be housed within the city limits, and that weapons were not to be carried upon city streets. While the decrees of the first emperor eroded elements of these laws, even in the time of Hanuvar, those walking the streets were not allowed to carry bladed weapons larger than utility knives. It was permitted to move privately owned weapons through the city, but only so long as they were not ready for use—bows were to be unstrung, spear blades wrapped, sheaths tied closed, and so forth.

Thugs and bodyguards took to carrying staves or canes, and some even equipped themselves with flattened cudgels like those employed by the city vigiles. The boldest criminals secreted large knives upon themselves, and faced stiff penalties whenever they were discovered. Some nationalities found the laws particularly irksome. The Ceori in particular believed it demeaning to wear no sword. Ceori visitors and citizens had caused so much turmoil each time they were challenged over knives only a little smaller than a Dervan gladius that vigiles and guardsmen relaxed the law's enforcement upon them so long as their weapon stayed in its sheath, a tradition mockingly referred to as the Ceori peace accords.   —*Andronikos Sosilos* find them there, and even then he did not feel fully relieved. It might be that some new owner had taken possession of the run of buildings and thought it unwise to part with the well-established symbols.

He didn't recognize the young man to whom he turned over his horse, but then he wouldn't expect that. Carthalo would never have survived so long at the hub of his intelligence network if he had employed obvious Volani, and this boy had probably been very young when Hanuvar last walked the Tyvolian peninsula.

He chose not to ask if Terrence, Carthalo's cover name, still owned the business, and, saddlebag on his right shoulder, war gear under his left arm, he walked past the street-side counter of the inn and into the shadowy restaurant interior. Most of the tables and low-backed chairs sat empty. A trio of old men were leisurely consuming a morning meal of eggs and bread, and they briefly eyed him before returning to a discussion about the merits of various drivers for the whites and who was best suited to win against the reds next week.

Two voices were engaged in a friendly exchange only a little further in. One was gruff and unfamiliar. The other was fluid and mild and Hanuvar permitted himself the faintest of smiles, for he recognized it on the instant as belonging to Carthalo.

An inner counter was illuminated by a low window and showed a stout Dervan vigile, or bucket man, of late middle years, leaning on a hairy arm with his nose pressed close to the open mouth of a wine amphora. He wore the blue tunic of his uniform and a wide belt from which hung a flattened wooden club. His helmet rested on the smooth, dark counter in front of him.

Carthalo watched the vigile. His dark, curly hair had receded from his forehead and his nose seemed somehow to have grown more pointed, but he otherwise looked just as Hanuvar remembered him from years of service; a medium-sized man with a rawboned strength invisible at first glance. His merry eyes were a warm brown.

"What do you think?" Carthalo asked. "Doesn't it smell as sweet as Fadurian wine? Tastes just a little less sweet but more complex; I always thought Fadurian was oversold."

"You're right about the smell," his companion answered.

"Do you want to try a cup?" Carthalo was already reaching for one, but the vigile raised a hand to forestall him and sighed with regret.

"I should get in and check on the lads. If I have one drink with you, pretty soon we'll be through the bottle and I'll show up half smashed."

Carthalo laughed and his eyes shifted to Hanuvar, who had stopped a few paces out. There was no missing the sudden shock of recognition and the greater shock of its impossibility. But Carthalo was a master dissembler and his easy smile shielded his surprise before the vigile had finished drawing in another sniff.

"That's fine stuff," the vigile concluded warmly. "Save me an amphora?"

"Surely. Tonight?"

"If things are quiet, I'll slip away." He slapped the counter. "Be well, Terrence." The vigile scooped up his helmet as Carthalo returned the farewell, then headed for the doorway. He sized up Hanuvar as he passed. He was heavy-set and powerful, with a square jaw and small eyes. He looked almost like a street thug himself. But then it took a strong man to wrestle with both criminals and fires, which the city's vigiles were sworn to do, by day or night.

Carthalo had joined the Volani forces when Hanuvar himself was older than he currently looked, and during most of that time Hanuvar had worn facial hair. But before embedding himself at the center of his intelligence network, Carthalo had seen Hanuvar in a variety of guises, and the man's perception was keen. He restored a cork to the mouth of the amphora, watching as Hanuvar advanced to the counter.

Hanuvar voiced the opening phrase of an old password exchange. Likely it had long since been abandoned, but he had no other phrase to offer. "My Uncle Cyrus says your red Divurian is best."

"Your uncle's a wise man," Carthalo replied quietly. He then added; "I'd heard he and his family were dead."

"They are. I'm glad you're still in business. And it looks as though your business is prospering."

"We do well enough. Are you an old friend's son I never heard about? The resemblance is striking."

"I'm older than I look. Is there some place we can talk? About a job?" he added, for the benefit of the old men. Although judging by their low chatter they remained so involved in their hippodrome race talk that they would hear nothing else.

Carthalo examined Hanuvar for a moment longer, then turned his head to call for "Horace." A handsome youth with Carthalo's curly dark hair emerged from a doorway in the rear.

"Take the counter," Carthalo said. "I'm talking to this young man about a job."

Horace looked at Hanuvar in mild interest, then said: "Of course, Father."

Carthalo beckoned Hanuvar to follow, stepped out from the counter, and headed through that same back entry way from which his son had emerged. He lifted a lantern from a crowded table, lit it from a low candle, and proceeded through a brick doorway and down an old stone staircase.

They emerged in a wide basement space supported by square pillars and stacked with barrels and jugs standing upon heavy wooden shelves with large numbered labels. One lower shelf displayed a jumble of urns and plinths and what looked so much like a human body that Hanuvar started until he realized he looked upon an exquisitely well-painted statue of an athlete—set aside for repair owing to a broken arm and chipped ear. There were yet more doorways; Carthalo ignored the first two and turned suddenly into a third, climbing two steps into a small, carpeted room with a central table, like a private booth at an expensive restaurant. He hung his lantern on an overhead hook and closed the heavy door.

He turned his attention to Hanuvar, and his eyes were piercing.

Hanuvar set the armor and saddlebag on the bench and spoke in Volani. "It is me, old friend. A spell went wrong and changed me thus."

Carthalo's gaze did not soften. "Prove it."

"When we were beside Adruvar's body you told me even headless he was a better warrior than any Dervan."

Carthalo's expression didn't change, so Hanuvar continued. "When you toasted Maharaval's wedding, you leaned over to tell me you just realized that you'd slept with his new wife's sister."

His eyebrows twitched at that, but he still looked unconvinced. "Tell me about the poem you wrote your wife."

Hanuvar slowly shook his head. "I wrote no poetry. I told you I only wondered if I should have."

Finally, there was a sign of Carthalo's discomfort, for he chewed his bottom lip. "It is difficult to believe. I heard rumors you had lived but I did not credit them. What are you doing here?"

"I'm looking up an old friend. I was afraid he wouldn't be here."

"They never found me out," Carthalo said quietly. "When Volanus fell I wondered for a time if papers from some of our correspondence would point my way, but I stayed. Strange as it may seem, I have a life here."

"Almost no one knew of your placement, and I assume you have been as careful as always, just as I assume our people would have taken time to destroy the most important documents as the Dervans marched in." Hanuvar's voice didn't break, but it had grown brittle.

"I worried they might have had other things to worry about."

A somber silence settled between them before Hanuvar spoke quietly. "When you know your time is nigh, I think duty may be the most important thing left you."

Carthalo nodded sagely, then stared at him, allowing a little wonder to show in his gaze.

Hanuvar wanted none of that. "Five years ago, you sat in the midst of a great web, gathering information. Do you still?"

"Most of my distant sources have gone silent. And why not? For whom am I gathering?"

"Can you rebuild your network?"

Carthalo set his left arm upon the table and leaned forward. "For what purpose? What can you even hope to do?"

Before he could tell him, he had to be certain. "Are you still with me, Carthalo? For Volanus?"

Carthalo sucked in a breath, and his head rose. His voice was cool, quiet. "You ask me that? Have I not given my life to Volanus?"

"Volanus is in ruins," Hanuvar said brutally. "Here you have a home. A family. A business that prospers. What I ask would have you risk it all."

"To slay the emperor?" Carthalo asked. The easy way he leapt to that conclusion revealed prior contemplation of the same path.

"No. I hope he lives long enough to suffer greatly. I plan to free our people."

Only someone who had known Carthalo for long years would have recognized his surprise. His expression was unchanged but his eyes took on an inward look of concentration. Finally, he reached a conclusion and it inspired a question. "You mean to transport them to your colony. It prospers?"

"Last I saw it, yes. I mean to buy the freedom of all survivors and send them to New Volanus. When they're released, I'd like to carefully contact all free Volani living in outlying lands, too. So that they know we still have a homeland."

Carthalo did not require any time to adjust to this new reality. He merely began performing new calculations about the requirements necessary for success in this new venture. Hanuvar could almost see him thinking. "You've ships?"

"I'm building a shipyard. And I have gemstones to finance our first efforts."

"Of course you do. You were always prepared well in advance."

"Not so much this time. I have had to improvise. We shall need more money. And we will have to find purchasers for the remaining gems. Using them exclusively as payment will present an obvious pattern."

Carthalo warmed to the topic. "And we can't just use one buyer for repurchasing our people. We'll need a sequence of them. Fake businesses, so the Dervans don't see what you're doing. That's in part why you need my network," he added.

"Exactly."

Carthalo stared at him then laughed and thrust out his arm. Hanuvar clasped it and found the grip tight as ever. "It's not just what you know, it's how you sound. It's you." He laughed incredulously. "How in all that's damned is it you? Like this?"

Hanuvar shook his head. "That's a long story and I'm only like this for a while. I'm quickly aging back." He forestalled further worry about where the end to the sorceries would leave him.

"You must tell me. How did you survive? Were you really there when Volanus fell?"

"I was. And I'd rather not go over that now." He suddenly felt leagues wearier. "Tell me about yourself and how you've managed here."

"I've had it simple," Carthalo said, as though building a successful business in an enemy metropolis while running an intelligence network could ever be an easy task. "I've been under no true hardship, nor has my family. I'm surrounded by people who've no

idea who I am or what I've done. I'm a fixture in the community, and
friend to vigiles, lawyers, and even a senator or three." His lip curled.
"I considered and discarded a variety of plans that might briefly have
made me happier, but would have jeopardized everything I'd built,
and the people I love."

"Movement against the emperor yourself?" Hanuvar sought
confirmation of his previous guess.

"And the circle that championed the destruction of Volanus. I
worked out a way to reach most of them and I might have done it, but
it would have exposed me. I didn't care about my own destruction,
but if they found me out, they'd have come after my family. My
employees. My friends."

"They will be at risk in this new venture," Hanuvar reminded him.

"This is different. This isn't an empty act of revenge that would
only clear the way for some new tyrant. That was about death. What
you propose is about life. The freedom of our people. However few
remain."

"Yes."

"I'm with you."

"I knew that you would be." He had never doubted Carthalo's
loyalty, much less his courage. The man had distinguished himself
from a very early age, leading scouting missions deep into Dervan
territory and returning with incredibly detailed information about
not just the enemy's movements, but the personalities of their leaders
and their internal disputes. Carthalo had a chameleonlike ability to
blend unnoticed into different groups of people, and a talent for
weaving disparate threads of information into surprisingly prescient
deductions about enemy intent. Hanuvar had reorganized his
intelligence service based upon Carthalo's suggestions. Carthalo
himself had been too fine a field agent to completely remove from
service, and at the end of the second war he had chosen to remain in
deep cover inside Derva itself to better monitor the empire's plans
for Volanus.

Carthalo anticipated the course of his thoughts. "I warned them,
you know. I was still in contact with Tanilia and some personnel in
the Ministry of Defense."

"I expected you were." Hanuvar could also guess that for some
reason Carthalo's communications hadn't been heeded. He knew

Carthalo well enough that he would never have considered blaming him for Volanus' fall.

But his old friend clearly faulted himself, at least a little. As he continued, his words took on a confessional note. "The Dervan senate debates about the war, and the build-up for it, were impossible to miss. And yet our councilors still thought the Dervans would be reasonable. They kept trying for peace." The pain in Carthalo's eyes was real. "Maybe there wasn't any other option left."

Not after the second war, when by the treaty Volanus had surrendered all but a handful of its warships and armaments, and had been forced to disband all but a fraction of its standing army.

"Maybe not," Hanuvar said.

"When the Dervans finally moved, it happened faster than I would have thought. I've been wondering ever since if I should have risked taking down one of their ring leaders. I would have loved to have killed Catius. I managed to bribe a few senators, to change votes, but the senate was mostly just a stamp for the emperor then, as now—"

Hanuvar cut him off. "You don't need to explain yourself. I've questioned whether things would have been different if I'd returned sooner. But there was so much to do finding and establishing a new colony, and I thought the city might draw less ire if I wasn't there. We can't dwell on what we didn't do. We have to move forward."

"I know," Carthalo said bitterly. "I know," he repeated slowly, but as if to unseen judges, or his own internal ones.

Hanuvar saw he needed to pull his friend back to the present. He tapped the table top. "Here, and now, there is no man I'd rather have at my side. No one is better suited to building and maintaining a network like this. You will be the one who sets our people free."

Carthalo's look was somber as he nodded acceptance—not to the compliment, for he was impervious to flattery, but to the idea of readying for the cause.

Someone approached the door to their booth, and a young woman spoke tentatively. "Father?"

"I'm in an important meeting," Carthalo answered without getting up.

"We've a problem upstairs," the voice said.

"What kind of problem?"

"You might want this private."

"Come in," Carthalo said.

The door was opened by a young woman in a yellow dress holding a candle. Her hair was wavy rather than curling, although it was the same dark color as Horace's. Her eyes were bright and inquisitive.

"This is Lucena, my daughter," Carthalo said.

Hanuvar nodded in acknowledgment. "I'm Postumus."

Carthalo broke into a grin at the assumed name[4], then addressed his daughter. "You may speak freely."

Lucena appraised Hanuvar for a few heartbeats, then addressed her father. "That man Cassandra's afraid of has turned up, and he's threatening legal action. He's waving a paper around and demanding she be turned over to him."

Carthalo's expression was sober as he turned to Hanuvar. "This must be dealt with." He climbed to his feet. "Lucena, can you get Postumus here some food?"

"I'll come with you," Hanuvar said. "This room's secure?"

"Indeed it is."

Hanuvar left his belongings on the bench and followed his old friend out of the basement and back through the halls to the central room of the tavern. Lucena trailed them.

The three old patrons had finally dropped their talk of chariot racing. They were turned in their chairs, staring at Carthalo's son, behind the counter next to a younger boy who was practically identical, and the patrician who faced him, flanked by two large guardians.

The character of some men was mysterious until you had spent long hours or days in their company, gradually learning their humors, their attitudes and preferences, and their special strengths and failings. The patrician was not one of these. The crux of his personality could be gained in a single glance. In his late twenties, his expensive orange tunic with its fine gold embroidery failed to

---

[4] By calling himself Postumus, Hanuvar was identifying himself as a child born after the death of his father. While he was young again, or reborn, both to a man long thought dead and to a vanquished city, it strikes me as a dry and rather convoluted joke, and a dark one as well, but Antires preserved Carthalo's reaction, so it must have taken place. I can only assume Carthalo possessed a somewhat morbid sense of humor and that Hanuvar, knowing him well, had anticipated how the name choice would strike him. Or it might be that Hanuvar himself was in a wry mood.

—*Silenus, Commentaries*

conceal his spindly frame, and his thin lips appeared permanently fixed in a superior sneer. The arrogance obvious in his stance was almost comically magnified by the backward tilt to his head so he might better look down his nose. His eyes glittered with something meaner; his was the malice of someone who believed wholeheartedly that he was an exceptional form of human and that all should acknowledge it. A large ruby glittered upon his citizen's ring and it flashed in the lantern light as he brandished a scroll at Carthalo.

Hanuvar's scrutiny shifted to the bodyguards. Their well-tailored tunics and sandals could no more have obscured their profession than they could have disguised the nature of upright bears. They had the thickset build and scarred, heavy limbs of gladiators, and their stares were practically unblinking.

Carthalo ignored the scroll and addressed the rich man. "What seems to be the problem here?"

As if determined to present himself as a stereotype, the stranger sniffed and spoke through his nose. "The problem is yours, for harboring an escaped slave, one Cassandra, whom my informants tell me is upon your premises. You'll turn her over immediately, if you know what's good for you." He again waved the scroll at Carthalo, who again refused to touch it.

Carthalo responded with flat disinterest. "You are mistaken."

The patrician blinked in astonishment. "You deny that she is here?"

"On the contrary; she is here. But she is a freed woman."

"You, citizen, are a fool or a liar." The rich man raised his other hand and wiggled his fingers. Both of the gladiators leaned closer, like hounds tensing on the leash. "Search this place and bring her to me."

Carthalo's sons and his daughter bravely moved into positions to oppose any forward progress, the youngest barely rising to the chest level of the brutes. Their father's voice rang with the sound of steel. "If you take another step into my establishment, you won't like what happens."

Behind Hanuvar was a heavy footfall. A quick glance showed him a hirsute man a head taller than Hanuvar, glaring at the two gladiators. He smelled of garlic and cooking oil, but his powerful frame and the look in his eye suggested he might have skills beyond the culinary.

"I am within my legal rights," the patrician sneered.

Carthalo answered without hesitation. "As am I."

"I have friends in high places." The patrician's voice was threatening, quavering with indignant rage.

"So do I," Carthalo countered.

At that the rich man laughed. "You, a tavern keeper? I count numerous senators among my close companions."

"That doesn't help you right now, though. Whatever's on that paper you're trying to hand me is horse manure."

The patrician eyed Hanuvar and the large man behind him and then sucked in a breath. His voice took on a wheedling, honeyed tone. "Let me make myself clear. It's possible that the girl deceived you. She is a notorious liar. She might even have procured false documents. If you turn her over to me, there will be no further complications, much less trouble and expense."

"I'm not turning her over."

The patrician's brief flirtation with cordiality ended on the instant. He shook the scroll. "The law will differ, citizen!"

"We shall see. For now, you and your men had best clear out. If any of you come at me or mine you're liable to get hurt. And I'd hate to see that."

Carthalo didn't sound as though he meant the last. The rich man's expression tightened; he crunched the paper in his fist. He turned on his heel and retreated so quickly his gladiators scrambled to part before him. He called over his shoulder. "You will rue your choice, tavern keep! You can depend upon it!"

The guards fell in behind him. The patrician continued ranting as he reached the door: "I'll sue you for everything you own! I'll buy out this whole measly property just so I can tear it down!"

The moment he stepped out of sight, a woman's voice, weary and hopeless, spoke from behind the big cook. "I'll never be rid of him. He's using sorcery. He must be."

At the same time, Carthalo was speaking softly to Lucena. "Follow them. See where they go. Don't be seen."

"Yes, Father." Her dark eyes flashed intently as she hurried quickly after. The younger son followed her.

Hanuvar turned to face the woman speaker, for whom the big cook had stepped aside. He loomed behind her like a sad giant, lifting a hand as if to pat her back, then lowering it as if he'd thought better of the idea.

She proved slender and solemn. The young woman's striking red-gold hair was styled simply, swept back from her forehead, exposing her fine brows. She looked toward Carthalo, though she did not quite meet his eyes. Her voice was sunk in despair. "How did he find me?"

Carthalo answered gently. "I don't know. Cassandra, this is the son of my best friend."

"I'm Postumus. What's your history with that man?"

She answered, matter-of-factly at first, but with growing speed and nervous passion, though she never met Hanuvar's eyes. "His uncle once owned my family. He grew old, and ill, and knew Titus was obsessed with me. On his deathbed, he freed me, because Titus and his mother were his heirs and he didn't want Titus to have me. But Titus followed me."

"What makes you believe he used sorcery?"

"He found me out, somehow, wherever I went. He left letters, telling how he watched me, though I never understood. He saw what I did in places where I was alone, where no one could see in. When I got here, I never went out, thinking he couldn't find me if he never saw a landmark. Although ... last week those boys were tormenting the cat, and I went outside to stop them. But I was only on the street for a moment ..." She put a hand to her head.

Hanuvar would have liked to have known more, but if Titus had led Lucena swiftly, he'd already be hard pressed to catch up. He faced Carthalo. "I'm going with your daughter."

Carthalo's eyebrows arched. "It's not your fight."

"It is if your business is in jeopardy. Take care of my saddlebag."

Carthalo would already have been sure to do that; by calling it out Hanuvar had ensured his old friend would personally inspect it and begin calculating how much money was left them, as well as how far it would go in freeing the slaves listed upon the scrolls hidden in another pocket.

With that subtle instruction delivered, Hanuvar dashed into the Dervan streets. Carthalo's younger son was stationed at the door and told him the direction Lucena had gone. Hanuvar managed to catch up just before she took an avenue to the right.

II

Carthalo's daughter accepted Hanuvar's presence with little question. As the young woman skillfully shadowed the patrician and his guards through the streets it was easy to imagine once again scouting terrain with a youthful Carthalo in the hinterlands before they'd crossed the Ardenines.

Titus' guards kept a wary eye on anyone crowding toward their master, but neither seemed alert for followers. Titus certainly wasn't. Every so often he would halt and lift a small rectangular object by its handle to peer into it. At first Hanuvar wasn't certain what it might be, but a growing suspicion was confirmed when the rectangle flared in the light.

"I think it's a mirror," he said to Lucena. They had stopped behind a vendor selling scrolls from a pushcart.

She snorted. "He must really be in love with himself."

Possibly he was. But there might be something more to the habit. Titus slid the mirror back into a belt pouch and headed forth.

Hanuvar stepped away from the cart, Lucena at his side. "It looks to me as if they're headed for the Tarkelian hill," he said. The destination seemed a likely one, given that the avenue led straight on toward the slope where many patricians made their home. But Hanuvar knew Derva mostly as lines on a map and wanted to consult someone more familiar with the streets. "What do you think?"

"I think it's a fair guess," Lucena replied. "But we shouldn't assume."

"I'm going to go a block over, make a run for it, and see if I can get ahead of them."

She eyed him skeptically. "Why?"

"I'd like a closer look at the mirror. It may be important."

She frowned. "Father said to be discreet."

"He'll want us to gain enough information to act."

Lucena's frown suggested she didn't like a stranger telling her what her father would want, but she said nothing as Hanuvar diverted at the next intersection. Once on the parallel street he ran flat out for the next three blocks. He was slowed by a line queuing up in front of a delicious smelling bakery he promised himself to revisit and nearly collided with a man stopping to shout a greeting at another leaning out a second floor window, but before long he was cutting back on a side street. Halfway along he stopped an old man and paid him two times the worth of his floppy brimmed hat, then slapped it over his head and turned the corner.

It wasn't hard to spot Titus and his gladiators almost two blocks away and strolling toward him. Now the only trick would be timing. Hanuvar proceeded slowly at first, hat brim pulled low, eyes fixed upon Titus. The aristocrat's mouth was turned down in a scowl, and he spoke energetically to the gladiator on his right from time to time, who replied with only short phrases. It didn't seem so much a conversation as an airing of grievances, to which the slave responded with studied sympathy.

When Hanuvar was only a hundred paces out Titus spoke to his bodyguards and veered toward a storefront. The aristocrat himself remained on the walk with the preferred bodyguard while the other stepped to the shop counter. Hanuvar couldn't yet see what was being sold, but he did spot Titus untying his belt strap, and hurried forward.

Titus lifted the mirror, then spoke a phrase to it, and stared.

Hanuvar abandoned all pretense and jogged ahead. He bypassed a trio of boys kicking a ball and raced past a woman who'd dropped her grocery basket.

At ten strides out he smelled roasting nuts and spotted a little sign dangling from the store's arch blandly labeled "Good Things." And he saw Lucena, who was closer than he was, walking up slowly, her eyes narrowed in warning to Hanuvar.

One of the gladiators was lined up to buy a bag of roasted, honeyed nuts. The other, though, was scanning passersby, and his eyes found Hanuvar, who slowed, clapped at his hat as if to adjust it, and came on, the arm he'd lifted obscuring his face, his head turned as though he were curious about the food. But his real gaze was focused to his side. He pretended distraction with the store so that he barely avoided the gladiator, then stumbled, shifting his attention to Titus.

The gladiator growled at him to watch himself; Hanuvar stared at the image in the mirror's rectangular bronze frame.

It should have showed him a reflection of the nut shop and Titus and maybe his wary guard. Instead, he saw a sad-eyed red-haired woman speaking to the big cook in some back room of Carthalo's inn, her mouth moving silently. Cassandra.

The mirror itself looked of standard make, the sort you could purchase at any upper-class boutique. Threads of hair were wound about the handle, and Hanuvar noted Cassandra's distinctive red-gold sheen among them.

The gladiator cursed and shoved Hanuvar, who apologized meekly and kept on.

He passed Lucena, who frowned. "Keep following," Hanuvar said. "I'll catch up."

"Discreet," Lucena whispered in disapproval.

There wasn't time to explain. He continued in the same direction until Lucena was a block ahead, then left his hat on the frowning bust of an ancient Dervan built into a wall recess and turned to watch from a greater distance.

Munching candied nuts, Titus resumed his disgruntled course until he entered a villa in the shadow of the Tarkelian hill, rather than upon it, suggesting he had less financial wherewithal than he pretended. It was abutted on its left by a weaver's shop with second story living quarters.

Lucena was waiting in a side street beside a restaurant, looking very much like an officer ready to scold a subordinate.

Hanuvar spoke first. "He was watching Cassandra in the mirror."

Lucena's brows drew in confusion; Hanuvar stepped to her side, his voice low. "He's using sorcery. Just like Cassandra thought."

The young woman's look was piercing, but she seemed to decide Hanuvar was both serious, and sane. He told her what he'd seen in detail.

"So can he watch anyone?" Lucena's voice rose in apprehension.

"I don't know the capabilities or limits, except that he can't seem to hear through it. And I'm guessing he can only watch those whose hairs are wrapped about the mirror's handle. These sorts of things usually have some kind of connection materials to link the subject with the sorcery, and I saw he had some of Cassandra's hair."

Her expression grew more quizzical, and he understood she didn't have the experience to accept the conclusion he'd drawn wasn't a wild guess. "What we should do now is scout the neighborhood to pick up gossip about Titus."

Her look said she still wasn't sure she trusted his judgment, but she nodded after a moment. "Getting more information isn't a bad idea. Why don't you wait here, and watch the villa, and I'll see what I can learn."

Hanuvar agreed, well aware that she was trying to keep him out of further trouble. She didn't know him, and she hadn't liked him breaking her father's instructions, even if it had yielded good information.

He took a seat at the restaurant counter. He ordered a large repast, eating very slowly while eying the villa's entrance.

This problem with the aristocrat needed to be brought to a close, and swiftly. Anything that imperiled Carthalo and his holdings imperiled the people of Volanus. That the threat originated from a self-entitled narcissistic boor was an especial irritant. Such a man held little value for Hanuvar, particularly when measured against the lives of his people. He found himself wishing the situation required a quick kill, but aside from the moral implications, the violent death of a man with connections would involve an investigation, then suspicion would almost certainly devolve upon anyone with whom the rich man was angry—the opposite of a swift and satisfactory resolution.

And thus he watched, and waited.

In less than an hour Lucena returned. Hanuvar gestured to the stool across from him and signaled for the server, then pushed the rest of the platter of sausages, barley cakes, and cheese toward his companion.

She waited to speak until the server deposited a new cup and left. Lucena chewed and swallowed one of the salty little sausages and waited further to ensure that the old owner was gossiping with some of the regulars at the back of the restaurant.

"What did you find?" Hanuvar asked.

The young woman's caution continued. "What's your stake in all this?"

She reminded him of his own daughter at that age and he couldn't help but respond warmly. "I'm the son of an old family friend. Any of your father's problems are now mine. But I haven't learned anything new sitting here, so what did you find?"

She didn't look entirely pleased about being pressed, but answered. "His full name's Titus Pira Vartius, and he's only recently taken possession of the villa, about a month back. He spends a lot of his time wandering around with those two brutes, staring at a little hand mirror."

"Go on."

"His slaves hate him, but are sullen and quiet. The local merchants say the slaves are terrified the master will find out if any bad word is said about him, then punish them severely."

Hanuvar hadn't expected kindness of him. "How often do the slaves circulate in the neighborhood?"

"The cook comes out every day in the morning, about this time. She's the only one with a regular schedule. Oh, one of the bodyguards is a slave, but the other one is a gladiator who won his freedom a couple of years back after he killed a lion in a single blow. His name's Nessus; supposedly the crowd went wild and demanded his freedom even though he wasn't well known."

"Anything more?"

"Not really."

"Well, that's a lot. Now, tell me about Cassandra."

She wiped her hand on a threadbare napkin, then rubbed the skin near her temple, still evaluating him. Hanuvar waited patiently.

She again decided to answer with apparent openness. "She's a freedwoman who's been working for Father. She's a potter, and a skilled one. She's been afraid of Titus for a long time. So afraid that she almost never leaves the building. I mean never. She never even visits the baths. The sad thing is that she's obsessed with cleanliness, and so she washes every day, sometimes twice or more, but she does it via a pitcher and a wash basin, like an old farmer."

"What does Titus want with her?"

"She really is a gifted potter," Lucena explained. "She invents finely detailed patterns." She sighed and looked straight at him. "But I gather he wants her for her body. Which doesn't make sense."

"Oh?"

She gave thought to her response, watching him the while. Her fine eyes were as perceptive as Carthalo's and he realized he had unintentionally presented himself as a mystery for her. His youthful appearance was out of step with his competence, or at least his apparent confidence, which probably seemed a bit different from that of an arrogant youth. She couldn't decide what to make of him. "Cassandra's different," she said finally. "She doesn't really like talking with people much. Father says that she communicates best with her clay. She doesn't seem to want to look at anyone, not directly, much less smile. And she hates to be touched. If this man wants to sleep with her, he doesn't understand her."

"There are legions of men who don't care about the understanding part," Hanuvar remarked wearily. He was tired of looking younger than he was. He was certain Antires would have been disappointed by his portrayal of a youth for the last few hours.

Lucena nodded sagely, liking his answer. "Exactly. If a woman looks a certain way, then they just want her."

"The way rich women want a bracelet," Hanuvar added, completing her thought. He swallowed a final swig of wine. "We should get back and tell your father what we learned."

III

When they returned, Carthalo was drinking at a back-room table with the vigile he'd been entertaining earlier that morning. He welcomed Hanuvar and his daughter with a glad hello. "I was starting to think something bad had happened to you."

"We're fine."

Carthalo addressed the vigile. "Julius, this is Postumus. His father was one of my best friends." He then turned to Hanuvar and his daughter. "Pull up a seat. Do you need some food?"

"No, thank you." Hanuvar took a stool on the vigile's right, away from the lone shaft of sunlight streaming onto the left side of the table. Lucena sat beside him, gilded in an outline of the beam.

"I told Julius about what's happened, and he's been making some inquiries for us. I've known him for ages. You wouldn't know it to look at him, but he used to be on the other side of the law."

"Before I got fat." Julius patted his belly. "I was a second story man and a first-rate street thief, if you can believe it." He chuckled.

Carthalo explained the vigile's change in professions: "He pulled some people out of a burning building and got offered steady work by the bucket brigade. Anyway, I told him you and Lucena were trailing the rich man. Did you learn anything?" He was implying Julius could be trusted to a limited extent, at least concerning their problems with Titus.

Hanuvar looked to Carthalo's daughter. "Lucena was in the lead."

She nodded at him before beginning a report on their findings and he found himself appreciating her physical features. A moment of self-reflection cleared up his confusion at being drawn to a woman more than half his age, who was the daughter of one of his closest friends. It was this young body. He snorted lightly at his own failings. While he hadn't stopped appreciating the charms of women as he aged, his body also hadn't been driving him to consider them at every turn.

Lucena finished her summation by offering Hanuvar's claim to have glimpsed Cassandra in the mirror as a partial explanation for why Titus had been seen wandering the neighborhood with it. She downplayed that he had broken her father's orders to remain out of sight.

At mention of the mirror being magic, Julius laughed. "That's impossible."

Hanuvar took no offense. "It ought to be. But I saw Cassandra in it. She was talking to that big cook in a back room about three hours ago."

"What were they saying?" Julius asked.

"I don't know. There was no sound from the mirror, and I only caught a glimpse. Cassandra told us that Titus seemed to always be able to track her down. In letters he's described where she was and what she had seen. So, she decided to remain totally indoors."

Carthalo nodded vigorously. "She's worried that Titus must have somehow learned where she was by a landmark on the street outside. I thought that a strange fancy."

Under different circumstances Hanuvar would have agreed. "It might not be. It's my guess that Titus has been wandering around the city trying to find something he saw her near when she was outside. Maybe it was your sign, or maybe it was a shop across the street, or the fountain. It's hard to know what all he sees. But that would explain why he's been in Derva for a month and only now approached you."

Lucena eyed him with respect. Carthalo nodded sagely. Julius' gaze was skeptical.

"Where is Cassandra?" Lucena asked her father.

"In back."

She slipped away, saying she was going to go check on her.

"What have you found?" Hanuvar asked. Carthalo wouldn't have been idle. Probably this vigile was a source, or he wouldn't be sitting in this private room.

"Julius, why don't you tell him?" Carthalo asked.

The vigile shifted in his chair. "Terrence here had me make some inquiries. It didn't take long. It looks like this Titus is in good with an aedile, who has examined paperwork proving Cassandra's a former slave, although there's no paperwork on Cassandra being an *escaped* slave. But there's no record on her being freed, either. The aedile's mostly honest but the word is he has a lot of debts."

Hanuvar accepted this information without comment. Dervan political offices could be prohibitively expensive for their holders, because many remunerated a pittance but required large outlays to fulfill their expected duties. As a result, graft and bribery were commonplace.

"Titus runs with a few senators. No one important," Julius added. He then named three men with whom Hanuvar was unfamiliar. It had been hard for him to keep track of all the Dervan senators even when he'd occupied the peninsula. The senate was composed of upward of three hundred landed members, the numbers fluctuating every few years from deaths, retirement, and the occasional removal of members demonstrating flagrantly abusive or morally repugnant behavior[5].

Julius continued, "My sources tell me the aedile's going to be presenting Terrence with an order tomorrow after he meets with his

---

[5] Even under the emperors, the official censors remained somewhat independent and could act with a measure of impunity, especially in regards to policing the senatorial class. Charged from ancient days with the maintenance of public good, they were well-known for closing theatres and drinking establishments frequented by rowdy youths, but they also kept their eyes upon the conduct of the empire's office holders. They tended to overlook bribery because the practice was so widespread, only decrying it when other charges, such as dereliction of duty, neglect of city infrastructure, or repeated instances of lewd public behavior could be leveled upon the accused. While to some the censors might have appeared in accord with the tightening restrictions over speech or atypical practices enforced by the revenants and the emperor's secret police, the censors at least seemed to labor in general for the health of the society rather than for the empowerment of the elite.

—*Andronikos Sosilos*

morning clients. He'll be coming with lictors, and he'll probably haul the woman away when he does." Julius looked soberly at Carthalo. "You need to hire a lawyer. A good one. Or simply give him the girl."

Carthalo emphatically shook his head. "I'll let no free woman become a slave. Much less to the likes of that man."

"Titus sounds like a first-rate ass, alright," Julius said. "But you can't just make one like him disappear. Not unless you've got friends higher up than I know."

"None that high up." Carthalo turned his attention to Hanuvar. "Do you have any thoughts?"

Julius' brows rose in surprise. But before he could ask why such a young man's opinion was being sought, a woman cleared her voice, and all three men turned to find Cassandra in the doorway, Lucena behind her.

Hanuvar eyed her as he imagined Titus might, trying to decide what about her inspired such obsession. Objectively he found her beautiful, but she did not possess any particular allure. He'd met women with far less refined features who were nonetheless more fascinating because they radiated an innate charisma this woman lacked. Or, he thought, more charitably, their manner invited engagement whereas nearly the whole of Cassandra's attention was focused inward.

"Hello," Cassandra said. "Lucena has told me that Titus has a magic mirror."

"It seems so," Carthalo said.

Cassandra worked her fingers together in a knot, struggled violently for a brief moment, then pushed them behind her back. "He was carrying a hand mirror when he came for a visit four months after the death of his father."

"I hope you don't mind," Hanuvar interjected, "but I think it best if you retreat into that corridor behind you. Is there something there you can pretend to do?"

"I don't understand," Cassandra said.

Quick-witted as he was, Carthalo gleaned Hanuvar's intention. "Pretend to straighten the shelf of oils," he suggested.

Julius eyed Carthalo and Hanuvar as though they were both demented. While confused, Cassandra complied, and was soon rearranging a shelf full of supplies in the dimly lit hall beyond.

Lucena looked undecided about whether or not she should be helping.

Hanuvar explained to Cassandra. "Titus doesn't seem to be able to hear through the mirror. You told me earlier that he had been able to send you notes. Think carefully. Did he ever suggest he'd heard you saying anything? Or was it only ever about what you could be seen doing?"

Cassandra paused in her work. "I . . . it was only ever about what I was doing. What I had seen. What was around me. He was always angrier if he saw me with a man. Any man."

"But was it ever about anything you said?" Lucena pressed.

"No. But what does it matter? You're saying he can always watch me? What am I to do?" Her voice cracked. "I'll never be rid of him. I will just have to kill myself. He will probably like watching that."

Lucena reached out with her hand, then withdrew it, just as the cook had done.

Julius looked as though he'd been gut punched. "Now you don't need to be thinking like that," he said awkwardly.

"I think we can help," Hanuvar said. "I've something in mind that may settle all of this. If Titus is obsessed with you, he must know your schedule. When do you usually bathe?"

Cassandra froze. Her shoulders stiffened. Her voice was anguished and remote. "Every evening. He has watched me bathe, hasn't he?"

"I am counting on him to watch you this evening," Hanuvar admitted. "And we can use that against him."

"How?" Julius asked.

"I need about ten people we can trust to play a joke, this evening."

Carthalo thought for a moment, then nodded. He didn't ask about details. "Alright. I can find them. Then what?"

Hanuvar explained his plan.

IV

The first time Titus saw Cassandra, she'd been shaping a pot at his uncle's farm, her hands filthy, her clear-skinned face marred by speckled red dots of clay and her stola strap slipped down one shoulder. He was so fired with desire he would have mounted her then and there if his uncle hadn't been standing close.

The old man had never liked him much and had deliberately ordered Titus to keep his hands off the slave. At first Titus thought it was because the old goat was keeping Cassandra to himself, until one day he'd sat him down on a bench beneath a shade tree. He'd explained the girl was fragile, and only suited for a handful of tasks.

"A slave should center her life on her master's needs," Titus had rightly pointed out.

"A good master knows his tools," his uncle had corrected with growing impatience. "Cassandra's a gifted artisan, and you'll ruin her if you have your way."

"If she cannot perform as required then she can be replaced," Titus said.

His uncle took a breath with visible effort. "I shall try one last time. Some tools have specific uses. Say you have an exquisite sword. You might be able to chop down a few small trees with it, but you'll dull it and might even break it. It would be a waste of a good weapon."

His uncle was an imbecile. "Women are for pleasure. They're nothing like swords."

Glaring, his uncle put his hands to his thighs, and rose stiffly. He departed without a backward glance and addressed Titus' mother, waiting near the garden pool. Titus had heard what his uncle said, and his blood still boiled in memory: "Your son is a complete idiot and a sorry sprig on this decrepit old blood line."

Titus contrived to obtain some of the old man's hairs. He'd thought it would be a pleasure to watch him breathe his final moments, but it had actually proved boring. He'd long since acquired Cassandra's hair and wrapped some around the handle—watching her had proved far more entertaining.

At first it hadn't seemed an impediment that he couldn't hear Cassandra, because she didn't spend much of her time talking. She certainly was amazing to watch when she disrobed and bathed, and once Titus understood that she performed this act at nearly the same time every single evening, he only missed a show when something irritating got in the way, like when his mother died, or when he got caught on the road in a rainstorm.

He felt sure if he watched her long enough he'd catch her kissing someone, hopefully another woman, or even pleasuring herself, but she seemed completely naive. Titus resolved that he would tutor her when he finally possessed her. The lack of sound from the mirror made tracking her down quite tedious, especially when she confined her activities to private spaces.

But now there was only one final obstacle. He'd thought that the aggravating innkeeper would cave once he had shown him the correct paperwork, but he hadn't. It didn't matter. Brencis the aedile had agreed to accompany him tomorrow, and then there'd be nothing the stupid tavern owner could do. There'd be an end to all of his difficulties very soon. If that contemptible plebeian didn't turn Cassandra over, he'd sue him into nonexistence and take everything he owned, including those miserable children of his.

For now, though, he went to his bath, had his body slave oil him down, and then reclined in the water with his mirror to await Cassandra's evening cleaning. At any moment, he would bask with his muse again in the bronze.

He rubbed the hairs tied about the mirror's handle, idly recalling the day he'd caught his father whispering strange words to it. Even when he'd sneaked into his father's office that first time and tried it, he hadn't understood how it really worked. He'd pried the information out of the old man's decrepit attendant.

He'd been told a Hadiran mage, indebted to Titus' grandfather, had ensorcelled a simple mirror so he could watch his home from afar when he'd ridden off to battle. Whether or not that were true, Father had inherited the thing and put it to more personal use. Titus eagerly sought it the moment his father died. His mother had been after it, too, and never believed Titus when he told her only someone of Father's bloodline could employ it.

You had to be special to use the magic.

His thumb caressed Cassandra's red-gold lock of hair, then he whispered the strange words. He closed his eyes to avoid the dizzying distortion when the device activated, and then turned over the mirror and saw Cassandra framed before him, almost as though he looked through an actual window at her. She was swaying down a hallway, her stola deliciously draping her backside.

Cassandra didn't turn into her private quarters, and he frowned at the thought he'd caught her early. She stopped to converse with the odious tavern keeper, who moved away to address a group of men seated in the tavern. The room was dark, for the door was closed and the windows were shuttered. Light strayed in through the slats, but most of it rose from lanterns.

Titus found that all peculiar, but not so peculiar as Cassandra's change from her reliable habits. It was downright frustrating, and he'd already had a frustrating day, so he cursed foully.

The tavern keeper in the mirror spoke silently to the men at length while Cassandra watched. Among those listening were a few he recognized, like the young man who'd stood at the tavern keeper's side, and the big fellow who'd looked so intimidating. Another wore a vigile's uniform, and from his command sash he could tell this was an officer. The tavern keeper's brats were nowhere to be seen.

When the tavern man finished talking, Cassandra carried a small bowl to each of the three tables, and one by one the men seated there reached into it. When their fingers emerged, they were black with ashes.

Each man then drew a symbol across his forehead—a circle with an opening along one side, and a slash through the middle.

Titus' frustration ebbed and his curiosity flowed. Over the year and a half he'd been watching Cassandra he had never witnessed any moment remotely like this.

The men appeared to be chanting something now, in unison, but Cassandra was walking past them. Rather than watch her, Titus found himself wishing she would turn, so he could better see what it was the men were doing. He supposed it was some ceremony of brotherhood, or even a religious ritual.

At the thought they might even be holding some kind of criminal covenant, Titus' jaw dropped open. It had never occurred to him to use the mirror to spy on malcontents, and then threaten to turn over their doings if they didn't pay him. While he had money, his family was not as rich as it once had been, owing to those upstart equites, so Titus was always alert to the potential for new revenue streams.

As he wondered how easily one might obtain hairs from the heads of criminals, Cassandra moved to a counter out of sight of the drinkers and mixed a variety of white powders from different vials. What could she be doing now?

Finally, she dumped all the powders into an amphora which she then corked and shook, vigorously.

So she was adding something to the wine? What, though?

Expressionless, Cassandra lugged the amphora through the doorway into the tavern, where she poured the dark wine into cups. She set the cups on trays, which she deposited on the tables.

Each man took up the cup but did not raise it. They were watching the tavern keep, still speaking at them. Finally, the proprietor took a cup himself, and lifted it, saying a few final words before downing it.

Every man drank but the big fellow.

The young man set down his cup then reached with one hand for his throat. Cassandra watched carefully as he appeared to be having trouble taking a breath. The man on his left then gagged and reached for his own neck.

As Cassandra looked about the room, every one of the seated men put fingers near their wind pipes, and one by one they toppled, some sliding to the floor, others across their tables. A few twitched when they landed, but momentarily all were still. Only the big man remained upright, and he did not look alarmed. He grinned. Cassandra reached behind a chair, produced a hand axe, and presented it to him. The owner must have consumed a separate draught, for he too looked unaffected, apart from a mad look in his eye. He raised his own axe and pointed the big man to the bodies on the left side of the room as he started toward those on the right.

Titus gaped. Cassandra and the tavern keeper had either murdered the men with poison, or rendered them unconscious so he and the big man could chop them to pieces. Titus leaned closer to the mirror, but Cassandra frustrated him once more, for she left the chamber before he saw what the tavern master meant to do. She returned to the counter. From behind it she removed a piece of papyrus and contemplated it.

Upon it was a long list of unfamiliar names. One by one she crossed ten off with an ash blackened finger. Titus realized just then that there had probably been ten men in the other room. Only one name was left, and that was his own. Despite the warm water, a chill spread through him.

Cassandra circled his name with her finger twice. Just then the big man came by and she paused to exchange a few words with him. They spoke casually, as though the big man's axe wasn't streaked in red. He opened a small wicker basket to show her bloody human hands and livers. One of them lay across the top half of a blood-smeared face.

Titus gasped in terror.

The big man wandered off with the basket, and the girl drew strange symbols around Titus' name on the papyrus. Finished, she headed for a tall cabinet near the tavern entry way and opened its door.

A pair of a pig's heads stared out at him from a high shelf, their eyes glazed in death, and he involuntarily pushed himself backward, so that he struck the back of his head against the stone rim of the bath. He swore in pain.

By the time he was paying attention to the mirror once more, Cassandra had rubbed the paper on the pig faces, looked carefully about the room, as if wary of being found out, then climbed into the cabinet beneath the heads. Once more she looked around, then shut the doors.

Everything then was black, for the mirror's view was restricted to her and her nearby surroundings. He had long since learned that he couldn't watch anyone very well while they remained in darkness.

He had seen enough this evening, however. He rose from the water, shouted for his slaves, and had started to towel himself off before they were there to aid him. He discovered his hands shaking, and realizing it was due to fright angered him. This was all that low class tavern keep's fault. Cassandra had been perfect until she'd gotten involved with him. The aedile's schedule be hanged. He would lead Brencis there tonight and carry her away. If she retained any strange beliefs, he could have them beaten out of her.

V

By the light of the lanterns they carried, one of Carthalo's lookouts noted Titus enroute with a man in a toga carrying the small gold baton of an aedile. They were followed by his gladiators and a pair of lictors with their staves. The news was passed to Lucena, who hurried to report to her father, sitting with Hanuvar and Julius in the central tavern room.

Hanuvar and Carthalo scanned the room and its two dozen occupants, relaxing at the tables with food and wine. All looked in readiness, meaning that the majority, who weren't in on the joke, were simply enjoying themselves. Julius toasted Carthalo with a cup of wine. "It won't be long now."

He was right. When the outer door was roughly thrown open, its bang was thunderous. The lictor in the lead stepped inside, his staff at the ready. As tall as himself, the pole was both an ornament of his office and a sturdy weapon for protecting the government official in his charge.

Like the few lictors Hanuvar had glimpsed over the years, this one was muscular. He wore a well-made white tunic with green scrollwork at its hemline. He took in the room full of citizens, among them three tables filled with uniformed vigiles, who looked back in curiosity.

The lictor addressed the room in a booming baritone. "Everyone stay where you are. The aedile Brencis Virgil Sertorius is here for official inquiry."

Another lictor entered behind him, followed by a small frowning man with a beard's shadow showing on his face. After him Titus pushed forward, leading his gladiators. The aedile turned to him expectantly.

Titus' eyes swept the room and widened as they settled on the cabinet a few steps beyond the front door. He pointed to it. "That's where my slave is hiding! Right there! Below the pig heads!"

The lead lictor advanced, his footfalls ringing in the stunned silence. He brandished his staff and threw open the door.

His body obscured what lay before him, but those nearest looked puzzled. The lictor stepped aside, looking back to the aedile for orders. Nothing sat on the cabinet's floor but a long row of stoppered amphorae. Various service dishes populated the shelves above.

Carthalo rose and started forward.

Frowning, Titus turned and jabbed his finger toward Carthalo. "There's the man! You, tavern keep! Where are the bodies? Arrest him! He killed them all! Including an officer of the vig—"

His voice fell, because at that moment Julius stood up. He wore his full regalia, including the sash with his officer's helmet-shaped sigil. A moment later Hanuvar came after.

"And that young man," Titus said, though his voice trailed off.

The aedile's brow creased.

Titus raised a shaking hand and pointed at both Julius and Hanuvar. "But you . . . you were poisoned, and then hacked with an axe!"

Julius stopped at Carthalo's side.

Carthalo addressed the frowning aedile low voiced, turned slightly away from Titus as though embarrassed by him. "This madman has been bothering us for the last few days. He complained initially that the donkey I left on his roof was making too much noise."

"I never!" Titus cried, and surged toward Carthalo, pointing his finger. "You're lying!"

Julius interposed himself and bumped against Titus, who stumbled. Julius, with a patient look, assisted him in righting himself.

Carthalo addressed the aedile. "Your honor, yesterday this man was back in my establishment and said he'd get the vigiles to arrest me because he knew Hanuvar was keeping elephants in my basement."

"It's true," Hanuvar said.

The crowd watched, and a few of them were laughing.

Titus had huffily separated himself from Julius and objected stridently. "I didn't! They're lying!"

"He threatened to beat me up so I couldn't marry his grandfather," Hanuvar volunteered, and more patrons chuckled.

The lictors looked back and forth at the crowd and Titus, and Brencis the aedile himself, whose frown deepened by the moment. The gladiators were slack-jawed in confusion.

Julius respectfully addressed the aedile. "Sir, how did he say he knew this business owner had killed someone?"

Brencis Virgil Sertorius answered slowly, with a hint of skepticism. "He said an informant directly witnessed a mass poisoning and preparations for chopping up the bodies. There were even some body parts carried away in a basket, apparently." He turned his head toward Titus. "I think there's been a misunderstanding."

Titus gnashed his teeth. He glared at Carthalo, then apparently came to a conclusion. "It wasn't really an informant. I was using a magic mirror!"

The vigiles chuckled at that, and then Carthalo quipped: "And I'm the ambassador from the moon!"

The tavern patrons roared with delight.

"This is all some trick!" Titus cried. "They staged it to make me look foolish!" He reached into the wide pouch tied at his belt and brandished the mirror. "I'll prove it!" He then pronounced Hadiran words Hanuvar recognized as "open to me" before crying: "Show me the girl!"

Titus waited expectantly, then stared at the mirror. "Show me!" he shouted.

"Is something supposed to be happening?" Julius asked.

The aedile traded glances with the lead lictor, whose stolid face betrayed weariness. The gladiators appeared equally confused.

"Show me!" Titus screamed. And then he stared at the object in his hand. "Wait! This isn't my mirror! One of you took my mirror!"

"Just like we took your slave?" Hanuvar suggested.

"She's mine!" Titus spat. "Where is she? She put you up to this trick somehow, didn't she?"

Everything had worked as Hanuvar had planned, better even, for he hadn't been completely sure how well Julius could play his role, much less whether the vigile's vaunted thieving abilities were as promised. But the man had switched out the magic mirror slyly enough.

It was then he spotted Lucena looking out from the doorway to the interior rooms. She motioned to someone out of sight, and Cassandra emerged.

Titus' eyes widened at sight of her. He screamed. "You! You foul little bitch! This is all your fault! You did this to me!"

"Calm yourself," the aedile snapped.

Cassandra's eyes were huge and white. She halted. Immediately after, though, came the cook, Brutus, his hands hidden behind him.

Titus backed away, gulping.

In his low, mild voice, Brutus said, "Cassandra asked me to show you something."

"He's got an axe!" Titus screamed. "Save me!" He ducked behind the gladiators.

The lictors tensed and interposed themselves.

Brutus halted. From behind his back, he produced a small lidded wicker basket. At sight of it, Titus let out a gasp of horror. "There's a face in there! A human face!"

Cassandra stepped to his side and lifted the lid. A pair of small gray kittens peeped out. They mewed softly.

The tavern guests roared with laughter.

Both lictors relaxed their guard stances and one of them audibly sighed in disgust. Cassandra retreated behind Brutus, her eyes still wide in alarm. While replacing the pig livers and statue parts with the kittens had been her idea, she hadn't felt up to the challenge of speaking to the odious Titus herself.

Titus' fists clenched and unclenched. Hanuvar could not hear what he said to the aedile, who glared at him. Finally, Titus could stand no more, and turned on his heel, shouting above the tavern noise that this was far from over. He tripped on the threshold as he exited, evoking another round of laughter. The gladiators left with him, one of them grinning.

Just as the laughter died, Hanuvar said coolly "I guess he doesn't like cats," which raised another loud guffaw from the crowd.

After the mirth trailed off, the aedile remained with his lictors, a solemn island. One of the lictors had striven hard not to chuckle, but the other had been unable to restrain himself and struggled still to stop smiling. He turned his face so Brencis would not see his expression.

The aedile addressed Carthalo in a low, calm voice. "In light of these ... revelations concerning the behavior of the accuser, I am no longer interested in investigating his charges."

"That's good to hear," Carthalo said. "He's been a pest."

"Can you see that this interaction is recorded?" Julius asked. "So that fool can't take his crazy claims to someone else?"

"I will make a note of it," the aedile replied. "But gossip spreads faster than fire in Derva." He looked pointedly at Julius, as if to intimate he knew how well the vigile was acquainted with fires. "By tomorrow morning I expect every official in the city will have heard of this disgrace. I'd be surprised if he stays in the city. He'll be a laughingstock." The aedile sighed heavily, probably anticipating that he'd be part of that punchline any time someone recounted the evening's events.

Carthalo invited Brencis and his lictors to stay, offering free rounds, but the aedile declined and departed with his men. After ordering another drink for the taverners, Carthalo motioned Hanuvar, Julius, Brutus, and Cassandra to the backroom, where they gathered at a table with Lucena.

Julius lifted the cup he'd carried with him in salute to Hanuvar. "That worked even better than I expected, boy. You got lucky."

"You and Terrence were fine actors."

The vigile shrugged. Hanuvar had the sense Julius had pretended to be many things over the years and that his job might require it— intimidator, confidant, criminal, and other roles besides.

"You played that just right, Brutus," Carthalo said with a laugh, then looked to Lucena. "Your timing was excellent. And that kitten idea was the perfect little sting on the end." He offered this last to its originator, Cassandra, standing just as tensely as she had before Titus. Brutus eased the basket toward her. She lifted one of the kittens and began to stroke its back.

Julius raised the mirror he'd procured. "Shall we see it working?" Without waiting for an answer, he mangled the Hadiran words Titus had used, then said, "Show me my son."

Nothing happened.

"I don't think it works unless you wrap the hair of someone you're trying to observe around the handle," Hanuvar said. "That's Cassandra's hair there."

"Don't use it to look at me," she said flatly.

"I wouldn't dream of it." Julius politely extended the mirror toward Cassandra.

Her expression suggested she'd just been offered spoiled eggs. She continued to stroke the mewing animal shifting in her arms. "I want nothing to do with that."

"We can work out the magic later," Carthalo said. "For now, some of the best magic is a good jar of wine shared between friends. Do you want to join us, Cassandra?"

"It is kind of you to ask," the young woman replied. "But no. Thank you all. You are sure he won't return?"

"I'm certain," Carthalo said.

Hanuvar gave him a searching look. It was unlike Carthalo to speak in absolutes he couldn't control.

His friend smiled at Cassandra reassuringly. "He won't trouble you again. Enjoy the rest of your evening."

She deposited the kitten she held in the basket, collected the other from the table, where Lucena had been engaging its attention with a shawl, and left with them both. Brutus said that he'd be back in a moment, then followed her.

Carthalo handed the mirror to Hanuvar. "I'd best get back out front. Put this some place safe."

"I'll be along in a moment," he said.

Carthalo and Julius left.

Lucena eyed him speculatively. "Well, go on. You want to try out the mirror, don't you?"

"It won't work without the hair of your quarry."

"Probably," Lucena agreed. "But we both know Julius didn't say the words properly."

He smiled lightly. After a moment, Hanuvar lifted the mirror and contemplated his own youthful reflection. He ran his fingers over the strands of hair tied about the mirror, almost certain that without one of Narisia's the spell wouldn't work. But, softly, he pronounced the Hadiran words that Titus had uttered, and asked the mirror to show him his daughter.

All that looked back at him was a young man with haunted eyes. He wasn't at all surprised. He had long since learned that the only miracles he could depend upon were those engineered by hard work, and the aid of friends. "Nothing." He set the mirror face down.

Lucena had lifted up a plain silver locket hidden by the collar of her stola and opened its face. From inside, she pulled a lock of silvery hair. "What were those words again?"

He repeated them and watched curiously as she lifted the mirror, carefully looped the hair strands around its handle, then spoke in halting Hadiran and asked to see her grandmother.

After a long moment Lucena let out a sad sigh. She lowered the mirror. "It didn't work. I don't understand. This is my grandmother's hair."

"There must be something more to using it that we don't know," Hanuvar suggested.

"Father knows some mages. Maybe they can help." Lucena took the hair from the handle and restored it to her locket. "How old is your daughter?"

"Impossibly old."

Lucena gave him a strange look, then replaced the locket below her collar. "I can't quite figure you out." A smile touched her lips. "Although I'm curious to try. Are you married?"

"My wife is dead."

Her brows drew down in sympathy. "I'm sorry. Was it recent?"

"It seems a very long time ago," he admitted. Or perhaps the sting of her loss was less noticeable amongst so many others.

She offered a tentative smile. "I'm going to put this mirror in storage, and then what say you join me for a meal? You can tell me where you're from and how my father knows you so well."

Were he the young man he'd seemed, he would have been flattered that a clever, pretty woman wanted to know him better. To some extent he still was, but he would not mislead her any further as to his nature or intentions. Whether or not his true identity should be revealed to her or any other member of Carthalo's staff was a decision best made in concert with Carthalo. For now, though, he had to simply, and a little regretfully, discourage her interest.

"I hope we can be friends," he said. "But it's been a long day. I think I'll have a quick chat with your father, and then turn in."

"Turn in?" She laughed at him. "The night is young! You sound like an old man!"

At that he could only smile.

⁂ ⁂ ⁂

Titus left Derva that night and was not seen again, a matter that might have looked more suspicious had he not so publicly embarrassed himself. I am inclined to suspect Carthalo's involvement in his disappearance, for he would not have wanted an ongoing threat to his security, but on this matter he refused comment.

Carthalo contrived to speak with some of Titus' household slaves before they were eventually passed along to the terrible man's remote cousin, and from one ancient learned the history behind the mirror, including the confirmation of the viewing subject's hair being required for use. Even with that information, however, the mirror's magic proved elusive and it was decided that the old slave's story about it only working for someone of Titus' bloodline must be true. Carthalo later melted it down.

It took long months for her to feel confident doing so, but Cassandra eventually began to venture from Carthalo's complex, journeying to the public baths and consulting with other artisans, and sometimes attending the hippodrome, although I gather she preferred watching the horses training rather than seeing them during actual races, which often involved injury and death.

More immediately, after that night, Hanuvar and Carthalo launched into action. With money and a list, the two began to plan the recovery of Volani slaves and reached out to former members of Carthalo's extensive network of allies and informants.

The majority of the slave liberation was handled with little drama, although, as will become clear, challenging situations presented themselves from time to time, some so difficult that Carthalo or Hanuvar had to personally address them. The first of these instances involved a renowned Volani theoretician who'd been forced by the Dervans to develop weapons of war.

Carthalo's informants learned where he and a Nuvaran sorcerer were being held inside Derva and arranged for an escape. Like all of Hanuvar's plans, it was well-laid and well considered. This one, though, through the intervention of an unexpected party, failed completely.

—Sosilos, Book Eight

Chapter 4:
The Shadow on the Stairs

I

The spear passed so close it set Varahan's beard waving. Startled, it took him a few heartbeats to understand that yes, someone on a Dervan street had hurled a weapon at him. The shaft was still vibrating in the door of the carriage he'd just opened, and the spearhead intended for his flesh was sunk halfway into the wood. He was still soberly registering that when he looked right to discover a man in the snowy road not fifteen paces away. The stranger's left arm was thrust back for balance, and his right arm was extended, as if he were an athlete modeling for a sculptor .

Varahan was used to long spans of time passing in blurs; he might sit in contemplation of an equation for hours at a time, belatedly realizing he was hungry because he'd worked straight through lunch and dinner both. But now, at this moment, time actually slowed. He became acutely aware of everything around him.

He scrambled into the carriage meant to convey him and Norok to the next phase of their imprisonment. To his rear, the praetorian shepherding them shouted to attack and another soldier screamed in agony.

Varahan crawled out the other side and looked back, calling for Norok to follow, but he didn't see the old Nuvaran, even though he'd been just behind. On his right a pair of cloaked figures struggled.

Neither was in legionary uniform. He could have sworn one of them shouted at him, in Volani no less, to get back in the carriage, but he saw an opening to a narrow lane and hurried toward it. He passed a crumpled body in the street, heard the scream of another legionary and the click of blade on blade, a sound he knew all too well from the fall of Volanus.

He ran into the dim alley, leaving prints in the thin snow with every sandaled stride. The pavers just ahead looked icy, so Varahan stepped to the left, breathing hard, before resuming his forward progress. The end of the alley was a bright rectangle opening onto a little marketplace. It seemed emblematic of safety and warmth, as though to pass through it he himself would be newly born into freedom.

But behind him the sound of footsteps came. He looked over his shoulder to see if his end would come via another spear throw or a sword to the back. A black-cloaked man snarled in close pursuit, a wickedly pointed knife raised in one hand. Varahan whispered a prayer to Danit, asking her to make it painless.

Then the assassin crossed onto the bricks Varahan had avoided, and his eyes flared wide. His arms flailed and his feet left the ground. He landed on his back with a loud splat and a painful sounding thunk.

He did not rise.

Just shy of the opening onto the marketplace, Varahan stopped and looked back at the downed assassin. So far there was no other pursuit. And while the marketplace might represent freedom, it was illusory, for Varahan had no money. He couldn't afford so much as a shave without any Dervan coins, let alone passage from this enemy city.

A sudden inspiration sent him back to his would-be murderer. Puffing, and thinking that he really ought to exercise more, he took the man's knife from the snow. Varahan sought and found the coin purse at the killer's side, then cut it free. The fellow groaned feebly in response.

Varahan looked back to the alley's empty entrance. Norok was probably dead. He hadn't realized how fond of his fellow prisoner he'd grown until he felt a catch in his throat. But there was nothing he could do for him, and more attackers might turn up at any moment. He turned and hurried for the end of the alley, his mind alive with plans.

First, he thought, a change of clothes, and a haircut and shave. After that, who could say? The coin purse felt as though it held a lot of money. His spirits rose. He glanced back a final time, only noticing then that his scarf had slipped off while he knelt. But he didn't need it anymore. He could buy another. He strode determinedly into the light.

II

Hanuvar pressed against the shutters of the second story window and peered to the north, as if he might see through the intervening buildings to the street where everything had gone wrong.

When he'd learned that the prisoners were shortly to be transported to speak to the senator sponsoring their experiments, he had quickly arranged what had looked to be a relatively simple interception. Matters had gone awry when a completely unexpected party intervened at the same time. And unlike Hanuvar, the Cerdian interlopers appeared to have had murder on their minds. By the time Hanuvar had dealt with them, his countryman Varahan had disappeared, and Hanuvar had been forced to depart in the carriage with only the Nuvaran. Four legionaries lay in the street, along with two Cerdians, and a passerby had been shouting for the vigiles. It hadn't been wise to remain.

The rest of their team scattered. He and Carthalo's son Horace left the carriage in a small warehouse a few blocks south set up as a hiding place. There they'd turned the horses over to Carthalo's daughter, Lucena, and retreated into an apartment above a fishmonger.

Hanuvar had removed the curly black wig he'd worn during the escape and traded out his black cloak for a brown one. He was still waiting on the Nuvaran to finish changing when Horace returned, stomping snow from his boots as he headed up the tight interior staircase. To Hanuvar's unvoiced query he only shook his head.

"They haven't caught anyone yet." Horace arrived at the landing and came through the doorway. The youth closely resembled a young

Carthalo, save that his face was leaner and longer, and, though the boy's mother had been a Dervan woman, the hook in his nose was even more pronounced than his father's. He was as dependable as Carthalo, as well, although more excitable.

The young man continued eagerly as he closed the inner door. "There's one thing in our favor. The Dervans believe the incident was a Cerdian attack. They haven't a clue anyone else was involved."[6]

Norok emerged from the back room, fussing with his abundant wispy white hair. He'd put on a light blue tunic and a black cloak, of flowery Herrenic style. He had complained that he looked nothing like a Herrene, and he certainly looked nothing like Antires, for he was old, wrinkled, and dour. He was also taller than the typical Herrene, and darker as well, but for his own safety his distinctive clothing had been discarded. He retained a necklace of colorful red and blue stones.

Hanuvar pointed to them. "You should hide those under your collar."

Norok did so as he spoke, his accented Dervan thick. "Why do the Cerdians want to hurt us?"

---

[6] Nowhere in *The Hanuvid* or within my ancestor's notes does Antires discuss how Carthalo explained Hanuvar's role or his rapid aging to his immediate associates and family. From statements later in his text it's clear Hanuvar's identity was not discussed beyond a core group, just as it's clear that a trusted few knew precisely who he was.

Fortunately, Silenus' researches supplied an answer. During her visit to New Volanus long decades later, she sat down with Kester, the youngest of Carthalo's sons, and asked for the details.

"You must understand," Kester said, "that we were schooled in keeping secrets from a very young age, and on reaching maturity were entrusted with greater responsibility. There were four of us in the immediate family, six if you count our two cousins. And there was an inner circle of trusted lieutenants who were either veteran spies from the war, or their descendants. Brutus was one of the latter, a half-Volani like myself, but there were old timers, like Farnus, who had been sneaking around behind Dervan lines in the war when he was younger than me. Anyway, the secret of Hanuvar's identity was shared only with those who were stationed in the central building in Derva."

Silenus asked: "How did your father introduce Hanuvar to you?"

"He was always direct. We'd been a little jealous that he seemed to trust this new young man above all others, and concerned that he seemed even to be giving Father orders, and so Father said something simple like: 'This is Hanuvar. Yes. He's encountered some magic so he looks younger than he really is.' Father then explained that everything we did from then on was to be dedicated to the recovery of Volani slaves. Hanuvar said a few words, and then that was that, and we got to work."

Silenus asked what Hanuvar had said.

"I don't really recall. I do remember that overnight we went from being jealous of him to being in awe of him. I also remember suddenly seeing Father in a whole new light. He was my father, so I had naturally respected him. But here was this living legend deferring to his judgment and closeting with him to lay plans. I began to understand just how important my father must have been back in the war, if Hanuvar depended upon him. And I tried to get Hanuvar to tell me stories, sometimes, but he didn't like to talk about the war very much."   —*Andronikos Sosilos*

"It doesn't make sense," Horace agreed.

Hanuvar explained. "If Cerdia is preparing for a war and learned you and Varahan are developing weapons, their movements make perfect sense. But then they may simply have been assassins who were Cerdians, rather than assassins sent by Cerdia. It could be they were hired by a rival senator to frustrate Senator Aminius' pet project."

"The Dervans would do this? Against their own government?" Norok asked in bewilderment.

"It's possible. Whoever they were, they seemed to learn you were out in the open, then moved against you."

"But how could they know?"

"Presumably the same way we did. Paid informers."

"And what about my colleague?" Norok looked at Horace. "I heard you say Varahan hadn't been caught by the Dervans. Is it possible the Cerdians captured him?"

"If they have him, he's dead," Hanuvar answered. "But I don't think they have him. I saw Varahan flee west. Where would he go?"

Norok let out a bark of laughter. "I think he ducked into the alley. But after that? How am I to know? He is a fluff headed idiot." His troubled expression belied his callous words.

Hanuvar had hoped for more insight into Varahan's likely whereabouts. The Volani scholar and Norok had been kept together by the Dervans for months. "He's relatively new to the streets of Derva, but he's a strategic thinker and well capable of improvisation. Did you ever discuss escape plans?"

Norok peered at him through shaggy brows. "None of any consequence. You speak as though you know him."

In fact he did, but Hanuvar merely shrugged. Varahan had helped design the dreaded Volani fire, a flame that burned on the surface of water, and when Hanuvar had held one of the two magisterial offices of Volanus he had consulted with Varahan dozens of times. So far as Norok knew, however, Hanuvar was a freelance mercenary working at the behest of friendly benefactors. That was a far more digestible lie than the truth that he was a de-aged general presumed dead but really leading a Volani liberation group.

"Stay with Horace," Hanuvar said to Norok, then threw on a blue cloak. "How well does Varahan speak Dervan?"

"Passably. But with an obvious Volani accent. And he has a beard like no Dervan wears. He could not possibly go unrecognized for long."

Norok was assuming Varahan would continue to act as he might normally. Hanuvar assumed a clever man would channel his wiles along new courses. "Stay alert," he said to Horace, then left the room, hurried down the steps, and exited the building.

He walked the few blocks to the ambush site and started down the sidewalk. Dozens of gawkers talked in little groups and pointed and stared at the bodies lying along the street. The masked priests of Lutar, swathed in their long brown robes and conical hats, were even now waving black wands over one of the corpses, ritually removing curses and sending spirits on their way so ordinary men could touch the bodies without fear of retribution from the angry dead.

A small band of praetorian soldiers kept onlookers back while their officers loitered, watching. All were distinctive in their white tunics, cloak, and helmet crests. But a group in black was drawing the most attention.

Hanuvar had expected the praetorians and the priests and the crowds, but he hadn't been certain the revenants would be called in. They were uniformed in full black armor and capes, complete with shining cloak tabs and helmet medallions. He was too far away to see the silvery decorative skulls inlaid upon their accouterments, but he knew they'd be present. Two of them were questioning a praetorian with a bandaged arm while a third studied the gray, overcast sky. A pair of black-cloaked, scholarly looking young assistants waited attentively to one side, and Hanuvar deduced they were some kind of adjunct force. Knowing revenants, they could be clerks with special knowledge, or even assistant spellcasters.

It was the smallest of the three revenants who'd drawn most of the crowd's scrutiny, a centurion, obvious from the way the horsehair crest crossed the officer's helmet from side to side. The onlookers seemed sure she was a woman. The men in the crowd of a half dozen actively mocked the notion, but the young man who'd seen her pass close insisted upon it, saying it was no beardless youth.

In no other Dervan military unit did women serve, but a handful of the most magically sensitive had been granted special status in the Revenant Order and been appointed to the rank of centurion so that common soldiers would be forced to treat them with respect. Most were kept out of sight of the public. This woman's presence in the field suggested she must formidable in several ways.

Hanuvar gave her and the rest of the soldiers a wide berth. He listened to the street gossip only long enough to determine there was no suspicion about Volani, then made for the lane a few dozen paces from where the carriage had sat against the curb. A pair of blue-cloaked vigiles stood with crossed arms in the alley's mouth, watching the activity but knowing better than to intervene. Vigiles might be charged with keeping the peace and fighting fires in the city, but when it came to investigating assaults and murders against praetorians, they were wisely hesitant to become involved. They gave Hanuvar scant notice as he sidled past.

Footprints in the street had been a muddle, but they were obvious in the narrow lane between warehouses. One man had fled this direction, his prints clear in the thin snow, and another had followed. A third had trailed later. Only two prints exited.

Eighty good strides past the opening, one of the men had lost his footing and slipped, landing on his back. It looked as though two others had knelt near him, one with smaller sandals. A wet scarf lay near at hand. Varahan's. Had he doubled back?

While Hanuvar considered the possible explanations, he noticed where two sets of tracks reversed course to leave the alley the way they'd come in. The other, smaller prints proceeded on for the far end. So Varahan had returned after the assassin had slipped, hopefully to take his weapon and money, then escaped before the second entered the alley. Hanuvar approved.

He glanced back to the alley mouth. The vigiles still had their backs turned. He followed Varahan's tracks out the alley and into a small forum with an abundance of market stalls. The scent of fresh baked bread helped obscure the more common, and less agreeable, odors of the city. After a cursory search Hanuvar spotted a pair of clothiers on his left. On his right lay a barber.

Norok had called Varahan a fluff-head, but even if he were absent minded, surely the scholar had seen the advantage of these resources. What he would have done after resorting to them, Hanuvar could not guess, but he hoped to narrow possibilities before the praetorians and revenants got their information straight.

III

Here in this neighborhood near the river Tibron, the lifeblood of the empire's capital, the apartment buildings climbed only a few stories, and much of this block was given over to old warehouses, many of them empty in winter. Dania been told the street was often deserted, but it wasn't now. A crowd of onlookers had gathered, and she'd ordered most of the useless praetorians to keep them back, dispatching the smartest to follow the carriage tracks, although she doubted his efforts would come to much. There were too many tracks through the snow already.

Like the crowd their subordinates kept at bay, the praetorian officers kept eying her as if they expected her to perform a trick.

She ignored them and thought about the battle site she walked. There were three dead attackers, one along the sidewalk, the others near where the carriage had stood. The survivor's confused recounting hadn't mentioned fighting a man on the sidewalk, and she bent to examine the corpse's wounds even as her junior companion Publius trudged up, two assistants following in his wake and complaining about the cold. Dania's look to him was meant to suggest he order them quiet, but Publius missed it because he was staring up at the empty windows.

Reedy and freckled, Publius looked more like a bewildered young priest than a revenant. He had come highly recommended from central, but so far today he'd only been interested in taking bird auguries, which would be of little to no immediate use even if Publius had mastered the difficult study, which she doubted.

She returned her attention to the corpse twisted in the snow. Like the other dead man, the body looked foreign. That was no mark of distinction here in Derva, the very center of the world, where people from all lands came to trade. Yet the corpse had the dark brown complexion and thicker eyebrows, not to mention the distinctive wide nostrils of his compatriot, and those were features common among Cerdian people.

Her optio, Vennius, led the praetorian over. While the optio wandered off, the trooper came to attention and saluted awkwardly, gingerly pressing his freshly bandaged arm to his white lacquered chest armor.

"At ease," Dania said. "There's something I want to ask you, Cassius."

"Yes, Centurion."

Dania walked him over to the driver, slumped in the snow, glassy eyes staring down the road, as if mystified by the absence of his carriage and horses. The true cause of his bewilderment was likely the gaping red wound in his throat. She pointed a finger at the black-cloaked figure crumpled nearby. Another likely Cerdian. "So you saw this man kill the driver."

"Yes."

"And you killed the Cerdian?"

"No, sir," the soldier corrected hastily. "I wounded him. Narses killed him." He pointed to a dead praetorian hidden by a crimson-soaked cloth. A pool of blood had stained the snow around the body and been soaked up by the fabric's edges.

"And who killed Narses?"

"The enemy was throwing javelins."

It had been hard to miss the javelin standing out of the other praetorian's head. Cassius himself had been wounded in the arm by one before slipping on the snow and spraining the same limb.

"So—how many attackers?" Dania had asked the praetorian the same question while the healer tended him, and Cassius hadn't been sure then. After revisiting the attack site, the praetorian looked even more puzzled.

"Three or four. Maybe five. I didn't see all of them. And it happened really fast."

"Come with me." Dania led him to where the third Cerdian lay in a doorway. "If I understand correctly, your attackers had assaulted the driver. At the same time, they moved against you praetorians, and all of you were in the street. You saw Narses caught from behind. You said Talcus was sliced open as he rushed forward, and that Tertius caught a javelin with his face. You were injured over there." She pointed back the way they'd come. "So who killed this man?"

Cassius' brow wrinkled.

Vennius returned, waiting expectantly. The handsome optio looked self-satisfied, as though he had news to report, but Dania held up a hand for him to wait.

"I don't think we got over here," Cassius said finally.

She sighed. "That is my point."

"Do you think one of them did it?" Cassius asked.

Dania rolled her eyes. "Why would they kill one of their own?"

"I'm just thinking out loud," Cassius answered apologetically.

"The tracks show the carriage horse moved off at a good clip. Did you see anyone besides these attackers?"

"I can't say as I noticed. I was watching the prisoners, keeping them safe while we walked them toward the carriage. The others were monitoring front, side, and rear."

"I don't think he knows much more, Centurion," Vennius said, smugly pleased with himself. "But I've found something."

Dania bade Cassius stay and then followed her optio, who said, "There are interesting tracks down this alley."

Vennius was arrogant, but he was also perceptive, and Dania tolerated him because he'd proven himself useful from time to time.

Publius and his assistants had already occupied the alley. The revenant knelt over a wet red scarf, contemplating it as though it held the world's secrets. She saw from his glassy, inward stare that he worked sorcery. What he expected to find she couldn't imagine.

Vennius adjusted his black cloak and leaned down toward the footprints in the lane to the right of Publius and explained what he thought they meant. If he was right, someone had run this way, pursued by one of the assassins. Then the pursuer had lost his footing. The running figure had returned, then headed out of the alley. Someone had dropped a scarf.

"And these other tracks?" Dani asked.

"Someone else wandering through, and me," Vennius explained.

"But our survivor said both the Volani and the Nuvaran were in the carriage."

Vennius scoffed. "Cassius isn't the brightest, though, is he?"

"That's certainly true."

"It might be coincidence," Vennius said. "Or it might be that one of our escapees ran this way."

As the wind picked up Dania pulled her cloak close about her shoulders and suppressed a shiver. The men were always looking for weakness in her and she worked never to show it to them. Instead, she absorbed the information and considered possibilities. "You think the prisoners weren't actively involved. That the Cerdians wanted them for themselves, and that one of them got away."

Vennius smiled in satisfaction. "Yes, Centurion. That's exactly it."

Publius cleared his throat then said, in a sententious voice: "I have determined the escapee's course." He lifted the balled, dripping red scarf.

"Yes?" Dania asked.

The sorcerer pointed down the alley, the way the footprints had gone.

"Oh, that's brilliant," Vennius muttered.

"There's more to it than that." Cradling the scarf against him, Publius lifted his other hand, as though he meant to throttle someone with it, then walked slowly forward. His fingers were outthrust before him, as though his hand was an independent entity and the rest of the body its mindless servant.

Vennius sniffed derisively. The young sorcerer did seem on the dramatic side, which was hardly unique among magical practitioners. Drama didn't especially bother Dania, so long as it got results. But she would not tolerate deceit. Over the five years of her service Dania had uncovered dozens of charlatans, three of them in the Revenant Order. If Publius was aware of that, he seemed unworried. But then fraudsters were well-practiced at being bold. And foolish.

They left the alley and emerged in a bustling marketplace. The sorcerer, led by his hand, moved blithely on before stopping at a booth displaying cloaks and shawls upon shelves under a sidewalk awning. At sight of the uniformed revenants led by one with a hand extended as if for strangling, a gaggle of shoppers turned heel, retreating into nearby shops or fleeing the square entirely. Dania was used to the respect her uniform inspired and wasn't especially suspicious of any of those who left. Most likely their true quarry had already vacated the area.

A wide selection of different colored cloth and a small assortment of finished garments were arranged on carts under the shop's awning. A middle-aged clerk was folding a red cloak at the counter just past the doorway. Her placid expression fell into one of dread when she beheld the strange, grim revenant and the others at his heels.

Publius stopped at a row of garments hanging on pegs just beyond the doorway, and the hand fell upon a plain brown cloak. He sounded weary when he turned to Dania, but relieved as well, as though he'd been able to set down a weighty burden. "This was with the scarf."

The woman had paled behind her counter. She pulled her hands back from the shawl she was folding and watched with wide eyes.

Dania lifted the cloak and walked toward her. "We're looking for an old man who was in this cloak. Either a Nuvaran or a Volani."

"I didn't know anything was wrong with him, I swear!" The wiry clerk paused to catch a breath then blurted: "That's just what I told his nephew."

"His nephew?" Dania repeated.

The woman stared as though she didn't understand the words.

Dania spoke slowly. "Tell me about his nephew."

"Yes, his nephew. He came by only a little while ago. He was looking for his uncle, whom he said was a little addled."

Vennius stepped up beside Dania. His voice was cold and remote. "What did this nephew look like?"

"Young. Friendly."

"Nuvaran?"

"Oh, no."

"Short, thin, fat?" Dania prompted.

"About average."

Vennius sighed in disgust. "This woman is useless."

Dania's temper had begun to fray but she still pretended calm. "Hair color?"

"Dark?"

"Are you telling me, or asking me?"

"I'm sorry—I was really more interested in the clothing. You know. That's my job. The garment selling."

Vennius curtly asked another question. "Did the nephew look like a Cerdian?"

"Well, no. I mean, I don't think so. He looked like a fine young Dervan man." She rattled on nervously. "I didn't know the old man was a Nuvaran—or Volani, I guess, I mean Nuvarans are dark, aren't they? Though he did have a funny accent. But a lot of people do." She briefly showed the tip of her tongue as she licked dried lips.

There was one last question Dania might ask. "Did either the old man or the nephew say anything about where they were going next?"

"The young man asked that same question and I didn't know, because his uncle didn't say. And he said he'd just go take a look around for him. Are they dangerous?"

"They're no one for you to worry about," Dania said.

The clothing seller gulped. Probably she was still afraid that she herself was in trouble.

Publius cleared his throat and Dania turned to face him.

"Centurion, I think I can find the Volani man." Publius pointed to one of his assistants, wringing water out of the scarf just beyond the doorway. "That garment wasn't important enough to him to be of any more use to me, nor was the cloak. I'll need access to his quarters. I need something that has more of his personal energy invested in it."

"You mean to work a more powerful spell," Dania said. "Can it be done quickly?"

"Regrettably, it may take some time. Perhaps an hour."

That was better than Dania had expected, though she did not show her relief. She looked to the sky herself, thinking that if she dared to use her own magics, it might speed the tracking. Unfortunately, the shadow would be very weak during the daytime. "It will have to be as it is. I think we've learned all that we can here." Her gaze fell on the clerk. "Stop quaking, woman."

The merchant watched with wide, fearful eyes until they'd left her shop.

IV

Varahan walked twelve blocks from the little marketplace where he'd effectively changed his appearance. Gone was the foreign bearded scholar with shaggy hair and in his place was a clean-shaven, prosperous older plebeian, with a tidy haircut and an ordinary off-white cloak. He'd purchased garments at a variety of vendors, the better to confound potential pursuers, then struck out in a random direction. He kept quiet, for his accent marked him as a foreigner. The weather let him keep his head down and nod politely if it was necessary to exchange a greeting.

Beyond the warehouse district lay an even wider mix of dwellings, with tenements and villas and smaller apartments above merchant shops on every hand, and it didn't take him long to find a clean, moderately empty tavern and then to settle in with a meal and consider the changed trajectory of his life. Only last week he'd planned to die in an explosion that would destroy his research and as many praetorians and politicians as could be lured in to witness the demonstration of Volani fire.

Senator Aminius had thought to foster a sense of gratitude by keeping them under guard near the river docks, where they could live in relative comfort with fresh restaurant meals. That they were also close to the warehouses where Varahan and Norok worked their experiments, and the riverfront, where Aminius had hoped his prisoners would demonstrate the secret weapons, had been a matter of convenience.

Varahan felt no more grateful to Aminius than he would have a guard dog who hadn't bitten him, and frowned at the memory of the oily promise to provide them with even greater luxuries, including slave girls, if they delivered for him. After Aminius had left, Norok had wished that the senator had provided a sharp Nuvaran axe and a brief moment to visit alone.

Neither in interest nor temperament had Varahan and Norok been well suited to work together, but they had found common cause in their captivity. The Nuvaran had stood a chance of one day being freed if he served his Dervan masters well, and he still had a home to return to. He had spoken about the wide valleys and distant snow-capped peaks of his country, and the bright songs of his people ringing through the clear air to cheer the sun.

Varahan made the sign of Danit over his chest, silently praying that the goddess had somehow protected Norok. And then he contemplated the smart course of action, which was surely to book passage to Surru or some other land. But he realized honor demanded he make a detour.

As far as he could tell, he was the sole surviving member of Volanus' scientific community. At his request, Aminius had provided a small library of scrolls liberated from Volanus' collegium, decades' worth of research he and his lost colleagues had conducted.

Those papers had inspired Varahan's resolve to destroy every scrap of Volani knowledge available before the Dervans could put them to use. He'd meant to have them go up in flames when he ensured his demonstration went wrong. He was free, now, but he could not, in good conscience, permit those papers to remain in Dervan hands. Someone clever could piece together the information they contained, and then the Empire would be spreading its misery with the aid of Volani science.

Varahan drank deep.

Resolved, he set down the mug, left a coin for the tavern keep, and stood. Pulling his cloak tight, he returned to the street. This course would probably get him killed, but then he'd honestly been surprised to survive the sack of Volanus. Maybe the gods had spared him for this purpose alone.

V

Lacking leads, Hanuvar returned to their safehouse, where Horace still stood guard by the upper window.

Norok crouched over a complex floor diagram he drew in charcoal. It had begun with a six-pointed star shape. He had then added a circle through its middle and a vast array of numbers and symbols written above and below the various lines.

"I am almost done. If he lives, this should find him." Norok looked up at Hanuvar, his heavy brows lowered as if in remorse. He spoke softly. "Do you think the fluff-head is still alive out there?"

"The fluff-head shaved, got a haircut, and an entire new set of clothes. He has money. He has a disguise. What do you think he would do?"

Norok shook his own curly gray head, which, now that Hanuvar considered it, was genuinely fluffy. "I do not know the man so well. He is ... unpredictable. But if I were he, I would get very far away as quickly as possible."

That seemed the wisest course. "How easy is it to perform this spell?"

"Easy? Does this look easy, young man?"

The mage had misunderstood his point. Hanuvar tried once more, this time with greater specificity. "How easy is it to track someone with magic? Can the Dervans do that to you or Varahan?"

"If you're worried someone's going to manage this with me or Varahan, rest easy. First, sorcerers of real skill are rare. Second..." He paused, his brow furrowing. "This is hard to explain in Dervan."

"I can speak Nuvaran," Hanuvar said in that language.

Norok's lips parted in surprise. "More than just a few curses?"

"Yes. I am a little out of practice, but I can speak it well enough." Hanuvar did not add that since he had learned the language from soldiers, he could reproduce a wide and colorful range of insults and imprecations.

"You speak with little accent," Norok observed.

Hanuvar was not nearly so fluent as he once had been, for his rehearsal opportunities with Nuvaran had been scant in recent years. "I'm a quick study. What were you wanting to tell me?"

Norok gave the head roll that was the Nuvaran equivalent of a shrug. "First, sorcerers of real skill are truly rare. Second, we either have to know the target fairly well or possess something that was important to him that was in his possession for some long while. Third, those who specialize in this kind of spell are rarer yet. Some mages lack the natural inclination. Just because you are a sorcerer doesn't mean you can manage every sort of spell. It's not like being a warrior, who could become proficient at every sort of weapon."

Hanuvar didn't correct Norok's impression about the ease of mastering a variety of weapons. He thought instead of a line from a Volani philosophy text; he translated the idiom into Nuvaran. "Like a musician born with a lovely voice who has no rhythm."

"A fair analogy," Norok conceded, and favored him with a penetrating look.

"Very well," Hanuvar said. "But can you find Varahan?"

"It will depend upon whether or not he has left the city. If he is within two miles, I should be able to do it quickly. But likely longer; if he's half as clever as you think then he's managed to get on a ship."

Hanuvar accepted a proffered wine cup from Horace and watched as the mage finished drawing his sigils. During the war, and while governing Volanus, he had staffed personal mages. Most had been employed in a defensive capacity, to help cancel the efforts of enemy sorcerers. He had never relied upon magic to turn the course of a battle, for sorcery was not just dangerous, it was notoriously unreliable.

Once complete, Norok's spell required almost a quarter hour of ongoing effort to activate. Even while he chanted, he had to adjust or add tiny squiggles to the diagram, move two small candles infinitesimal degrees, and sprinkle powder in the air. Finally he sat back and lit a larger candle beyond the circle.

At first, nothing seemed to happen. And then the flames began to rotate. Horace let out a low oath.

Norok sprinkled fresh gray powder around the central circle. That which dripped down to the northeast sparkled as it touched the diagram. He sighed. "Well, he's not dead, but he's still a fluff head. He's within two miles."

"Can you tell if the revenants have him?" Hanuvar asked.

Norok fixed a withering look on him.

Hanuvar couldn't help sounding defensive. "I don't know the limits of your power."

Norok spoke with asperity. "Shall I conjure you up a gold chariot, or a pretty lover, or a giant made of stone to smash your enemies?"

"The third one might be useful."

While bent over his diagram, Norok's necklace had slipped outside his collar. The little blue stone hanging between the red ones began to glow with a ghostly internal light. Norok lifted it in one weathered hand, his expression troubled.

"What does that mean?" Horace asked anxiously.

"Someone's tracking me."

"You said that skill was rare," Horace pointed out.

"It is." Norok swore in Nuvaran about the improbable digestive practices of Dervan mages, then looked over to Hanuvar, still speaking Nuvaran. "I should have bathed. Some fiber of my real clothing is stuck to me, or they've some garment of mine with my hair in it. A spellcaster could make use of that."

"Revenants," Hanuvar said grimly. "They have a sorcerer. Can you tell how far away they are?"

Norok climbed unsteadily to his feet. It had not been obvious until then that he'd been weakened by magic use. Hanuvar gripped his shoulder to steady him.

"It should take them a while to hone in on us." Norok stared at the soft blue glow. "It will get brighter when they are closer."

"How do we counter their ability to track you?"

"I have time for a fast towel off. And I may have you cut my hair."

At mention of the Nuvaran's hair, Hanuvar brightened. "You've given me an idea."

VI

Dania had sent one praetorian to walk ahead of their band as they maneuvered through the streets. Publius, his assistants, and another praetorian brought up the rear. She would have thought a pair of revenants and a pair of praetorians would send crowds scurrying, but these streets were so narrow it was impossible for people to give them a wide berth.

Each time someone bumped the assistants, the wooden platform they carried between them wobbled, and then Publius cursed at them, for on the platform's rimmed surface lay a complex pattern of symbols and materials the sorcerer had arranged with laborious care. For his tracking spell to work, everything had to remain precisely as he'd arranged it, which took incredible care on the uneven stone streets. To make the progress of the assistants even more challenging, thick snow was drifting down out of the graying skies, and snowflakes too would interfere with the tableau. One of the assistants had removed his cloak, and one of the praetorians used it to shield the platform from the snow, walking backward the while.

Dania was aware that their entourage looked comical and guessed that if she had not left Vennius behind to sort the paperwork of the prisoners he would be constantly scoffing. The situation was nothing to laugh at, however, for owing to her gender her superiors were always ready to assign blame, no matter her long string of successes. She would not fail.

Publius took their efforts seriously. He followed his assistants, hand cupped over a ruby he'd covered in his own blood. It glowed with inner fire that seemed to have brightened as the skies themselves darkened. The mage halted at the intersection with a little side street, snapping at his assistants to stop, and he stared at the patterns of powder on the platform. He placed the blood crusted ruby at its center. Golden lines glimmered along its every edge.

"Why are we stopping?" Dania demanded.

The mage shifted a pinch of gray powder into a pile of blue powder in a little cup to the left of the ruby, then looked up at her. "Something's gone wrong. First I thought he was moving, and now it seems he's in multiple places at once."

Dania addressed him with quiet severity. "You've made an error."

Only then did Publius seem to realize he might be in trouble, and his eyes sought Dania's own, pleading. He actually gulped. "No, I swear, Centurion. I would never act with anything but the greatest—"

"I don't care about your excuses. I want you to find them. Either of them. You said you could get a better fix on the Nuvaran." Though her own magic skills were of a different sort she had understood the younger man's explanations. The Nuvaran simply had more emotionality invested into his belongings. Apart from Varahan's writings, the Volani had left almost nothing behind that had not been given him by his captors.

Dania still had a hard time believing Senator Aminius' folly. Aminius had wanted the prisoners kept near the Tibron river, so they could perfect their Volani fire experiments on actual boats. He'd also subscribed to the theory that his prisoners would be more inspired to cooperate if they were provided with comforts.

The coddling hadn't produced results, and only made it that much easier for Cerdians to get wind of both their location and the very date and time Aminius had summoned them to explain their lack of performance. Sooner or later that security gap would have to be explored. For now, though, locating the prisoners was the matter of gravest import. And until a few moments ago, Publius had seemed to feel they were very close.

The mage shifted some of his powders about, then pointed down the lane. "This way."

They diverted down a diagonal alley then climbed a short set of steps to turn sharply onto Dolus street, which, a half mile distant, would wind up Campion hill and the fine homes upon its rounded height.

"We're getting close now," the sorcerer said, and Dania wished she could know for sure if that was real or feigned confidence in his voice.

They turned a corner into a fountain square surrounded by old two-story buildings sheathed in flaking gray plaster. Young women were fetching water from a basin fed by a broken-winged swan sculpture. A small crowd looked over a grocer's wares, and dozens more huddled under the awning at a neighborhood restaurant. The smell of frying meat and uncounted decades of wine was somehow sharper and more distinct in the crisp winter air. Nearby a band of young boys tossed a black ball while two smaller boys and an eager brown dog tried to intercept, unbothered by either cold or snow.

"He's right here," Publius said. He raised his finger without directing it toward any of the dozens who eyed them warily.

"Where?" Dania snapped. "Make it quick!"

The mage paused an agonizingly long time and Dania bared her teeth, willing him to get on with it. She searched for a Nuvaran, wondering if those two near the weaver's shop in heavy cloaks might be the escaped prisoners, or if the Nuvaran might be one of those darker skinned men staring at them from the back of the restaurant line. She was readying to order her men forward when the mage finally spoke.

"He's by the children!"

Dania pointed. "Secure the children and anyone near them!"

The praetorians trotted forward, happy to have something to do, and shouted for the boys to stop. The seven youngsters, none of whom could be older than ten, halted their game. Most of them had the sense to look alarmed.

Publius' assistants advanced more slowly, burdened now with both the platform and the cloak shielding it from the snow.

Dania ordered them to watch their step then followed the praetorians. She thought the situation would grow clear as she drew close, but no one near the boys looked remotely Nuvaran, unless she was to count a dark-skinned woman looking down from a window above a leather worker's shop.

Frowning, Dania scanned and discovered no Nuvarans anywhere close, and certainly not among the patch-cloaked boys or their dog, panting beside the skinniest of them.

"You," she said to the gangly boy holding the black leather ball, "have you seen a dark-skinned old man? A Nuvaran?"

His eyes wide, the boy slowly shook his head, as though his very life depended upon his answer. It might.

Publius lifted his hand, and Dania gave him space, waiting to see where the fingers led. Might the Nuvaran be hidden someplace nearby, in that barrel, or even behind some secret door?

The sorcerer halted before the skinny boy, shifting to left and right in time with the dog, who seemed frightened but unwilling to run off. It was a medium sized shaggy mutt just this side of a puppy, a little dirty and mostly brown. Animals were especially sensitive to magical doings, and the pup was probably uncomfortable with the mage's spell, and her own aura.

"The dog," Publius shouted. "Seize the dog!"

One of the praetorians bent and snagged the animal's ruff. It whimpered and fought the soldier's grasp, growling as the mage bent at its side. It was only then that Dania observed a small brown pouch tied about its neck. The mage grabbed hold of the pouch, lifted a broad knife—eliciting a gasp from the onlookers—then cut the bag free without harming the animal.

He rose with it in his hand.

Dania's lip curled. "What are you doing?"

The mage showed his teeth in a grimace, then opened the little bag. He closed his eyes and passed it to Dania.

It had been stuffed with curly gray hair.

"You've been following a hair bag," Dania said with a groan.

"Yes, Centurion," Publius said softly. "The Nuvaran must have cut his hair and tied some on stray dogs. All over the neighborhood."

"You've figured that out, have you?"

The mage's voice rose in a whine. "But how did he know I was watching him?"

"Clearly he's created some kind of ward." Dania stalked to the board that the acolytes still held, ignoring their apprehensive looks. The one who'd given over his cloak was shivering. She peered over the complex symbols and the arrangement of the power web. She understood what Publius had done but felt no affinity for the lines he'd manipulated. Below the bloody ruby lay a tiny piece of fabric torn from the Nuvaran sorcerer's belongings.

"If we replace the garment with a some of that paper that Varahan handled, can this same spell work for him?" she asked.

"It will not be as powerful." The mage had said as much earlier. "We will have to proceed far slower."

"Perhaps not." Dania reached within her cloak and withdrew a small, flattened jar, all of black, with a gold-threaded stopper.

Even with it unopened, Publius sensed the jar's power. Fascinated rather than repelled, he took a single step forward. "What is that?"

"The help we need." At least, Dania hoped it was. She glanced to the clouds, wishing they were even darker, or that evening was closer. The circumstances were far from ideal, but she was tired of relying solely upon the other mage. She could not afford to fail. She passed over the scrap of papyrus she'd torn from the most handled of Varahan's documents. "Reset the spell with this as a focusing agent, and I will ready my own magics to assist."

"But what kind of magic is that? It feels like . . . many heartbeats."

"A special project. I haven't quite perfected it, but . . . Stop staring, man. You, Praetorian! Clear those people away from that restaurant so we can set this down out of the snow and make adjustments!"

VII

Only a few hours before, Varahan had fled down this lane. Now he peered out from its mouth, studying the door to the building where he'd been held. Apart from some stained snow, no sign of the struggle itself remained, and the street itself was empty save for a lone cart. When its driver finished guiding it slowly through an intersection, the scholar started across the street and along the far sidewalk.

The snow had been descending in sheets, but it died back as Varahan reached the door.

He fully expected the place to be locked, but when he walked up to try the latch the door swung inward. The gods were smiling. He entered cautiously, stopping only a few steps into the atrium. He could have sworn he'd heard the creak of a floorboard above, as of someone moving, but it overlapped the sound of him swinging the door closed, so he couldn't be certain. He stepped into the shadows and watched the balcony overlooking the entry, expecting to see a face.

No one appeared. It might be that an old building like this was just shifting in the winter wind. He flexed his fingers, eying the dark archway to right and left that had led to the quarters kept by the ground floor guards. No sound could be heard apart from his breathing and the bark of a distant dog. He started up the stairs. He had never before noticed how much the boards complained at someone passing over them.

The upstairs apartments were centered around a single common space open to the balcony and mostly taken up with the desks Varahan and Norok had used. Shelves holding Norok's jars of foul liquids and colored powders rose along the east wall between the doorways to their tiny bedrooms. Most of Varahan's papers were stored along a shelf upon the west wall, right up to the edge of the closed doorway to the right of the landing, leading to the upstairs guard bedroom. Most of the south wall was papered over with his equation covered sheets of papyrus. The only breaks in the run of calculations were a single window shuttered on the south wall, high on the left, and the sealed door to the roof, on the far right.

In a single glance Varahan saw that someone had been rifling through the papers. Not only had they been piling things up beside a satchel, they'd left a heavy lantern burning on the desk.

He didn't see the body until he'd walked a little further in. A man in a dark tunic was stretched out on the floor on the other side of a chair.

The floor creaked further under Varahan's approach. As he nudged the man with the heel of his new boot he noted that a helmet with a black crest sat on the edge of Norok's table, near a gladius in a black sheath. He swore in his own language. The man was a revenant. Varahan had seen more than his share of dead bodies during the fall of Volanus and recognized that unfocused stare in a face frozen with pain. The pool of blood was small, but originated from a rent in the revenant's black tunic.

While he was still wondering who had left a dead revenant on the floor of his detention apartment a hinge squeaked behind him.

Varahan whirled. A pair of men in brown tunics and cloaks eased from the guard's bedroom at the top of the stairs. Both held swords. The one on the left was the man who'd knocked himself senseless in the alley.

So it wasn't oversight that had left the front door open. These men had forced their way in, killed the revenant, and then looked over the papers. He should have known his luck was going to run thin eventually. Varahan pulled his knife, but it looked pitifully short in comparison to the weapons of the opposition. The Cerdian he'd stolen it from frowned.

"You do not want to fight us," the other Cerdian said, his Dervan so fluent that his accent was virtually unnoticeable. "We can make this nearly painless, if you cooperate."

"If you're afraid I will give secrets to the Dervans, why kill me? I'm planning to escape."

The Cerdian inclined his head, his mouth shifting into a doleful frown. "Regrettably, I have my orders. My superiors do not like us to take too much initiative, and you have already proved a complication. I do not lack compassion, however. I shall be swift. Where is the other?"

When Varahan saw the shadow of a man upon the stair to the Cerdians' right he naturally assumed it was cast by someone climbing stealthily for their position. The figure glided swiftly on, soundlessly and without the lurch from a person shifting their weight on each stair, Varahan realized, as his blood chilled.

No one was casting the shadow.

Alarmed as he was by the thought of death on a Cerdian blade, the shadow on the stairs terrified him to the very core of his being.

The head assassin was faced away from the stairs, so that all he noticed was Varahan's reaction. He looked pained, as if disappointed the scholar would attempt a well-worn ploy. But his companion turned in time to see the shadow reach the landing. The second assassin cried out in horror and tripped over his own foot as he fled for the door to the roof.

By then chief assassin had turned to behold the man-shaped blot of inky darkness floating above the floorboards. He shouted in alarm, then stabbed at the shadow. His blade passed through without doing any apparent damage.

The thing thrust its hands for the Cerdian's neck and closed around it.

The assassin-turned-victim wrestled with black wrists no longer insubstantial, but he might as well have pried at stone with his fingertips. The shadow proved unyielding. The Cerdian's eyes rolled, and his face was a ghastly mask of terror. A tremor passed through his body, and then he dropped, motionless, fainted or dead. His sword clanged against the floorboard and slid next to the leg of the revenant's corpse.

The shadow glided over the body and toward the remaining Cerdian. Finding the door to the roof locked, the other assassin had been kicking it frantically, and had just managed to break through the lower panel when the creature fell upon him. He screamed, once, and struggled fitfully.

In desperation, Varahan snatched the lantern, thinking it might be of use against a creature made of darkness. He had just lifted it when the shadow left the limp body of the second assassin and drifted toward him.

He opened his mouth, wondering what he might say to it, and found himself only capable of gasping. He had read accounts of men stricken by fear, and that scholarly part of his mind that was always dispassionately observing was fascinated by his reaction.

He lifted the lantern to the shadow and the thing halted only a few paces out. Varahan gulped, staring up at where its head would be. He perceived a dim face floating in the murk. Disturbingly, it appeared familiar.

The ground floor door opened.

If Varahan took a step or two to the right he could have peered over the balcony and down at the door. But he dared not move.

"He is up there," Norok's voice said. And two pairs of footsteps hurried up the stairs.

Wonderful as it was to hear a friendly voice, Norok's approach awakened Varahan to action. "Get away, Norok," he cried. "There's a spirit here!"

It was not Norok who reached the landing first, but a young man. Varahan did not recognize the bald Nuvaran just behind him as his colleague until Norok shouted something in his own language.

The shadow rotated to face both newcomers, then extended its hands and flowed forward.

Norok lifted a charm from his neck and thrust it stiff armed before him. Chanting, he placed himself between the shadow and the young man.

It was only then Varahan glimpsed a future in which he might not have to die. He surprised himself when he plodded forward, lantern held high and blazing against the shadow.

As he neared the thing its form wavered, fading to a lighter gray through which he saw not just Norok, but the three red stones of the Nuvaran's necklace, dangling from the sorcerer's hand and burning with such intense inner light Varahan could not bear to stare directly at them.

The spirit cared for the stones even less than it liked the lantern. It shivered in its place, then sank slowly, narrowing as it did, sliding finally between a dark gap in the floorboards.

Breathing with effort, Norok restored the necklace to his throat. The stones dimmed, fading to black.

Varahan beamed. "Norok!"

The young man with Norok was talking quickly. Norok had his hand to his blue stone, the only colorful one left to him. He rattled on in what sounded like Nuvaran and the young man responded in kind. Their exchange continued, and then Norok pointed toward the door along the back wall, and the young man rushed to it, kicked the broken panel the rest of the way open, and squeezed through. Varahan heard him pounding up the steep flight of stairs to the roof.

"Who's that?" Varahan asked. "What did you tell him?"

"That the shadow is going back to its master. It was weak in the daylight, and poorly formed, or we could not have hurt it."

"And what's your friend going to do?"

"Disrupt the spell used to find us, if he can. Now thank me, you fool! Of all the places to go, you came back here?"

"I had to get the papers."

"Papers," Norok snorted. "You and your numbers."

Varahan laughed and threw his arms wide, and then Norok grinned at him and did the same. The next moment, they were clasping and thumping one another's back.

"Do you know how many years I put into those stones I burned?" Norok said to him. "It is a good thing I like you, fluff head."

"What happened to your hair?"

VIII

Norok had told Hanuvar the shadow wasn't dead, just weakened. He'd said further the workings for any spell so powerful would be obvious, and fragile. And that whoever controlled it was drawing closer.

Hanuvar hurried up the dark, narrow stairwell, unbolted the door and headed into the cold air, striding through the slush and snow gathered on the building's flat black roof. To the north was nothing but the empty street below, and Horace, standing watch outside. To the south, behind their building, he found a similarly deserted lane and a line of warehouses, and beyond them docks projecting into the mighty Tibron itself, a murky channel winding through the city.

He stilled, listening, at slowly advancing footsteps. A strange procession came slowly into view on the back street. Among them was the woman revenant centurion in black, two praetorians in white, their uniforms tarnished with mud, and a rangy revenant plodding behind the two black-cloaked assistants, who carried a wooden platform holding a collection of painted diagrams and powders. Flitting in front of them was something that might have been a bit of dark mist. Hanuvar knew better—it was all that remained of the shadow thing.

The gangly revenant was manipulating some ingredients upon the platform.

So far, none in that procession were looking up. Hanuvar crouched at the rail, digging into the snow at his feet.

Below, one of the praetorians remarked that the neighborhood seemed familiar.

When Hanuvar rose again, his left arm cradled a half dozen compacted balls of snow. He'd sent the second hurtling through the air before the first one struck the mage in the side of the head. The sorcerer staggered with a grunt that transformed into a cry of anguish as the second snowball hit the platform. Unguents and powders spattered widely and what looked like a ruby slid to one side. One of the bearers stumbled and then the third snowball hit him in face and he and the table dropped. Powders wafted into the air.

The misty shape in front vanished entirely.

By then the revenant centurion was shouting that they were under attack. Hanuvar dashed for the exit.

His father had taught him that neutralizing an enemy didn't always require lethal force. Hanuvar wondered what Himli Cabera would have said to see how his son had just eliminated this particular threat of Dervan sorcery.

It was a hard dash then for a better hiding place, but Hanuvar managed to guide his charges to freedom at one of Carthalo's safehouses four blocks distant. Varahan had insisted on dragging a big bag along with him, and once Hanuvar understood the importance of the papers it contained, he had shouldered it himself.

They had access to a water pump in the courtyard behind a bakery, and, after consulting with Norok, arranged for both Varahan and the Nuvaran to scrub themselves thoroughly in the cold water, and for the Volani to shave his head down to the scalp. Neither of the old men were especially happy to be so wet on such a cold day, but after they dried off, Norok grudgingly agreed this would probably put the Dervans completely off the scent. Through a sorcerous lens, the cleansing would be like granting them new identities.

By then Lucena had arrived with a new cart, and they climbed inside. Soon they were rumbling away toward the city center.

"What happens next?" Varahan asked.

Hanuvar, seated across from him, answered easily. "That depends on what you want. If you wish to go to safety directly, I can arrange that. A place with free Volani."

Varahan blinked in surprise at this idea, obviously curious, but didn't ask for the details Hanuvar expected. "What's the other option?"

"I mean to free more Volani. And I can use your help."

"And what about me?" Norok asked.

"I can supply you with the funds to return to your homeland."

The Nuvaran's brows rose in wonder. "Just like that?"

"My money isn't endless," Hanuvar admitted. "And if you wished to help me with a few things before you left, I'd be grateful. But I wouldn't require it of you."

Norok cleared his throat, his expression thoughtful. "What sort of things do you need help with?"

"I'm only interested in getting Volani free. But there will be more revenants, and more mages, and from time to time I may need to consult with a sorcerer to counter their spells. Like that shadow."

Norok nodded. "We were lucky to fight that thing in daylight. And it seemed, somehow, unfinished. Like the spell was not complete."

The cart rattled over a low spot and all three men quickly grabbed the side of their seats. Up front, beside Lucena, Horace swore.

"The shadow monster," Varahan said. "It had a face. Did you see it?"

Norok gave him a sharp look. "You should not look into the eyes of such evil."

Hanuvar had not seen a face in the creature and looked to Varahan for further information.

"Its face looked familiar, and it took me a while to realize why, though it made no sense."

"Go on," Hanuvar urged.

Even with that encouragement, Varahan still needed a moment to explain. "I could have sworn that the face looked like one of the seven Volani councilors."

Hanuvar's heart sank. He thought he could guess. "Tanilia?"

The scholar gaped. "How did you know?"

He wrestled with the weight of the ramifications of his deduction as he answered. "A few months ago I learned the revenants had some high-ranking Volani in their custody. She was one." He did not add that one of his cousins had been another.

"Then they have warped living spirits to make a monster." Norok's face was drawn. "That shadow was powerful because it was held by the life of many. Whoever they are, they are trapped, and controlled by this mage."

Long years ago, during the second war, Hanuvar's own band of mages had almost been wiped out by shadow magics, until his brother Harnil had rooted out the Dervan sorcerers behind the attack. It had seemed the entire school of them was finished forever, for they'd encountered no further such dark sorcery during the rest of the conflict. He hadn't personally faced them or their powers before, but he remembered what Harnil had relayed to him, and something in Norok's words gave him further pause. "You mean we didn't destroy the shadow when I broke their spell?"

"No. I think it was dismissed only. You broke their tracking spell. To fully eliminate an abomination such as that . . . this will require some thought." He met Hanuvar's eyes. "Such a thing is a blight upon humanity. I will stay, and I will think hard, and I will find a way for you to send those spirits home."

Hanuvar inclined his head and spoke formally. "I am grateful."

His sincerity seemed to embarrass the Nuvaran. "Well, I can't really imagine travelling in the winter anyway," he said. "Especially crossing mountains."

"I've done that a few times," Hanuvar said. "I don't recommend it."

※ ※ ※

We did not know it at the time, but Dania's superiors were displeased with her failure, pulling her from active command and sending her back to the remote prison fortress of the Revenant Order. There she brooded and labored in the darkness upon her monster.

All that winter Hanuvar and Carthalo worked their miracles, reinvigorating the old spy network and empowering middlemen to handle the negotiation and purchase of dozens of captured Volani. This swiftly grew expensive, and not just because coins had to cross so many hands. Too much attention would have been drawn if it became obvious interested buyers were combing the country and purchasing only Volani slaves. Sometimes entire domestic staffs had to be obtained, at exorbitant fees, just to acquire one or two slaves.

Once, to free a single slave, every wretched man working a small silver mine had to be liberated. Many of these workers were in terrible condition, and required nursing, and others were hardened criminals, rightly sentenced to hard labor for terrible crimes. Their fates had to be handled with great delicacy. The most violent had to be killed after they attacked the men who had freed them. The untrustworthy had to be sent far away after we had revealed as little about ourselves as possible, for some would have sold out their own brother for a few extra coins.

Despite these and other trials, a small but steady stream of freed Volani was being guided north to me. Though I had little experience in management I did not fare too badly. I had to pay at first for the labor that saw to the felling of trees and the construction of buildings, but before much longer I had a host of free assistance, some of it skilled and all of it grateful. This eased the strain on finances but did not alleviate it, nor did it solve our most pressing issue—we needed trained shipwrights, and navigators.

Hanuvar knew this all too well, and so, one day in late winter, he made the day's journey from Derva to the port of Ostra, there to call upon Izivar Lenereva for assistance.

—Sosilos, Book Eight

Chapter 5:
A Ring of Truth

I

Hanuvar often heard the voices of the dead when he dreamed. In some ways such dreams were a solace, but they inevitably left him feeling fragile and alone on waking, for long months had passed since he'd been in the presence of people freely conversing in his native tongue.

This day, though, the air was rich with the speech of Volani as late season olive oil, and wine, and lumber were carried by deck hands who alternately cursed at one another or made jests, or simply shouted orders.

That these were ordinary words made them all the more remarkable. The last time Hanuvar had been near so many Volani speakers, the surviving Eltyr had been succoring the wounded and the dying, and eying the storm-tossed waves as they prepared to cast off into the ocean. Today, these workers carried on ordinary duties, almost as though nothing had changed. The mundanity tore at his heart— that so simple an experience should be so extraordinary. For here, within this little Dervan coastal town, a little over two hundred Volani lived free.

It was not that their existence had gone unnoticed. It was that Tannis Lenereva, merchant-prince of Volanus, had publicly broken with his own city in the contentious months before the third and final Volani war, relocating himself and his immediate family to his

153

holdings in the port of Ostra, the naval gateway to Derva itself. Originally only a few dozen of his retainers and employees had elected to accompany him, followed by a few dozen more Volani from other enclaves in the Inner Sea.

And then, after the war, when the pitiful few survivors had been auctioned off on Dervan slave blocks, Tannis had purchased the finest ship builders, and then his daughter had bought almost fifty others—family members of the ship builders and still more Hanuvar assumed were their relations or friends. He couldn't be certain; he had inferred much from a few unguarded phrases he'd overheard and from information in the paperwork detailing the sales of the men, women, and children of Volanus.

He listened with eyes closed and head rested against the shuttered window of a small tavern, a warm mug of cider cupped in his hands. He was alone, for the rest of the patrons huddled about the braziers further within the building. He couldn't bring himself to feel gratitude toward Tannis Lenereva for betraying his homeland to nest cozily in the enemy's bosom, but he could be grateful for this moment.

He had come to speak with Izivar Lenereva, but before he did so he had wished to observe the Volani under her family's care. Now, watching them through the slats, hearing their voices straining to be heard against the cries of seagulls and the slap of waves, they seemed little different than other folk who were free. If he squinted, this place almost felt like home, although only in the worst of winters did the weather of Volanus grow so cold.

Far-sailing ships were rare in most Dervan ports, and absent on this day, but commerce continued from the nearby isles and from up and down the Tyvolian coast. The dock workers wore heavy, sleeved tunics and leggings and caps, and had traded out their sandals for boots.

He could not long pretend this was his home. These workers were unloved by Dervans, only grudgingly tolerated because of the wealth and connections of their employer. Even from Hanuvar's limited vantage point it was easy to spot locals casting frowns or suspicious glares toward the Volani.

Tannis, and his father and uncle before him, had struggled so determinedly against Hanuvar's family it sometimes seemed they chose opposing viewpoints out of sheer contrariness rather than genuine ideological differences. Under Tannis, the Lenereva had always favored a different course, whether it was opposing the "Cabera war" or opening a second and useless resource-draining front in Icilia. When Hanuvar had led his army over the Ardenines, the Lenereva faction had followed the precedent they'd established in the first war, meaning Hanuvar's victories were proof no additional support was needed and setbacks were evidence of imminent failure so funding should not be risked.

After the war, when Hanuvar had returned to Volanus and risen to hold one of the city's twin magisterial posts, Tannis had objected more loudly than anyone else as Hanuvar and his allies remade the state, raising taxes on those who could afford them and eliminating traditions of comfortable corruption. Finally, Tannis had leagued with the Dervans to arrest and deport Hanuvar. Only a warning from Ciprion had alerted him to the approaching net.

The wind rattled the shutters and shook him from his ruminations. He hadn't meant to be lost in thought. A consequence of growing old, he thought, then smiled wryly as he flexed hands no longer crossed with wrinkles or scars.

Now that he better understood the condition of the present, it was time to contemplate the future. Challenging conversations lay before him. Beyond his personal distaste for interacting with the Lenereva clan, his presence here was an enormous risk. So long as he lived, his plans could grow, and the network that Carthalo had once overseen would expand to become an instrument of freedom. Much like a tree, when it was firmly rooted it could survive the loss of its gardener. But at this point, that tree remained fragile. He was low on funds and desperately short on skilled labor. He needed experienced hands to build ships, and to sail them. And here, in this community, those hands could be had. But at what price? He had many times weighed the risk-to-benefit ratio of pursuing his contact with Izivar, and even now was uncertain he measured correctly.

In the months since Hanuvar had last seen her his appearance had gradually changed. Gone was the youth just this side of puberty. Now when he looked in the mirror he saw a young man in his middle twenties, which was almost the same age he'd held when he'd led his expedition over the Ardenines and into the Tyvolian peninsula. A lifetime ago. Then he had been bearded and uniformed. This time he was beardless and dressed as a simple Dervan of the middle class, his dark hair cut straight across his forehead. The Dervans themselves would be unlikely to recognize him.

But Volani might. Izivar had thought he resembled Melgar when she'd met him earlier, perhaps because Melgar had often gone beardless after the second war and had been a common sight in Volanus. Others he passed here might also note the family resemblance.

He stood, raised the hood of his cloak as if against the chill, and tucked one hand into his dark robe. He left the inn and headed into the street. The leggings were welcome, though he'd have preferred good Ceori boots rather than his lighter Dervan ones. They would have made him distinctive, and Hanuvar worked not to be.

As he turned up a sloping side street someone called accented taunts—a Volani speaking Dervan. The distinct smack of flesh against flesh came after, followed by laughter.

Someone up ahead said, in Volani, "He doesn't look like so much now, does he?"

"I am a friend to Volani," a counter voice said, though in Dervan, and Hanuvar, who'd been uninclined to intercede, paused just beyond the sounds of conflict, at the entrance to a narrow street.

"Are you?" the first voice asked. "You going to tell me how nice you are?"

"I don't want trouble," the Dervan voice answered, and Hanuvar swore softly to himself. That was the voice of Enarius, favored nephew of the emperor. What he was doing in a side street in Ostra without bodyguards or friends Hanuvar could not guess.

Hanuvar had no love for the Dervan royal family. But if the emperor's favorite was injured or killed by Volani, retribution would be certain and deadly not just for the perpetrators, but for this entire Volani enclave, and likely even beyond.

Scowling, Hanuvar walked into the side street. Three men circled another huddled against a wall, one to front, one to the side and one with his back to Hanuvar, a short youth pulling back to kick his victim.

None of the three were older than their early twenties. If Hanuvar hadn't had to maintain his disguise in front of Enarius he might have scolded them in their native tongue and reminded them of better manners.

Instead, he swept his cloak from his shoulders and ran at them. The one facing away started to turn. With a boot to the rear Hanuvar sent him tumbling over the crouching Enarius, to sprawl on the dirty bricks.

Hanuvar tossed his cloak over the man who'd been at Enarius' side, doubling him over with a punch to the gut that brought the youth's chin into Hanuvar's upthrust knee. The man cried out as he sagged.

Enarius, his cloak and tunic dirtied, pushed to his feet and stumbled toward Hanuvar. The third attacker was the largest, broader than Hanuvar and half a head taller. He snarled and advanced with clenched fists. Hanuvar backstepped, ignored a feint from the left, then slapped the right hook away and staggered the brawler in the cheek with a backfist.

"More are coming," Enarius warned.

Three more men hurried in from the far end of the street. It might be they were coming to break up the fight. But they might also be reinforcements. Hanuvar hated to leave a good cloak, but discretion was better warranted, and he and Enarius backed away, then ducked around the corner. They sprinted uphill then turned down a larger avenue. Footsteps clattered behind them until they neared a small square crowded with Dervan merchants. From behind came curses, and Hanuvar looked over his shoulder. The big ruffian put thumb to nose and flicked it at them while one of the others shouted his thanks for the cloak and waved it in the air.

Enarius bent to catch his breath, both hands on his knees, and regarded Hanuvar. "It's you, isn't it?" he said between gasps. "I can't believe you helped save my life a second time."

Hanuvar stared as if confused, then smiled as though a thought had just struck him. "Ah, you must think I'm my younger brother. We look a lot alike."

Enarius' brow furrowed. The look of concentration seemed out of place on his open, hearty features. He was a handsome young man, with bright blue eyes. He pushed back his black, wavy hair from his forehead, and straightened. "I see it now. The resemblance is striking, but you're clearly older."

"My brother saved your life?"

"Well, he helped save my life." Enarius offered his hand in a clasp. Hanuvar took it while Enarius lowered his voice. "I'm Enarius Marcus Avonius."[7]

Hanuvar let his eyebrows climb but Enarius made a shushing motion with his lips. "Keep it quiet. I'm just a man you saved from a beating, nothing special."

"It's an honor to meet you," Hanuvar said. "My brother mentioned you."

"But he didn't say he'd helped me? He must be a modest young man. Well, it seems I owe you a cloak. At the least."

There were two cloak sellers obvious in this marketplace. "Normally I'd say no, but it was pretty new. If you're . . ." he pretended to rethink what he'd started to say, "who you are, what are you doing here, away from your guards and servants?"

Enarius smirked. "Guards and servants are such a bore. I sneaked away."

"Why did the Volani attack you?"

"Because I'm a rich Dervan on his own, I expect. I don't think they recognized me, or I'd have heard the usual slanderous insults about being my uncle's lover." Enarius stopped beside a rack on a street counter beside a selection of hats and scarves. "What do you think of these here? Do they seem thick enough?"

Hanuvar allowed the emperor's son to buy him a replacement garment, watching the while for the Volani attackers. They must have decided further harassment wasn't worth the effort. He acknowledged his thanks, pulled the brown cloak over his shoulders, then said, "Let's get you back where you belong. What were you doing in a back lane, anyway?"

Enarius smiled as if amused by his own antics, then started down

---

7 Enarius was the son of Cornelia major, the oldest daughter of the Cornelian line; he did not assume the Cornelius cognomen until he was formally adopted by the emperor. Gaius Cornelius was a confirmed bachelor, like the first emperor, his older brother Julius, neither of whom were able to sire children. Enarius was one of four nephews who survived to majority but was the favorite by a considerable margin. His older brother had broken a leg as a young boy and it was permanently stunted, such that he did not like to be seen in public.

　　I had the opportunity to engage with some who had known Enarius' cousins and they were described to me as pleasant nonentities conceited by the luster of their name. By all accounts, Enarius' charm won the emperor's affection very early on, and there was little to no competition from his relatives for the post of favorite. —*Silenus, Commentaries* the street. Hanuvar fell in step beside him. "Truth to tell, I've grown fond of Volani wine. It's probably some kind of heresy of me to say so. But then there are a lot of sweet things I like about Volani." He glanced sidelong at Hanuvar, as if admitting a great failing of his: "The way the women dress..." He shook his head.

If he meant the scalloped blouses that bared shoulders and the flounced calf-length skirts and winking ankle jewelry, Hanuvar understood, for he thought the garb far more becoming than that of Dervan women.

"I didn't see any on the streets dressed like that," Hanuvar said.

"Too cold for it. I tell you, I've never been much interested in older women, but there's a Volani widow under my protection. She's aged well and has these huge, sad eyes, and quick wit, and such grace. She knows a lot but doesn't shove it in your face."

Izivar. Hanuvar pretended ease with the concept of discussing the subject. "What does your uncle say about your interest in such a woman?"

Enarius laughed. "I'm not talking about marrying her."

Hanuvar braced to hear the young man say something lewd. That it would be uttered by the relative of the ruler who'd ordered the extermination of the Volani people almost made him break the character he pretended. He struggled to maintain an expression of polite curiosity.

"It's just..." Enarius' voice trailed off, and then he spoke in an open and charmingly vulnerable way: "I rather care for her. She's the sister of a good friend, and I promised him I'd look after her. He died, trying to help me."

Hanuvar nodded as though he understood. So Enarius knew that Izivar was not for him and yet pined for her and felt protective over her all the same. His opinion of the younger man rose a little. "Is that why you're here in Ostra?" Hanuvar asked. "To see her?"

"In part. There's also a fantastic boxing ring here and I'm in for that. That's how I made friends with the Lenereva family in the first place."

"I assume you've been referring to the lady Izivar," Hanuvar said. "I'm to meet with her myself, to convey a note from my brother."

"I should have known we hadn't met by chance. So does your brother mean to court her?"

Enarius really wondered if he, Hanuvar, meant to court her, in his current guise. Hanuvar shook his head. "She's too rich for our blood. My brother said she was striking, though."

"I can deliver his letter for you." Enarius strove to sound helpful rather than defensive.

"If it's all the same, I'd like to meet this beauty myself."

Enarius laughed. "It's my own fault for talking her up."

They had arrived at a street fronting a wide building with old square columns. A row of food vendors had set up beneath its entablature and patrons lined up before them. Merchants with pennants and scarves and hats shouted to purchase colors for favorite boxers, calling out their names and associated hues.

The arches opened onto a wide, well-lit gymnasium in the round, though he could only see the backs of the spectators' heads poking above the top row of the sunken ring.

As they closed on the main entrance Enarius spoke rhapsodically about watching a boxer ascend through the ranks, and how his success was much more about personal skill than the whims of a mad promoter. "You never see a boxer suddenly destroyed in a pairing against a leopard or something ridiculous like you see with gladiators. This is a real sport, not a bloodbath. I don't understand why it doesn't have a larger following in Derva. Here's where you can find some of the best fighters in the world."

While Enarius discussed the virtues of boxing, Hanuvar expressed polite interest with a nod, wondering why so many of those fascinated with sport shared the delusion others liked to hear them expound upon it. He happened to agree with Enarius' opinion of gladiatorial combats, and thought he raised some intriguing points, but he had no more interest in a lecture about the merits of boxing than he had in gargling salt water.

"Are some of your friends here?" Hanuvar asked.

"My minders, you mean," Enarius said with weary bitterness. "Most of my friends died in that grisly assault your brother helped me with. I expect Metellus and his people are off searching for me. Or they might not have noticed I'm gone yet—"

"Enarius, praise Jovren you're well."

Hanuvar and Enarius turned at the sound of the patrician voice behind them. Its source was a distinguished older man with silver hair, a highly arched Dervan nose, and a dark green robe, which he clutched closed with one gloved hand. The quality of the garment and the glimpse of the tunic beneath suggested wealth, as did his emerald studded citizen's ring and familiarity with Enarius. A patrician, then, but not a senator, for his tuni lacked a edging stripe. The man's formal decorum suggested religious vocation.

His eyes were a bright clear brown. They shifted from Enarius so that Hanuvar now faced the full force of their scrutiny. The stranger quickly masked his amazement.

Hanuvar had no memory of meeting him before and concealed his worry he'd been recognized. Might they have met some year long ago? Hanuvar debated his options if the man should address him by name.

"Forgive my manners," the stranger said, not unkindly. His attitude was not so much suspicious as supremely curious. "Good day to you."

"And to you." Hanuvar masked his concern with bland politeness.

"We should talk, you and I," the man said further.

Hanuvar gave him a bemused look.

"Lucius Longinus, this is . . ." Enarius faltered and turned to Hanuvar. "Do you know, I don't think I asked your name!" He laughed then looked once more back to Lucius. "He's the brother of the man who helped Metellus and me save the lady Izivar."

That wasn't how Hanuvar would have described the incident, but he did not correct Enarius, who continued his introduction: "Not only does he look a lot like his brother, he's just as helpful. He pulled me out of a scrape close to the docks."

"You're a fortunate young man, then," Lucius said, "and I am fortunate old one, because your uncle would have had my head if anything happened to you."

Enarius leaned toward Hanuvar. "My uncle put Lucius in charge of my moral instruction. He's a priest of Jovren."

"And who are you?" Lucius asked Hanuvar.

"I am Decius." Hanuvar bowed his head. "Decius Marco. It's an honor."

"It seems his family and yours are wound together in some fashion," the priest said. "As if the gods themselves sent you and your brother to help safeguard Enarius in his times of need." Lucius peered so keenly at Hanuvar he had the sense the man was somehow looking through him.

"That may be," Hanuvar allowed with a polite head bow. "Or it might be that my brother was passing on a common road, and I was in a large port city delivering a message to a mutual acquaintance."

"Much more than an acquaintance," Enarius said with dignity.

The priest ignored him. "I've been told your brother wished no aid from Enarius. Most people would seek out the company of a wealthy patron and make excuses to be around them."

"Ah, well." Hanuvar cleared his throat as though he were embarrassed. The continued attention of the priest alarmed him and he strove to keep his voice level. "Enarius bought this cloak for me, which is more than enough thanks. It's been a pleasure to meet you both, but I must deliver my letter."

"If you're looking for Izivar, she's probably in the offices." Enarius pointed beyond the arches. "The Lenereva family runs most of their business from inside, and she's taken over the largest share of it these days. Her father's been feeling poorly."

Tannis Lenereva had been complaining publicly about his health and advancing age for more than twenty years without ever seeming to lose energy or the ability to command his mercantile empire. This time, though, according to Hanuvar's sources, Izivar really had assumed many of the day-to-day administrative duties.

"Thank you again, Decius." Enarius offered his hand. They clasped one another's forearms.

Hanuvar bowed his head to him, and the priest, and started for the arches.

He heard Enarius say behind him, quietly. "What a curious fellow. A nice one, I mean, but curious. Quiet."

Hanuvar felt the priest watching him until he stepped out of his line of sight into the stadium itself.

II

Though Hanuvar explained he was at the stadium only to speak with the Lenereva family, the ticket master forced him to purchase entry, then pointed vaguely toward a back wall.

Much lay between Hanuvar and that back wall, though. A crowd milled about a restaurant tucked in the side of the gymnasium. From a balcony those eating could look down and watch the fights. Like the gymnasium itself the restaurant was open to the air, though its pillars supported a roof to protect its diners from precipitation. Bench-lined tables were grouped around smoking braziers.

A small crowd of well-groomed men in expensive tunics and cloaks had gathered at one of the nearer tables, waited upon by a phalanx of servants and presided over by gray-haired Tannis Lenereva. The old man wore a fine blue tunic, and his well-oiled gray-black beard bounced on his expansive chest as he laughed at some jest. Hanuvar swung wide so he would not be noticed.

Tannis had lost weight in the years since Hanuvar had seen him last, although his cheeks were flush with health. In strongly accented Dervan he was telling those with him that despite his infirmities, gods willing, he hoped to keep going for a little while.

Naturally the surrounding sycophants praised his constitution and assured Tannis he had long years yet. The stink of men gathered about another with power was the same, country to country. Seeing the beaming delight of the old man to hear such reassurances, Hanuvar fought to keep his mouth from twisting in disgust. He had loathed Tannis Lenereva for decades, and hearing him speak once more left Hanuvar questioning the wisdom of his visit. Tannis could never be trusted to look out for anyone's interest but his own.

But then he hadn't come to speak with Tannis.

Beyond the restaurant's tables a long counter stretched, and here crafty plebeians gathered, sipping their wine and weighing the expressions and clothing and manner and coin purses of all who neared. He knew them by look: the most primitive, like the little man leaning too close to the wide-hipped woman with kohl-lined eyes, hoping to improve his current mood by the simplest and most immediate of means. The woman and others of her kind looked to profit from men of his ilk. Those with slightly more complex motivations were mixed in among them: gamblers and down-and-out managers and washed-up fighters with creased and battered faces hoping for an opportunity for glory or at least a small prize purse.

Hanuvar passed them and the back row of benches surrounding

the square pit below. He doubted the seats would have held more than a thousand spectators. Today that number looked to be in the low hundreds, watching with limited interest as a troupe of clowns tossed balls back and forth while singing a bawdy song. The performers were actually quite skilled, but the audience hadn't come to appreciate their ability to catch the balls with feigned carelessness. The gymnasium was between fights.

On the far left, beyond the back rails, a sign hung, lettered in several languages, declaring that there was to be no traffic beyond it, and, if that were not clear, a figure with a line drawn across him was depicted below the words. Somewhat surprised there was no actual guard, Hanuvar stepped through the curtain, and under a stone arch. A long hallway stretched out before him, lit by a single lantern burning in a recess halfway along. He supposed that the Lenereva clan was so secure in their position they feared little. If that was true, they should know better.

As he rounded a corner he came upon a better lit hallway with several doors, one of which was being closed by a surly mouthed man with a broken nose. His immense muscular arms were all the more obvious in his sleeveless tunic. At sight of Hanuvar the stranger squeezed his hands into fists. He hadn't looked to be in a good mood to start with, and he now glowered. "What are you doing back here?" His voice was a low rumble, and his Volani accent was strong.

"I'm looking for Izivar Lenereva." Hanuvar wondered if it were vanity or simply insensitivity to discomfort that enabled the boxer to wear such a shirt on a cold day.

The boxer raised one scarred fist and extended his pointer finger. "I know your type. She needs not to see you."

"I have a message for her."

"I'll take it back to her."

"I've been paid to do that," Hanuvar said reasonably.

"It's not about the message, is it?" The boxer sneered. "You wish to see her, do you not? You Derva boys are all the same. To court a Volani woman, after you gut her city. After you blood her people. She is not for you!" He emphasized this with a step forward and another shake of that pointing finger.

Hanuvar understood the boxer's sentiment and was faintly amused by the situation. Coming to blows with Volani while pretending to be Dervan was the obstacle he'd least anticipated, and now it threatened a second time in a single day.

He was saved from further comment by the opening of one of the hallway's doors. A young lady emerged in one of the blue and white flounced skirts Enarius had remarked about, though she wore leggings and boots as a concession to the cold, and a blue scarf graced her neck. Her blouse bared her prominent girlish collar bones. Hanuvar was reminded of an old Volani folk song about the beauty of sparrows. She was a coltish thing with the same curling dark hair and slim hooked nose as Izivar, and similar almost imperious confidence. Her eyes, though, were green.

"Maravol," she said in exasperated but unaccented Dervan, "let him be! You know Izivar has been expecting a messenger."

"You do not know this is him, Julivar." The boxer's defensive, injured tone in response to the smaller, far younger person was faintly comical.

Julivar possessed a strange name, one neither Dervan, nor Volani. She was likely no older than fourteen. She rocked her jaw back and forth as though agitating it helped her to think.

"I am the messenger," Hanuvar explained. "My brother met the lady Izivar in the marshes, in the company of the emperor's nephew."

"He passes," Julivar said firmly. "You can go, Maravol."

"I should stay."

"You can come back later."

Maravol wagged his finger at Hanuvar as he passed, warning to watch himself, then stomped around the corner.

"Don't mind him," Julivar said. "He's just trying to protect us. He says it's a bad idea to leave the halls unguarded."

"It is."

"Father used to say if you can't be approached, how can you do business? Izivar says it should be the same way as always, but Father says it shouldn't, not when women are in charge. But Izivar disagrees and I'm not sure." She shifted conversational subjects without pausing for a breath. "Izivar said your brother was handsome." She headed for the door at the far end of the hall. "Does he look like you?"

Hanuvar was surprised that he enjoyed hearing Izivar found him appealing. He didn't think of himself as a vain man. "There's a close resemblance."

"Men say my sister is beautiful." Julivar faced him as she reached the door and put her hand upon the latch. "But I don't look much like her." Her eyes tried too hard to look nonchalant.

"Who cares what men say?" Hanuvar asked. "What do you say?" He reached past her to knock on the door.

The question appeared to have befuddled her.

"Who is it?" Izivar called from within.

"That messenger you wanted is here to see you," Julivar said. "Maravol wanted to fight him, but I sent him away. Maravol, I mean. I sent Maravol away."

Hanuvar wondered if she were always this talkative, or if Julivar were nervous for some reason.

"Send in the messenger," Izivar said.

"It was nice to meet you, Julivar," Hanuvar said. "You have a lovely name."

"Father gave me a Dervan name. It's Julia. But everyone calls me Julivar, which isn't a real Volani name, but sounds better. At least to us, I mean."

"I am Decius," said Hanuvar. "And I have enjoyed your company, whatever your name."

She smiled at that. Hanuvar opened the door and found himself in an office cramped by two desks and a long rectangular display table on the right wall seated just under a shelf jammed with square cubbies from which the tips of loosely rolled scrolls protruded. The table overflowed with trophy statuettes crafted of bronze and wood. High rectangular windows threw light into the room, though Izivar and Serliva, seated at the smaller desk, employed bright candles as well.

Hanuvar gained only a fleeting impression of the maid, Serliva, who looked up at him in surprise, for his eyes settled on Izivar.

At his first sight of her she'd been travelling overland in Dervan garb, and had experienced long days on the road, as well as shock, and grief. Today he had found her in her environment, with her curling hair brushed carefully, with a sapphire necklace upon her slender brown throat, with fine lines of kohl about her eyes and bangles below the cuffs of her blue and white striped blouse. Her elegance stopped his breath.

She smiled, and then her expression grew slightly bemused; she had noted his changed appearance.

"It's good to see you," Izivar told him. "I was afraid you weren't going to come."

She had decided he was the same person, and before Hanuvar could protest she shifted her attention to Serliva. "We'll finish later. Why don't you grab a bite to eat?"

The maid said that she would and then passed Hanuvar, smiling in droll amusement, as she might at leaving two lovers alone. The inference troubled Hanuvar, who was sorting through his feelings as the door closed behind him.

Hanuvar opened his mouth to tell Izivar he was not actually the man she thought him, but she then said: "You look older than I remember."

He closed his mouth. He could still lie, but the sense of connection that lay between them had been visible in her eyes and he was not a fine enough actor to have kept it from his own. It would be impossible to deceive her. As he walked closer she frowned. "I don't understand. It is you. But . . ."

"Are we alone?" Hanuvar asked.

"Yes," she assured him.

"Do any listen in? Servants? Your sister?"

At that, Izivar smiled. "No one is listening in." She gestured to one of the chairs before the larger desk. He saw now that a black band was hidden in her hair, a sign that she mourned her brother.

Her smile was open, but still confused. "I don't understand. Were you disguised to be younger, earlier? Or are you disguised to be older, now? If so, your camouflage is impressive."

He had not planned to have this particular conversation with her, nor to discuss his true identity so soon. And he questioned his judgment as he considered his motivation. His eagerness to engage with her was not because he found her appealing, at least not solely. She had impressed him with her kindness and her intelligence. In her he'd seen an honest concern for their people.

If they were to work together, they would have to learn to trust one another. And thus he spoke the truth. "I was caught in sorcery several months ago. An accident, with some fortunate and unfortunate effects. I was briefly granted youth, although I am rapidly regaining my true age."

She tilted her head as though trying to get a better angle to see him by. She opened her mouth, then closed it. When she finally managed a response, she spoke with awe. "That's an astonishing story. If I didn't see the evidence in front of me, I would say you lied. Not because I doubt you, but because this sounds like something from a fable. How did it happen?"

"A wizard had left a snare on some property that suited our needs."

"And you destroyed it?"

"No. Another wizard tried to use its power to save himself, and the sorceries affected me as well."

"But not him."

"He was already dying. He wasn't a good man." At her pensive look he added: "I don't mean to be evasive. It's not a nice story."

By her nod Izivar acceded to the unspoken request to cease prying for details about the event itself. "What's your true age?"

"I'm about ten years older than you."

As this idea sank in, her face subtly transformed. Gone was her warm engagement. Kindness ebbed like the tide from her eyes, and her mouth. By a matter of only a finger span she pulled back from the desk, but it was as if she stared at him now from across a great chasm. "You are Hanuvar."

"I am."

Her lips twitched into a sneer, then settled into cool disapproval. "How did you survive? Another miracle?"

"Are you angry I did?"

"I'm angry you deceived me."

"I spoke what truth I could, in the camp of an enemy. I thought I had found a friend."

"So had I."

"We are after the same things, Izivar."

"Are we? You led our people to destruction. The war was your idea." That she meant the second war was made perfectly clear as she continued with asperity. "You provoked the Dervans so they were satisfied with nothing less than our whole city! And now you come to me, a Lenereva, thinking I will help you?"

He shook his head, sadly. "This is not about me. It's about our people."

"It was always about you."

"I am the same person you met upon the road. Not some stranger."

"Oh? So this is no act? Or do you seek for a weak point in your old enemy, my father? By coming to his daughter?"

"I'm looking for an ally."

She apparently expected a more detailed answer and gave him silence to contemplate it. When he said nothing, she blinked in astonishment. "That's all you have to say? Have you no defense? No spirited debate about how they would have come for us, in the end?"

"Leave it for the historians. I am concerned with the present."

"Were you concerned with my brother?" she asked spitefully. "He said you nearly killed him."

Hanuvar kept his tone level. "I spared him when he reminded me he had followed the teachings of his father. Who was I to kill him, when I had followed my own, and there are so few of us left?"

Her lips twisted in scorn. "I will not risk our people in some stupid war against the Dervans."

"A war would be foolish. That is not my plan."

"And you are not foolish? You squandered our resources and manpower in a war that only hastened our destruction."

"So you said," he replied wearily. "I've no interest in listening to you parrot these points. I heard them and their like dozens of times in Volanus after the war. I know what I did, and I know who I am. At each instance I made the best choice I had."

"So did my father. He meant to protect his family."

"He meant to protect his family and his wealth. But not his people. And you admitted as much to me. You've done more for them than he. I have seen the records."

She shook her head. "Your family protected your wealth, just like mine. You Cabera always pretended you were better than us, but you counted every coin—"

"I needed every coin for the fight. One way or another the Dervans meant to finish us. The best we might have hoped for was an existence like the Herrenes, a client state, beholden to Derva. But if I had smashed their power—"

"And ruled their land, as an emperor?"

She was smarter than this and was letting her rage and her prejudices outpace her judgement. "That war was never about conquest. It was about smashing the machinery of empire. Taking it down in size so there was room for the rest of us. So that the Inner Sea would be something more than a great Dervan lake."

"Now you will tell me it almost worked, and that I should be grateful."

"I don't want your gratitude. You're focused on the past."

"There's little else left our people." Her tone had shifted. Though still laced with anger, she sounded remote and resigned.

"No, there is a future. And it can be far brighter for those who yet live in slavery. You have saved some of them. What would you say if I told you we could save the rest?"

"I would say you're deluded."

He showed her empty hands. "I came to you, in peace, so that our families might work together for the betterment of those who are left. I will not wage another war, and I will move discreetly. But I will see them freed."

"An uprising?"

"No."

She looked intrigued despite herself. "And where will they go?" She paused only a moment, and a light kindled in her dark eyes. "The colony. You really did found one."

"Yes."

She gulped. "... how many are there?"

"Only a few thousand. I would give them a thousand more, if you aid me."

She stared at him, and he had the sense she was looking at him, once more, as a human she tried to gauge rather than as a vessel full of outlooks she despised. From her expression she was having a hard time reconciling two incongruent conceptions.

"I didn't realize the depths of your own hate for me," he said. "Or the shock that learning my own identity would bring. I will give you time. And I will seek you tomorrow."

"What will you do if I can't help?"

"Do? I will find a way to free them, without you. I had planned to do that from the start but with your aid the chances of success improve immensely. Our people need help, Izivar, and so I ask for yours. But I do not need an enemy at my throat. The wrong word to the wrong person and every last one of them is doomed." He climbed to his feet. "If you wish to see me tomorrow, tie a ribbon about the rightmost column archway up front, at eye level."

There was no knowing what she thought of that suggestion, for her expression remained grave. She rose as he reached for the door, but she did not bid him farewell.

He had misjudged the situation, perhaps badly. But then he had counted too much on the connection he'd thought forged between himself and Izivar, one too easily shattered once she had learned his true identity. He should not have been surprised.

Still, he had seen a glimmer of hope there, near the end. He would give her the time he had suggested. Judging by her own interest in the security of her people, she was unlikely to turn him over to the Dervans, but he felt exposed and vulnerable as he passed back through the gymnasium. He neither saw nor heard Tannis on his return trip, but then he deliberately walked along the side furthest from the restaurant.

He retreated to the little dockside inn and sat this time by the braziers and nursed a very good crab stew, along with some sweet Volani wine.

As he was nearing the bottom half of the meal, a young man ran into the counter and shouted stunning news.

Tannis Lenereva had been murdered.

III

Hanuvar finished the meal slowly and soaked up the information around him as he used the dark Dervan bread to sop the broth at the bottom of the bowl. Details were scarce, but the old man had been found in his office.

The Lenereva patriarch was a lynchpin of the community, for he was not only the owner of a gymnasium central to the sea-side town, he was the man behind the shipping empire employing almost all the Volani in Ostra. His death might presage irrevocable changes as outside rivals fought for his markets and connections. Some worried a Volani woman couldn't actually run a powerful business in Dervan society without a man acting as her screen. They feared that business contracts and other connections might wither overnight.

Hanuvar had never expected to feel remotely troubled about the death of Tannis Lenereva. His current circumstance changed that. Yes, now he would not have to contend with Tannis in any way. But Izivar's father's death would take a toll upon her that would almost surely sour any tenuous dialogue they'd begun. Not only would she have to concentrate most of her attention upon funeral and business matters, there was the very real chance Izivar would think him behind her father's death.

He considered the paths open to him, left coins on the table for his food, and departed, wrapping the new cloak about him.

A band of grim, scarred men loitered outside the gymnasium, the heavy black doors of which had all been closed, apart from one pair on the farthest right that opened directly into the restaurant seating area. As Hanuvar neared it one of the guards moved toward Hanuvar and showed him his palms, saying the gymnasium was closed.

"I heard the news." Hanuvar peered over the guard's large shoulders and spied an open air conference under way within the restaurant. Among those in attendance were Enarius, Izivar, Lucius the priest, and a scarred praetorian centurion Hanuvar recognized from his first meeting with the emperor's nephew. Metellus, he recalled.

Hanuvar addressed the guard. "I spoke with Lady Izivar only an hour ago and forgot to relay some information to her."

The guard shook his head dismissively. "She's busy."

"I'm certain she'll want to speak with me."

"Come back later. Her father's just died."

Hanuvar was readying to counter that when the priest caught sight of him. The older man froze in surprise then rose and started forward.

The guard stepped into Hanuvar's personal space. "Back up and leave. I don't want to cause a scene today, but if I do, it'll be your fault."

The guard hadn't heard Lucius come up behind, but he froze as the commanding voice addressed him. "Let that man in."

The guard turned, sizing up the priest, then looked Hanuvar over doubtfully.

The priest nodded to him. "Decius. You've returned. Is there something you wanted?"

"To express my sympathies," he said, "and to offer my services."

Lucius accepted this proposition without question and bowed his head as if in polite thanks. "I think they will be glad to have them both." He turned, motioning Hanuvar to follow.

While Hanuvar didn't understand the priest's affection for or acceptance of him, he didn't gainsay it. He stepped past the bemused guard and walked at Lucius' side.

"That was kind of you," Hanuvar said.

"Think nothing of it."

He was inclined to inquire about the priest's help, but Izivar had seen him and raised her brows. Though her recovery was swift, her expression had been noted by Enarius and Metellus, who turned to watch him. Enarius still looked pleasantly disposed toward him. Metellus' expression was muted and grim, as though he observed the return of an unwanted rival.

The last time Hanuvar had seen him, the young praetorian had taken a grievous wound to the side of his head. In the intervening months the wound had begun to heal, but his handsome face remained marred along one side by three jagged parallel lines, the longest of which stretched nearly from his ear to his upper lip.

"What are you doing here?" Izivar demanded.

"I came to offer my condolences," Hanuvar replied with a head bow. "And my assistance."

She opened her mouth to respond, then thought better of whatever she'd been about to say, and closed it, frowning. The display clearly confused Enarius and intrigued Metellus, watching with considerable interest. That man would bear careful monitoring.

"Will you excuse us, please?" Izivar said coolly to the others. She stood without waiting for a response, and beckoned Hanuvar to follow. "Come . . . Decius."

He felt the scrutiny of the others upon him as he passed. Metellus remarked to Enarius that he was right, the family resemblance was truly remarkable.

Izivar did not look back to him, but strode along the side of the empty ring and on for the back hall, thrusting the curtain aside. She only advanced a few feet before rounding on him, her voice an icy whisper.

"Did you kill him?"

"No."

"You've lied before. It must come easily to you."

"I am only here to get help for the Volani in chains."

"Gods. You brought our people to this."

He ignored the barb. "I have the means to free them. And your family can help. I would not have jeopardized that to take revenge on your father."

"No? Or maybe it was an opportunity you couldn't resist, since it would leave me in charge of his business and you'd far rather try to manipulate me. You wouldn't have been able to manipulate him."

"No one could ever manipulate your father," he agreed, though he might have made a dozen different and less charitable observations. "I am sorry for your loss, if for nothing else because it makes our own arrangements that much more problematic."

"We have no arrangement! Do you think I mean to throw in with you? Do you know how 'problematic' our position already was before this?"

"Problematic," he repeated. "Shall I tell you of the Eltyr, and how they had been sent to the arena to spill blood to amuse the Dervans? Should I tell you of the Volani garrison in the Isles of the Dead, tortured into digging up the bodies of our ancestors to enrich the coffers of the empire?"

That gave her brief pause, though it did not dull her anger. "Do you think I have had it easy?"

"I think you've had it far easier than many. And you will disappoint me if you fail to acknowledge it."

She sighed. "Fine," she said tersely. "But that does not mean my life's a simple one. I must constantly balance the needs of my employees and their loved ones with the pressure from the empire, and the attentions of Enarius himself, a vital friend whose displeasure could doom us."

"All the more reason for us to move swiftly. And we must do that in any case because every day our people live in slavery is another day some horror is forced upon them. You know this."

He had her full attention now. She was listening rather than waiting for an opening to voice counter points.

He continued. "New Volanus lies far across the sea. It is not large, but our people live free there, beyond the shadow of Derva and the whims of its rulers. I need ships to get our people there. Deep, ocean-going ships. And that means ship builders."

She shook her head. "That can't be done here. You know how much attention that would call to what you were doing?"

"I don't mean to do it here. The more carefully we move those we recover, the better. I've purchased land with a deep harbor, but I need craftspeople. Your craftspeople. Your sailors."

She spoke with sharp finality. "Then find his killer."

"What?" Hanuvar had heard her. It was her reasoning he didn't understand.

"If you want my help, learn who killed my father. And prove that it wasn't you," she added with a snarl.

He had gravely misjudged her. "That is your condition? That you will help our people if I find who murdered your father?"

Even in the darkened hallway he felt the impact of her gaze. Her voice, too, was penetrating. "Prove to me I can trust you."

He was saved from the formulation of a response by the sound of approaching footsteps. Both turned at the sound of them and a moment later the curtain was swept aside.

Metellus was the one holding the curtain, but behind him was Enarius and, once again, Lucius. All three halted at sight of Hanuvar and Izivar beyond the entryway. Enarius looked especially curious, as if uncertain whether he should be jealous. Even an idiot could have seen the fires of Izivar's rage in her stance and eyes, no matter that she had quickly banked them.

"Is this man bothering you, Izivar?" Enarius asked.

She shook her head, slowly. "I've asked him to help find my father's killer."

"Him?" Metellus asked. "Why? Leave things to the professionals, milady."

"Him," Izivar emphasized. "And you." She looked past Hanuvar at the priest.

Hanuvar briefly believed she had chosen Lucius at random, but then the priest spoke with solemn dignity. "As I told you, I will be happy to assist."

"Lucius is pretty clever," Enarius said, then looked again to Hanuvar, clearly wondering why he should be involved.

Before his question could be asked, Hanuvar explained. "I

mentioned to the lady earlier today that I'd helped clear a relative falsely accused up north."

"That seems an odd topic to come up in conversation," Metellus observed sardonically. "Are you one of those who likes to spout on about their family?"

Izivar took the lead and ran with it, lying expertly. "I pried it from him. Decius is no more forthcoming than his brother. It's as aggravating in some ways as the men who won't shut up about themselves."

"I hate to ask," Hanuvar said, "but I've heard nothing but gossip. How did your father die?"

"I had suggested we go look at the body," Lucius said.

"I will show you." Izivar turned so quickly her cloak swirled in her wake.

Enarius put a hand to her arm, halting her before withdrawing his fingers. Her eyes didn't quite blaze, but it was clear she hadn't welcomed the touch.

"Forgive me, Izivar. Do you really wish to see the body again?"

"If it helps lead to the man who killed my father? A hundred times." She started down the hall.

Hanuvar followed directly on her heels, the others trailing. "When was he found? Do you know who was last to see him alive?"

"A boxer went back to see him," Izivar said. "My sister tells me you met him."

"Maravol," Hanuvar said.

"Julivar saw him leaving the backroom looking angrier than usual, which is saying something."

"I've seen Maravol," Metellus said. "If you ask me, that's our man."

"Maravol was asking for my hand in marriage," Izivar said. "He would have been an idiot to kill Father."

Metellus' response was slyly amused. "Your pardon, but it doesn't take a great deal of wit to stand up and get punched over and over."

"It actually takes a great deal of wit and skill," Enarius objected.

"But does it take self-control?" Metellus asked, his tone skeptical but no longer mocking. "A boxer is used to thinking with his fists. He might have lost his temper when the lady's father refused to turn her over to him. Assuming that's what he did."

"I doubt it," Izivar said stiffly.

They rounded the corner, and Izivar walked for the office door and pushed it open. She gestured inside.

Hanuvar noted the condition of the room and the open window on the far left, a shifted chair, some upset clutter on the desk edge, and then walked in to stand over Tannis Lenereva. The priest knelt beside the body.

Izivar waited just inside the door with arms crossed, biting her lower lip. Neither Metellus nor Enarius advanced past the threshold, evincing the usual Dervan squeamishness around the dead, a paradoxical predilection, given the Dervan penchant for blood-letting.

Conscious that he should pretend to share that mindset, Hanuvar peered at the body but did not touch it. Tannis' remains lay with arms outstretched. There was little doubt as to the wound that had caused his death, for the side of his head was bloodied. His bearded face was turned toward the left side of the room, the slackness of death already rendering his features waxlike and inhuman.

Izivar choked back a sob. Despite his sympathy for her, Hanuvar could conjure no pity. For if Tannis Lenereva had contrived to get himself killed in the early stages of the second Volani war, the world might be a very different place.

"Who found him?" Hanuvar asked.

Izivar just managed a reply, her voice tight. "My sister."

"See if there are additional wounds," Hanuvar said to the priest. His eyes had already taken in a blood smear along the pointed desk edge, and he stepped around the body, careful not to walk upon the outstretched hand. In life, it had been studded with rings. Now it wore none, and their absence made obvious by lines of lighter skin.

Hanuvar scanned the tables and the scroll cubicles, checking their contents against his recollection, and then he moved to the back wall.

"Did any of you have call to move this chair?" he asked Izivar.

"I didn't."

"I hate to point this out," Metellus said, "but it might be that the old fellow simply slipped. Old people do that, sometimes. He could have struck his head all by himself."

"His seal ring and the ring my mother gave him are both missing," Izivar said. "And so's his necklace."

"There's a smudge here, on the wall," Hanuvar said.

"A smudge?" Metellus mocked.

"It wasn't here earlier. Nor was the chair."

"I understand you remembering if there was a chair there," Metellus said. "But you noticed a smudge?"

"Someone positioned the chair here and then their sandal rubbed against the stone as they pulled themselves up to the window." Hanuvar might have leapt to the sill and pulled himself up, to demonstrate, but he climbed the chair instead and looked over the sill and down on a back alley. Because the building was built on the edge of a low hill, the drop was a good sixteen feet. It would have been nice if the assailant had broken his neck on the way down, but no corpse obligingly lay crumpled upon the turf.

"I find only the one wound," Lucius said, rising, and then joined Hanuvar as he lowered himself. "Did you see anything?"

"Not from here. We'll look outside. But our attacker was short, or he'd not have needed the chair. He might not have been especially strong, either, although he was probably in a hurry." He turned to Izivar. "This suggests a crime of opportunity rather than a deliberate plan. It might even be that Tannis was pushed and lost his balance. Obviously expensive material, like that gold goblet there, and that medal next to the statue, were left behind. The killer was focused only upon what was immediately in front of him. He'd noticed the jewelry, so he took that, and then he fled."

Enarius appeared reluctantly impressed. Metellus looked less pleased, but it was Izivar's opinion that mattered most.

She wiped moisture from her eyes. "Very well. Now what?"

"We'll look at the ground below, though there may not be much to see. Then we'll talk to any of those who might have a motive."

"Like the boxer," Metellus said. "You mentioned an unplanned attack."

Enarius shook his head. "The boxer's not short." Hanuvar liked that he'd been paying attention.

"I understand, sir," Metellus said. "But I'm not convinced that wall scuff means anything, and that chair could have gotten shoved there if Tannis Lenereva was wrestling with his killer."

"Huh." Enarius looked momentarily pensive, then turned to Hanuvar. "What do you say to that, Decius?"

Hanuvar shrugged. "I'll talk to Maravol. Who else was mad at your father, milady?"

Her eyes fixed him with burning intensity. "There's always Hanuvar."

Metellus chuckled and Enarius smiled weakly, as though discomfited at the bad timing of the jest.

"In all seriousness, milady," Lucius said, "I think Decius is on to something. We can question the boxer, because he seems to be the last to have seen him alive. But who else is currently, angry with him?"

Izivar suddenly looked very tired. "I'm afraid it's a long list. There's an unhappy ship captain, but I don't think he's in town. Father was getting ready to fire his recruiter, and the man knew it. I've heard them shouting at each other." She raised a hand as if warding away a host of possibilities. "My father argued a lot. It was in his nature. He just had a fight with my sister earlier today," she admitted. "But that doesn't mean Julivar or anyone else wanted to kill him. He was volatile. He liked a good fight."

"Why was your sister quarreling with him?" Lucius asked.

Izivar looked irritated for him having asked. "The battle of every father and daughter as she approaches maturity. He thought she should keep off the docks, because she was engaging the attention of some young sailors. My sister's not boy crazy," she added. "She loves ships."

Lucius turned to Hanuvar. "None of those people sound quite right. Not if it's a crime of opportunity."

"Maybe it's someone clever." Izivar's gaze was pointed. "Who wanted the attack to look like a crime of opportunity."

Lucius frowned. "I think that's supposing a little too much. Decius, I like your suggestion. If there are any signs below it will confirm at least that it wasn't the boxer, won't it?"

"Probably so," Hanuvar agreed.

The priest turned to Enarius. "Perhaps you could help milady determine if there are any items inside that are missing that she hasn't noticed."

Enarius seemed to think that was a good idea, for he nodded.

Hanuvar asked where the recruiter and Maravol were likely to be found, and after receiving curt answers from Izivar he followed the priest from the room. He waited to speak to Lucius until they had turned the corner. He still wanted to know why Lucius was so welcoming to him but dared not ask. Better to learn more about him. "What are you really to Enarius?"

"His uncle thought he lacked guidance."

"The young man seems to like you well enough, given that you're a kind of nanny."

A smile briefly brushed the priest's lips. "He possesses the capability for self-reflection. His choices cost him his closest friends. At such times, wisdom is more appreciated, even by impetuous youth."

"And what wisdom do you give him?"

"Whatever tired lessons he needs. With many men, especially the young, the right course is often clear, but temptations present themselves."

"You mean to keep him from marrying the Volani woman," Hanuvar suggested.

"His uncle would not favor that match."

"He knows it. He told me himself."

"Yet he loves her."

Hanuvar stopped at the curtain and faced the priest, hoping to assure him Izivar was no threat. "He told me that he knows she does not love him."

"I've seen that, and I'm glad of it, because I like her, and her family's suffered enough. I'd hate to have to report to the emperor that she had designs on him."

Hanuvar was surprised by the man's empathy, though he pretended Lucius' conclusions hadn't occurred to him. "I don't suppose that would go very well for her, or her sister."

"I can't imagine it would. That there's a Volani family tied to his own has already been a political stone about Enarius' neck for some time, even with Tannis' boisterous support for the emperor." Lucius pushed through the curtain and held it for Hanuvar. "You're a very interesting young man, Decius. I should like to meet your brother, some day."

"You meet me, you pretty much meet him."

To access the back alley was not so simple a matter of walking around the side of the building. They had to maneuver around most of the block and then come up an angled side street.

Rotting wooden crates, barrels, and occasional piles of garbage lay along much of the alley's length. The land beneath the gymnasium's back windows was steep and weedy. The fates hadn't left them the murderer's body, nor a very visible set of tracks, but careful examination showed them a few partial prints of heels and toes and a single outline of one side of a left foot.

"He seems of ordinary size," Lucius said. "I'm not sure how much this little exercise helps us."

"We can discount anyone with really large feet or small ones," Hanuvar said.

The priest thought for a moment. "And we can eliminate the boxer. For clearly this person dropped from the window, as you surmised, and the boxer was seen leaving the room. I suppose we will have to talk to the other people who disliked poor Tannis. I don't imagine many of them will obligingly be wearing muddy sandals."

"Even clever men make obvious mistakes," Hanuvar said.

"It is a bit of a drop. Ten feet, do you suppose, if you're hanging from the ledge? But survivable without injury. Unless he had a rope. But he wouldn't have had a rope if this was all improvised. What's that you're looking at?"

Hanuvar had discovered another print only a few paces further in, one clear smaller sandal shape, and a partial scuff in the mud beside it. "Someone was sitting here, on this crate. Recently."

"Waiting for our thief?"

"It's hard to know."

"That looks to be a youth's sandal," Lucius added after a moment.

"Or a small woman," Hanuvar said reluctantly.

"Oh, I hope this does not mean Julivar is involved."

Hanuvar nodded agreement to that.

"We will have to question her, now," the priest said grimly.

"Perhaps. But I'd like to continue this investigation without the involvement of Metellus. And if we go back inside the gymnasium, he'll intrude again."

"Wisely said. We could send in word for Julivar to talk with us outside."

Hanuvar shook his head. "Let's see what else we find, first."

Lucius eyed him sharply. "I hope you don't mean to set justice aside because you find it inconvenient."

"No. But I don't want to give Metellus the simple solution he's after. He'd as soon be done with this, and he'll do his best to shape Enarius' opinion as well."

"I'm afraid you may be right. Very well."

Against his better judgment Hanuvar was coming to like the priest, who seemed not only to possess a solid, moral center, but an able mind. He still didn't understand the man's interest in him, but he had begun to suspect Lucius wasn't suspicious of him as a threat at all and was sizing him more as one might a potential employee. He found that darkly amusing.

Hanuvar hoped he was making the right choice as far as the investigation. It was possible that the second prints had been made by Julivar, and that she had been in league with the murderer. Her active involvement would completely change the spontaneous nature of the crime he had assumed. But then the prints might be those of someone else, or Julivar might have been back here for some unrelated reason.

The recruiter Tannis had been arguing with was named Balthus, and they found him running sprints in the courtyard at the nearby bath house. He was alone apart from a trio of younger men practicing wrestling pins.

Hanuvar and Lucius watched him race back and forth at high speed four times, then approached when he paused to wipe sweat from his brow and swig from a wineskin.

The gymnasium recruiter was a short man of pale, almost gray skin and had tightly coiled black hair. He was in his early thirties and exceptionally fit.

"Balthus?" the priest asked as they walked up.

"That's me." His voice was low and gruff. "Who are you?"

"I'm Lucius Longinus, and this is Decius Marco. We're doing a favor for the lady Izivar."

At mention of that name, Balthus' lips twisted peevishly. "Are you here to fire me, then?"

"No, my good man. We're wondering if you heard anything about her father's death."

Balthus gave them a lizard-eyed stare. "Of course I heard about it. Everyone has. But you think I killed him, don't you?"

"We're looking for information on who might have killed him," Hanuvar corrected. "We thought you might be able to tell us a little more about his enemies."

The little man could hardly wait to get started on that subject. He chuckled. "A lot of people wanted that bastard dead. Oh, he talked a fine game, but he was always looking for an angle that would help him out. Saying he was your friend, telling you what high esteem he held you in, but always keeping his eye out for a better deal. Well, his family's in for it now. A woman's going to be in charge of the boxing. A woman! As though a woman can appreciate a good boxing match. They might like the muscles, but they just don't understand."

He opened his mouth, probably to list additional character failings of women in general or Izivar Lenereva in particular, but Hanuvar cut him off. "You say a lot of people might have wanted him dead. Do you have any idea who?"

"Maybe." Balthus wiped his brow again. "How did he die? Was he beaten to death, or stabbed?"

Hanuvar debated whether to get specific, and checked with the priest, who seemed to be wondering the same thing, for Lucius arched an eyebrow as if to ask what the harm was.

"It looks as though he was pushed," Lucius said.

"Pushed? You mean like out a window? Or onto a knife?" Balthus chuckled at his own joke.

"He hit his head," Hanuvar said. "But it doesn't look like an accident."

Balthus took another sip. "You want to know what I think, I'd check with his daughter. The youngest one. She may look all sweet and light, but she's got a tongue on her. And you know how young women are. He was angling her at some stuffy patrician when she got old enough, but she wanted nothing to do with it. I've heard her screeching at Tannis. She wished he was dead."

Lucius gave Hanuvar a significant look.

"We've heard you've done some yelling with Tannis yourself," Hanuvar said. "Where have you been for the last few hours?"

Balthus smiled in disbelief. "I've been here. You can check with anyone." He waved toward the wrestlers. "I took the whole day off today. I'm looking in on some other opportunities and might hire on as a private coach to some famous athletes. I talked with people all day long. There's lots of ways Balthus can make a better living without having to suck up to a rutting Volani. Looks like I'm getting out just in time. His whole little business empire's going to swirl down the drain and I'm going to be happy to see it happen."

"Some people think Maravol might have been after him," Lucius said calmly.

"Do they? I'd hate to see that happen, but I guess it could. He has it big for the prissy older daughter. Last night he brought out the ring he was going to show Tannis, to prove he'd made money and could keep it. A big old sapphire. Gaudy and about as bright as he is dim. I told Maravol it would take more than a sapphire to court that woman, and that she's going to be trouble, but he thinks with his other head, if you see what I mean."

"We see," Hanuvar said.

"He was going to talk to Tannis with the ring today," Balthus went on. "And if it didn't go well—and you can bet it didn't go well—he coulda lost his temper. One good punch from Maravol might have been enough to drop the old man for good."

They left him to his exercises and returned to the street.

"Where does this leaves us?" Lucius asked. "Do you really believe it might be Julivar? What a tragedy that would be. She was the one who found him." Lucius paused thoughtfully, then added: "But she might have dropped from the window and come back around and pretended to find him."

"Possible. But why would she have taken the jewelry?"

"To make the accident look like a robbery," Lucius suggested. "She seems a smart girl."

"We need to talk to the boxer."

"You said it couldn't have been his print outside the window."

"It's curious that all of Tannis' rings were missing, and that our boxer was going to show him one."

Lucius considered that for a moment. They turned down a quiet side street. "An interesting observation. What do you think it means?"

"Right now, I'm just scouting for information. We'll have to assess it when we've gathered it all."

IV

If Maravol were a guilty man he certainly wasn't a clever one, because he hadn't the sense to run. He hunched at the counter of a tavern one street over from the gymnasium, a platter scattered with meat and cheese crumbs his only company, apart from a small amphora and a wine cup. The establishment was dimly lit, owing to the closed shutters, probably meant to help retain the heat from two braziers burning near the counter.

The tavern's patrons talked in low voices over their own sausage, cheese, and flatbread. The smell of garlic and wine and the ubiquitous fishy garum sauce was heavy in the place.

The five sailors stared at the priest as he and Hanuvar walked past. The slim, lantern-jawed barkeep asked what they wanted to drink, but Hanuvar only pointed to Maravol. The barkeep moved off along the wooden counter, applying his shabby cloth to some smear only he could see.

Maravol drank deep before turning his head to consider them. His eyes had the glassy, unblinking focus of someone stewed in wine. He stared for a moment at Lucius, nonplussed, before shifting to Hanuvar. He scowled.

"You," he said. "The messenger. You have a message for me, messenger?" Drink had thickened his accent. "Izivar send you to me?"

"In a way," Lucius said. "She asked us for help finding her father's killer. And we believed you might be of assistance."

That wasn't how Hanuvar would have started the conversation, but it did give the boxer pause.

"He was a bastard," Maravol said, though he spoke in Volani.

Hanuvar was startled to hear the priest reply in the same, though his Dervan accented Volani was a little clumsy. "He did not deserve to be murdered."

"Why did Izivar choose you, messenger man?" the boxer asked, speaking Dervan once more. He straightened in his seat. "A Dervan. Tannis hopes to arrange a Dervan for his little girl. Does he want a Dervan for his big girl?"

He climbed off the stool and looked down on Hanuvar from several inches.

"What happened to your sapphire?" Hanuvar asked.

"You going to help with that now, too? What I think is the guard stole it."

"What guard?" Lucius asked.

"What business is it of yours?" Maravol rounded on him.

Hanuvar interposed himself. "He's a priest of Jovren. And he really does want to help."

"I don't want his help, and I don't want yours either." He glared. "I ought to kick your ass."

"Why don't you tell us about the guard," Lucius suggested.

Surprisingly, Maravol obliged. "I was getting ready for the fight, see. Tannis said it was a nice ring but he'd have to give it some consideration. I knew what he meant. I was getting ready for the fight and I asked Torstis to hold it for me. Why are you looking at me like that?" he said to Hanuvar.

Hanuvar wasn't aware that his expression had changed in any way.

"You think I'm stupid, don't you?"

"No." Maravol was drunk and frustrated, but not necessarily stupid.

"Come on. I'll show you. Come on." Maravol stepped away from the bar and raised his fists. His snarl turned into a fierce grin. "Come on, messenger."

"I don't want to fight you."

"No fighting in here," the bartender called.

"You Dervans can't take it, one on one," Maravol said. "Come on!"

"I'm not a boxer."

Maravol grunted. "Tell you what. Score on me, and I'll tell you what you want to know. One good hit."

"No fighting," the bartender repeated, his voice rising stridently.

But Maravol didn't hear, and the band of sailors murmured excitedly and dragged tables and chairs aside, moving with such practiced speed Hanuvar suspected they'd done the same thing before.

Maravol had several inches over him as well as a good forty pounds and a longer reach. He also had expertise in the very specific field in which he'd just challenged Hanuvar. Moreover, he was angry at the world and needed to punch out his ire.

Hanuvar rolled his neck and shoulders as he had begun to do in his late thirties. There was no crackle of ligaments now, though, just as there was no intermittent knee pain. He had the speed and resilience of youth, as well as experience Maravol couldn't anticipate. It wasn't the specialized knowledge of his particular style of combat, but it might serve.

"Who referees?" Hanuvar asked.

"Your priest."

"This is a terrible idea," Lucius said. "Is this really necessary?"

"Shut up, priest. We're going to fight. Aren't we, messenger?"

Hanuvar lowered into a fighter's stance and curled his fingers into fists.

"Say when," Maravol told the priest.

Lucius shot Hanuvar a questioning look, and Hanuvar nodded.

The first part of the word "begin" hadn't quite left Lucius' mouth when Maravol exploded forward with a right hook. Hanuvar leaned as he sidestepped, arms shielding his face. Maravol followed the hook with two jabs Hanuvar took on his forearms. They struck like hammers.

Hanuvar drove a hard right into Maravol's heart and the big man let out a groan and stepped back, momentarily rattled.

The priest yelled for pause, since Hanuvar had delivered the requisite blow. The onlookers shouted, wondering how long the Dervan could hold out against the Volani, and then the bartender said he'd take one of those bets.

"That wasn't a good hit." Maravol weaved in a fighter's crouch while grinning boozily. "That was a love tap. Come on, boy. I'm open. Come and get me."

Hanuvar had expected something of this kind from the start, and advanced to meet it. The boxer would give him nothing until he'd well and bloodied him.

Thus began a bruising battle. Maravol's footwork was practiced and smooth, no matter the wine muddying his brain and reeking on his breath, but Hanuvar had speed and a warrior's instinct. He took a strong blow to the shoulder and another to the chin before he caught on to the tell-tale twitch that signaled Maravol's right on its way.

This time he brushed it aside as it was half extended and then drove in from the left with a powerful blow to Maravol's nose that sent the bigger man reeling. Were this a normal fight, Hanuvar would have pursued and finished him, but he waited, only then realizing just how sore his chin and cheek and knuckles were. He had come to prefer backhand blows for any number of reasons, one of them being less damage to his fingers.

Maravol recovered against the counter, shaking his head, wiping blood from his nose.

One of the onlookers called out to him. "Come on, Volani! You gonna let this weak Dervan kid take you out with a lucky hit?"

"You said one good blow," Lucius said, stepping between them and lifting his hands. "And that was a good blow. No one could doubt that."

"No one's going to doubt Maravol's a pansy," one of the onlookers called.

Until that moment Maravol's resolve had been wavering. With that insult, the boxer shoved Lucius aside and came on with the subtlety of a hurricane.

He smashed in with lefts and rights and Hanuvar could only cover and shift against the onslaught. It was as though all the vitriol the man had stored against the Dervans was being directed against this lone representative.

A fist grazed Hanuvar's temple and opened a cut above his eye. He tucked in a blow that caught Maravol under the chin so hard it clicked the bigger man's teeth.

The onlookers chuckled, and Maravol's eyes blazed.

He thrust out an arm, and this time, rather than delivering a blow, he closed on Hanuvar's neck as he drew back with his right.

Until that moment, Hanuvar had played by the rules as he understood them.

When that hand closed he shifted his approach. He ignored the press of powerful fingers wrapping his throat and snagged the pinky and index fingers of that hand, pushing back and twisting the wrist in a sudden jerk. Maravol's grip eased. The boxer still sent his other fist piling in but his concentration had been shattered and his aim and power were less certain.

Hanuvar ducked but even with the blow poorly timed it still snapped him hard in the forehead and he flailed backward. He threw one leg behind to root himself, realizing how dizzy he was when his balance left him and he went down to a knee.

Lucius shouted to stop the fight, that they weren't playing by sporting rules. Maravol ignored him and steamed in with one leg reared back to kick.

Hanuvar pushed up and tackled Maravol. The boxer fell

backwards onto the black and white floor tiles with an explosive gasp and a meaty smack. Hanuvar's head smashed into Maravol's stomach as he landed atop him.

Even dizzier now, Hanuvar forced himself to his feet. Maravol's eyes were glazed as he sat groggily upright, his eyes at Hanuvar's belt.

The spectators had gone silent. Hanuvar grew aware that Metellus had entered and now watched with the others.

"I just want to know about the ring." Hanuvar was a little surprised at how much effort it took to make that statement.

Maravol's gaze settled on him but the boxer didn't seem to see Hanuvar. Then, in a finger snap, his concentration was back, along with a look of fierce determination. The boxer grabbed for Hanuvar's calf.

Hanuvar leaned over and slugged him, hard, on the cheek. Maravol cursed and reached again, and Hanuvar dropped a second punch. This one struck the boxer's chin and sent him to the floor.

Hanuvar, panting, wavered while looking over him.

Maravol still wasn't out, but the fight seemed to have left him at last.

Hanuvar sank to a knee at the fighter's side. Maravol's nose was mashed and bleeding, and his face was purple and black and beginning to swell.

"Tell me about the damned sapphire," Hanuvar said. "You gave your word."

"Tougher than you look," the boxer slurred.

"My dad was a fighter," Hanuvar said. "I spent years training with him." If he'd been able to speak to the man as a Volani from the start this whole battle might have been avoided. But that hadn't been possible, and so this admission was the only face-saving salve he could offer.

It seemed to work, for the big man nodded. Hanuvar offered his hand, and after a moment, Maravol took it and sat upright, propping himself on his left hand. Hanuvar continued to crouch beside him.

"Why do you want to know so bad about the ring?"

"I think it's important. Just tell me about it."

The boxer shrugged his huge shoulders and wiped blood from his mouth. "It's for Izivar. Beautiful. Like her. Been saving the money. Making the money, not drinking it."

"Did you give it to her?"

"I showed it to Tannis, but he didn't approve. I was going to show it to Izivar and just ask her straight out, but my match was coming up. So I gave it to the arena guard, Torstis, but he told me this one woman kept nosing around for it, asking him about it, and so he took it back to Tannis for safekeeping. That's what he says. But it's gone now."

"I've been talking to Torstis," Metellus said. "You beat him up pretty bad."

"He stole my ring."

"What did this woman look like?" Hanuvar asked.

"One of the harlots," Maravol said. "I know her. Short. Brown hair, wide hips. She's at the arena all the time."

"Her name?"

"You think the woman murdered Tannis?" Metellus asked skeptically.

Hanuvar ignored him and said Maravol's name to get his attention again.

The boxer's rolling eyes looked back to him. "The woman's name?" Hanuvar asked.

"Nelivana."

Hanuvar pushed to his feet and discovered his own footing was unsteady.

"It's him that did it," Metellus said, nodding down to the boxer. "I saw the fight, and how he lost his temper. He did the same thing with Tannis."

Hanuvar shook his head and felt it. The dizziness was ebbing, but still troubling. "It's not him. Someone dropped from the window. There were prints there. And everyone saw Maravol leave."

"Decius is right," Lucius said. "You're fixated on the wrong man." Metellus crossed his arms.

"I think I know where to find the right one," Hanuvar said.

Lucius eyes swept him in disapproval. "You look terrible."

"It looks worse than it is." Hanuvar felt just as bad as he appeared, but he recognized that his body was already aging through the injuries. To cover up what was likely to be a strangely rapid healing process, he said, "Give me a few moments with a wash bowl and I can get myself cleaned up."

"Then what?" Lucius asked.

"We're going to talk to Nelivana."

V

After Hanuvar splashed some water on his face and rubbed it with a cloth everyone remarked that he really did look a lot better. Maravol, more ashamed that he had lost his temper than that he had lost to an untrained fighter, tried to offer Hanuvar a drink, but Hanuvar bought one for the boxer instead, and left with Lucius. Metellus insisted on following. They headed down the street, Lucius walking at Hanuvar's side and Metellus a step behind.

"So was your father a boxer, then?" Metellus asked. "Maybe I've heard of him. You're pretty handy."

"He mostly fought in the provinces," Hanuvar replied.

"I really didn't think you had a chance," Lucius said. "You might have a future in the ring if you can fight like that."

"I'm not interested."

"What are you interested in, if you don't mind me asking?"

"Is this a job interview?" Hanuvar countered.

Lucius admitted as much with a nod. "The young master seems kindly disposed toward you, and you've a level head and can take care of yourself. I think that you're a much more solid companion than what's left of the last batch, don't you, Metellus?"

"I suppose." Metellus sounded underwhelmed by the prospect, then added, with grudging respect: "The whole lot would have fainted if that Volani boxer even waved a fist at them."

"That's kind of you to offer, but I have other people depending on me," Hanuvar said. "Family business."

"Oh? What does your family do?" Lucius asked.

"Transport," Hanuvar replied. "We move goods. Mostly to the south," he added.

"A merchant who fights," Metellus said. "Don't they just hire guards?"

"A merchant who knows how to defend himself doesn't have to hire as many mercenaries," Hanuvar said. "I don't know this city. Are we headed the right way?"

"We'll need to turn right at the next intersection," Metellus said. "But what is it we want with this woman?"

"Do you think this Nelivana will have the ring?" Lucius asked. "Is that it?"

"Yes."

The priest looked doubtful. "If she's the thief, or the thief's lover, won't she be in hiding, or have the ring in hiding? Or won't she just have sold the ring?"

He was trying to communicate something more with his sharp look, likely wondering about those prints in the alley but not wanting to say anything about them in front of Metellus.

Hanuvar acknowledged his look with one of his own. "We'll see." If he could have explained, he might have said it was possible the lady was the one in the alley, but that they still lacked enough information to know for sure.

Nelivana was a working woman, and they found her plying her trade at an upscale tavern. A beefy brown-haired sailor had her on his lap.

"Is that her?" Metellus asked. "That looks like a sapphire on her finger." He swore. "Look. She's showing it off right now. Like a Hadiran waving a fish for her cat."

"I stand corrected." Lucius sounded dumbfounded. "Apparently the woman's not at all worried about capture."

"You make the mistake of a lot of smart people in assuming everyone will plan and anticipate," Hanuvar said.

"You're saying people are base and greedy."

"He's right about that," Metellus agreed.

"I'm saying some only live in the moment."

"I'll go arrest her and we'll get some answers," Metellus said.

Hanuvar shook his head no. He was scanning the crowd at the counter. And before very long at all, he spotted what he'd sought. "There. That's the man we want. See how he's watching her?" The little man he nodded at was the one who'd been cozying up to the harlot when Hanuvar had seen them at the gymnasium's restaurant counter earlier that day. There was no missing the intense gaze he fixed upon the man holding the woman in his lap.

"So we grab him, then," Metellus said.

"Let me talk to her," Hanuvar suggested. "You two move in on him while he's distracted. Wait for my signal."

Metellus grudgingly watched him go.

Hanuvar walked up and stood at the table where Nelivana sat laughing. She and her holder looked up at him with a similar exasperated expression, almost as though they were one entity with two faces.

"What do you want?" the sailor asked sourly.

"Nelivana's time."

"Get in line." The man grinned at his own joke.

Hanuvar addressed the woman directly. "I have a friend whose father was murdered by a thief who liked rings. Do you know the kind of penalty a murderer gets around here? Is it crucifixion? Or just hanging?"

"What's this all about?" the man growled.

Hanuvar ignored him. "Of course," he said to Nelivana, "I'd hate to see the wrong person arrested. If, say, you didn't know where the ring had come from."

"This was a gift," the woman said, covering the ring with her other hand. "And it's mine now."

"It looks just like a ring that could get a person executed. Even a woman. Or maybe buried alive. I forget what the penalty is, really. If you happened to know who did the murdering, it might not end as badly for you."

"It was a gift," she repeated stupidly. "Who are you, anyway?"

"I'm the one working with the praetorians to find the murderer of Tannis Lenereva," Hanuvar answered. "And the praetorian centurion is right over there at the counter."

She and the sailor looked to the left and Hanuvar moved to the side so he could observe with them. He lifted his hand.

The little man had noted Metellus coming up on his left. He shot off the stool only to bump backward into Lucius, approaching from his right. The priest seized his arm.

Quick as a cat the thief slipped a short knife from his tunic and slashed. Lucius threw himself out of the way and his attacker darted for the door, but Metellus snagged his weapon hand and clouted him in the side of the face, then tripped him when he stumbled. It was accomplished with brutal ease. Hanuvar hadn't expected Metellus to be quite so efficient.

Nelivana pushed to her own feet, but before she could run

Hanuvar grabbed her wrist and dragged her forward. The rest of the bar had fallen silent. "You'd best explain your part in all this," Hanuvar said to her ear.

Metellus had disarmed the thief and dropped him onto the floor, shouting for the alarmed patrons to get back and stay clear. Hanuvar guided the woman forward but kept tight hold of her. He stopped beside Lucius.

The thief looked up with eyes that showed mostly whites. At closer look he proved younger than Hanuvar thought, no older than his late twenties. His face might have been handsome if it were not lined with suspicion and bitterness.

"It was him," the woman said huskily, pointing at the thief on the floor. "He gave me the ring. I didn't realize he'd killed for it until you told me!"

The thief's face lost any semblance of attraction as it twisted in fury. "You bitch! You told me you'd want me forever if I got you that ring!"

"You?" She scoffed. "A weasel like you?"

"It was her," he said, frantically searching Hanuvar's face for any sign of fellow feeling. "She made me do it!"

"So you killed Tannis?" Metellus demanded.

"I didn't make him," Nelivana shrieked. "I just said I sure liked the ring. The rest was him!" She pointed again at the little man on the ground, as if her meaning wasn't clear. "I didn't tell him to kill anyone!"

"Give me the ring," Hanuvar said.

She did so with great reluctance, even as the thief shouted it was all her fault.

"I didn't mean to kill him!" he cried. He started to push to his feet, but Metellus pressed his foot to his chest. That didn't discourage the man's efforts to plead his case. "That part was an accident! My girl liked the ring, that's all! The old man tripped when I was trying to get it away from him!"

Metellus smacked him again in the head and told him to shut up. He grinned at Hanuvar. "I've got it from here. You can take in the girl if you want."

Hanuvar didn't want. He let her go. Nelivana glared at him, then Metellus, and rushed from the tavern.

The crowd watched her leave, then shifted their attention to Hanuvar and Lucius. They left together.

It was nice to be in the street away from the crowd and the stink of the taverns. He'd spent too much time in taverns today. It was good, too, to be away from Metellus, grinning eagerly at the little doomed man.

"That was well reasoned," Lucius said.

"Thank you."

"I was supposed to be the one doing the reasoning, but you really didn't need me, did you?" Lucius didn't wait for a reply. "You know Metellus is going to take all the credit, don't you?"

"I don't care."

Lucius grunted agreement. "Metellus' aura is terrible."

Hanuvar looked at him sidelong. "You can see auras?"

Lucius eyed him sharply. "You know what one is?"

"I once met a woman who said she could see them. She thought her power a curse. Does all of your priesthood see auras?"

"That woman may have been right. Occasionally it seems a gift. And no, my order can't see them and it's probably a good thing. Most wouldn't like what they saw when they looked in the mirror."

"Do you?"

"I've learned to live with it." He stopped in the street, and Hanuvar halted beside him. "You know," Lucius said, "usually when I tell people what an aura is, and that I see them, they want to know what theirs is like. I assume the woman you met told you, since you're not asking."

"She said something about it. So is this why you stared at me when we first met?"

"I so seldom encounter one like yours. You must have devoted yourself to the welfare of others your whole life, young man."

"I help where I can."

Of unvoiced accord, they started forward together. "What about Enarius?" Hanuvar asked. "How is his aura?"

"There's hope for him. His uncle thinks I will be a good influence upon him. And I think you would be, too. Are you sure I can't change your mind and have you join his staff? Wealth, security, and social standing honestly don't interest you? Any family obligations can be taken care of with this kind of patronage."

"You're very kind. And I am truly honored. But I cannot accept. What about the emperor's aura?"

Lucius let out a grunt that might have been a single laugh. "What do you think? It brightens somewhat as he begins to look toward his legacy."

"Most men in power hold more tightly to it as they age. Their view constricts."

"You're an interesting young man. You sound much older than your years. But then I sense yours is an old soul."

"A curious expression."

"What about that extra print in the alley?"

"Two possibilities are likely."

"That they were made before or after by someone completely uninvolved," the priest said. "It's a secluded spot—a young person might come there to hide, or to play."

"Yes."

"What's the other?"

"That the woman was waiting for the thief. But she'd never admit to being involved."

"And that would mean that the murder hadn't been an accident. I think it was. Do you think that the thief still has any of Izivar's family's jewelry?"

"He might. If not, I bet he'll be willing to tell to whom he sold it."

Metellus must have known a more direct route, for they found him inside the gymnasium's restaurant, presenting the thief to Enarius and Izivar, who once more sat beside a brazier. This time a red-eyed Julivar sat beside her, and Serliva waited behind. The two sisters listened, stony eyed, as the praetorian positively brayed about the murderer being behind it all.

"Think of it," Lucius said quietly to Hanuvar. "Here was Tannis, this powerful man, one who was friendly with senators and generals and magistrates and even two emperors, not to mention princes of industry. He was a giant of the world. Yet was he brought down by assassination, or betrayal, or some ancient grudge? Or by the prejudices against his people?" Lucius slowly shook his head. "No. He was killed by a tawdry fellow who hoped to impress a woman who could never be his."

"Death comes to us all," Hanuvar said. "The mighty usually forget that. And how small it all looks at the end." He bowed his head to the priest. "Good luck to you, Lucius. I hope you shape Enarius well. The empire needs wise leaders at its head."

"Where are you off to?"

"I'm going to consult with Izivar and give her Maravol's ring. But then I'm on my way."

"If you change your mind someday, ask for me at the court. The offer stands."

"Thank you."

Hanuvar truly hoped Lucius' efforts with Enarius would succeed. It might be he could steer the future emperor onto a better course, and his disposition would mean a great deal to the fates of hundreds of thousands of people.

Metellus, accompanied by two of the arena guards, led off the thief. Izivar noticed Hanuvar and motioned him over.

He and Lucius stepped forward. Hanuvar glanced at Serliva, trying to judge from her look whether Izivar had confided his identity to her. If she had, Serliva was doing a fine job hiding her curiosity, for she was giving most of her attention to Julivar, talking to her in a low voice.

"Metellus says it had something to do with a ring that you found," Enarius said, "and that it led all of you to the thief."

That was one way to interpret it. Hanuvar supposed it was true enough, and nodded.

Lucius extended a hand toward Hanuvar. "Decius here did all of the reasoning. He used me as a sounding board and Metellus as the muscle."

"Well, good for you, Decius," Enarius said. "You're a handy man to have around. But what happened to your face?"

"Maravol was drunk and angry about his ring being stolen," Hanuvar said. "This ought to cheer him up." He opened his palm, where the sapphire lay winking, and then passed the ring to Izivar. She examined it with curiosity but no love.

"It's all solved," Enarius said to her. "Your father's spirit can rest easy now. The right man will be punished."

Izivar smiled tightly, with no great pleasure. "If you don't mind," she said, "I think I'd like to be alone now. I just have a few questions for Decius."

"Of course," Hanuvar said.

"If you'll come with me?" She nodded to Enarius as she stood. "Thank you, Enarius. I'm grateful to you and Lucius both for all of your assistance."

"Of course." Enarius still looked confused about Decius and his role, but apparently decided against further inquiry.

Hanuvar followed Izivar to the empty counter of the restaurant.

Izivar wrapped her shawl about her shoulders as she sat, then shooed a questioning attendant away. They were alone.

"You found the murderer," she said. "And quickly."

"I needed to find him fast."

"I knew it wasn't you," she said. After a moment, she added, softly. "I'm sorry I made you go through the steps."

"Why did you?"

"Because I was angry. It was spiteful and small." She looked over at him. "But I also wanted to make sure I could trust you, and your word. You're . . ." she paused to find a word, "complicated."

"Not really."

"Your plan . . . You're not going to try something . . . vainglorious and stupid?"

"It may be stupid," he conceded. "But it has nothing to do with glory. That's a young man's game. I want to work with your shipbuilders, and your navigators, and your designers. Just as I said."

She nodded once. "Then let our families work together, at long last. For the good of our people."

"Yes."

She fell silent and rubbed the smooth wood along the counter. When she spoke again her voice was wistful. "What is New Volanus like, truly?"

He could picture it as it looked last year when he'd left. It felt like a century ago. "Small and warm. The bay is crystal clear, and there are snowy peaks in the miles beyond. The soil is rich and well-watered and crops are abundant. We've laid out the city in a grid, and the walls rise high. Someday," he added, "there may be great towers. They might even be silver."

"And how many live there?"

"Four thousand and some."

"Not so many."

"No."

"Father thought that there must have been a few thousand free Volani scattered around the Inner Sea. Are you going to let them know?"

"When we're further along, yes."

"And how do you mean to free the rest?"

"For the most part, I mean to pay for them."

"With what money?"

"I liberated some from the islands of the dead."

"From the tombs?"

"We have protected the dead for so long. It seemed time for them to protect us." He would have recovered even more riches if it would have been possible to transport the wealth clandestinely.

"So you plan no uprisings? No murders?"

"Nothing that will draw attention to us. Not when we have so many to free. Attention will bring an end to all our efforts."

She offered her hand. "I will help you."

He took it. "I'm glad. We need all the help that we can get."

※ ※ ※

Until the moment Izivar Lenereva arrived at our north harbor I had been pleased with our progress. With her, however, came even more workmen, and they soon put our earlier progress to shame. Over the next weeks buildings rose by the score. Roads were laid down, piers stretched into the water. And, perhaps most importantly, ship construction was underway at last.

In the mornings I used to go down to the warehouse near the shore and watch them shape the curved ribs of what looked like the skeleton of a great wooden beast.

Izivar was skilled at administration, and employed loyal, talented laborers. With her was a grim and quiet foreman with a scarred and weathered face. He limped, and his left arm was crippled with a deep red slash. I later learned that these were wounds earned during the defense of Volanus and that truly heroic efforts by his fellow prisoners had kept him alive during his recovery in captivity. His name was Himli, and while I'm told he bore no similarity to Hanuvar's father of the same name, he became like a father to the enterprise, and bent all of his energies to the construction of our settlement and its ships.

Though the arrival of these reinforcements was an immeasurable help, between the twin strains of the first stages of construction and the costs of the slave repatriation, our funds were at a low ebb.

And so Hanuvar devised a scheme set in Derva itself, summoning me to assist. It was the first time I had been to Derva, and the first time he and I had shared an adventure in many months.

I had seen Hanuvar plan tactical situations on the spur of the moment, and make do with the material at hand, but until that enterprise I'd never seen what he was capable of when he had complete knowledge of the enemy's movements, numbers, capabilities, and even personalities. What might have been an insurmountable challenge to any other man became almost like a dance to him, or—and you will forgive me if I fall to what must seem the most obvious metaphor for me—the directing of a play. For he had those of us in the know rehearse our parts unto exhaustion, so that we could skillfully bend those who had no idea of his manipulation to aid his designs.

He gave me a starring role in the production, and it proved one of the most challenging I had ever played.

                                                        —Sosilos, Book Nine

Chapter 6:
The Cursed Vault

I

Most actors held that one assumed a character the moment the mask was donned. Since meeting Hanuvar, none of Antires' acting had taken place under a mask, but he still held with the adage. He assumed the mindset of his character as he dressed, adding elements of personality as he added each element of the costume.

When he pulled on the fine tunic, he luxuriated in the thread density. The man he pretended to be deserved only the finer things in life and did not yet have enough of them. There was no eques's ring on his hand, for example, which would rankle, despite the bejeweled citizen's ring that glittered in the lantern light as he slipped it onto his left hand.

His sandals were plain, slightly worn but of good make, brown and sturdy. Here, too, he imagined the man he played expected one day to have the mark of an eques upon the footgear, the little hoof symbol that from time immemorial meant the wearer could supply a horse and serve as a mounted warrior. In the modern era the emblem more likely meant you had the money to hire someone to serve for you on a horse, but it still meant whomever had it was worthy of notice and probably had more money than most who would be observing it. And the man he pretended to be would want that, very much.

Once he had dressed, he left for a well-lit room within Carthalo's complex. Carthalo's oldest son Horace waited for him there, quiet and intense. His black hair was naturally curled almost as tightly as Antires' own and his long-lashed eyes would nicely compliment the whole ensemble.

Antires addressed Horace in something like his own voice, but with the pressured arrogance of his role creeping into his delivery. "I'm going to want to look as though I have many slaves to tend me, though I probably only can afford one or two."

"The man you're playing, you mean?" Horace asked.

"The part. Me. I am playing the role," Antires explained. He hated having to break character. "I'm getting into character now. And as my assistant, you need to be in your role."

"I'm only pretending to be your body slave," Horace reminded him. "Do you expect me to hold your mirror?"

Antires passed it over. "If we're to be convincing, then our actions must feel natural. If we are not convincing, then we fail. And if we fail—"

Horace finished the sentence reluctantly. "We will die. Painfully."

"Yes. And betray the cause, and—"

"Yes, yes. I'll hold the mirror." Horace's voice grew eagerly servile. "Shall I trim your nose hairs as well, sir?"

"I will handle the nose hairs. But perhaps you could attend to these eyebrows."

"Your eyebrows seem fine to me. Sir."

"The man I'm imitating is one of those obsessed with the detail. He's a perfectionist that should always look his best when he can be observed by anyone who matters. Does that make sense?"

"Of course, sir. I shall trim ever so neatly."

"Excellent. See that you do," Antires added in a clipped tone.

Horace lifted the small scissors and set to work. "Now you have me wondering if maybe I should have my own eyebrows looked at."

Antires responded with dismissive arrogance. "We shall see if another slave has time to attend you."

Horace chuckled.

It took almost an hour before Antires was thoroughly satisfied with both his appearance and that of his servant. This left them ready well in advance, another point Antires had insisted upon. Hanuvar seldom required his specific talents, and while their lives depended upon a convincing performance, he more urgently hoped to demonstrate to Hanuvar that he was a master of his craft.

In the time remaining to them, he and Horace rehearsed various lines and substitutions. Horace was naturally reticent, but in his role grew even more so, adopting a subdued affect and a humble readiness. Antires coached a respectable aplomb as well. He couldn't resist reminding Horace, as he had several times in their weeks of rehearsal, that something always goes wrong in every performance, but that as long as they remembered their lines and, briefly failing that, their characters' motivations, they could sail though.

Finally, Hanuvar called them to a private meeting in the tavern basement. Hanuvar already wore his revenant's uniform, though he had not yet put on the helmet. So facile had he become with makeup that he had created a convincing scar running along one side of his cheek. Carthalo was with him, though he was not yet in costume.

Hanuvar looked to be about Antires' age, in his late twenties. At that time in his life, he had been leading a Volani army across the length of the Tyvolian peninsula, a fact Antires still found amazing. Unlike then, he was now clean shaven, and his hair was square cut straight across his forehead. It had also been dyed a vivid black, to better match his somber garments, although the scar was probably the most masterful touch. It would also draw the attention of anyone encountering him so that it would remain the dominant feature in their recollection.

"You know what you need to do," Hanuvar said. "Aleria[8] sent word that she's ready and heading off to the rendezvous. We'll be behind you shortly."

Antires nodded confirmation. He would have advised against relying upon the thief for anything, but Hanuvar had tracked her down and invited her into the scheme before Antires' arrival. While involved in their plans, Hanuvar had held all rehearsals and conversations that involved Aleria beyond Carthalo's tavern complex. He relied upon her to carry out her part, but said he'd be a fool to trust her with information that could endanger the future of his people.

---

[8] This is the woman thief Hanuvar encountered in the provinces during the events Antires described in his tale of "The Autumn Horse."   —*Andronikos Sosilos*

For the fourth or fifth time, Carthalo repeated his warning. "Remember, if for any reason you feel that you must abort, drop the red scarf you've been given on the stairs as you exit."

Antires bowed his head, formally.

"Go and make us proud," Carthalo added.

"We will, Father ," Horace answered. The two embraced. Antires, in character, frowned impatiently.

"Do you want a hug?" Hanuvar asked him.

"From a revenant? Thank you, no."

"You look like a miscreant anyway," Hanuvar said, suddenly sounding like a judgmental martinet. Then, more warmly, he said: "Off with you, then. And good luck."

They had practiced the route three times and Antires had it memorized as well as Horace, though he doubted he could have navigated it blindly, as Horace claimed his father's key operatives could do. A small run of tunnels lay beneath Carthalo's complex, and they had been expanded over the decades so that some intersected with the vast Dervan sewers and a partial cave system running even more deeply. Antires wished that they had even more tunnels and more exits, but Carthalo had laughed and told him there was only so much digging you could manage without bringing buildings down on top of you.

Outside the tunnels, small hideaways lay scattered through the city. Antires had been shown to some of these as well, should their project veer wildly off course.

He and Horace travelled the tunnels for what seemed an interminable time, although Antires knew objectively their route required less than a quarter of an hour. In the end, they emerged from stairs hidden in the cellar of a small bakery owned by one of Carthalo's lieutenants. The baker's back rooms were allegedly closed all day for a private function, so that when Antires and Horace emerged the few people sitting at the counter must have assumed the haughty Herrene and his officious tablet-bearing slave had been part of some important gathering.

Outside, the afternoon was fading toward evening. A blue, cloudless sky domed the city. Winter ebbed but still clutched with chilly fingers. Those abroad in the streets wore leggings and cloaks to protect themselves and many walked in boots.

Antires hardly felt the cold at all, so fixated was he upon their goal. In a few blocks they veered left onto the Avenine way and made for the forum. Its stalls were populated by fewer vendors than usual, owing to the lateness of the day. Antires and Horace were just one more pair of well-dressed figures walking through the center of the Dervan Empire.

A single bored guard stood at the bottom of the dozen wide stone stairs to the colonnaded temple of Savernus. The praetorian[9], in the white cloak and tunic of his order, warmed his hands over a smoking brazier. Antires ignored him and the guard glanced at them without suspicion. To his eyes, they probably looked like functionaries, not Cerdian spies or thieves or any other threat.

Soon they were up the grand stairs and past the wall of six pillars fronting the huge temple. Both monumental bronze doors were closed. Each towered three stories high and were likely large enough for Savernus himself to pass without stooping, should he happen to take possession of the statue inside and decide on a stroll through the forum.

A human-sized wicket door was inset into the left portal and opened to Antires' touch. In moments they were walking through the cavernous space. It was cold, dark, and austere. At one end of the chamber, an enormous and stiff depiction of the god stood in the gloom. As usual, the ancient carving was lit with candles on nearby plinths and from mullioned windows below the soaring roof line, so that all but his stern face and sandaled feet was cloaked in shadow. It surely impressed the Dervans, but then few of them had seen the masterwork of the Herrenic sculptors in their native element.

The marble floor was well-worn by the passage of feet through countless years, black and cracked in places as the ground beneath had settled. Two doorways opened to dim chambers, one to the left and one to the right. Familiar with his destination, Antires bore left

---

[9] By ancient decree, armed forces were not allowed within the city limits of Derva, for the citizens of the Republic had wisely not wanted armed bands determining the course of policy or selecting their rulers. With the accession of the first emperor and the creation of the Praetorian Guard, laws were passed excepting the praetorian soldiers from such considerations, and while this set many to grumbling, it was widely acknowledged that some public spaces would benefit from having an official protective guard force. The Revenant Order, created later, were likewise exempt from the laws that kept militias and ordinary legionaries from walking the streets with weapons, and there was even louder grumbling about them, at first, until the revenants became the organization most efficient at silencing dissenters.   —Silenus, Commentaries

and was soon headed into a stairwell lit by lanterns hung in scalloped recesses. The stairs were wide and deep, and turned back upon themselves at a large landing. Light glowed beyond the archway at the stair bottom, where they stepped into the warren of bureaucracy that was the Dervan treasury department, markedly warmer than the temple above. A half dozen tunic-clad slaves of the civil service sat at lamp lit desks, scribbling on parchment. Sturdy bronze doors stood in their casings up and down both sides of the wide hallway and a smaller set of bronze doors sealed a service entry down the hall and to the left. Other bureaucrats walked along the corridor, and a pair of armored praetorian soldiers lounged on cushioned chairs toward the middle of the chamber, beside another smoking brazier.

Antires was intercepted within a few paces by a large nosed, heavy-set man in an immaculate white tunic, the head slave of the treasury. Slaves owned by the civil service took immense pride in their positions and, in recognition of their dedication, lived far better than the average Dervan citizen. They could look forward to generous pensions and citizenship upon their retirement at age 45.

He'd never personally met Antipater, but Antires had been fully briefed on him. The slave was only two years from freedom and was always skeptical of requests from senators, whom he seemed to feel had nefarious political motives for any interaction with the treasury department. Antires suspected he was right.

"Good afternoon, citizen," Antipater said. "I am afraid this is a restricted area."

"I am well aware of the nature of the area," Antires said stiffly. "You must be Antipater. I have been appointed by Senator Starsis for an inspection of certain materials held here within the treasury."

Antipater frowned at this news. "I have not been informed of any inspection."

"That was entirely the point. The senator wished mine to be an unanticipated survey."

The senator had requested no such thing. Elderly and retiring, Starsis had once been a minor power with ancestral ties to the priesthood who ran the religious duties carried out in the temple above the treasury. He had also been a vocal proponent of launching a war of extermination against Volanus. Starsis was currently out of the city in the warmer, southern climes. There he could not be easily contacted for confirmation about the activities of any supposed subordinates.

Antires snapped his fingers without turning his head and Horace, acting the part of a dutiful slave, crisply produced a stamped document from his case. Antires passed it to Antipater.

The treasury functionary accepted it with grave dignity then slowly moved it out from his face, squinting.

In case Antipater should be familiar with the senator's handwriting, Carthalo had acquired several samples of the senator's letters.

Unlike many men in positions of power, Starsis insisted on continuing to write out his own letters rather than dictating them, and his was a shaky old man's hand. Carthalo, long used to fabricating documents, had practiced until he had a fine approximation of his scrawl, and he and Hanuvar had cooked up the appropriate phrasing, authorizing the senator's rrepresentative to investigate as he saw fit. So as not to inconvenience the hard-working staff Antires as agent was to limit himself to three randomly chosen areas. The letter went on to ensure the reader that he, Starsis, had no doubt that the treasury was as well organized as ever, but that certain malcontents sought to increase their own standing by suggesting the department was poorly administered, and this fact-finding expedition would be used to counter their efforts.

Antires waited stiffly, affecting boredom. He followed Antipater's eyes as they swept over the page. Carthalo and Hanuvar had imitated the old senator's prose well, beginning sternly and bluntly and then moderating before sounding almost apologetic by the close, as if Starsis lost confidence in his own authority as he went. Antipater's expression hardened near the midpoint of the letter then softened as he reached the end. He returned the letter. Horace stepped forward to receive it, then retreated smoothly.

"You must pardon me, sir," Antipater said with grave formality, "but do you possess any additional credentials?"

Antires motioned Horace forward again with a crooked finger. The pretend slave produced a small sheaf of papers, attesting to Antires' citizenship, family holdings, and character. Antipater considered the citizenship papers most closely and merely skimmed the rest. He returned them to Horace. "Everything appears to be in order. You must pardon my thoroughness, sir."

Antires replied briskly. "No pardon is necessary. I'm told you must ask for such identification no matter how famous the visitor."

"That is quite true, sir, unless they are personally known to the attending clerk. It sounds as though this spot inspection is to be conducted swiftly, which suits us both."

"Yes, two to three places." Antires turned to consider the hallway doors stretching right and left. "Felix," he said to Horace, "pick a number between one and eight."

He didn't watch Horace, but he knew from their rehearsal that the young man was furrowing his brow and wrinkling his smooth forehead, though not for very long. Horace wished to appear dutiful, not imbecilic. "Five, master."

Antires turned to Antipater. "The fifth chamber it is, if you please, clerk. Upon the left," he added.

"Very good, sir. Follow me." So saying, Antipater turned down the hall, his shadows shortening and lengthening between lanterns. They passed clerks of varying ages copying or inspecting documents, most of whom were too involved in their work to glance up. Antipater gestured to the Praetorian Guards. Only in government service might a slave pass orders along to a member of the armed forces without causing insult, so ingrained were the complex hierarchies of the Dervan state.

Up rose the praetorians, a young muscular one and a lean man with prematurely silvered hair. They left their helms on their bench. Hanuvar's inquiries had found the details about these men as well. The first was a ranker finishing his fifth year of service and recently appointed to this relatively cushy position, the fourth son of an unimportant eques likely destined for a minor governmental post. The praetorian centurion was nearing the conclusion of ten full years of service. This was Catullus, a man who had risen slowly but steadily through the ranks by following every rule to the letter and making no particular waves. Sources said that when he left the service he planned to run for public office under the wing of Senator Epulius.

Antipater halted as the two soldiers drew close.

"Who is this man, Antipater?" Catullus demanded.

"A representative of Senator Starsis, Centurion. This is Entirion." He indicated Antires.

"And what has the senator sent him here for?"

Antipater quickly explained their story while Antires waited. The centurion motioned for the papers, which Horace provided promptly. He was unworried about this particular challenge. So mired was the Dervan state in bureaucratic process that as long as you presented the appropriate paperwork you could get into nearly anywhere without sustained questioning.

Catullus frowned over the introductory letter, his expression clouding. He then visibly relaxed and flipped through the rest of the documents before passing them back. "It seems in order. You couldn't have come earlier in the day? I have a dinner engagement in two hours."

"My apologies, Centurion," Antires said. "The senator suggested I arrive late in the day when attention to duty might be expected to be more lax."

The centurion frowned. "It is never lax here in the treasury."

"Indeed," Antipater agreed.

"Let's get this over with, then." Catullus sent the other soldier running for a lantern, then both praetorians walked with them for the fifth door on the left. Antipater stepped forward and lifted a heavy ring of keys from his belt. He thumbed through them with elaborate care.

Antires retained his bored affect, though he worried about the length of time everything was taking. Had Hanuvar calculated this finely enough? If he were to burst in too soon, everything would go awry.

Finally, the slave produced the proper key, fitted it to the lock, and turned it. There was a click. Antipater pushed open the door, removed a lantern hung in a small recess beside it, and walked into the vault.

Antipater lifted the lantern so its warm glow illuminated the space ahead. No deeper than twenty-five paces, the vault was stacked with heavy wooden chests, three high. They lined the walls, and much of the floor, with three wide aisleways providing access. This was but one vault housing a small portion of Derva's treasury, though it alone held more coinage than many a small country.

"You shall find everything quite secure," Antipater reported. "Every chest is individually locked. The holdings of each, large to small, are carefully accounted for, twice before being placed in storage, and counted again upon every access. Each time by a different attendant."

"Let me see for myself," Antires said. "Soldier, give my slave your lantern. Felix, try the latches along the far aisle."

"Yes, master," Horace replied.

The praetorian obligingly passed across the lantern even as Catullus stared in disbelief.

"You wish your slave to test the finances of the empire?" the centurion asked.

"If these lockboxes are in danger from my slave's fingers, then the empire is in far more peril than the senator suspects." Antires finished the declaration with a sniff. "Proceed, Felix."

Horace bowed his head. "Yes, master."

"I'll follow the slave," Catullus said gruffly to the other praetorian. "You stay with this one and Antipater."

"Yes, sir."

That, Antires thought, had worked beautifully. Now the more observant of the soldiers would be away from him. That still left Antipater. Antires contemplated the chests to right and left, as though his course had not been predetermined for the middle and smaller aisle, where chests of ordinary size were stacked. He began to bend and examine the locks, rapping on the wood as if to confirm their solidity. He tried to open all of those to right and left at waist height. As he had expected, each chest was completely solid. All he intended was to make the two keeping pace with him comfortable with his handling of the containers.

What he wanted was the tenth chest topmost along the left-hand side. He coughed as he neared it, patting his chest and palming the stub of charcoal he'd hidden in the folds of his tunic. The cough was the signal for Horace.

From the other side of the aisle there came a muffled slap as of a sandal hitting stone and Horace suddenly cried out. The light of his lantern wobbled. Horace had pretended to stub his foot and steadied himself against a bank of chests.

The attention of both Antires' companions was diverted. As the two men craned their necks to peer toward the other aisle, Antires sketched a tiny symbol upon the lower side of the top chest, then covered it with his hand.

Horace, meanwhile, was apologizing for his clumsiness.

"What have you done, Felix?" Antires called, which was their agreed upon signal his part of their deception was complete.

"I'm just clumsy, master. I tripped."

"Pull yourself together. You yipped like a little girl."

"Yes, master. Sorry, master."

The praetorian with Antires chuckled, and for his benefit, Antires shook his head in exasperation.

Hand still braced over the tiny symbol, Antires looked across the aisle at the chest on the right and stepped there. Neither the soldier nor Antipater appeared to notice the charcoal sign drawn upon the sturdy banded wood, and he proceeded with a cursory examination of the chests along the right side, although he stopped looking at every one of them. He made a pretense of checking some along the back wall and the far aisle, then declared he had seen enough, though he made sure to advance down the far aisle, rather the central one where his marked chest sat.

Horace returned to report that all the chests were locked.

"Nothing to alarm yourself about then, apart from your sandal?"

Horace looked down as if abashed.

Antipater showed them to the doorway, and Antires and Horace emerged first into the hall, followed by the soldiers. The slave shut the door after them, locked it with elaborate care, and held the key ring in one sturdy hand as he looked down his nose questioningly.

"I have seen a vault," Antires said. "Perhaps a document room. Are those further down?"

"No, sir. They are on the right. Doors seven on."

"If you please then. I will pick—" He lifted his hand as if he were choosing at random, then turned to Antipater. "There are more doors on this side."

"Yes, sir. Twelve total."

"Then I shall select door number eight."

"As you wish, sir."

"Eight," he added, "has always been my lucky number."

"Indeed, sir?"

"Do you need us for this part, Antipater?" Catullus asked.

Naturally the soldier had little interest in accumulated papers. Hanuvar had anticipated as much. There might be some important information within the vaults, but it was the more physical manifestations of wealth that the centurion would think needed protection.

"No, Centurion," Antipater said. "I think matters are well in hand."

Catullus nodded to them as a group, motioned his underling to follow, and the two walked toward the cushioned bench where they'd been sitting.

Straight-backed and dignified as a priest, Antipater led Antires and Horace past a half dozen more clerks with heads bent over papyrus. One sat inking and stamping documents a younger clerk presented to him.

Some of the chambers on this side held offices. Behind door number eight, however, were documents that could forever change the lives of dozens of Volani living in Dervan captivity.

Antipater stopped before it and once again sorting carefully through his keys. Antires, feeling the rising tension, did not check with Horace, though he felt an impulse to do so. He did not look to the arch that led upstairs, afraid he would see Hanuvar already on the way. Not yet, he prayed silently to Caleva, muse of theatre. Not when things had gone so well. Let us get to the other side of this door and perform a few more minor steps, and then let it all go as willed.

Antipater found the proper key at last, fitted it ever so carefully to the lock, turned it with dignified calm, and then pushed the door open. Liberating the lantern that hung in the alcove beside the door, he led the way inside. Antires fought and won a final impulse not to look over his shoulder and followed.

II

When he'd first been posted to his current assignment, Catullus had thrilled to the responsibility. That he should be entrusted with the safety and security of the empire's chief treasury certainly sounded impressive, and he had fantasized about uncovering some flaw or inventing some security plan that would earn him acclaim.

But his enthusiasm had long since abated. Odd as it seemed, the government slaves held all the real power over a system that had been set in place generations before. Neither they nor the praetorians who stood watch could make any change without convoluted and laborious processes, even to the smallest of procedures. Both Antipater and himself were but new mortar in an old wall, and sooner or later they would be replaced with other mortar, while the wall remained.

He would never have identified himself as a friend to any slave, but after so many years serving amicably with Antipater, he trusted him to maintain the drudgery of the agency to which he had dedicated the rest of his career, just as the slave trusted him to maintain security.

Not that he ever had much security to trouble himself with. There were the occasional senators who demanded accountings over various things, and several mobs had formed in the forum over the years, though none had ever dared to storm the treasury. The slaves even served as the initial security, greeting those who entered the lower hall. As a result, Catullus spent most of his time lost in idle thought. So deadly dull were his service days he had sometimes imagined bringing in a scroll to amuse himself with, but he sensed that sort of thing simply wasn't done, and it certainly wouldn't look very good during one of the rare inspections his superiors ran.

He so often longed for something interesting to happen, a chance to distinguish himself in this role, that he was startled to realize how annoyed he'd been with the Herrene's interruption. He puzzled over his reaction after he returned to his bench and supposed he was too used to comfort.

"What's the strangest visit you've had here, sir?" Lentullus asked him.

Catullus thought briefly, then smiled to himself. "There was that senator who came in with two whores. He had a letter with an official stamp claiming he needed to perform a personal inspection of one of the vaults. He got irate when Antipater wouldn't leave him alone with some open chests. It turns out he just wanted to get laid surrounded by a horde of gleaming gold."

The young soldier laughed. "Some old men need extra help to get a rise."

"This was a young senator." So many senators, he had come to learn, were simply idiots. He had resolved that he would never be an idiot himself. He would follow the rules and keep his mouth shut. No one would make a spectacle of him.

The clatter of footsteps rang in the stairwell and a helmeted figure in dark armor emerged into the light.

Lentullus gasped, and Catullus barely restrained his own surprise. There before them was a centurion of the revenants, in full gear, complete with shining ebon helmet fronted by a silver skull emblem and crossed transversely by a black horsehead crest. The man was scarred, with grim black brows. One step behind him was a woman in a dark cloak, her stola black as his armor, her brown locks crossed with a silver circlet.

"Who's in charge here?" the revenant demanded.

Antipater's assistant Pullo was already hurrying toward him, and Catullus shot to his feet, clapping his own helmet to his head. He didn't have to tell Lentullus to get a move on, for the younger man was already in motion.

Pullo introduced himself and gestured to Catullus as he strode forward.

The revenant's dark brows were clouded; this, Catullus sensed, was a dangerous man. The woman beside him might have been pretty were she not so somber and oddly pale. From the skull-faced necklace at her throat and her presence beside the centurion he guessed her for one of those rare witches used by the state to stamp out sorcery.

"I've ordered your man above to secure the building," the centurion said to Catullus. "He's confirmed that a Herrene entered the temple a short time ago, accompanied by a slave."

"He did. What's this about? Who are you?" Catullus asked.

"I am Centurion Claudius Fulvo," the stranger replied impatiently. "And I am in search of an impostor. Where is the Herrene?"

"The Herrene's paperwork had to be in order," Pullo said, sounding flustered. "You saw it, didn't you, sir?" He looked to Catullus for help.

The revenant cut in before Catullus could offer any assurance. "He's a mercenary paid by Republican rabble to weaken the empire. He and his boy must be taken alive, for questioning." The revenant scanned the hall, but Catullus was already staring toward the vault where Antipater had led them. Curiously, the door had been closed, and Catullus' heart sped. And here he had been wanting something diverting to take place.

Catullus slapped his hand to his sword hilt. "They're in there." He pointed and started forward.

"Alive," the revenant hissed. "He knows vital secrets. And we move quietly."

Pullo held up a hand. "I am very sorry, Centurion. But protocols must be followed. I must insist ... that you ..."

The revenant officer scowled and thrust folded papers at him. "You think someone would dare to impersonate a revenant? Do you know the penalty?"

He was right, and Catullus frowned at the slave, even as he realized Pullo had longstanding instructions that could not be bent, just as he himself did. He was a little annoyed that the slave had done a better job of remembering than he had. His eyes strayed again to that closed door. Gods, what had he allowed to happen on his watch?

While Pullo nervously scanned the revenant's paperwork, Catullus sought clarity. "What's this Herrene's plan?"

"He's planning to curse the treasury so that nothing in here can be touched for a generation, which his backers think will drive up the value of their own holdings —"

He was interrupted by the woman. "Centurion Fulvo!" Her voice was low, breathy. The revenant whirled on her as though she had pulled his dark cloak. She steadied herself against his armor and Catullus watched in growing worry as her eyes rolled. She wobbled.

"What's wrong?" the revenant snapped.

"Magic has been activated." Her voice grew stronger and she blinked, regaining her equilibrium. "I sense its power. Growing. We have to stop him before it worsens!"

"You heard her," the revenant glowered, his gaze fixing on Pullo. "Unless you think my paperwork needs to be inspected further?"

"No sir," Pullo stammered. "It looks to be in perfect order."

"Quickly then," the revenant said. Catullus dashed ahead, fearful now that he had overlooked something, something he would be blamed for.

The revenant kept pace with him.

Catullus started to place a hand to the door, but the revenant slapped it out of the way. "Lydia and I move first," he said. "There's no telling what sorceries may have been wrought in there."

"They haven't been in there long," Pullo squeaked, then said to Catullus: "Oh, I hope Antipater is alright."

The revenant thrust open the door and swept inside, the woman coming after.

They found a strange scene within. Entirion's slave had backed Antipater into a corner and held a knife upon him. Entirion himself squatted on the floor, where he was in the midst of drawing a white chalk arc surrounded by strange symbols and intersected by lines and circles and triangles. The Herrene gasped and started for his knife, but the revenant leapt forward without hesitation and caught the man's wrist, dragging him to his feet.

The woman advanced on the slave—Felix, the Herrene had called him, one hand outstretched. The slave turned, threatening her with the blade, but she spoke to him in a quavering, haunting voice, one hand pressed to her forehead. "Lower the weapon."

The slave stared at his hand in disbelief as it shook. It dropped suddenly to his own waistline, seemingly without his volition.

"You can't command me so easily," the Herrene spat.

"Silence." The revenant's voice was icy.

"Drop the blade," the woman commanded, and the slave did so. It clanged against the stone floor.

"You," the revenant said to Lentullus, and pointed to the slave. "Keep him still. And watch him. He may be a magician as well."

The junior praetorian seized the young slave and shook him a little, to let him know he was in charge, but the young man must still have been under some magical influence, for he flopped at the shaking and barely held to his feet.

"Just keep him still, man, or you'll break the trance," the revenant commanded.

The woman drifted along the edge of the arc the Herrene had drawn. "This spell focuses dark powers," she said in a sepulchral voice. "I pray we interrupted him in time. It appears energies were directed there." She waved her hands over a wall lined with cubbyholes, filled with documents.

A wide-eyed Antipater sidled away from the Herrene and the

slave. "He was mumbling strange words under his breath and gesturing there before he began to draw upon the floor."

The woman nodded. "Centurion, the energy's intensifying."

The revenant scowled and turned upon Antipater. "You. Arrange these documents for transport. They must be disenchanted."

Antipater started to object, but the woman cut him off.

"It's not just the documents, Centurion." She placed one hand to her head again, as though she were weary from magical effort. "There's more."

Then the Herrene laughed. It was startling and eerie. "It's too late," he cried.

"You lie," the woman said coolly, and spoke to the revenant. "It's not too late if I act quickly."

"Has he been anywhere else?" the revenant demanded.

Shamefacedly, Antipater answered. "He was in one of the treasury vaults."

The revenant's eyes widened in disbelief. "Did you allow him to touch anything?"

"He and the slave touched a lot of chests," Catullus admitted. He gulped. "Does that mean he's already cursed them?"

Rather than answering, the revenant gritted his teeth as if experiencing enormous pain, or the stupidity of fresh cadets.

"Forgive me, Centurion," Antipater pleaded. "He had the proper paperwork! He said he was on an inspection!"

The revenant looked as though he were ready to slap Antipater, for he raised his hand. The Herrene resumed laughing uproariously and the revenant slapped him instead.

That silenced Entirion for a moment, though he continued to chuckle.

"You," the centurion said to Lentullus, "take his slave out of here. Wait by the doors in case I need him." He turned again to Antipater. "You heard me. Find a chest and get all of these scrolls on this upper quadrant into it."

"What about the curse?" Antipater asked warily. "Are we cursed, or just the papers?"

"You're already affected," the witch said. "But I can clear it with some effort. These papers, though, are too far gone. It will take more magic than I can currently muster to clean them."

The revenant appeared frustrated by the delay but was icily cordial to Catullus. "Centurion, did you see what chests were touched?"

"Antipater, Lentullus, and I did. Are all of us cursed?"

The revenant scowled at him. "Lydia will see to that. The empire's treasury is in danger, soldier. Show some backbone."

Lentullus shamefacedly looked away.

Antipater quickly relayed to his assistant Pullo to ready the scrolls for transport, then hurried from the room, struggling for some of his customary dignity while fumbling with his keys. The revenant pushed the Herrene, arm twisted behind his back, ahead of him. Entirion still smiled maniacally. Lentullus had pulled the stunned slave into the hallway, looking pale as a cadet waiting for a dressing down.

Catullus trailed after Antipater and the revenants and the prisoner. "How much damage can they have done?" he asked. "None of the chests were opened. Were they, Antipater?

"No, sir," the clerk confirmed. He hurriedly sorted through the jangling keys, found the proper one, and inserted it into the lock.

Catullus looked to the Herrene, who smiled archly. He seemed awfully pleased with himself for someone in the hands of the pitiless revenants, and that only added to Catullus' concern.

Antipater opened the door at last, took down the lantern with a shaking hand, and headed into the vault.

Catullus searched in vain for any sign of disaster and found only closed and sealed chests. No underworld monsters capered atop them, and no arcane symbols were drawn upon the floor.

"Where was he?" the revenant demanded.

"He touched all of these," Antipater answered.

"Touching is one thing." The witch put a hand to her head, wincing as she closed her eyes. She faced the middle aisle and lifted a hand. "Did he go this way?"

A chill ran along Catullus' spine.

"He did," Antipater confirmed with a gulp. "He handled many of the chests."

"But did he make a mark?" the revenant asked. "So long as he made no mark, we may yet be well."

"He made no marks," Antipater said. "I had my eyes upon him the entire time."

"Are you sure?" The woman advanced into the aisle, one hand

outstretched, one hand still to her head. She waved taut fingers across one chest, then another.

The Herrene no longer smiled and watched with hatred in his eyes.

"Here. This one." The woman stopped by a chest of medium size. "Do you see?" She pointed to a small, strange wavery triangle symbol inscribed upon the chest, though she was careful not to go near it.

Antipater moaned. "I don't know how he did it. I swear I thought I had my eye upon him the entire time."

"He's clever. He already tricked two of my colleagues as they were closing in on him," the revenant said.

"Why mark this chest rather than a really large one?" Catullus asked. "If he wanted to do the most damage? Wouldn't that harm more gold?"

"This one is centrally placed. The spell must be powerful enough to affect the chests around it. It may even amplify the curse he launched in the other room."

The Herrene muttered something, and the revenant shook him once.

The woman waved her hands over the symbol, speaking under her breath in a hoarse, sibilant voice. She stopped after a long moment, breathing heavily. "He built threads here but it hasn't expanded yet. It's confined to this chest. And everything inside it."

"What do we need to do?" the revenant asked, speaking as if the others were entirely absent.

"We've got to treat it, carefully. And I'm already weak after using so much magic. It needs to be evaluated by the tribune in any case. The Herrene dared to use the symbol of Abruses."

The revenant centurion sucked in a breath, then turned to Antipater and Catullus, his eyes narrow. "We will need to take the chest as well."

Antipater cleared his throat. "Sir, I can't let you do that without, well, a number of forms and permissions—"

The revenant showed his teeth. "Fine. I'll just leave it here to spread like mold over everything in the treasury so that none of it can be used for decades. Would your superiors like that?"

"I'm sorry sir. But my superiors—"

"Antipater," Catullus said. "It's not as though the revenants are going to steal it!"

The revenant laughed once without humor. "We can't even safely touch the contents while it's cursed!"

Antipater wouldn't quite relinquish his duty even then. "But what about after?"

"You're the head clerk, aren't you? Each of these chests must be numbered and counted in triplicate, so you know exactly how much is inside. Write out an accounting and I'll sign it myself."

"Yes, sir," Antipater agreed reluctantly.

The woman turned to Antipater and placed a hand upon his arm. Perhaps it was meant to be comforting, for her look was, even though the slave shivered at her touch. "The order will endure every hazard to ensure these coins will be useful once more."

"You heard her." The revenant shook the scowling Herrene again and spoke to Antipater. "Ready men to carry the chest."

"I will begin a counter spell," the woman said. "To protect against any effects that may yet linger in this room." She exchanged a look with the revenant and spoke softly, though Catullus overheard: "You should keep clear, in case things go badly."

She was trying to warn him, which meant she was putting herself at risk, but the centurion didn't acknowledge it. He just turned and shouted for the rest of them to clear out. Catullus looked back at the brave woman as she began to mumble over the symbol.

The revenant didn't seem to be concerned with her in the least, because he shifted immediately to the subject of transportation, explaining that he'd requisition a carriage near the service entrance. "We'll load up there." He then passed over manacles he'd carried on his belt and ordered Lentullus to put them on the prisoners.

"What about the curse on us?" Catullus said. His skin still crawled with the thought of it. "You said she could clear the curse placed on us." He looked back at the open doorway to the vault. From where he stood, Catullus could not see within. He wondered if the young woman was still alive.

"If she's successful then she can work her magic in the central chamber," the revenant said. A faint trace of empathy could be heard in his voice. "It will be a protective circle. I've sat in them before. You won't feel anything, and after an hour's time you should be able to safely leave it."

As he finished talking the woman emerged wearily and called for everyone to gather. Catullus sent Lentullus upstairs to retrieve Julius, who the revenant had ordered to bar and guard the front door.

By the time Lentullus returned with his fellow praetorian, Antipater had drafted a document that the revenant had signed, and the clerks had opened the reinforced inner and outer service doors opening to the side street, built for those occasions when large monetary transfers had to be made. The clerk oversaw the carrying of a chest of papers and the much heavier treasury chest into a passenger carriage outside. A frightened patrician and his very young wife spoke softly to one another, casting worried glances at their requisitioned conveyance before resignedly setting off on foot. Lentullus and Catullus himself escorted the two sullen prisoners while the revenant spoke sharply to the huge carriage driver about watching them closely. The revenant then returned with the praetorians to the temple interior.

Desks had been dragged aside so the revenant's woman could chalk a large white circle in the chamber's center. She did not seal its final portion until she had all the clerks and praetorians seated within. She then wiped sweat from her brow and sprinkled the outside barrier with powders.

She stepped back, then dully intoned a long prayer to Jovren and Hecalia, goddess of the moon and witchcraft, and used a candle to set the powder alight. A number of the clerks gasped in shock, for the fire burned green.[10] Catullus managed to keep his own reaction muted.

The woman sagged against the revenant centurion, who steadied her. She addressed those within the circle, her voice utterly drained. "Take your ease here for another hour. By then a full trio of revenants will arrive to look over the area. You are safe so long as you do not leave before then."

"I should have gone pee," Lentullus whispered.

Catullus hushed him. "You'll be fine."

The revenant announced, "We've acted swiftly enough to contain the danger. I will return tomorrow to personally complete the inspection."

---

[10] Green fire was a secret of the Volani priests, and Arbatean magicians. While known as bluestone, in the single demonstration of its use that I witnessed, it was oddly enough a white powder, and said to be poisonous if consumed or even handled over much, and is laboriously harvested from a crystal found in certain mountainous regions.   —*Silenus, Commentaries*

"Thank you," Catullus told him.

The man nodded gravely. "I merely serve the empire, like yourself."

Many of the clerks and the other soldiers gave their thanks to both the revenant centurion and the woman, who leaned heavily against him as they departed. It wasn't until they had shut the inner set of transfer doors that Antipater remarked they had no way to lock either the inner or outer doors for the next hour.

Catullus laughed at him. "No one's going to even think to try to break in here. And besides, they're cursed if they do."

They all laughed then, and Antipater smiled in chagrin. "I suppose you're right."

III

Aleria stayed in character until the man she knew as Helsa[11] returned to the carriage, climbed inside, and removed his revenant helmet. The Herrene and the younger one had already undone their manacles. Helsa leaned forward to address the cart driver through the little window to the front bench. "Any trouble?"

The driver's deep voice came over the clop of the horse hooves on the brick. "A patrol came past shortly after you headed back inside. I showed them the paperwork, but they still seemed suspicious."

The carriage had been there from the start, naturally, and Helsa had only pretended to requisition it from confederates dressed as patricians. He'd also arranged official looking documents for the driver to present in case he was questioned while parked in the lane beside the Temple of Savernus.

Helsa closed the window and put a finger to his artificial scar.

"Don't mess with it," the Herrene chided him. "A man with a real scar would be used to it and wouldn't fuss with it."

"We're not under watch anymore," Aleria reminded him.

Ahead of them the horses neighed and came suddenly to a halt.

Aleria looked out through the narrow window to the front and

---

[11] When interacting with Aleria, Hanuvar apparently retained the assumed name he had used when they first met. —*Silenus, Commentaries*

gulped. A band of six praetorians blocked the street, a broad-chested centurion in their lead.

The whole plan had simply gone too well. Bad luck had finally caught up to them.

The praetorian centurion was advancing on the driver. "My men tell me you have revenant paperwork," he said crossly. "Revenants don't have jurisdiction here."

Helsa stepped out of the carriage, pushing back his cloak.

"Centurion," he said with icy formality. Aleria couldn't see him, but she heard him continue. "Revenants have jurisdiction everywhere. We've just completed a special investigation. You need to stand aside. We have prisoners aboard for questioning."

The centurion frowned. "If you're a revenant, where are the rest of your men?"

"One is incapacitated; the other led a unit another direction. I cannot stress to you—"

"This seems suspicious to me," the centurion growled. "Where are *your* papers?"

Aleria swore under her breath.

"It's alright," the Herrene whispered. "He's got this."

He sounded so certain Aleria eyed him with renewed skepticism.

Helsa pretended outrage at being challenged and he and the centurion postured about their particular jurisdictions. She only half listened, thinking back to the circumstances that had brought her here and wondering why she'd gone along with it. A much younger looking Helsa than she remembered had presented himself last week, explaining the difference in his appearance as the skillful application of makeup. She would have had a harder time believing him if he weren't so clearly the same man she'd met last year on the other side of the Ardenines.

He'd told her then that were she interested, he had a caper that would net them a tidy sum. When he'd proposed this scheme and laid out the information about the temple's schedule and its staff, she realized just how carefully he'd analyzed its flaws and opportunities.

And until this moment, everything had gone according to Helsa's carefully detailed plan. She had been about to congratulate him on his cleverness, but then doom had arrived with the praetorians. She eyed the door, wondering how far she could get if she made a break for it. Probably the soldiers would be kept busy with the men.

The two on the carriage seat across from her remained tense but expectant, as if they had information she lacked. The praetorian centurion was demanding for a third time to see some papers when an armored figure rode into view, resplendent in black armor and a black horsehair crest. Now they were really done for, because he was clearly some kind of revenant tribune or legate, judging by the gold gilding upon his cuirass and helm.

His voice was crisply challenging. "What seems to be the trouble, Centurion?"

The praetorian centurion drew himself to attention. "Sir! This carriage was loitering outside the treasury."

"This man is an officer of the revenants under my personal command. Do you have a problem with that?"

"No, sir!"

Now the young man beside the Herrene grinned, and Aleria realized that whomever that man on the horse was had to be a final protective measure put in place by Helsa. The phony revenant officer continued to flex his rank as Helsa climbed into the carriage and closed the door. The others grinned at him, but he remained in character, ordering the driver to move ahead.

It was not until they rolled into a side street that she breathed a sigh of relief. "By the gods, that was close."

"I told you he had things taken care of," the Herrene said, and then flicked an admiring glance at Helsa. He nodded slightly to her. Another man might have looked immeasurably pleased, or cocky, but he seemed only satisfied. As though he were already thinking about further obstacles.

"Is there something else we need to worry about?" she asked.

"That's the end."

"And you anticipated that final challenge?" she asked. "Why didn't you mention it? Who was that?"

"Another ally. You did well, all of you. I picked the right people."

The boy was laughing. "Dad always said you were amazing, but I had no idea. I mean, he told me stories, but . . . that was incredible!"

The Herrene smiled and nodded enthusiastically. "If he chooses the terrain and can plan ahead, he'll be ten steps ahead of nearly everyone."

"You make it sound like he's a general," Aleria said, and the

Herrene and the young man fell silent, casting guilty glances toward Helsa, as if suddenly aware they had spoken out of turn. She looked at Helsa. "Who are you, really?"

"We," said Helsa, "are the people who just walked out of the Dervan treasury with a chest of gold, some of which is yours."

"That's all you're going to say?"

He smiled. "That's all that's important."

"And the papers? What are those for?"

"They're valuable in a different way."

She would have liked to have heard more about them, but she sensed he would reveal nothing else, and the other two looked uncomfortable, so she let the matter drop.

"I wonder how long those men are going to sit there in that circle," the young man mused.

"Probably a full hour," the Herrene said. "You two were very convincing."

"So were you," she said, and he smiled at that. Like most men, he seemed to need the praise. She then looked through her lashes at Helsa. "That was the best executed plan I've ever seen."

"It worked well," he agreed. "But no plan can succeed without skilled participants."

So much for that gambit. But then she had seen before that he appeared to be immune to charm. It frustrated and amused her at the same time. "Is it always so hard to give you a compliment?"

He laughed. "Sorry about that."

"At least tell me what this is all for. Obviously you aren't going to go spend this in sybaritic luxury."

"I need to help some people," he said. "Leave it at that."

She shook her head.

She was only a little concerned that he might double-cross her. A woman had to be wary. But when they parked the wagon in the rented warehouse and changed into new garments, Helsa counted out a tidy sum of gold for her as the driver and the younger man loaded their gear into a worn-down tradesman's wagon, and she placed it into a metal reinforced wicker basket and then covered it with empty packages. The Herrene oversaw the transfer of the gold and the chest with the papers while Helsa scrubbed off the scar. Without it, years seemed to have dropped from his face. Garbed now as an ordinary workman, Helsa walked her to the door. She had donned a bright pink dress and darker cloak, washed the pale makeup from her face, and brushed out her hair.

"This is goodbye, then?" she asked.

"Resist our mystery," he said. "Enjoy your gains. For your own sake, steer clear of us."

It was as if he was daring her to be interested in him; the fact that he understood her curiosity both irritated and intrigued her. "If I need to find you, how can it be done?"

"I'm hard to find. Can I still leave word for you at that tavern near the fountain of the two swans?"

"If I'm in Utria it will be hard to reach me fast, but, yes."

He opened the door for her. She was only halfway down the street when their carriage passed her. Helsa waved and then the vehicle turned and headed south, toward the river. She lost sight of it when she took another street toward her home, tucked up above a bakery. She was just laying hands to the door latch when several disparate thoughts dropped suddenly into alignment, and for a brief moment she thought she glimpsed the truth. Helsa was a meticulous planner, and followed by a cadre of loyal, devoted men. He had the air of a veteran officer rather than a thief, and if she had read the young man and the Herrene correctly, he had achieved many notable successes.

Then she laughed at herself. That famous enemy general, here, in the capital of Derva, robbing a treasury? She shook her head. No, that was outlandish. And he was too young, even if he weren't dead, as many claimed. He must be some disgruntled former serviceman, maybe an adherent of one of the emperor's enemies.

She opened the door and started up. She'd lay low here for a few weeks and then do just as she'd promised, and head for Utria. Twice now Helsa had done right by her, this time more lucrative than the last. But both times his motivations and his identity had remained mysterious. She promised herself that if there were a third time, she would find a way to learn his secrets, one way or another.

※ ※ ※

While the influx of gold was welcome, it was the treasury papers we'd recovered that were most vital. We might have found our way to wealth through a dozen other methods, but the treasury was the only place where the sales records of Volani nationals to foreigners and government institutions was stored. We had deliberately cast our net wide with those documents so that our interest in the Volani would remain obscured. Carthalo discovered useful information in some of the additional paperwork as well, for the man had a gift for assembling fragments into revealing and even compromising wholes.

You might think that the Dervans would have been up in arms after our escapade, sending guards boiling through the city like ants after a child kicked their nest. The praetorians and the revenants did arrive at the treasury in force, but they weren't left with useful leads, much less physical evidence, and their investigation proved useless. The government quashed rumors there had been a break-in at the treasury, as well, and gossip about it was wildly inaccurate. Carthalo's sources suggested that the emperor and his advisors believed the theft the work of Herrenes, Cerdians, or merely homegrown thieves. Not even the revenants suspected Hanuvar's involvement.

I remained hidden within Carthalo's quarters for a week, collecting tales from his family and staff, then reluctantly started the long journey north to resume what was left of my managerial duties, for Izivar Lenereva was swiftly making me irrelevant. Construction had continued in my absence and had advanced remarkably fast. And Carthalo's agents made steady progress so that a small trickle of Volani were continually being purchased from amenable owners.

Not all were willing to sell, of course, which would eventually require drastic action. That winter, however, the efforts of Hanuvar and Carthalo were circumspect. Any procurements that would draw particular attention, especially in or around Derva itself, they decided to leave either for ideal circumstances, or until the final moments of their campaign.

For weeks, everything flowed smoothly. And then, just before the spring festival, Hanuvar received word that Ciprion wished to speak with him, in person. Through hidden channels the men had exchanged an occasional note, but this was the first time they were sitting down face to face since their meeting the previous year. Ciprion was well known and might be under surveillance both by enemies and alleged allies. Hanuvar understood that if Ciprion had requested a meeting, it must be for an important reason. And so he disguised himself and headed forth, never guessing the heartache that lay before him.

—Sosilos, Book Nine

Chapter 7:
Mask of Beauty

I

Ciprion's jaw was still slack in amazement, and he examined Hanuvar's face with the focus of a man readying to paint it.

Unlike Hanuvar himself, his friend and former adversary had changed very little in the months since they'd last met. His dark hair was just starting to gray. His thick eyebrows lent him a deceptively stern appearance only partially belied by the care lines about his mouth and eyes, which were exaggerated and deepened by the faint light of the lantern hung over their table.

The two men sat across from each other in a curtained booth at the Antyrian Bath, just north of the Dervan forum, a rambling complex of courtyards, gymnasiums, restaurants, and different sized pools offering a wide selection of temperatures. Volanus, too, had maintained public baths, but nothing on such a scale, and Hanuvar still found it strange that so much business was conducted within. The meeting point provided a fine screen. Even if Ciprion had been recognized, no one would be overly suspicious about the identity of a citizen in a private consultation with him here, for this bath house was frequented by both plebeians and patricians, and remained a neutral ground where different social classes and political factions freely intermingled.

Though the spring festival was only a day away, winter's chill still clung to the capital, and both men wore cloaks over long-sleeved tunics, and boots rather than sandals. The mulled wine Ciprion had ordered was hot enough that steam drifted from their cups.

Ciprion blew across the rim. His voice was low in awe. "It's uncanny to see you like this."

"Don't be too impressed. It's a mixed blessing." Hanuvar hesitated, then decided on full candor. "My muscles aren't stiff in the morning, and I'm more alert at night, and I can see better. But there are other differences you forget about. My temper's shorter, and I feel like I'm too eager to react. I have to force myself to slow down sometimes. The right words don't come as easily." He smiled wryly. "And I'm easily distracted by women."

Ciprion laughed shortly. "Surely you're not going to tell me you never thought about sex when you were older."

"Of course I did. Just not constantly. There are other things, too. It's strange, not recognizing myself in the mirror. My scars are gone. And some of those were reminders of where I've been, and what I've done."

"Forgive me if I pry, but how did this happen?"

Hanuvar had not looked forward to explaining the story again but had known it would be necessary. "Accident. A sorcerer was trying to heal himself and when his spell struck it affected us both."

"An agent of the revenants, or someone else?"

"No. Someone preying upon an old woman." He didn't want to dwell on that part of the story. He turned over his hand. "The effect isn't permanent. Look. No callouses."

Ciprion peered with interest. "I assume that you haven't been living the soft life for the last few months."

"Not exactly. I'm aging too fast to form them. Last fall I looked like I was seventeen."

"Seventeen," Ciprion repeated in disbelief. "I'd gauge you for your mid-to-late twenties now. So you've changed a lot in just a few months. And you'll keep aging this fast?"

"So it seems. At this rate I should be back to my real age by summer or fall." He did not admit to his growing concern on that account.

Ciprion lightly raised his drink to him, the lines about his mouth shifting into the suggestion of a smile even if his lips did not quite reach it. "Here's to your luck, though. I should like to taste youth once more, while I've the wisdom to appreciate it. I hope you enjoy it while it lasts, mixed though its pleasures are."

Hanuvar lifted the cup in appreciation. "I'm doing my best."

The wine was warm and sweet. Hanuvar had accustomed himself to the drinking of heated wine, although he'd never come to enjoy it.

Both of them stilled as a group of men walked past their curtained alcove. The strangers talked loudly about what masks they meant to wear at the Festival of Vanora and debated which sort women liked best.

Ciprion's lips ticked up in a rueful smile. "I don't suppose you're planning on taking in the festival?"

"I may." Attendance at the city-wide Festival of Vanora, a raucous celebration of spring's return, wasn't high upon Hanuvar's list of priorities, but moving around while masked might prove useful. He waited until the men had moved completely past, then continued in a low voice. "I will never be able to properly thank you for the information you left me. I am deeply grateful for your courage and skill."

Ciprion passed off the compliment with the lifting of his wine cup in salute. He had somehow obtained and copied most of the recorded sales of Volani slaves, presumably without drawing the scrutiny of the revenants or other suspicious parties.

"I assume that was your work on the treasury a few weeks ago?" Ciprion asked.

"Yes."

Ciprion looked faintly amused. "I thought as much. Executed with extreme precision, and no one harmed during the entire operation. Starsis questioned and left looking like an impotent fool. You also made a laughingstock of the praetorians and the revenants. The legates of both groups were livid. Did you find what you needed?"

Indeed he had; the paperwork he'd recovered had information on the whereabouts of those few Volani sold by Derva that Ciprion hadn't been able to track down. "I know where almost all of my people are. Now it's just a matter of finding a way to them."

"My heart is with you."

Hanuvar inclined his head graciously. "What about your own

challenges?" He referred specifically to the plot Aminius had hatched to assassinate Ciprion. "I was surprised you had moved again into the emperor's confidence."

Ciprion spread his hands as if acknowledging an oversight or failing. "It seemed the simplest way to outmaneuver Aminius. I can't move against him overtly, but I can help wedge out his relationship with the emperor. He's no longer the favorite."

"Enarius is," Hanuvar said.

"Yes. A few years ago, the emperor asked if I'd like to serve as an advisor to his nephew, and I declined. This fall I asked if the offer remained open. I expected the emperor to be skeptical or even suspicious of my inquiry but he seemed delighted, even though he knows I favor the republic. He told me it's refreshing to have someone nearby who dares to speak his real opinion. There are only a few who will."

"Such is the fate of tyrants."

"Yes. I thought I'd just be shielding the throne from Aminius, but I'm honestly growing fond of Enarius. He seems curious and eager to learn. He's a far cry from what I'd seen of him previously."

Hanuvar almost added that he, too, found Enarius forthright and likable, though far too trusting. He said only: "He's learning from adversity."

"I think you're right."

"What are you going to do about Aminius?"

Ciprion grew somber and his voice lowered, likely not because he feared being overheard, but because he spoke on deeply private matters. "I must be patient. For now, my family's safe. He can't move against me when my star's risen with the emperor, and I think he's more worried about Enarius than me. He's angling for a governorship and I'm encouraging the emperor to give it to him."

"That's a lucrative post. What's your reasoning?"

"The emperor's been ill. He's about to formally adopt Enarius and announce him as his heir, which will help secure the situation, but if the emperor were to go to his ancestors while Aminius is far from Derva, all the better for the empire."

Hanuvar tried not to dwell upon the fate of the old man who had ordained the murder of the Volani people. The emperor had lived into old age surrounded by luxuries, with a chosen successor to follow in his steps. Tens of thousands of Hanuvar's people had perished without anything close to that satisfaction.

He forced his thoughts onto more convivial subjects. "What of your family? How are they?"

"It's kind of you to ask. My daughter and her husband have returned to their home in Derva and Amelia and I are staying with them while a new home's being readied for us. My finances are not what they were, but the emperor has been generous."

"And your grandson is well? He fully recovered?"

"He did, thank you. He's become fascinated with lizards and snakes of all types. He's more interested in reading, at least. Especially about snakes and lizards."

Hanuvar chuckled. "And how is Amelia?"

"Quite well. She's thriving back in Dervan society. She's a more adroit politician than I ever was and manages a lot of diplomacy without ever having to hold office. I would have liked to have brought her to meet you today, but the circumstances didn't feel appropriate."

He knew then that Ciprion was finally nearing the reason he had invited him to this meeting.

"What are those circumstances?"

Ciprion seemed to choose his words carefully. "I do not wish to know the details of your operations. But I hope you will tell me truthfully. Are you working with the Eltyr?"

The elite, all female fighting corps had originally been established to protect the gate to the Volani military harbor. Hanuvar had helped to free some surviving Eltyr in the far-off city of Hidrestus, and he sought information about his escaped daughter and her friends, all Eltyr, but he wasn't working with anyone from the corps. "I am not."

"I was almost certain you were not; I'm glad."

"Why do you ask?"

Although relieved, Ciprion's brows were still drawn. "Over the last few months someone has been murdering prominent Dervans. I see from your expression you haven't heard of this. It's nice to know that some state secrets don't leak."

"And you think it's one of the Eltyr?"

"The symbol of the corps is drawn beside the bodies, in blood."

Hanuvar had seen that symbol on standards borne by troops and flown from battlements for as long as he could remember: a half-circle above a horizontal line, contained within an arch, symbolic of an ocean moonrise viewed though the Volanus River Gate.

"Whoever leaves the mark has slain prominent citizens," Ciprion continued. "Senators. Bankers. Businessmen."

"Do they have anything in common?"

"They encouraged or profited from the Third Volani War."

Hanuvar had no love for such men, but he had less love for drawing official attention to Volani. He wondered if he needed to express condolences. "Are they men you knew?"

"Not most of them, at least not well."

"How many have there been?"

"Six."

"What does the emperor plan to do about it?"

"I've told him that there would be someone eager to take revenge, and I've even pointed out it could be someone using the Eltyr as an excuse to settle scores. The revenants think it's your daughter. They keep trying to get the emperor agitated about you anyway, although he's starting to question them. I think that's Enarius' influence. It doesn't help them that no one can find you, and that no one's claimed to have seen you for months."

"Is there any sign that the Eltyr is my daughter?"

"There's not nearly enough information. For your sake, I pray she's not. What do you think?"

Hanuvar wished he could definitively say he was certain she was uninvolved. His own sources had found no word of her, but if she were laying low, that meant nothing, for she hadn't known about the existence of Carthalo's intelligence network to seek it out. "This doesn't sound like her," Hanuvar said, finally. "But ... her city is dead. And her husband. And her children."

"I had not heard that you had grandchildren," Ciprion said solemnly. He took a deep breath and said, with great care, "I grieve for you."

"I never met them," Hanuvar confessed.

A pensive silence followed before Ciprion spoke haltingly. "If one of your people is this murderer, whoever she is, she will have to be stopped."

"I understand. And my people might be scapegoated if these

attacks continue, so if the murderer is one of my people, she jeopardizes the lives of those few who remain."

"Then we are in agreement."

Hanuvar was readying to ask further details about the murders when they heard a man cry for help. Running footsteps echoed on the tile, and someone shouted for a healer.

II

Hanuvar and Ciprion rose as one, Ciprion sweeping the curtain aside, and then both hurried into the hall. A trickle of men and women were running from the restaurant area into the courtyard where little knots of men and women gathered. A man's body lay with his head in a shaded colonnade, his feet extended into the courtyard's edge. A small crowd of onlookers watched as a middle-aged man in a plain white tunic knelt and pressed two fingers to the body's neck.

Hanuvar saw no obvious sign of mortal injury, and as he and Ciprion started forward he shifted his attention to their surroundings.

The nearby onlookers appeared stunned and were talking in hushed awe. One of them was saying something to his companion about a goddess.

The prone man shifted and mumbled a little.

The man checking for a life pulse lifted his fingers and shifted closer. "I'm here, sir." His accent was Volani. Hanuvar examined him, finding a pleasant-looking intellectual of early middle years that he did not know.

The paunchy nobleman he tended wore only a loincloth. He lay beside a towel. The Volani helped his master to a sitting position.

"Did you see her, Adherval?" the nobleman asked weakly. "She was a goddess."

"She spoke," Adherval said in a quiet, reverent voice, "and it was as though my mind went blank."

The rich man's eyes settled upon Ciprion and lit with recognition. "Ciprion, old friend! Did you see her?"

"I'm afraid not."

From around a corner came a man in a formal toga, followed by a pair of lictors, tall, strong men with austere expressions who each carried a heavy ceremonial staff of office. And behind them, Hanuvar saw a woman in a blue stola who could not possibly be here.

He touched Ciprion on the arm. "It was good to see you."

He did not wish to remain in an area where Dervan lawgivers were in abundance, but more than that, he had to make sure he had really seen who he thought.

Ciprion nodded his farewell, and Hanuvar left him.

Disaster drew interest, almost always, and most who felt it near came closer to learn the details, unless the threat was still ongoing. But some retreated, and one of those was the small, fair-faced woman. Hanuvar left the courtyard for the central hall, trailing her as she moved for the exit. He questioned his own vision and wondered if he were simply imagining a connection that hadn't been there. Surely, it could not be her.

And then, as she threw on her cloak, she glanced warily over her shoulder, and immediately made note of his watchful gaze. Recognition struck him like a thunderbolt, and he saw in her eyes she felt the same thing, although her smooth brow was clouded with confusion, as if she refused to believe what she was witnessing.

She was Senanara, former wife to his brother Melgar, a beauty in early middle age, with wispy brown hair, a heart-shaped face with broad full lips, and a fine figure, well suited to the Dervan dress. She should not have been here, in a Dervan bath house, and it was nearly impossible to credit that she lived at all. At the door, a blaze of sunlight obscured all but her shapely outline.

He followed her into the street.

Two attendants walked with her, one a young woman, the other a young man. Senanara glanced back when she was a little way into the crowded street, but he contrived to bend and adjust his sandal as he saw her turn and didn't think she'd noted him. He waited until all three had disappeared across the busy forum and then kept a block distant as they turned down a side street winding around the foot of the Kaladine hill.

Derva always bustled in the late morning, but with the festival tomorrow, out-of-town visitors swelled the usual numbers. Everyone seemed in a lighter mood. Merchants hawked their wares, women and slaves wandered to and from the market with baskets, and messengers dashed through the open space with set, purposeful expressions and flat, short-strapped shoulder bags held tight to their chests. Hanuvar passed a band of workmen pushing wheelbarrows loaded with hammers and saws and dodged a band of rustics too busy staring at the buildings to pay heed to passers-by. Further down the way a band of tall copper-skinned men in orange robes walked the street, visitors from far-off Ilodonea, hard-eyed as veteran centurions, the turban-wearing diplomat in their midst the sharpest of all.

He tracked Senanara and her companions for the next quarter hour. Occasionally he delayed his pursuit when they turned into an empty lane, and then he'd be forced to jog to catch up. At some point the two women lost their male escort. Possibly he'd been dispatched on an errand, but Hanuvar had a different suspicion, and remained alert for him.

Finally, Senanara and her female companion arrived at a small square. Typical of Dervan construction, a wide fountain bubbled in its center. A trio of young women stood beside it with buckets on its ledge, less interested in water filling than making each other laugh.

Senanara approached a recessed red brick doorway to a two-story building squeezed between a garment maker's shop and a pottery market.

The confrontation he anticipated took place the moment she advanced into the dark alcove.

He'd been listening for the pad of feet to his rear, or he'd have never heard the light footfall. He whirled, ducking as a burly man swung a flattened club at his head. The strike barely missed. Hanuvar drove a blow deep into his opponent's diaphragm and folded him with a gasp. He pushed him into the younger man a pace behind.

The second attacker was the one who'd been walking with Senanara. The collision with his comrade threw him off balance. Hanuvar grabbed the younger man's wrist, pulling him forward. He brought the fellow's arm tightly up behind his back, paused to kick the first man in the stomach when he started to rise, then pushed his prisoner into the square.

"Keep moving or I'll break your arm," Hanuvar said into his

charge's ear. His captive had little choice but to cooperate, and received no aid from his companion, still moaning in the street.

Very shortly they were before the door through which Senanara had vanished.

"Open it," Hanuvar instructed. When his prisoner resisted, Hanuvar pushed up his arm and the young man groaned, then reached for the latch. As the door swung wide, Hanuvar pushed him stumbling ahead then came in and stepped to the left.

Senanara and her female companion waited inside a small atrium, though neither had taken advantage of its couches. Both stood, as if waiting upon a report or the delivery of a body. And both gasped as one of their own tripped inside. Their eyes rounded on Hanuvar, who kicked the door shut and then stepped further to the left, taking in the room.

The young man recovered quickly, turned, and brought his arm in front of him, where he massaged it and glowered at Hanuvar.

"Senanara," Hanuvar said, "we need to talk. Alone." His eyes shifted to her companion. She was comely but surely not so radiant that she would have been remarked upon by the men of the bath house in such a glowing term as "goddess."

"You barge into my dwelling?" Senanara's voice was strained and husky, her lightly accented Dervan well-educated, distinctive more in the rise and fall of her phrasing than actual pronunciation. "And tell me what *you* wish?"

"You will want to speak with me," he said, in Volani.

Her pretense of outrage was subsumed by the wary curiosity he'd detected in her from the start.

"Who are you?" she asked in their shared language. He again saw recognition in her eyes, although it had not quite fit into place for her. "You're a Cabera." She spoke as she came to the realization. "I can see it in your face! But I thought I had met you all. Who are you?"

Both his attacker and the other woman eyed him with increasing curiosity. He could tell they were following the conversation. They, too, understood Volani. The door rattled open to his right and the other man entered, club in hand and murder in his eye. He favored his right leg.

"Hold," Senanara commanded, then repeated the order when the man insisted on advancing. The limping movement seemed a habit rather than a recent injury. At Senanara's word he stopped and lowered the weapon.

"I may not be who you think," Hanuvar said to Senanara, addressing her still in Volani. "But we should talk. In private."

"You'll talk to all of us," said the man with the club, also in flawless Volani, then spoke to the room at large. "He's some kind of Dervan spy."

All of them were Volani. He could see it now: their garments were appropriate for upper middle-class Dervans, but their hair styles weren't quite right, and the women's jewelry was smaller but brighter than the Dervan norm. The men lacked citizen's rings[12].

"You think we'll let you speak to her, alone?" the other woman asked.

"I don't think any of you are in charge of her," Hanuvar replied with brutal honesty. "No one has been in charge of Senanara since she left her parents' home. And probably not even before that."

That acknowledgment of Senanara's well-known willfulness coaxed a faint smile from her. He felt the scrutiny of those rich brown eyes even more intently. He wanted to get her alone before she announced the oncoming conclusion of his identity to the others. She had always been smart, but she had rarely been subtle. She had both delighted and exasperated Melgar.

"Alone," Hanuvar insisted.

"Very well."

The others objected, and she snapped: "Quiet! You, stranger, with me." And without a backward glance she stepped for the door to a back room. She paused to one side while he opened it for her, for it was her habit to be waited upon. Hanuvar remained alert for someone to creep from behind. No one did.

She passed him and entered the small dining room, arranged Dervan style, with a selection of couches around a low central table.

---

[12] This is not to suggest that all citizens bothered with a ring, or even that those who possessed them wore them every day. The citizen ring was not, strictly speaking, a necessary status symbol, for some aristocrats wore gaudy ones and others wore nothing, thinking it gauche to advertise what was obvious from their clear wealth or well-known features. The old maxim is that freedmen and the lower classes were most determined to demonstrate that they were not slaves, but that didn't hold true either, for many of the poor didn't expend the resources and those involved in manual labor, be they freed or lower or middle class, didn't want to risk damaging or losing their rings during their work day. Thank goodness that in our current times such jewelry is no longer necessary.   —*Andronikos Sosilos*

But she did not stop there. After Hanuvar closed the door, she allowed him to open another, then advanced through an archway and into a tiny courtyard, more the feeling of a waterless well bottom than a garden sanctuary, for the building was small and the walls stretched two stories high all around. A little square of greenery stood out from the center tiles, along with a half dead evergreen bush. An empty waist-high pot stood in each of the four corners, and benches faced the center.

"It's not much, compared to what I once had," she said. "But most of our people have nothing at all." She gestured to one of the benches and sat on one end, pulling her cloak tight. He sat down on the other, turned toward her.

He had not been in Senanara's presence in more than five years. She was one of those whose appeal was somehow stronger than her objective beauty. Whether it was a matter of her carriage and confidence or what the poets described as inborn charm he had never been able to tell, but he was keenly aware of her physical presence and that it was distinctly feminine. He couldn't help wondering if he would have noted her quite so acutely if he were in the body he'd had last year.

"You look an awful lot like Melgar," she said, softly. "But you move and sound like Hanuvar. And that can't be, unless he had a son I never heard of."

"Do you trust your people?"

"With my life. Can I trust you, nameless Cabera?"

"Yes. What is it you're doing here?"

"Why should I tell you?"

"So I know how your plans will affect my own."

Her eyes glittered like sharpened knives. "I do what I must, to recover a pitiful handful of our people."

It might be that, against all odds, he had discovered another useful ally. He would have thought Senanara one of those who would die with sword in hand, even if she had no practice wielding one. She was a fighter. She had survived, and so, like himself, she would find a way to continue the struggle. And it sounded as though she had a similar vision about how that might best be done.

To gain her trust and learn her aims, however, he would have to take a risk. She watched as he debated, and he felt her fascination.

Sooner or later she would convince herself of his identity, no matter how strange it seemed, whether he told her or not. Better then to reveal it and use the declaration as a tool to leverage her acceptance.

"What if I were to tell you that I, too, am here to recover our people?"

"Who are you?"

"The first time I met you, Melgar was so proud to have you on his arm he dribbled wine when he tried to toast you. And the last time I saw you, you two were divorced. You loved him still, and I saw his eyes burn when he looked at you. But he remained angry, after the war. You wanted to move past it. And he couldn't. He told us all he wanted to let go, but I'm not sure he really did."

Her lips gaped, though there was less surprise and more confirmation in her look.

"Hanuvar."

She sounded certain as she said his name, then looked confused again. "But how? Our own people saw you die! And you're so young!"

"I didn't die. As for this," he said with a short gesture that swept across his chest, "it's a temporary effect. I'm using it while I can to help our people."

"How?"

When he hesitated, she laid a hand across his forearm. Her touch was cool and unmistakably charged with sensuality. "I've obtained a small amount of money, and we're using it to buy and free some of our people. Is that what you're doing? It's something more, isn't it."

He knew that she wasn't lying. He just wasn't sure he could trust her judgment. "And you, a Volani, are allowed to buy them openly?"

"But, you see, I am not openly Volani. I claim to be from Surru. There are many mixed folk there."

The island city-state of Surru shared ancient cultural ties with Volanus, and remained nominally independent, although it was now a Dervan client state. At one time there had been a thriving community of Volani residents there. "I'm told that the Dervans arrested many of the Volani in enclaves around the empire."

"Many, but not all." She moved her hand at last, and it amused him that he wished she had not. "Some of our people live free in Surru. And there are more in Ostra. Did you hear Tannis Lenereva died? Bastard." She spat, an astonishing gesture from a woman of high breeding. Her head rose nobly, as though by that action alone she restored her dignity. "The free among us have pooled our resources. We don't have much, but it's enough to set us up in respectable accommodations for the brief time we're here, and to seek out and negotiate for the release of our people."

That she was concerned about the social status of her dwelling place disappointed him, for surely her money would go further if she and her entourage stayed at a humble inn, or some apartment, but it might be that her cover story required certain appearances to be maintained.

He was even more troubled by her overt efforts to seek out Volani slaves.

But he put that worry aside and permitted himself the luxury of sitting beside another free survivor, one who was part of his extended family.

She reached out to squeeze his hand. He looked across at her, then asked, quietly, "How did you escape Volanus?"

"I wasn't there when it fell," she said with strange regret. "I was on a pilgrimage to the temple of Danit in Etessus."

He could not conceal his pleasure and felt a surge of hope. "Was your daughter with you?"

Her chin lifted minutely; her voice was level as an ice field. "My daughter was in Volanus."

He should not have allowed his hope to rise, but for a brief moment he'd thought kind young Edonia, who couldn't be older than nine, might still be among the living. His remorse was heartfelt. "I'm sorry."

She slid her hand away to flick something invisible from her stola, as though casting off her anger.

He opened his palm as if showing a wound, or a span of exposed flesh analogous to his heart. "My daughter lives. At least she did, recently. She escaped Dervan custody, and they haven't found her yet."

Her enormously expressive eyes widened. "Narisia's alive?"

"I think so. I haven't located her." He did not add that she might have become a vengeful killer.

"The not knowing must drive you mad," Senanara said. "Sometimes, I think, perhaps Edonia might live. But in what conditions?" She fluffed her fine hair with her fingers. "I bribed a man to let me look at sales records of the Volani slaves, and her name wasn't on them. But she's a clever girl. She might have given a different name, don't you think?"

"She would have known that the name Cabera would have meant trouble for her," Hanuvar agreed.

"But then how would I find her?" There was panic in her voice. She stilled it and straightened. "I must assume she's dead. Only a handful live, and many of them in situations I wouldn't wish upon an enemy." Her eyes were dark. "But I wonder what I might do to Derva, had I the chance."

"What were you doing in the bathhouse?"

"I was there to visit my husband. My second husband," she added.

"When were you married?"

"Almost three years ago. He's alive and tending some rich, spoiled Dervan. Eletius Empronius," she added with distaste.

"Tending?"

"Adherval's a physician." Her voice grew bitter. "And his fat bastard of an owner won't sell him. At least not for what I can afford."

"Others have had it far, far worse," he reminded her gently. "He's apparently healthy and well fed."

"Should I be grateful to the Dervans?" Her voice was sharp even though soft.

He didn't bother answering. "Eletius seemed to have suffered some kind of attack at the bath today."

"I heard. It looked as though he lived." She sounded disappointed.

"Did you have anything to do with it?"

"If I'd wished to kill him, I'd have done a better job of it. Now tell me, what is it you're planning? You know you can trust me, or else you'd never have confided your identity to me."

"I trust you." She was loyal to the Volani people, but she remained the same tempestuous person he had known for years. He had already risked much by confirming his identity. To share anything about his own operations would be sheer folly. He could not tell her that, so he played to her pride, and vanity, and self-identity. "But to protect our people, you must trust me and wait."

"Wait? We're in negotiations right now. My associates have a mother and father who've both survived, as well as a young cousin, and they're reaching out to the men who've purchased them. If you want them to wait, you shall have to tell them yourself."

He made direct eye contact with her, to press home his point. "I'm in the midst of very delicate operations, and there are other events going on, connected with the Volani, that might make things even more dangerous."

"What kind of events?"

"I can tell you when they're complete."

She sighed in frustration. "We are not made of money, Hanuvar. We can't just wait in the city indefinitely."

"I'm not asking for an indefinite wait. Supply me with the names of those you're seeking, and I will see what I can do to help."

She eyed him shrewdly for a long, quiet moment. "You're planning something really big, aren't you." When he didn't reply she smiled and answered her own question. "Of course, you are. You never do anything small. I can help. You know I can."

"I'm certain you can. But first let me see who you're trying to buy, and then I need to get to know your people."

"You can count upon them."

"I'm sure I can. But you must not tell them who I am."

Her soft lips parted in surprise. "You must be joking. Telling them about you will give them hope."

"Let their work give them hope. The few Dervans who think me still alive need to continue seeking an old man, not a young one. They assume I'm dead set on killing the emperor. If I've any luck, they also think I'm missing an eye and am about a foot taller than I really am. I want them to keep seeking *that* man. And if any one of us is caught . . ."

She sagged a little in acceptance, then smiled playfully. "You do know that somewhere there's a tall, one-eyed middle-aged veteran being interrogated by Dervans right now."

"That may well be," Hanuvar conceded.

"You're really not after vengeance?"

"The living must come first."

"You're right," she said, although he heard a note of disappointment in her voice.

"I can't be more clear," Hanuvar said. "Please hold off on any other efforts. Your plans may jeopardize my own. Do you understand?"

"Are you so close to moving forward?"

He nodded, unwilling to say more, and she sighed at him. But her quicksilver mood changed on the moment, and she beamed. "You are still exasperating. If I had any doubt it was you, there could be none now. You used to drive Melgar mad. Where is he? Is he with you?"

His expression must have revealed all.

Theirs had not been an amicable parting, but her grief was genuine. "How did he die?"

"It was a brief sickness. Not battle. The last time he woke, he found the irony of dying in bed darkly funny. You could almost say he died laughing."

"Not spitting bitterly at his enemies? Had he changed, in the end?"

"He had, a little."

"I would like to think he had known some happiness."

"He had."

"And what of the colony the two of you sailed off to found. Does it prosper?"

"Someday, the Dervans will hunt for it. Maybe they already are. The less known about it, the better."

"They've their hands full with Cerdia and another Herrene rebellion."

"For now."

"You're so cautious. I thought you were the most daring of all your brothers!"

That had likely been Harnil, but he did not say it.

"Very well, then. Caution. What shall I tell my people? Especially since I said you looked like a Cabera." She spoke again without waiting for a reply. "Perhaps I should not have said that."

He allowed that with a shrug. Melgar had loved her not just because she was beautiful, but because she was bright and fiery and clever, which at one extreme meant she could be rash and impetuous.

"Tell them I'm a remote cousin, if you must. Everyone knows Hanuvar had no sons, and that he is dead."

III

She told him the names of the three Volani her associates were trying to free and offered to write them down, but it wasn't necessary. Through dint of long study, Hanuvar had memorized all the enslaved

Volani. What he did not know was the extent to which Carthalo's efforts to free many of the particular individuals had proceeded.

Senanara offered to feed him, but seemed almost glad when he refused, saying he had to leave. She escorted him past her curious underlings, and then Hanuvar returned to Carthalo's tavern by a circuitous route. If anything, the streets were even more crowded with out-of-town visitors than they had been earlier in the day. Probably the numbers would continue to swell through the afternoon and evening, as long-distance revelers arrived in anticipation of tomorrow's festival.

Carthalo's entire complex was overflowing, but Carthalo himself had turned over the running of his cover business to his daughter Lucena. With an influx of strangers through the streets, masked along with Derva's populace throughout tomorrow's festival, Carthalo was presented with greater than ordinary opportunities to spirit Volani house slaves away from owners who'd proven unwilling to sell. He was hard at work in his back rooms, arranging final time tables, routes, and assistance for the liberation of fourteen Volani from eight separate households.

Hanuvar almost hated to interrupt, but Carthalo turned the calculations over to his top lieutenant, sturdy, soft-spoken Brutus, and joined Hanuvar in the same small room in the cellar where they'd conferred upon Hanuvar's arrival.

Carthalo had recently had a haircut, so that his receding black and gray hair was almost a military length. His dark eyes were grave as he listened to Hanuvar's recounting of his meeting with Ciprion, and his talk with Senanara. His intelligence chief might have insight over anything that was said or even intimated, and so Hanuvar did his best to relay every interchange exactly as it had taken place.

When Hanuvar had finished, Carthalo asked for several clarifications and then sat drumming fingers on the table edge. "I haven't heard back from our contacts in Surru," he said after a long moment. "I still think it's Narisia's most obvious destination. Your daughter could blend in there relatively easily."

"If she wants to hide," Hanuvar agreed. "If she wants to fight, she could have taken up with one of the Herrene city states. Or the Cerdians."

"Or the Arbateans. Or even the Hadirans or the Ermani, I

suppose. I know." Carthalo turned over his hand, as if to show it still held nothing useful.

They'd debated Narisia's possible whereabouts again and again, and it was frustrating that they'd made no headway. But it took a long time for messages to travel across the Inner Sea, and they hardly had a surplus of reliable intermediaries. The majority of their efforts had gone into seeing to the men and women who weren't free, rather than trying to find someone who was.

Carthalo's look was grim. "You know how closely I considered going after the emperor and his top advisors. Only my love for family and friends kept me from acting. If Narisia doesn't have that, there's no knowing what she might do. But then I don't know her." He looked to Hanuvar.

"I've a hard time imagining it's her. Even if she were motivated by anger, I'd like to hope that she had a better plan. Unless she has some longer game we can't see."

Carthalo nodded agreement. His gaze fell to the tabletop between them, though his thoughts were elsewhere. "I'm bothered by the coincidence of Eletius falling ill at the same time Senanara was present, at the same time she's angry with him."

"Exactly. I can't help thinking she's doing something she hasn't told us."

"Do you think she'll follow your instructions about waiting?"

"I want to think so. I'd like to speak with her husband myself and ask what she's told him. Have you been in contact with him?"

"Not directly. I'm aware of him—Horace has even watched him and looked into his situation. Adherval's owner doesn't want to sell him. But he's on my low priority list." Carthalo had assessed the conditions of all the Volani slaves who were readily observable and ordered them by the relative safety of their circumstances. Those on lower priority were much less likely to suffer mistreatment or abuse and would be left in place until those in far more dire circumstances could be freed.

Carthalo explained further: "If you're wanting to speak with him, it should be simple. He's at relative liberty to move about the city to seek supplies for cures. Etulius even hires Adherval out to consult about medical affairs—so long as the prospective patient isn't riff-raff. If you were to dress as a patrician and call today between meal times to ask for help with some minor complaint you'd probably be let in. The question is how you'll get useful information out of him."

Hanuvar had a few ideas in mind, though he'd have to improvise depending upon Adherval's responses. "I'll find a way."

"I bet you will." Carthalo's eyes flashed in amusement. "I'm tempted to come with you, but I should really finish here." He scratched the side of his nose. "Why don't you let me send Horace? A proper patrician ought to be followed by at least one slave, and he might learn something."

"Fair enough."

IV

By early evening, Hanuvar was walking along the forum's edge in an expensive long-sleeved tunic and cloak, Carthalo's oldest son Horace following a few paces behind, like a proper slave.

Green and yellow banners had been strung below the pediments of the city's temples. The forum was always crowded with market stalls, but dozens of brightly colored tents blossomed along them like flowers, and the stalls themselves were freshly painted and decked with garlands.

They passed beyond the forum and a short while later were up the gentle slope of Campion Hill. The villa of Eletius Empronius lay only a little way from its summit. A clean, wintery breeze swept down from on high. Mixed in with the city smells of roasting meat and boiled cabbage, the stench of packed humanity and the faint reek of sewers, was the unmistakable trace of incense, borne by the wind from some nearby rich man's private shrine.

Eletius' dwelling was of the old school, with all of its wealth hidden behind a bland two-story front. From the outside it was ostentatious only in its width.

A stooped old house slave opened the door to Hanuvar's knock, saw by his clothes and amber citizen's ring that he was a patrician, and bowed his head politely. After Hanuvar explained that he hoped to consult the physician he was asked to wait upon the stoop.

Before long he and Horace were ushered inside and led through a wide atrium decorated not with the traditional masks of ancestors, but with goods from Volanus. One high shelf was lined with diminutive blue and green glass perfume bottles, and another with small, delicate, smiling, terra cotta figures, but the greatest space was allotted to stunning bowls of silver and bronze depicting figures both fanciful and real; griffins bowed to coiling asalda, and winged men flocked to hear the music of women lyrists.

He could not help staring at the display, nor could Horace, which was surely the intention, though a defeated enemy general was surely not the expected audience. He wondered if the boy understood that every item displayed here had been ripped from a Volani home.

He shook his head to clear it and left his feelings unvoiced.

The slave conducted them to a small library, one wall of which was covered in scroll-filled cubbyholes. Adherval sat in a short-backed, blue-cushioned chair, and climbed to his feet at their entrance, steadying himself against one of the two desks.

On second meeting Hanuvar thought the physician younger than he'd initially assumed, likely in his late thirties. His hair was prematurely gray, his face lean and handsome. As before, there was the sense of intelligence in his gaze, along with the slight squint that often denoted long hours spent pouring over scrolls. His fingertips were lightly stained in yellow by some chemical substance. Adherval bowed his head respectfully as the old house slave announced Hanuvar by his assumed name, Relnus Calpurnicus.

Hanuvar said that his own slave would be staying for the consult, and then waited for the old man to withdraw. Someone within the villa was languidly strumming a harp, as if he or she sought to put himself or those listening to sleep.

Adherval stood with one hand upon the desk, watching as the house slave slowly retreated across the atrium. He faced Hanuvar. "How may I assist you?" His accent was clipped, his pronunciation of the Dervan vowels just a little drawn out. "You do not look ill."

"I'm not the patient. I've come to consult about someone else. It's a private matter and I'm sure the woman would not like to chance her situation being overheard."

"Of course. Please, be seated." Adherval stepped past to shut the door. With a hand wave Hanuvar indicated Horace stand nearby, then moved toward a pair of chairs, but did not take either.

Adherval started back toward the desk.

"I'm here regarding a woman who's facing some difficulties," Hanuvar said. "I encountered her at the bath. You may know her."

Adherval stopped at the edge of his desk. His mouth thinned. "I'm not sure what you mean."

"I think you do."

His head rose. "What is this? I already explained to the revenants that I didn't know anything about what happened to the master in the baths."

Hanuvar wished that he'd known about the revenants. "I am a friend," he said, adding, more quietly, "to Senanara as well as yourself."

Adherval breathed out and put a hand to his head. "I've told her she's got to be more careful with her messages. She's going to attract attention. Tell her I'm fine, but that Eletius doesn't want to sell. For any reason."

The physician clearly wasn't used to thinking like someone who must act covertly. By assuming that Hanuvar was a messenger in disguise Adherval had left himself wide open for disclosures, so long as Hanuvar acted wisely.

A man shouted from deeper in the house, a call of alarm that shuddered to a halt.

Adherval rose and started for the door. Horace looked as though he was thinking about interposing himself, but Hanuvar motioned the youth aside even as a second cry of alarm rang out. A man called for help. Hanuvar followed on Adherval's heels, and Horace hurried after. The old house slave stumbled past, pointing over his shoulder, speaking incoherently. He did not look frightened so much as awestruck.

They raced on, and into a courtyard. The physician passed through the open doors to it and slid to a stop just beyond. Hanuvar halted beside him, gaping.

He was only vaguely conscious of the courtyard's ordinary aspects: a garishly painted stone satyr pouring endless water from a stone pitcher into a pool alive with huge yellow and orange fish. A brazier bright with crimson coals, beside a couch under a shade tree where stout Eletius lay. After that, things were stranger and stranger, for the patrician lolled, a vacant, beatific smile painted numbly over his lips. His harper lay crumpled in the corner by his instrument and stool.

And the goddess who'd stood over him turned at their entry.

She radiated sensual energy. She seemed small, yet somehow mountainously tall. So lovely was her face Hanuvar could not truly fathom it, only the faint suggestion of a corona of hair about her features. She was burning perfection.

Adherval choked on the start of a word then fell silent as the woman lifted a single hand in a fluid, feminine gesture, then pointed it in their direction.

Her voice was like a shimmer of sunlight, a lover's burning fingertips across the brow. It was smooth as the finest wine on a dry throat. Hanuvar could not stop smiling, to experience it, and to be in her presence.

"Lose yourself in thought of me," she said. "Close your eyes, and I shall be with you."

Hanuvar's lids felt heavy, and he tottered unsteadily. But he retained enough presence of mind to throw a shielding hand before Adherval as he raised the other before himself. He heard the pad of sandaled feet, and at some level he was conscious that she left and that he should follow, but his mind's eye overflowed with images of her perfectly formed body pressed tightly to him, her garments so light he felt her every curve through them. He imagined his hands in her hair, her cool lips against his face, the fragrance of her in his nostrils.

When he at last shook himself free, he found the woman fled.

"See if you can find which way she went," he said to Horace, whom he discovered behind him, stupefied. The young man shook his head to pull himself together, though he tripped over his own sandals as he left. Surely there were only a few exits. Surely someone had allowed her in. Unless the woman truly were a goddess?

Adherval had recovered as well. And, seeing him, Hanuvar wondered if his own forehead was as slick with sweat as the healer's. The physician hurried for his master, lying with that same ecstatic smile. Eletius' heavy chest rose and fell.

The harper lay motionless. Hanuvar turned for him, wondering why the woman might seek to harm this slave, and not the Dervan master.

The musician still breathed, though he was slow to respond. Hanuvar helped him rise and he blinked, his face still transfixed by awe.

"What did she say?" Hanuvar demanded. "Did she say why she was here?"

"She was beautiful," the musician said. His voice was reedy and thin. "Did you see her?"

"Did she say what she wanted?"

The musician blinked and shook his head. "She . . . she was talking to the master. About Adherval."

Hanuvar looked over to Adherval, whose brows were furrowed in worry.

"About me?" The physician looked up from his examination of his senseless master. He sounded genuinely worried. "Why?"

The musician didn't answer.

"What was she saying about Adherval?" Hanuvar asked.

"She told the master to free Adherval and that she would reward him with all the dreams he could imagine about her."

Hanuvar groaned inwardly. He no longer had any doubt as to Senanara's involvement. "And what did Eletius say?"

"He couldn't answer." The musician's chin swung toward his master. "The drug was in him. I've seen him like that before—he may look like he hears you, but there's no one home."

Hanuvar joined Adherval beside the perfumed bulk of the Dervan nobleman, slack jawed and dreaming wondrous dreams. "You drugged him?"

The physician sounded irritated to be questioned about his treatment regimen. "With the pain from his gout and the overall excitement today, he requested it. He won't be answering anyone for the next hour or so."

"What do you know about this?" Hanuvar demanded.

"Nothing!"

Though the healer was obviously frightened, his denial seemed genuine. "You didn't see the goddess at the baths? With the woman I mentioned?"

"No!"

Either Adherval was a better actor than he seemed, or he was speaking the truth.

Adherval's anger had turned him indignant. "Who are you, really?"

"A friend." It was a poor answer, but he left without explaining further and hurried after Horace, whom he found at a servant's entrance, speaking with an older female slave and a younger male with sleepy eyes.

"She came in through here." Horace pointed at the door. "She knocked for entry and then used her powers to put the answerer to sleep and work her way through the villa to the courtyard. One slave boy saw her and ran and hid."

Hanuvar understood why.

"She's a goddess," the young male slave said, face flushed. "Vanora come to us."

"We should go," Hanuvar said. The house slave started to guide them toward the main entrance, but Hanuvar pointed to the servant's exit and the bemused slave opened it for them. He and Horace left without a backward glance and started down the back street, past the long high walls of other villas.

"You know something?" Horace said.

"I know she's not a goddess. A goddess wouldn't have to knock at a door."

"But you saw her!"

"I did. But she was no goddess. I'll have to explain later. You need to return to your father and tell him what happened. Tell him that I'm going to call on Senanara again."

"I'm supposed to go with you," Horace objected stubbornly.

"You're supposed to follow orders. Go on. I'll be along presently."

Glumly, Horace headed off to the right. Hanuvar turned left.

It would have taken too long to make things clear to the young man, especially since Hanuvar was unsure of the method Senanara used to wield such power. What he did know was that she had recently visited the temple in Etessus, sacred to Danit, and that there had been many priestesses of Danit among her ancestors, for the goddess of prosperity, love, and fertility was the chosen of their family, just as Varis was the chosen of Hanuvar's. That Senanara happened to be in the baths the first time the goddess was seen, and that the goddess was asking for the very thing from Eletius Senanara herself wanted could not be coincidence.

V

Dusk was giving way to night by the time Hanuvar neared Senanara's dwelling. Normally, many Dervan neighborhoods were empty at night, for few streets were lighted, and the vigiles patrolled only the more wealthy and important districts. Tonight, though, most avenues remained crowded, for celebrations had already begun. Taverns overflowed into the public spaces, and impromptu gatherings were underway around many neighborhood fountains, with dancing and music and, naturally, drinking.

Senanara's neighborhood remained more subdued. With fewer pedestrians present, Hanuvar more easily noticed the Dervan watchmen.

They did their best to blend. Two sat by the fountain in the square beyond Senanara's home, pretending to be in conversation. Another petted a stray dog in front of the closed tile shop. A fourth watched from the upper window of an apartment across the way. Each was clean shaven and had a military haircut. They were keen-eyed, muscular men too slim to be gladiators, and wore ordinary citizen's tunics and heavy cloaks, the better to conceal weapons. They were almost certainly members of the emperor's secret police.

Hanuvar stopped two paces into the square, scratched the side of his head thoughtfully, as if just remembering something, shook his head in disgust at his forgetfulness, then retreated. He felt certain the watcher in the window had seen him, but no cry was given, and he did not hear anyone in pursuit.

He forced himself to retreat without haste, imagining the sentinel in the apartment still watching. What he couldn't know was if they were aware of him, specifically, or if they were intent upon Senanara or some member of her entourage.

Senanara's female assistant walked hurriedly along the other side of the street toward the square, a covered basket on her arm. Her eyes flicked warily to Hanuvar, gauging him for a potential threat before she approached the intersection. She hadn't recognized his face in the shadows.

Hanuvar darted for her.

She gasped at his approach, but he whispered at her in Volani. "Soldiers are waiting."

It took her a moment for his words to sink in, and even then she raised the basket as if to thump him. She seemed to recognize him, though there was little warmth in her eyes.

"Dervan soldiers are there. You can't go back."

She hesitated, then fell in step beside him as he retreated, searching his face apprehensively.

It wasn't until they reached the closed shoe repair shop at the end of the block that a pair of men stepped around the corner. In the twilight their features were uncertain, but by shape and size and the cut of their hair they could have been brothers to the band waiting in the square. They must have been following her at a distance. Both stepped out to block their way.

They were still twelve paces off and striding forward. "What's in your basket?" Hanuvar whispered to the woman.

She hesitated, more from surprise than the desire for secrecy, he thought. "Food."

Before she'd finished the word, he was pulling it from her arm.

Six paces out. One of the men raised his palm while the other slipped a hand behind him, doubtless on the hilt of a truncheon or sword.

Hanuvar tossed the basket at the one in front and ran as the man threw up his hands to block. The other charged. The moment the wicker handle struck the first man's shoulder Hanuvar drove the knife he'd pulled from his cloak into his opponent's chest. He'd delivered seven blows with blinding speed before the second man could even come up.

The first hadn't the breath left to scream. Blood poured from his mouth as he reeled, arms waving ineffectually. The second man presented a gladius, the short sword of the legion, so highly polished its blade edge gleamed in the fading light, as though a fragment of dying sun were caught upon it.

Hanuvar slung his cloak with his off hand even as the attacker with the gladius shouted "Man down!" He punched the sword point at Hanuvar, who swatted it aside with his cloak-wrapped arm; the sharp blade tore into the cloth though it did not cut through. He stepped in close, driving a knee into the soldier's groin. An armored legionary would have had protective gear about his loins; his opponent, in civilian clothes, did not, and he grunted, leaning forward with a gasp that lowered his head. Hanuvar drove his knife deep into the exposed neck. The secret policeman dropped with a gurgle.

Both men were down and dying. The threat was hardly dealt with, though, because a slap of sandal on pavement sounded from Senanara's square.

"Hurry!" Hanuvar thrust his dirty blade into its hidden sheath. He grabbed the woman's hand and sprinted ahead.

They'd only advanced half a block before the woman stumbled, crying out in pain.

"My ankle," she said. "Go on without me!"

He swept her into his arms and hurried on.

"I'll slow you down!" she said in Dervan. Unlike Senanara, she spoke the language without accent.

"No one gets left behind."

She tightened her arms about his neck and he ran, ignoring his body's reaction to the press of her flesh against his own. He dodged onto a side street that curved along the hillside, heavy in shadow. He wanted to ask if Senanara and the others had been waiting inside, or if she had any suspicion they'd been watched before now, but he saved his breath. When they got clear, he could ask for details.

Throughout the winter Hanuvar had walked Derva so he now knew the city not just by the maps he'd long since memorized but by the character of its avenues, and he recognized the entrances to the safe spaces kept by Carthalo. None were close, but beyond the next intersection lay a maze of smaller streets, and if he could reach them, he'd easily lose his pursuers.

Up ahead he heard a curious wailing, the clangor of trumpets, the beating of a drum. It reminded him of a Ruminian ceremony he'd witnessed to banish demons from a sick child. While there must certainly be Ruminians living in Derva, such a loud clamor made no sense to him, and it took a moment for him to sift through the possibilities.

Lantern light glowed from poles ahead. A crowd waited on either side of the street intersecting their own, and it was only then that Hanuvar understood. This was a Dervan funeral procession. That shrieking was no one under attack, but the wail of professional mourners. A mass of people followed the lead women along the cross street, accompanied by pipers and drummers. Hanuvar slowed as he came up, casting a single glance behind him. As yet the soldiers were lost in the dark, but could not be far away.

A trio of young men surveyed a cart hung with festival masks that some enterprising merchant had rolled onto the street. They turned at Hanuvar's approach, appraising the woman as he sat her down and steadied her. Probably they wondered at her disheveled stola, and the way she leaned against Hanuvar.

"A jest for you," Hanuvar said, with a grin. This younger body was so fit he wasn't even out of breath.

"Oh?" the nearest boy said. He looked just this side of earning his man's toga. His two companions took their eyes from the woman and considered Hanuvar.

"Cause some mischief." His hand extended with enough coins for a fair day's wage. "All you need do is run straight through the funeral procession, and on for two blocks."

Just audible over the commotion of the procession was the pounding of feet behind them.

"Alright," the boy said. He looked a bit confused, but grinned and scooped up the coins. He turned and started forward.

"You're really going to?" one of his friends asked.

"You bet!" And, laughing, he pushed straight into the crowd and cut into the procession. His two companions came after.

The wake they left would have been obvious from far back up the street.

Hanuvar carried the woman to the side of the mask seller's wagon and slipped into the shadow of a doorway, putting her behind him.

Four more of the emperor's finest tore into the intersection, following the obvious disturbance through the observers and the crowd. The moment they had moved beyond, Hanuvar turned back to the woman. "We have to keep moving."

"Very well," she said, a little hesitantly.

He swept her into his arms, then passed into the crowd, chuckling as though he were drunk, muttering slurred endearments and promises. The throngs lined the street side for many blocks, and he walked parallel to them as the long procession wound past, lanterns swaying. Bystanders muttered at their interruption. He overheard enough of their conversation to understand they witnessed the funeral of a priestess of Cerica, the moon goddess, which explained both the timing of the procession and its length.

Finally, Hanuvar was able to duck into another side street and drop the charade of a drunken lover. The young woman introduced herself as Diravel and thanked him, and when he told her they would be safe with friends, she did not object. Soon they were secreted in the backrooms of Carthalo's tavern.

Carthalo's daughter Lucena treated Diravel's ankle and instructed her to keep it elevated and to stay off it. Hanuvar set a pillowed stool across from her so that she could prop her leg.

Diravel looked no older than her middle twenties, with light brown eyes, a short nose with a rounded tip, and a slim, pointed jaw. She said she was too worried to be hungry, but once the spiced sausages, hardboiled eggs, and nuts were placed in front of her she set to them with vigor, downing cups of Carthalo's wine.

After a while, she blushed, apologizing for being such a glutton.

"No apology's needed. Diravel, Senanara is likely in danger, and I need to know what she's capable of."

The young woman's gaze grew guarded.

"I saw her. I was at the villa of Eletius when the goddess came and demanded he release Senanara's husband from slavery."

Diravel's eyes were huge and white and young.

"I think it was Senanara, and I think it was Senanara at the baths. And I think you know it." Diravel didn't answer, so he gently pressed on. "What kind of power is this? How does it work?"

She hesitated only for a little longer before confessing all. "She stole the sacred mask from the temple of Danit. In Etessus."

Of course she had. "Tell me about the mask."

"Do you know the story of Sedeno?"

Hanuvar humored her. "I do. His lover had been imprisoned in Etessus by an evil queen."

"A queen who was the daughter of Danit herself," Diravel added.

Hanuvar knew that and encouraged her to continue with a polite roll of his hand.

"She ruled men by her tremendous beauty and presence. She thought she could command Sedeno as well, but so pure was

Sedeno's love for his missing princess that the queen's powers had no effect upon him."

"So he killed the queen and freed the princess," Hanuvar finished succinctly, waiting to see if Diravel would correct him. "But from the queen's blood an ash tree grew. It became sacred to the people of Etessus, who built a temple around it."

"Yes."

"But how is this connected to the mask?"

Diravel pushed a strand of hair behind an ear. "The tree was struck by lightning and died. Its wood was used to create an altar to Danit, and many other artifacts."

Now he understood. "Including a mask."

"Yes."

"What are its powers?"

"It enables the wearer to . . . to channel the powers of Danit, or at least some small part of them, for limited times. Not just any wearer, though. You have to be schooled in the rites of Danit, and it's dangerous to wield such power."

"I can imagine. And Senanara's learned the rites."

"She planned to use the powers only if we couldn't work things out ordinarily. That's how she got access to the slave records," Diravel added, proudly.

Hanuvar imagined the pained expression Carthalo must be wearing as he listened around the corner. He worked not to let his own exasperation show. "Did she tell you I suggested she refrain from any further action until I looked into trying to free the people you were after?

Diravel bobbed her fair-haired head reluctantly. "Yes."

He let out a sigh of disgust, although it was anger he felt. "And did my advice give her any pause? Or was she just telling me what she thought I wanted to hear?"

"She said she couldn't stomach seeing her husband in slavery one day longer, and that she would go quiet after she freed him."

That willfulness was typical of Senanara, who assumed she always knew better than everyone around her. Although, were their positions reversed, would he have done any different? "Do you have any idea where she might be?"

"No. I don't. She's very smart, though. She's probably safe. I just hope Matho and Hinelcar are with her."

Hanuvar leaned back against the chair and rubbed his forehead. Very briefly he'd thought he'd found another ally. Instead, he'd encountered a dangerous liability. If Senanara and her people were rounded up and captured, the Dervans would be alerted to the existence of a small group working toward the same goals as Hanuvar's own. It didn't matter that they were two separate organizations; the Dervans would thereafter be alert for similar activity. And that might be the end to all of their carefully laid plans.

He bade Diravel to be comfortable and take her rest.

He retreated to counsel with Carthalo. Their forces were already stretched thin by the operations planned for tomorrow, so Hanuvar changed clothes again and returned to the streets himself, accompanied by the only two operatives Carthalo could spare, and together they kept watch on both Senanara's home and its sentinels.

Neither she nor her followers returned, and some member of the secret police seemed always to be watching, which meant Senanara's band had not all been apprehended by the authorities.

When Hanuvar finally returned to Carthalo's complex in the early morning, he learned grim news. One of their informants had passed along that Adherval the physician had been carted away by revenants for interrogation. Rumors were already flying through the city that he'd been arrested for practicing sorcery in a bath house and might even be behind a series of dreadful murders.

VI

Another Volani was in danger, and likely slated to die, one whose fate had been completely avoidable. That dawn Hanuvar pushed through his anger, more frustrated by his own helplessness than anything else. Senanara had to be found.

Today was the Festival of Vanora, the Rite of Winter's Unmasking. As the city was overflowing with people in full or partial masks until midnight, Senanara could be anywhere amongst tens of thousands. It was the one day every year where social station meant almost nothing. House slaves were traditionally granted a small gift and twenty-four hours of freedom. Masked men and women alike wandered in clothing that would normally be scandalous. Not for nothing was there a famous joke about Vanora's second festival of delivery, nine months later.

Almost surely Senanara would know of her husband's capture, and how impossible Adherval's recovery would be. Even if she were to charm a revenant into cooperation, they were unlikely to know what cubbyhole her husband had been thrust into. She, too, would be feeling helpless, and angry. But unlike him, she had extraordinary power.

At that thought, he guessed what she must be planning.

He would have liked to have run his conclusion past Carthalo, but his old friend was directly overseeing today's rescue plans. His youngest son Kester was one of the few left in the inn, and from him Hanuvar obtained a brown cloak and a half mask with wide, laughing eyes and outrageous eyebrows, a gaily painted thing of pressed fibers and resin with a long pointed nose and small cut outs to see through. He gave the boy a note, telling him to have his father open it if he didn't return.

Kester eyed him in alarm, then promised that he would.

Inside the sealed paper Hanuvar had instructed that if Senanara drew undue attention to the Volani, Carthalo was to lay low. If there was no way to carry on, he was to implement their contingency plan to deploy the rest of their financial resources evacuating with everyone they'd recovered so far and attempt to free the others at some future date.

He prayed it would not come to that.

There was enough of a nip in the air that heavy cloaks were perfectly comfortable, which suited Hanuvar, though it probably disappointed a whole host of those who would have preferred to head forth in more daring attire. The garment allowed him to conceal a sword in a shoulder sheath, a weapon illegal for any but praetorians and revenants[13] to carry within city limits.

Carthalo's headquarters lay only a few blocks from the forum.

---

[13] And the secret police, whom no one was supposed to acknowledge. Even today it is hard to be precise about the numbers of the emperor's private security force, because so few records were kept about their organization. Estimates range from as few as fifty to upward of five hundred, a number that seems difficult to credit. Their duties were different from those of the praetorians, who were conspicuous guardians of state buildings, the emperor's holdings, and the emperor's family, as well as the revenants, ever vigilant for enemy sorcery. While the revenants were alert for more mundane threats to the empire as well, they were not as adept at monitoring the general public as the secret police, who were based primarily in Derva and Ostra, although rumors persisted that they were to be found in all of the empire's largest cities. —*Andronikos Sosilos*

Normally Hanuvar might have reached the city center quickly, but with parties under way on every street, nearly a quarter hour of constant effort was required. Musicians stood in every other doorway, surrounded by dancers, almost all masked and many already blind drunk. Heedless of the weather, the younger men and women had stripped to revealing garments. Some of the men went shirtless, their skin dimpling in the cold. The women were wiser, donning heavy cloaks that swirled as they danced, permitting tantalizing glimpses of flesh barely hidden by thin scraps of material.

Many of the masks were simple affairs of leather or cloth, but others were painted to look like gods and goddesses or even famous Dervan soldiers, politicians, and entertainers. Hanuvar did a double-take at one mask, so fine was the representation of Ciprion's proud nose and sad thick eyebrows, but the man wearing it was too tall, and too young.

He demurred numerous invitations to dance or drink or eat, pushing his way through one raucous party that had encompassed an entire lane. Finally, he turned the corner into the forum itself.

Never before had he seen the space so crowded. When he'd first arrived in the city, it had amused him to stroll through the very center of the Dervan Empire, though he had never made a habit to do so, thinking such hubris invited the wrath of the gods. The famed spot had proved smaller than he'd anticipated, even after long familiarity with the city's maps, a rectangle of five hundred yards total length and two hundred in width, lined with shop stalls and fronted on every side with pillared buildings. Some were temples, one was a law court, and one was an extended wing of the imperial palace. Today almost all were hung with banners and decorated with greenery.

He kept to the forum's edge, circulating past the busy vendors selling steaming mugs of mulled wine and cider and the ubiquitous spiced meats. Normally the steps and pillar footings and porches of the great buildings were occupied only by important dignitaries, but on festival days plebeians and patricians alike took their ease upon them, some crowded about warm braziers, gathered to watch the entertainments and the running of the supplicants. By age-old tradition the race's runners bore willow reeds with which they would slap the offered body parts of women who wished the special blessing of Vanora.

Those women were now gathered in little groups near the runners, who stood in a small, cleared area at the foot of Vanora's temple. Many of the athletes stretched their calves, but others oiled their bodies or simply stood and drank wine near a big brazier. The waiting runners went maskless. Here were the most famous of the young and near young among the equites and patricians, vain of their looks and eager to curry favor or simply attention. The more muscular and handsome preened for admiring onlookers.

All of this Hanuvar took in from behind his own mask. He had not seen Senanara at any of the merchant stalls. If she meant to work her magic, any of the temple fronts could serve as a platform, but he could guess which one she would find most attractive. So far there was no sign of her upon the steps or peristyle of the temple of Vanora, Danit's Dervan counterpart.

He paced slowly among the merchant stalls and their supply tents. Here and there he saw praetorians, and they, too, were masked, though by bronze faces attached to the visors of their helmets. Probably there were secret police and revenants among the onlookers somewhere, or at least their informants. Nowhere, though, did he spy Senanara.

He was halfway through a second circuit of the forum when he spotted a limping man.

There were a small number of limping figures to be seen, of course, for veterans were in attendance, but this man favored his right leg in just the same way as one of Senanara's male protectors.

His back was to Hanuvar, who followed him, pushing through a crowd lining up for wine.

From the rear the man was nothing remarkable—just a dark-haired plebeian in a brown cloak with old boots. He stepped beyond one of the vendor tents, wineskin in hand, pausing at the last moment to look behind him. He wore a half-mask, so his eyes and forehead were obscured, though not the aggressive thrust of his chin.

He didn't seem to recognize Hanuvar behind the mask or understand that he was being followed. He turned on his heel, lifted the flap of a small tent to enter, and then dropped it behind him.

Hanuvar maneuvered through the crowd to the back side of the tent, found a different gap in the fabric, and stepped inside.

He hadn't accounted for a rope placed at ankle height. It sent him sprawling, though he tumbled smoothly and came up in a crouch. Unfortunately, the mask had slipped and obstructed his vision. Even though his knife was in his hand, he was at a grave disadvantage. He tore the mask free and climbed to his feet.

It was good that he had, for two men were there, and the limper had the same flattened cudgel he'd meant to use the night before. He halted with the weapon half raised. "You," he said.

Hanuvar heard Senanara speak with weary rancor. "Drop your blade."

She sat on a stool on the far side of the little tent, her booted feet resting on its support strut. She wore a dark green cloak and a light green stola with a low neckline. Her eyes were hard and sad.

"What will you do if I don't?" Hanuvar asked.

"You mean to stop us," she countered.

"It depends on what you intend."

"Put up your blade, Hanuvar. I won't have them kill you, but they'll certainly hurt you."

The two young men exchanged a confused glance and then considered him in perplexity. She had casually mentioned his name as the secret seemed no longer important to her.

He could take them both, but not without killing them. And too many Volani were dead already. He slowly eased his knife away then adjusted his tunic, covertly ensuring his gladius was in place in its shoulder sheath. He'd felt it as he rolled, but it had not come loose.

"Diravel's safe," he said. "I got to her before the Dervans did."

"I'm glad of that." Senanara's stiffness modulated only slightly.

The two men looked surprised, and the limper's shoulders visibly eased. "Praise Danit," he whispered.

Hanuvar took in the tent with a look. "Were you planning this from the beginning, or did you use your powers to steal this hiding place?"

"How long have you known it was me?"

"You should not have lied to me. I understand your rage. But this will help nothing."

She shook her head. Though she looked toward him, her gaze was inward. "You ask me to be slow, and patient, and clever. But I've never been patient. You know that."

"You shouldn't have tried to free your husband."

Her eyes flashed and she cast off her mood of weary resignation with an imperious lift of her head. "You wanted him to fester there, in a home stuffed with looted Volani treasures? Jumping at his master's every whim? Adherval was one of the finest physicians in all Volanus. And here he was following the fat fool around like a dog, having to ask permission every time he had to urinate."

"His position doesn't seem that bad."

"Says you, walking free. How long were you going to wait before you got my husband released?"

"Compared to some, he was practically in a vacation home. But now the revenants have him. Because you drew too much attention."

She climbed from the stool, her eyes flaring, a small woman towering in her anger. "Is it my fault my husband is a Dervan slave? They will kill him, as they killed my daughter! And yours! Oh, don't look at me like that. You're deluded if you think you'll find Narisia alive. They would have killed us all, if they could. All!" She was working herself up, like an actor, although her words were sincere. She suggested the forum beyond the tent with a grand sweep of her arm. "I'm going to show them what it's like to face destruction!"

He spoke quickly. "I will try to find a way to free Adherval—"

Her laughed cut him off. "Even you can't get a man away from revenants. Maybe at your prime. But now you're afraid to take risks."

"I was always afraid to take the wrong risks. We have to pick our battles carefully. If you call more attention down on the Volani you'll make the rest of our rescues impossible. More than a dozen are under way right now."

"So you're saving them. I thought as much. Probably slowly, cautiously. Nicely." She said the last as though it were a deadly insult. "What does any of that matter, Hanuvar?"

At the second mention of his real name her two followers traded another bemused look.

She struck her chest with a fist. "They have destroyed us! Saving one or two doesn't save our people! There's not enough of us left to matter."

"That's not true."

"You've deceived yourself. Do you honestly do this for their sake, or your own? You fight for them to stave off the emptiness. The sense of failure. Because you cannot bear to see yourself in the mirror." He opened his mouth to object but she spoke over him, saying "There's no point in anything, apart from vengeance!"

He called her name, but she stepped over the trip wire and left, a plain wooden mask clutched in her hand.

The two men kept wary eyes upon him.

"Let me stop her."

"Are you really Hanuvar? The Hanuvar?" the limper asked.

"He can't be, Matho. He's too young," the other man countered. He, then, was Hinelcar.

Hanuvar spoke directly to Matho. "I've been disguised by sorcery. If a Volani sets the Dervans at each other's throats, what do you think the Dervans will do to the Volani slaves? Or any others they can lay their hands on?"

They stared at him. He was about to tell them he didn't want to fight them, but Hinelcar waved his cudgel toward the exit. "Go. She's headed for the temple of Vanora."

Of course she was. Hanuvar grabbed his mask and hurried into the forum. He heard the others behind him and turned to find they followed, wearing simple cloth masks.

He didn't see Senanara, yet. Far away, on the temple of Vanora's pillared portico, a short fat man in a ridiculous orange toga and a half mask with a bulbous nose finished a sentence about a senator that sent waves of laughter through the crowd.

Hanuvar thought about the chain of decisions that had brought him to this moment. If he had told her more about New Volanus sooner, might he have changed her mind? Or would even that have been enough?

Maybe nothing was enough when your people's goods decorated their conqueror's walls, and their crafters were murdered or enslaved, when your daughter was presumed dead, when your lover was in the hands of torturers. When nearly all you cherished was as less than dust and those who'd made it thus ruled the world.

He understood her, and how enervating it was to try to root strength in the anger and the hate. In the darkest watches of the night, he had even asked himself the kind of questions Senanara had demanded of him. He wondered sometimes if he always wore a kind of mask, pretending everything he did was rational and sane because if he were to pause, he'd be overcome by rage and despair. And he had wondered, too, what difference to his people one or two or even ten more could mean.

Yet after lengthy consideration he had arrived at an answer different from hers, and he wished she'd given him time to explain. He could have reminded her that if you reduced men and women to numbers, losing one or two or ten or a thousand became an abstraction you could measure against another, like the numbers needed to till a city's fields, or assemble an army. By that reckoning, the thousand he fought for meant very little.

But it mattered to every one of them. And each mattered to him.

He saw the commotion she caused before he spotted her. There to the right of where the comedian addressed the crowd a mass of people suddenly parted, and then Senanara was climbing the steps. She looked over her shoulder once, her features disguised by a roughhewn wooden mask with red lips and huge eyes and arched brows. When she arrived upon the portico a blue-cloaked man reached to pull her away.

Senanara slipped from him, faced the crowd, thrust back her shoulders, and transformed. No longer a curvaceous woman in a strange mask, she was beauty incarnate, a vision of Danit. The man who'd tried to pull her off staggered as if physically struck. The comedian faltered to a stop, turned, then tottered backward down the temple steps. No one tried to steady him: everyone stared at the vision as she lifted her arms.

She was glorious.

Hanuvar could not take his eyes from her. He forced himself to breathe and fought his way forward. No one paid any attention to his jostling.

Senanara spoke, and her voice was smooth and sweet and shining like warm honey. It rang through the forum. "Look upon me, people of Derva! Behold my beauty. It is without parallel. I am everything you wish for!" She lowered her arms and opened her hands to the crowd. "I am tender, and sharp. I am demure, and passionate. And I am skilled and giving and soft and warm."

Only forty feet separated Hanuvar from the steps now, but it might as well have been forty leagues.

Her voice rose. It struck as a wave, to reverberate through him like the heaviest drumbeat. It lingered with the potent sting of desire. "All my love can be yours," she promised.

Hanuvar hoped it could be so, for he craved to possess her love above all things. Those around him shifted and he could feel it in them as well, men, women, even the children. They had eyes only for her. What they each saw he could not guess, for he could not have hoped to describe it himself.

"Prove yourselves deserving!" she cried, spreading her arms wide. "Only the greatest among you is worthy of my embrace!"

The fighting began immediately. Some called that she would be theirs, and others mouthed insults and slurs to their neighbors, but everywhere fists rose.

Hanuvar struggled on, fending off blows, consumed by the craving to earn the love of the magnificent vision.

Senanara called to the throngs, enflaming them further. "Am I not more magnificent than any other? I will transport you to greatness!"

Before Hanuvar an old man bludgeoned a boy with his fists and sent the child down in a rain of blood. A scream of agony rose behind him. Hanuvar was struck in the shoulder and arm. He blocked a kick to his groin and maneuvered one of his attackers into a group of fighters on his left. On his right, three women bit and scratched at one another while a fourth fought them with fists.

Step by step, Hanuvar advanced. He was no stranger to setting impossible goals and working to reach them. He found a way ahead, his eyes set, though he wasn't fully sure what he intended. He had never wanted anyone as much as he wanted the goddess at the temple. Unbidden, images of the women he had loved rose before him. He examined and dismissed them as though each were nothing more than their physical attributes. How could any compare with the peerless perfection before him?

Rank after rank of the crowd he diverted or defeated until there were only scattered knots of figures left upon the temple stairs ahead. He felt her eyes. She had recognized him.

"Only the most worthy earn the power of my pure love!"

One of her words struck reason even as lust warred to rule him. Pure.

His instinct was to prove to her that he was the best of all possible lovers, and he was turning to fight the muscular man winning the brawl on his right when he halted with fist raised and considered her again.

Yes, she was unutterably beautiful. And he did wish to love her. But this love wasn't pure; it was all consuming. It was like a drunkard's thirst for the bottle.

He had known a purer love.

He had seen the sea beating against the quays as twilight fell and the silver towers gleamed in the sunset. His city had not lacked troubles, but from humble beginnings his people had forged a society in which men and women chose their rulers. A city where they could speak their mind to power, and where laws were not tools of the mighty. Volanus had been a bastion of learning, and art, a great city of the world. As his fleet had sailed away in the pre-dawn gloom, off to found New Volanus, he had heard the priestesses in the seaside temple welcoming the sun with song, and his heart had ached, knowing it might be long years before he'd hear them again.

Now those voices were stilled forever. Their song had vanished with his city.

He started up the stairs.

She addressed him directly, her voice rising with wonder. "How do you resist? Do you not wish to prove your love by triumph? Do you not love me?" He felt the full force of her power, and his heart raced. Yet with him still was the vision of that shining city, forever lost. Tears tracked down from behind his mask.

"Stop him!" she shouted.

Those behind grabbed for his legs and his arms, but they were enthralled still by her beauty, and he was free, and he was Hanuvar. They came high and low, swinging and kicking, and he blocked and weaved and threw them off and emerged at last at the height of the steps.

She pulled back, her confidence wavering, and he saw her again for just a woman in a mask.

"There is more to love than this." He tore the mask from her.

The woman who had been a goddess covered her face with her hands and shuddered. Hanuvar looked down at the thing in his hands without daring to meet the blank gaze of it and broke it over his knee into two pieces. The resounding crack echoed through the forum like a thunderbolt.

Senanara slumped. Behind him the sounds of conflict continued, although it seemed to him the noises had already begun to change.

Her eyes fluttered, and he bent to scoop her into his arms. He had little time. The fights were breaking up and people were shaking off their confusion. He darted to the left and dropped off the side of the portico. Not so long ago his old knee injury would have made such an act challenging, but even with her in his arms his legs absorbed the drop without complaint. He was soon passing through a group assisting each other to stand after knocking each other bloody and bruised. He hissed to make way for a wounded woman and pushed on through other groups, some bent beside the injured. He passed into a side street.

When he finally reached Carthalo's tavern, Senanara was stirring fitfully in his arms. Kester and Lucena eyed him strangely as he worked through the celebratory crowd, and then he had passed into the back rooms and found the small chamber he'd made his own. He closed the door and was readying to lay her gently upon the couch when she feebly whispered his name.

He tipped up his mask so that she might see his face.

She was spent and drained. Whatever she had done with the mask that day had left her with nothing more. She was empty.

Her grip upon his arm was weak. Only a short while before her voice had been molten gold. Now it was the barest whisper. "Adherval," she said.

"I will find him," he pledged.

Her lips moved toward a smile and never reached it, for her expression went blank in death.

He stared down at her placid face and discovered he was weeping. Whether it was for who she had been, or who she might have grown to be, or for Melgar who had loved her, or for all the vanished past and impossible future he could not have said, but he crushed her body to him and rocked her and kissed the top of her head, wishing she had found a different path.

※ ※ ※

By the next day, rumor on the street held that Vanora herself had appeared at the festival. The priests announced that her manifestation had been a blessing and that it boded well for the health of the empire in the coming year, despite the carnage. More than a dozen had been killed and hundreds were injured.

The Dervans remained blissfully unaware of any connection between what happened at the temple and Senanara herself, especially since all Adherval knew of his wife was that she was free, as had been learned by the emperor's spies, for she had been too bold. Fortunately, Hanuvar had rolled up any of her connections before the secret police could learn her true aims, and Diravel and her compatriots were welcomed into Carthalo's organization.

At some other time any hint of Volani involvement might have drawn greater scrutiny from the authorities, but with news spreading about Enarius' coming adoption by the emperor, and his well-publicized support for the Lenereva family, any outright slander against Volani was seen as an attack against Enarius himself. Not even the revenants were that daring, especially with the emperor growing increasingly frustrated with them.

As for poor Senanara, she was interred after a private ceremony in a courtyard in Carthalo's complex. I myself observed the grave, and once saw Hanuvar standing with head bowed before it.

Carthalo's carefully crafted festival escapes came off with near perfection, although one had nearly been ruined by the commotion in a street beside the forum. I'm told that the festival inspired hundreds of slaves to attempt escape every year thereafter. Most of these later ones were caught; the Volani slaves, though, were not, and before too long were well on their way north to Selanto, accompanied by guides and carrying forged identity papers.

Though determined now to find the Eltyr, Hanuvar had sworn an oath to a dying woman. And so over the next few weeks he and Carthalo bent their considerable intellects toward a single, impossible objective: the recovery of Adherval, and the liberation of the Volani prisoners in the hands of the revenants.

If he had shared his plans with me, I'd have told him they were lunacy. For Hanuvar meant to take the fight to the empire's most dangerous and magically skilled defenders, in the very heart of their remote fortress.

—Sosilos, Book Nine

Chapter 8:
A Shadow in the Chamber
of the Lost

When the Revenants led Hanuvar inside the prison's main building they searched him carefully in the entryway, removing even his personal knife. That didn't surprise him, but it didn't please him. The slim, pale revenant considered him at length from behind the counter, employing the glassy stare Hanuvar had seen in the look of sorcerers. The older man who'd searched Hanuvar retreated behind the counter, watching with only mild interest, and brushed a brown hair from his black tunic. Neither man was armored, though the skull-faced emblem of the Revenant Order gleamed upon their rings.

Finally the mage blinked his glassy look away and pointed to the gold pendant at Hanuvar's neck. "What is that?" The mage's voice was as cold as his black eyes.

"A gift from Enarius, the emperor's nephew." Hanuvar lied, but his examiner couldn't know that.

His questioner was unimpressed. His tone was accusatory. "It possesses a dweomer."

Hanuvar touched it protectively. "I was told to always keep it on my person. The emperor wished it to be used by Enarius' chief agents."

The revenant's frown deepened, and he looked to his older companion for orders.

"Confiscate it," the older one said. Weathered and wrinkled, he possessed the tired eyes of a serious drinker.

Hanuvar stood straight, as though he were a prim patrician used to being obeyed. "Enarius will not be pleased."

The older one shrugged. "You can have it back when you leave."

Hanuvar frowned but slowly removed the pendant. As he lifted it with his right hand, he twisted its back free with his left, concealing it in his palm as he passed the front on to the younger revenant.

"I will keep it here, with your weapon."

"Be careful with them both." Hanuvar played the role of an aggrieved, upper ranking servant, hands balled on his hips. "Both were gifts."

The weathered revenant grunted without any great interest.

"If you will come with me?" The ashen younger one almost managed to sound welcoming, though there was something funereal in his delivery.

Hanuvar's black clad escort led him through a bland atrium with clean red tiles and a circle of plants dying about a scummy pool and took a doorway toward the four-story tower jutting above the wall. Hanuvar could not view the sea, but he smelled salt in the air, and heard the slap of the waves against the nearby cliffs. The sky was bright blue graced by lacy clouds.

Beyond the doorway lay an arch to what looked like a mess room or meeting hall, but his escort diverted left and up past the closed door on the first landing. While they climbed Hanuvar slipped the back of the talisman into a hidden pocket in his tunic. His guide halted before the closed door at the second landing and knocked loudly, then drew himself to attention and announced: "Centurion, I have brought the visitor."

"You may enter," came the answer. It was a woman's voice. Hanuvar's sources had informed him about what little was known of the woman temporarily in command in this remote outpost, and when the door opened, the consort led Hanuvar in to meet her.

Dania stood up from behind a camp table, a small woman with a receding chin and auburn hair pulled back in a loose bun. She wore a black stola and a silver circlet. Both the circlet and the pendant about her neck showed skull's heads. She was a fiend with pretty teeth and pretty brown eyes flecked with spots of gold. "I do not normally receive guests, much less on such short notice," she said.

With her was a thick-necked brute of a revenant with heavy sideburns, and red hair. He sat the papers he'd been examining on the centurion's desk and Hanuvar saw at a glance that they were the carefully forged identity documents he'd been separated from at the dockside entrance. They identified him as Minucius, a highly placed intermediary within the government bureaucracy.

Dania vacated her black cushioned stool and advanced around her desk to stop in front of him.

"Centurion Dania," Hanuvar said with a nod of greeting. "I've heard that you are a fascinating and capable woman."

"Now who says that?" she asked. "I have many detractors, Minucius."

"I have heard the hatred spewed by jealous critics," Hanuvar explained, "perhaps amplified by the guilty who have reasons to fear the revenants. Or the foolish, who lift a blade by its edge rather than its hilt. But your corps has many admirers among upright citizens."

Dania looked past Hanuvar to his escort. "You may go. Marcus, you as well."

The brute gave Hanuvar a sour look, then turned it to Dania before following the young revenant out the door, just managing not to slam it behind him.

Dania waited to speak until their steps retreated. "Our superior is in Derva this week and Marcus feels he should have been placed in charge rather than me. I don't know what infuriates him more—that a woman commands him, or that he sees I'm better at the job. Please, sit. I seldom have interesting visitors."

"Thank you." Hanuvar moved toward the bench facing the desk.

"Shall I offer you wine, or food?"

Hanuvar held up his hand. "Kind as you are, this isn't a social call."

"I hardly thought it was." Dania returned to her desk and sat.

Through the window behind her Hanuvar saw the docks, where his small swift ship, known by the Dervans as a catascopus, sat at anchor. So far the revenants had left it alone. He took his seat.

"You're here on some sort of government errand," Dania said, "but one without a truly official stamp of approval, unless I miss my guess."

"Wisely reasoned. Rumors have spread of an Eltyr killer, but my employer is tired of rumors."

"He wants action?"

"He wants information."

A pleased smile ticked up the corners of her lips. "You haven't come from the emperor, or you'd already be throwing his name around. And you're not one of Ciprion's representatives. Or Aminius."

"I'm from Enarius."

She nodded as if she had guessed that from the first. "Then you know you have no true power to command me."

"Yes. Just as you know that Enarius is heir apparent."

She agreed with a small bob of her head. "The emperor requested information about the Eltyr killings be kept strictly confidential."

"Who's to say that the emperor didn't tell Enarius to seek this information?"

She weighed the information without expression. "Are you telling me that's what's happened?"

"I'm merely advising you about what questions you might consider asking me."

"You are being circumspect. Enarius wants information, and the emperor may or may not have authorized him to seek it."

"I honestly have no idea what the emperor told him. But the emperor's health is failing. Enarius looks forward to a long and fruitful partnership with the revenants."

Her small chin lifted slightly; her eyebrows arched.

Hanuvar paused a beat before explaining. "Enarius has little lust for the throne. He wants to ensure the emperor's survival for as long as possible."

"—and so he wants to know about the threat posed by Eltyr to the emperor himself," she finished.

"Yes."

"I don't suppose it would do me any good to explain to you we have matters well in hand."

"Those are words. I must verify."

Her gaze had softened; there appeared to be an actual human expression in those light-colored eyes. "Very well. Ask away."

Hanuvar inclined his head in polite affirmation. "Do you have the killer?"

"Alas, no."

"How many deaths have their truly been?"

"Seven."

Hanuvar pretended surprise. "That many?" As the centurion nodded yes, he asked: "Is the murderer truly an Eltyr?"

"She is a skilled killer. She may be Herrene, or Cerdian, or a criminal element pretending to be Volani. But I think it's the Volani. I'm sure you know that three Eltyr remain at large. Along with Hanuvar himself."

He scoffed. "You believe Hanuvar is in command of the Eltyr?"

"He may be."

"And you're sure he's alive?"

"He lives," she declared with caustic certainty. "Witnesses have confirmed it."

"One of them was Indar, Enarius' friend," Hanuvar said.

"I'm well aware of the report."

"Then you're also aware that Indar was a drunk. Enarius honors him, for the man perished protecting him, but Enarius has reasons to doubt his judgment."

"Others claim they saw him as well. Caiax."

"Who managed to get himself killed in some kind of strange personal venture against the Ceori tribes."

Dania didn't seem to like the line of argument. "Are you here to ask about Hanuvar, or the Eltyr?"

"The Eltyr. It's you who brought up Hanuvar. Enarius isn't concerned about him. The Eltyr, though . . . he wants a full briefing. Enarius heard that you have retained more than twenty Volani prisoners. No one's told him a word about them. Were any of them working with the Eltyr?"

She placed both elbows on her desk and tapped her fingertips together. And she changed the subject. "You're far less nervous than most visitors to this office."

The centurion was testing him, so he boldly met her eyes. "Do you like that?"

She drew back and lowered her hands. "Are you flirting with me, Minucius? You do realize how many men have assumed I am weak willed and malleable? Are you another?"

"On the contrary. I was told you could be frightening."

Her teeth flashed. "Do I disappoint?"

"Not in the least. Perhaps you are more appealing because you are a little frightening."

She laughed. "You *are* flirting with me. You waste your time."

"I'm just being honest." He sat back. "I'd like that drink now, if it's still available." He nodded to the wine bottle on the sparsely decorated shelf behind Dania and she started to rise.

"Allow me," Hanuvar said with a smile.

"I am self-sufficient."

"Even those of us who are self-sufficient don't mind being attended to sometimes." The bottle sat on a shelf with a row of red goblets. He retrieved two by their stems, set them on the desk, and poured out a half measure for them both.

Dania stood, and they raised their goblets together. "To what shall we drink?" she asked. "The emperor?"

"To the identification of the Eltyr."

They saluted each other with their goblets and then drank. It was light and dry, undiluted by water.

She returned the goblet to the table. "Do you know, my adjutant Marcus was suspicious of you."

"Me?"

"He's suspicious of everyone," Dania said dismissively. "There have been some peculiar impersonations of late, and Marcus is sure some of them have been Hanuvar."

Hanuvar chuckled.

"I think he's out there but ascribing every strange event to him is credulous. As for you—"

"Me?" Hanuvar asked.

"It would be immensely foolish to attempt to impersonate someone in the heart of our fortress. And you do not strike me as foolish." She eyed him speculatively.

"I try not to be."

"You wish to see the files on the Eltyr? I will have them brought to you. But I think I'll give you a tour first."

"I'd hoped to see your domain."

"Did you? The cells aren't a pretty place."

"I've seen ugly things before. And I'm curious."

"You're curious about the Volani," she guessed.

Hanuvar offered his palms. "Not so much me as Enarius."

"You do know that he is sweet upon a Volani doxy, don't you?"

It should not have astonished him that Dania disparaged the elegant and accomplished Izivar Lenereva. It wouldn't have bothered the man Hanuvar pretended to be, so he shrugged it off. "I've heard rumors."

"Only rumors? Don't you think she's the reason you're here, looking in on these prisoners? I can guarantee that she has him wrapped about her wrinkly finger. She's much older than he, you know."

"I haven't met her."

"And you don't wish to speak ill of her. Especially to a revenant. I understand. We do gather information for the emperor, after all." She took another sip, then shrugged, as if casting off an unpleasant garment. "We can select our underlings, but never our officers. But we can choose our friends. Let us be friends, Minucius." She set the goblet aside. "When we get back you can pore over the papers as you wish, although there's little there. The first few victims were vocal allies of Catius. Warhawks, you might say. The last two have been children."

"Children?" Hanuvar had reconciled himself to the idea his daughter might be murdering enemy civilians, but the notion some of them were children startled him.

"You think the enemy has any moral qualms, Minucius? You've led a more sheltered life than I'd have guessed. Yes, children. The Eltyr knows she has power only through fear, and brave Dervans do not fear so much for themselves as they do seeing their own progeny die before them."

Hanuvar shook his head. "That's low. Even for Volani."

"Volani," Dania said with a sneer. "Come, I'll show you those we have in custody. I had twenty, but we were down to four." She laughed shortly. "I am down to three, as of last night."

"Oh?" That the revenant's tone was dismissive, as though the lives of Hanuvar's people were of no more concern than children's toys, stretched his acting ability to its utmost.

Fortunately, the centurion was moving toward the door, and Hanuvar was able to master his expression. "We had an old Eltyr," Dania continued. "A retired officer with some knowledge of magics." She started down the stairwell.

He wished he could ask her name. Hanuvar left the goblet on his desk and followed. He had to take a breath to keep his voice level. "What happened?"

"She refused to discuss how the Volani dragons were controlled."

That was likely because the asalda had never been controlled. From the start the great serpents had been guests of the city, grateful for the shelter and aid they had been granted when very young.

Dania continued: "The punishments we inflicted upon her finally took their toll. Do you want to know what they were?"

"I don't believe I do," Hanuvar said, and his revulsion was genuine. The truest measure of his acting was the mastery of his compulsion to slay Dania with his bare hands. "Who are the others?"

"No one of real consequence. An old priestess who may know some secrets. An apprentice sorcerer." They reached the first landing and passed it. "And our newest, the husband to Melgar Cabera's former wife. He's a physician. I'm hoping he can help keep other prisoners alive after some of our more intense sessions. He does seem quite talented."

Hanuvar affected approval. "The wise use all the tools available."

"Exactly."

They passed through the courtyard and into the office building, where the red-haired brute and the dark-skinned revenant were looking over a letter delivered by a soldier in standard legionary's uniform.

Hanuvar glanced at the soldier with indifference, despite the fact he was Carthalo.

"Is this man anyone I should be concerned with?" Dania asked his underlings.

The older one answered, his voice a low growl. "It's just a letter from a senator who thinks he's found some Volani witchcraft artifacts."

"That sounds important," Hanuvar said.

Dania laughed. "Every other week someone thinks to impress us with a gewgaw or slander or secret information. Most of the time it's crap." She faced Carthalo, looking taciturn and grim in his legionary's armor. "It's crap, isn't it? Just some old clay pots or something?"

"I'm afraid so, Centurion," Carthalo said.

"How much of it did the senator have you send?"

"A wagon load of it," the older revenant reported.

"I'll have the boys give it a going over, just to be sure," the revenant mage said.

She shrugged. "Come, Minucius." Dania pointed him to a lantern, took one for herself, and headed for a sturdy door set into the wall behind her underlings.

She opened the way, moved onto the landing beyond, then shut the door behind them. He heard the click of a lock.

"You were so dismissive of the possibilities there," Hanuvar said conversationally. He pretended no concern that he was trapped underground with a murderess.

Dania paused to open the lantern and hand over the candle so Hanuvar could use it to light his own. "Don't you find the same uselessness when you have to talk with politicians? People desperate to impress, wasting your time and energy? You may think we're on this lonely coast because of security, but it's in part so we're further away from the petty place seekers. The most determined find us anyway, but if this stronghold remained in Derva they'd be pestering us every day."

Showing her light down a dark, winding stone stair, Dania gestured for Hanuvar to precede.

Hanuvar pretended nonchalance as he started down, lantern in his off hand. He spoke with his head half turned. "I'd think you'd want to humor these requests. Enarius says that the emperor has grown frustrated with the revenants. He wants more results."

"Some of my superiors are too eager to report success, or its proximity, so that when they fail it appears a setback rather than slower than expected progress."

Hanuvar had known true fear and did not project it upon places owing to expectations. Its smell here was real, as certain as the scent of wet earth and old stone. People had suffered and died in this place, and their experiences had left an imprint.

Dania apparently felt it as well, though she found it amusing. "Still eager to see my domain?"

Hanuvar chuckled like a man trying to hide his nervousness.

They arrived at last at a solid floored chamber, fifty steps below the surface. To right and left were stone archways. Through a single left one Hanuvar observed barrels and crates and the red wink of rat eyes. The little creatures chittered alarm and scattered into the darkness. From further ahead someone coughed weakly.

To the right were additional open archways. Through one he glimpsed a rack, and a row of chains and pointed implements. The stone floor was dark and stained, and a pair of cockroaches scurried along the edge of the light, fleeing their sudden exposure.

"Hang your lantern in that niche, there, beside the locked door."

This he did. Dania, though, did not advance toward the door. It had no bars, nor a window. Someone on its other side coughed again.

She advanced another step. "Have you observed my shadow, Minucius?"

He had. That it was larger than Hanuvar's own had nothing to do with the angle of light. The blackness of the sorcerer's shadow was more pronounced, as though it were an oily body of water fed by tributaries of lamentation and pain.

"You say that you have heard of me. There are sorcerous centurions in the revenants, but I am the only one who truly commands. Do you know why?" Dania was too eager to wait for an answer and continued: "It is because I am their most powerful sorcerer. I don't just sense magics, I build them."

She cast two shadows now. One was no more remarkable than Hanuvar's own, and the other flowered behind her, a thick, winged ogre's shape from a light source that wasn't there.

"Finally you look worried, Minucius. Here is where you tell me why you waited until my superior was absent before you came to visit."

She did not wait for a response, continuing: "Here is where you tell me why you dared to sneak a magical shield into my fortress. Yes, I sensed it. If you had heard about me, surely you knew I could sense such things."

"The most powerful mages always can."

"But only when they're obviously working? Is that what you were told? That's true of weaker mages. But then you've had a spell cast on you, too. And now your stance shifts, as if you think to fight. It won't do any good against my shadow, but I understand your impulse."

"Do you? What's this about?"

"I don't yet understand. It may be that you're just who you say, and that Enarius gifted you with a tool because he did not trust the revenants."

"Or?" Hanuvar offered.

"Or you may be something else. In which case, no one will have to drag you down the stairs and into the cell behind you. My shadow will do it."

The thing flowed to the revenant's side, casting darkness and cold as it oozed forward into an upright bipedal shape. In the place where the suggestion of its head rose, Hanuvar saw a face.

Months ago, the first time he had glimpsed the shadow, he had seen no features, though the scholar Varahan had. This time Hanuvar perceived a succession of them. The first was a young woman with mad, rolling eyes. A breath later she had receded like mist and a groaning, bearded man stared at him; Hanuvar's breath caught in his throat for he recognized the face, and he swore it recognized him as well. The mouth opened and the shadow started to turn.

"Steady," Dania said, her hand outstretched toward the thing. It halted its progress. "Your shield? It might protect you from spells I throw. But the shadow is not a spell. Do you understand? It is something I have created and command. Your magic will not protect you."

"You think I'm defenseless."

"I want you to understand your position, Minucius, so that we can start speaking truth. You are an enigma to me. In your place, anyone else would be quaking. There is fear on you, but there is something more, and I think it must be related to an odd aura you cast. What is it? Are you a sorcerer yourself?"

"I have my secrets."

"I will learn them, one way or another."

"Perhaps we can trade a secret for a secret, then," Hanuvar suggested.

A laugh of disbelief escaped her. "You still think you can bargain?"

"You risk Enarius' displeasure if you act against me."

"If you do work for him. But I will humor you. A secret for a secret if you go first."

"I am far older than I seem. I've taken stolen lives to regain my youth."

She studied him for a long moment and then her mouth dropped open. "Gods! It is true—I do not believe it! How did you do it? And why keep the lines unsealed? Is that so you can shift your age as you like?"

He didn't know what Dania meant by unsealed lines, but despite the question worrying him Hanuvar managed to smile and shake his head, as though he possessed more information than he let on. "Now tell me what this shadow is. My power is useful only to me. Your shadow seems like a weapon fashioned for the empire."

"It is—and my power over it grows. I've a few more experiments to perform," she said eagerly, then stopped. "But that is more than you asked. You wanted to know what it is. This is the death of nearly two dozen Volani left in my charge. One of the Seven. Some girls. A dragon keeper. One of Hanuvar's cousins. None of them could tell me much that was useful, not now that Volanus is leveled. But I've made them useful. At night, and in the darkness, their power is unstoppable. And I'm almost ready to show the emperor what I can do with it. Shall I show you?"

She pointed and the thing flowed toward Hanuvar, who felt rather than heard a moan of its pain. As it advanced he saw Dania through it as though it were a dark gauzy drapery. He backed toward the wall.

The revenant's voice was stark and certain. "Now you will tell me why I have not yet received clearance about your ship. I sent a message by sun telegraph the moment you pulled up beside the dock and it's gone flashing across the countryside all the way to Derva. If you were authorized, I should have received a response by now."

"Maybe Enarius is occupied and can't respond."

"Or maybe you are not who you claim."

"That might be."

"Might it? Then who are you, really?" Dania was enjoying herself, and at her gesture the arms of the shadow thing lifted and moved toward an embrace of Hanuvar. A second back step brought him beside the locked door.

"Now you fear! Oh, I shall wrest the secrets from you, Minucius." Dania was all but breathless with excitement. "Or whomever you really are. A Cerdian sorcerer, I think. A powerful but limited one. Who's not quite as clever as he thinks."

The shadowy hands stretched for Hanuvar's neck and the face of a sad young boy stared out at him.

"I'll tell you a final pair of things," Hanuvar said.

"You'll tell me everything." Dania's voice was shrill with joy. The hands of the shadow came to Hanuvar's neck. They were cold and cloying. He felt the pressure of an ice-like thumb against his trachea.

He placed the stone that he'd palmed against the shadowy hands upon his throat.

Dania laughed at him. "I told you! Your stone can only shield you against my spells, not against my creature!"

"I'm not shielding *me* from your spells." Hanuvar forced the back of the medallion into the inherent wrongness and its glacierlike cold.

Over the monster's left shoulder, he saw her expression shift as Hanuvar's meaning dawned upon her.

"Throttle him," she cried. "Throttle him now!"

But the creature's fingers had closed upon the stone, and the hand upon his neck drew no tighter. Hanuvar met the spot where its eyes shifted and addressed the dead in the language of his people.

"I am Hanuvar Cabera," he said. "And that stone shall set you free."

The faces flashed one by one past him and there was dawning awareness in those horrified eyes. The hand dropped from his throat and then the thing turned on its heel, advancing for Dania.

Hanuvar followed in its wake. Dania shrieked command after command that it was no longer compelled to obey. Though he had no sorcerous sense, even Hanuvar felt the revenant's magic stir the air. She began to mutter an incantation, but it was cut short by a gurgle as icy hands closed upon her slim throat. The revenant fumbled with her lantern and shone it at the thing.

The proximity to the light burned a hole in the shadow but did not stop it. The monster's hands tightened on her, and she dropped the lantern. It rattled when it hit and the candle slammed against the side, sputtered briefly, then went out. She scrabbled at the shadowy arms she couldn't fully grasp, and her eyes rolled pleadingly at Hanuvar.

"There's been no response from the sun telegraph because my men captured the next station," Hanuvar said. "And by now my men have won through your walls and past the soldiers of your garrison, for my officer came through to open the way. When I give the word, your fortress will be rubble, with your bones at their very bottom."

The revenant's eyes bulged and her lips worked, though no sound came.

Hanuvar watched the woman's eyes roll back, watched her go limp, watched the thing let her slip lifeless to the floor. His expression did not change until the shadow turned once more to him.

"You are free," Hanuvar said sorrowfully. "Would that you were free always in life."

A girl's face appeared to him, pleading, mouthing words he could not hear. And then he saw Tanilia, one of the seven high councilors of Volanus. His name was on her lips, and her eyes shifted toward the lantern hung beside him, and then back to him, with longing.

"You wish destruction?"

She confirmed this with the solemn closing of her eyes.

"Because you are trapped," he said. "In an abomination. Trapped as a monstrous tool in the space between life and death."

Her mouth firmed. She even reached for the lantern but the hands withdrew and the faces fluttered. Perhaps the creature could not seek its destruction, or it might be that not all of the individuals that comprised it were in agreement. Or sane.

He lifted his lantern from the rung and pushed it into the dark body as the face of a frightened boy looked out at him. The boy closed his eyes and bit his lips as the bright light ate into the thick shadow body. A bearded man with rolling eyes seized control of the form and drove a shadowy arm at him.

The cold seared through his shoulder and left him gasping but he held to the lantern and opened the glass plate, thinking more direct heat might aid the process.

The man's face blinked away and then Tanilia returned, her features strained. She lowered the arm.

The little boy's face replaced hers and he smiled sadly at Hanuvar. And then he faded, and with him the shadow lightened.

The remaining souls appeared, one after the other, the shadow growing less substantial as each departed. A trio of little girls. A young woman with a sweet smile. The old man who had looked so wild eyed, then another calmer one so similar in appearance they must have been brothers. Tanilia bowed her head to him, and then, as she disappeared the body of the shadow faded to just a wisp supporting the face and extremities.

A few others acknowledged him and left. Finally, when nothing remained but the faintest of outlines, his cousin Olmares took command and tried to speak. Hanuvar couldn't hear him, but thought he understood the words. He was asking if he would free the others.

"I will free them all," he vowed, his voice shaking.

"I know," his cousin mouthed. And then he was gone, and the only shadows in the room were his own and that of the dead revenant slumped on the floor.

He wiped tears from his face, bent to retrieve the stone left by the shadow, then tore the keys from Dania's corpse. With them he opened the door to the round room beyond, more a pit than a cell, where eight prisoners were crowded, their hands manacled. They were grimy and smelly and malnourished and had been bedding down in filthy hay.

Adherval the physician came forth first, weeks of beard on his cheeks. Though his eyes were slitted even to the feeble lantern light, they were bright with wonder.

"We heard," Adherval said to him in Volani. "We heard everything." His eyes found the dead revenant, and he spit toward her.

Hanuvar took the keys to his manacles. "Not all of them can walk well," Adherval said, looking back over his shoulder. "And not all of us are Volani. But all are victims of the revenants."

"I will leave no one in this place but revenants," Hanuvar promised.

And he kept his word. His men had already overpowered the little garrison. They helped transport the weakest of the prisoners up the inner stairs, and then carried them down to the dock and onto to the ship. All were blinded by the sun and half were weeping.

Though weak himself, Adherval followed, urging one of Carthalo's followers to be careful of a prisoner's arms, and reassuring the others there would soon be food and water. Seeing that they were in good hands, Adherval came and stood near him along the prow, smiling and shaking his head in disbelief. "You are really Hanuvar?"

"I am," he said gently. Soon, he would have to tell the man that his wife was dead. That, though, might wait a little longer. "You are free. And you will remain that way."

Horace hurried past with a large wicker basket stuffed full of scrolls. Carthalo descended from the tower height to report the barrels had been placed, and the final signal had been sent.

"That," Hanuvar explained to Adherval, "means that the signal tower my men captured, next up the chain, has just relayed a message to Derva. The last message ever received from this tower will be that they were under attack from a Cerdian warship."

Carthalo clapped Hanuvar on the shoulder. "Time to be going."

As the rest of their force boarded, Hanuvar's final orders were carried out. Only a few months before, the Dervans had hoped to learn the secrets of the so-called Volani fire, but Hanuvar had freed Varahan, the man behind its creation, as well as his companion, a talented Nuvaran sorcerer. The latter had devised a spell breaking amulet, and the former had refined the weapon he had never divulged to the Dervans. Carthalo's men had placed barrels of the incendiary in key spots within the small fortress and its tower.

At Hanuvar's signal, runners lit tinder beside the barrels. The last of them had reached the docks when they heard a muffled blast. Before long, red and blue flame raced along the fortress's exterior wall, and as the ship weighed anchor, the tower height collapsed, taking its sun telegraph with it, shining until it fell into the stone. Hanuvar watched with unaccustomed satisfaction as the outer wall tumbled into the sea. Red flame and black smoke soared into the heavens and Carthalo, at Hanuvar's side, cackled with joy. The destruction was even more complete than they had hoped.

They were at full sail very quickly. When Hanuvar looked back he beheld a further surprise. Weakened by the internal collapse, the cliff upon which the fortress had stood crumbled at its edge and then much of the supporting escarpment crashed into the water at its base, sending up an immense fountain of water. Hanuvar grinned with savage pleasure.

Carthalo, divested now of his legionary's armor, laughed in delight. "Oh, that went even better than I dreamed! And look at that." He pointed out to sea. "No sign of other ships. That's what the Dervans get for wanting their secret revenant prison far from prying eyes."

"Every strength can be a weakness, if you know how to find the chink."

"The mission was a complete success," the spy master continued. "We didn't lose a single man. And that physician we rescued thinks everyone we brought out has a fair chance."

"That is good to hear."

"It should be. I know you were hoping to find more of our people."

Hanuvar nodded slowly, his gaze still upon the distance.

"But we freed many who had no other chance. And we found all the papers they had on the Eltyr."

"I don't know that they'll help us much. I don't think the revenants had many leads."

"I know that look. Something else is troubling you."

Many things were bothering him, including the intimation that there was something wrong with the spell that had restored him. It was probably past time to look more closely at its effect. But chiefly his thoughts were turned upon those long-suffering faces.

"Did you have to deal with the revenant's sorcery?" Carthalo asked.

"I did."

"And was Norok right? There were people inside the monster? Our people?"

"Yes. They set me free and I returned the favor," he said. "And they killed the monster."

※ ※ ※

It was not that Hanuvar had assumed too much about the aging spell's effects, but that those gifted with sorcerous sight who were members of our network did not understand its magic. Skilled though he was, Norok had no knowledge about life magics or auras.

Carthalo had reached out to other contacts and one had been called to our little naval yard just south of Selanto. Hanuvar expected her to be waiting for him when he returned from his mission against the revenants. Dania's comments about his lifelines left him uneasy, but the matter was beyond his control, so he spent most of the short journey going over the records stolen from the revenant stores.

Eventually I had time to study them myself, and they were dire in the mundane way in which they cataloged evils. I will not trouble your minds with the matters they recorded, though I will share that Hanuvar's suspicions were correct. The revenants had scant information about the Eltyr apart from the names and ages of the victims and when and where they had been found. Nor had they any more information on the whereabouts of his daughter Narisia or her companions than we had learned already.

At some point during the journey Hanuvar shared news of Adherval's wife's death with him, and I know only that the story left him partly broken, for he was somber long weeks. I came to know him well in the ensuing months and understood then how deeply the death touched him, for he was by nature an optimistic man, even in the face of the adversity he had experienced.

The voyage to our base was not a long one, and fairly soon it was explained to the recovered prisoners that, for their own safety, they would need to leave the ship in packing crates padded with blankets and pillows, and, naturally, air holes. Two of them were terribly frightened by this, but there was nothing to be done, for it was not as though our little enclave in Selanto was completely secret. Someone might well be suspicious of the influx of pale, malnourished travelers turning up within a day of the destruction of the revenant coastal prison.

As it happened, no one caught wind of their arrival, but other, more dangerous developments loomed.

For the emperor, concerned about the future of his bloodline, had ventured north on a fact-finding mission that would take him to Selanto itself.

—Sosilos, Book Ten

Chapter 9:
Bloodlines

I

Back in Ostra, Julivar's father had forbidden her seaside visits and even Izivar had cautioned her to stay clear of the wharves unless she travelled with bodyguards. But here, in Selanto, she could watch the new ships growing in their dry docks every single day, beautiful, long, deep-hulled vessels designed for the outer ocean. She could talk to the sails master and the foreman and even help out with the carpentry if she wanted. It was a dream.

The little port bustled with far more energy than she would ever have guessed. It wasn't just the ships, but docks and warehouses and apartments. Antires had told her there'd been nothing on this land only a few months before, and that it had all gone up with incredible speed.

She still wasn't entirely sure about the reasons behind the move, or the construction, but Izivar had confided a handful of secrets to her and had finally admitted that some of the Volani hidden among them were escaped slaves. Not only would they be in jeopardy if found, so too would everyone giving them shelter.

Julivar heard how badly some of them had been treated, and she pledged her heart to the cause with the zeal of a religious convert. She had also decided that she would have to watch out for her sister, who seemed too enmeshed in the day-to-day struggles of management to truly be cognizant of dangers.

And so Julivar had sneaked through the kitchen cabinet and into the hidden observation cubicle, banging her knee in the process. She hadn't liked the look of the visitor Izivar had agreed to meet privately. He'd been short and powerfully built, with an evil mouth and pointed eyebrows. He didn't seem like a man who laughed much.

Now, as she pressed her ear to the wall, he was bluntly speaking to Izivar about his aims.

"... know you have a small enclave here that can't possibly bear the emperor any love," he said. Sometimes Julivar had to press in close to hear the speakers, but she had no trouble overhearing him, for his voice was loud. "And yet somehow you have the protection of the emperor's heir."

Izivar's voice was clearer still, for she sat closer to the panel behind which Julivar hid. Her sister sounded coolly polite, calm, and masterful. Sometimes Julivar wished she could speak with such measured grace. "We've been quite fortunate," Izivar said. "And blessed in our friends. We seek no enemies."

"But what if the enemies seek you?" the man pressed. He seemed as though he were in a terrible hurry.

"No enemy is seeking us now," Izivar countered reasonably.

"You pretend to be foolish and I know that you are not. With a snap of his fingers the emperor might decide that you all are done for. That he has no use for you, or your people. What would you do then?"

He was right. Julivar liked Enarius, but the emperor had sent his legions to destroy Volanus. And if a big city like Volanus couldn't withstand him, these buildings would fall in an instant.

Izivar's voice had grown cool. "You said you wished to discuss a business venture. This strikes me instead as talk of treason."

"Treason," the man said, his voice speculative. "Against whom? Treason can only be against a government that is your own."

"The treason of one ally against another."

"I will be blunt."

"You have hardly been subtle so far."

"We of Cerdia mean to stop the Dervans before they finish us. Just as your Hanuvar attempted, but without such wasteful expenditure of men and material. We need only a little help."

"You will not have it from me." Julivar heard the sound of chair legs scraping across tile and imagined her sister standing. She couldn't believe she was so dismissive of a potential ally, especially one that sounded so dangerous. "Leave. Do not darken my doorway again."

"You are either an ally, or an enemy," the man said with a warning tone.

"In this, I am your enemy. And I can act against you if I must."

Julivar gulped, afraid for her sister. This listening post didn't have a door, and it would be a long way around to reach Izivar's office.

"You will regret this," the fellow promised.

"I doubt that very much."

Julivar risked sliding the little eye panel aside for a look. But the Cerdian had already turned and stomped toward the door. He slammed it closed behind him. She clambered from her listening post and ran at full speed for her sister's office.

Izivar left off massaging her forehead and looked up at the sound of the door reopening. The dust mote laden sunbeams streaming in from the high window behind illuminated Izivar's desk but hid the woman in shadow.

Julivar closed the portal behind her and addressed her sister in a loud whisper.

"Why didn't you hear him out?"

"You thought he was a man to trust?" Izivar asked in disbelief.

Julivar smote her heart, as she had seen an actor do before he declared his undying love. "The emperor killed our people. Our blood cries for vengeance."

"And our blood would flow if we joined that man," Izivar said. "A wise leader thinks more about her people than herself. You would have me throw all our lives away to see one old man dead."

"Maybe." Julivar was no longer as certain as she'd been a moment before, then, hating the sound of vacillation in her voice she straightened so she looked more confident. "A leader must be decisive."

"And a leader must choose her allies. That man was so obvious he's either going to get everyone working with him caught and killed, or he's some agent of the empire trying to root out traitors. You were listening, weren't you? Did you like the way he sounded, or the volume of his speech? Did he seem like a careful planner?"

"...no," Julivar admitted.

"I'm glad you see that."

Worried now about her lack of understanding, Julivar spoke quietly. "You really think he might have been a spy for the emperor?"

"I don't know. But we must remain wary. People will try to take advantage of us. To use our connection with Enarius. If we lose sight of our mission and focus on revenge, we will only end up getting our people killed. We have to protect those who are left. Don't let anyone get you talking about plots or plans or revenge. Do you understand?"

"It doesn't seem right," Julivar said.

"It isn't," Izivar agreed. "Life isn't fair. But it's been much easier for you and me than it's been for others. We've been lucky. And because the gods have blessed us with fortune, we will use it to help those around us."

Izivar had shared that particular axiom a thousand times. Adults ended up repeating some of their stock phrases so much she had sworn to herself that when she got older she'd only say things once.

There were footsteps outside and then a knock upon the door.

"Lady Izivar," said Antires. "The ship has returned."

Julivar didn't ask which ship; her sister had asked to be informed the moment the *Lion* reached port. It had left yesterday at dawn, and Izivar had asked after it several times already.

She saw Izivar's eyebrows twitch at the news and a nervous alertness possessed her face. She looked expectant and pleased, but troubled at the same time.

"What's wrong?" Julivar asked.

"Hopefully nothing." Izivar pitched her voice louder. "Thank you, Antires. We'll come right out. Is our friend well?"

While Izivar sounded completely calm her expression remained tense. Her sister liked the mystery man central to all of their efforts more than she let on. Everyone referred to him as Decius, but he spoke Volani like a native. Izivar had warned her to keep any observations about him to herself.

"He's fine," Antires answered, the sound of a smile in his voice. "I saw him moving around on deck."

Izivar pushed out from the desk. "We're clear, aren't we?" she asked Julivar. She started for the door.

"Everything's clear." Julivar followed her sister through the doorway and down the hall.

Antires had waited for them and fell in step beside Izivar. He was very handsome, with dark creamy skin and a dazzling smile. He wasn't as muscular as the men Julivar usually admired, but he was well-spoken and always stylish, even when in casual clothes, and he told wonderful stories. Today he wore brown sandals and an off-white tunic with red, lined sleeves, tied at the waist by a twisted brown leather belt featuring a Ceori hound-faced buckle.

As they exited the building and moved toward the docks, she shielded her eyes from the sun. It hung low on the horizon, throwing a brilliant white path across the ocean.

Off on her right, just up from the shore, stood the wide warehouse where the ships were being built.

She spied one of the omnipresent watchers on a distant rooftop platform. A squadron of sentinels kept watch for any unwanted visitors. Word had been allowed to leak that the Lenereva family had invested in an innovative shipping venture to explain away the security of their outpost south of the village and the large number of Volani in residence. Even if many of those here in the complex had no knowledge of ship building or involvement in the vessels' construction, the Dervans widely believed cultural stereotypes, like all Volani possessing an inborn love of the sea and knowledge of ships.

Her sister and Antires paid no attention to the gorgeous natural environment around them, looking at neither the sheltered hilly cove and the calm blue sea in its arms nor the deep green of the encircling pines and spruce. They had eyes only for the sleek, high-prowed vessel at the dock. A band of sailors unloaded crates large as coffins with such incredible care they must have contained priceless statues or very tender fruit. Other sailors were already dangling from ropes alongside the hull and painting the ship's trim a bright green, while still others touched up the ship's eyes, lengthening them and making them blue rather than brown. The flag, too, had come down.

Himli, Izivar's scarred foreman, was supervising the cargo transfer, gruffly cursing the men to carry their burdens even more carefully than they already were.

Izivar stopped at the bottom of the dock where Decius oversaw the unloading himself. He had seen her and Antires approach but was so busy with orders about the ship he didn't greet them until they were at his side.

Antires looked joyful enough to embrace him—just like a Herrene, or a puppy—but Decius simply nodded. When he'd first appeared in Izivar's life, the same day that horrible little man had killed their father, Decius had looked young and interesting. He appeared to have aged a lot in the last few months, either because of worry or lack of sleep.

"Was the venture a success?" Izivar asked. Though her sister was clearly troubled, she asked about her worries in a way that struck Julivar as rather bloodless, and she wondered if she meant more than what the words said.

"The journey was a success." Decius' answer was flat, and his eyes slid over to Julivar before he returned his attention to Izivar. "The cargo's substantially smaller than I had been led to believe."

"Oh." Izivar's expression fell. She looked as though she wanted to know more, but her eyes shifted to Julivar.

"What?" Julivar asked. "What are you talking about?"

When her sister's lips parted, Julivar expected she was going to be told to move along as though she were a little girl, but Izivar's mouth clamped shut at the sound of running footsteps Everyone turned to their source.

Panting, one of the watchmen came to a halt in front of them. He passed a scroll case to Izivar. "A legion messenger just delivered this," he said, winded but not fully out of breath. He added, "It has the emperor's seal."

Izivar blankly accepted the thing, then traded a concerned glance with Decius before prying off the cap. She shook out the scroll, then studied the unbroken wax upon it as she handed him the case. Julivar tried to crowd close, because she'd never seen the emperor's seal before, but Izivar broke it and unrolled the paper.

Julivar watched her sister's eyes rove over the document and then saw her brows arch. Her sister tilted it toward Decius, and Antires read over his shoulder.

"The emperor's on his way," Izivar summarized. "He'll be here by early evening. He's coming for an unofficial visit and writes we shouldn't worry about any pomp or special consideration."

"He can't possibly have heard about...the venture, can he?" Antires asked.

"No," Decius said. "If that's what this was about, he wouldn't be coming himself."

"You need to get out of here." Izivar's gaze shifted to the last of the crates, still carefully being carried off, then swept over the changes being painted upon the ship. "And this needs to be finished, fast." She called to her foreman. "Himli!"

Antires turned to Decius. "She can handle all of this. We need to get you hidden."

As Izivar launched a series of orders, Julivar followed Decius and the Herrene, running to catch up as they reached the end of the dock and started for the residential buildings.

"What's in all of those boxes?" she asked him. "Are those weapons?"

Decius answered with incredible calm. "No, not at all."

She kept with them as the two men arrived at one of the three cottages near the office. When Antires opened the door and entered the atrium the smell of fresh paint was still strong.

Antires put a thumb over his shoulder toward her as they advanced through the atrium. "Should she be here?"

"It's fine," Decius answered.

They arrived at a plain brown room with a bed and a table set with pitcher and bowl. A mirror hung above it and a door opened onto a little courtyard. Decius poured water into the bowl.

Julivar couldn't contain her curiosity. "Why is Izivar so worried about the emperor seeing you?"

"Shaving first?" the Herrene asked.

"Yes," Decius answered.

"Why do you need to do any of that?" Julivar asked. "Izivar doesn't want you seen at all."

"Neither do I, but in case I have to be, I want to be prepared." Decius turned to pull a shaving blade from a drawer and sharpened it briskly on a whetstone.

"Why does the emperor scare you?" she said. "Will he recognize you? Are you Melgar?"

Antires gave her a searching look, then turned to Decius, now soaping his hands and spreading the lather on his face, dark with a day's growth of beard.

Decius' answer held an air of cold finality. "Melgar is dead."

"You look like him," she said.

"How do you know what Melgar looks like?" Antires asked.

"I saw him. And," she said, "my sister used to have a bust of him she thought I didn't know about."

Antires grinned. "Izivar had a bust of Melgar?"

"I mean my other sister, Celidra," she said, keeping her voice even. "She's dead, too."

Antires' expression fell. "I'm sorry."

Julivar didn't want to dwell on that. "But Izivar found it one day when Celidra was still living in our house, and Celidra was so embarrassed Izivar confessed that she always thought Melgar was handsome too then said that they should never tell Father."

"And you were there?"

She shrugged, proud that she often managed to be on hand when the interesting things were happening.

"What did Izivar think of Hanuvar?" Antires asked casually.

Decius ignored the entire conversation, studying his reflected face in the bronze mirror as he worked.

"Izivar said he was an arrogant man, risking others when he was too stubborn to admit he was wrong."

Antires absorbed this without comment, then turned his attention to his companion, dragging a blade through the lather on his face.

"Are you actually a Cabera?" she asked him. "You look like one."

"Pretty soon he's going to look like a Ceori," Antires spoke up. "Just as soon as we can spend a little time with his hair and wardrobe."

It was strange that there was such familiarity between the two of them, and over personal matters like grooming and fashion. "Are you two lovers?"

"No," Antires answered with a laugh.

"That's good," Julivar said, seeking the reflection of Decius' eyes. "Because I think Izivar likes you."

She was disappointed that got no reaction, but Decius did speak to her. "You should go now. And I suggest you stay hidden; don't answer any questions from the emperor or his men, no matter how friendly they are."

"You sound like Izivar," she said crossly. "I won't tell anyone about our secrets."

Frustrated by their lack of trust, she left them to their preparations. The mystery of Decius' real identity could wait. For now she was curious to learn what had been transported in those boxes and to catch a glimpse of the emperor himself. What could he possibly want?

II

The red cushions Pellas sat on within the emperor's carriage were as plush and comfortable as the purple ones decorating the bench upon which the emperor reclined across from him. Pellas knew because during one of the emperor's bathroom breaks, he'd slipped over to try them out. But no matter the cushion color there was apparently no way to render this carriage truly comfortable. Pellas' entire backside was sore from the constant rattle over the roads. He remained astonished that the emperor had wished to extend his inspection tour to this remote outpost at the last moment, but then there was no knowing what the emperor might do day to day or hour to hour, not anymore.

Pellas was starting to wonder if the emperor's entire explanation about visiting the lumber yards of the north had been a screen, for he'd looked extremely disinterested during the presentations, and only appeared focused when he decreed there would be a detour.

That focus had waned. At the moment, the emperor sat looking out the window, coughing.

The old man's white mane of hair still looked impressive, but his skin had paled over the last months. He'd been a bulky, powerful man for long years and he still had the frame of one, although his shoulders were hunched and the weight had dropped away.

"You can stop staring, Pellas." The emperor slowly turned his head away from the view of the screen of pines and the flat sea occasionally visible beyond them. "I'm not going to die in the next hour."

"I wasn't thinking about that, Excellency, but about how thin you've become. This travelling can't be good for you. You need your bed, and your chef. And the sun of your garden."

The emperor regarded him through drooping, bloodshot eyes. He covered his mouth and coughed. Lightly, this time. "I do need some wine," he said.

Pellas quickly poured some from the decanter cleverly ensconced in a delicate wall cabinet. The matching cup he used was deep, so it wouldn't disgorge splashes of wine while the carriage bumped.

The emperor managed not to spill any as he took a long drink. Yesterday there had been curses and a long delay and a change behind a dressing screen that had to be pulled off one of the trailing carts. And then, after two hours had been added on to the trip, the emperor had been furious with everyone but himself at the delay.

He handed the cup back and adjusted his toga.

There were some who thought Gaius Cornelius insisted upon the toga owing to dignity of his office, but Pellas suspected the emperor wore it constantly because he was always cold. Additionally, he draped a wool blanket across his shoulders.

Pellas had assumed the conversation over, but the emperor resumed it. "This is about the future."

"Your eminence?"

"Enarius is smitten with this Volani woman. He says she isn't similarly enamored. He swears it by all the gods and the soul of my poor sister and had told me not to worry about her."

"But you're worried about her," Pellas said, putting just the right amount of warmth into the observation.

"I'm worried about the future. I don't have much longer, Pellas, and I don't want my son mooning over some Volani, much less marrying her once I'm with my ancestors."

"Which I'm sure is many years away."

The emperor growled at him.

"Why don't you just have her killed?" he asked.

"That would upset my son."

The adoption of Enarius was still strange to Pellas' ears. He would adjust to it, just as he had adjusted to so many changes over the course of his tenure. He'd first been elevated into the emperor's inner circle because of his talent with the same board games the emperor enjoyed, and because he was, perhaps foolishly, not afraid to win. When it came to his gaming, at least, Gaius wanted an actual competition. As the emperor had aged, Pellas' position had somehow evolved into personal confidant and occasional nurse. It was in the former capacity that he smiled reassuringly. "He loves you, sire. He would get over it."

The emperor let out a grunt that managed to convey disparagement and his disdain for the idea. Sometimes that would have been enough, but the emperor was in a talkative mood. "He has been fascinated with this woman for years, but her father and my spies have always reported she has no designs upon him. And he has told me that he knows he cannot have her. Now would that be fair of me to kill her, out of hand? Especially when my son tells me that he pledged—" he paused to cough without covering his mouth—"to her dying brother he would protect her? The brother he claims was slain trying to save him?"

"They're all just Volani, sire."

The emperor sighed. "We're not at war with all the Volani any more than we are at war with all the Herrenes. It was just those in the city who posed a threat. It will destabilize the empire if our enemies imagine we're out to exterminate them all. Besides, laborers in this shipyard are supposed to be working on some new designs that will benefit the empire."

That, Pellas thought, was already the sound of Enarius speaking through the emperor's mouth. "But who's paying attention right now to whether or not Volani are running this new shipyard?" Pellas asked. "It wouldn't hurt to have a citizen in charge of these shipyards, would it? Instead of this woman?"

The emperor's eyes then were barbs of fire, and their burning malignance served as a stark reminder that the old man across from him had the power to kill in a finger snap. "Some relative of yours, perhaps?" he asked slowly.

It would have been folly to answer, so Pellas kept silent.

The emperor looked toward the window without actually peering through it. "I don't know back end from front when it comes to ships, but the Volani do, and the empire can use that knowledge if we're to grow."

"Of course, sire."

"Of course," the emperor repeated darkly, under his breath, and fell silent.

Pellas was well acquainted with his master's moods. Further

conversation initiated on his own would only anger the man and drive a further wedge between them.

He better understood the emperor's aims. Gaius was skeptical of the woman, but disposed to let her live and, if the intelligence reports from his own sources were accurate, the woman was as disinterested in Enarius as a lover as the emperor's own reports had publicized. She was no fool.

But that didn't mean that there weren't actions to be taken. Aminius had advised him to think on his feet, and that he intended to do. Just because Enarius had been adopted as a son didn't mean that there wasn't still room for Aminius to rise. Especially if a wedge were driven between the emperor and Enarius. The death, say, of the lady Izivar during or immediately after the emperor's visit. The young man would be unlikely to believe any of the old man's denials if she were to perish around the same time as their interaction. The trick would be arranging it so that Pellas himself remained clear of suspicion.

But then, as the emperor's personal companion, he had unprecedented access to the emperor and all others who came in contact with him. How hard would it be to arrange for an accident? He would assess the situation when he arrived.

III

Izivar told Julivar she was not to be seen by the emperor, much less heard, and ordered her to keep away from the listening post.

She'd kept to the letter of the first part of the order, staying well clear of the emperor's sight, but she'd been on hand when the dozens of cloaked, armored praetorians rode into view. They looked rather dashing with their white lacquered armor and black cloaks, and she wondered how they kept their kit so clean on the move.

The praetorians had wandered around from the moment of their arrival, standing guard at intersections and the road to the village. While more of them were taking up posts in front of key buildings and Izivar was still rushing around ensuring everything was more neat and organized than it already was, Julivar took advantage of the bustle and crept through the kitchen into the pantry. From there she slipped into the cabinet with the concealed door and the listening post. She hadn't actually responded to Izivar's barked instructions so no one could rightly accuse her of breaking any promise. Once ensconced, she wondered again why she hadn't bothered to bring a cushion. Izivar, she thought, would have remembered to do so.

The space had been modeled after the one their father had built into the side of his old office at the boxing arena, but it wasn't as comfortable, perhaps because the whole building had been thrown together so quickly. It was supposed to be set up so that important advisors could listen in, but Izivar hadn't been putting people in it at all.

The other side of the office was quiet for a long while, and Julivar began to wonder if maybe the emperor was meeting Izivar somewhere else. She'd been told she was terrible at waiting, though, and it was true. She resigned herself to being patient, because if she were to emerge now the kitchen staff would see her—she heard them banging around in there.

After a while, she realized that she actually could hear the sound of Izivar, and a man talking in a gruff, whispery voice. But she couldn't understand what they were saying, and she swore quietly, using words Izivar would have frowned at.

Izivar must have deliberately rolled the shelf over to block access to the listening post, so that she could have absolute privacy. She'd done that every time she met with Decius.

The exchange with the emperor seemed to go on interminably. At one point, Julivar was certain she heard Izivar laugh, but she had no other indication about how her talk was going or what its subject was.

She was bored.

The sounds from the kitchen staff died out at last. She decided she would go find something more interesting to do. Carefully she slid from the concealed section, closing the hidden door behind her. She then peeped out of the pantry.

A man she didn't recognize stood with his back to her. He was wearing an expensive red tunic with gold threads. A gilded goblet sat on the counter beside him, next to a slim blue amphora of wine, uncorked. Nearby was a goblet she recognized as her sister's, dark red, with a wide base that faded to gold. The stranger, his dark head hunched, dipped a small cloth into a little unguent jar, just like the kind older women kept make-up in, and rubbed the inside of her sister's goblet. Rings shone upon nearly every one of his fingers.

Julivar spoke without thinking, demanding loudly: "What are you doing?"

The man whirled, his eyes furtive, his hands wrapped secretively about the goblet and the unguent. She couldn't tell his age but he didn't have any gray in his hair.

"That's my sister's goblet," Julivar said, advancing. A part of her wondered why she wasn't frightened, but she couldn't seem to shut up. "What is that? Is that poison? Are you putting poison in her goblet?"

"Keep your voice down," the man hissed. "Who are you? This isn't poison—"

"What is it then?" Julivar's voice rose, which may be why the kitchen door suddenly banged open. Once again the man with the goblet whirled, this time away from her. In walked one of the praetorians, a tall man in lacquered white armor shaped into chest muscles. A shorter man with a broken nose followed on his heels, his eyes bright and dangerous.

"What's this?" the first praetorian demanded.

"I'm Julivar Lenereva," she said. "And that man—"

"The girl's shouting about poison," the man said. "She's just excitable—"

"He's holding poison behind his back!" Julivar pointed. "He was putting it in the goblets!"

Perhaps they immediately took her seriously because the praetorians were extremely cautious about threats upon the emperor's life. Or perhaps it was because she sounded so confident and the stranger looked so very suspicious. It might even have been a consequence of the protective instinct she had noted among some well-bred men. They could be lecherous and demeaning to women at other times but leapt to shield them when they were threatened. The stranger spun to her and raised his hand to slap her, shouting to be silent, and the tall praetorian seized his hand as she backstepped.

"Let go of me," the stranger whined. "I am the emperor's personal companion!"

The tall praetorian wrenched the stranger's arm behind his back and the broken-nosed one pried the tiny jar from his fingers.

"What's this you were holding, Pellas?" Broken-nose demanded.

The man struggled vainly in the unyielding grasp of the tall soldier. "Unhand me!"

"What's in the jar?" the other repeated through clenched teeth.

"I took it from the girl!"

"He's lying," Julivar said.

She saw from the look the tall praetorian gave her that he believed her.

"I demand to see the emperor!" Pellas said.

"I was just thinking about taking you there," the tall soldier holding him said. "Elgius, take the goblets and the little pot. Who are you, girl?"

"I'm Julia, Izivar's sister." She remembered to use her Dervan name hoping it would further communicate trustworthiness to the emperor's soldiers.

"Where did you even come from?" Pellas demanded.

She didn't answer that, and the praetorians didn't seem interested in learning. "Come with us, please," the one holding Pellas said. The one named Elgius had placed everything on a serving platter and pushed the door aside with his hip.

Pellas' voice rose in protestation. "Unhand me!"

"Eventually," the praetorian replied.

It was only after Julivar was following the praetorians and their prisoner that she realized how heavily her heart beat and how much danger she might have been in. Suppose those praetorians hadn't been nearby? Pellas was a lot bigger than her. And there were knives in the kitchen he could have grabbed. Suppose the praetorians hadn't seen right through him? And what was going to happen if the emperor didn't believe her, or them?

The praetorian loosened his hold on Pellas but kept his arm behind him, and as they drew near the office, he told a muscular, friendly faced soldier on guard outside that they had to interrupt.

Pellas had worked himself into a frenzy. "You will regret this," he told his handler venomously. "I will see that you're busted down to the lowliest frontier legionary, cleaning latrines on the gods-cursed, fly-infested Cerdian border!"

Elgius knocked on the office door, and to a gruff voice demanding what the interruption was, he replied. "There's been a situation, sire. We need to report."

Pellas continued his imprecations, and Julivar couldn't hear an answer over them, but there must have been one, because Elgius pushed open the door.

It was strange to see the emperor seated behind the desk, but he was, and he proved disappointing, an old man nearly lost in his toga, with white fluffy hair and big fuzzy eyebrows. He didn't look like a monster, just a curmudgeon. Izivar waited in the seat across from him, looking up in surprise and then shock as she spotted Julivar following the praetorians and their prisoner. Her sister gave her a searching look, as if she somehow expected Julivar to explain what was going on by motioning with her hands.

A side table overflowed with desserts that should have set her mouth watering, including puddings and four separate kinds of cakes. She paid them scant attention, her focus centered upon Pellas.

The poisoner proclaimed this was all a misunderstanding, but Elgius advanced with the wooden platter and the goblets. Izivar's had fallen over. The unguent jar sat beside it.

The emperor's brows lowered. He raised a white, wrinkled hand, and eventually Pellas shut up.

"Release Pellas," the emperor said.

"I don't trust him, sire," Elgius said.

The emperor's mouth twisted irritably. "What's he done?"

Pellas answered before the praetorians could. "I was simply polishing the goblets and inspecting them, as I always do, eminence." He shook his head as if in consternation. "But these—"

"He's lying," said a voice, and Julivar was astonished it was her own. She started forward and the praetorians both gave her a surprised look. Elgius even looked amused by her, in a friendly way. She continued: "I caught him rubbing something from a jar on the inside of the goblet."

"She was trying to rub it," Pellas said. "I took it from her—"

"I wouldn't put poison in my own sister's goblet!" Julivar objected shrilly.

Once more the emperor held up his hand. He faced Izivar. "Your sister?"

Izivar's reply was so measured she managed to look completely untroubled, as though the entire situation were the merest trifle. "By my late father's second wife."

"Ah," the emperor said.

"We believe the girl's telling the truth," the tall praetorian said. "Elgius and I were posted in the central room. We heard the girl shouting at him about poison and he denied having any. He was trying to hide that little jar behind his back when we went in to investigate."

"Silvo's correct, eminence," said Elgius. "The girl was right in your secretary's face, pointing at him, and he was acting like a man with a secret."

"Well, well." The emperor reached for Izivar's goblet.

"Be careful, sire," Silvo cautioned.

Ever so carefully he lifted Izivar's goblet to his nostrils and sniffed. He looked at Pellas, nervously licking his lips, then returned the goblet and considered the unguent jar. He bent to sniff it as well and withdrew quickly.

"They smell identical, Pellas. Are you going to tell me this isn't poison?"

Pellas said nothing.

"I could have you prove so," the emperor said, a biting, dangerous note in his voice, "by licking it up."

Pellas gulped and spoke with a great show of subservience, complete with lowered eyes. "Perhaps if I could speak to you alone, sire, I could clear all of this up."

"No, Pellas, I don't really want to hear it. You were trying to poison me, weren't you?"

"You? No, sire!" He shook his head adamantly. "Just the woman."

"I see. Just the woman I've dragged my weary body all the way north to talk with. Because you thought I might like that?" The emperor's voice quavered. "I've a mind to have the praetorians force the goblet and jar both down your throat! Tell me why I shouldn't!"

"Sire, this is all a misunder—"

He pointed at Pellas. "Get him out of my sight!"

Each praetorian grabbed the poisoner by his arms.

Pellas pleaded as they dragged him out, even choking down a sob. With his free hand he caught the door jamb and tried to hold himself there, still shouting to be heard. But then Silvo smashed him in the nose and blood splattered onto the wall, and Pellas wailed and let go. The guard outside closed the door after them.

The sobbing continued along with the tramp of hobnailed sandals and the sound of Pellas' feet being dragged across the carpet outside.

It was only then Julivar realized that she remained in the room with her sister, and the emperor, whose eyes were rooted upon her.

IV

An untrained observer might have said that the praetorians were everywhere. But Hanuvar had carefully noted their positions. He had discarded his initial plan to disguise himself as a Ceori and dressed instead as a simple workman, the better to lose himself among dozens busy about the complex of buildings that evening. He had been eyed by one pair of praetorians with special care, but not halted. He imitated the stride of the other workmen moving about the site with tools or lumber or buckets of nails. They had their own places to be and didn't pay him any special attention.

So far none of the praetorians were investigating the buildings with care, which suggested they were here for exactly the reasons they had stated. Their task was to secure the emperor's immediate environs.

And that meant they wouldn't be examining the very solid looking false wall in the back of the warehouse built into the hillside, where the survivors they'd liberated from the revenant prison had been moved in crates and were under medical care. There too was Carthalo, who did not wish to be linked in any way with the Volani naval venture, and the sorcerer, Norok of Nuvara, and Varahan, who'd designed the Volani fire that they'd used to such devastating affect against the revenant holdings. With them were a few others who had been freed extra legally. It was best not to chance any of their false paperwork against scrutiny unless it proved absolutely necessary.

Bucket in hand, Hanuvar neared the end of his survey, pleased that his charges were secure and that his goals remained a secret.

That left his concern for Izivar front and center. If the emperor meant to destroy them, he would have sent more soldiers. If he meant to pry into their technical achievements, there would have been naval architects and scholars in his entourage.

But he remained closeted with Izivar, which meant the emperor's interest was a more personal one. Surely it was Enarius' attachment to Izivar, a woman of the wrong ethnicity and age. She was a liability to the emperor and his political allies, especially after Gaius Cornelius had done so much to vilify the Volani.

The emperor's measure taking of Izivar Lenereva would be conducted under the guise of a friendly visit, but it was in actuality a court case with but a single judge. How Izivar answered and portrayed herself, and how the emperor reacted to her, was the thin line between life and death. At this point her survival was directly linked with the welfare of their people, but he found himself troubled over the threat to her. Over the last months she had more and more regularly been present in his thoughts. At first he had passed this off as him being the prisoner to a younger man's biology. More recently he had admitted to himself he made foolish excuses and that her true nature had been visible from their first meeting.

Yes, she possessed an air of entitlement. She was the product of an environment that had denied her almost nothing. And yet she had been shaped by trying circumstances and risen to meet them. She was astute and tenacious. She had suffered loss, and adeptly navigated her way through a hostile political situation. She thought long term and had committed herself and her family's fortune to the ongoing enterprise to recover their people.

That her dark curling hair smelled always of a floral scent, or that she had light brown eyes flecked with gold and a warm smile that pierced him, and that she sometimes wore the flowing, layered ankle-length skirts of her foremothers... all of those things should only have been incidental considerations. More and more he found that they were not. He was so used to thinking of himself as an instrument self-shaped for his mission it was sometimes a surprise to discover he was as human as the next man.

This amused him, and as he finished his circuit of the complex he was smiling faintly at his self-deception. No matter Julivar's teasing, he did not expect Izivar would ever see him as much more than a convenient ally, for she had been raised believing him an arrogant instrument of their culture's destruction. Many Dervans thought him implacable and inhuman, so he was well-used to shrugging off the myths others would make of him, yet her sentiment stung. He might play many roles, but he was still only Hanuvar. And he naturally felt attracted to an intelligent disciplined woman who shared his goals and labored cleverly to reach them.

Though he weighed these concerns his attention never fully left his patrol. So when he turned a corner and spotted two praetorians leaving a path behind the warehouse he slipped back into hiding.

They passed Hanuvar's hiding place without notice, as their attention seemed occupied with how they may be viewed. One of them brushed at his cloak. Leaves and petals fluttered from its edge. The other looked over his shoulder at the way they'd come, not once, but twice.

Something back there troubled them. And as the first one continued fretting with his cloak, Hanuvar noted neither man looked as if they fit their uniforms. On one the sleeves were too short and on the other the helmet sat high. Neither looked so ridiculous they would have drawn comment from a centurion, and neither would have been completely out of keeping with standard issue legion garments. But these men were praetorians, and while they weren't the absolute cream of the crop they thought themselves, all dressed as though they were. Many were the pampered sons of patricians, and tailored their uniforms and employed skilled artisans to resize armor so that it didn't just fit but flattered them.

These two walked with a typical legion stride toward the flat-fronted main office building. The moment they stopped looking back, Hanuvar slid around the corner and followed their track to the weedy patch running between the first warehouses and the rocky slope that lay below a stand of pines.

Their trail led to a staggered line of myrtles. The ground was heavy with scattered rock and weeds, and decaying leaves from autumns prior.

The sole of a motionless human foot protruded from behind a bush. After only a few more steps Hanuvar determined it was attached to a motionless human leg. It would have been a waste of time to verify the man was truly dead, and that his companion lay beside him. That was far less important than the fact two men were disguised as praetorians. The pretenders had boldly slain two of the elite force just now and left the bodies less than well-hidden, suggesting they did not have a long-term goal. Whatever they meant to do must already be underway. And Izivar was in discussion with the man who was almost certainly their prime target.

Hanuvar cast down his bucket and dashed back the way he'd come, rounding the corner at a run. He arrived in time to see both men disappear into the central office building where the emperor was meeting Izivar. The bored praetorian on the steps appeared not to have noticed that there was anything odd about them. But he keyed in on Hanuvar as he ran up, stiffening to alert and putting his hand to his sword.

"Halt right there," the praetorian commanded. "Come no further—"

"Those men weren't praetorians," Hanuvar said. "Did you recognize them?"

"Who are you?"

"Listen to me, soldier," Hanuvar snapped, the parade ground in his voice. "Those are impostors! Did you recognize them?"

His words gave the young man pause, but his small brown eyes hardened.

"The emperor's in danger," Hanuvar said, starting forward.

The soldier was still on guard but he didn't draw. Hanuvar had already judged there was no convincing him, so he faked with his right and slammed his left into the knuckles of the praetorian's sword hand. That slowed the young soldier's pull, and the stamp on the man's sandals left him cursing. As the praetorian's head came forward, Hanuvar's elbow slammed into his throat, and then he punched the tip of his heroic chin. The praetorian slipped nerveless to the stairs. From behind came shouts and the slap of sandaled feet. Other praetorians were on the way.

Fine with him, so long as they didn't stop him. He needed backup.

He ripped the sword from the sheath of the groaning man at his feet then pushed into the building.

V

Izivar watched the emperor's gaze shift from the objects on the platter before him and back to her little sister. She was certain her own surprise showed on her face and fought to mask her expression.

Julivar stood straight and tall and proud, looking very much like her mother. Izivar had never been fond of Julivar's mother, but there had been no ignoring her when she decided to take a stand, no matter how petty her chosen battlefield. Julivar was far more intelligent than her mother and, Izivar suddenly realized, more courageous than she had ever expected.

The emperor's gaze softened. "What is your name, young lady?" he asked.

"Juli—Julivar," she said, defiantly using the name she preferred rather than the official Dervan name her father had given her. "Your eminence."

The curious nature of her name made no impression upon him. "You are very brave," the emperor told her. "You saved the life of your sister today, and since I'm not entirely sure that Pellas spoke the truth, you might have saved my life as well. Do you know that?"

"I suppose so," she said softly.

"You don't need to be shy now," he said, and then coughed. His coughing fit lasted several moments, and Izivar started to rise.

The emperor waved her back. "I'm fine. It seems your entire family possesses great reservoirs of strength. I of course know of your own brother's brave sacrifice defending my son. And it occurs to me now that your father required a certain courage to stand against the popular opinion of his people for so much of his life." His eyes briefly settled upon the bust of Tannis she'd placed on the desk earlier that evening. "I know so many of your people were deceived into following ruinous policies. But your father, and his father before him, were always ready to defy the Caberas. It's a shame that they couldn't have convinced the rest of the populace to hear them. We might not have ended up with such a tragic situation."

Once, Izivar would have agreed wholeheartedly with that assessment. It had been easy to believe it when she was surrounded on every side by those who agreed with her father. But in the years after Hanuvar and Melgar's departure and in the months after the war, an old seed of doubt had sprouted. Her father had possessed courage, it was true, but some of his resolve was rooted in avarice. He had wished to protect what was his, including his earnings.

It might still be that her father's positions during the second and third Volani wars had been right and it was the action of the Caberas that had brought Derva down upon their city. But she had come to see Hanuvar was right as well, for the empire had finally destroyed Volanus, just as Hanuvar, and his father before him, had warned. It had been easier to lay that blame at Hanuvar's feet before she had become acquainted with him. He was not the vainglorious man her father and his adherents had claimed.

The emperor was staring at her and she realized that she had lost track of her own thoughts. "I'm sorry, your eminence." She bowed her head. "I'm afraid this left me more shocked than I realized." She faced her sister. "Julia may have saved my life, and I can't help wondering if I'd have been as bold as she was in my own youth."

The emperor's smile at this was kind. He was saying something complimentary to them both, but she didn't fully hear, for there was a shout from outside and what sounded like a scuffle and a cry of pain. Then the door was thrust open and a new praetorian shouldered his way in, a bloody blade in one hand.

"Your time's up, emperor," he announced gleefully, and advanced upon the desk. Another praetorian slipped in after him.

Julivar gasped. Izivar reached for the bronze vase in the niche to her left.

"Who are you?" the emperor demanded. He climbed to his feet. The praetorian in the lead charged.

Izivar pitched the vase. She'd been aiming for the man's head, but she was no marksman. It fell short, striking the man in the leg, which fortunately sent him stumbling; he slammed into the desk, upsetting the goblets and the poison unguents and the plaster bust of Tannis Lenereva, which plummeted from the desk and crashed into pieces. The emperor leapt back with surprising speed and steadied himself against the rear wall.

The other assassin spun with sword leveled at Izivar, and it was only then she recognized him for her earlier visitor. Four feet lay between them. Julivar stood by the wall behind him, and Izivar feared she was about to do something that would get her killed. The praetorian who'd stumbled pulled himself upright.

Hanuvar burst through the open doorway. The soldier facing Izivar turned to confront him, then threw up the sword to block a fluffy green pillow flying toward his head.

Hanuvar, dressed in a simple workman's garb, launched forward.

The assassin had brought his weapon to the right as he swept the pillow clear. Hanuvar locked the weapon with his own sword and with his other hand drove a knife deep into his opponent's neck. Blood spurted.

Izivar gasped in horror.

The dying assassin clapped a hand to the terrible wound and struck out sloppily. Izivar felt sure the blow would kill Hanuvar, but he slid away with preternatural grace and then the man fell, gurgling.

The first assailant put one hand to the desk, as though he meant to vault it. "For King Mithran!" he cried.

Much happened at the same time. Hanuvar lunged as the man pushed off the floor. Julivar leapt for the assassin, who got midway up the side of the desk, his body twisting just as her fingers closed around his ankle. Her leap brought her head into the front of the desk with a crack as she slammed into the floor. The assassin landed half on the desk edge with a grunt of his own, his sword clattering to one side, and then fell across Julivar, who cried out.

Hanuvar dragged him off Julivar. The assassin grabbed for a knife, but before he drew Hanuvar split his skull straight through to the teeth, spewing blood and brains and gore.

Only then did more praetorians turn up, calling for the emperor and advancing with bared weapons.

The emperor shouted for them to stop, but they came on.

Izivar threw herself in front of Hanuvar and her sister, only realizing after she did that she was unlikely to give the soldiers pause. Their swords were raised and she was but a woman, a Volani woman at that, and there were dead praetorians on the floor.

The emperor found his breath. "Stop, you fools!" he shouted. "Stop!"

The praetorians halted, uncertain, and the emperor was overcome by a coughing fit. He leaned against the desk, speaking through the cough. "These people saved me from..." he paused, coughing, "assassins!"

"But this one attacked me!" The lead soldier waved his sword at Hanuvar.

"I tried to tell that guard these two were impostors," Hanuvar said. "He refused to listen."

"They're assassins," the emperor spat. "Do you know them?"

The praetorians gave Hanuvar another wary look, then, gazing down at the bodies, appeared more confused.

"No, sire," one of them said.

"They're Cerdians," the emperor spat. "That one there said he was going to kill me for their king!"

Julivar quietly climbed to her feet behind Hanuvar, one hand holding her head.

"Drag their bodies out of here," the emperor said, and then he swore. "A stranger and a little girl saved me. What happened to the soldier at the door to the office?"

"These two killed him," Hanuvar answered.

"And how did they get past the one posted outside?" the emperor demanded of him.

Hanuvar shook his head. "I'm not sure, eminence."

The emperor addressed the praetorians waspishly. "Stop staring! Drag them out of here!"

The one who Hanuvar had stunned outside pointed at him. "But that man has a blade in the presence of the emperor." He sounded indignant.

"He just risked his life to save me!" the emperor's voice rose in a screech. "You think he's going to kill me now? You heard me! Get the bodies out! Out!"

With mumbled apologies, the praetorians sheathed their weapons and dragged the bodies away, each taking one by their arms. Both left a long smear of blood on the carpets. None closed the door behind them, and Izivar noted that the sweet-faced young praetorian she'd seen posted outside the door earlier did indeed lie dead, on his back, just past the threshold.

"Close the door!" the emperor demanded. Izivar did so.

The emperor leaned against the desk, panting.

Julivar crept across the floor, carefully sidestepping all the blood and the spatter of brains, and stood behind her sister.

Hanuvar remained beside the desk, looking at the emperor. His hand was tight upon the sword, and blood dripped down its runnels.

Izivar experienced an entirely different fear. Surely Hanuvar wouldn't act. Not now. And yet . . . there, within reach, was the man who had commanded the destruction of Volanus and charged his followers with the sale of the pitiful survivors. What must Hanuvar be thinking?

Julivar, either frightened by the terrible events or aware of the tension, reached to take her hand. Izivar squeezed it without looking at her.

The emperor struck his chest with his fist, coughed a little longer, then collapsed into the chair behind the desk. He looked out at Izivar and Julivar, as if seeing them after a long absence, and then considered Hanuvar.

If he saw anything in that blank, thousand-yard stare, he did not acknowledge it. The emperor's gaze was inward. "Twice, in the span of a half hour, your family has risked their lives to save me," he said to Izivar.

That wasn't entirely true, but Izivar wasn't about to naysay the emperor when he spoke in her favor.

"They may think I'm old, but I see things," he continued. "I know you threw that vase. I know your little sister grabbed that man's foot." Again he flashed a smile to Julivar. "By Jovren, girl, if you were a man, I'd commission you a tribune on the spot, because we need courage like that in the ranks. And who is this man? One of your slaves?"

Izivar started to explain that the Volani had no slaves. The emperor surely would remember that if he took a moment to think.

Hanuvar answered. "I'm one of the family's personal guard," he said. And then, with elaborate care, as if he were weary and the sword was an incredible weight, he knelt and placed the bloody blade on the floor before him.

"Well, you certainly know your business," the emperor said. "Were you a legionary?"

"I have been a sailor, sir," Hanuvar answered.

That seemed to befuddle the old man, and then he nodded. "I suppose you have seen your share of pirates."

"I've faced a lot of bloodthirsty men."

"I can tell you have. If not for your quick thinking, well." The emperor cleared his throat and stared at Izivar. He knocked on the table. "Izivar Lenereva, I came today to measure your character. You have earned my honesty. I wished to learn if you had designs upon my son. You have denied it, and I believe you. Fully. More than that, what I have seen this day has convinced me that you remain a true friend not just to the empire, but to my family. From this day forward you and your communities are inviolate and will have my protection and blessing. However long I may live." He smiled weakly at that. "And I am certain that my son will continue that tradition."

"I am honored, eminence," Izivar said, bowing her head. Hanuvar did the same.

"Further, I shall have a gift made to this man, and your sister, and shall have sacrifices made in their names in the temple of Jovren upon my return to Derva. If I had not just now had my assistant dragged away, I would have the decree written up this moment." He coughed. "It occurs to me that if Pellas hadn't been up to no good, there would have been two more guards on duty and then those assassins could not possibly have gotten through. He has much to answer for."

The emperor's mouth curled, and Izivar realized that much of his ire was going to be directed against the one surviving enemy of the day's events.

The emperor pushed to his feet. "And now, young lady, if you do not mind, I am weary. I am in need of some wine, and a bed."

"You are welcome to stay here, your eminence." Izivar stepped around the desk, past her father's shattered bust, and he leaned heavily against her. He smelled of mint and garlic and, faintly, of urine.

"No, no. I think my visit is already memorable enough. If I press hard, I can reach Carasus just after nightfall. My chefs are there and will have my food ready." He patted her arm. "But if you would help me to the door, I would be grateful."

She assisted him past the two long smears of blood. He didn't notice tramping through some gray matter but frowned at the terrible stains on her beautiful carpet. It had once decorated her mother's office in Volanus.

"I shall send you a new one," he said.

The crimson stains continued across the floor tiles and down the outside stairs, as though they were a line for the emperor to follow. Once outside Izivar turned him over to some nervous looking praetorians and a huddle of slaves. Early in the visit the old man had told her he didn't like being fawned over by slaves, but he seemed comfortable being assisted by them now.

She waited on the steps until he had climbed into the vehicle. By the time she'd returned to the office her hand maid Serliva had appeared to supervise workmen scrubbing the tiles. Two were carrying the blood-soaked rug from the office, rolled on their shoulders. She stood aside as two more praetorians solemnly removed the body of the soldier who'd died defending the door.

At sight of Izivar, Serliva fired off a rapid spate of worried questions, but Izivar assured her she was fine, that they would talk later, and retreated to her office.

Hanuvar remained inside, seated on the desk edge. Julivar sat in the chair before him. They appeared to be speaking intimately and fell silent as she drew close. Izivar couldn't help feeling she had intruded upon a private moment.

"I'm sorry," she said.

Hanuvar shook his head. "There's nothing to apologize for."

"Are you alright?" Julivar asked her with a depth of care and maturity she hadn't used before.

"I am. Thanks to you. And Decius. You were very brave today, Julivar."

"So were you." Her sister stepped close and hugged her tight around the waist.

Izivar felt a great surge of affection for her little sister and held her tight.

"I'm glad you're all right," Julivar said.

Izivar kissed the top of her head. She wanted to ask how she was after seeing two grisly deaths and multiple bodies, but Julivar smiled at her, saying, "I'll leave you two be." She stepped around Serliva, standing distraught in the doorway, and called her away. Julivar glanced back once, her eyes straying to the cakes on the side table, then closed the door.

Izivar had wanted a moment alone with Hanuvar, but now that she had it, she felt uncomfortable. His eyes held a peculiar, haunting gray quality today, as if he could see right through her, and she didn't want to be held up for scrutiny when she already felt fragile. She looked away. There on the floor lay his bloody blade, and there, to the left, lay the shattered bust of her father. Probably that signified some message from the gods. She stared down at two fragments of her father's forehead, then looked back at Hanuvar.

His gaze had softened. A complex blend of sorrow and deep-seated pain was writ large upon his face, as though he had suffered some terrible injury that had never fully healed.

She understood that. "Thank you," she said finally.

"For helping you? Or for not killing him."

"For both."

"I could have," he said. "It would have been easy."

"I know."

Though he was a mature, powerful man, and she had just seen him kill two heavily armored assassins, as he stood there with empty hands and empty eyes it struck her how very vulnerable and lonely he was. She took a step toward him, hand outstretched. He took it in his own and suddenly he was holding both of hers and she felt an electric charge that both pleased and alarmed her.

"He was right there, in front of me. With the blood of our people on his hands." Hanuvar fell silent. She squeezed his fingers in her own and then found herself gently brushing his hands with her thumbs.

"If I could have struck him down last year, or, gods willing, twenty years prior, I'd have done so without hesitation. But now..."

"Now would have brought an end to our people."

"The dead cry for vengeance. I have heard them."

From the look in his eye, she wondered if he spoke figuratively.

"But you were acting for the living," she said.

"Yes." And then, quietly, he added: "I am glad you're one of them."

She felt herself blushing like a maiden and looked down at the fingers she stroked. "Well. Somehow we made it through the day."

"An eventful one."

She released one of his hands and tugged him toward the door with the other. "You've travelled a long way these last few days. Let's see you fed."

"I would like that."

He left the room with her. If he thought about the bloody sword, or the shattered bust, he said nothing of them, and neither did she.

※ ※ ※

Many of us had noted the invisible bond growing between Hanuvar and Izivar, though neither of them had discussed it. When they finally relented to their mutual attraction and could be glimpsed in public touching the other's shoulder or hand I nearly shouted with joy.

Other developments proved far less uplifting. Carthalo's mage, an older Turian woman, examined Hanuvar's aura for more than an hour and pronounced his lifeline broken. The spell had shattered it. Worse, she informed him that his accelerated aging would not slow when he approached his true age, which meant Hanuvar would grow to be an ancient and give up his ghost before the year's end.

The magic worker said only a more powerful mage might be able to set things right. Unfortunately the Dervans had actively hunted witches and sorcerers for the last decade. Carthalo suggested another woman, one who had helped Hanuvar's army in the final years of the second war, and messengers were sent out both to her and to the Ceori seer, Bricta.

Carthalo promised to use his network to make urgent inquiries about other sorcerers, but until we could consult with them, there was nothing to be done.

Hanuvar didn't like dwelling upon his looming mortality. When I asked him about his subdued reaction, he merely said he was surprised he had survived so long.

"You sound remarkably resolved," I said. "Don't you want to see your daughter? Spend time with—" I paused, starting to describe Izivar as the woman he loved, and decided against using words he hadn't publicly uttered "—a charming woman? See New Volanus once more?"

He gave me one of those hard looks which is what he did rather than roll his eyes. "Life is sweet, and I do not welcome death. There is much still to be done."

Sometimes he could be quite open about his thoughts and feelings, but in this instance he remained closed. I managed to get him talking about it a day later, when he said he did not regret the gift of restored youth, because without it there were people he might not have saved. The first of these he was thinking of, I am very certain, was Izivar, valuable not just to him but to the entire enterprise.

Another might have been pleased with what he had accomplished, or worried over his own fragility, and left his duties to other men while he waited for assistance. Hanuvar, though, refused to pause, and when a series of difficult situations presented themselves, he rode forth to address them personally.

—Sosilos, Book Ten

Chapter 10:
The Last Hunt

I

Almost, the villa had grown to be one with the encroaching forest. Before time had inflicted a stream of minor wounds no one had properly mended, it must have been a handsome country getaway for some minor aristocrat. Now, many of the red roof tiles were cracked. Moss lay thick along others. Leafy vines draped two-thirds of its front, and the plaster upon the exposed stonework had crumbled badly. One of the three outbuildings sagged under rotting timbers.

But despite its fading grandeur the home was not yet abandoned. Horses grazed behind the dilapidated fence, and a half dozen middle-aged slaves worked the field near the wood's edge in sleeveless tunics, two clearing while the others planted. As Hanuvar left his horse along the narrow dirt track that disappeared into the dark woods, he scanned those slaves, though he was certain none were the ones he had come for.

He advanced up the villa's stone walkway. Though not free of weeds it had at least been recently swept.

The young house slave who swung the door wide at his knock was of Ceori stock, his hair reddish blond, and he stared in clear surprise, for Hanuvar had dyed his own hair blond, and wore it combed back like a Ceori warrior even though his finger bore the iron band of Dervan citizenship and he himself wore a beige Dervan calf-length tunic and blue traveling cloak. To the young slave he must have appeared a countryman, and he saw the youth's eyes flick enviously to the ring.

Hanuvar addressed him politely, his Dervan favored with the trace of the Ceori tongue. He had served with so many Ceori that their distinctive rolling pronunciation was simple to mimic. "Good afternoon. Is your master at home?"

"Who shall I say is calling, sir, and on what business?" The boy's look suggested he was curious to know far more. As Hanuvar opened his mouth to answer, a balding Dervan man in an old gray tunic stepped up behind the boy. From somewhere in the back of the house a weak female voice called:

"Natius, who is it?"

The Dervan turned his head and shouted back. "I don't know yet, dear."

"What?"

The man raised his voice and repeated the information then offered an apologetic smile. "Please pardon. How may I help you?"

Natius looked to be in his early fifties and held himself in that stiff way of old soldiers used to standing at attention. His shoulders were wide, and what hair he had was closely cropped, like many a legionary after leaving the service.

Hanuvar bowed his head politely. "I'm seeking the home of Drusus Ontoles. I thought I had the right way, but I'm afraid I've turned too soon."

The man smiled ruefully and he stepped outside past the slave boy. He pointed toward the track Hanuvar had traveled and then with that arm straight, swung it toward the woods. "You're nearly there. Drusus lives further along the road, down that way."

Once past the villa, the "road" looked little better than a deer trail, scarcely wide enough even for a small wagon. And the woods that lined it were close and still.

"It's really nothing more than a hunting lodge," Natius continued, "but he's lived there for years. If you mean to visit, you'd best get on with it. He doesn't like strangers on his property after dark."

"Not a friendly fellow then?" Hanuvar asked.

"No," Natius said. "Not anymore," he added resentfully, then changed the subject. "Served with the legions, have you?"

The stranger had detected the more subtle signs of Hanuvar's assumed identity. "Is it so obvious?"

"A Ceori with a citizen's ring? And you hold yourself like a soldier."

Hanuvar bowed his head formally. "You found me out. I see you served as well."

Natius drew himself up proudly. "With the Glorius Twelfth. Centurion Natius Braxtus, at your service. I heard a few of the Ceori had sided with us during the war, but I never met any. Tell you what, Drusus isn't one for company, and it's more than an hour to a good inn. When you've made your visit to him, I'll put you up for the night and we can swap old lies about the legion."

"That's kind of you, Natius," Hanuvar said. "I'm Katurix, but the lads called me Katius so much I almost had it changed when I signed my citizen papers."

The old soldier laughed. "Well, make your visit. My cook's no gourmet but he sets a fair table."

"Until later, then."

Hanuvar lifted his hand in farewell and departed. The door shut behind him. He had little interest in returning to talk about Dervan legions, but depending on the conclusion of his business in the woods, he might need to remain in the area for a time.

He climbed into his saddle and reviewed what little he'd learned about the Volani slaves he sought, and their mysterious master. Like his neighbor, Drusus was another soldier who'd mustered out at the rank of centurion. Regional gossip said Drusus had never left his wilderness estate except to purchase these slaves, all members of the same family, whose adult professions had been listed as foresters. He had bought the family's minor children as well, a kindness not always practiced by Dervan masters. And kindness might well be the stumbling block to their freedom, for one of Carthalo's agents had reported that Drusus was unwilling to sell at any price, moreover that the slaves seemed not only well-treated, but uninclined to leave.

"As far as I can see," Carthalo had told Hanuvar, "these aren't especially valuable men and women. It's not like forestry is a truly rare skill, so he hasn't made an unrecompensable investment. And I can't fathom why the Volani would owe him any allegiance."

Hanuvar and Carthalo had discussed the matter one evening after dinner in a tavern south of Derva owned by one of Carthalo's agents. They had been taking stock of their most challenging cases.

"Has he fallen in love with one of them?" Hanuvar asked. Old masters falling for pretty slaves was so common a trope that it turned up again and again in Dervan theatre.

"It's hard to say, but Farnus visited twice, and the Volani were especially cold toward him the second time, when they seemed to know why he was there. They were a united front, and you wouldn't expect that if one of them was being abused."

"So it's that rarer saw, of someone who's purchased slaves and come to cherish them," Hanuvar suggested.

"It happens. The Dervans will drive their galley slaves and their mine slaves and their farm slaves until they drop—although some of the slaves on family farms get treated decently. But household slaves sometimes have cordial and even pleasant relationships with their owners, and many of them are freed when they reach an advanced age."

Hanuvar nodded his understanding. Carthalo continued: "Sometimes bonds of true affection form on both sides, and it can get a little strange if you have an old Dervan with a household of loyal slaves. The master starts thinking of them as confidants, almost like family. Dervans may think they want good things for their slaves, and might even have manumitted them in their will, but they don't want to lose their only friends. So they keep them in bondage."

"And you think that's what's happened in this case," Hanuvar suggested.

"I don't really know, I just surmise. Farnus is one of my best men, and he couldn't make headway with this one."

"It sounds as though one of us needs to see to it."

"Probably you. We've a big influx coming from a farm estate and arranging all that paperwork is going to take days."

"Say no more," Hanuvar said.

Scouting out the situation had sent him a few days south, through a sleepy little village and now past a dilapidated villa and onto a narrow dirt road into what felt like a haunted woodland.

Hanuvar's horse snorted as they passed into the shadows, as if to comment that they were once again journeying into some place they were unwanted.

"Well," he said softly to him, "we should both be used to it by now."

The trees further in were tall and stately, mostly silver leafed holm oaks with vast understories, their spaces sprinkled with red-orange barked maritime pines. The track beneath them was a shadowy tunnel flush with the pleasant scent of loam and pine needles, but the atmosphere itself was somehow foreboding.

There would be no bandits hiding on a minor lane, but there might be sentries, and there might be boar, so he eyed the darkness with care. Apart from the songs of distant larks and a few scuttering insects, the forest was silent.

The path wound on across little slopes and down gullies, and after what Hanuvar reckoned was a quarter hour he heard a woman singing. At first her words were more a sensation, scarcely distinguishable over the sound of his horse's steady tread. Before long, the sound resolved itself into a melody he recognized. This was a song of his people, and more than one voice sang it. Moreover, it was no threnody, but a folk tune about the gathering of berries, and the sweet drinks they would produce, like the kisses of a beautiful youth.

The trail turned and a blaze of light set the track in stark relief beyond the branches ahead. He had almost reached a clearing. Hanuvar slowed, peering through a screen of low hanging branches. A wide cabin of dark wood sat on a rise amongst a cluster of smaller cabins and a sprinkling of outbuildings and fenced fields and orchards. There was even a henhouse. In all there was perhaps three thousand square feet of cleared space. A young woman and a boy sang as they picked berries at the field's edge. A man sat in the shade of a solitary oak honing arrowheads. Smoke curled from the largest cabin and one of the smaller, and with that smoke came the scent of cooked meat and baking bread. It struck Hanuvar that he had come upon a homey oasis.

The woman's voice faltered as Hanuvar rode from the woods. The boy sang boisterously for a moment more before noticing the woman had stopped, and then he too fell silent and looked up at her. At the same moment the man set down his work and started down the little rise for Hanuvar, his expression stern.

Hanuvar reined in, his hand raised in greeting. He would have given much to have wished them a good afternoon in Volani, but he kept to his assumed identity. "Hello," he said in Dervan, accented as though he were Ceori. "I seek the home of Drusus."

"You have found it," the man said. He continued his advance, polite but hardly welcoming. He was muscled trimly, no more than thirty summers, a dark-haired, hazel-eyed man with a flattened nose. His garb was Dervan, though his boots were decorated with a spiraling Volani flare, much as his Dervan words were decorated with a Volani accent. Here, before him, was a countryman, like Hanuvar sundered from a land the Dervans had burned and butchered. Though this forester had surely suffered, he did not seem to be suffering now, nor did the woman who watched with her basket of berries. She was fair-featured, no more than twenty years, and there was an honest, happy glow to her cheeks.

"Where's your master?" Hanuvar asked.

"He is out hunting. Who are you?"

"I am a friend." Hanuvar climbed down from his horse and scanned the little clearing.

The man took a cautious step forward but remained a good two sword lengths clear. Beyond range of a sudden draw and slice, or the kick of a warhorse.

"The master did not mention a friend was coming."

"That is because I am a friend to the Volani," he said in his native tongue.

The man's eyebrows rose in astonishment.

"I would speak freely," Hanuvar said. "But not if there are Dervans near."

The man stared at him. "Who are you? Why are you here?"

"Are there Dervans here, or not?"

The man shook his head no and stepped closer, still awaiting the answer to his own question.

"Call me Katurix. My real name's not important now." It would invite a long series of questions.

"You speak my tongue like a native."

"I am a native," Hanuvar said.

"I can see it, in your face," the man said slowly. "Though you could be Ceori. If you are Volani, that cannot be your ring."

"It is my ring now. I would like to arrange for your freedom. Are you Levemar?"

His expression widened in surprise. "How do you know my name?"

"Because I looked at the sales records."

"Why?"

"I want all remaining Volani to be free."

The man looked at him sadly. "Free? And what will we do with freedom? Where would we go, and who would have us? The master is kind and leaves us to our work. We do much as we did outside Volanus—"

"For a master."

"Yes. But we have food, and shelter, and we know how blessed we are for that."

"Only one in twenty survived the siege of Volanus," Hanuvar said. "How did you come here, with the whole of your family?"

The woman had drawn up to the man's side, and now that she stood close Hanuvar saw a familial resemblance in the shape of the forehead, though the woman's nose was not so broad, and her hair was dark and curling. It had been cut short and pulled back from her cheekbones with a black cord. He guessed that this, then, was Elava.

Her scrutiny of his own face was intense, and her brow furrowed, as though she saw something familiar in it. It might be that she had seen him, bearded, speaking to a crowd, or witnessed his brother Melgar in one of his own public engagements. She was too young to have seen and remembered Adruvar or Harnil, who had seldom been in Volanus during the second war and died before its conclusion.

"We were the first to fall," Eleva said, with the quiet of a shy person. "We lived in the wilds of mount Erydus, in the forest of the slope. A Dervan advanced patrol came through, scouting an overland route before the dawn. They had us before we even knew there was a war."

"We know what they did to some of the prisoners. But these troops were...gentle by comparison," Levemar said, almost as though he were ashamed of his good fortune. "We lost our homes, and our freedom. But we remained together, and they did not harm us. And the master, when he bought us, let us stay together. Where might we find a kinder fate? The gods have guided us here, as though it's the last safe refuge. Can you think of any other place where my sister might sing in her native tongue? Where my son can run and play in the woods, as I once did?"

Hanuvar had helped build such a place. "I would like to offer you a berth on one of the ships heading for a new Volani homeland."

The man stared at him.

The woman's jaw opened slowly. "They say that Hanuvar went to found a new colony."

Levemar countered her hope. "They also say Hanuvar died in Volanus, and that his ghost walks Dervan lands, killing the leaders and their children."

"He lives," Hanuvar said curtly. "And he has no interest in killing children and lacks the incentive to hunt the Dervan leaders. All he cares about is preserving what is left of his people. I've been charged with finding them and giving them a way out."

Levemar was having none of the good news. "This is a trick. Like that man who said he was here to buy up Volani slaves."

"That man works with me."

Levemar frowned. "And how do we know who you work for?"

"Why would a Dervan hire someone to speak Volani and pretend he wishes to free us?" Eleva asked her brother.

"Who knows why the Dervans do anything?"

"I think he speaks the truth," the young woman insisted.

Levemar turned to Hanuvar. "My family will have to talk about this."

Hanuvar had to confirm he'd understood clearly. "You have to decide whether you wish to be free?"

"No. My brother must be told, and my wife . . . it's complicated."

"The master needs our help," Elava explained, as though that would provide clarity.

"Money is generally helpful to most masters," Hanuvar observed.

She shook her head. "It's not about money. He trusts us, but that's not it, either. He's close to his final hunt. We shouldn't leave him until it's done."

Levemar agreed with a vigorous shake of his head. "We wouldn't want to abandon him when he's so close."

"So close to what?" Hanuvar asked.

The man and woman exchanged a look, then seemed confused about how to answer. "We should not say," she managed at last.

It was hard to make sense of them. He tried another approach. "I have some experience solving difficult problems. Can I help?"

The man made a cutting motion with his hand. "It is not for your ears."

They had begun to irritate him, and he reminded himself how little reason they had to trust him, or to risk anything at all when they had miraculously found an island of safety amongst terrible circumstances. "How long do you need?"

"Only a few days," the woman said. "A week at most."

"You wish to live on as slaves for another week?"

Elava responded to his obvious confusion. "We know that we have been blessed," she said. "And part of that is because of our master. We owe him our thanks."

There was a twisted truth to what they both said. "I can give you a few days only," Hanuvar said with reluctance. "Can I stay here?"

The man quickly shook his head. "No. You should come back, in the morning. As a matter of fact, you should leave, now. It will be dusk soon."

Hanuvar sighed in frustration. He would like to have pushed to learn the truth, but he saw now they were distracted by the oncoming night and whatever strange threat that presented. "Very well. I'll return in the morning. Talk among yourselves."

"We will. And to the master."

Hanuvar froze. "You don't mean to tell him about your homeland, do you?"

"Should we not?" Elava asked.

He stared at her in disbelief, doubting her intelligence for the first time. "The Dervans know of the colony only as a rumor." He might have said that the new colony was small, and while hardly defenseless, could not yet endure an invasion from a fully committed Dervan expedition. But he was almost as wary of her good sense as they were of his promises. He finally added: "It needs to remain nothing more than a rumor."

Elava turned to her brother. "We could invite the master with us, when the hunt is through."

While Hanuvar was not opposed to men and women of good character joining the colony, he was stunned by her matter-of-fact assumption. Elava must truly hold Drusus in high regard. "No," Hanuvar said, "I would rather you not do that, until I at least take the measure of the man. For now, tell him I represent a free Volani man you once knew who learned that you were still alive."

"I don't think we should lie to the master," Elava said.

Her stubborn insistence astonished him almost as much as her brother's silent agreement. "Any mention of the new homeland could place all surviving Volani in jeopardy. Do not speak of it. If it is that you do not wish to lie, say whatever you like, so long as you leave out the colony or mention of me as a Volani."

Elava mulled his information silently.

Levemar looked nervously at the sky, as though he expected the sun to plummet down from it. Hanuvar bade a gruff goodbye, mounted his horse, and turned back to the road.

Levemar hurried to his side. "I should come with you."

"I can manage."

"You don't know these woods."

Levemar surely understood that all Hanuvar had to do was reverse his course on the single road, which lacked any divergent paths or byways. But it seemed Levemar knew more than he was saying, and Hanuvar wondered if he should be alert for ambush. He supposed it was possible the slaves meant to ensure he would not backtrack to spy upon them, but he sensed some other explanation. He worried that he had risked too much by being open with them and it troubled him that he must fear treachery from his own.

Levemar led the way, walking a few feet in front of Hanuvar's horse. He neither volunteered information nor invited conversation. Hanuvar did not bother questioning him, for he sensed no more answers would be forthcoming today.

On either hand loomed the vast, primordial woodland. It felt quieter than it should have been in the late afternoon, as if even the trees were poised with expectation. Somewhere out there the peninsula's red chested warblers exchanged greetings in their distinctive burbling; all else was still, with not even the swish of a squirrel's tail in evidence.

When Hanuvar recognized they were not far from the forest's edge he caught a flash of movement on his right. He glanced first left, to see if an attack were being readied, then back right, and a slim female form in a flowing Turian dress disappeared behind a trunk. His heart hammered, for that woman had been his lost Ravella, and that could not be. He had known the way she moved, the shape of her head among the curls, the proud heft of her shoulders.

A trick. A sorcerous trick. Ahead of him, Levemar had not broken stride, and Hanuvar glanced once more in the other cardinal directions. His horse faltered, then kept on with a little huff.

And then he glimpsed a high, silver tower through the woods, as though a thin screen of leaves separated him from vanished Volanus. The westernmost tower gleamed in a shaft of sunlight, and he would have sworn he heard the song of morning prayer rising from the island temples.

This time he stopped, hand to sword, staring. The image had been blotted out by a tree branch. The singing ceased.

Levemar halted and faced him, considered his guarded searching for a moment, and finally spoke. "You've seen it. Whatever you saw, don't go after it. It's not real."

"I know it's not real," Hanuvar said sharply. "But what is it?"

"That which the master hunts," Levemar replied grimly.

"You could speak with more precision."

Levemar answered reluctantly. "It is a spirit of the deep woods, cursed and vengeful. She means to cloud our minds with what we desire most. Were you to dismount and pursue, we'd be unlikely to find you. Or, if we did, you would be maddened, or broken, or a dead husk."

"And you're safe from it?"

"So long as I keep to the path."

"Suppose it presents a path that looks like the one you want."

"I know the way. And the master has taught me its signs. But you do not know them." He stepped to Hanuvar's side, and his voice was considerate. "What did it show you?"

"A woman lost to me. And one of the silver towers."

Levemar's face registered a solemn compassion. Quietly, he revealed a trouble of his own. "It shows me my mother." His eyes were dark with the shared sorrow of loss. "She did not survive the slave pens. If she could have lasted but a few more weeks I'm certain the master would have bought her too."

"I'm sorry for your loss."

"I think we have both had losses," Levemar said. And then that brief feeling of fellowship vanished and he grew hard and stern once more. "I tell you this now—stay clear from the woods until the sun is high tomorrow. We can talk then."

Hanuvar spoke as Levemar started to turn. "I've faced and defeated more strange magics than you might believe. I'm no sorcerer, but whatever you mean to do, I can aid you, if it will help win you free."

The man gravely considered this, then bowed his head. "I believe you. I will talk with the others, and the master. For now, though, we must keep moving."

In only a few hundred feet the waning light was a welcome amber glow on the road ahead. Levemar raised his hand in farewell and Hanuvar guided his horse for it.

He looked back only once, but his escort was already lost in the darkness beneath the trees.

II

"I expected that you'd be back by nightfall." Natius repeated himself over the dinner, for he'd said it at the doorstep when Hanuvar presented himself. They ate Dervan style, lying on couches across from each other while an elderly house slave and the boy presented them with food and wine. They were alone, and there was no sign of a third couch; the aging soldier said his wife wasn't well and preferred to eat in her room. He'd also said he preferred to eat outdoors, and they did so now, on a dilapidated veranda. Two wings enclosed the north and south view, but the west looked out upon a small garden and the dark bank of woods below.

The meal was warm and fresh and simple. It started with hard boiled eggs and sweet dipping sauce that was better than usual garam, although Natius apologized for the flavor being thin. It then moved on to venison.

"Drusus keeps us supplied with deer," he explained. "I don't see him very often anymore, but he's mad for hunting. One of his Volani slaves brings a deer by every now and then; sometimes a boar."

"He sounds generous."

"He feels guilty that he won't let me hunt there. He says it's dangerous."

"Do you think it's dangerous?"

The old warrior looked up from his plate, rubbed some flat bread around in the sauce, then considered his response a moment longer. "You've passed through those woods. What do you think?"

Instead of answering, Hanuvar asked, "Have you seen things there?"

Natius smiled in triumph. "Ah! You've seen her too, then."

"I saw something," Hanuvar admitted.

"The woods have an uncanny feel, don't they? And in the dusk Drusus says they're deadly. I used to hunt with him, right after we mustered out."

"You served together?"

"We did. Best friends, we were. Saved my life more times than I can count, back in the day, and I had his back as well. We bought adjacent plots."

"But you're not friends now?"

Natius frowned. "He's got secrets. There's magic in those woods. I don't understand it, but he keeps it for himself. To use himself," he finished bitterly.

Hanuvar considered telling him something of what the slaves had said, about the master getting ready to destroy the beast, or spirit, once and for all, but held off until he better understood Natius. "You're saying he's a sorcerer?"

"He must be in his mid-sixties now, but I swear, apart from a little gray at his temples and a few wrinkles, he doesn't look much older than when we settled here. You know, I've been a poor host. I haven't asked you much about yourself. What is it you're doing here?"

Hanuvar masked his frustration, for Natius had seemed ready to divulge the interesting details about his former friend. "You've been a perfect host. I hesitate to disclose my employer's aims. But I suppose there's no harm in telling you if I don't mention names. Some of those Volani slaves come highly recommended. They're supposedly great hunters, and a senator's son has it in his head he's going to take them on an expedition."

"And there aren't any good Dervan hunters?" Natius asked huffily.

"A fine point," Hanuvar said, inwardly grinning at his predicament. "Or Ceori ones, for that matter. We know which end of the spear is sharp!" He accentuated the point by waving his finger at him.

Natius was proud of his people but conceded that the Ceori could field worthy hunters as well by means of a polite nod.

"I said all that to my employer," Hanuvar continued. "But the boy wants to go hunting on old Volani land and wants Volani guides. And so here I am. I get paid either way, but if I can convince Drusus to sell, my employer's apt to give me a bonus. Sadly, Drusus was out hunting. The slaves said to come back around noon tomorrow."

"When the sun is highest," Natius said, as though he had heard the information himself. "I think they know what Drusus is doing."

"I'm certain they do."

"Volani are sneaky. You know that. You served against them, didn't you?"

"I've dealt with a lot of them," Hanuvar admitted.

"Can you believe that Drusus doesn't even have an overseer? He trusts the Volani more than he trusts a Dervan of ancient stock. I'm no blue blood, but my people have been on Dervan land since the days of the founding."

Hanuvar nodded sympathetically. "I am a soldier, as was my father, and his father before him. I sense the same in you."

"It's true. A man can tell." Natius gulped his wine, sloshed the dregs in his cup, and seemed to reach a decision. "I hate to tell you this, my new friend, but I don't think Drusus will sell. He's mad for hunting. He does it every day, summer, fall, winter, or spring, and he needs those slaves to help him."

"What is it they're hunting?"

"He says it's a special beast. But it's magic, I know it. He's never been the same since his nephews died. Kids. They were killed by a bear when they were visiting, out in these woods. He got that bear a long time ago," Natius added. "But that didn't change anything. He's been strange and solemn ever since."

"You were best friends," Hanuvar said. "Did he never explain himself?"

"No."

Hanuvar sipped at his wine. "A while ago you asked if I'd seen her too. Who did you mean?"

Natius opened his mouth and for the first time he didn't speak right away. "You want to know what I saw?" he asked, and then, before Hanuvar could answer, said, "My wife. When she was young, and fair. But it wasn't her."

"No," Hanuvar agreed.

"It was what used to be her," Natius went on.

"What do you mean?"

"You know how I think Drusus stays young? I think he keeps hunting down his youth. In the woods. That's why he's always there, because he needs to drink it down, all the time. There's something there. Something keeping Drusus young."

Something Natius himself wanted, by the look of it, and he was jealous his old friend wouldn't share.

"What would you do if you could catch it, Natius? Assuming it's real?"

He spoke without hesitation. "First, I'd give it to my wife. I don't know how long it lasts, but . . . even if it gave her a few years, how happy she'd be. How nice it would be, to hold her again."

"And then?"

"Well, if he can catch it again and again," Natius said, "then so could I. Imagine what it would be like to spin back ten or twenty years? Or even just three. To have three years back? You ever think what that would be like?"

"Not really," Hanuvar said.

"Of course not. It's the kind of drivel Herrenes lie around and wonder about instead of getting things done, like a good soldier. Like a legionary."

"I'm surprised no one has called the revenants on him."

Natius grimaced. "Don't be daft. Nobody wants to get their attention, not for anything."

"Have you ever asked him directly about it?"

"I have." There was that in Natius' voice that hinted at deep fury held in check. "He refused to own up. Said that the woods were more treacherous than I would believe. He said that there are some things that legionaries don't know how to fight, and that this battle was his alone. And he refused to talk about it further. So. I just sit here on the outside, growing fat on his game, and my dear Lavidia wastes away, growing thinner and fainter every day." His right hand was tightening, as though he gripped the hilt of a gladius.

Hanuvar had learned more than he expected from Natius, and now sensed he'd be hearing few new details, just some that the old soldier would want to circle back to. He complimented him again on his food, and then the two fell to talking about campaigns and battles.

Natius had been stationed against the Herrenes during most of his time in service. Hanuvar pretended to speak of some of his own final battles in the peninsula as though from the Dervan perspective. Twice Natius staggered off to check on his wife, drinking with dark resolve after each venture, as if he fought to stem a tide of some onrushing enemy.

Finally, Natius began to slur and grow maudlin. Hanuvar excused himself, and a slave conducted him to a small spare room. It was clean enough, though the walls were cracked and the mediocre frescoes needed touching up, especially where a leak in the ceiling had obscured a pastoral scene.

As Hanuvar settled into bed, he sorted through what he'd been told and what he'd seen but came to no conclusions. Following the sound of the slaves tidying up after supper, he heard the distant sounds of his hosts speaking, Natius drunkenly loud but awkwardly tender, the woman's voice weak and curious about their guest. Their voices grew too soft to hear, but just before Hanuvar drifted off, he was surprised by the sound of a man weeping, and surprised further by a woman making soft soothing noises: "It's alright Natius. I'm still here," she said. "I'm still here."

III

Hanuvar rose early. A few of the slaves had done so too, although those out in the fields weren't laboring with any great urgency. The house boy told him the master usually slept late, but that if he wished there was leftover bread and eggs and some berries, which suited Hanuvar fine. After that light meal he went out to care for his horse, then to clean the saddle and bridle and other gear. Garbed in a sleeveless work tunic, he stretched and practiced some martial stances, feeling stiff after so long a ride the day before. It was nothing like what he'd felt as an older man, but very different from the easy way he'd shrugged off physical effort only a few months earlier.

Some of the slaves watched from a distance. As he was pausing to drink from a jug of water, he heard the clop of horse hooves and turned to behold two mounted figures turning up from the woods. The one to the rear was the same flat-nosed Volani he had spoken with yesterday, Levemar. The other could be none other than Drusus. He was muscular and broad through the shoulders, narrow through the hips. His hair was dark and lustrous and worn long, parted in the middle, and graced with touches of gray at the temple and near his ears. His face was clean-shaven, tanned without being weathered, bright-eyed, even and pleasing. As Natius had suggested, his years lay light on him, for he appeared in his late forties at best.

"I bid you greeting, Katurix of the Ceori," Drusus said. "My slaves speak well of you, and Levemar is a good judge of character."

"That is kind of you, and of him."

"He has spoken to me, and I would speak with you."

"Please, join me. Forgive my appearance."

"It is I who should apologize for interrupting your training." Drusus climbed down from the horse. Levemar did as well, and then his master passed off his horse reins to him. On the ground, Drusus proved half a head shorter than Hanuvar. "Levemar told me you witnessed something in the forest yesterday. So you may have an inkling of what I do."

"I saw something, but I've no idea what it is you do."

"It was something you desired? Yes?"

"Yes."

Drusus breathed out decisively. "And yet you did not succumb. Levemar told me you said little. Most are compelled to chase it." He looked toward Natius' villa.

"I saw things that could not be," Hanuvar said simply.

"It tempts you with things you desire most."

"There are things I wish for, but I know the difference between dream and flesh."

"You sound like a man who's well rooted."

"Perhaps I have grown inured to loss. I'd offer refreshments and ask you to sit down with me, but this is not my home. I do have water."

"Thank you, no. Levemar says you have come to purchase his freedom, and that of his people, where they may live among other survivors."

Hanuvar did not give Levemar the look he was owed, for saying too much.

"It is a lofty goal," Drusus said. "If you help me, I will help you."

Hanuvar did not betray his amazement. "How can I help?"

"Spoken like a man determined to see a goal through. Katurix, here is my challenge. There is a curse upon my land."

The door to the villa creaked open and Natius himself stepped out. His close-cut, receding hair had been hurriedly brushed, and he'd thrown on a rumpled tunic, which emphasized his protruding gut. He himself appeared hardly ready for an upright stance, nor to have his eyes open, and they were shielded from the light with a hangover grimace and a hand visored at his eyebrows.

Drusus' handsome features showed brief displeasure before widening in a smile. "Hello, old friend. I've come for a short visit, and a minor favor."

"Drusus," Natius said, his voice hoarse. He cleared it then started forward, legs stiff but loosening as he drew close. "You're an early riser, Katurix. Well, you're younger than me. What's this favor you need, Drusus? Another hand at the hunt?"

"No, no. If anything were to happen to you, who would look after Lavidia? I need a witness. I've prepared a document, but I need someone to see me sign it."

Natius' expression had grown sour, though his tone remained cordial. "What are you changing?"

"I am manumitting my slaves this morning."

Natius' lips formed a circle of surprise. "All of them? Why? How will you hunt without them? How can you afford to free them all?"

Drusus accepted the assault of questions with weary impatience. "If all works out, this will be my last hunt. I hope to survive it, but if not, well, I want the slaves rewarded for their faithful service. One was injured just last night."

Hanuvar frowned but read nothing in Levemar's expression.

"Your last hunt?" Natius asked. He did not wait for a full answer. "So you're finally going to stop the magic?"

Drusus shook his head. "It's not like that."

"What is it like? Why don't you tell me?"

"I'm sorry. I pledge that if all works as I hope today, tonight I will tell you everything. I swear. It's not a pretty story, though, Natius. You may not want to hear."

"If it's something you need help with, you know you can depend upon me."

"I do need your help. With the will."

"Why not ask Katurix?" Natius asked peevishly.

It seemed to Hanuvar that Drusus spoke with great patience. The man possessed a strength of character he could not help but respect, and he was coming to understand why the Volani foresters held the man in such high esteem. "I would ask Katurix, but since he is going to accompany me, it is better that someone who will surely survive bear witness. If I fall this night, I want the Volani to live without legal challenge to their status. Will you help?"

For a long moment Natius stared, and Hanuvar thought to hear him erupt with the rage obvious from his lowered brows. But then, slowly, he nodded.

"Good," Drusus said. "Thank you."

After that, Levemar removed a small portable desk strapped to his saddle and held it steady with his forearm while he carefully removed a parchment from a scroll case.

Though curious about what was to happen next in the day, Hanuvar was immensely pleased that the freedom of these Volani had been secured. He watched as Drusus signed the emancipation document, and Natius signed a letter saying he had been present as witness. Drusus handed both papers over to Levemar, who rolled them up, fitted them into the scroll case, and capped it. The Volani bowed his head in gratitude.

Drusus thanked them, then urged Hanuvar to ready himself. Natius quietly wished them good luck and watched as they rode into the forest.

Once they were beneath the tree boughs, Drusus spoke to Hanuvar, riding at his side. "Levemar tells me he trusts you. I want you to trust me."

"You have acted honorably. I will do the same. But what is it you wish me to do?"

"I have tricked the spirit I hunt into smaller and smaller confines. Through misdirection and lures, and trial and error and study, I have learned the old signs that give it the greatest pain and placed them."

Levemar, riding behind them, spoke up. "Fencing it is not as simple as building a wall. It has to be tricked to circle against the shadows, not with them."

"That's essentially correct," Drusus said, "though there is more involved even than that. It must be lured to move in the right way, at the right time, while the proper rituals are being performed. While all the wards are maintained. The larger its area, the harder it is to maintain the wards. But now, finally, I have it penned to a very small section of grounds."

"Your visit yesterday distracted it at just the right moment," Levemar said. "It backtracked when it detected you and that allowed the master—"

"Drusus," his former master corrected graciously.

"...that allowed Drusus to close it in. The moon will begin to wax in two more days, and then its power will grow. But right now, it is at its weakest, in its smallest area."

"The weapons have been ritually purified," Drusus continued. "It can be brought down at last."

"But not without some danger?" Hanuvar suggested.

"Yes." Drusus breathed out, slowly. "It's my fault it's here. If I die, that's the price that must be paid."

Hanuvar understood his sentiment. Drusus had an objective he had set, and the man suspected he might not live to see it resolved, just as Hanuvar had long suspected he would eventually take one too many risks in furtherance of his goals. "Tell me what it is we're facing."

"It's a dark forest spirit. It prospers upon ... intense feelings. It will show you what you most want. It will sear your heart, and try to twist you, so you crave what it offers."

"It can talk," Levemar said.

"What does it say?"

Drusus' smile was thin and bleak. "Whatever you most want to hear."

IV

Drusus spent much of the morning taking a mixture of liquid that was clear spring water and the blood from fresh animal hearts and pouring it across elaborate spirals incised into the tops of boulders scattered through the woods. These, Hanuvar was told, were the rituals that had to be performed at least once every week, no matter oppressive heat or cold so intense it chilled to the bone. If the spiritual magic was not maintained, the creature would escape.

Hanuvar memorized the feel of the half mile space that they walked, where the hills were, where the gullies and creeks ran, the location of a lone dead fall, and other land features.

While Drusus retreated to his cabin for final preparations, Hanuvar sat down with his countryfolk at a wooden table in the shade for a mid-day meal heavy with meat and light on vegetables. He had expected a more celebratory atmosphere, but their manner was oddly somber.

He was introduced to the other two adults of the group, Levemar's sturdy wife, Sophonia, and tall young Nelcar, who'd sprained his right arm when he'd slipped last night. Beside them were three children, two dark-haired girls of eight and ten, and the curly-haired boy Hanuvar had seen earlier.

All were as curious of him as he was of them. The children eyed him surreptitiously. The looks from the adults were more probing, even after Hanuvar spoke of New Volanus and explained to them that their ocean voyage would be arranged.

"This opportunity seems too good to be true," Nelcar said, frowning.

Hanuvar might well have pointed out that the opportunity was only available because he himself had survived long months of hazardous trials and had been joined by others now risking their lives to make liberations like theirs possible. But the young man probably wouldn't be capable of understanding that. While he was still framing an appropriate response, the older of the two girls spoke up.

"Can the master come?"

"Yes," the younger said. "What will happen to him? Can he come with us?"

"What do you think?" Eleva asked Hanuvar. Her clean-featured face was so bright with hope she looked almost as young as the children. "Once the hunt is over, can we invite Drusus?"

Hanuvar understood how they could come to respect so forthright a man, but the peculiar intensity of this devotion puzzled him.

"You've seen he's a good man," Lenereva said. "In everything that he does."

"I've seen that," Hanuvar conceded. He almost spoke to them of the lives put at risk every time someone was told about New Volanus and the efforts to reach it, but their steady scrutiny disturbed him, and he couldn't know if it was their natural disposition or a byproduct of their current environment. "Tell me more about the spirit you're hunting."

They repeated that it was deceptive and very dangerous.

"Has it killed?" Hanuvar asked.

"It killed the master's ... Drusus ... nephews many years ago," Lenereva said.

That was interesting, for Natius had told him a bear had done that. "Has it hurt any of you?"

Nelcar winced as he lifted his sling-restrained right arm.

Hanuvar wanted to point out to them how strange it was that a dangerous entity that Drusus had been hunting for years hadn't managed to do anything more than deliver an injury that could have been the result of carelessness. But he decided against disputing the preconceptions of his audience. "What does it try to lure you with?"

The girls said that they had seen and heard other children in the woods.

"It's a little boy," the boy corrected. "And he always wants me to chase him. But I never do."

Elava elaborated. "It wants to lure us deep into the woods. Sometimes, I swear I've heard the marketplace, and the laughter of the couple who used to run it."

"They were upland from the coast," Sophonia explained. "We passed the market they ran when the Dervans brought us out. The soldiers were hauling all the goods away for themselves." Her voice grew heavy. "We didn't see what they'd done with Cerona or her husband, but we never saw them with the other slaves."

"What do you see when you're hunting it?" Hanuvar asked.

"The Dervan general," Sophonia said finally. "Striding around with an arrogant scowl, his head thrust out like a vulture. But alone. Unguarded."

Hanuvar would have recognized that description anywhere. "You see Caiax?"

"Yes."

"He's dead," Hanuvar said with grim satisfaction. He'd seen the blow that had finished him.

Sophonia's tight expression eased ever so slightly. "That's good to know. How did it happen?"

"Violently. One of his own men killed him."

"Good."

One by one the others told him what they saw when they hunted the spirit; enemies, friends, potential playmates, even, in Nelcar's case, a young woman that he'd hoped to love. The spirit, they said, was wily, but they knew better than to pursue, not unless they were with Drusus.

Though the reverence for Drusus and almost obsessive alignment with the hunter's goals troubled Hanuvar, he could not help but like the foresters, and not simply because they spoke his own language. There were strong, loving bonds between them. They were kind to one another, and generous to him, even if they remained somewhat cautious. After surviving the destruction of Volanus with but a single loss in their immediate family, could he fault them for being suspicious of him, a stranger, when he meant to take them away from not only their zone of safety, but their protector?

It might be that there was nothing wrong with them that couldn't be explained by the trauma they'd endured. But something still felt off.

Near the meal's end, Drusus emerged from his cabin. The handsome hunter insisted on serving himself, then sat down at the table's head and ate prodigious amounts of venison and tubers. When he was finished at last, he asked his former slaves to gather in a half circle, then brushed back his tresses and thanked them for their loyalty and vigilance.

"It's nearly time to take our stations," he said, and his eyes flicked to Hanuvar. "If you see the spirit, call to me and get ready to advance. Remember, whatever you do, don't touch the boulders. You will disrupt the energies collected there."

Every adult but Nelcar was assigned a post beside a boulder and instructed to patrol to its left and right without crossing the invisible barrier, as though they were sentries. If they perceived the entity, they were to drive it forward and call their position to their fellow hunters. The purified metal on their spear points, Drusus explained, would inflict terrible pain if it even neared the creature.

Hanuvar wasn't fully pleased with the plan and studied the serious faces of those around him to gauge their reactions. None raised objection.

Before long, they headed to their respective places and sat their glowing lanterns beside their stones. It was dark beneath the trees, and the gleam of the lanterns of their allies was all but obscured by intervening tree boles.

One by one the calls of the forest denizens faded, as though they were candles being snuffed, and an eerie stillness settled over the woods. The light dropped as the sun sank beyond the forest edge. Shadows lengthened and merged until the land beneath the tree boughs was heavy with primordial menace. It had become a land where gods might walk.

Hanuvar had just begun his third back and forth patrol when he spotted someone seated upon his boulder. This startled him, especially when the figure waved. The entity, he'd been told, could not approach the rock, but this person sat upon it.

It wore Hanuvar's daughter's shape, not as she would be now, but as Narisia had been when he'd seen her upon his return from the war, a gangly teen with long hair and dark sad eyes.

He had heard how great the creature's power was but seeing it thus and experiencing the depths of the great longing to be near it he understood its power.

"Harken," it said, advancing softly along the invisible line that lay between its grounds and that of the greater forest. It pressed against its edge, looking with Narisia's eyes. "I know his plan. And I know what they have told you. There's more."

He stood ready with his spear, his lips parted to call Drusus. And yet he waited and tried to decide whether his hesitation was inspired by his desire to learn more, or the creature's effect upon him.

"You know I am not your daughter," it said, though it spoke with her voice. "But I am not a ravening monster luring you unto death."

"You wear my daughter's shape."

"And you do not like that." Its form blurred and shifted until it was a woman he did not know, a fair lady with creamy skin, with a pretty corona of black hair. She was broad hipped and small breasted, the Dervan ideal. "Here," she said. Her voice was sweet and light. "Is this better?" She did not wait for an answer. "You are different. You crave a city, a people. You know that I can help you, don't you?"

"How?"

She laughed, softly, as if sharing some intimate secret. "I know you long to put them on the ships, but that you fear for them. The way is long. There are enemy vessels, and pirates, and terrible storms. You have wished there was some other way."

What she said felt truer even than he had believed. Her words sank deeply into his perception of the world, and he fought against the weight pulling down his own convictions. "And you have one?" he suggested.

"Do you know how wide these woods are? And how many people they could hold?"

"You think I could put my people here?"

"With room to spare. And the forest would provide. Does it seem to you as though the ones you came for suffer? All their needs are met. And their health is assured. Perhaps it's harder to tell with the new ones, but surely you see Drusus. He used to be more grateful," she added with a frown.

These points, too, seemed reasonable and oddly attractive. He sought for flaws in her arguments and found the largest. "What do you wish in return?"

"Merely that the game continue."

"The game?"

"The hunt, silly man. All you would have to do is hunt for me."

"What if we do not want to hunt?"

Again she laughed. "Everyone hunts for something, don't they?"

"You would have me lead my people here and keep them separate from their fellows."

She stared at him and slumped a little as she sighed. At the same moment any appeal of her strange proposal left him.

"Oh, you are not like the others," she said sadly. "Your longing is just as great, but the *kind* of wanting is different. Drusus craves forgiveness. And vengeance. Natius desires youth and the intimacy he once had." With a distinctly feminine gesture she brushed one clothed thigh with her left hand while stroking the left shoulder with her right.

"Why do you do this?" Hanuvar asked.

"It is my nature. Just as it is yours to shepherd."

"So it is your nature to toy with humans?"

She laughed and shook her head. "No."

"That's not an answer."

"Perhaps you have asked the wrong question."

He had any number of questions, and he still doubted whether any of them would get him truth. And he might not have long before it tried some other ploy. So he turned to a topic that might shine the light in a different direction.

"How did you become the quarry of Drusus?"

"Many seasons ago, he sent his nephews into the forest to gather berries. He had seen bear tracks a few days before, but decided the animal was passing through, for he had found no other sign. He wished to dally with his brother's wife. The nephews discovered the bear, and it killed them. Drusus found their bodies and begged the gods to tear out the part of him that hungered so that he would know peace again."

"You are that hunger?" he asked. She simply stared at him. Then he said: "Why do you run from him? Don't you wish to be rejoined?"

She shook her head. "It is only he, chasing himself in circles."

"Whatever his mistake, he has paid for it. The circle must be broken."

"If the circle is unbroken, it is because he refuses to break it."

"Riddles," he said disparagingly. "Why do you remain? He would cease to hunt if you were not here."

"We revolve around one another, he and I, though he cannot see it. The hunt grants him purpose. And he gives me life. Although he means to end it. He does not see how important we are to one another."

"Lividia!"

It was a choked cry of rage and dismay. Hanuvar stepped apart before he turned to confirm it was Natius who'd shouted; he wished to avoid putting his back to the thing, or to the man charging through the brush.

Spear in hand, the retired centurion raced forward, scattering forest detritus with every stride in his forester's boots. His face was tense with anger and anticipation. The young Ceori slave trotted on his heels.

The creature with Lividia's shape changed so that her clothes slid away to mere tatters; her form grew more voluptuous. Her hair streamed behind her in a wind that was not there and she chastely drew her arm across hard nipples as if suddenly embarrassed by them before running fleetly away.

"He lied!" Natius cried. "That's my wife's youth!"

"No, Natius," Hanuvar said. "It takes whatever shape is wanted."

Natius made a shoving motion at him as he swept past, calling for Lividia, the boy hurrying after. Hanuvar guessed then that it must have sensed Natius approaching for long moments. How much of what it had said been true, and how much merely a ploy to distract him, he could not guess.

The Volani foresters called out questioningly.

Whatever the thing truly was, it played a game, and whatever he was, Drusus at least wished to stop it. "Drusus! It's here, and Natius chases it! East by southeast!"

"East by southeast," one of the foresters repeated, and there was the sound of running feet. He went after Natius and the spirit, his own spear ready. He heard others closing in, and then something pale and swift swept back the way they'd come, and Natius panted after. Hanuvar pursued in time to see young Lividia reclined upon a boulder, a young maiden who pretended modesty while staring with coy eyes.

"Hurry, you fool," she said. Natius rushed to embrace her, his spear point heedlessly endangering the Ceori boy at his side. It was not just Hanuvar who shouted at him to halt, but Drusus as well, for he was running with great bounds, and three of the Volani were behind him.

A foot shy of the woman spirit and the boulder, Natius stumbled and landed gracelessly in the bush, his hands striking the stone's sharp edge.

To the rear, Drusus cursed him.

Natius rose, staring at the smear of blood on his hand, and his partial handprint across the spiral upon the boulder.

The Lividia-shaped spirit let out a peel of laughter and cast back her head, impossibly beautiful, then she leapt over him, danced past one of the Volani with a spear and hurried free of the broken ward into the deeper woods.

Drusus spun on his heel and hurried after. "Levemar, refix the seal! You two, head east and west! The rest of you, fan out!"

Hanuvar ran with them. Dusk had fallen and the gloom was deep, but from time to time he spotted a pale glowing shape ahead. From somewhere on his left he heard Natius shouting for Lividia, and the little slave boy calling "mistress!"

"It's not her!" Drusus shouted, apoplectic with rage. "You've broken the seal! If we don't catch her now, years have been wasted! Years!"

As if summoned by his voice, the pale form, somehow retaining the failing light, glided toward Drusus. Natius turned on his heel with surprising speed and sprinted after. The veteran's breath was labored, but he ran as though a life depended upon it, perhaps his own, heedless of roots and tree trunks and the treacherous ground. Hanuvar came after. He shouted for Natius to slow, then gave up, understanding the creature had the man ensorcelled. He did call to the young Ceori, but the boy was as keen as a hound in following his master.

They plowed headlong into Drusus at the top of a rise. Over the crash of feet through the detritus rose a cry of pain and then silence descended.

By the time Hanuvar arrived, a ring of people looked down a small, steep drop of six feet, where a little ridge looked over a creek bed. A figure lay twisted in the water. Natius stood over it, breathing heavily, his weapon low, and the little boy was near him. Hanuvar carefully worked his way down.

Natius staggered away from the body. His face was pale to the crown of his balding pate, and his spear tip red. Red too was the tunic covering Drusus' still body. When Hanuvar descended with his lantern and found no pulse, he saw that the hunter's face was strangely peaceful.

"We both slipped," Natius said, panting. "I didn't mean to do it. She tricked us! It *looked* like there was a path there! I . . . I fell into him—"

"You killed him!" Levemar shouted. He dropped, landed heavily on two feet and drove his weapon toward Natius.

Hanuvar interposed his spear shaft, blocking the blow.

Levemar's eyes flashed in fury. "He wants the hunt for himself! He's come hunting her before!"

"It's tricked him, as it tricked Drusus," Hanuvar said.

"He's lying!" Levemar pointed at Natius.

"Leave him be," Hanuvar growled.

The forester cursed, glaring, but Hanuvar urged him back with the spear haft and the man finally relented and stepped away.

"Come," Hanuvar said. "We'll carry Drusus back."

"But . . . the creature," Elava said. Her voice was heavy with sorrow. "It will get away."

"I'll avenge him," Natius vowed. "I will carry on his hunt. You can rest assured."

No one said anything to that, but as they bore the dead man back through the woods, Elava sobbed and young Nelcar openly wept. The little Ceori boy followed, fearfully scanning the wood, as if a legion of spirits hid just out of sight.

"You can show me the spells, can't you, before you leave?" Natius pleaded. "Teach me how to seek it?"

No one said anything for a long time, but Sophonia said, softly, that the master had many papers and she supposed Natius would be welcome to them. So eager did Natius prove to see them that he headed directly into the main cabin after asking where those papers were.

Hanuvar watched while the Volani dug the grave, at the garden's edge, wondering if he had chosen the right course. Rightly or wrongly, he had wanted more information before he acted, and it might be that they could have brought the creature down if he had not delayed. But then he sensed that this spirit played an ancient game that had no true finish, and that it would never be caught.

After they had buried Drusus, the Volani sang a traditional song in his honor and laid flowers upon his grave. Hanuvar remained outside as they gathered their belongings from their cabins, watching the lantern shining in the central building and sometimes looking off into the wood. He thought he saw a pale form beside a tall oak, but before he could fasten on it fully, it faded into the woods.

Levemar kept shooting angry glances toward his dead master's cabin but said nothing. As they started for the road, the cabin door opened and Natius stepped out, a sheaf of papers in his hand. He appeared bright, almost hopeful, more vigorous, as if the struggle were already restoring him. "Take the boy back to the manor with you," he said. "He can tell my wife I'll be back in the morning."

Hanuvar said that they would, and then Natius raised a hand in farewell and closed the door.

"He thinks he will capture it," Levemar said softly. "You know he killed Drusus. You should have let me kill him."

"It tricked him," his sister Elava said. "What we should do is help him, so that we can avenge the master."

Their step faltered and the children looked back.

"The creature needs someone to hunt it," Hanuvar said. "Do you want that to be you?"

Apparently that hadn't occurred to any of them, for his words were followed by a shocked silence.

"Unless you want to be trapped here, forever, we need to go," Hanuvar said. "Now. If this is its power at its lowest ebb, you will have no better chance."

They hesitated, then seemed to decide as one, and resumed their forward course.

For a long while there was only the sound of their feet and the clop of hooves from Hanuvar's horse. The lanterns showed the way along the dark forest road.

"So was it all for nothing?" Elava asked, finally. "All those long years of his struggle? The mast... Drusus was trying to do good."

"A least, he thought he was," Hanuvar said. "He was kind to you, and for that we can be thankful."

"He was trying to stop an old evil."

"Or trying to blot out a mistake he'd made. His obsessions consumed him, and the creature distorts the understanding of all who meet it. In a few years, Natius might not even remember how he became the hunter."

"Will my master be hunting for years?" the Ceori slave asked.

"For long years," Hanuvar answered. "One dance has ended, and a new one begins, with a different partner."

When they arrived at last at the manor house beyond the woods, the sounds of lamentation reached them. Lividia had died. The mournful slaves said she had been calling for her husband.

Hanuvar led his people away from that dark place and on down the long road north.

❊ ❊ ❊

The family of foresters were just one small band adding to the steady stream flowing by multiple routes into our hidden enclave at Selanto. By that time in late spring, nearly four hundred Volani people had been recovered. That so many had been rescued in a half year was the result of Carthalo's extensive contacts and field agents, many of whom weren't aware of their employer's true identity or aims. They were simply skilled individuals well paid by a distant merchant to make purchases and would have been just as happy seeing to the transport of fruits, or carvings, or rare plants.

The vast majority of the former slaves had been restored to freedom without Hanuvar's intervention, though that is not to say no cleverness had been involved, for Carthalo and his operatives and a small number of skilled smugglers they paid knew just where to apply money and influence to achieve their aims.

When my children were old enough to appreciate the finer details of these stories, they asked why Izivar did not simply ask Enarius to free the rest of the Volani, especially after the emperor himself had expressed his undying gratitude to her.

I wish matters had been that simple. To ask for slaves to be freed from hundreds of households across the empire would have struck the Dervans not just as absurd, but incredibly suspicious. To their way of thinking, the enslaved had been handed their fate by the gods; they had lost their freedom because they were weaker than the Dervans. Some few might eventually prove themselves of so much worth to their owners that they would be manumitted, but they would have to win their freedom with their own merits.

For all that there was goodwill from the throne for the public face of Izivar's ship building venture, we had to move with the utmost care in the recovery of Volani, for if the emperor were to discover he had inadvertently been aiding a plan of Hanuvar's, his retribution would have been swift and merciless.

Hanuvar himself did not return to Selanto, in part because three of Carthalo's best men sought in the Turian hills for Rokana, a sorcerous ally from the war, and he wanted to be close if she were located. But his driving reason was that a series of complicated recovery efforts all came to a head at about the same time in the regions just south of Derva. The old maxim is that bad news travels in threes, and the Volani had run into three separate slave owners who refused to sell in the span of several weeks, within a few day's travel of one another. I've already shared the story of the hunter and the foresters. I myself was with Hanuvar for the second of these problematic situations, and it is not one I shared with my children for some years, for it is among the more distressing of our exploits.

—Sosilos, Book Eleven

Chapter 11:
In a Family Way

I

The sinking sun had drained the world of color. The leaves on the olive trees around the little villa were almost black, and the bright red tiles along its pitched roof had shifted past maroon and darkened to mahogany.

From the wooded hillside Hanuvar watched as the field slaves were called in for their evening meal. For a short time the sounds of cutlery on plates, the low gabble of voices, and an occasional shout filled the air. After that came a crash of breaking crockery, and silence. Only then did he motion three of his people down slope. They entered the building and joined the silence.

Antires crouched beside him, hand pressed to the trunk of an oak. The playwright had left soft beds and warm meals behind when he'd officially turned the management of the harbor to Izivar Lenereva, and he had insisted upon accompanying Hanuvar on this mission into the wooded foothills southwest of Derva.

"I need to actually see your efforts if I'm going to bring them to life on the stage," Antires had told him over a dinner in a private tavern room. He still possessed a young man's craving for adventure, even though he had surely learned by now that any exciting moments lay between long stretches of hard living and incredible boredom, and not uncommonly were marked by horrifying violence. Hanuvar had reminded his friend of this, then pointed out that this particular mission was hardly a standard one.

"But none of them are really standard, are they?" Antires had asked. "Any time you or Carthalo are handling things personally it means you couldn't simply buy or trade your way clear."

And so he'd rejoined Hanuvar, grumbling only a little when their expedition had been caught in the rain on an open road.

Carthalo had sent his oldest two children along, both to assist, and for seasoning. Hanuvar was particularly glad to have Carthalo's daughter Lucena accompany them, in part because she was clever and capable, but also because these particular slaves would likely feel more at ease if at least one of their liberators was female. Four more of Carthalo's long-time operatives rounded out their force and helped manage the two horses and the wagons as well as security on the night watches. Three of them waited a quarter mile out with the animals.

From time to time, faint voices from the villa reached the ridge where Hanuvar and Antires waited. That was all to be expected. Hanuvar was more concerned that the sedative with which the conspirators had laced the food might be discovered, or simply not be heavily enough imbibed by the rest of the household. A slighter danger was that it might be too heavily consumed.

The evening stretched on. The sun in the trees sank further, until the shadow of the oaks merged with the ground in the growing murk. The roof tiles transformed from mahogany to black.

Finally Carthalo's son Horace emerged, his features lost in the twilight, for he was only a darker outline against the grayer villa behind, identifiable only by height and the shape of the curling hair his father had passed on to him. He raised a left hand and waved it three times; the all clear.

Two more followed him out, one tall, one short, then another pair, holding close to one another. A sixth walked with the unmistakable waddle of a woman far into pregnancy. That left only one more, apart from Lucena and sturdy Brutus, one of Carthalo's best operatives, but an additional slender adult emerged, walking with two children holding hands.

"Is one of them Lucena?" Antires asked. "This is more people than we planned for, isn't it?"

"That's not Lucena," Hanuvar said, for he had seen a more confident female figure emerge, followed by wide-shouldered Brutus.

"Who are the extras?" Antires asked.

"We'll find out soon." Hanuvar replied. As Horace drew close Hanuvar stepped to the slope edge, hands extended to assist over the final feet.

Horace anticipated Hanuvar's questions as he came up, saying sheepishly: "The ladies brought a few more. They insisted."

The old maxim held that few plans survived contact with the enemy, and while that was true, in Hanuvar's experience a plan was just as likely to go awry in the hands of allies with motives of their own. In this case the plan had depended in part upon their contacts in the household, and they'd apparently altered his detailed instructions.

The extent of those changes wasn't fully clear until all of them were in the little clearing just beyond the wood edge. Horace introduced them by the light of a lantern unshuttered by Brutus.

First were the two Volani women, slim and pale and very young. Bruises stood out along the arms and shoulders of the older, and from their tight-fitting tunics it was clear that both were a few months along in pregnancy. One of the smaller figures was the third Volani that they'd been aware of, a sad-eyed girl of about eight, who clung tightly to the hands of the other girls.

Then there was a ruddy, sharp-featured Ceori woman with light brown eyes and red-gold hair. She too was bruised, but there was nothing shy in her manner. Her gaze was challenging. Near to her was the woman furthest along in her pregnancy, a darkly tawny beauty of Ruminian extraction, to judge from her coiled black hair. If the Ceori was challenging, the Ruminian's stare showed that she was downright angry. Finally, there was a shapely Hadiran, with thick straight black hair, wide-hipped and deep-bosomed, whose dark-eyed gaze kept shifting between confusion and fear.

Three others were there, including their first unexpected guest, a shy little blond boy. The other person, whom Hanuvar had taken to be a child, proved to be the last of their intended guests and their principal contact, Marcella, a short, buxom woman in her early middle years scarcely as high as Hanuvar's chest.

Most of Marcella's attention was upon the woman standing

defensively behind her. And this refugee was the biggest surprise of all. The rest of the women were garbed in plain white tunics and sandals. This last, also visibly pregnant, wore a finely tailored blue dress. A delicate azure necklace hung about her slender throat, and matching earrings dangled from her ears. Even her sandals were elaborately tooled.

"This," Horace said, "is the lady Helena."

Antires voiced Hanuvar's own astonishment. "You brought the master's wife?"

Little Marcella's head rose swiftly. Her sharp, nervous movements suggested she were a stout bird. "Please, you don't understand. The mistress was just as badly treated as the rest. I had to tell her." Her gaze shifted to Hanuvar. "Please, lord. Take her and the boy with you."

"I'm no lord. You delivered the drug to all of them?"

"Yes, lo . . . yes. They sleep, just as you promised. But the master is away, visiting his father."

"It's all that saved him," the Ruminian said in fluid Dervan. "I would have killed him if I could have." The fire in her dark eyes suggested she spoke the truth. And her words inspired no change of expression in the serious young wife.

Hanuvar sighed inwardly and shifted his attention to Horace and Lucena. "Was there any violence?"

"One of them kicked one of the overseers a few times," Horace reported. "But no deaths. Everyone else in the villa is asleep."

"We moved a few to their sides so they could breathe more easily," Lucena added.

Any deaths during the escape would increase the chances of pursuit. For all that she was new to field operations, Lucena seemed to have a better instinct for thinking on her feet than Horace.

Hanuvar faced Helena. "We can help these slaves. We can give them new homes and new identities. But what can we do for you? Where will you go?"

The wife's voice was tired but fierce. "Anywhere but here. Anywhere without him."

"The master is a terrible man," little Marcella vowed, and the other women agreed in a variety of languages. Only the Hadiran said nothing, but she nodded vigorously.

"And there's another matter, lord—sir." Marcella pressed her hands together and tilted her head sharply. Her fingers intertwined, wrestling out her anxiety. "My husband is away, with the master. If we could wait until they return, and free him too, it would be . . . I would be very grateful."

"I told her we can't do that," Horace told Hanuvar, then turned back to Marcella without waiting for an answer. "None of us like slavery. At all. We'd wipe it from the peninsula if we could. But we can't. We can't save everybody."

Hanuvar stilled him with a hand on the shoulder. By talking too much, he was making it obvious that they were not true members of Dervan society. "We can't wait," he told the women. "I'm sorry."

Marcella's eyes were pleading. "The master will be terrible to him."

"I wish we could help him. But we've limited room, and resources. And time. We must leave now."

Marcella's face sagged with sorrow. She had to have known what the answer would be.

Helena rubbed her maid's shoulder in sympathy, which elevated Hanuvar's opinion of her on the instant.

Antires still looked to Hanuvar, an unasked question in his gaze.

Taking a Dervan patrician's wife was trouble. But then there had been ugly complications all along when it came to freeing Volani women, many of whom were in horrific circumstances, owned by brothels and bathhouses and inns. Again and again Carthalo or his agents had been forced to pay extravagant prices to purchase entire female slave holdings so that no one would get to wondering why so many Volani were being singled out.

But what might they do for a Dervan matron?

"Let's get moving," Hanuvar ordered. With a few quiet words Brutus got the expedition sorted and led them deeper into the woods. Only a short hike would deliver them to the back road where the wagons waited.

Horace trailed, and Hanuvar brought up the rear. After a time he realized Lucena's brother deliberately hung back because he wished to speak privately. The young man said, at last: "I'm sorry about all this. I wasn't sure what to do with them. I didn't think it was wise to leave any behind who wanted to go. They'd have told people what we'd done."

"You did the right thing," Hanuvar assured him.

Horace seemed to take some solace from that but remained apprehensive. "Are we going to be able to find room for them?"

"We'll think of something."

Horace relaxed, apparently pleased that someone else would have to solve the problem. After a time, his mind turned to another concern. "Did you see their bruises?"

"Yes."

"Calchus beat them, him or the overseer. All those women."

Hanuvar didn't feel a response was needed. Horace was just a dull shape in the darkness beneath the trees, but his manner and voice were quiet and wistful. "He had all these pretty young things in his home. All he had to do was be kind to them, and he would have been the luckiest man alive. Living a dream."

"Some men need better dreams," Hanuvar said.

Horace might have been considering that comment for the rest of their hike, for he remained silent.

II

The master had finally stopped shouting, but his face remained mottled with red splotches. Ironically, he had handsome features, with a fine nose and broad cheekbones and a strong chin. But his mouth was often twisted into an ugly sneer, pinched with meanness, or rapaciously open and acquisitive. Calchus seemed capable of few other expressions.

The head overseer abased himself on his knees, pleading that he had beaten the remaining slaves already and assured the master they'd have confessed if they knew where the women had gone.

All the women of the household had fled. Every single one of the master's bed slaves, his wife, the little girl, and then, of course, Florin's own wife, Marcella. The little house boy had wandered away with them as well.

As Florin listened to the recounting of it all that morning he felt at a strange remove. His Marcella had left without him. How could she have done that? And where could those poor women be thinking that they could go?

He listened while the burly overseer, Monto, said he suspected one of the slaves had poisoned the food. Monto repeated again and again that he had questioned everyone, told how he and the others hadn't awakened until the morning, a few hours before the master's return. Some had been hard to rouse.

Calchus' father Plautus waited silently with his two Hadiran bodyguards, grim, hatchet-faced men who spoke only when their master asked questions of them. Plautus was an older replica of his son, virtually identical save for a few streaks of gray in the black hair, some wrinkles, and a mouth permanently drooped into a scowl. And whereas the master had three principal expressions, the father had two; the angry one he wore when at rest, and one of unbridled contempt when facing anyone who displeased him. Plautus' hands were knotted about his twisted oak staff. His eyes roved over the frightened and uncomfortable male slaves gathered in the courtyard. Many bore bruises or gashes, no doubt from the chief overseer's interrogation.

"Where are my women?" the master shouted. "They had to have talked. Women always talk!"

The slaves stared back in abject fear, and shook their heads, quickly.

"Good money was paid for those women," Calchus continued.

Florin wondered why the master mentioned that, because the slaves could hardly be expected to appreciate it, or care.

"My money," Plautus interrupted. "Your shouting's doing no good. We need answers."

Calchus scowled and his blank-eyed gaze searched among the slaves. Finally it shifted to Florin, standing to the right of Plautus' Hadirans. "You," he said.

"Me, master?"

The master advanced so that he stood with his face only inches from Florin's own. "You know something. Your woman had to tell you."

"No, master."

"Liar!" The blow to Florin's face sent him stumbling. He raised a hand to his stinging cheek as the master advanced, motioning the overseer toward him. "Give me your whip!" he shouted, then once it was in hand turned to Florin again. "You had to know!"

"No, master. I would have told you!"

Teeth bared, the master brought the whip down across Florin's shoulder, striking at too close quarters to cause any lasting damage, though the blow still stung.

"Liar! Lower your hands!"

Florin had raised them to protect his face and head. Shaking, he forced them down, and the master lifted the whip.

"Enough!" Plautus cried. "Value a man who speaks the truth."

The master swore silently and lowered the whip. "We will have to contact the slave catchers," he said with a scowl. "I'll be a laughing stock."

"Forget that. Slave catchers will not be gentle enough with the women," Plautus countered, sneering.

"The women deserve whatever manhandling they get."

"Fool. If they're treated too roughly, they could lose the children."

Calchus looked abashed and lowered his head. "Yes, Father. I do want them alive. The punishments I will give them..." His eyes glittered. "But how will we find them without the slave catchers?"

His father must already have been contemplating that, for he answered without hesitation. "If we were in my sanctorum, it would be simpler. But here we must make choices. I will need one of your slaves. The one you will miss least. And I shall need a bit of your blood."

"My blood?" Calchus asked.

"Family blood," the older man said. "You know how it works."

"Yes, Father," the master said dully. Without much reflection he pointed out old Titus, the farm hand. The assistant overseer ordered the rest of the slaves out. Florin briefly hoped he too could leave but it was not to be.

The gray-haired man laboror watched wide-eyed as the Hadirans carried forth one of the battered wooden tables the field hands ate from and sat it in the weedy courtyard. He pleaded only a little when the Hadirans ordered him to the table, then lay face up when Monto cracked his whip. He lay shivering as the Hadirans bound him to the wood, with his hands stretched above his head.

Plautus, meanwhile, contemplated a black prism he'd pulled from his cloak. It seemed ill suited for the daylight, a black turnip-sized hunk of darkness daring the sun to counter its majesty. Plautus made no effort to calm the frightened old man. He seemed scarcely aware of him as he drew squiggles on Titus' forehead with ashes. He looked to the Hadirans and pointed vaguely at the slave's chest.

Titus and Florin gasped as one of the Hadirans whipped up a knife and stepped forward. But when he brought the knife down it was only to rip open Titus' tunic from collar to waist.

While Plautus drew more squiggles on the exposed gray-haired chest, Titus pleaded a last time with his master, watching uncomfortably from the side.

"Please, master. I never gave you no trouble. I always did whatever you asked."

"You were always slow," Calchus said. "Silence, unless you want the whip. You'll disturb my father."

"But what will he do with me, master?"

Calchus' voice rose. "Do you want the whip?"

"No, master," Titus said in a small voice, still trembling.

He fell silent, and in a few more moments Plautus seemed satisfied with the strange spiraling symbols with which he had ornamented the aged farm hand. Only then did he look up from his work. With the same carelessness with which he had signed the Hadirans, he waved his own son forward.

Florin rarely saw the master dismayed, and at any other time he might have enjoyed just how uncomfortable Calchus was to present himself to his father. When the master offered his bare left arm, Florin finally understood the cause of the long line of old scars he'd long since noted. With a sharp, hooked knife, Plautus gouged a new line in his son's flesh below the elbow. Blood flowed freely. It splattered the grass, and the master's sandals, and his father's prism. Against that strange surface the blood did not drip but sank inside almost as though it had been suctioned.

One of the Hadirans tended the injury with brusque care, as though it were a task with which he had long familiarity.

Plautus had already turned away, whispering strange words to the prism while he rubbed the knife against it. He loomed over Titus and lifted the blade.

The old man screamed when Plautus drove the knife into his stomach and kept screaming as Plautus thrust his arm up through the wound and deep inside his body.

Titus didn't stop making noise until a few moments after Plautus pulled free a pulsing, dripping human heart and held it against the prism.

Florin had seen goats sacrificed, but never a man, and he had to gulp down his bile. He traded a look of disgust with Monto that was a brief, and rare, moment of fellow feeling.

The heart stilled and paled and diminished, as though it were an olive left long days in the sun. Plautus too, had changed, for, at long last, he was smiling. He sank to his knees beside the corpse and began to chant into his prism.

III

Their wagons were stopped mid-way through the morning by a half dozen bored horse troops. The leader of the cavalrymen was a grizzled optio with sharp eyes who pulled up beside the first wagon, driven by Antires. The other horsemen eyed the wagon's armed guards with casual care, alert but unconcerned about the visible weapons. On back roads, only foolish merchants travelled without guards.

Hanuvar sat in the back of the covered wagon, amid the barrels of wine and the crates of goods. Larn, the little blond boy, sat across from him, and a portable wooden game board that Brutus had carried lay on the crate between them, populated by blue markers. The optio peered in at them before returning his attention to Antires.

"Where are you headed?" the optio asked.

"Clusia," Antires answered.

"Transporting wine?"

"And leather for sandal making. I always carry some wine samples if you're interested. Nothing fancy, but pleasant enough."

The optio didn't react one way or another to the offered bribe and waited for his junior to return from his onceover of the second wagon. Hanuvar heard him report: "Looks normal enough."

"We appreciate the legion watching out on the roads," Antires said.

"They've got us spread thin these days." The optio made no mention of fugitives or escaped slaves. One of the women hidden in the compartment below the wagon bed moved with a thump but the optio didn't seem to notice. Hanuvar shifted a half breath later to cover.

The optio was more old-fashioned than some, and only accepted two wine skins after Antires insisted he and his men deserved their thanks. The veteran politely raised the skin in salute, then just as politely praised the wine and passed it to his second. The officer waved the wagons on, and both vehicles rumbled forward, followed by their own horse guards. Outside, the cavalrymen gathered to pass the skins around. Inside, the little boy's eyes were round in fear.

"There's nothing to worry about," Hanuvar said with a smile. "They weren't even looking for us. They were just a normal patrol."

The boy seemed uncertain, but the pretty painted board soon captured his attention again and they returned to the game, a rudimentary tactical exercise highly governed by chance.

They stopped only twice before making camp, and each time the women emerged from their cramped hiding places sweaty and uncomfortable. This, Hanuvar thought, was just one more dreadful trial for them.

If they'd cared to travel further into the evening, they'd have reached a nearby village. But a village would mean being seen by a host of fellow travelers, and so they camped off the roadside in a burned-out peasant's cottage with partial walls. The dried horse manure and the ashes in the firepit pointed to its recent use by others for the same purpose.

In only a few days they would arrive at a safe house, and from there the women could be scattered as they wished. But for the next few days, pursuit remained a possibility. Slave catchers had almost surely been alerted. His people remained watchful.

The women stayed mostly to themselves, preferring the company of Lucena to their male escorts, as Hanuvar had thought they might.

He had just finished his evening meal of oat and dried fruit when Lucena walked over from the fire where the women sat and stopped before him. Antires and Horace, seated nearby, looked up.

Lucena's young, fresh face was solemn with responsibility, as though the news she was about to relay was a grave burden. Her look was apologetic, but her tone was certain. "The women are pressing for silphium."

Horace finished chewing and swallowed then bluntly stated the obvious. "That would make them sick for days!"

"Tell them I'm sorry," Hanuvar said. "But they need to wait. We didn't bring near enough for the use they want. And we don't have someone trained to help if something goes wrong, nor can we manage the delays necessary even if all goes well. Have you seen the effects of silphium?"

"No," Lucena admitted.

"They're going to be feverish, and needing to void themselves, probably multiple times as the the drug works through their body. Suppose that would happen while we're being stopped by another patrol."

"It was bad enough when Helena needed us to stop for urination the third time, right after that hay cart passed us," Antires said.

Though with her youth and finer features Lucena little resembled her father, when she frowned the family resemblance grew more obvious. Her attention to detail was similar as well. "What about those who are close to the cutoff point? Helena's worried that even a few more day's delay will be too late."

"The cut off?" Horace asked.

"There's a point where no matter how many silphium leaves you eat, you're stuck with the baby," Lucena explained. "Ontala is past that day. Some of the others are close."

"I wish it didn't have to be this way," Hanuvar said gently. "Once we reach our refuge, we will have the help needed." Their collection of fugitives included several experienced midwives and a world class physician.

"Hold on," Horace said. "Are our women wanting to lose their babies too?"

"Our women?" Lucena asked.

Horace seemed not to have noticed the warning disdain in his sister's voice. "The women from Volanus," he explained.

"The girls? Yes." Lucena's dark eyes flashed challenge.

Horace, being young, either missed it or ignored it. "We can't let them do that," he said to Hanuvar. "Those are Volani children."

"It's not your business," Antires said coolly.

"Well, is it yours?" Horace returned heat. "These are Volani." He faced Hanuvar. "Isn't that what we're risking our lives for, every day? To save Volani lives?"

"This isn't our concern because we aren't the ones to live with the consequences." Hanuvar thought the note of finality in his voice would discourage Horace from further inquiry, but the young man insisted on pressing ahead.

"I know their father is Dervan, but their mothers are Volani. Are they worthless because they're only half Volani?"

"It's nothing to do with that! You would make the women bear these children, against their will?" Lucena seethed with fury. "You, who speak so passionately against slavery? Will you keep them in manacles until it is time to deliver?"

Horace didn't have an answer to that. He could not meet her eyes.

Hanuvar returned his attention to Lucena. "Explain to them that for their safety, and ours, we have to wait. It will only be a few more days. You could tell them I sympathize but it may not mean much."

"It may not," Lucena agreed. "But they want to talk with you."

"Why?"

She looked astonished at him. "To thank you."

"Have you told them who he is?" Antires asked.

"Of course not! They've heard rumors that Hanuvar wanders the countryside killing wicked Dervans, though, and some of them think you might be him."

Antires grinned as Hanuvar groaned. "With a lyre and a garland in his hair," he suggested.

"Very well," Hanuvar said wearily.

Lucena nodded politely, fixing Horace with a pointed look before moving off.

"Why's she so angry?" Horace asked quietly.

"If you haven't figured that out," Antires said, "you might need to reflect a little longer."

"Why don't you leave me to speak with the women?" Hanuvar suggested to Horace. "They seem nervous around most of us."

"They do," the young man agreed, then nodded his chin at Antires. "Is he staying?"

"I've been trying to get rid of this Herrene for almost a year now. But he keeps coming back."

"It seems a shame to throw me away now," Antires added.

Horace looked confused by the answer but noting the return of Lucena with some of her charges, he wandered over by Brutus on the north side of camp.

Lucena arrived with the two Volani women and their even

younger companion—Meravar, Callena, and Sanava. Even with their noticeable pregnancy bumps the two older ones looked incredibly young, likely no more than fifteen. Their eyes were wide as they bowed formally to Hanuvar and Antires, sitting along the edge of the broken wall. They stammered out a broken, accented thanks. The youngest was more certain in her speech, but also more wooden in delivery. Her gaze was wary.

But then she had been subjected to terrible brutality.

"You are welcome," Hanuvar replied in Volani. The young women perked up at this, and even the girl eyed him with greater interest.

"Where were you born?" he asked them in their language.

They told him that they had lived in the Talon, a claw shaped promontory north of Volanus' central harbor. One of them had been a perfume maker's daughter, the other a carpenter's. Despite their similar features, they were cousins, not sisters. The smallest one had been an officer's daughter who had sometimes gone with her mother to the perfume shop and had recognized one of the young women in the slave pens and immediately latched onto her.

"The Talon was lovely in the mornings," Hanuvar said. "And all along the quay you could clearly hear the songs from the island temples."

At this, Meravar sang quietly, haltingly, and then her cousin joined. Their confidence grew with the paired sound. Both had pleasant voices, but Meravar's was truly beautiful, clear and sure. It was a happy song she sang, of the sun's rising and its gleam upon the ocean, and the departure of the morning fleet on their hunt for fish, but their features were haunted by memory of the harbor and ships that were no more. The little girl began to cry without making a sound.

Beside Hanuvar, Antires wiped tears from his cheeks. Hanuvar nodded slowly in appreciation, then praised their singing. "You will be free to sing as you wish," he promised. "You need fear no longer."

The young women hugged him then, but the smallest looked as though she would believe in freedom only when she saw it personally. The three departed, and then Lucena presented the Hadiran, Calakanel. She possessed a lost doelike quality that diminished her otherwise striking features.

Hanuvar's Hadiran was as rudimentary as Calakanel's Dervan, but they managed to exchange greetings. He had the sense she still didn't fully understand what was going on but was happy to be away from Calchus. He lamented no one on this expedition could communicate with her but assured her he had friends he'd introduce later that spoke her language well. She at least understood that she was safe and that things looked better for her future.

Next came the Ceori woman, who Lucena introduced as Maeve. On release last night she had worn her hair pulled back from her forehead, like a Dervan. Tonight it cascaded loosely about her face. She was pale and fierce, sharp and beautiful as a well-made sword.

"I thank you," she said to him in accented Dervan. To save him from Antires' questioning later he responded in kind, rather than speaking Cemoni, for he recognized her region of the Ceori lands from her accent.

"It is said that you are a father of battles," Maeve continued, and Hanuvar did not reveal the inner wince. It appeared that this woman at least was confident in his identity. "I wish you had taken the battle to the master." She spat to her left after she said his title.

"If we had killed your former master, the pursuit would have been more vigorous and certain."

"He deserves death. I am the daughter and granddaughter of chiefs. I would have given it to him."

"I'm sure you would have."

The woman rested a hand upon the slight protrusion of her belly, and she saw the direction of his gaze. "I will raise my child as a Ceori and teach him to hate the Dervans."

"You don't have to keep the baby," Hanuvar told her.

Her eyes burned. "The child is mine," she declared with the hint of a snarl.

"The child is yours," he agreed.

She wanted to know if it was true they would be freed with Dervan papers, and he assured her they would be. Maeve accepted the largesse with a grave nod, thanked him once more, and departed.

The Ruminian passed her as she walked forward, and Lucena said her name was Ontala. Her gaze was as fierce as the Ceori's, though their looks were otherwise different, her eyes dark and long-lashed, her body full and rounded with at least six months of pregnancy.

She shook her head at the Ceori's retreating back and said to Hanuvar, though not without affection, that Maeve was a fool. "A child from such a man will be a monster. Calchus is a monster, and so is his father. If I had the means, I would rid myself of this one."

"Some say it's blood that makes a child, and others how the child is raised," Antires said.

"So says the philosopher," Ontala said, and looked to Hanuvar. "What do you say?"

There was the shine of bright intelligence in her dark eyes. Hanuvar gave her the complex answer she deserved. "I have no great experience with such matters but suspect both can be true. Do not judge your child harshly."

Her full lips pursed at his words. "Something grows in me I do not want. My aunt died when her child came. My grandmother was never right again after her third child." She rested her hand on her belly. "You men think it is easy."

He shook his head gently. "My wife died giving birth to a son who lived only a few hours. I loved her, and I would have loved him." He felt Lucena's eyes upon him as he continued. "I do not wish this upon you. But since you cannot change it, I wish you peace."

She seemed to weigh his words for falsehoods. "And what will you do for me, and the child? The others say you will set us free. Why?"

"Because I swore an oath. I would tell you more, but if I'm to help others, my reasons must remain my own. Do you understand?"

"Not fully, but I respect an oath. Where will you take us?"

"First, to safe houses. But then we can arrange transport wherever you wish to go."

"You're a strange man," she said, "if all that you promise is true. Are you a mystic, or religious man?"

"No."

"All the stranger," she said. "Well, then, mystery man, I shall wait to see what happens. If you speak the truth, my blessings will follow you forever after."

"I could stand a few more blessings," he said truthfully.

She left him.

"I didn't know that about your wife and child," Lucena said softly. "I'm sorry. I should have realized what you said that day we met was true. About your family."

"You're kind," Hanuvar said, and was glad that the tone in his voice discouraged further comments.

Finally Helena arrived before him. The other women had looked fresher despite their long, uncomfortable day, as though even this restrictive freedom in hiding invigorated them. Helena looked more mussed and less settled, although the swelling along the side of her face had gone down. She had removed her jewelry. Mud stained one sleeve of her stola.

She thanked Hanuvar politely then got right to the question that must have been burning at her. "Why are you helping all of us? Oh, I know what the others say. But they're just foolish slaves. I know you're not Hanuvar. And I know you're not doing this out of kindness. There's profit in so many healthy young women. I just hope you'll be kind to the boy and Marcella."

Antires bristled. "Haven't we been kind to you?"

Hanuvar stayed him with a lifted hand.

"You've been pleasant enough, but let's be honest. You'll clean us up and have us at a bordello. Possibly a high class one. I'm sure our lives will be better there," she added.

Lucena gasped.

"What makes you say that?" Antires asked.

Her face clouded. "Any place would be better than where we were."

"So you've said," Hanuvar responded. "Where do you want to be?"

"I've no home left. My father might as well have sold me to Calchus. Mother and her sister have been dead for years."

"So you've no close family. What about friends or relatives in provinces?"

"Why do you ask?"

"Because it's hard to know how to help you. These others are simpler. They'll be able to fend for themselves. But you're a patrician."

"And you're not sure if you can trust me," Helena added. "Because you're afraid I could tell people about your group. Don't worry. I'd never tell. Just so long as you can get me away from Calchus. I'd even work at a whore house. At least then I'd be getting paid for sex, and I could save the money for something better."

She apparently had a misconception about how most whorehouses operated.

"I don't believe most women working there are well treated," Antires said.

Worry furrowed her brow. "But yours will, won't it? You don't seem to be evil men."

"I swear to you that I am not taking you to a brothel, of any quality," Hanuvar said.

"We wouldn't do that," Lucena assured her.

Helena looked doubtful, so Hanuvar raised his hand and swore an oath by his ancestors that he was not selling them off. The woman looked confused but thanked him and bade him a good night. Lucena followed her, mouthing additional assurances.

"I'm still not sure she believes you," Antires said quietly.

"Can you blame her? If I told her why we we're doing this she might understand better."

"But you can't," Antires said. "What are you going to do with her?"

He'd been wondering that himself. "I'm just not sure. I don't think she'd give us away on purpose, but she might let something slip someday. Or decide like Maeve that I am Hanuvar."

"It doesn't help that you talked about Volanus with the young ones. Was that a good idea?"

"It was a good idea for them."

"Fair enough. But what about Helena? It would take a great deal of money to set her up with a small household, and that would require the purchase of slaves as she likely can't do much for herself. We've no spare money and I know you won't buy any slaves unless it's to free them."

"You're right. I'm thinking about putting her on one of the ships."

His brows rose precipitously. "You're going to put a Dervan on one of the ships to New Volanus?"

"I've done it before," he reminded him.

"If you're talking about the gladiator, and those others, they were former or current slaves. They weren't patricians."

"It's not her fault she was born in Derva any more than it's her fault she was born into a family that married her off to that terrible man."

"You can't expect your people to welcome her, though."

"And why not? They're no strangers to suffering. She's suffered. It's not as though she was remotely involved in the decisions that led to war."

Antires shook his head. "You're so used to looking further than other men you sometimes forget most can barely see past their feet."

"Basic empathy shouldn't be such a hard ask."

"Yet you know that it is."

He was right, and Hanuvar sighed. "And that may be our greatest failing of all. Not as Volani, or Herrenes, but as humans."

"Now who's being philosophical?"

"Did I accuse you of being philosophical?"

"Not today."

A chorus of female voices lifted in overlapping screams.

Hanuvar leapt to investigate. His sentinels had responded too but he shouted to hold their posts and went forward only with Antires.

Lucena lay on her back near the second campfire, struggling dazedly to rise. Maeve stood protectively over her, a knife in one hand. Perhaps it was Lucena's. The other women had gathered behind Ontala, who held a burning brand.

They faced a man's shape of dripping darkness. It thrust one clublike limb toward Maeve, who struck it skillfully and sent drops of shadows spraying like blood. The thing withdrew its arm and slid to the left.

"What is that?" Antires' voice rose in consternation.

"Shadow magic." Hanuvar grabbed an unlit lantern that stood near Lucena. "Grab something on fire and circle it so it's surrounded by light! Quickly!"

He stepped to the right, snatched up tinder, stuck it into the campfire, then used it to set the lantern blazing. He shone it at the creature, which quickly shifted backward. Ontala shouted for the other women to go. Helena, Marcella, and Calakanel hurried off with the boy, but the others snatched up burning wood. Lucena staggered upright, still dizzily shaking her head, and Antires helped her get clear.

The shadow man slid to the right, after the women, until Hanuvar directed the lantern beam toward it. The thing flowed to the other side, raising the same limb. While the majority of its form shifted like fog inside its confines, the one arm remained solid. It sidled back and forth between the threat of light from Hanuvar and the fire, and the flaming brands waved by the five remaining women and girls. From its movements it looked to Hanuvar as though it was tempted to slide all the way along the axis to its right, through a little gap and on toward the trees, but Horace raced to block it, opening the shutters of his lantern directly in its path.

The thing careened toward the women and girls, no matter the flames at the end of their tinder. Maeve brandished the knife and Antires returned to chuck a burning log at it, halting its progress. Hit then from the direct light of the two lanterns it shrank in upon itself until it was a black ball of darkness no larger than a gourd lying on the ground. Bits of shadow bubbled off it as though it were submerged in boiling water.

"Steady now," Hanuvar ordered.

As he spoke another woman screamed from behind. Hanuvar heard a male shout, and other cries of alarm. He distinctly heard Marcella yell, "Let her go!"

He couldn't give any of that his full attention until they'd finished burning down what he now knew for a distraction. The little ball of blackness steamed away into nothing over a dozen heartbeats. Then it was gone. Antires was at his side as he hurried toward the second combat. And as usual the Herrene had questions. "Was that like the shadow monster the revenant made?"

"A little," Hanuvar said shortly. He didn't add that the Dervans had employed shadow magic against his men in the second war, and that Harnil had ruthlessly stamped out the practitioners and their acolytes. Until his encounter with the revenant sorcerer, he'd thought the practice lost, for it had never been used against his people again.

One of Carthalo's men bled from a deep slash across his shoulder. Hanuvar snapped his fingers and set another to tend him. Brutus pointed toward the tree line west of the camp. There Hanuvar heard the unmistakable sound of crashing brush through the dark woods. Something out there moved heavily through the foliage.

Marcella was looking up at him, her face bleeding from two parallel gashes that stretched from forehead to cheek. "It took the mistress!" She pointed. "Just took her up in its arms!"

"What swept her up?" Hanuvar demanded of Brutus.

For once the big man proved garrulous. "It looked like it was built of bloody feathers. It was about the size of a man, but with wide shoulders, and huge arms with claws. And . . . it didn't have a head. I swear. Nothing. It was the ugliest damned thing I've ever seen."

"How about that?" Antires asked. "You deal with anything like *that* before?"

"No. Marcella, is this your former master's doing? Is he a sorcerer?"

"No, sir. It must be his father."

Ontala and Maeve came up beside them. The Nuvaran had dropped her brand, but her companion now clutched a sword, possibly Lucena's as well.

"He bragged sometimes that his father had powers," Ontala offered. She blinked long lashes in disdain. "But he bragged about all kinds of things."

"What did he say about his father?" Hanuvar asked. "Did he talk about the kind of his magic? Was he part of a group? Was he a revenant?"

"He'd surely have threatened us if that were so," Ontala answered. "No. His father lived alone. He didn't even like his son to visit him."

Marcella bobbed her head. "It's true. My husband told me of the master's father's home. It is an old, crumbling place with only a few servants. He was always too busy to speak to his son, unless he was shouting at him. But he gave him lots of money."

"We need to get your face tended. Once you've relaxed that's going to hurt."

"Is it bad?" Marcella asked, raising a hand to her cheek. She blinked at the sight of blood on the fingertips she pulled away.

"I think it's likely to leave a mark."

"What about my mistress?" Marcella asked.

"I'll deal with that."

"I can tend Marcella," Brutus said.

"See to it." Hanuvar called the rest of them together and saw that no one else was missing. Lucena still looked shaken. "Antires can come but I want two more volunteers."

He settled on Horace and Maeve as he needed Carthalo's agents to protect the rest. "Brutus, you're in charge. If we're not back by midmorning, get everyone on to the safe house."

"I want to go," Ontala said.

"I will slay him for us all," Maeve promised.

"That will have to be good enough," Hanuvar said.

Ontala scowled but embraced Maeve fiercely.

They grabbed a few waterskins, and Antires rigged a lantern at the end of a short pole. They then headed into the woods in the wake of the headless feathered monster.

IV

Monto's snores were gentle as those of a sleeping baby, and Florin wondered how such a vicious man slept so comfortably. He supposed it was due to his removal from responsibility. The man's entire moral compass was given over to following orders.

The master tossed and turned while he dreamed, sometimes raising his voice, though the words were incoherent.

Florin himself couldn't sleep.

When he'd been very young, he'd been the child of simple farm laborers, but his first master, a kindly man, had recognized his intelligence and brought him into the household, where he'd been given duties that were more socially than physically demanding. Then, at the man's sudden death two years ago, his cousins had sold off his slaves, and Florin had found himself a personal assistant to Calchus. It hadn't been long before he'd wished that his first master had not been so kind. For the first few months, Calchus had spent most of his time in a small house in Vorsini, or, more properly, the nearby brothel. But then the rich young man's father had gifted him with a bevy of slave girls as well as a young wife and a country villa. As a farmhand Florin might have had a harder life, but a farmhand would not be witness to the cruelties, both physical and mental, constantly on display inside the master's home.

Marcella told him that each slave woman kept the master occupied as long as possible whenever they were selected for his company, so that their fellow sufferers would have as long a break as possible from his attentions. Marcella. His heart ached at the thought of her. What would the master do to her once he caught her? And what could have possessed her to go along with this scheme? The master hadn't been especially mean to her, since she was beneath his notice. Short, round, and loquacious, the master had thought it the height of amusement to house her with Florin, tall, slim, and quiet—he dark skinned, she light. But they had found that after long stressful days, holding one another was a healing balm in their meager lives. They would lie entwined, listening to the sobs or stifled screams rising from other parts of the house and praise the gods for the whim that had brought them together.

Now . . . now she was probably doomed. They would catch her. The master would likely torture the women he slept with. When done he would have no more use for Marcella than he'd had for poor Titus.

Florin turned his attention to the slump-shouldered figure seated by the fireside. Plautus still stared into the black prism, endlessly whispering to it like a demented lover. The light flickered ruddily along the side of his face, casting him in outline and painting him with wavering red and gold lines. The ebon crystal took no reflection and stood out only in its resistance to light.

The old man had grown older. Yesterday his hair had been black, with a few gray lines; now the conditions were reversed. So there was a price for working evil magics. That was some consolation.

Dawn's light birthed in the surrounding trees. Florin gulped and rose, casting an eye toward the master, still tossing. Monto yet slept.

But Plautus' Hadiran bodyguards were up. One or the other had been awake all night long, and they watched Florin as he wandered to the camp edge to relieve himself. Theirs was the gaze of hunting dogs trained not to kill the master's livestock.

Florin returned to the camp to wash his hands, then, quietly as possible, readied the breakfast skillet and dug through their packs for supplies. He deliberately stayed on the far side of the fire from Plautus, which brought him into direct proximity to the Hadirans. The thicker of the two obligingly threw in some extra tinder, which was far more solicitous than Florin would have anticipated. He'd assumed the guards typical of the kind who thought themselves above other slaves, owing to their master's own superiority. The Hadiran even managed to be gracious about his assistance, gesturing politely to the fire. Florin offered a nod of thanks.

There wasn't warmth in that severe, emotionless face, but perhaps the fellow was not the unfeeling monster Florin had assumed. While he began to steam some water for the porridge, he quietly asked a question of the watching Hadiran. "What is it your master's doing?"

"He keeps the beast in his heart." The man's accent was strong.

"I don't understand," Florin said after a moment.

"He works the magic through his mind, and his heart. But it is dangerous to have it in your heart for so long, so he has to give of other hearts, first. The more like his own, the better."

Florin mulled that over as he added in the oat flakes and tossed in a few golden raisins. "Is that why he wants the women so much? Because the pregnant ones have two hearts?"

The Hadirans exchanged a laugh.

"No," the nearer one said. "A mage must spill his own blood to work the great spells. The ones that affect him. But how can you spill enough of your own blood, and live?"

"The babies," Florin said slowly. The abhorrence he experienced did not seem shared by the Hadirans, whose expressions had settled once more into unemotive masks. It was all clear to him now. Plautus had only twice visited the home after the women had arrived, and each time had asked if any of them were pregnant. Then, just the other day, he had mentioned wanting to see how their pregnancies were coming along.

To think that Florin had imagined some kind of grandfatherly interest from the fellow. He shivered. Plautus' had been the curiosity of the owner of a plot of fruit trees checking to see if the produce was ready for harvest.

Florin had just decided the porridge looked thick enough when the footsteps crashed through the forest.

Though there was no trail from that direction, Florin heard no break in the steady stride. Just the sound of branches yielding to a crack, the crushing noise of sticks and old leaves, and, oddly enough, an occasional feminine moan of terror.

Fear advanced before the sounds, much like a perfumed messenger before a wealthy man and his entourage. The morning birds didn't just quit their songs, they fled the nearby treetops. Squirrels who'd been silent chattered alarm and dashed away through the upper branches, the leaves shaking in their wake.

And Florin's heart fluttered.

The overseer and the master woke and sat up blinking with worried eyes. The implacable Hadirans rose and stared alertly toward the oncoming sounds.

Almost too late Florin wrapped a cloth about the skillet handle and pulled it free of the fire. In the master's current state, burning breakfast might get Florin killed. Or worse.

When the headless feathered thing stamped out of the darkness of the forest Florin was drizzling honey into the porridge from a shaking hand. Probably too much honey, but he could not look away from the thing. He could barely think.

It moved almost like a man, but its strides were too long. Wet feathers red as blood sheathed it. It reeked like a dead animal left too long in the sun. And it had no head. Its unnaturally long arms ended in clawed hands. Currently it cradled a female bundle with fear-maddened eyes. As the monster came to a stop before Plautus, only now rising with his black prism, Florin realized it bore the master's wife.

Plautus breathed heavily; the creature breathed not at all. Its body came to a complete stop, as though it were a statue erected to the god of primal horror. Helena whimpered and tried to pull away, but she was held too tightly.

"You found her!" Calchus cried and stepped to his father's side before laughing at his wife. "What do you think of that, you bitch? Did you think you could escape us? You just wait and see what I have in store for you!"

"Silence," Plautus commanded, then whispered words into the prism. The thing knelt, setting the woman upon the ground. At more quiet commands it stood and stepped back, then was motionless once more.

"Father, where are the other women?" Calchus asked.

Still brandishing the prism, Plautus faced his guards. "Bind the girl to a tree. She must be secure."

Helena stirred as the Hadirans hoisted her up but her struggles were ineffectual.

"Are you going to send it back after the others?" Calchus asked. "Father? Do you—"

"Silence," Plautus' voice was icy and Calchus fell quiet. As uncomfortable as the atmosphere remained, Florin felt some small pleasure in seeing his master put in so servile a position.

The old man fixed his son with a baleful stare. "The women have warriors with them. I had planned to have one spell hold them while the other creature chased the women my way, but the warriors broke my magic."

"But you can still catch them?"

"Yes. I feel the call of their blood. But it took more power than you know to summon creatures to our world, and then to have my spell fail. I need to spend more blood. Much blood. And it must be of my line."

Calchus gulped and looked down at his arm; Florin looked over to where the men tied Helena's hands. Her eyes wandered over toward her husband and stared with bleak coldness.

Finally Calchus seemed to register his father's meaning. "You're going to kill her?"

"I need the child's blood," he said. "And I can't very well wait for her to give birth, can I?"

"But she's carrying my child."

Most of Calchus' slave women were carrying his child, but like many Dervans, he didn't care about those who weren't from Dervan bloodlines. Many masters sold off their slave-born progeny for a profit, and Florin had originally assumed his would do the same.

Plautus' voice had grown grating. "I need the blood. We'll find another wife."

Calchus stomped over toward Helena as the Hadirans led her stumbling toward a nearby tree.

Monto followed, a confused expression on his homely face.

Calchus directed his anger at the woman as the Hadirans pushed her next to the straight trunk of a tall pine. With great care, watching his every footfall, Plautus followed, hand still holding his eerie black prism. His right hand slipped to his waist and he drew the hooked blade he'd slain Titus with, laying it against the black crystal.

"None of this would be happening if you'd been true to me," Calchus snarled to his wife. He stomped up to her and shook a finger in her face as the Hadirans raised her bound hands.

She kicked out, cursing, and caught Calchus either in the genitals or near them.

He yipped and stumbled backward, hands shielding his privates, and bumped into his father.

The blade spun out of Plautus' hand. He floundered for balance and scrambled to hold the prism. The thing seemed to take on a life of its own, falling from one hand to the next as he fought to keep it from striking the earth. His eyes were wide in alarm.

"Master!" the burly Hadiran cried, and both dashed to help.

Helena was suddenly free of their attention. Too late Monto started for her; she darted past Florin and snatched the blade dropped near her feet. Her wrists were bound, but the blade was sharp, and she pointed it toward the overseer.

Plautus, on one knee now, had finally steadied the prism. He eyed it as though it were a lion, ready to eat him.

The Hadirans looked over at the feathered thing at the camp's edge.

"Don't just stand there," Calchus said to the overseer. "Take the knife from her."

"It's a sharp knife, master."

"Use your whip, idiot!"

Monto unlimbered the whip. "Now lay down that knife, mistress," he said. "I don't want to have to use this on you."

Her eyes shifted to Florin. He'd never seen so despairing a look, though he had seen Titus' eyes only a day before. This was different. He had been helpless. She found strength, and not just in the sadness in Florin's eyes. She turned the blade upon herself and drove the blade into her stomach, deeply.

Plautus screamed for her to stop.

She gasped, and shook, then, as the overseer advanced, she stabbed herself again and again, and again, until the blade and her hands and her dress ran with blood. She sank to the ground.

Calchus swore at her as he ran up. Weakly, she dropped the knife. Weakly she laughed and cursed him.

Plautus hurried to stand over. To Monto he said: "Cut her open."

"Master?" The overseer turned to Calchus.

"Surely the child is dead," Calchus said to his father.

"Its blood is still rich with life if we cut quickly! Move, man!"

Monto looked down at the knife as though it were a serpent.

Florin didn't see the moment the prism was struck, but he heard the clink and saw a small metal blade soaring off to the left. Plautus had yanked back his bleeding hand, and the prism plummeted. When it hit the ground something inside audibly shattered.

The feathered thing heaved into motion, arms outstretched, and gathered speed toward Plautus, who shouted in panic.

The Hadirans drew their curved blades and interposed themselves.

And from Florin's left a figure burst from the undergrowth. He didn't recognize Maeve at first, for her hair hung wild and she'd painted her cheeks with muddy lines.

She shouted something in her own language, and then Monto drew his blade and blocked her progress, lifting his whip in his other hand.

The monster shredded the Hadirans with its terrible claws, leaving them twitching and moaning and dying, and had advanced as far as Plautus when he shouted, bloody fingers raised. He sketched symbols in the air.

The beast turned then, seemingly under the old man's control and just in time, for three men had emerged from the undergrowth, a Dervan youth, a Herrene, and a muscular man in early middle age. The last one sent a javelin hurtling toward Plautus. The red beast intercepted the weapon with its body. The javelin drove all the way through, the point sticking through its back.

If the thing felt the injury, it showed no sign, for it rushed ahead as Plautus shouted in his sorcerous language. His hair had turned completely white now.

The javelin thrower ordered the others to split up.

The monster honed in on the man in charge and swiped, but he'd put a tree bole between him and its attack. The tree vibrated under its assault. The leader called for the others to move against the sorcerer, but the youth instead swung his sword at the beast and took a clawed swipe to the shoulder. He was hurtled backward with a splatter of blood.

The creature then advanced against the older man, and Florin could pay that battle no further mind because of the one going on nearer him. Monto lashed once with the whip, catching Maeve in the thigh.

She gasped, then hissed at him. "You're first." She limped to the right. Monto followed. He failed to note Florin, who rose with the skillet. Maeve saw him and taunted Monto.

The overseer didn't hear Florin coming behind until he was only a few feet away. Monto whirled, raising a small blade in his off hand.

Florin had meant to catch him in the head. He struck Monto's meaty arm with the skillet instead. The overseer's skin sizzled, and the stench of cooking human flesh filled the air with his scream. Oatmeal sprayed widely.

Maeve dashed in and cut halfway through Monto's whip hand. Her second blow tore through his chest. The overseer dropped, dead or dying.

Her features now painted by a vivid splash of blood and eagerness, Maeve turned to the master.

Calchus backed toward his father. Plautus had called back his beast because he'd noted the Herrene advancing upon him. He continued to mutter strange words under his breath.

And that was Plautus' undoing, for the leader dashed on its heels and into the clearing. In one smooth move he flung a knife the short distance to its target.

Plautus turned in time to receive the blade in his cheek. His chanting halted, and all that came from his throat was a rattle. He sagged.

The beast dove at his summoner and tore Plautus into bloody shreds.

Calchus screamed and ran headlong into the woods.

The leader paused briefly to take in the scene. Plautus lay dead; the feathered thing was disintegrating in a rain of red feathers that fell across the body. Florin stared in horrified wonder.

Maeve sprinted after the master. A moment later, Florin followed. He'd never thought himself a bloodthirsty man, but he found himself hoping he'd arrive in time to see Calchus die.

The leader of the strangers caught up and passed him. Ahead, a startled Calchus cried out. When Florin came up, he spotted him lying prone at the bottom of a muddy hill. Maeve was climbing gingerly down the muddy slope to reach him. The leader descended via tree roots that separated the dirt almost like stair steps, and Florin followed on his heels.

By the time the stranger reached the master, Calchus had lurched to his feet. His rich tunic was slathered in mud, and so was his face, and the front of his legs.

The leader waited with bared sword.

The master caught sight of Florin, who halted on the stranger's left. "Help me, Florin," he said. "Help your master. This man means to kill me."

Florin shook his head.

"I don't intend to kill you," the stranger said. But he did not lower his sword.

"I'll reward you handsomely." Calchus' voice shook in relief. "Anything in my power. You want the rest of the women? You can have them. I'll just buy some more."

"No," the stranger said, "I don't think you'll be doing that."

Maeve arrived at last. She panted slightly, but she smiled widely. She raised her sword.

"Are you going to let her kill me?" Calchus demanded.

The stranger nodded. "Yes."

Maeve moved forward, every step an oath. "This is for your wife. And for Ontala, and me, and all the rest of us."

Calchus' voice rose in desperation. "I can set you free! I can give you money—"

"There's not enough gold in all the world," Maeve mouthed, but not to him.

The master's scream rose even before the first blow hit. It reached a crescendo on the second as he desperately threw up his hands to block her swings. He was still whimpering a little on the fourth. By then, the stranger had turned away. Maeve kept hacking at Calchus long after he'd stopped moving. Florin watched it all.

After a while she sat down on a fallen tree, and Florin brought her some water.

Once they returned to the hilltop, he learned that the youth had been wearing leather armor that had kept his wound from being mortal, though the cut along his upper chest was deep. The leader said he'd probably be feverish soon and that they needed to get back to the camp.

Florin wondered if maybe they should bury the mistress, but the leader of the men said they didn't have time for that. He allowed Maeve to say a few words over her in Ceori.

Maeve looked tired now, but said she was up for the walk back, no matter that the Herrene complained it was going to be a long one.

"You need to get back and tell the others we've been delayed, but that all is well," the leader told the Herrene. "And you'd best move fast."

The man sighed something about always getting the best jobs, then hurried off.

"Is Marcella well?" Florin asked. "She's with you, isn't she?"

"She's well enough," the leader said. "And she's been worried about you from the start. You're Florin, aren't you?"

"Yes, master."

The man shook his head. "I'm not your master."

"Who are you then? Why are you doing this?"

"That's a good question. I pressed hard, thinking we could save Helena. But it turns out we came to rescue you. Marcella will be very happy to have you back."

Florin helped the leader drag the bodies into a clearing, along with all the equipment he had no interest in, which included Plautus' powders, tools, and scrolls. Likely they were rare and expensive, but the leader packed branches and leaves and kindling around them at least as carefully as he did the corpses, then set everything aflame. Once certain the fire was fully established, they watched for a while downwind to verify that the bodies were being consumed, then retreated. Florin followed the others into the cool, soothing safety of the woods, and the promise of the company of the woman he loved.

With the assistance of midwives, both Ontala and Maeve gave birth to their children, but I regret to report Maeve did not survive. Ontala suffered no more than is normal for women giving birth, but the death of her friend grieved her terribly, and she vowed she would raise her friend's baby boy as an enemy of Dervans, pledging she would do the same with her newborn daughter. What the character of their children proved to be I cannot say, for Ontala left our company to return to Ruminian lands.

The rest of the women successfully terminated their pregnancies, with no lingering ill effects, so far as I am aware. Calakanel, the Hadiran woman, left with Florin and Marcella and Larn, the little boy, and opened a bakery in the very south of Utria. As for those three young Volani, I like to think that they found fine homes and healed their deep hurts in New Volanus, but I cannot say with any certainty.[14]

---

[14] I was able to speak with the youngest of these women, who had grown to be a leading statesperson in New Volanus. Her name was Sanava, and she remained close with the other two, whom she described as her sisters. Even though she knew I worked to clarify the story of Hanuvar's war of liberation, she preferred not to discuss her experiences while in Dervan captivity. I found her austere and dignified and faintly sad, though I do not mean to suggest that she was incapable of humor. She spoke eloquently about the great gift Hanuvar had given to her and so many of her people.

—*Silenus, Commentaries*

Long before their safe passage, though, we travelled to join Carthalo, who had been overseeing a difficult assignment of his own. His had been resolved with far less turmoil than ours, until the final moment, which drove him out into the road to intercept us before we were caught in the same trap that had nearly snared him. For, as it turned out, there was a traitor in our midst.

—Sosilos, Book Twelve

Chapter 12:
The Man at His Back

I

They had almost reached the village that evening when two cloaked figures rode out of the dusk.

Hanuvar, on horse a few hundred feet ahead of the wagons, stopped on the woodland roadside and watched the oncoming horsemen. The rider in the vanguard flashed the correct hand signs, but Hanuvar didn't relax until he recognized Carthalo. That evening the spy master wore simple traveling clothes and a light hooded cape. His face was stubbled with a day's growth of gray-black beard.

Once they'd exchanged greetings, Carthalo wasted no time getting to the bad news. "Our way station has been compromised. Dervan slave catchers rounded up most of our people and marched them out."

Hanuvar's hands tightened on the reins. "How far ahead are they?"

"They came in the middle morning."

"How many slavers?"

"Six."

"How many of our people did they get?"

"The three slaves I freed from Taron. And Farnus. He managed to get the rest out a hidden back way while stalling. If Corven and I hadn't been out scouting for you, they might have snapped us up as well."

385

This was terrible news, and not just because lives were in danger. "How much does Farnus know about the network?"

There was the crucial question, and Carthalo's own worry for it showed in his face. "Up until now the Dervans didn't even know we *had* a network. I don't think he'll talk easily. But when he does our days are numbered."

Hanuvar looked back to the two wagons. Disguised as simple merchant transports and filled with goods, between them they housed nine escaped slaves, three of them Volani. He had planned to have them rest a few days at a small farm just beyond the village before they were separated into alternate, and more comfortable, traveling accommodations. "Where can my people be sent?"

"They'll have to head for the coastal road. Two days, then travel by boat to Ostra and thence to Selanto. It'll cost more."

"What do your sources say about the slave catchers?"

"Local gossip doesn't know anything about Volani emancipation. So far they assume our people were either escapees or headed for illegal slave markets. I think the Dervans lucked into this."

"Luck," Hanuvar said, wishing his people had more of it. "All right. One of ours is healing from a nasty facial injury and is feverish. The majority of those we freed are pregnant, of course—a couple pretty far along. Your son and Antony were wounded. Antony's feeling better, and Horace is over the worst of it, but he's going to be sore for a while." He bowed his head, calculating quickly. "We can leave Lucena in charge of the wagons. We'll take Brutus and Antires. Five of us against six slave catchers. If we strike at night, we ought to have it simple. How far ahead of us are they?"

"The slavers spent so much time searching the farm for additional hiding places they didn't get out until midafternoon. So, they're probably camping by now. They shouldn't reach Vorsini until tomorrow evening."

"Then we'd best get moving."

"Right."

While Carthalo checked with his staff and children, Hanuvar asked Antires if he wanted to come along and the playwright answered with an exasperated look that meant it was absurd to ask.

Hanuvar then bade a farewell to the people he had helped rescue, regretfully passing along the news that they'd have to camp out again tonight. After, he selected official-looking credentials from his available false paperwork, on the unlikely chance he could bluff his way into freeing the prisoners. Then he gathered his gear and rode off with the others.

They passed the little farming village that would have been their night's reprieve, then took the northwesterly road out of the community. The sun was most of the way down already and soon the stars hung bright overhead.

They pressed their horses to a good walking speed. Any faster on the dark road would have endangered them. The land grew more hilly as they travelled further west. From time to time, they passed isolated shacks and farm spreads, some of which lay behind high walls.

Riding beside Carthalo while Brutus took point and Antires and Corven brought up the rear, Hanuvar told his intelligence officer about their own mission and the dreadful encounter with a sorcerer. Carthalo, too, had been forced to rescue slaves a master wouldn't part with, although he'd faced fewer trials. They'd drugged the man's wine and slipped away without issue. Everything seemed to have gone perfectly until the slave catchers had somehow learned about Farnus' inn.

Hanuvar remembered Farnus well. He'd been one of Carthalo's most reliable field agents during the war and now oversaw a number of small way stations along key travel routes. If Farnus were forced to reveal what he knew, Dervans would learn about most of their network, from Derva to Selanto. All would have to be abandoned.

Carthalo had additional bad news. "The Eltyr's been active again. Two more Dervan nobles are dead. Children."

Ciprion had pledged to keep them informed about the Eltyr's activities. Hanuvar had hoped that there'd be nothing to hear. "Who were they?"

"A remote cousin of the Marcelli, and a niece of Senator Ervonus."

Reading Hanuvar's brooding silence, Carthalo said: "It might not be your daughter. It might not even be one of ours."

"It probably is one of ours," Hanuvar said. Their people had tens of thousands of reasons to seek vengeance.

"Yes," Carthalo agreed, and fell silent.

They rode for long hours. And then, finally, reasoning that the slavers couldn't have gotten much further before they'd needed to stop for the night, Carthalo urged them to advance more cautiously, warning that an old camping site lay nearby.

Hanuvar ordered the others off the road and left them with the horses, including Antires. The playwright was resourceful, but he was no woodsman, and they needed stealth.

He took Carthalo ahead with him. They crested one hill carefully to discover only more landscape, then reached another and spotted a campfire on level ground a good spear toss back from the road. The camp itself seemed quiet, although the susurration of crickets drowned out softer sounds.

Carthalo breathed a sigh of relief. "Got them," he whispered. He, too, had worried that the slavers might have pressed on, or moved further off the road. But he wasn't in the habit of talking out his fears.

"Let's go verify."

When they crept closer, they spotted a sentry nodding at his post.

Hanuvar and Carthalo sank down behind a juniper bush and watched, working out a sense of the camp. Hanuvar searched in vain for an outer sentry. Carthalo pointed to the lumpy shapes lying around the fire. One had shifted and there'd been the unmistakable rattle of chains.

Hanuvar nodded in acknowledgment. "Does Farnus have a pick?" he asked in Carthalo's ear. Carthalo had insisted his field operatives, including Hanuvar, wear sandals modified to conceal a small set of lockpicks in the heel. Hanuvar had yet to master their working, but Farnus was a practiced hand with such tools.

"If he wore the right sandals," Carthalo whispered back.

A figure on the other side of the fire sat up with a groan, then hurried for a bush at the end of the camp and crouched. The sound of explosive flatulence ripped through the night, momentarily quieting the nearby crickets.

"All the niceties of Dervan society," Carthalo whispered.

The Dervan continued his business for some time, cleaned himself, then moved at a foot-dragging hunch back to his sleeping roll.

Mockingly the sentinel asked if the man had worked everything out.

"You're funny," the other man said with a curse.

"I'm dead sick myself," the sentry admitted.

"At least the two of us can still walk." The first sank onto his bedroll. "Jovren's balls. This is dreadful."

"I told you that lamb was off," the sentry said fiercely.

Hanuvar decided on his course of action. "This may be easier than we thought, but I'm going to scout the rest of the perimeter before we close in. Slide back and get the others. We'll rendezvous at that rock. Leave Antires with the horses."

Carthalo acknowledged the orders with a pat on Hanuvar's shoulder and crawled off.

The situation was almost ideal. Several hours of darkness remained, and the Dervans were not at their best. He wondered if Farnus and his three were afflicted with a bad stomach along with them.

Staying low, Hanuvar circled a short spear's toss from the camp's edge. As he arrived at its northern side his diligence was rewarded, for a figure was briefly outlined against a slight rise. He would have to be eliminated before Carthalo returned.

Hanuvar advanced, his progress masked by the ever-present drone of Tyvolian crickets. He lowered to his belly and crawled forward along the side of the steep slope. The man crouching ahead of him cursed softly to himself. He thought he knew why; this watch point lay closer to the side of camp chosen as the latrine, and the stench of human waste had swung this way as the breeze changed.

A horse whinnied in the camp, and the figure Hanuvar closed upon cursed quietly once more.

And Hanuvar, already tense, felt the blood drain from his face. He had misread the situation. A sentry wouldn't be troubled by the horses making noise, but an enemy scout would. He pressed himself flat, senses stretching taut.

Below, the camp sentry called out for one of his men to check the animals. A grumpy, sleep-fogged voice told him not to worry about it, but the sentry insisted and the grumpy man swore and said he'd look into it.

The man Hanuvar watched chuckled quietly to himself, as if pleased by the enemy's weakness.

For what force did this man scout, and how many were with him? Hanuvar eased back until he had a better sense of what was going on.

"Chenat," a voice whispered to Hanuvar's left, "is that you?"

"Here," whispered the watching scout.

"Then who's that?"

Hanuvar wasted no time, shooting to his feet as the questioner came forward. He backed from the thrust of the shadowy figure's dark blade, then drew and swung his gladius in a single motion. The attacker leaned out of the way, misstepped, and fell forward.

Knowing he was close to the hill's drop-off, Hanuvar stepped right, only to have the earth give out beneath him. He dropped only half his height, but his feet went out from under him, and to keep from striking his head he had to drop his weapon. A moment later he was tumbling down the grassy slope. He struck knee and elbow and back on roots as he rolled, landing finally on his belly close to the stinking latrine. He'd lost his sword.

Gasping, and a little stunned, he lay flat until he could catch his bearings. Someone outside the camp was shouting "Go, go," and Hanuvar presumed an attack from the mysterious second group was under way. Chains rattled on his left. He was close to the prisoners. He didn't feel like moving yet, but he dared wait no longer. He was starting to rise when a lantern light pinned him. A man was shouting at him to lie still unless he wanted a spear point. He obeyed, frowning, uninclined to act until he could better gauge the position of his enemies.

He heard the clack of swords and a scream of pain, and the unmistakable sound of a death rattle.

A woman's gruff voice called out of the darkness for a report. Men replied, relaying that the slavers were down. One reported the capture of two patricians, and then the spearman behind Hanuvar called out: "I've got one over here, and he doesn't smell like shit. I think he's another noble."

"Bring him over," the woman called.

"Up, you," the spearman said harshly. "Hands away from your belt."

Hanuvar climbed slowly to his feet, arms raised.

Four men sat off to one side, manacled hands lifted in surrender. A pair of guards watched them, and one barked to lower their hands. Hanuvar wasn't put with them, though.

The spearman jabbed him toward two Dervans sitting hunched

and miserable on the bare ground. One of their new captors tossed more tinder into the campfire and it blazed up, revealing the limp bodies of the rest of the slavers, dragged into a line. Bandits searched the corpses while joking about the stink.

The two dejected Dervans said nothing to Hanuvar when he was told to take a seat next to them, though their curiosity was palpable. Neither resembled the scarred, brutal slave catchers he'd seen on the streets of Derva. One was a slim man barely in his majority, wearing a light green tunic that emphasized the sickly green in his pale face. The other was a young patrician, with a proud, sharp nose, pointed chin, and honey-colored hair. The one in green opened his mouth as if to question Hanuvar but the other silenced his companion by putting a hand on his leg.

A muscular woman stopped to the right of their campfire. She wore a helmet, leather cuirass, and a soldier's baltea and boots. The fire cast her face in deep shadow and outlined her high cheekbones. "You're no shit-eating slaver, are you?" she asked casually of Hanuvar. "How much are you worth? You a noble Dervan?"

He answered with a patrician accent. "The noblest. My patron will reward you handsomely for my safe return."

"Fabian, search him," she said.

A large, freckled man patted Hanuvar down, discovering his regular knife, two throwing knives, coin purse, belt pouches, and paperwork, which held the most interest for them. The woman tilted it toward the fire, which fingered her helmet with shifting brightness as she read. "Quintus Claudius Marcellus," she said slowly. "There's something in small letters here about a quaestor."

"I'm a special emissary of quaestor Lentullus."

"You sound important." The woman lowered the paper and shoved it roughly back into its waxed pouch. "Lucky thing for you." She gestured vaguely toward one end of the camp. "A couple of my boys say they wrestled with a Dervan on the hill. Was that you?"

"Yes."

"Well, well. He said he figured you broke your neck on the way down."

"I'm a fortunate man."

She turned her attention to the other Dervans. "Who are you?"

The obvious patrician spoke first, his voice weak from his illness.

"I am Alosius Magnus Senrilla." He indicated the man beside him with a nod. "This man is in my employ."

"I didn't expect to find any noble among slave catchers."

The young man's head rose proudly. "I'm doing what I can to help the empire."

The bandit queen mocked him with a downward mouth twist, imitating a lackwit, and her men laughed. "Help the empire," she repeated slowly. "Let me guess. An old family with a proud name, but low on money, right?" She smirked. "I hope your people have enough to pay a good ransom for you. Do they?"

"They do," Alosius said grimly.

"So let me see. You lot are moving captured slaves, aren't you? What are they?"

"A clerk, a cook, and a gardener."

"Huh. They could earn us a little coin. And the little fellow with you?"

"My father will pay for him as well."

"How fortunate for him. He doesn't look as prosperous. Do you know, I heard you mention three slaves, but you have four there. Have you miscounted?"

"One of those men is under arrest for moving slaves illegally," Alosius' companion said.

"Oho! But that's what we're planning to do. Does that mean you would arrest us?" She tapped her leather armored breast. "Go ahead, Alosius Magnus. Arrest us."

"You have us surrounded," Alosius said, adding, "but had I the means, I would."

Her tone shifted to one of cutting anger. "I know you would. It's good that I have some use for you that might make me money."

"Once our ransoms are paid, I will hunt you down," Alosius vowed.

Hanuvar kept from wincing.

But the bandit queen seemed to expect that level of arrogance. She laughed. "All right, Dervans. You'll have new quarters for a few days. Until your people pay your ransoms. If they pay. For now . . . get used to wearing manacles. It's always such a shame to see them on rich folk."

Her people came forward with heavy chain-linked wrist cuffs

they had found amongst the Dervan gear and forced Alosius and his assistant to their feet.

Hanuvar watched as those two were fully made prisoner, then, resignedly, stiffly, held out his own hands and felt the iron fastened about his wrists. He had long dreaded such a day; these were not Dervans marching him off for a show trial, and his fate was far from settled, but he was not remotely reassured.

After he was manacled, he and the two Dervans were linked by a long length of chain with those he assumed were Farnus and the other Volani. Hanuvar, at the far end of the line, could barely make them out, much less engage or even exchange looks with them in the poor light.

Shortly thereafter the bandits gathered the rest of their booty, including four horses and several heavy bags of goods and weapons. There were two dozen men in all, and five stood guard at all times. The troop was capable and seasoned, and Hanuvar was glad his own people had so far held off an attack. The right time would come. Carthalo would assess the situation and plot his move for the most opportune moment. For now, he himself would have to remain patient.

II

The two Dervans remained weak throughout the hour-long march over forested hills. By the time they arrived at the bandits' camp, they were wobbling on their feet. The three Volani looked only a little better, their faces downturned and hopeless. The man at their head, though, was alert, taking in his surroundings like a professional. Hanuvar couldn't see him as more than an outline but was certain this was Farnus. There seemed to be no good way to communicate discreetly with him in the dark, with so many others listening, and so Hanuvar stayed quiet.

Over the course of their overland march, the bandit queen twice called one of her companions by the name Fabian. He seemed to be her second-in-command, for he relayed her commands to the rest of the bandits and travelled up and down the line to check on their underlings.

They finally reached their destination as a sliver of moon sunk low beyond the looming trees. The bandits' settlement was situated at the base of a limestone cliff beside a sandy beach and wide stream. A fire burned low along the bank, where the two sentries must have been warming themselves. They had risen to report to the woman leader. A denser forest loomed on the stream's far side.

The captured horses were led to a rudimentary corral at the cliff base and the captured belongings were removed and cataloged. Fabian took charge of Hanuvar and the prisoners, ordering them to sit at a fire and warning them they'd best cooperate with the recording of their names and the information needed to ransom them. He looked a formidable opponent—large, well muscled, and keen eyed—a ruddy, freckled man in his middle thirties. He said something about being back in a moment, ordering a sentry to stand over them while another bandit passed out stale flat bread and waterskins. All the men tore into the bread, but the Dervans were especially thirsty, leaving the bandit presenting their food to joke that they acted more like fish than men.

Hanuvar finally got a better look at the Volani slaves. The young heavyset fellow with his head in his hands was almost surely Melquarn the chef. The other two looked just slightly less unhappy. Both were lean, somber men in their early thirties, and both stared blankly as they wolfed down bread scraps. The more weathered one was likely the gardener. Even imprisoned himself Hanuvar couldn't help feeling badly for them, being thrust suddenly back into captivity only shortly after experiencing a few brief hours of freedom. It was no wonder they looked dejected. And Hanuvar wondered if the slavers hadn't bothered to feed their prisoners the evening before.

Farnus sat on their far end, and as he returned Hanuvar's scrutiny his eyes widened. It was small wonder. With a full day's growth of beard, Hanuvar imagined he looked very much like he had during the war, when Farnus had last seen him.

The spy remained stocky and powerful, though his dark hair was dusted with gray. His square face was puffed with bruises. His eyes were dark and alert and searched Hanuvar's face for some kind of confirmation that he really was who he seemed.

Carthalo hadn't passed word to his contacts that Hanuvar still lived and that he looked younger than he should, which explained

Farnus' confusion. He was surely wondering if he imagined things, or if Hanuvar was some unknown Cabera relative.

Hanuvar shifted through the three signals denoting membership in Carthalo's organization as he lifted his waterskin.

Hanuvar saw a return signal in acknowledgment. Professional that he was, Farnus hid any further reaction. That, unfortunately, was the extent of the communication they could exchange, for Fabian returned with a companion who looked more like someone's secretary than a fugitive or bandit. The wiry older man proceeded to ask each of the Dervans, Hanuvar included, for their full names and where their relatives or sponsors might be found, recording everything on browned papyrus.

Hanuvar named Senator Aminius as his sponsor, which prompted curious stares from both Dervans.

When their questioning was finished, Hanuvar, Alosius, and his assistant were separated from Farnus and the Volani, handed some threadbare blankets, and herded into a low cave. They were told that guards were stationed and that they'd be beaten if they made any trouble. He wondered if there was much difference between these accommodations and those accorded non-noble prisoners. Perhaps the others didn't receive blankets.

Hanuvar kept his hand lifted to feel the ceiling, so he would not strike his head. The jangle of the chains at his wrist was a constant reminder of his situation. The air of the cave was cool, and when he sat, he found the dirt floor cold. For all that, it wouldn't be the worst environment he'd ever slept in. He might have used the picks in his sandal to try the lock, but at the moment he had other concerns.

The questions from the Dervans came as they divvied up the blankets. Each man took one to lie on and another to cover with. Hanuvar bequeathed the two extras for his companions to use as pillows.

"That's kind of you," Alosius said as he lay down close by. "How did you come to be in my camp?"

"I appreciate you not raising suspicion about me." Hanuvar had invented a reasonable explanation during the long march. "I was travelling late at night, and my horse went lame. I saw your fire and decided to approach cautiously. I thought you might be bandits."

"That's funny," the assistant said with a tired chuckle. He had introduced himself as Cassius to the bandits' scribe.

"Not especially," Alosius said sympathetically.

"Yes," Hanuvar agreed. "I was just approaching the camp to learn whether you could be trusted when I came into contact with the bandits. I know your names, but I don't know who you really are. Neither of you look like the typical slave catcher."

"I take your meaning." There in the dark cave, Alosius was little more than the suggestion of a shape with an exhausted voice. Cassius, on his other side, could not even be glimpsed. The young patrician's tone was bitter. "That bandit woman isn't too far off the mark. My grandfather wasn't wise with his investments, and didn't leave Father with much, but Father's a clever man. He bought an interest in a slave-hunting outfit, and when he saw how badly managed it was, he took over himself."

"I see," Hanuvar said. His interest in the topic was already spent, but the younger man continued, a note of pride in his voice.

"While the playwrights have you thinking slave catchers are all heartless men hunting fragile girls mistreated by abusive masters, the reality's very different. Our group doesn't bother hunting any but the dangerous ones. Murderers, rapists, and mad men. One of my first cases was tracking down a barbarian who'd caved in his master's son's head with an axe and fled into the hills. He'd turn up every few days to kill some other villager at random. Women, children, freedmen, even other slaves. Sheep, too. He didn't eat the sheep, mind you. He just liked to kill."

"A mad dog," Hanuvar suggested, though he did not add that a society that enslaved people might engender some anger, or even madness, amongst its victims.

"Yes," Alosius agreed. "And there was a rough band that escaped from a mine. They had been sold into slavery because they were trouble. They were put to work, but they escaped. It took a while to track all of them down, and they cut a swath through the region. They liked to set things on fire."

"So you're protecting the empire," Hanuvar suggested.

"Yes." Honest passion could be heard in the young man's weary words. "My father is trying to build a real organization instead of this scattershot thing we have now. So that different regions can communicate and track the escapees and do a better job keeping everyone safe. What good does it do if someone flees Turia for Utria and the locals don't know they're an escaped slave because the regions aren't in contact?"

"Those men you were transporting don't look so dangerous."

"They're Volani," Cassius said, as if that explained everything.

Hanuvar replied as if the notion amused him. "Does that make them dangerous automatically? I thought you said they were domestics."

"It's the fourth fellow, Farnus," Cassius explained. "He's the one who's behind the whole thing."

"The whole thing?" Hanuvar asked. Now they were finally closing on the information he most desired.

But Alosius grunted discouragingly. "I don't know that we should go into that."

"Is this Farnus dangerous?" Hanuvar asked. "He looked as though your men had worked him over."

"He's lucky he's still alive," Cassius said. "Or, maybe in his case, unlucky."

Alosius cut him off. "That's enough, Cassius." His tone softened as he returned his attention to Hanuvar. "I'm afraid you haven't told us why you were riding through the dead of night."

So the young man was feeling cautious, which said something about his presence of mind. Hanuvar would have to be careful pushing him for information. What he most needed to know was how many people were aware of the Volani slave liberation network.

"It's best I not go into too much detail," Hanuvar said, as if he were reluctant.

"Why not?" Cassius asked.

Hanuvar explained with the condescending patience of a Dervan patrician to a social inferior. "If the bandits get word of what I was doing they may well press for details, and no one else should be put at risk."

Cassius wasn't dissuaded. "You're some kind of courier, aren't you? What kind of messages were you carrying?"

Alosius snapped his response. "Mind your manners. Quintus is trying to shield us. Little good it will do. You must forgive him, Quintus. He is Volani."

"Oh?" Hanuvar asked.

"Half Dervan," Cassius asserted quickly. "My mother was a Volani slave before she was freed. But I'm not like the Volani. I've helped you out, haven't I, Alosius?"

"You have," Alosius said, "but you need to know when to keep quiet." To Hanuvar he said: "We should sleep. Especially if we're to be alert for opportunities tomorrow."

"Do you think we'll have opportunities?"

"We can hope that the gods will provide them."

"I suppose you're right," Hanuvar agreed. "Let's get some rest."

Both wished him a good sleep, and Hanuvar laid back, trying to ignore the rough iron around his wrists. Though he was no great lockpick, he guessed that with steady effort he might free himself. He longed to give it a try. But he should take advantage of his circumstance to learn just how much the remaining Dervan slaver had discovered about Carthalo's network, and who else he might have told. He could do that best if he had Alosius' trust as a fellow hostage.

Much as he loathed the discomfort and vulnerability of confinement, he was in a far better state than others similarly held—he knew allies were nearby working to secure his release. Carthalo would have followed, assessed the camp, and observed the interview the bandits' clerk had held with them at the campfire; he would have deduced Hanuvar was being held with the other nobles for ransom, a common practice with captured patricians. Seeing that Hanuvar was in no immediate danger and that his own forces were outnumbered, Carthalo would likely watch the camp's routines and confirm their numbers by daylight so he could identify weaknesses and options.

Or he might be waiting for Hanuvar to slip away, knowing that given time even Hanuvar's rudimentary pick skill could overcome simple locks. Maybe he was wondering why Hanuvar had not already escaped.

There was no way to communicate with Carthalo without drawing dangerous suspicion, nor any way to free Farnus and the three men without loss. There was nothing he could do to resolve the entire situation without more rest, and this night he welcomed it without the usual stretches beforehand. He took a few deep breaths and, once he closed his eyes, sleep came swiftly.

When Hanuvar woke to light at the cave mouth he saw from its quality the time was well past the early morning. Low voices muttered outside. Someone cursed about rust spots on a helmet, and water splashed, intermixed with the laughter of children. He supposed that a large camp was likely to have family groups.

Alosius lay on his side, still soundly asleep. Cassius had vanished.

Hanuvar slid from the blankets, brushed grit from his feet, and slipped into his sandals, his hand passing across the metal stud he could remove to access the picks. Not yet.

In a few moments he stepped to the cave edge. The guard posted outside heard the crunch of his footsteps and the jangle of his chains and was turned toward him by the time he drew close.

"If you need to piss, come outside the cave," the bandit said with disinterest. "Your grub will be ready soon, and we'll have you eat and wash up before. There are a couple of waterskins there on the left."

Hanuvar saw that indeed there were. He wasn't surprised. Their captors understood that they needed to keep their prisoners in fair shape if they were to get their money for them.

"That's good to know," Hanuvar said. "Where's our companion?"

The pockmarked bandit eyed him without comment for a count of five, then said, "Mind your own business."

Seeing no need to antagonize him, Hanuvar took up the waterskins, lingering at the entrance to slowly drink while he searched the stream front for a clue to Cassius' whereabouts. He saw only a half dozen children of varying ages gamboling along the edge of the water near some women washing clothing.

He retreated to the rear of the cavern, where Alosius was sluggishly waking.

"Here you are." Hanuvar handed over a waterskin. "Feeling better this morning?"

The young man sat up. His eyes looked small and tired and somehow his nose looked even larger than it had yesterday, as though it were a feature he hadn't grown into. "Thank you." His voice was raw and soft. "My stomach's finally settled, if that's what you mean." He blearily took in his surroundings as he drank, then lowered the skin. "Where's Cassius?"

"The guard won't tell me."

Alosius chewed on that, frowning, and took another drink.

"Do you think he's telling the bandit queen what I told you last night?"

Alosius' frown deepened. "He might be."

"Why would he do that?"

"He needs money. But he'd be a fool if he thought the bandits would pay him."

"Maybe he thinks his ransom won't be paid."

"I promised him my father would pay for his release, but . . . he's worried about that." He sighed. "I shouldn't trust someone who betrays his own people."

"What do you mean?"

"He turned the Volani over to me. He said it was out of duty, but he was clearly in it for the reward. I gather he has some debts."

"I don't understand. He said his mother was freed. So he wasn't involved with these escaped slaves."

"No." Alosius hesitated a moment before deciding to explain. "Someone's going around and buying up Volani slaves, and Cassius heard about it and alerted me."

At last, Hanuvar had an opening to the conversation he most wanted to have. "Why would someone buy Volani?"

"I don't know. I didn't believe him, but when Cassius told me those slaves that couldn't be bought were being stolen, and that he knew where some were going to be . . ." He let the thought trail off. "Well, we found them, in a hidden room in that Farnus' inn."

Hanuvar's composed expression hid his anxiety. How many people might Cassius have approached before coming to Alosius? And how many people had Alosius spoken with about the Volani liberation? And how had Cassius found out about Carthalo's organization?

He turned his discomfort into a question. "Who would want the Volani?"

Alosius shook his head. "I don't know yet. But I'm worried it's something dangerous. That maybe someone's trying to build up an army of angry Volani."

"You said these men were no real threat."

"Well, you can train men, can't you? And the Volani always hated us. You think they'd know by now that we're their betters." The young man shook his head in exasperation, as though he pitied the Volani for not understanding their place. "If they'd just given up sooner, they wouldn't have ended up slaves."

"That's a good point," Hanuvar said. "I blame Hanuvar."

"Well, he has a lot to answer for, but I tell you this, we're lucky his people didn't listen to him better, or they'd have given him a bigger army. Then we'd have been in even worse trouble." There was no missing a note of admiration in the young man's voice. "My father met him once."

"Did he?"

"My father was in the Mighty Sixth. His patrol got captured by some of Hanuvar's scouts. When they were surrounded, he figured they were done for, but Hanuvar himself showed them around the camp and even drank wine with them before setting them free."

Hanuvar remembered the occasion and wondered which of the five men had been Alosius' father. "Why would he do that?"

"Father thought it was because Hanuvar wanted to convey just how confident he was of victory. He had every right to be," Alosius added. "He won that battle." The young man hesitated a moment, then went on: "Father said he wasn't at all like he expected. He even had a sense of humor."

"It's easy to be gracious when you have the upper hand," Hanuvar suggested.

The younger man bristled, as though taking offense at the slight to Hanuvar's honor. "It wasn't like that."

"My apologies," Hanuvar said, disguising his own amusement. "Put aside Hanuvar. Cassius came to you and told you someone was moving a bunch of Volani slaves. And he said others were being moved?"

"He did. And I know what you're going to say."

"Do you?"

"He might have been lying just to get my interest. But he says Farnus is a Volani agent, working with some kind of Volani organization freeing the slaves. I didn't believe him at first, but then we found the slaves. It has me wondering if Hanuvar is involved."

Hanuvar chuckled. "You don't honestly believe the rumors he's still alive, do you?"

"You don't?"

"I suppose anything's possible," Hanuvar admitted.

"Hey, you two!"

The guard was calling to them. He was backlit by sunlight less bright than Hanuvar would have supposed, as though it were already evening. "You want your grub, get out now. You can also wash up in the river. If you're not assholes, I'll even let you clean upstream." He laughed at his own wit. "But hurry it up. I'm hungry myself."

Jangling, they came to the cave entrance. Hanuvar was close to getting the confirmation he needed about the extent of the slave catcher's knowledge; he just needed a little more time.

Outside the sunlight was muted. A wind buffeted the trees at regular intervals, and the earth itself felt tense, as if it cringed in expectation of a blow the sky might give.

Hanuvar noted the position of the bandits. Four kept constant watch. Others ate at two cookfires, or cleaned gear, or tended horses, or just took their ease. A trio of women worked further upstream, wringing out clothes, assisted by some of the older children. The younger ones had been herded away from the stream and the prisoners.

Probably Carthalo had intercepted the bandits' clerk and his escort when they were sent forth this morning with information about their prisoners, in which case Carthalo possessed a better idea of the bandits and their capabilities and their defensive positions even than Hanuvar.

Hanuvar and Alosius were pointed to the stream. Guards with spears stood on either side of the water, disinterested but alert. Farnus and the Volani were washing in the waist-deep water. They'd been permitted to remove their manacles, which were piled on one side of the shore. The four men scrubbed with lumps of soap placed on a flat black rock in the stream's midst.

"Don't cause any trouble, if you know what's good for you," Fabian instructed them. In the light of day his ruddy skin made his northerly Ermani heritage even more obvious. "Those that fight don't get fed." And, watching them carefully, Fabian removed their manacles. Hanuvar couldn't help but rub his wrists as the hateful things were pulled away. He also couldn't help thinking of the three nearby Volani slaves and how many times they'd had to don chains.

The big freckled bandit eyed him suspiciously. He turned away.

Farnus and the others had stripped bare and were working up a lather with the soap. The one he'd identified as the cook still moved despondently. The other two looked tired, but more alert, and they returned Hanuvar's scrutiny. Good. They weren't completely cowed yet. He needed all them ready to move when the time came.

Farnus' face was puffy and purple but his eyes were sharp. Of Cassius Hanuvar saw no sign.

When he disrobed it was strange still to see his body without the prominent scars to which he was used. Almost all had faded to nothing, even the line from that near fatal attack the previous winter. He advanced into the stream, lagging behind Alosius, and was soon waist deep. The water was cold.

The Dervan pointedly kept his distance from Farnus. Hanuvar asked the younger man if he wanted him to get soap.

"That would be kind of you."

Hanuvar pushed through the water, his toes spreading against the cool mud.

He stopped just short of the rock where the soap lay.

Farnus stood beside it, scrubbing his hair. He spoke scathingly. "It did me good to see a Dervan in chains."

"I'm just here for the soap," Hanuvar said. "It's an important key to health. That and good footgear."

Farnus grunted. "Don't worry about my sandals or my health, Dervan." He watched as Hanuvar lifted the soap, finger and thumb in his hair briefly shaping the affirmative signal.

"Get as clean as you want," Hanuvar said. "You'll still end up crucified. Even if you had a whole band of allies out there, they wouldn't bother trying to free you. You Volani are wily, but you're all cowards in the end."

Farnus absorbed that with a sour look then replied with a sneer. "Rut a goat, Dervan." He glanced at the watching guards, flashed another affirmative signal, and turned away.

Pleased with the communication, Hanuvar took the soap and returned to Alosius, lathering his chest as he went.

Alosius thanked him, then lamented the inability to shave. He thought nothing of Hanuvar's growth of beard. But then no one in this particular camp but Farnus would recognize Hanuvar from his campaigning years.

After they'd finished washing, they had no choice but to pull on their sweat-soaked garments and submit once more to the manacles. They were served a fish broth heavy with vegetables that proved better fare than he'd expected. He was nearly done with the bowl when Fabian returned to stand over him. "Captain Olisia wants to see you."

Hanuvar hadn't yet heard the woman's name, but there was no point in pretending he didn't understand. He set the bowl aside. "I'll not keep her waiting."

Fabian led. The other guard followed, spear at the ready, though he wasn't pointing it at Hanuvar's back.

Olisia's cave lay off to one side, up a steep slope. Someone had piled some rocks along it as rudimentary steps. Why the cave was worth the extra trouble to reach became obvious when they arrived. Its ceiling stretched high overhead so that even a man as tall as Fabian didn't have to duck.

A mishmash of clashing red and green rugs were strewn over the cave floor, spread out before a pair of couches thirty paces back from the entrance. Twin lanterns burned on two small tables beside the one facing him.

He'd halfway expected Cassius to be on hand bearing witness, but Hanuvar saw only a single seated figure. Olisia. Fabian advanced to wait at her right hand and crossed his arms over his broad chest, like a gladiator ready for review. "Stand right there," he said, pointing to a space in front of his captain's couch.

He did as ordered.

Olisia's arms were far more toned and muscular than the Dervan ideal, and her jaw was long and sturdy. She'd removed her armor, but still wore a man's short-sleeved tunic rather than a stola, and military boots. Her eyes were flat and black.

She didn't bother with preliminaries or pretend to play the part of a host. "I've been told you weren't originally a part of the Dervan camp."

"News travels fast."

"It leaks faster. So you're some kind of night courier. Working for whom?"

To sound realistic, he would have to sound reluctant. So he did. "I'm a messenger for a faction of senators."

"And you didn't think to tell me that?" She shook her head as though he had disappointed her. "You do know your chances of survival rise the more valuable you are to me, don't you? And I assume your news is valuable, or you wouldn't be travelling at night."

"I'm routinely after valuable information. The people I work for know it and will pay for my release."

"You sound quite certain of yourself."

"Many men can be messengers." Hanuvar raised an open palm, and perforce had to raise his other hand along with it. His manacles rattled. "Only a few can be good information brokers. I'm certain you understand the value of the right kind of news."

"I do. Are you going to share your news?"

"I will if I must. It probably won't be of interest to you, though. You'll get the value out of me regardless, because my employers know my worth."

It wasn't that her expression warmed, but he saw in their depths she was reassessing him. Before she could come to a new determination or refocus upon obtaining a story he had fabricated about his imaginary message, he spoke again. "I wonder if we might have some other use for one another."

Her brow furrowed. "What do you mean by that?"

"I mean that in your line you're sure to come into contact with information sometimes. I could pay you for it."

A bark of laughter escaped her lips. "Now? The money you carried is already mine."

"I mean in the future, once this particular arrangement is concluded."

She sat back against the couch.

Fabian spoke softly to her, his eyes on Hanuvar. "He's trying to angle for release."

She thought that over, then answered without taking her own gaze from Hanuvar. "No, I don't think so. He's not afraid." She addressed Hanuvar. "Maybe you should be."

"So far you've treated me fairly. Better than I might have expected," Hanuvar added. "I think I've no reason to fear so long as I cooperate, which I will, and so long as my people come through for me, which they will. So. I see the potential for a more profitable future with you."

She pulled at a thread on the couch. "Shouldn't you be boasting how you'll find your way back to this camp and hunt me down? You're not insulting my men, or the fact that a woman leads them."

"That's not my job. And if I were stupid enough to try to hunt you down in a few weeks, when this is all over, you'd have moved on to some other place. This is clearly a temporary camp."

She absorbed this without reaction, although he felt the intense scrutiny of Fabian, who seemed troubled that Hanuvar had reasoned so far.

"Where do you think I'll go?" she asked.

"Another region entirely. Probably you only swing through here a few times each year. You lucked into what happened last night because you were just out on patrol. Like a good warrior, you pounced when you saw that the camp was poorly defended by a band of slave catchers with stomach maladies."

The lantern light seemed to brighten as the daylight behind him grayed. Thunder rolled.

"You have to be ready to seize opportunities when you're presented with them," Olisia said. "I do sometimes hear things, although I'm not sure how interesting it would be to soft people like you."

"I'm not soft."

"Your hands are."

"I've recently recovered from a long illness."

"That explains your manner. You talk like a man who's been around."

"I'm older than I look."

She stared at him for a long moment, her expression closed. Then she turned to the man beside her. "Fabian, undo his bonds."

Fabian started but did not object. "Hold out your hands," he ordered, and untied the key at his belt.

The bandits had politely permitted their prisoners to bathe without manacles, so they could remove their clothes to do so. He had hoped, but not been certain, Olisia would exchange the same small courtesy if they were talking business. Outside rain began to patter on leaves.

In a moment the big man had undone the manacles. He dropped them on the faded red rug just a foot to Hanuvar's left. His eyes held a warning look.

"That was kind." Hanuvar brushed rust and sand from his wrists.

"This is just temporary," Olisia told him. "And only because you didn't look like you expected it."

"I appreciate the courtesy."

"Sit. Tell me about how this would work. If we were to meet up later to trade information, how would I know you weren't laying a trap for me?"

Hanuvar sat on the edge of the couch across from her. "I wouldn't lay a trap for someone in my network. You supply me with useful news on people's movements and doings, and I pay you good money. There's no mystery."

"So what are you wanting? Dirt on political opponents? Rumors about movements in the criminal underworld? Are you after contacts for services your men don't want to do?"

"All of those. I handle a few of those kinds of contacts myself."

"Do you?"

He shrugged. Sooner or later he'd have to provide her with more details. He had no idea if someone in her position could really be useful to him later on but it wouldn't hurt to test the waters. Outside the rainstorm increased its assault. He heard the wind's whistle. If he were Carthalo, he'd be putting aside any plans for a night assault and taking advantage of the conditions for a rescue right now. Easier to see during the rainstorm than at night, and discern where opponents hid. Farnus would also be preparing to escape. Events could easily twist any plans he made out of his control.

Olisia turned to the low table at her side. Her hand closed on the handle of a beautiful blue amphora with a single chip along its mouth. She filled a cup, handed it to Fabian, and pointed to Hanuvar. She then poured a draught for herself.

Hanuvar took the cup with a nod of thanks to the lieutenant, who frowned at playing the part of a servant.

"You can go, Fabian," Olisia said.

"You trust him?"

"You think I can't handle him?" she asked. "Besides, he's serious about all this."

Fabian frowned at Hanuvar then departed for the cave mouth. Hanuvar heard a second pair of footsteps retreating with him. Both guards were going to be out of close range.

Olisia drank without preamble.

Hanuvar raised his own goblet toward her and took a minute sip. Not top shelf. Probably Mervisian wine, with a faint back note of clove.

"Quintus, speak true. What service would someone need to provide to someone such as yourself if they wanted to rise above their past?"

For the first time her eyes shone with an inner light. This topic was her dream. The woman wasn't just a clever manager of this group of bandits, she had ambitions, and was aware that the limitations of her current venture would be reached sooner or later, probably bloodily.

"I find with enough money one can rise above nearly anything," he said. "You strike me as a careful planner."

The air crackled with thunder.

"I'm talking about rising into respectability."

"So am I. Wander into some small seaside town with a chest of coins and buy yourself a wine shop or inn to keep money rolling in. Hire someone else to manage it. Live off your gains and continue to buy other businesses with a public front. In a few years you'll be a respected member of the community."

"You think it's that simple? For a woman?"

"It's hardly simple. But it's possible, especially beyond Derva itself."

"I've been thinking about such things." She sounded unguarded, almost exposed. Likely she seldom spoke so openly about her dreams to any of her followers.

"I've seen far less clever people than you accomplish such changes," he said honestly.

"You didn't begin life as a patrician, did you?"

He laughed. "You couldn't have been further from one than I was."

"Is that how you did it? With money?"

"I haven't done it yet. I'm still pretending. If I'd succeeded in my aims, I wouldn't be riding through the dead of night on a chancy mission. I've a lot of work to do before I can rest in a villa by the sea. I'm not likely to make it. I think you might manage blending in better than me."

"What makes you say that?"

"Who would suspect a woman merchant of once having been a bandit queen? Whereas a man who accumulates secrets accumulates enemies."

"I've my share of those," she mused. "Bandit queen," she repeated. "No one's ever called me that."

"No? It suits you."

Her smile was slight, but it touched her eyes. She looked as though she had another question in mind, one that obviously came with concern, for her brow furrowed, and she hesitated in its asking.

Fabian ran up, shouting about an attack. He repeated the information several times as he neared before it actually registered with Olisia.

"What?" She stood. "The legion?"

"I don't know—but men are attacking!"

"Well, form up our boys!" Her gaze shifted to Hanuvar. In a moment she'd tell him to get the manacles back on. Already her eyes had hardened.

Fabian turned and hurried toward the exit even as she whipped out her knife. "Get the manacles back on."

Hanuvar climbed down from the couch, frowning that his time was up, then swiftly dropped to one hand and used it as a pivot point to kick her legs out from under her. She fell into the table with a shout, sending the beautiful amphora off its side. It smashed to pieces and splattered wine. Hanuvar pounced on her knife.

Fabian charged back, slowed only briefly by the manacles Hanuvar slung at his thigh. When the taller man stabbed with his gladius, Hanuvar turned the blow with an expert knife parry. From the corner of his eye, he spotted Olisia rise and lift her hand with a throwing knife clasped. He backstepped, gauging his time, then shifted to Fabian's right. The big man turned with him, and Olisia's weapon struck the back of his neck.

Fabian stumbled, clutching for his throat while she gasped in dismay; Hanuvar whipped his knife at Olisia and snatched up Fabian's sword.

She flung herself aside, tripping against the couch and sprawling.

He didn't wait to see how she recovered but sprinted for the exit.

The rain sliced out of the sky at a slant, only a little hindered by the leaves. Hanuvar dropped out of the cave. He paused briefly to take in the shouts from his right and splashing footfalls from his left. As he headed downslope a trio of bandits rushed from the wet. Two carried swords and a third held an axe, snarling at Hanuvar: "Take him!"

Hanuvar had faced better odds. And he was all too conscious Olisia might slip in behind.

He slashed the blade in front of him to warn them off.

At the same moment a figure rushed the three from behind. The axe bearer half turned and received a blow on his chin from a wrist-wrapped manacle. He shrieked, shattering the confidence of the other two. Hanuvar struck the sword aside from one and both turned tail and dashed into the rain.

Alosius had leapt back from the man he struck; Hanuvar drove his blade through the injured man's chest. As the bandit dropped, clawing at the mortal wound, Alosius scooped up his sword.

"Thank you," Hanuvar said. "That was well timed. Come on." Hanuvar hurried away, Alosius at his side.

Alosius asked him what was happening and how he'd gotten his manacles off, but Hanuvar was too busy evaluating the environment to answer. The bandits fled in every direction. There must have been a separate exit from Olisia's cave, for she was out ahead of them and shouting for her boys to rally. No one heeded her.

A huddle of men was heading across stream, Farnus at their head. From somewhere on the south side of camp the rattle of swords could be heard even above the roar of rain, as well as the sound of Carthalo calling for him. "Quintus!"

"You have friends out there?" Alosius asked.

"Yes." Hanuvar spotted a slim man in a green tunic splashing into the water. Cassius. "I want him." Hanuvar followed the traitor, Alosius at his heels.

Cassius looked back when he was halfway across the stream. There was no missing the wide whites of his eyes in his rain-slick face. He froze for a moment, and Hanuvar bounded for him, splashing up a white sheet of water when he landed calf deep.

The traitor had just reached the far shore when Hanuvar snagged his tunic. Cassius lost his balance and splashed into the shallows.

"Don't hurt me," he cried.

Carthalo, meanwhile, still called for Quintus.

"By the stream," Hanuvar shouted back, then dragged his sodden prisoner to the shore and flung him down near the roots of an elm.

Cassius repeated his protest, his narrow face twisted in fear. "Don't hurt me! I'm on your side!"

"Which side is that?" There was more ire in his voice than Hanuvar meant to share. "You turned your own people over to the enemy. And you shared my secrets with the bandits. How could anyone trust you?"

The young man's face was a tragic mask of self-pity. "You don't know what it's like! I had nothing, in a land where no one trusts me!"

Alosius had advanced to Hanuvar's side and waited, dripping. The rain had slackened to a drizzle. "Why should they?" he asked.

Cassius' eyes found Hanuvar's. "I'm valuable. I know more than I told Alosius."

"Do you?" Hanuvar asked. "Who did you learn the information from?"

"Farnus. He took me into his confidence. He's not just a Volani spy. He's been one of Hanuvar's agents for years. And the Volani have big plans!"

"Quintus," Alosius shouted, "on your left!"

Olisia must have crossed downstream. Her face was twisted into an ugly sneer, and she came at them with five spear-bearing bandits. Her cheek bled from a long gash. "Kill them!"

Hanuvar crouched and swept up some sand. He'd thought her a better businesswoman than this. But then she'd been showing her vulnerable side to him, so his betrayal might have been a deep strike.

Cassius crawled off to the right. Alosius stepped to Hanuvar's side, weapon ready in his manacled hands.

The bandits approached from the front and right.

Hanuvar slipped out of the way of an eager but overextended spear thrust and stepped in with a deep slash. He leaned away from a second man's lunge to his throat, then stabbed the thigh of one of those moving on Alosius and sent the screaming bandit down in a spray of blood.

"Stand aside," Olisia roared, and rushed him with a bared sword.

The others gave space as she swung with measured strength, right and left. Hanuvar backed off, conscious of the tree roots to his rear. He feinted and as she leaned, he went right.

But her eyes followed, and a desperate jab drove her sword into his forearm below the elbow.

She let out a cry of triumph, but he ignored the stinging pain and switched the weapon to his left. He was merely competent with his off hand, but like many facing a left-handed opponent she wasn't fully sure how to defend. She stretched too far to parry and exposed her belly.

He didn't want to take the strike, but he followed through. Blood welled from her mouth almost the same moment he pulled his blade free.

Her eyes were more alive than they'd ever been as she sank to her knees near the tree roots, and they told a story of shattered dreams and astonishment. Her sword slipped from nerveless fingers, and she put hands to the bloody rent in her garment, as if she couldn't quite believe death had come for her. After only a moment she lay as still as her bandit companion.

Her surviving comrades had fled before Antires and Carthalo, who formed a half circle around the battle site, next to Farnus. The three Volani were still manacled, but the young chef held a spear.

Alosius' face wrinkled in confusion when Farnus and Carthalo exchanged a hearty hand clasp.

"What's going on?" Alosius demanded warily. He seemed to realize, suddenly, that maybe Hanuvar wasn't who he seemed, and turned to him with blade half lifted.

It was then Cassius rose behind him.

"Alosius, look out," Hanuvar called.

The young Dervan whirled, but he wasn't fast enough to ward Cassius' knife thrust. The young man followed it with a second jab to the Dervan's chest. At the same time Alosius buried his blade in the younger man's chest, then hung onto the hilt to keep from dropping. Cassius' eyes widened in pain and shock and he looked at Farnus. His mouth moved, but no sound came forth.

Blood sprayed widely as a staggering Alosius ripped out his blade. Cassius pitched forward, his dying breath wheezing in his throat. The Dervan cast the blade aside and dropped to his knees. Olisia lay only a body length away, looking strangely young, for her expression was open forever now.

Hanuvar hadn't wanted to kill her. And he hadn't particularly wanted the traitor or the slave catcher dead. But then he hadn't wanted any of this.

Noting Hanuvar's bloody arm, Antires asked how badly hurt he was. Hanuvar raised his good hand to them in a sign to stay clear and knelt beside the failing Dervan.

The young man's expression was grave, and paling. His eyes were sharp. "You're with the Volani," he said. It wasn't a question.

"I am," Hanuvar said with a nod of respect. "You're a brave man. And you may have saved my life today. I will see that your ashes[15] are delivered to your father, and that he knows you died honorably."

Alosius lowered his head once in thanks. He gasped, swaying on his knees, and looked at the tree roots, though he was surely looking past them toward his final end. Somehow he managed to find the strength to look up. "Who are you?"

"A man trying to save his people. I'm on no campaign of revenge. I just want to see them freed. If Cassius hadn't been a traitor, no one would have had to die here."

Alosius was fading fast, but he fought fiercely to stay kneeling. He weakly nodded his understanding.

"Did you tell anyone else about us?" Hanuvar asked.

He wondered if he would hear a curse, but Alosius was honest to the end. "No one who wasn't with us." His voice was losing strength. "That's all you really want to do, to free them?"

"I mean to take them to a new home."

His look was searing. "Are you Hanuvar?"

He nodded once. "I am."

"I thought you'd be older." Alosius slowly put out one bloody hand, though it nearly sent him sprawling.

Surprised, Hanuvar clasped it, and the young man steadied himself against him.

"I wish you luck, Hanuvar. I wish my father could know . . . I fought at your side." He smiled mirthlessly.

He died shortly after Hanuvar eased him to the ground. And despite his own injury, Hanuvar knelt beside him for a long moment.

He rose, his hand still red with the other man's blood.

Antires, as usual, had something to say. "We thought you'd know we'd attack once the rainstorm started," he said.

"It was the smart play." He looked down at his stinging gash. Owing to his rapid aging, the blood had already stopped flowing. "I need to get this cleaned."

---

15 In Hanuvar's time, especially in warmer months, when men and women died far from home the people of Tyvol often cremated their dead and carried their ashes in grave urns rather than transporting corpses.   —*Andronikos Sosilos*

While Carthalo dug into his pack for supplies, Farnus came forward and saluted, shaking his head in disbelief. "I can't believe it's really you," he said. "You barely look older at all."

"It's a long story. Did you make the men sick at the original camp?"

Farnus smirked and traded an amused glance with the chef. "They had Melquarn cook, and he managed to slip something into their broth that made them a bit uncomfortable." He chuckled. "Maybe too uncomfortable, because they weren't going to sleep. I was waiting for the guard nearest us to start snoring. Another quarter hour and we'd have been able to run for it. We needed better timing. But then this whole thing was bad timing. And bad judgment," he added. "I shouldn't have tried to recruit Cassius. I'd known his mother, and I thought he had the same character."

Farnus had taken a risk, and it had almost gone terribly wrong. That's what happened in war, even if it was a covert one. "The important thing is that we all got out of this alive, and the Dervans still don't know about our organization."

"It was a close thing," Farnus said, "and I'm grateful for your help."

Hanuvar nodded, then gave his attention to Carthalo's lieutenant Brutus, arriving to report that the area was secure and that the bandits were on the run, though he was concerned they'd return before long.

Hanuvar had no wish to remain. They paused only to treat his wound, recover their gear, and retrieve a small cache of coins in Olisia's cave. They wrapped Alosius in one of her rugs and bore the body with them.

Antires fell in at Hanuvar's side as they headed off.

"What would you have done, if the young Dervan hadn't been dying?"

He met his friend's gaze unflinchingly. "I hadn't worked that out."

"He was a slave catcher." Antires' mouth twisted upon the word.

"Yes." Hanuvar rubbed the edge of the white linen wrapping his lower arm. The wound throbbed in time with his heartbeat. He wondered if he'd take a fever from it, or if his accelerated healing would skip past the discomfort. To Antires' questioning look he said: "Alosius didn't choose to grow up in a society inured to slavery. But Cassius chose to betray us. He gave the bandits my false cover story, and before that, he turned over his own people. And at the end he tried to curry favor by murdering Alosius. I can tell you which one I trusted at my back."

※ ※ ※

With those men recovered, we started north once more, but were only a few days along before one of Carthalo's couriers caught up to us. Rokana, the sorceress who'd aided Hanuvar in the final stages of the Second Volani War, had been found, and was ready to assist, if she could.

It is true that while I respected Carthalo, I never fully warmed to him, for he was so layered an individual it was generally impossible for me to tell which was his real personality. But that day I glimpsed his true face and could tell that he was torn. He wished to ride south with Hanuvar and care for his security and learn his fate. Hanuvar ordered him north instead, saying that Carthalo had more important things to concern himself with, for there were many others still to save, and Carthalo's being there or not would have no bearing on what was to happen with Hanuvar's health.

Carthalo then met my eyes and addressed me shortly. "Take care of him, Herrene." He didn't actually pledge to kill me if I failed; his eyes conveyed his meaning well enough.

I promised I would, and then Hanuvar and I turned south once more, and on for the wildlands just north of Turia, after three days arriving at a lonely hut beyond the remotest of old farming towns.

—Sosilos, Book Twelve

Chapter 13:
Land of the Fallen

I

"You were right to be afraid," the witch said to Hanuvar.

Just as her home was not a dark pit of infamy from myth, Rokana herself was neither a hideous crone nor a blinding beauty. She was merely an even-featured older woman with a mix of brown and gray hair. After her assistance against the Dervans during the war, she had feared their retribution but had not wished to leave her native lands for Volanus. And so Carthalo had found her a new identity and she had retreated to this dwelling on an out-of-the-way hilltop. The city-born woman seemed to have adapted well enough to the countryside. She kept her practices to herself, and neither the Dervan legions nor the revenants had ever found her.

Hanuvar sat upon the hearthside chair across the table from her and watched her unfocused gaze, directed at whatever unseen supernatural information surrounded him. Her eyes were crinkled in concern. She did not explain her statement, and he did not pry. She would report when she was ready.

He heard Antires fidgeting behind him in the closed doorway of the stone cottage. A beam of sunlight slanted in through the shuttered windows, and another streamed past the open doorway that led to what was presumably the woman's bedroom. Rokana owned a small, comfortable dwelling, aged and sturdy, surrounded by a well-tended garden of herbs and vegetables and guarded by a pair of dogs. She possessed a small flock of chickens, and, fenced in back, a smaller herd of goats. Inside, her home was cluttered but tidy, full of pleasant scents of drying mint and stewed goat meat and old fires. In different circumstances, Hanuvar might have found it restful.

Finally, Rokana looked away and with a prominently veined hand reached for the steaming cup of tea beside her. Hanuvar's still rested nearby, untouched. She sipped from hers delicately, then rested the cup in her hands. "Your years are galloping out of control," she said. Her voice was clear and unburdened by the husk or quaver of advancing age. "How did this happen?"

"A sorcerous entity stored life force," Hanuvar said. "When it died, the force flowed into me."

Rokana lowered the cup to the table and closed her eyes once more. She leaned toward Hanuvar, her hands stroking the air to either side of his head. "Whoever wrought this spell was incompetent. Any healthy effect is only temporary, at expense of measured lifelines. They're no longer fixed."

"What does that mean?" Antires asked.

She answered while still exploring the invisible beside Hanuvar's face, as if she combed tresses she alone could see. "It means that his own body has lost sight of its proper cycles. The general's natural limits look as though they've been magically burned away. I've never seen anything like it."

"What can be done to fix it?" Hanuvar asked.

Rokana sat back, blinking, and put her hand once more to her tea cup. She touched it as often as the devout brushed their sacred talismans. "Your lifelines must be modeled after another Hanuvar."

Before Hanuvar could ask for explanation, Antires spoke up.

"That . . . that doesn't make any sense." Antires walked further into the cottage, a few steps shy of the little table. There the Herrene was mostly in darkness, a slim man hungry with questions and pent-up energy.

"I am sorry that I have no more chairs," Rokana said. "What visitors I have usually see me one on one."

"I don't care about that," Antires said. "There's only one Hanuvar. What do you mean about modeling off of another one?"

Hanuvar had an inkling of her thought process, but said nothing, waiting as the woman marshaled her thoughts.

"There are a thousand, thousand worlds, tapestries beyond counting where things are perhaps only a little different from what you know here. Or vastly different. I need to model his lifelines off of another Hanuvar from one of those tapestries if I wish to do it properly."

"That sounds complicated," Hanuvar said.

Antires agreed. "Why can't you just . . . shore up what's already in place here?"

"He's not a building," the woman said with tart good humor. She faced Hanuvar. "Your lifelines are broken. If I alter them without a proper model, I could cause you terrible harm. And I cannot shape it based on your friend's lifeline, or mine, because our lines are very different." Seeing that her audience still looked uncertain, she thought for a moment, then seized upon another analogy. "Think of me like a tailor. I need to have the same kinds of threads and needle and pattern if I'm to make a similar garment."

Hanuvar looked down at his hands and flexed them. "How long do I have?"

"The condition appears to be worsening. In a few weeks or months, you will be old and gray. Or dead."

"So. We need a magical tailor," Antires said. "Are you one?"

She looked across the table at Hanuvar. "I think I can be. But there will be risk for us both."

"Have you done this before?" Antires asked.

Hanuvar had been wondering that; he waited for her answer, then saw it in her eyes.

"I have not," she said with a quiet sigh. "I don't think anyone has."

"How great is the risk?" Antires asked.

The witch didn't answer the Herrene. She looked to Hanuvar. "Do you fear?"

"I would not risk you, or myself, without good reason. I have already lived far longer than a man like me can expect."

"Yet few of us wish to die," she said kindly.

"That's true. And there are things I would live to do."

She spoke decisively. "You present an interesting challenge. I have always been curious about the other tapestries, but too cautious to look long at them. You may be able to glimpse them yourself as I work. You must prepare for visions that may disquiet you."

"I am ready," Hanuvar said.

"You speak without hesitation."

"My people have searched for a solution for a long while. You are the first person to offer a cure. I am prepared to act, for with every hour, weeks are passing from my life."

"I'm not sure the magic flows in a steady stream like that, but you're essentially correct. There is no time to waste." She patted the table. "Drink the tea. I will ready the incantations."

The spellworker rose and passed through the doorway to the backroom. After a moment she could be heard unrolling a stiff sheet of papyrus.

Antires stepped into the light, his handsome face twisted by a frown. "You didn't ask her what could happen if it went wrong."

"I know what will happen if we do nothing," Hanuvar replied evenly. He lifted the cup to his lips and drank. Mostly he tasted water, with a pleasant mint overlay.

"You should ask for more detail about the risks."

"Since she's endangering her own life to aid me, that would be disrespectful. It is enough to know if we don't act, I will die soon."

"So she says."

"It's not as though we can go find another mage for a second opinion, is it?" he asked with gentle humor. While many pretended knowledge of magical powers, most were charlatans. A majority of those who were not were allied with the Dervans or had long since been rounded up by them. Likely a few others lived on in remote parts of Tyvol, and it was possible his old Ceori friend Bricta might be able to help, for she had spoken to him last winter about tapestries. But she was far away still and had not yet responded to Carthalo's message. Besides which, Rokana was expert with the magics of life. For the last few years of the war, she had aided his surgeons and helped save hundreds of wounded.

Hanuvar lowered the tea and met his friend's eyes. His voice was measured and serious. "If something does go wrong, you will have to carry on without me." He did not welcome his end, but he no longer feared his people were doomed if he himself fell. With Carthalo and

Izivar helping to carry out his vision, the safety of his people no longer rested as heavily upon his shoulders alone.

"Things will run better if you're involved," Antires objected. "You know it."

"Nevertheless. The plans must unfold even if I am not able to direct them."

"I can guess what your orders are," Antires said crossly.

Rokana returned bearing a browned scroll wrapped around a pair of time-blackened wooden rolls.

Hanuvar wasn't sure what he expected next, but it was not that she would begin chopping ingredients—among them oregano and lavender, a tiny bit of rue, and some flower petals—and then brew them.

While the ingredients steamed in a pot she burned incense, and after that, she turned to Antires.

"Are you staying inside, or going?"

"Staying inside. Why, is it dangerous?"

"Not to you. But you must not interrupt. *That* would be dangerous. For the two of us. Do you understand? Once the spell begins, you must not interfere."

"No interfering," he said, hands raised and empty.

She grunted doubtfully at him.

Rokana didn't bother with any theatrical flourishes like colored fire or speaking to unseen spirits. With charcoal she drew a few runes on the stones above and to the side of each window and the single door and even the doorway to the bedroom. She then did the same thing above the entrance to the little hearth. She turned to Antires. "There are blankets folded on the shelf near the bed. Bring four of them in here in front of the hearth. Oh, and we will have to move the table to the right, there."

Antires retrieved the blankets, helped Hanuvar move the table, and then the three of them folded the blankets so that two lay beside one another on the hardpacked dirt floor, and a second lay on top of each.

"It's not going to be comfortable to lie there, even still," Rokana said to Hanuvar.

"I'm unaccustomed to much comfort."

She nodded, then sat and picked up her scroll. She studied it for another hour and then said they would be ready shortly, and it was time to consume the brew. Hanuvar drank a mug of the concoction along with her. The mint and lavender and floral scents couldn't completely obscure the rue's astringency.

She instructed him to consume everything served to him, including the leaves and little grains or seeds, some of which were sweet as honey, and others of which delivered heat.

Antires paced and eyed the pot from which the tea had come, looking irritated he couldn't be more closely involved, or be better able to help.

At last, Rokana set down her scrolls and told Hanuvar he needed to lie at her side.

As he stretched out upon the blankets, she sat down beside him, smoothing out her stola, then lay back. "It may take me some time. Whatever you hear from me, do not fear on my account. We are tethered to our world so long as you are with me. And I can find our way back because of the strong roots I've used to anchor myself here." She looked into his eyes. "Do you feel the tea taking affect?"

"I feel at peace."

"I don't think I've ever heard you say that," Antires observed. Hanuvar smiled wryly at him, noticing as he turned his head that the motion seemed too rapid, as if his body moved faster than his soul. He rotated more slowly back to Rokana and experienced the peculiar sensation a second time.

"Breathe easy," she instructed. When she reached out to take his hand, he found her grasp warm.

His body felt light. She told him he was apt to see strange things but that he should not be alarmed. Her voice was like the steady drip of a water clock. Calming, certain.

He realized he was looking down at his body, but even this was not alarming. His chest rose and fell. His eyes were closed. The world blurred as though he perceived it through drunken eyes, and the cottage vanished.

He was aware of the woman beside him in this experience, and that he held her hand, but he did not feel her so much as perceive her presence. About them lay a blue-gray fog, swirling and cool, and through it strange images swam. At first, they were simply disjointed shapes, but he and Rokana drifted closer to them through the fog.

The images grew clear. He looked upon himself once more, and marveled. There he lay in a stone hut by Rokana, but with a single arm, and it was Carthalo waiting in the doorway, not Antires. The mist swirled and he saw himself striding through a gray countryside toward a promontory. One of his eyes was filmy and sightless.

That image rippled and he again looked on a version of himself, though this one had an eye patch, and a beard. He seemed untroubled by the disfigurement, though, for he smiled broadly and sat with a toddler clasped to his shoulder, patting the child's back while speaking to someone on his left. Who? Was it his child? Where was he?

Other Hanuvars came and went before him. There he was with a scarred face. There he marched in Dervan armor at the head of a band of legionaries. There he toiled with a pick in some dim place against a wall of rock. His frame was shrunken, and his neck was collared. Immediately after that he stood upon a battlement overlooking a stormy sea while a flotilla of triremes flying a banner that wasn't quite the flag of Volanus drew near.

"You're at the center of so many places," he heard Rokana say, her voice surging around him like a tide.

The images gathered faster, and then one hove into view that did not waver.

He lay on his side upon a bed, looking perhaps a little grayer, but whole and more at ease. Propped up on one arm beside him, her other arm distractedly playing with her own graying hair, lay lost Ravella.

His heart skipped in a pain that was both sweet and striking.

Beside him here in this spirit place the witch released his hand and lifted her own. He could not see what she did, but he felt it, as though she stirred the waters of his bath. In some unseen way, he thought, she was measuring his duplicate, or at least his energies.

And then she turned her attention upon him and her hands stretched apart, as though she separated yarn. The more she manipulated these invisible strands the more he realized that with each shift he felt a slight tingle. One change left him suddenly breathless and constricted and he put hands to his throat. The witch worked rapidly then, as if untying a knot, and the impediment eased, then vanished altogether.

After that her adjustments were minor, though she shifted behind him and to his side, floating now here, now there. The while, Hanuvar looked down on this other version of himself, lying peacefully with a woman he had loved. In what version of his life had she lived, so that the two of them reclined comfortably together? This other Hanuvar laughed with his lover. They were relaxed; two intimate friends. Were they talking about people they knew? Or the war? Or might their war be long since over? Could they be talking about children?

Someone called his name.

It sounded so much like Rokana that he turned to her. Her face was obscured by mist, but her mouth was closed and she looked intent upon some final adjustment. He was watching her as his name rang out through the ether, and with it he heard another female voice.

"Father," the voice called, and it was achingly familiar, though he could not be certain.

Rokana let out a sigh of relief and lowered her hands. She studied her work with the satisfied air of a master craftsman until she too heard his name called.

This time Hanuvar recognized the voice as his daughter's.

"No," said Rokana, but he turned toward that sound, and apparently in this strange place to focus attention keenly was to move, because suddenly the voices grew louder and more certain and the fog scrolled past him and behind him the spell-maven called to him, telling him no . . .

And then he was lying once more beside Rokana. At some point they must have stopped holding hands in the real world just as their spirits had.

But he realized he was no longer on blankets as he propped himself up on his elbows—nothing lay beneath him but grass. The woman blinked blearily and rose up at his side.

From his left came a feminine gasp.

He saw then that he did not lie in a stone house. A canvas awning peaked above them, supported by tent poles. The same rune that the witch had drawn beside the doorway was etched to the right of the closed tent flap.

And there, standing where Antires had been, his own daughter stared at him as though he were a ghost.

II

Narisia looked much as he remembered her, dark hair touched by red, and shorn short. An unfamiliar scar stood out along her forehead, just below where the line of a helm would lie. She was dressed like a warrior, complete with breastplate engraved with entwined, winged serpents, leather pteruges hanging skirt length, metal shin greaves, and worn soldier's boots. A sword hung at her side, not a Dervan gladius, but a falcata, the long blade of his own people, convex as it lengthened and tapering to a point.

"How—how are you here?" his daughter asked.

"I'm not sure." A wave of dizziness struck him as he climbed to his feet and she was there, supporting him.

To have her at his side was almost intoxicating, and she seemed just as shocked to be in his presence. A grin spread slowly across his face even as he took in the environment. "This isn't right," he said. "Though you can't imagine how pleased I am to see you."

"And I you," Narisia said, though she still looked stunned.

Rokana sat up, breathing heavily, her eyes wide as they fastened upon him. She looked different; her dress was of finer quality, and her hair was professionally arranged. About her wrist was a bracelet in a serpentine shape he recognized for a stylized depiction of an asalda.

Before she could speak, the tent flap was thrust open and in stepped a broad, heavy figure, a powerful man in similar armor to Narisia's, his beard graying, his neck corded with muscle.

"What's happened?" he asked, and then his eyes widened and he roared out a question. "Hanuvar?"

His brother Adruvar. Alive. They surged toward one another in delight and the next thing Hanuvar was being enfolded in his brother's great arms. He laughingly slapped his back.

"By the gods!" Adruvar stepped back and beamed at him. To Rokana, now supporting herself on a chair to the side, he said: "You said you two were only going to consult with him—but . . . you've brought him back!"

"He is not your brother," Rokana said. "Or your father," this to Narisia, "though he will be much like him."

"He looks like him," Narisia said, staring at him with huge eyes.

"I've slipped into another tapestry, haven't I?" Hanuvar asked of Rokana.

"Yes. Very good," she added.

"But you didn't expect me? I heard you calling my name."

"Rokana was going to consult with another you," Adruvar explained. "You weren't supposed to come back." He laughed in joy. "This is fantastic!"

Hanuvar nodded agreement. There was so much to ask his family, but first he looked back to Rokana. "In my tapestry you were trying to heal me of a magical accident. But not in a tent."

"You were working with me?" she asked. "Interesting. But then similar threads appear in similar tapestries."

"Are you sick?" Narisia asked him, then, before he could reply, she curtly demanded of the woman, "Is he well?"

"He appears healthy, both in this world, and magically."

"We need your help," Adruvar told him. "The Dervans are marching on Volanus."

"Only now?" he asked.

Adruvar's look was curious. Hanuvar gently patted his arm and stepped past to push aside the tent flap.

The tent was pitched in the shade of an oak, on a rise overlooking an armed camp and ordered rows of tents. Beyond, low clouds scudded in an evening sky.

A sentry stood beyond the tent. He turned and gaped at Hanuvar. He was approaching middle age, a bearded man in Volani armor with a deeply scarred forearm.

"General?" he whispered.

"Gisco?" Hanuvar asked in response. Gisco had climbed through the ranks, starting out as a clown of a soldier until he was a steady veteran and a signalman who could almost intuit the commands Hanuvar meant to relay. He had died at Mazra, taking a spear while struggling onto his horse when they prepared to retreat.

Both men stared as though they looked upon a ghost, and their smiles flared at the same moment. Hanuvar laughed and offered his hand and the two men clasped forearms warmly, slapping each other in the shoulder.

Gisco looked bewildered. "I saw you die, General! But you're real as me. You're no ghost!"

Adruvar spoke behind them. "With my brother at our head, we'll finish those Dervans, Gisco."

"I am sure of it, sir," Gisco agreed. He was still grinning widely, vigorously shaking Hanuvar's arm.

"It's good to see you." Hanuvar wiped at tears and couldn't tell if they were of sorrow for his lost companion or of joy in seeing this living duplicate of him; he had the same trouble when he looked upon his brother.

Narisia waited with the tent flap open. But Hanuvar turned and considered the camp again, seeing where the horses were picketed. There were mahogany-skinned Ruminians at work feeding them. And there, he saw a separate contingent flying standards from the Herrenic city-states, including Orinth, in his world leveled by the Dervans as thoroughly as Volanus. He also spotted bands of Ceori among the armed host, readying equipment.

This, though, was not Tyvol. While these same kinds of trees could be found in the southern coast of the peninsula, he instinctively knew that he was north of Volanus, not far from the coast.

Hanuvar clapped Gisco's shoulder and walked toward his beckoning daughter. Adruvar followed. Rokana sat at the table, drinking tea, and his daughter regarded him with wary optimism, as though they were estranged. Seeing her manner, he kept from pulling her close, though it pained his heart. He tried to remind himself that this was not truly his daughter.

"Gisco says he saw his Hanuvar die," Hanuvar said. "How long ago?"

"Sixteen years," Narisia answered.

"How?"

"You fell against the Dervans, at the battle of Mazra." Adruvar stepped behind Rokana and rubbed her shoulders. She closed her eyes and relaxed under the care of his huge hands. That was an interesting development. In his world, the two had never met, for Adruvar had died before she joined forces with them.

"In my land," Hanuvar said, "I survived Mazra. Though I lost the battle."

"In this world, you won but died of your injuries," his daughter said. "And Ciprion?"

The furrow on his brother's brow suggested his surprise that he cared. "He was killed in the battle."

"And then what happened?" Hanuvar asked.

"Well, there was a big funeral for you," Adruvar started, and looked as though he meant to say more.

"Not that. What happened in Volanus?"

His daughter answered. "We've had an uneasy truce with the Dervans ever since. The Herrenes and Cerdians have been keeping them distracted, but they put down a rebellion in Ethenis last year and Caiax is marching on Volanus."

"Caiax." Hanuvar's lip curled as he said the name. "In my tapestry he sacked Volanus. Tens of thousands were slain and only a few live on under the Dervan yoke."

They swallowed his words but could not digest them.

He spoke on, slowly. "Narisia was one of them. You escaped, but I've no idea where you went."

"What about me?" Adruvar asked.

That reply came hard. "You've been dead a long time, brother. One of Catius' sons intercepted a message you sent me."

Again that great brow furrowed. He repeated the name as though he mentioned a Herrenic health tonic. "Catius?"

"How fortunate for you," Hanuvar said. "A world without Catius. What of Melgar?"

Narisia answered. "He's marshaling our forces in Volanus."

Melgar lived. He let out a shuddering breath. "Volanus stands. Adruvar and Melgar live. My daughter is free. What of Harnil?"

Adruvar grinned. "He's one of our shofets."[16]

Hanuvar laughed in delight. All of his brothers were still alive. "And what of Imilce?"

Adruvar shifted sheepishly and cleared his throat. "Melgar . . . married Imilce. You've been dead a long time," he added apologetically.

---

[16] The shofets were the two elected magistrates who ruled Volanus. Originally one had focused upon internal matters and the other upon external concerns, but over long centuries it was not uncommon for one of the shofets to be subordinate to the other, acting as a trusted right-hand advisor and executor. Such had been the case during Hanuvar's tenure, when he had been ably assisted by the wise former councilor Sophonisba.   —*Silenus, Commentaries*

Hanuvar laughed.

"What happened to Mother in your world?" Narisia asked.

It was a bleak answer, but he did not blunt it. "She died in childbirth. We thought we were blessed, that she would bear another child of ours, but it proved the death of both."

She nodded slowly. Almost he asked after Ravella. But it might be that Narisia didn't know of her, or that this Hanuvar had never met her.

Narisia straightened, as if making a mental shift in the adjustment. "We need to focus on the tactical situation."

That sounded so much like something he would say that he nearly smiled. "Tell me about the Dervans."

Clearly, soberly, succinctly, Narisia described the problem they faced. Caiax, eager to prove himself, had marched in advance of the other consul, Aminius. "We lured Caiax forward to cut him off. He's retreated into a highly defensible position, on a rocky hillside. They have enough water, and food, to hold out for a few more days. Our scouts tell us we have two days before Aminius' legions rejoin him."

"Tell me more about their positioning."

"It's a decent natural fortress. The hill is sectioned off almost like giant steps, with the main camp on the upper level and skirmishers on the lower."

"Troop quality?"

Adruvar answered. "A core of veteran legionaries, but almost half are recent levies."

"Sorcerous adjuncts?"

"The Herrenic uprising played havoc with their sorcerers. Eledeva burned down their ship shortly before arrival."

Hanuvar brightened at that. Maybe it wasn't the great winged serpent who'd been his friend, and given her life to swim him to safety, just as this really wasn't his daughter, or his brother, but . . . he felt a fluttering in his chest. Of course Eledeva lived, if Volanus hadn't yet fallen, for the asalda had called the city home for centuries. "She's alive. What of her sister?"

"Eledeva was wounded during that attack and is still recovering," Narisia reported. "Merontia's broody again and isn't leaving the city. Or even taking to the skies."

That there might be asalda eggs in this Volanus was astonishing, even thrilling, but not germane to their current concerns. He returned his attention to the disposition of their forces. "How good is the Dervan intelligence about your army?"

"Adequate," Narisia answered. "We're not aware of any large leaks, and use the small ones to feed misinformation."

Hanuvar asked about the quality and numbers of their own troops, how experienced their own skirmishers were, whether the Ceori were new recruits or better intercalated, and the composition of the Herrenic levies.

All but the Herrenes had served with the united forces for a long time, and Hanuvar learned to his surprise that many old friends survived in this tapestry, and commanded units. The fates had been far kinder to his people in this world.

While Narisia briefed him, Adruvar departed and returned with a map. Rokana left them, saying she had some matters to look into. Hanuvar had questions for her, namely how he was to get back, but right now his attention was devoted to the needs of this family, so much like his own.

Someone on staff had drawn a fair map of the countryside, carefully noting the placement of the military divisions. Elevations and likely ingress and egress points along the rise where the Dervans camped were well detailed. He would expect nothing less, for these were the same kind of precise maps his father had taught his army to work from.

"Our plan was to pretend a retreat, and hit their flanks when they come down," Adruvar said. "But Narisia isn't sure Caiax can be lured out before it's too late. Caiax thinks he's safe, and together the two Dervan armies outnumber ours. He means to crush our army between the two of his."

"The trick would be to make it seem like we're almost clever enough. And there's a matter of timing, as well." Hanuvar leaned over the map, weighted on each end by a small stone carved with a horse's head with wide brows. Part of his brother Adruvar's standard. He could not help glancing at the big bluff man drinking beside him. He would never, he swore to himself, take this moment, or the memory of it, for granted.

Then he looked across the table at his daughter, still watching him as though he were a stranger, or possibly a magic trick. He returned his attention to the map and the lines of their own troops. He asked their proximity to a road, and the density of trees, and several other topographical questions before arriving at a decision. He tapped the land in front of their camp. "First, we make a big demonstration of pulling out. We'll kick up dust. And cause lots of commotion. But at the same time, we close off this valley here, with two thousand, and here, with another two thousand. The rest of us stop our advance behind this tree line. While all that's going on we deploy skirmishers against them, as though we're actually screening a retreat, but then we use them to push, hard."

"Our skirmishers are veterans," Narisia said. "They know how to push."

"And then?" Adruvar asked.

Hanuvar smiled tightly and explained his plan.

III

Hanuvar remained upon the hilltop as the army quietly waited for orders to depart. They'd eaten well that evening and would now rest until the early hours of the morning. Probably word had spread among the army that some miracle had been worked and a new Hanuvar was among them, but a small band of sentinels kept anyone from climbing the hill. Apart from Rokana, who had just reached the height.

"Are you all right?" he asked. She looked tired.

"I'm well enough. And you? From what you've said, this must be an incredible shock."

"I cannot express how good it is to see them. Even if they're not my family, they feel like them." He met her eyes. "How do I get back?"

She shrugged wearily. "Why should you want to? From what you say, this world is a far better land for you and yours. I have seldom seen your brother so happy. And I can see in your eyes that you feel the same."

"I do. The circumstances are different, but the people are like mine."

"You must have come from a very similar tapestry."

"You don't know?"

"No. I tried to reach out to get advice from a Hanuvar in a tapestry close to ours. But you were between. Maybe that still means you came from one close. I think you should embrace your good fortune."

"It's very tempting. These people need me here, at this moment, and I am glad to help. But the people of my world need me, too."

"I worried you might say something like that."

An armored figure had started up the hill. It was Narisia, her hair burnished by the sinking sun so that it gleamed almost the same color as the helm beneath her arm.

"I've studied my books," Rokana said, "and all my own notes, and . . . I'm sorry. I've no idea how I can find a way back for you."

Narisia arrived and stood waiting while they finished.

Rokana explained further. "I can keep thinking. I can even look at tapestries again, with you. But I don't know how to tell which one is yours, and I do not know how to send you there."

"Why not stay here?" Narisia suggested. "Volanus dead, every one of your brothers dead, Mother dead . . . your world's a terrible place."

"Were I to choose a better land, I could do far worse," Hanuvar conceded. "Maybe there's somewhere I was triumphant in Tyvol and there never was a Mazra. Maybe I might have known you growing up. I wondered, when I first arrived, at the distance I saw in your eyes. But I understood as we kept talking. You never really knew your father, did you?"

"We met once, before Mazra," she said. "I was thirteen."

Hanuvar nodded. That echoed his meeting with his daughter in his own world.

"It was nice," Narisia said hesitantly.

She was awkward because their meeting had been awkward. That day they had met for the first time. She had been reared in Volanus while he'd spent the entirety of her life marching back and forth across the Tyvolian peninsula, trying to bring the Dervans to heel. When he'd finally spoken with her, a Dervan invasion was imminent, and his forces were few. He'd had other things on his mind, and no good way to suddenly tighten bonds with the strange young lady who shared his blood. That's all she would have seen of him. The Hanuvar from this land hadn't had the pleasure of later years to get to know his daughter as a person.

Rokana raised a hand in farewell to them and stepped away. They both returned the gesture. As she started down the hill, a distant trumpeter in the Dervan camp sounded the call to retire for the night.

Narisia's eyes somehow held the light, and they searched his own. "What am I doing in your world?"

"You and a few Eltyr escaped imprisonment. I don't know where you went. I'm searching for you. Someone is murdering high-ranking Dervans and leaving an Eltyr symbol behind. It may be you."

"So I'm fighting back against the Dervans?"

"It may be. Someone is killing children so Dervan parents can suffer, in the name of the Eltyr."

Her entire face showed the same revulsion he felt. "And you think it's me doing that?"

"It doesn't seem like you. But seeing your city destroyed, your husband killed, everyone you know dragged off in chains, or dead... I've met people who've been terribly warped by what happened."

"What did it do to you?"

The question, cutting and sudden, was so much like something his own Narisia might have said that it startled him. "I'm not sure yet. I've kept busy so I don't have to think about it."

"Busy doing what?"

"I was away from Volanus when it fell. I founded a new colony, weeks away. I'd returned to recruit more colonists and arrived just as the walls were breached. Eledeva died getting me to safety. By the time I got back, the Dervans had sold the few survivors. I'm buying them secretly, or freeing them, and getting them on ships."

"How many?"

"A little over a thousand. That's all that were left."

Her eyes widened in horror. "By the gods. I can see why that would drive someone to kill. Do you think it did to me?"

"I don't think so. That's not the woman I know."

"How well do you know me?"

She strove to sound self-possessed, but there was no missing the longing there. A desperation to hear of something positive. He told her the truth. "After the war, you and I became friends. I ruled as one of the shofets for almost seven years, until Ciprion warned me the Lenereva faction and the Dervan military were conspiring against me."

She looked bemused. "Tannis Lenereva," she said. "I wouldn't think even he could sink so low. But Ciprion warned you? A Dervan?"

"He's a good man. He spent all of his political capital trying to stop the third war and then spent most of his money buying Volani children so they wouldn't end up in far worse circumstances."

She assimilated that and ground her lips together. Beyond the camp, the final rim of sun had vanished, though the clouds were still stained red in its wake. Volani trumpeters now called their own soldiers to their bunks, a lonely sound that cut through the night. Narisia spoke quietly. "I suppose things can be worse than losing your city and parents and being sold into slavery. What was I like there, before the war?"

"You were tempted to come with me to found the colony. But you were an officer of the Eltyr and wanted to continue to mold the corps. You and your husband thought you might be pregnant." He wondered if he should ask if she had children.

"My husband," she repeated. "Who is he?"

"An artist."

She laughed.

"Are you married here? Do you have children?"

"Three, and yes. But he's no artist. He's a friend of Melgar's. An admiral."

"Bomilcar?" he suggested.

She laughed. "Yes! How did you know?"

"He was smitten with you in my world. Melgar kept telling him to court you, but he couldn't get up the nerve."

She laughed, then sobered. "Is Bomilcar alive there, too?"

"Yes," he nodded. "In the colony."

She seemed pleased that her husband's counterpart still lived, but she was curious about another topic. "Tell me about this colony."

"A little over four thousand live there. It lies past the Lesser Lenidines, east and further east, almost two weeks beyond the isle of Narata, in an archipelago. There is a deep, sheltered bay, and the air is rich with the scent of flowers at nearly every time of year. Fruits grow in abundance, and the fishing is plentiful. It is not Volanus, but there our people live free. They must labor hard, but they are happy. And they are far from Dervans."

"I named one of my boys after you," she said suddenly. "And another after grandfather. You can meet them, after we win."

"That would be a fine thing."

Her gaze had softened. It was wistful now, clouded with imagined moments she had never had with her own father. "You seem just like him."

"And you seem just like her."

"Rokana said that we had to find a tapestry close to ours, or you wouldn't be similar enough to offer the kind of advice we needed."

"I hope I do not disappoint."

"Not so far. We should see you fitted for armor. Are you ready to dress for war?"

"I am."

"Come with me then. Father," she added. She didn't sound entirely comfortable saying it, but a warmth had kindled in her eyes.

"I will come, daughter. And we will fight together. For Volanus."

IV

The Volani tried to be secretive as they pulled out in the predawn hours, but the scouts had noted the dust plumes against the stars.

Marius peered out from the height where the majority of the legion was bivouacked. The enemy had left their tents in place, and skirmishers had been trading spears and slingstones with their own force through the night, on the lower, east side of the hill. That the enemy had recently increased the tempo and the ferocity of their attack was meant to suggest that an assault might be imminent, but they had failed to count upon the excellence of Derva's best scouts.

The general was up. He hadn't emerged from his tent, though, because he was sulking. Caiax had been trapped and only by chance had Marius discovered this excellent defensible spot before Adruvar's army closed in.

When he neared the consul's tent, Marius saw candlelight from under the canvas barrier. He had the sentry announce him, and then Caiax gruffly bade him enter.

The consul looked worn and angry, and his gray head craned out over the map in his quarters. Marius wasn't sure what the old man searched for, given that the map was of the coast, but Caiax studied it for a good long while before finally looking up. "First Spear," he said, addressing Marius by rank rather than name. "You look happy with yourself. Have my messengers returned from Aminius?"

"No, sir. I have other news. The enemy's retreating and trying to conceal themselves. I think Aminius has gotten too close for their comfort."

Caiax grunted. "There are reports that the Volani have redoubled the assault of their skirmishers."

"Yes, sir. I believe that's an attempt to deceive us. They want us to think that they're not really leaving. After all, they wouldn't leave their skirmishers behind."

A rare smile ticked up the corners of Caiax's mouth. "You're certain it's a trick?"

"They are not nearly so clever as they think, General. Every one of them thinks they are Hanuvar—"

"—And none of them are. Yes. Good. Turn out the men. We'll move fast."

"Yes, sir. Should we feed them?"

"We need to hit the enemy hard and fast. It's no time to coddle the boys. They're tough. And they're itching for a fight."

"Yes, sir." Marius saluted and left. Caiax's confidence was a salve to his own worries. In good spirits, he passed along his general's orders. He, too, was eager for the fight, but he wondered if it was truly wise to send out the men before breakfast. An additional half hour's delay surely wouldn't prove too advantageous for the Volani, and while he agreed that the men were ready for a fight, men always fought better well fed.

He ordered the signalmen to call the men to arms, and soon they were falling out of their tents and their optios and centurions were shouting them into gear and into line.

On the lower step of the hill camp, some thirty feet below, he heard the occasional shout and the clatter of arms, and, sometimes, a scream. Soon, though, an optio came puffing up to report that the skirmishers were starting to retreat.

Dawn's light sharpened the sky. To north and south, on either side of their flattened hilltop, the growth was thick and forested and dark, and Caiax startled him when he appeared at Marius' elbow.

"We'll get them this time," Caiax said. "Full on their heels, Marius. Do you hear?"

"Yes, sir."

He set their skirmishers after the enemy's. Then, as the sun began to scale the trees, the first cohort crossed down from the lower level and moved onto the plain, in hard pursuit. Soon half their force was either on the lower hill or moving forward. Runners came in that the enemy skirmishers were digging in behind fortifications beyond the tree edge at the edge of the plain below. Scouting reports from flankers from north and south were late returning, which was a little concerning, but not nearly as troubling as the sun now shining straight into their eyes. It would prove an impediment, and one Caiax should probably have thought of. After all, it wouldn't be quite as pronounced when the sun was higher, and a delay to eat would have seen to that.

Beside Marius on the lower step of the hillside, Caiax shielded his eyes and watched his men marching out and forming up. Their skirmishers could be seen further ahead, exchanging slingstone and javelin with the Volani, sheltered behind wooden barricades hastily thrown up in front of the distant woods. He shifted his attention to Marius and frowned. "I know that look. Do not whine like an old woman, Marius. The men will be at a brief disadvantage. But speed is our advantage. Fortune loves the bold. The Volani light troops can't long hold those positions. We'll soon have them flanked."

The unmistakable ululating cry of the Eltyr Corps erupted from somewhere to the south.

It wasn't one voice, or ten voices, it was hundreds. And they were very close.

Caiax's beak of a nose swung first toward the noise, then swiveled to poke at Marius. "You said the defile to the south was too steep to bother with!"

"I said it was an impediment," Marius objected. "I placed sentries there."

"Well, they've done a bang-up job, haven't they? The Eltyr have doubled back around and are trying to flank us!"

V

From his family, Hanuvar had confirmed that the Caiax of this tapestry was just as confident and heedless as that of his own. Caiax, embarrassed by his mistake, was eager for a victory, especially if he could claim it without having to share accolades with Aminius. Now his forces were strung along the ground below the stairstep hill and split upon its two levels.

While the Eltyr held the attention of the Dervans with their attack up the southern slope, Hanuvar's contingent advanced from the dark screen of trees and started up the steep northern side with little opposition. Dervan sentries spotted them just as the advance slingers brought the foremost sentry plummeting thirty feet to sprawl dead a horse length to Hanuvar's right. The nearby Volani soldiers laughed, and then Hanuvar shouted at them to move.

And move they did. A picked force of warriors charged on the double, falcatas in one hand and their notched oval shields in the other. A screen of thirty slingers advanced before them, bolstered by a small cadre of Adruvar's best spearmen, held back from the main force of light troops. They reached the north edge of the higher hill and fought to hold it.

All of the Dervan slingers had scattered across the plain below; there was nothing to counter the advancing Volani skirmishers but the Dervan reserve, which he knew from intelligence reports to be the greenest troops, sprinkled with a handful of veterans. They came scrambling to counter the Volani assault, and slingstones and spears sent them tumbling to the earth and down to the underworld.

Veteran rankers rushed up to push back the invaders, better armed men, in better order. A few dozen of Hanuvar's heavy infantry had joined the advance, and at his command the skirmishers slipped back through gaps. The heavy troops surged ahead while the Dervans still struggled to form a line. The next few moments were the crucial ones. The Volani were outnumbered, but the Dervans were on the wrong foot, disorganized. Hanuvar shouted at his soldiers to hurry to reinforce, and up they clambered over near vertical spans of slope.

He was exhorting the next line to follow when a wave of dizziness staggered him. He steadied himself against a rock. For a moment he thought a fog had risen, and then he understood that the strange mist of the lands between the tapestries had been superimposed across the battlefield. Rokana, the Rokana from his world, floated within it. Her eyes were bright and her hands sought his. "Come with me," she cried.

"I can't. Not yet."

He backed away from her. The mists faded but clung to his vision like cobwebs. Stepping back from the slope, he saw the band of Dervans tightening in an arc, holding their own. Dervan reinforcements were closing. No more Volani could reach the ground, and those that had taken it were sorely pressed. Unless he acted quickly, those soldiers would die, and their attack would fail.

But he spotted another path up the hillside. Steep, yes, but unwatched. He motioned for the men to follow and started up through tough grass and rocky ground. He scraped a knee on a sharp gray stone and bashed an elbow against the steep side, barely feeling either. He vaulted a boulder then raced up a final four feet of slope and saw that as soon as he advanced, he'd be behind and to the left of the Dervans. He held position until six more men were with him, then eight, then twelve, and then, with others close on his heels, he lifted his falcata and charged.

A grizzled centurion turned at the sound of their footfalls and opened his mouth as if to shout warning, then gaped. His eyes widened in recognition. "Hanuvar!" he cried. "It's Hanuvar!"

Belatedly the centurion cried for his men to swing about, his eyes alive with fear. Hanuvar brought the falcata swinging down. The blow swept the Dervan gladius aside. The broad front end of his blade struck more with an axe's force than a sword's, shearing through the centurion's collarbone. It was only when he yanked the falcata free from the sinking flesh and armor that he registered the man as one of Ciprion's standard bearers.

Other Dervans had turned then, with his name on their lips, and it spread through their ranks with a note of hysteria.

But the Dervans had not yet cracked. Optios and centurions shouted to hold the line, and Hanuvar led his men ahead, swinging his falcata into a shouting face and transforming it into a screaming red horror before it dropped away.

All then was madness and ruin, with enemies before him and allies to right and left. He fought and slew and ducked and heaved, shouting until he was hoarse. The old instincts were still with him, and his little band smashed through the invaders on the rise. Those few Dervans not caught between the two bands of Volani fled for the main body of their troops, shouting that Hanuvar was back from the dead. Both of the Volani routes were open now, and he motioned his soldiers on, screaming at them to hurry.

And once again Rokana was before him, her forehead creased with worry. "Soon it will take too much energy to pull you back."

"A moment," he said. "I'm needed here."

Her eyes were accusing, and he hated to turn from her.

Before him the Volani line advanced. He heard the call of the Eltyr, and frantic horn blasts of the legion, trying to form into some coherence. He clambered onto a boulder for a better view and saw where the two sides of the Volani line had caught the Dervan column in the open. Adruvar's command had reached the lower hill and crashed forward even as the first of Hanuvar's band was hitting from the rear.

"The center!" Adruvar called. "The center!"

His brother's distant face was blood streaked, but he grinned through it, a warrior's fierce smile.

The Dervan standard beyond the helms on the lower hill wavered. Those few left on the higher hill were perishing between the remainder of his force and the Eltyr.

Seeing that the upper hill was all but won, Hanuvar followed with his contingent. He paused for a moment before descending, looking over the wave of allied troops overwhelming the column on the plain, and advancing on every side against the shrinking center on the first level of the stairstep hill.

There about the shining eagle standard an armored figure sat upon a horse, his mouth opened in a shout, his long neck stretched forward. The Dervan officer pointed frantically, then swung his horse about, as if he searched for a line of retreat while his men screamed and faltered and died.

It was this tapestry's Caiax. And as the Dervan leader looked upslope his eyes settled upon Hanuvar, motionless upon the upper rim only a few hundred feet away.

Caiax froze. His head lifted, and Hanuvar would have sworn that the man gaped. Hanuvar pointed down at him.

The moment seemed suspended in time, as though it stretched for hours, but then, with a finger snap, the main Dervan line shattered and the center caved. The few survivors retreated to a tiny circular core, about the standard, the crush so great Caiax was forced to abandon his horse. Hanuvar lost sight of him in the savage flurry.

He spotted his brother, directing troops on the lower level, and started down for him, calling his name.

The big man heard, and broke away from his soldiers, though he still pointed them forward toward the final knot of enemy soldiers.

Adruvar stepped apart, eyes bright, and waited for Hanuvar, wiping his face of some other man's blood.

From beyond came an exultant shout, for the Dervan standard with its gleaming eagle had fallen.

Adruvar grinned and laughed at him. "Your plan worked perfectly! Just like always, my brother!"

Hanuvar smiled back, but his brother recognized his heartache, and his expression fell. "What's wrong? Are you wounded?" He stretched out his hand.

"I'm fine. But I have to go."

Adruvar snorted in disbelief. "What are you talking about?"

"You don't need me anymore."

Adruvar shook his shaggy head. "Of course we do! Your plan won the day!"

"And now you can face Aminius and squeeze his army between yours and Melgar's."

"With you at our head we will be victorious."

"My brother." Hanuvar gripped Adruvar's arm. His warm, living arm. He blinked tears away. "There's nothing I would like more than to sit again with you and Harnil and Melgar and my daughter. To see my former wife." His voice broke. "To walk the streets of Volanus. To hold my grandchildren." He shook his head and forced himself together. "But the people of my own land need me more than you. Tell Narisia I'm sorry I can't be there for her. I'm sorry her father wasn't, and I know, from the depths of my heart he would have been, in a better world."

Adruvar bowed his head, his eyes filling with tears. He clasped Hanuvar's shoulder. "I understand. So will she."

They clung tight to one another.

"Live long, and well," Hanuvar told him. "Tell our brothers the same. And give my best to Imilce."

"I will. Good luck to you, my brother."

Then, Hanuvar turned at last to Rokana, waiting at his shoulder. He thought that Adruvar must have caught sight of her, for his expression clouded.

She smiled sadly as her grip tightened around Hanuvar's fingers. He turned to see his brother raise his hand. Then the world faded and they were once more amongst the mist and the drifting darkness.

VI

"You should not have done that," Rokana said wearily and with a touch of asperity that was practically a shout in this liminal space. "I nearly lost you. I nearly lost my own way."

"I apologize," he said, head bowed "I hadn't meant to go. I heard my name, and when I sought its source, my body travelled to that place."

She frowned. They hung suspended in the shifting fog. Her free hand stirred the air as her other held to his, and then stilled, as though she had grasped hold of something. For a brief moment, Hanuvar perceived a shining thread between her fingers, and then her hand tightened around what looked empty air.

But she pulled once, twice, and the gray mists whirled and faded and spun, or perhaps the two of them did, so dizzy was he. Suddenly he lay looking up at the wooden rafters of a stone hut. It took a long moment for his head to feel like it had stopped its rocking.

"Hanuvar?" Antires asked. Then, exultant, he repeated his name. "Hanuvar!"

He sat up, hand to his head, still unsteadily.

"You just . . . vanished!" Antires said. "Your whole body! And I couldn't raise Rokana all night!"

There was a growl in her voice as she pushed up on her hands. "You should not have interfered. When you shouted at me it just made things worse. But I found him. And somehow I found our way back."

"And he's healed?" Antires demanded.

"He is."

"Why is he covered in blood? Where did you get the armor?"

Hanuvar looked down at his armor, and his arm, and the falcata he clutched. The sword that his daughter had given him. "It's Dervan blood."

He lay down the sword and undid the strap of his helm. Less than twenty-four hours before, Narisia herself had presented it to him, her eyes alive with pleasure.

Confusion was heavy in Antires' voice. "I don't understand. What happened?"

Hanuvar released his tight grip upon Rokana's hand and turned to her. "I can never thank you fully for what you did. You not only gave me my life back, but you helped me save an entire people. You gave me moments with loved ones forever lost, and others I might never see again. Whatever is in my power to grant you, I shall."

The consternation in her features dulled, eased by tenderness. She patted his arm. "First," she said, "I mean to sleep for days. But I have all that I need in this humble place. If I think of anything else, I will let you know."

He wanted to tell her of Adruvar and the love he had seen between them both. But what good would that story do her? "Is there anything I can do for you, now?"

"Would a general care to fix me some eggs? And ready some tea?"

"If the lady will permit me a moment to clean up, I will prepare whatever my feeble skills permit."

Antires belatedly moved to help Rokana to her feet, then guided her to the chair.

Hanuvar started for the door, taking the falcata with him.

His friend was a moment behind. "You still look a little younger than you were last year. Like your early forties."

Hanuvar looked down at his bloody hands while he called up the water from the old pump outside, then washed them clean.

Antires stepped to assist him with his armor. "Are you going to tell me what happened?" he asked, working the buckle on the right shoulder. "You look a little like you've seen a ghost."

"Not ghosts," he answered. "They weren't ghosts there."[17]

---

[17] In amongst Antires' papers I found the following fragment, which seemed directly related to the moment of Hanuvar's return. Why he cut it from the published versions of *The Hanuvid* I cannot say, but I present it to you for your entertainment.   —*Andronikos Sosilos*

> When Hanuvar told me of the many people he had met, I could not help lamenting that he had not encountered me, and wondered where I was in that tapestry, and what I might be doing.
> "I saw you," he said, and while he smiled, I could tell he was not joking.
> "Where?" I asked.
> "You were pulling on a shield and addressing a band of Herrenes, readying them for battle."
> "So I was an officer?" I asked.
> "Indeed you were, weathered and scarred and battle hardened. Your arm looked half again as thick."
> I flexed my arm, which was by no means puny, and wondered what course my life had taken in that place that I had ended up a warrior. But then many of the greatest Herrene playwrights were soldiers. "Did you say anything to me?" I asked.
> "I was tempted, but you were busy, and would not have known me. There were so many others I would have loved to have spoken with, but there wasn't time before the battle. I didn't know I wouldn't have another chance."

※ ※ ※

There are some who like to speak constantly about their hopes and fears and their inner thoughts and dwell constantly upon things they cannot change. Hanuvar was not one of these, and so I rarely heard him discuss his daughter. I am sure he thought often of her, especially in the months after he first learned about the Eltyr and the murders alleged to her.

With his condition normalized Hanuvar had a brief reunion with Izivar, south of Derva. None of Carthalo's contacts had yet turned up any information about Narisia or her Eltyr companions, though we were still waiting upon word from informants beyond the peninsula.

In the meantime, Hanuvar and Carthalo prepared to address a spate of challenging situations in the south, where slaveholders of Volani were stubbornly intransigent. He was only hours away from leaving when we received word from Ciprion, who requested assistance. I'm sure Hanuvar would have lent it on the instant regardless, but he had additional impetus to do so, for the Eltyr had returned to Derva, and Ciprion himself had been tasked with stopping her.

—Sosilos, Book Fourteen

Chapter 14:
Line of Descent

I

The movements had grown rote. Cough, and cough again, willing what felt like invisible pulleys to bring up the sticky stuff from deep inside. Then, taste the blood and raise the cloth to his lips.

Gaius didn't know why he looked at the cloth afterward, as if to confirm that there was blood on it, because there always was. It astonished him how much blood he'd been coughing up. Surely one man shouldn't lose so much, yet he kept on going.

He looked across his desk as he lowered the fabric.

Sarnax sat primly on the facing chair, his old brown face struggling between three equidistant points of solicitude, pity, and disgust. In a fit of petulance Gaius crumpled the cloth and tossed it at his old friend. He regretted the action the moment it left his hand.

The soiled napkin went no further than the edge of the ridiculous wide expanse of the desk separating them.

The struggle on the old Hadiran's face was won at last by pity, and Gaius scowled. "If you're going to keep looking at me like that, you can just go now." He knew his voice still conveyed power and was disturbed that the effect was lessened by the hint of old man quaver on the final word.

Sarnax's more customary imperturbable mask slid into place, smooth and bland from his chin to the top of his long round head, shorn close overall. Hair that had once been jet black was gray, and sparse along the sides, as though it were a legionary's helmet. The freedman and now chief advisor would have made a spindly, pathetic legionary. Even in his prime he had never been capable of feats of brawn, but his agile mind had any number of uses.

Gaius sighed at him. Sarnax, as usual, refrained from responding to the temperamental outburst. In his own way he was as unyielding as the fluted columns built into the wall of the study behind him.

"I hate this room," Gaius said. "All this marble. It looks like a temple, or a tomb. Which I supposed I'd better get used to."

"We need to get you south," Sarnax said. "I don't see why you won't go."

"Not until this matter with the Eltyr gets cleared up. The revenants seem to have botched it thoroughly."

"Surely we should blame the Cerdians."

It was the Cerdians who'd brought down the revenant outpost where many of the records on the matter had been kept, but Gaius shook his head. More and more often he'd come to doubt the revenants. "My brother put too much faith in them. And so did I. I'm starting to think they engineered all this talk of Hanuvar just to make themselves more important."

Sarnax countered with reported facts. "There were the testimonials from the Isles of the Dead, and those who say they saw Hanuvar in that arena in Hidrestus. And there have been other instances—"

Gaius raised a hand as Sarnax spoke. It was wrinkled, but he thought it still looked strong. Especially for a man his age. He shook the hand and cut off his advisor. "Who knows what really happened, and how reports may have been exaggerated by the revenants?"

He continued as Sarnax opened his mouth to object. "And don't talk to me about Caiax claiming he saw him. Caiax was a vainglorious fool. Marching off without leave for some ridiculous vendetta against the Ceori. He'd clearly lost his mind."

"We could have followed up against the Ceori more forcefully afterward."

Gaius snorted. "And waste more men chasing them through their valleys?" He pointed with his hand to the floor, only then noticing a spot of blood on his thumb. He couldn't see the space in front of his desk without craning forward, but there was a bright tiled mosaic of the Inner Sea with Tyvol central before him, and the emperor's sigil fastened to the front of the desk hung directly over it. "You believe what the maps show—that we control every spare inch of land in Tyvol. It's not like that. We control the cities and the hubs of transportation. It's not worth it to control every flea-bitten desolate mile."

"We Hadirans have some familiarity with empire, sire."

"As you've mentioned. But it's easier when you've got a long strip of land on the side of a river and nothing but sand-blasted desolation everywhere else. Who cares if there's some criminals or unruly bits hiding out over there, as long as they keep to themselves and leave off our commerce?"

"If they don't become too numerous, I suppose there are better things to waste our resources upon," Sarnax agreed with visible reluctance.

"But to my point. Caiax. What did Caiax expect to find? Hanuvar and a ghost army, crossing the Ardenines again?" He sputtered his lips in disgust. "I'm tired of all of it. Fools, the lot of them. I'm starting to regret that entire Volani debacle."

"And then you'd have had Cerdia to the west and Volanus to the east and the Herrenes and the Ceori setting fires everywhere else?"

"You're being especially argumentative today, Sarnax. Are you enjoying your Volani riches? Now no one trusts us."

"But they fear us. You yourself said that was important. And if my Volani riches shame you in any way, I will part with them."

Gaius shook his head and waved his hand.

"I think that the Volani women charmed you," Sarnax said.

"They did, and rightly so. Izivar and her little sister, both. And the revenants are full of shit if they think the entire matter was engineered to impress me. Idiots. Those two girls were desperate to help me. And that younger was the bravest of all. I swear, if I had a legion of men as brave as that one girl..." He let his voice trail off because he suspected he repeated himself, and the patient look in Sarnax's eyes confirmed it.

He sighed. "Forgive me that comment about your riches."

Sarnax bowed his head.

"I am so tired all the time now," Gaius said bitterly. "My temper is short. Like my time. Anything now is just a delay."

"Yes. But will the delay be a few months, or a few years?"

Gaius liked the sound of that. "You are a good friend. The most important thing is to prepare Enarius for what's to come. I don't think we can manage the Cerdians before I pass, but with luck Aminius will get himself killed fighting them, and get them bloody at the same time. He'll never be able to ingratiate himself with the legions."

"I think you're right on the latter point, and we can hope for the first."

Gaius liked the sentiment, but there was a touch of pity again in the shape of that thin old mouth across from him. Gaius swore. "I'm doing it again, aren't I. Saying the same things over and over. I feel as though I'm making a list in my head and have to keep going through it to make sure my choices are sound."

"There's the matter of the Eltyr, sire."

Good old Sarnax. He'd remembered what they were really supposed to be talking about, and brought it back around. So many other courtiers would let him wander from topic to topic to keep him happy, but Sarnax spoke the truth, even if it got him growled at.

"Yes. I've made a decision. I'm done with revenants. I've placed the matter of the Eltyr into Ciprion's hands."

Sarnax's black eyes stared into the middle distance as he composed a response. "He is an avowed republican, sire. He has publicly stated, on many occasions, that he feels the power to run an empire is too much for a single man, no matter how talented. Do you think it wise to trust him with the safety of you and your son?"

Gaius laughed derisively. "People said Catius was the most honest man in Derva. But Catius' 'honesty' was always self-serving, and shallow. Ciprion also tells you what he thinks, but his thinking is deeper. His ambition is only for a steady state. He's no revolutionary, and he's not in it for himself or his family. He will help shape the rule of Enarius. And Enarius will profit from his guidance. With Ciprion for military matters, you for societal and political ones, and Lucius for spiritual concerns, Enarius will be in good hands."

"Ciprion is an honorable man," Sarnax conceded.

The general had confounded Sarnax for years, just as he had Gaius himself. But as his life closed, Gaius had come to understand some topics in a different light. Most around him thought mainly about increasing their intake of the state's treasures. But through inclination or schooling, a very few were defenders of the whole, thinking of the treasury as vital for the empire as though all the people in it were one large family. Ciprion himself had explained his concept of duty to Gaius over the winter, and it had struck a chord with him.

Sarnax was waiting patiently, and Gaius finished. "So. Ciprion is taking over the investigation. If he needs resources—"

"Of course, sire. I shall be happy to assist. I suppose it is fortunate you retained copies of records of the Eltyr's depredations."

"It is. The revenants are nearly useless."

"Their leaders do seem more concerned about their hold on power than they do the welfare of the state."

"That is exactly what Ciprion said. Do you know, Enarius wishes to speak with me this morning. I've a mind to assign him to assist Ciprion's search. It would do him good to see our master strategist at work."

"I imagine you're right. Especially since the only military man he spends time with is Metellus. Which, if I may, brings up a point of concern Lucius and I have."

This again. "Metellus is a brave man. And a good observer."

"Lucius doesn't trust him. He says there's a darkness to Metellus."

"He's a soldier. Of course there's darkness. And he's ambitious. But he's kept his head and kept Enarius protected."

"And he also reports on Enarius to you. Yet Enarius thinks him a boon companion. If he can fool your son, who else might he be fooling?"

"Metellus just reports to me because it's a soldier's duty to report to his emperor. Enarius has gotten a stiffer spine around Metellus. A stronger character. And Ciprion won't last forever—Enarius will need someone younger to counsel him, eventually, someone he can trust."

"Perhaps your son's developed that character in spite of Metellus, sire. If I may, Metellus may feel that he's more important than he has a right to be. There's the matter of that special banner he's had made, and the way that he actually drinks with Enarius. As if he thinks himself an equal."

"We've been over this. A man has to have a few around him who aren't always bowing and saying *sire this* and *sire that* and telling him what he wants to hear."

"Which is why you long ago advised me to be blunt. You wish to build for the future. I do not trust Metellus. I advise you, strongly, to separate him from Enarius."

Through their long years together, Gaius had learned when Sarnax believed something passionately. It didn't show in his eyes, but in a slight twitch along the left side of his mouth. His thin lips twisted now, though his voice remained level. "Send him to Aminius, to report on him. Let Metellus gain more seasoning, if you mean him to be the military expert he thinks himself. He's never seen actual warfare."

Sarnax had a legitimate point. A military advisor to leadership had to have experienced more than a few small combats. He dimly recalled that the young centurion's record consisted of typical praetorian work shepherding members of the royal family from place to place. Gaius lightly tapped the desk with his knuckles, spotted more dried blood flecking them, and scraped it clear with his thumbnail. He looked up at Sarnax. "Good enough. A little time on the frontier should make him more useful."

"Exactly, sire."

"Or maybe you want him killed."

"I find him unsavory, sire."

That Sarnax, after seeing and hearing so much over the years, should take exception to one bawdy young officer, struck Gaius as amusing. He laughed, but that turned into a long, racking cough.

Sarnax stretched across the desk, picked up the bloody cloth, and passed it back to him so he could wipe his lips.

The blood was shining red, bright and winking like a sword point.

II

After the aged house slave admitted Hanuvar to the atrium, Ciprion was swift on the scene. Like Hanuvar, he played a role, and thus his welcome was formal, appropriate for greeting an old underling with whom he was fond rather than a peer. He showed his approval of Hanuvar's disguise only by a brief uptilt of a thick eyebrow. He remained as Hanuvar had last seen him, a handsome aging soldier with dark thick hair and bushy brows, his stern demeanor belied by faint lines of humor about his mouth and eyes. He wore a red tunic with a plain black belt and sturdy brown sandals.

When he was not concealing his identity, Hanuvar now appeared closer to his true age than he had in months, although owing to a lack of weathering, wrinkles, and scars that his newly regenerated body had never accumulated, he could still pass for a younger man. For all that, though, he was more easily recognizable as himself, which was why he had dressed head to foot as a Ceori veteran of the legion auxiliary. A gaudy citizen ring shone on his finger, as though he were proud of the right granted him by his service. Like many aging Ceori he had dyed his hair blond and combed it back. He had also grown and dyed a thick mustache, though his chin and cheeks were cleanly shaved.

Antires had suggested he apply makeup to lighten his skin, but there were enough half-breed Ceori serving in the Dervan ranks that Hanuvar had decided against that more involved and more easily detectable step. Instead he relied upon long experience among the Ceori to inform his walk and manner. A Ceori who'd risen through the ranks and won the regard of a famed war leader like Ciprion would be proud of his acceptance, and therefore wear a fine Dervan citizen's ring, but would retain enough pride in his heritage that he would style his hair and mustache traditionally and prefer a piney-green tunic too earthy for most Dervans. As final elements of his assumed identity, Hanuvar had donned Ceori boots, and a woven Ceori belt holding a knife almost large enough to be challenged by the city vigiles.

There was no knowing what servants might be listening in to spread gossip, so Hanuvar greeted Ciprion with his Ceori accent and an effusive raising of his arms, though, as a Ceori would know, he did not expect a Dervan patrician to actually embrace him. Instead he smiled and took his friend's offered hand in an effusive shake.

They then went through a pantomime of health inquiries before Ciprion finally ushered Hanuvar formally into his home. He told the house slave that they were not to be disturbed and led Hanuvar forward.

Masks of ancestors hung upon the walls, and Hanuvar was certain two were of Ciprion's father and uncle, who had battled against him and Adruvar both. There were lovely paintings of temples and seascapes and ships in encaustic wax, and a few fine Herrenic sculptures. Though he couched his appreciation in Ceori phrasing, the pacing huntress with a lion was honestly masterful and Ciprion informed him that his brother Lucius had acquired it for him.

Much as he would have liked a proper tour of Ciprion's home, all this was prelude to the true purpose of the visit. Ciprion conducted him through a courtyard with a fountain that featured a stern helmeted warrior pouring water from a pitcher. The statue's other hand held a spear, and it wasn't entirely clear what the tableau was supposed to portray.

Ciprion sensed his curiosity and said apologetically, "This villa was a gift from the emperor. I'll get that replaced, eventually."

"Is he readying to spear a fish?" Hanuvar asked in his accented Dervan.

"I think that's the intent, although the spear's pointed at the bush, and why is he pouring water into the pond?" Ciprion shrugged, a Ceori gesture, and Hanuvar chuckled and mirrored it.

Stopping before the left of a set of double doors closed to the courtyard, Ciprion knocked the bottom of one with his foot, as was Dervan custom. "Amelia," he said, "our guest is here."

Ciprion had not said why his wife so wished to meet, though Hanuvar inferred she meant to take the measure of him. A woman's alto voice with a slight rasp bade them enter.

Opening the door, Ciprion gestured for Hanuvar to precede him.

Amelia was rising from behind a desk in a small, tidy office. Behind her was a shelf unit partly given over to the display of potted plants and busts and partly to the tidy storage of documents. Family portraits of her daughter, grandchildren, and son-in-law hung upon the wall opposite the courtyard.

Hanuvar paid only scant attention to the surroundings. He advanced into the space and presented himself with the formal dignity of a Ceori, bowing from the waist before rising to meet the shrewd brown eyes of Ciprion's wife.

Hers was an appealing face, with high cheekbones. Her nose was small and rounded and her brunette hair was well tended without being elaborate; from the way she presented herself, Hanuvar had the sense she liked things just so, and wished them to be pleasing to the eye, so long as no truly extravagant expenditure of time was involved. Her hair hung in flattering loose curls, and had surely taken some effort, but not the labors of a half dozen slave women. Her stola was a soft green with brown-gold tracing that called out a similar shade in her eyes.

"I've brought our guest," Ciprion said, and closed the door behind him. Light still flowed through open windows above the walls to the courtyard.

Hanuvar kept his accent but left off the Ceori gestures. "I am honored to meet you. Thank you for welcoming me into your home."

"I have hoped to meet you for some time," she said. The rasp remained. Ciprion had not mentioned her being ill, and he did not wish to immediately inquire about her health.

"Why don't we sit?" Ciprion indicated the two cushioned chairs facing the desk.

Amelia retreated to her short-backed chair behind the desk. Ciprion had probably told her that Hanuvar would be disguised as a Ceori, but he felt her attention upon his mustache and hair for a long moment before she chose to speak at last. Her diction was formal, almost stilted. "I wish to thank you for your help with that unpleasantness in the provinces. You saved the lives of my grandson, and my husband. I am grateful."

He bowed his head to her. And here, quietly, he dropped his accent at last. "I am grateful to you both for your help safeguarding Volani orphans. If it is not too much trouble, I'd like to see them in the coming weeks."

She acquiesced with a graceful inclination of her head. "Ciprion mentioned your interest. He said there's a possibility that one of your nieces might be among them."

"I do not hold high hopes, but I would like to meet them regardless."

"I'll be happy to arrange a visit. We . . . acquired Volani tutors for them. We wished them to be as comfortable as was possible. Given the circumstances."

"So Ciprion said, and I am immensely grateful." Ciprion and Amelia had nearly bankrupted themselves buying all the young Volani children they could afford to house and care for, and it was a debt he would never be able to repay. That the boys and girls had been indelibly traumatized and were being raised in a culture in many ways antithetical to their own were worries for another time. Under the aegis of these two, the children at least were safe from abuse or exploitation.

"And how do your liberation efforts proceed?" Amelia asked. She seemed to be warming ever so slightly.

He answered honestly. "Better than I feared. We have recovered nearly half of them so far. Slightly more if I account for the children under your protection."

"And you are taking them away from our lands?"

"I am."

"How far off is . . . your new city?"

She had come very close to naming New Volanus. Ciprion had assured him that they could speak openly here, so her reticence likely had more to do with the desire to refrain from mentioning certain topics by name. Hanuvar appreciated that, for it was easier to not speak of the wrong things in the wrong places if you were practiced in never mentioning them at all.

"Half a world. While I've some Dervan friends, it seems best to keep our peoples separate going forward."

"That may be true. Are your people in no danger there? There are no other nations?"

He wondered if she were merely being polite, or if she was honestly curious to know just how distant he and his people would be from hers. Probably she wanted to ensure that they would cause no more trouble in the future, either for Ciprion or her family. "There are some city-states on the mainland, and a few tribal cultures on some of the islands, something like those living among the Lenidines. But there are no great powers. As of now, we all have room."

"That is good to hear." She folded her hands and her gaze sharpened. "I don't know if you're aware of this, but my brother and my father died in your war."

Hanuvar felt rather than saw Ciprion tense beside him.

"I did know that," Hanuvar replied. "I'm sorry for your loss."

"They didn't have to die when they did. They were good men. Kind men."

And did she blame him for those deaths? He couldn't fully read her, though long-banked anger was clear in the way she held her head.

"If the good and the kind were the ones who led us, we might never come to blows," Hanuvar responded.

Ciprion approved of this with a grunt. "Fairly said."

Amelia eyed her husband for a moment, her expression still guarded. She returned her attention to Hanuvar. "If you had won the war—if you had beaten the Dervan legions, what would you have done?"

He would neither apologize, nor make excuses. "You want to know if I would have leveled Derva. Sold the survivors into slavery?"

His bluntness did not surprise her; perhaps she even appreciated it. "I know that you Volani do not keep slaves."

"We do not level cities, either."

"But you kill. I'm told more than fifty thousand perished that day with my father and brother, at Acanar. Ciprion was there. He might have died as well. You started the war. How would you have ended it?"

It was Derva that had started the war, by making their plans for domination manifest, and by gobbling up, taxing, subjugating, and otherwise interfering with Volanus' formerly free trading relations. But this was not a time for debate. By starting the war she meant that he was the one who had invaded their lands. And by that reckoning she was correct.

"I thought I could bring Derva to its knees, and it would have to make terms. I was young, and hopeful, and a little arrogant. I didn't know how stubborn Derva would be. But then I didn't know how changeable my own government would prove, or how undependable the Herrenes would remain."

"Would you do it again?"

"Invade Tyvol? We knew you would come for us, too, sooner or later. What other option did I have?"

She had grown more somber still and sat frowning. "It might have been different if you had not spilled so much of our blood."

"We might have lived on under Dervan governorship. With Dervan rules, intolerable to most. My people have been free as long as yours. We did not want to wear your yoke."

She breathed out slowly. She looked over to the door, but not at it, as though at some distant landscape. He wondered if she were imagining the past, or the future, or was remembering her father and brother. "You are the enemy of my state," she said at last. "There was a time when I would not have suffered you in my presence. But here I sit, knowing that having you in my house is tantamount to treason, and yet I will not report it. My husband has taken immense risks for you and continues to do so. And he risks more than himself."

"I know it."

She shifted her attention to Ciprion. "Do you honestly think he will be seen for a Ceori?"

Her husband answered smoothly. "There are many half-breed Ceori in the ranks of the auxiliary, and they frequently dye their hair. Especially the older ones. And his mangled Dervan is perfect."

Hanuvar addressed his friend with a thick Ceori accent, rolling his *r*s and lingering on the hard consonants. "But I have been working so hard on my Dervan. Do you think I have an accent still?"

Ciprion chuckled.

"You two are amused by yourselves," Amelia said.

Her husband showed empty palms in concession as he replied. "Amongst such grim duties, we must look for humor somewhere."

She faced Hanuvar. "I can see why my husband likes you. Can you explain to me why his efforts on your behalf are worth the risk to my family?"

"They aren't." His answer seemed to startle her, though she recovered as he continued. "If I had other options, I wouldn't ask him to make such efforts."

"If anyone were to learn that he had assisted you, it would be not just the end of him, but our entire line. Not just me, and our daughter, but our grandchildren, and our brothers and sisters and cousins. Do you understand that?" Her gaze transfixed him. This, he thought, is a mother lion, declaring a warning from her den.

"I do. I will never be able to thank him adequately, and you, for the aid you have provided me."

"I do not want your thanks," she said curtly. "I want you to keep him safe."

Beside him Ciprion shifted in his seat. Hanuvar guessed that he had not anticipated this particular line of conversation.

Amelia continued. "My husband seems to think that you are the cleverest man in the world. Well then, make sure that you use that cleverness to shield him, and our family, and that your tracks are so carefully covered that even were you to fail in some scheme nothing could be traced back to us."

Hanuvar bowed his head. "He has been a true friend to me. And I hold true to my friends and allies. I pledge what you ask with my life."

She held his gaze for a moment longer. She looked as though she meant to say more but remained silent. Finally, she gracefully inclined her head to him and spoke to her husband. "What are the two of you going to do first?"

"We're trying to narrow down the Eltyr's possible hiding place based upon the locations of the murders," Ciprion said. "We're expecting the delivery of an important map today that should help. After that, we're going to personally visit each of the murder sites ourselves."

"And you think you can stop this murderess?" Amelia asked.

"I know that we will try," Ciprion answered.

"Even if it is your daughter?" she asked Hanuvar.

"I do not approve of her actions, whoever she is. There must be no more."

Ciprion climbed from his chair. "And time speeds. We should be on our way."

Hanuvar stood with him.

"You do not want to host your friend for a meal?"

"Few things would please me so well," Ciprion said. "But there is work to be done."

"He's right, and I've already eaten," Hanuvar said. "But milady is kind."

She rose. "Thank you for agreeing to meet with me." She offered her hand. As was Dervan custom he took her fingertips and squeezed them gently before releasing.

"It was an honor." Hanuvar bowed, and when he straightened, he spoke once more with his Ceori accent. "It is time, yes?"

"It is time," Ciprion agreed. He exchanged farewells with his wife, who wished them fortune, and then they left the villa and started into the city streets.

"I hope that was not too uncomfortable," Ciprion said after they had advanced to the opposite curb. They started downhill past expensive neighboring villas.

"Her concern is entirely warranted," Hanuvar answered. "I like her. She's smart and dedicated." He held off saying that if her society had accorded her the power to match her intellect, she'd likely be as formidable on the battlefield as her husband.

"She is."

III

This time the old man had summoned him to a small office to the rear of the palace. Wide doors were thrown open to an inner courtyard Metellus had never seen, one where a riot of greenery thrived, and where a gorgeous, garishly painted nymph statue with one cocked hip leaned over from her pedestal to stare into a rectangular pool. The sun was so bright it was almost blinding, but he saw the outline of a butterfly flitting in one of the beams.

The emperor sat behind a high-topped desk. There was a remarkable contrast between the courtyard and the empty desktop, the gray of the emperor's skin, the room bare of decoration apart from a solemn bust of Gaius' predecessor and older brother.

The sour old Hadiran, Sarnax, sat in a backless chair to the emperor's side.

The emperor's gaze was stern, by which Metellus understood that Enarius' meeting hadn't gone quite so well as he'd suggested. But then Metellus had prepared for just this moment. If he could get the old tyrant to hear him out, he might still be able to turn things the proper direction.

The emperor frowned. "My son has told me of his ridiculous scheme. He tells me further that you support it."

Metellus bowed his head. "Your Excellency, Enarius seemed bent upon the enterprise. He said, 'No more children should be put at risk while I walk shielded.'"

"He is my only heir!"

"That is what I told him, Your Highness!" Metellus nodded fervently. "But Enarius was insistent. He said a ruler had to protect his people and that he would put a stop to this child murderer."

Enarius had said something of the kind, but Metellus had forgotten the wording. It didn't matter.

"And you have spoken to Ciprion about this? He is in the midst of bringing a stop this matter right now."

"Is he, sire? Enarius worries that he's taking too long already. And I do not mean to malign Ciprion—he deserves honors. But his thinking may be too conventional in this instance. Enarius will draw out the killer."

"Ciprion would not risk exposing my son," the emperor said sharply.

The Hadiran continued to watch, his expression masklike.

"I advised him that you would not like the plan, Excellency," Metellus said. "But he told me if I did not want to help him, he would find someone else. And I do not trust someone else."

"If I may, sire," Sarnax said quietly.

The emperor coughed as he turned to him. He raised a cloth from his lap, coughed thrice, then lowered it as the attack subsided. "Speak."

"A successful venture like this will only enhance your son's popularity, especially since it was his idea."

"It will kill him if it fails."

Sarnax received this objection placidly. "We can take steps to ensure his safety. Make Ciprion a part of this planning. No offense to this young officer here, but your son is likely to be far safer if the plan is overseen by the master of Dervan strategy. And you did say you had been thinking about having your son assist in the investigation."

Metellus didn't like that at all; if matters weren't arranged just so, then the entire operation would be for nothing. And yet he saw the emperor's expression softening. Gaius turned to the wrinkled advisor as if by scrutiny he could weigh the worth of his advice. "My son did wish to use Ciprion's anniversary celebration as the opportunity for a lure. I told him that Ciprion has no interest in celebrating that occasion, though. He's made that perfectly clear."

"Another of Ciprion's peculiar habits," Sarnax said. "He is not one keen to sound his own horn. But if you order Ciprion to attend the celebration and place him in charge of your son's safety—"

"Your pardon, Minister," Metellus said, and pretended as though he were not dismayed by the sudden intense attention his interruption brought. "I have pledged to protect Enarius."

Sarnax looked as though he were about to speak, but the emperor launched into a prolonged coughing fit, and the old Hadiran clamped his mouth shut.

The emperor dabbed at his lips with the cloth then lowered it. His gaze was watery and ill-defined and Metellus wasn't sure what the old man was looking at or thinking about.

"If I may, sire," Sarnax began, but the emperor held up a hand to him.

The silence stretched on.

"I trust Ciprion," the emperor said finally. "And I must allow the boy to make his own decisions. But heads will roll if anything happens to him." He looked pointedly at Sarnax.

"I will let nothing happen to him," Metellus vowed. "I shall be there every step of the way."

The emperor rubbed at one bloodshot eye. "I think not. You've done such a fine job keeping tabs on my son that I have another task for you. You're to be posted to the border. Greater hostilities with the Cerdians are certain, and I want someone I can depend upon to keep a close watch on what our legions are doing."

The old windbag hadn't come up with this idea on his own. He never had any ideas of his own. Which meant that it had likely come from the ancient Hadiran, whose expression was remote and superior.

Metellus bowed and kept the anger from his voice. "My emperor, have I disappointed you in some way?"

"On the contrary, Metellus. I am pleased with you."

"Surely you already have other agents monitoring Aminius. I think that I am more useful here."

"If you are to advise my son you need more seasoning." The emperor spoke as if relating well-established fact. He continued irritably, "And you need to learn better how to follow orders. You will pack your bags and prepare for departure tomorrow morning."

Metellus bowed formally. "I hear and obey. But, sire . . . grant me a small request."

The emperor's heavy jowls quivered. "You tax my patience."

With head low, Metellus offered his open hands. He spoke quickly and worked to demonstrate heartfelt passion. "Permit me to see this operation through to completion. I have been charged with Enarius' protection this last year, and he is knowingly putting himself at risk. I would never forgive myself if something were to happen to him when I was not here. It is true that Ciprion knows far more about strategy than I. Let him plan the larger details, but allow me to learn from him, and stay at your son's side through to this mission's completion."

The emperor still glared.

"Sire, I have saved him in the past. I will make sure he is safe now."

The emperor sat there unmoving for a moment, but, like winds pushing through thunderheads, his expression cleared. For more than anything else, the emperor cared for his legacy, and right now his adopted son was that legacy personified.

"Sire," Sarnax said, "Ciprion has a whole host of veterans he can assign to help Enarius."

"Metellus is right, though, old friend. He personally saved my son's life once already. How many other men can say that? Very well, Metellus. I grant your favor. See this operation through before your reassignment. For the sake of my son."

"Thank you, sire. I shall not fail you."

That was the wrong thing to say, for the emperor's expression clouded once more.

"Fail me, and it will be the end of you. Now go."

Metellus bowed deeply, aware of the deadly look from Sarnax as he departed. He felt it against his back as surely as he felt the sun on his face as he left the palace.

IV

A young slave from the civil service finally arrived with the map, and then he and his assistant unrolled it across the long table in Ciprion's office, in the rambling government building near the forum. It was an impressive piece of papyrus that stretched nearly the entire two spear lengths of the table and came within a handspan of its other sides.

The slaves weighed down the corners with curios. Some artisan had labored long hours to carve warrior faces framed in helms out of sizable chunks of amber, conjuring stunning personality, and now they served solely as paperweights. They grimaced at the detailed map of the city of Derva like angry golden gods.

The slaves left, and Ciprion set to work, assisted by Antires. The Herrene needed no disguise, for Herrenic servants and slaves were ubiquitous throughout the empire. The young playwright wore a well-made tunic and a freedman's ring, less ostentatious than Hanuvar's. And he held a sheaf of papers, from which he read off the location of each of the recent murders identified as the work of the Eltyr.

Ciprion leaned out across the table, and, impervious to the scornful gazes from the ferocious little amber heads, darkened the beautiful map with tight text where each of the murders had taken place. Volani maps tended to be more colorful and impressionistic, conveying essences more quickly, but Hanuvar appreciated the stark precision in the detailed line drawing beneath his hands.

The room's last occupant waited to one side, the most obviously incongruous of them all. Izivar today wore Dervan garments, and her curling ringlets were pulled high. The soft saffron stola sheathed all but her ankles and sandals. She might have passed for a Dervan woman if she held herself with less open curiosity. She was engaged, and contemplating the work of these men, in a man's office in the sprawling government building, as though she were an equal participant. Dervan women might command a household, but few would have looked so comfortable at a conference in so masculine a setting.

She had arrived separately, for her quarters were removed from those of Hanuvar and Antires, to maintain the illusion of their respective identities.

"It seems a shame to mark up that map," she said. "It really is quite beautiful."

"It is a work of art." Ciprion's voice was strained from his stretch across half the table. He finished his notation. The mark was in black, and to differentiate it from the detailed roadways, he had enclosed each of the murder points with a precise, thick rectangle.

Ciprion straightened. His thick dark eyebrows were drawn as he contemplated his handiwork.

"What's the goal of this?" Izivar asked. She had arrived only a few moments before.

"He's trying to pinpoint a safe area for the killer's retreat," Antires explained, "based on where the murders have occurred. And the times when they occurred, when known."

She nodded impatiently. "But Derva's huge. Even if this gives you some kind of pattern, how much help can that be? Suppose it points to the north; the northside of the city is vast."

"Milady has a point." Ciprion allowed a trace of his famous charm to show in his smile. "This is only a humble start."

"If we organize the information, connections may stand out that aren't immediately visible," Hanuvar said.

Her look to him was that of one upon hearing surprising words from a stranger. He had promised her he would maintain his cover constantly, warning her not to show any sign of a personal connection between them, but realized from her reaction that he hadn't mentioned he would maintain his accent. She might have expected him to dispense with it in private.

"It's like a tile picture designed by some artisan that you have to assemble on site," Antires finished, probably pleased with his metaphor, although it was obvious from Izivar's look that further explanation was unneeded.

"So you're hoping to understand the ground and then see if there's another way to get close," she said to Hanuvar.

"Yes," he agreed, amused that she had spent enough time with him to speak of taking ground as a tactical matter.

Ciprion directed a question to Antires: "Is that the last one?"

"One more."

Izivar fingered her bright blue necklace and walked closer, studying the map, then each of the locations marked by Ciprion. The majority occurred in a rough crescent in the city's central north, and slightly west. Beyond the forum, beyond the apartments, rooted around the moneyed neighborhoods.

"Five in the last two months," she said, as Ciprion was making note of Antires' final information. "And three were children?"

"Yes," Ciprion answered grimly.

Hanuvar let out a slow breath, remembering how the Narisia from the other tapestry had recoiled at the thought of slaying children. He hoped his Narisia, even impacted by misfortune and tragedy, would never have chosen this course of action. It might be one of the other

Eltyr who had escaped with her. But then what if Narisia had seen her own children die by Dervan hands? His grandchildren?

Hanuvar discovered he had balled his hands at his sides and forced himself to unclench them.

"This is strange." Izivar tapped the second location.

Ciprion had bent across the table with a notched measuring stick but looked over to her and straightened.

Once more she tapped the location, and the bracelets upon her slim dark wrist made soft, jangling music. "Are these the dates found, or the actual dates of the murders?"

"Day discovered," Ciprion answered. "All were children under ten. They were not left unattended for long."

"I wished to be sure," she said. "I thought I had heard that some of these were found the day after their death. That they had been slain in the night."

"Most of them were likely slain in the night," Ciprion confirmed.

"Well, then, we have a conundrum." Again, her slender fingers played with her agate pendant. "This was a high holy day. Some Volani are more observant of religious traditions than others, but this is the day that Danit stepped from the ocean to take up with a human lover, before they met, again and again, at the site of the sea gate. The Eltyr especially hold this night sacred. If the child's body was found the next morning, that means an Eltyr could not have maintained an all-night vigil before a ceremonial bath."

"Well reasoned, lady," Hanuvar said.

"And do you happen to know if Narisia was devout?" Ciprion asked the room at large.

"According to my sources," Hanuvar said, "she practiced the traditions with great solemnity, and found them spiritually cleansing."

It felt strange to speak of his daughter with such a remove, but fictions had to be practiced, lest he drop his guard at the wrong moment. And there was no knowing when they might be secretly overheard. This old capital building could contain hidden passages or spyholes.

Ciprion set his measuring stick aside.

Hanuvar continued: "But we must also remember that a warrior, given an opportunity to achieve some important goal, would not put it aside for a religious day. The more so if she thinks their gods have abandoned them."

"And do you believe she thinks that?" Ciprion asked.

Hanuvar replied with a question of his own. "How could she not?"

"It depends upon the strength of her faith," Izivar said. "But it is curious."

"So the date may or may not mean anything," Ciprion said, and to Izivar's raised eyebrow he added: "But it may be important. I just don't know how to use the information. At this point it's hard to know what information is useful and what isn't."

As he finished, a loud knock sounded on the outer door. Ciprion glanced toward it, checked the room, and then said, simply, "Enter."

The door was pushed open by a man in a glittering white praetorian uniform, minus the helmet, but complete with lacquered white chest armor. As a praetorian Metellus was even permitted to wear a sheathed sword on his hip within government offices. His was a noble profile, one with a proud nose and dark eyes. A trio of scars traced down the left side of his face. He swept the room with his eyes as though assassins or plebeians might be lurking in every shadow.

On his heels came Enarius, in a plain red tunic, his wavy hair recently trimmed, and after him an older man in a long, old-fashioned toga: the priest, Lucius Longinus, walking with a staff tipped with a falcon's head, though he did not seem to require its assistance, for his tread was certain.

Months had passed since Hanuvar had been in the company of any of the three, and then he had looked decades younger and Dervan as well. But he didn't care to encounter any of them, much less all at once in a well-lit room.

Ciprion greeted them by name, apart from Enarius, whom he addressed as "Excellency," then asked what had brought them here. He had been promised privacy for his investigation.

Metellus was staring at Hanuvar as if he had discovered a rotting fish among the table fruits. "Who's the Ceori?"

"This is Acunix. He's an expert on the Eltyr. His unit tangled with a small contingent of them during the second war, and he was involved in a prisoner exchange."

Metellus' brow furrowed but he must have decided that he didn't know the man disguised before him or that the explanation made sense, for he lost interest and walked toward the map.

Enarius greeted Izivar brightly, complimenting her hair. Antires, playing the part of a servant, stepped to the back, and Ciprion made no effort to introduce him.

Lucius, though, stared at Hanuvar with growing curiosity.

This same man had seen his aura and commented upon it months before. Was his scrutiny owing to recognition, or that he had found another man with a certain kind of aura?

"Father told me you were in charge of the hunt for the killer," Enarius said to Ciprion, who managed to look only a little startled by the pronouncement.

Metellus peered down at the map. "How do you expect to find the killer with this?"

"These are the locations of the attacks," Ciprion explained. Metellus and Enarius both drew closer, and Ciprion told them he was using the murders to determine a point from which the Eltyr could advance and retreat in a single night. He meant to create expanding circles to surround the neighborhood of the killer's likely headquarters.

As the general explained his reasoning and rattled off details about the deaths, the priest stepped to Hanuvar's side and pretended to watch the cluster at the table.

"We have met before," Lucius said softly.

"Have we?" Hanuvar asked, just as soft, but with his strong accent.

The priest's lips twitched toward a smile without reaching it. "There is no mistaking your aura. But you are decades older. And wear another nation's garb. How is this accomplished, and what are you doing here?"

It was pointless to dissemble, although he did not abandon his accent, or his own whisper. "It is as Ciprion says. I have experience facing Eltyr and I am here to help find the killer."

"Why are you in disguise? Does Ciprion know?"

"Justice cannot always be delivered openly. And Ciprion trusts me. I thought I had your trust as well."

"You did. But I find this troubling. Your transformation is, frankly, confusing and concerning."

"These are confusing times. But my motives remain the same."

"Your aura does," Lucius said doubtfully. He returned his attention to the others. Izivar and Antires both watched Hanuvar's quiet conversation with veiled concern. Ciprion had deployed his measuring rod amongst the murder sites while the other two questioned him about security at the attacks.

"I would be your friend," the priest said softly. "Why must you be evasive?"

"I am in need of friends," Hanuvar replied with grave patience. "But now is not the place, or time, for this discussion."

"If it were not for your aid to Enarius and the profound strength in your aura, I would demand an accounting, now. Your changed appearance cannot be managed with cosmetics. You must be a wizard, and that troubles me. Greatly."

"I am no wizard."

"You will explain, later?"

"At some point. You can rest assured that I am here to help."

The priest grunted. "Were you helping Enarius in his earliest difficulties, or was that truly your brother?"

Hanuvar answered with a look and the priest delivered a slightly more optimistic grunt. It was likely the best reception to be had at the moment.

Ciprion had finished his presentation and Enarius stepped back, hands at his hips. "This is all very clever, but how are you going to draw her out? There's a lot of places she could be hiding."

"We're still early in the investigation," Ciprion admitted. "We finished notating the map only moments before you arrived."

"So you need more time to plan?" Enarius asked. To Ciprion's polite, neutral smile, he turned to Izivar. "And you, my dear, have you been able to provide any useful insight into what an Eltyr might think?"

"Not very much, I'm afraid. But then I only arrived a few moments ago myself."

"We need to stop planning, and act," Metellus said, with the sly arrogance of a youth.

Enarius was more diplomatic. "I mean no disrespect, General. But we can't have more children dying. We know that she means to kill the children of the powerful, but we don't know where she'll do it. We need to draw her out."

"With a tempting target?" Ciprion suggested, and then at Enarius' head bow the same realization must have come to him as it came to Hanuvar, although Ciprion hesitated a moment before voicing the disbelief visible in his gaze. "Please tell me you're not thinking of yourself."

Enarius' head rose, as though he imagined himself speaking before a multitude. "I am thinking of myself. Why should I be shielded when infants are being slain?"

If his pose was dramatic, his expression at least seemed honest.

Ciprion objected, although Hanuvar was grudgingly impressed by the young man's sense of duty. He said, quietly, to the priest: "A ruler must put the people before himself. Have you taught him that?"

Lucius inclined his head ever so slightly, saying, "He has some inclinations in that direction already."

"Did you know they were going to suggest this?"

The priest's answer was dour. "The emperor has already approved the basics of their plan."

Metellus, meanwhile, had lifted placating hands. "It could work. Without that much risk. We put out word that Enarius is going to be doing something that would suggest he was exposed. But then we don't actually have him as exposed as he seems. We could even have someone dressed up like him."

"You two have been planning this for some time," Ciprion said.

"My father has given us permission," Enarius said. "But only if you oversee the overall strategy."

Ciprion digested this with an expression just shy of nausea.

Metellus looked almost smug. "We mean for Enarius to be supremely well protected, of course. We were thinking that a celebration of the anniversary of the Battle of Mazra would serve as a fine opportunity for him to appear in public at a specific time and place."

Ciprion's frown deepened. "I don't celebrate that."

Hanuvar saw Antires' eyes flick over to him as if he tried to gauge Hanuvar's reaction on the mention of the battle he had lost to Ciprion years ago. But Hanuvar wanted no connection made between himself and Antires by the priest, and so ignored the attention.

"I'll throw the celebration for you," Enarius said. "We should remind the city why you're so well honored. And we'll annoy Aminius as well."

Ciprion glanced over to Hanuvar as if in apology but also to invite his input.

Metellus continued: "We thought that we would create the appearance of a small security breach. It seems as though the Eltyr is an opportunist who takes advantage of those. Except this time, it will be deliberate."

"But suppose they come in disguised as a Dervan lady, or a slave, or a servant?" Ciprion asked.

It was a fine question, but Metellus answered it.

"However they come in, they will have no access to Enarius. He's going to give a public speech from a distance, then we'll get him away to a private room. He'll never be near anyone we don't know. We'll have a decoy dressed like him to further complicate matters."

Hanuvar wasn't entirely sure a decoy was necessary, but he wished to draw no attention to himself, and remained silent.

Ciprion rubbed his forehead. He seemed to be reluctantly coming around to acceptance of his role in Enarius' rash plan. Recognizing this, Metellus looked ready to rub hands together in satisfaction. Izivar's eyes were deep with worry, which did not go unnoticed by Enarius, although he seemed to interpret her meaning differently.

"Bowing out seems rather cowardly on my part," he said finally.

Metellus' surprise looked honest. "No one expects you to remain and stand toe to toe with a trained killer with decades of fighting experience, Excellency. You're our next emperor. The general and I have studied to be warriors."

"He's right, Enarius," Izivar said softly. "No one here doubts your bravery. Especially since this plan smacks of something you would think of. But it's your duty to rule. You have tens of thousands of men who can stab other people."

He accepted this counsel with a slight smile.

"But I still don't think you should do it," she added. "This Eltyr is very determined and obviously a little mad."

"We can protect him," Metellus insisted.

"And we have to lure this woman out into the open so we can finish her," Enarius said. "She's out to hurt the empire by killing its children—how could she resist a chance to murder the son of the emperor?"

Hanuvar was struck by the conviction with which the young man spoke. While there was excitement in his manner, he radiated dedication to his ideal rather than a thirst for glory. It reminded Hanuvar why he had grown fond of Enarius, against all natural inclination.

He leaned to Lucius, speaking softly. "He may do well, at that."

"I think he may," the priest whispered back. "Will you be fighting to safeguard him again?"

While the priest recognized him, he still had no idea as to Hanuvar's true identity, for there was no irony in the question. And while there was considerable irony in the situation, Hanuvar answered with a single, solemn nod. A real Ceori would have boasted and sounded elaborate, but now was not the time for loud gestures. Ciprion, Metellus, and Enarius now discussed fine points. "Like you, I think that he is the future of the empire. A more benevolent future."

"Whoever you are," the priest said, "I believe that you have the empire's best interests at heart. I would prefer to learn the truth from you sooner, rather than later."

The only interest in the empire Hanuvar had was to keep it from murdering his people and allies, but because it seemed clear their safety was far more likely with Enarius' hand upon the tiller, Lucius' assumption was essentially correct. As to that in-depth conversation, Hanuvar would delay as long as possible, for he had no idea what he would say. But his expression remained closed, as if he thought for a long moment over the answer he had already formulated. After a time, he spoke. "When this crisis is resolved."

"Very well. Let that be soon."

V

Metellus didn't permit himself a true smile until he was well clear of the government offices. Gods, but he was brilliant. He'd managed not just to turn the emperor to his needs, but outwit Sarnax and outmaneuver Ciprion, the alleged master of strategy.

He laughed out loud. One by one he'd steered all of them into place, starting with Enarius. It had by no means been easy, but he had done it.

Now there remained one last sticking point, but with the report he was about to make, surely even they would come around to his way of thinking.

He wandered the streets for a time, imagining he might be followed, and passed through an inn he partly owned, seeming to settle down and joke with some of the regulars and drink a little before telling them he had to visit the Cerdian throne room.

But rather than heading to the private piss hole he slipped into a backroom, threw a cloak over his distinctive features, and slid out the back. Evening was on its way, and he hurried through narrow streets with his face concealed. His stride was purposeful, and the young bravos readying their nightly scourings let him be.

Finally, he made his way into a tavern in the shadow of the Kaladine hill, flashed a hand sign to the clerk behind the counter, and retreated to a rear area almost completely absent of the reek of sour wine and cooked goat meat which had soaked into the stone and wood in the rest of the building. The scowling attendant warding the private room opened it to his knock, let him in, and then promptly closed the door and sat down beside the portal on a cushioned stool.

Cerdians were almost universally courteous even as they plotted against you, but they also kept rigidly to their assigned roles, and this fellow was a doorman, not a chaperone, or a host. Metellus started toward the table where three men waited, already drinking. They shoved a cup toward him and he reached over for the pitcher. He poured himself a draught.

They watched, keen-eyed murderers that they were, to make sure he drank deep before they said anything.

It was fine wine, though flavored with some exotic spice the Cerdians cared for overmuch, and dry as his throat was it took no great effort to down it and prove his trust in his companions.

He set the cup down.

"You said that you would have news, and we have waited," said Taricon, seated in the middle.

The three Cerdians possessed straight dark hair, and a complexion of a dark sepia. That skin tone in itself would not have rendered any of them suspicious, for Derva was a melting pot of freedmen, citizens, slaves, and merchants from dozens of far-flung lands. And merchants from Cerdian lands and Cerdian-adjacent lands had been present in the east for generations, so even given the current paranoia about Cerdians Taricon's accent would have given few pause. It was the flat-eyed stare employed by all three that was worrying, as if they had little patience and examined Metellus to consider where best to insert their blades.

He smiled. "Cerdian wine. A gift to the world."

"You promised you would have word on who was behind the destruction of the revenant fortress in our name."

He reached for the pitcher and poured out more wine, then beckoned to the others, offering to fill.

They simply stared.

He set the pitcher aside. "I don't know, and I don't care, and neither should you."

The three men were completely different in appearance apart from their hair, skin tone and murderous stares. The shorter one with the cheek mole cursed him. The one on his left, his face cratered with acne scars, smiled unpleasantly. But both waited for Taricon, who had a long, slim nose. His skin was clear and smooth, almost feminine, as were his soft eyes and long lashes. His voice too was smooth. "I do hope, for your sake, that you have better news on our other front."

"He has none," said the one with the mole. Metellus had forgotten his name because it was a mouthful of strange sounds and because he rarely spoke. "He said he would reward us for our help, and he does nothing but drink our wine and smile his smiles and promise things that never come to pass. And we stain our honor with the blood of children."

Metellus had always prayed to Ericol, the swift and subtle. The plump ewe he'd sacrificed at his temple earlier this week must have pleased the god, for mole-face's objection could not have been a better prelude for Metellus' news.

"If I'm smiling today, it's because I bring news that will please all of us." Metellus took a long drink, silently praising Ericol. The first Dervan child murder had been unplanned—the Cerdian assassin had been unable to locate the target and the boy had been about to raise alarm. Only Metellus had seen the possible advantage, and he'd convinced the Cerdians to change their campaign to target the offspring of the powerful.

The skepticism of the Cerdians had been growing, but he'd known it would require multiple attacks before he could shape the opinion of Enarius into taking a stand.

He set his wine cup on the table side. "Enarius is planning to offer himself as a lure so the Eltyr can come for him. And guess who's helping manage security for the alleged trap?"

That set their heads turning, and the three quickly exchanged words in their own language. Metellus drank more wine.

Finally Taricon silenced them with a look and faced Metellus. "So you have delivered upon your promise. What are the details?"

Metellus hunched forward across the table and lowered his voice. He didn't fear they would be overheard, but he wanted to stress the secrecy of the information he was about to share. "In a few days' time, Enarius is throwing a commemoration for Ciprion's victory over Hanuvar. I'm going to get you in there and the Eltyr's going to kill off the priest, Lucius, Sarnax the Hadiran, and Ciprion himself. Anyone else who has Enarius' ear but *me*. I'm going to get him out of there alive, which will make him even more inclined to be grateful and listen to my advice."

Taricon's lips slid into a sardonic smile. "So we'll be helping you. That doesn't do anything about the emperor."

"Did I leave that part out? He'll be there, too. And the Eltyr gets to kill him as well." He smiled and sat back, then spread his hands. "Enarius ascends the throne. The Volani take the blame. The Cerdians make some kind of gesture—claim the tower was destroyed by a rogue captain or a pirate—or even some disguised Volani or something—and send a big basket of royal gifts, so Enarius can get back to partying and leave the border."

"Just like that."

"Just like that."

Taricon glanced at his advisors, then, finally, poured himself another drink before adding more to Metellus' cup, the ultimate sign of Cerdian accord. "Tell me more."

VI

The child's death had so disturbed the slave that her expression remained fixed in horrified regret when she showed Hanuvar and

Ciprion around the room of the murder. She was small and sturdy, with an age-seamed face and apple cheeks and bright blue eyes that roved constantly toward the window through which the attacker had vanished.

"I was the first one here," she said, repeating herself.

It was too much to ask that any real evidence remained in that upper room where the little boy had been killed only a few evenings before. Marta, the slave and nurse, had already told them how he'd been playing with toy legionaries while she swept the walkway overlooking the courtyard.

She'd heard a scream and come running, only to find the boy twitching in a rapidly expanding pool of blood among his scattered soldiers. A woman in armor, her long dark hair hanging in a ponytail behind, had been escaping through the window.

Ciprion was still trying to extract information while Hanuvar moved to the window. "You said she looked back at you. Did you see her face?"

"I'm sorry, my lord general. I did not. It was dark outside—it was raining. That's why the boy was playing upstairs."

Ciprion had already instructed her twice that such a weighty honorific was unneeded, but Marta had returned to it in her nervousness.

The floorboards had been well scoured, naturally. Of the Eltyr symbol and the blood with which it had been drawn there was no sign, nor were there footprints or even toppled toy soldiers. There were only the storage chests and some old furniture. Hanuvar walked to the window, undid the shutter, and pushed open both sides.

The afternoon light streamed into the space. The sun was lower than Hanuvar would have liked. The last few days had moved too quickly. Ciprion had fervently hoped that their map triangulation would prove more useful than it had so far, for he had no liking for Enarius' plan and would just as soon find the murderer before the heir risked himself.

But it had as yet done no good to have expanding circles of possibility as to where the murderer might be retreating after each killing. Over the last two days Hanuvar and Ciprion had traveled to each of the murder sites in an attempt to gather additional information, learning only today that this one had a witness.

Unfortunately, Marta hadn't been able to tell them much more than they already knew, and in not too many more hours their efforts would be for naught, for Ciprion's celebration would be under way.

Ciprion joined Hanuvar and both men carefully examined the sill. The blank wall of another building lay less than five feet away. There was no mystery about which way the murderer had gone, for part of the reason the slave's story had been believed was that muddy footprints had been found not only in the room, but in the dirty alley below where the woman had dropped and run away.

Hanuvar ran his hand along the sill and looked over the edge.

Ciprion braced himself against the sill so he could lean out and inspect the right shutter's front, then pulled it towards him. He rapped his fist against one slat marred by a long, recent scratch through old red paint, and Hanuvar nodded his agreement. That was the point where the invader must have inserted a tool to open them. "Do you see anything else?" Ciprion asked.

Behind them, the woman continued lamenting about what a sweet child little Lentullus had been, and what a tragedy his death was.

Hanuvar touched more damage on the weathered sill. "I believe this is where a hook must have landed. A strong climber could have been up in a few heartbeats."

Ciprion's mouth thinned. "That doesn't tell us anything useful. I'm afraid this whole trip may be a waste of time."

"There's something that strikes me as strange," Hanuvar said.

Ciprion met his eyes. "Go on."

Hanuvar turned from the window and spoke to Marta, his Dervan still touched by his Ceori accent. "You say she was armored. But not in a helmet."

"No, sir."

"What armor did she have?"

"On her chest." Marta touched her solar plexus. "And she had a soldier's leather skirt. And the leg armor."

Hanuvar nodded his thanks, then faced Ciprion. "So she was wearing baltea and greaves and apparently a cuirass. It smacks of theater, doesn't it?"

Ciprion grunted. "You're right. There's no need for armor like that on this sort of mission. It would make climbing harder."

"The master keeps armed doormen in the house, though, my lord general," Marta insisted.

"Yes," Ciprion agreed politely. But his look to Hanuvar said what both were cognizant of: the presence of seasoned fighters didn't explain away wearing stiff, heavy gear on a mission of stealth. "Did she want to be seen?"

"She wanted to ensure that if she was seen, it would strike fear. It seems a peculiar risk to take." Hanuvar considered the window, through which it was just possible to climb if a person crouched and kept their head low. "I assume she might even have worn a helmet if it could have fit through here."

"Let's examine the ground."

The sad-eyed matron waited on the main floor, eager for information, or the promise that justice awaited the boy's killer. Ciprion had to delay while speaking with her, so Hanuvar left through the servant's entrance and headed into the alley by himself.

As he had expected, any prints were muddled by previous investigators. Hanuvar hadn't the skill to separate who might have been wearing what sandal.

He looked up at the window, already reshuttered by Marta, and calculated where the murderer's rope would have lined up. A row of neglected shrubs had taken root along the foundation, and those beneath the window looked as though they had suffered recent damage.

Hanuvar knelt in the moist earth beside them and began a painstaking examination of both vegetation and ground.

He hadn't expected to find anything of use, so he was intrigued when he discovered a scrap of cloth caught in the lower limbs of a prickly bush. He extricated it carefully and lifted the dark fabric to the light.

Threads trailed from its edge. It had been torn, possibly, but not certainly, when it had caught on the bush and someone in a great hurry had pulled away.

He was lifting it to his nose when Ciprion joined him.

His friend looked dour. "Something?" he asked.

Hanuvar passed him the cloth. "What do you smell?"

Ciprion sniffed it, looking thoughtful, then smelled it a second time. "Goat dung."

"Our murderess might have torn it when she landed and left in a hurry."

Ciprion took in the trampled bushes and the mess of prints. He gently cradled the fabric in his hand as though it were a weighty thing. "We might make something of this," he said finally. "If we had more time. There are a lot of taverns in Derva, even in the area we've centered on. Even assuming we're right."

"Not all of them will sell goat meat."

"No." Ciprion swore. "Pardon me."

Hanuvar stood. "I share your sentiment. We can put Antires on this. He's sharp-eyed. Send him out with a couple of your men and he'll have knocked on half the right doors in the next few hours."

"What we need is a few days."

"But we don't have them. A general should be familiar with the press for time."

"Is it wrong of me that I never came to like it? Also, this..." He lowered his voice before continuing. "This upcoming operation did not need to be forced. Not yet." He lifted the cloth. "Not when this might lead us on to victory."

"Or it might be an old cloth a goatherd was wearing as he staggered drunkenly down this alley. Come. We have to turn it over to the scouts. They'll seek out the truth and report back in. We've got to get you to your party. We can't have the guest of honor turning up late."

"I don't suppose we can, at that."

They returned to their headquarters, explained their instructions to Antires, who couldn't seem to decide if he was pleased to be so instrumental in their plans, or disappointed to be absent from the celebration. But he hurried away, accompanied by a squad of legionaries, and Hanuvar and Ciprion retreated to their respective quarters and dressed for the occasion. Before very long, they had arrived at the appointed villa, one of those situated in the sprawling grounds north of the city, below the low rise sometimes called the sixth hill of Derva. Both wore ornamental, though still functional, armor. It was a look both normally would have disdained, but they had agreed it appropriate in light of the potential for danger this evening.

"We'll feel very silly if nothing happens, won't we?" Ciprion asked.

Antires had taught Hanuvar never to fiddle with the accoutrements of his disguises, because that would draw attention to his unfamiliarity with them. But Hanuvar had long since learned that there are few absolutes. He'd seen enough Ceori playing with their mustache ends over the years that he had adopted the fingering of the left side of his own over the week he'd maintained his new identity, and it had grown into a habit.

That evening, he pulled at the mustache as he stood with Ciprion on a balcony overlooking the central garden of the great feast. Expensive glass lanterns hung in abundance, painting everything beneath them in warm amber. An army of slaves finished placing reclining couches about long tables. At the garden's far end the slaves wheeled in a life-sized artistic depiction of a warrior bowing before another in Dervan armor. The resemblance to Ciprion was more implied than definitive because the scene had been fashioned from flowers and plants: Ciprion's eyes were dark blue periwinkles.

The bowing figure before Ciprion Hanuvar guessed for himself, from the green crest rising from the Volani helmet.

"I am sorry for this," Ciprion said softly.

"I've long since gathered that if the gods are paying attention to mortals, they love irony." He had grown so used to using his Ceori accent he had joked with Izivar he might not recognize the sound of his actual voice. For a variety of reasons, she was not in attendance this evening. Ciprion's wife, Amelia, was making the rounds and speaking with the serving staff, hoping to minimize potential embarrassments.

Both men turned at the sound of footsteps behind them. It was a pale-skinned slave, a pretty blonde who bowed her head and offered a platter of baked goods topped with honey and fruit, cut into shapes someone had thought appropriate for a military celebration.

"Don't feel so bad," Hanuvar told Ciprion. "Have an elephant cookie." He selected one himself and bit into it. He nodded thanks to the slave.

Ciprion demurred and the girl departed.

"It's good," Hanuvar said.

"I think you're enjoying this," Ciprion said from the side of his mouth.

"You sound like you're in a Herrenic tragedy." With a slight gesture of his cookie, Hanuvar encompassed the garden arranged for Ciprion's benefit. "Surely you can enjoy the hard-won victory in defense of your people. As for me..." He smote his chest, armored in a bronze Dervan cuirass, decorated with images of laurel leaves and curling vines. "We Ceori know to drink deep and eat all the elephant cookies we can, for life is short."

"Oh, very nice. Is that your original gem of wisdom, or did you read it on a bathhouse wall?"

Hanuvar grunted and spoke with stuffy dignity. "I think you civilized folk forget the simple truths."

That finally broke Ciprion's reserve, and he laughed. "All right, my barbarian friend." He spoke with a dramatic flourish. "Tomorrow we may die, so we must seize the cup with both hands."

"Or at least the elephant cookies. One in each fist, I say."

Ciprion snorted. "Are they really that good?"

"You ought to try one."

A movement on the far end of the hall caught both men's attention. One of the domestic slaves was conducting a gaggle of well-dressed Dervans into the central chamber.

"It looks like the celebrants are arriving," Hanuvar said.

"I suppose I ought to go press the flesh. But if I start now it's going to be interminable."

"Would you rather wait until you're announced?"

"Perhaps. It will be difficult to appear relaxed and welcoming. The less time I have to do that, the better."

"I was going to double-check the security postings," Hanuvar said. "Join me?"

"Yes, I think I will."

They left the main hall by a back stair. At the end of a long corridor, they spotted Metellus scanning in their direction, and the men raised hands to one another in greeting.

With twilight deepening, the plan would be for the slaves to light the outside lanterns, and then be called away from a point on the east before they completed their job. This would leave a defensive gap that it would seem they forgot to return to address.

With Ciprion following, Hanuvar walked the outside grounds, keeping to the shadow of the sprawling villa, knowing that the sentries were posted in obvious places. A trumpet fanfare rang from the front of the building, signaling the emperor's arrival. Hanuvar glanced at Ciprion, wondering if that meant he would wish to return, but he made no comment.

Ciprion appeared even more reluctant to attend than Hanuvar would have guessed, for he lingered over the various sentry posts, examining things in far greater detail than Hanuvar expected.

Finally, they passed the point where the gap in lanterns lay, closer to the outer wall than any other locations. An ideal advantage for enemy exploitation. So far no one seemed to be moving on the opening. The villa sprawled unevenly, with long wings thrust out from the central quadrangle. As they rounded a corner of the right wing, they saw that someone had left a barrel-laden wagon against one of the walls.

He halted, and Ciprion came to his side, whispering, "This is nowhere near the kitchens."

He answered with a single nod. Both men were intimately familiar with the positions of troops and outside forces. There should be no wagon here.

A pair of praetorians patrolling the grounds with a lantern drew close to the wheeled conveyance, and Hanuvar expected that they would soon express dismay and send one of their number running for assistance. Instead, the one in the lead set down his lantern and both raised their hands to the clear heavens, looking as though they were trying to shield themselves from the moonlight.

But Hanuvar deduced their true intent. They were measuring the height of the moon above the trees to gauge time.

"I don't like this," Ciprion said softly. He took the lead and strode forward, Hanuvar following. He announced himself with the penetrating snap of a commander. "Soldiers!"

They jumped at the sound of his voice and turned to face him.

"You have no orders for stationing here."

The one who'd brought the lantern had a long square chin and large ears that stuck out from his helmet. "We have them, sir."

Ciprion raised his head imperiously. "Show me."

The two looked confused for a moment and exchanged a look. The shorter one reached toward his belt.

There had been no written orders to anybody tonight. Hanuvar called warning and ducked the sword blow of the man he'd heard creeping from behind. His own blade slashed through the dangling pteruges of his attacker and into his thigh. Blood splattered the nearby shrubbery.

The wounded man screamed, even as the big-eared one dashed forward and swung wildly at Ciprion, who drew and struck in a single motion, taking the soldier's overextended arm off at the elbow, then drove his sword tip through his screaming mouth.

The third man rushed Ciprion's side, but Hanuvar interposed, swaying away from a deadly head blow. He pivoted left, and Ciprion drove his own gladius under the man's arm. The Dervan general had to throw himself backward to avoid a return blow, but then their adversary sagged, saying in surprise, "You've killed me."

The praetorian sounded both startled and accepting of the situation, as if he were a philosopher disengaged from worldly concerns. He dropped with a groan and lay still beside the armless man, trembling in shock as he bled out.

Hanuvar scanned the surrounding environment. Beyond the dying man's gurgling, he heard distant laughter and music, and the moan of the man who'd come at him from behind, crawling determinedly toward the lantern. He left a long smear of blood across the grass in his wake.

Ciprion trudged after him and Hanuvar, blade ready, followed. As they neared the wagon there was no missing a faint reek of oil.

The wounded man was so determined to reach the lantern, Hanuvar almost felt bad for him when Ciprion stepped past and lifted it out of reach.

"Who sent you?" Ciprion demanded.

The soldier cursed him. Something flared to the east.

A red tongue of flame lapped at a corner along the other wing.

The man at Ciprion's feet chuckled. "Stupid Dervan," he said. His voice was weak with death, but it rattled with the trace of an accent, one Hanuvar identified as Cerdian when the man kept talking. "Your emperor and his nephew will die now." His chuckle turned into a death rattle.

Either the Cerdians had slain and replaced some praetorians, or some of the praetorians themselves were part of the cabal.

Ciprion swore and spoke quickly to Hanuvar. "Get inside and get Enarius to safety." He started away at a run.

"What are you going to do?"

Ciprion shouted over his shoulder. "Rouse the troops!" With that, he increased to a sprint. Hanuvar would have preferred a longer consultation and hoped Ciprion had in mind that if these praetorians were impostors, others might be.

But he trusted his friend's judgment and understood the need for haste. Well-briefed on the building's layout, he dashed for the nearest entrance, his thoughts turning through various scenarios as he searched the gloom, alert for more attackers.

He'd been concerned that he'd arrive at a locked door, then was more troubled when he found it open. No praetorian was stationed on its other side, and he supposed that meant one of those supposed to be there was among the three he and Ciprion had fought.

From further along in the building a man shouted a warning about the fire.

Hanuvar ran on toward the backroom where, if the schedule was accurate, Enarius should be waiting to emerge and present his speech.

It was then he saw the emperor, surrounded by a security entourage, being escorted through the doors ahead.

VII

Gaius had insisted on a final change in the plans, so that he'd speak before Enarius, promising the crowd his son would be out shortly. He'd planned to thank Ciprion in person, but no one seemed quite sure where the general had gone. The guest of honor's absence had irritated him, but Gaius had plunged ahead. His words were well received and he managed to get through the whole speech with his back straight and voice strong.

He'd expected to retire to a backroom where refreshments waited. He had thought all the violence would take place far from him and his son, so the sight of dead bodies in the back corridor came as a shock. Two were praetorians and the third was a young dark-haired man in purple tunic. Enarius.

Gaius threw himself to his knees, his heart thundering, blood trailing from his lips as he coughed. He touched the prone body of his son, found it warm, but discovered by pressing hand to his neck that there was no pulse.

With an agonized cry he shook the body, careless of spirits, shouting that he could not be dead, that he must come back to him. It was only when the young man's head flopped around that he saw it was the stand-in, a slave with a similar build. He'd been supposed to come out after Enarius had given his speech and wave from the balcony, so everyone could be certain his son was still nearby.

Someone was shouting about a fire, and Lucius put a hand to his shoulder, telling him that they had to leave.

Gaius climbed unsteadily to his feet and then hurried away with his escort and advisors, wiping tears and straining to breathe while he fought off a coughing fit. Sarnax assured him Enarius' own security detail would see to his son's safety, but the praetorian squad leader advised finding him, and Gaius agreed.

Neither Sarnax nor Lucius cared for that, and Gaius swore he'd have all of them crucified if they didn't find his son alive. And so they relented and moved on into a small courtyard. Two of the praetorians entered boldly into the space and started across it. The moon shone on statues and sent long shadows down from the second-floor loggia.

The lead praetorians were halfway across when spears rained down. The praetorians cried out in alarm. Two were shouting to protect the emperor; another called something strange to the attackers: "Not us, you fools!" But he died with a spear in his throat.

"Down, my liege," Sarnax shouted, and then a spear struck him through the chest. His hands cradled its haft like a lover and then he dropped groaning to the pavers. Gaius gasped in horror.

The ululating call everyone knew for the sound of the Eltyr rang out nearby, and another man cried, "Death to the tyrant! Long live Hanuvar!"

A half dozen warriors closed in against the final pair of praetorians, and with them was a dark-haired woman, shrieking her strange warrior call. Lucius brandished his staff and stood before his liege.

The praetorians fought bravely, taking out two and sheering through the Eltyr's cuirass. She staggered back and collapsed. One of the assassins broke past the praetorians, slid by Lucius, and came at Gaius.

He saw the hatred in the man's eyes. The actual spear thrust seemed to take a hundred years; Gaius was acutely aware of its slow plunge toward him. He willed his body to move but it seemed reluctant. He had barely leaned away when the spear tip took him in the belly.

It struck him deep and hurt more than he would have guessed, almost like a burn. Even after the spear was withdrawn, he felt it inside of him, as though part remained to block his breathing.

A praetorian cut the spearman down before Gaius was stabbed again. Gaius retreated, wobbling on his feet. Dimly he was aware of Lucius crying out in worry for him.

The last two praetorians tried to ward him and the priest both, but couldn't fend off so many determined attackers, and fell in short order.

Gaius sank to his knees, dizzily noting that it was his blood staining his toga. The three final assassins closed in. Lucius interposed himself with energetic swings of his staff. Gaius didn't know why he fought so hard. Didn't he see that they were finished?

And then a Ceori warrior came, moving like a ghost, slaying one of the attackers as he turned. The assassin fell so swiftly it was as though the Ceori had only to touch a man to kill. He moved with a dancer's grace, blocking a spear thrust with a casual tap of his own spear before plunging it through his attacker's loins.

The last assassin tried to run, but the Ceori flung his spear, and the tip hit the man's back with a sturdy chunk, as of a knife delivered through an apple. He was dead before he hit the pavement.

Lucius limped over to the victorious warrior. "Help the emperor," he pleaded.

But the Ceori strode for the downed woman in warrior garb.

VIII

The runner reported there was still no message from optio Munius, who was supposed to be alerting Metellus to the arrival of the Cerdians. Metellus didn't care for that at all. Had the Cerdians been admitted in their disguise as entertainers? Where were they?

The emperor was gone and Enarius hadn't appeared, but that

didn't matter. Ciprion's wife was talking to the crowd, saying that her husband was doubtlessly seeing to the emperor's security before he could be bothered with a celebration, for duty always came first for him.

Rolling his eyes in annoyance, Metellus slunk away and started through the backrooms. With any luck, Ciprion was already dead.

A few partygoers lingered in nearby chambers to flirt or talk politics. Metellus ignored them and kept on, as he suspected a man charged with security would do.

He'd thought the Cerdians would understand the advantage of the plan he'd laid before him, but he felt a presentiment of disaster and called for one of the real praetorians to accompany him. He'd taken his assistant Munius and a small inner circle into his trust; all the rest were loyal to their oaths.

It was then someone called warning about a fire, and Metellus, cursing, realized he might just have given the Cerdians too large of an opening. He threw himself into a flat-out run for the room where Enarius was supposed to be safe. One of the emperor's personal guards, an amiable ex-gladiator named Belbo, came alert as Metellus slid to a stop at the chamber door. "Is Enarius all right?"

"He's in here, and he's fine." Belbo's face wrinkled in consternation because screams and shouts filled the hall beyond the two praetorians.

Belbo threw open the door. Metellus snapped at him to stand guard and brought the soldier in with him.

Enarius looked up from a chair, sulking. Across from him was a pretty slave girl and between them was that stupid Hadiran board game with the pegs and stones.

"Metellus!" Enarius cried. "Am I my father's prisoner now? He insisted I—"

"We have to get you out of here," Metellus said. "Something's gone terribly wrong. Up, sire. Up!"

"What's gone wrong?" Enarius climbed to his feet. The nervous young slave rose with wide eyes.

"The building's on fire," Metellus said.

"What?"

Metellus didn't bother repeating himself. Enarius motioned the girl to come with him, which was just the sort of useless thing he supposed the heir would do.

Then the door burst open, disgorging a trio of men dressed in garish tunics, like circus entertainers. Two of them were Metellus' Cerdian table companions, and they bore bloody blades.

Metellus' curse was drowned out by the slave girl's scream.

Apparently the Cerdians had decided it more advantageous to kill Enarius along with the emperor. Enraged by the betrayal, Metellus ran at them, blade in hand.

He ducked the swipe from the longer sword and drove the gladius deep through Taricon's chest. He felt it punch clear through.

But the blade was caught on a rib and he struggled to pull it clear. The other Cerdian brought his weapon clanging against Metellus' helm.

It was as though a burning brand had struck him in the side of the face. He didn't remember falling, but suddenly discovered he was on the floor, and something was wrong with his right eye—he couldn't see through it. He tried to shield himself with upraised hands as the mole-faced Cerdian cried out death to the tyrant, long live Hanuvar. He advanced with his companion, and Enarius retreated, warded by the praetorian ranker.

Other men came at the Cerdians from the rear. But Metellus could not focus upon them. He heard the clack of swords and the screams of men. Dully through the pain and the shaking vision he realized the man in the lead was Ciprion. Thrice cursed Ciprion, who told Enarius to come with him.

And Enarius, loyal, stupid Enarius, was talking of Metellus. "Help me get Metellus! He's been wounded, fighting to protect me."

Rough hands grasped him and the jostling shook out a fresh wave of pain. The last thing he heard was a gasp and final phrase from the slave girl. "Master, his eye!" And then, mercifully, he lost consciousness.

IX

Hanuvar bypassed the emperor, who clasped futilely at the dark stain on his toga. He ignored the priest.

He had seen the woman fall, and he went to her.

Time always passed slowly for him in combat, as if he could take measure of every single breath while they ticked on. Usually, it snapped back to normal when the fight finished. This once, though, that awareness of individual heartbeats remained. He smelled burning wood, heard distant cries of fear and the steady bleat of the priest's remonstrations. Then, too, there were the groans of the wounded emperor.

But Hanuvar's eyes were only upon the outstretched body and the feebly moving leg that might be his daughter's.

He couldn't be sure. He doubted. But he still feared. And it was a terrible thing to fear for her, who had lived despite great odds and might be dying now before his eyes.

When he reached the woman, he didn't recognize the face below him, paling with blood loss in the courtyard's bright moonlight. Her eyes flickered.

The blood was thick about her. Whoever she was, she did not have long.

He spoke to her in Volani. "Hail, Eltyr," he said. "You fought bravely. It is almost time for the final sleep."

She groaned and gritted her teeth.

"You escaped with my daughter," he said. "Do you know where she is?"

The woman only stared blankly, cursing him in Dervan. Her accent was Cerdian. Her words lost steam and then she began to mumble in her own language, one he understood passably, enough to recognize that she spoke a prayer.

He stepped away.

Behind him rose the voice of Lucius, speaking in flawed but practical Volani. "She's not an Eltyr at all, is she?"

"No." Hanuvar turned to face him.

The emperor still breathed. He was turned on his side, hands pressed to the dark rent in his garment. The dead lay everywhere around him, macabre lawn ornaments.

The priest fought for breath and used the staff too support himself. "You're Hanuvar, aren't you. I don't understand. How did you trick me?"

Hanuvar gave him a pitying look, then looked down at the man who had killed his people.

"Please," the emperor said. "Help me."

The words that left Hanuvar's lips came out shaking. "You beg me, for help."

The emperor looked up, wide-eyed and wheezing, and Hanuvar stared down at him. There was so much he might have said. When the thousands had braced themselves behind the walls of Volanus, waiting for their deaths with swords in hand, who had been there to help *them*? After the city was razed and the fire swept through the slave pens to claim the lives of even more Volani, who had rushed to free them from the manacles?[18] What of all the predations, thefts, pain, indignities, much less the beautiful things lost to the world because of this man, who had done nothing to abate any of the suffering, before, during, or after?

For once he could not contain the rage, and he bared his teeth, as though he were an animal.

"You are a good man," Lucius said. "I . . . I don't fully understand, but I have seen it from the first. Do not allow him to die, in here. I cannot move him, and I cannot leave him."

Lucius leaned heavily against the staff, his eyes pleading.

Hanuvar's gaze swung back to the emperor. Easier, he thought, to kill this man. But he did not move. Lucius would probably not depart without this hated old man. And the place reeked of smoke. Soon it might choke them all.

He bent and rose with the emperor. The dictator was lighter than Hanuvar expected.

He headed for the doors through which he'd entered, Lucius walking with him.

The emperor groaned. Hanuvar's hands were wet with his blood.

"What is it you've been doing all this time?" Lucius asked.

Hanuvar said nothing.

The priest answered his own question. "You've been saving people, haven't you?" His voice was soft, but certain.

Hanuvar looked over to him.

Lucius explained his conclusion. "The revenants coat their reports with lies, but Sarnax passed along the rumors that did not fit. That

---

[18] During several talks with Olmar, upon the Isles of the Dead, Hanuvar had learned how thousands of those who'd survived the siege of Volanus had perished in a fire of indeterminate cause the night after the battle. More than four thousand men, women, and children were overcome by smoke and burned to death. —*Silenus, Commentaries*

Hanuvar was the one who set fire to the amphitheater to kill an underworld demon. That Hanuvar wandered through a village and killed a creature that was trying to kill many others."

"I have done what I must." They passed under a flickering lantern and in its light the priest was almost as pale as the man Hanuvar carried. The priest leaned upon his staff to help him walk, and his breath was rapid and shallow. Hanuvar hadn't been heeding the signs that Lucius had been injured. "How badly wounded are you?"

"Worse than I thought."

"The emperor is dead." Hanuvar halted and faced Lucius.

The priest's eyes were searching. "How does that make you feel?"

"I'm no child in need of a parable on the emptiness of revenge. I'm saying I should set him down and carry you."

"No. You must bear him out."

"We must honor the dead but care for the living."

"Bear him out. There is a favor I can do you yet."

"Why should you help me?"

"Because my people let him murder yours. And because a lesser man would have left me to die, with him, or slain me once I confessed I knew you."

"Come, then."

The fire roared somewhere behind them.

"You really weren't involved with the Eltyr murders, were you?" Lucius asked. "Why are you here? Why are you, of all people, trying to protect Enarius?"

"Because your empire needs a good man at its helm. And because I like him. And I was trying to stop the Eltyr murders. Your people took my daughter from me." He forced his voice to cease its shaking. "I feared you had made her into a monster. But she is gone, still. All I found was a Cerdian playing dress-up."

The empire had stolen his daughter. But she was not yet a monster.

They arrived at last at the little side door through which he'd entered, and walked clear. The sky was red with the fire that ate at the villa and threw crimson light and flickering shadows upon the crowd that encircled the dying building. Hanuvar bore the dead man toward them and raised his voice, remembering once again to employ a Ceori accent. "We need a healer!" he cried. "Where is a healer?"

Limping at his side, Lucius shouted on his own. "Where is Enarius? Enarius, attend! Lucius calls for you! Your father needs you!"

Folk pushed toward them, but Lucius weakly swept his staff to right and left, crying for all to hold back until finally Enarius arrived. A mix of slaves and guests and scattered praetorians kept everyone else at bay while the young man came forward.

Hanuvar knelt with the body and lay it in the grass, staring down at the blank face, empty and foolish and waxen. All had left it, sense, and evil, and love, and hate, drained away with the mistakes and the triumphs and embarrassments and worries and hopes. In the end, good or bad, there was nothing left but this empty vessel.

Ciprion arrived, Amelia at his side in an elegant creamy white stola, her hair this night elaborately curled. With them was a Herrenic healer, who knelt by the emperor's body. Hanuvar tried to turn him toward the priest, but he insisted on inspecting the dead man. Enarius, his face ashen, stared down into the empty gaze of his adopted father.

Lucius eased painfully down near the emperor, saying, wearily, but carefully, "It was not Volani, it was Cerdians. In their guise." He raised his voice. "They dressed a woman as an Eltyr, but when addressed in Volani, she could not understand!"

Ciprion succeeded in turning the physician's attention to Lucius, and the gray-haired Herrene ripped open the priest's robe to show the bloody gash in his side. The fire painted both in ruddy shades and highlighted the stark black stain along the side of the priest's robes.

Enarius turned from the body of his adopted father and gasped at sight of his advisor's injury.

Lucius muttered something about Jovren under his breath, blinked slowly, and looked up at the new emperor. "The Cerdians were behind it all," he said.

"I heard." Enarius' voice was quiet as the grave. "They will pay."

Lucius blinked. "Heed Ciprion, sire. He is the last of the advisors your father chose for you. Select the next batch well. And 'ware Metellus."

Enarius shook his head minutely without taking his gaze from the dying man. "He lies gravely wounded and may perish. He was injured trying to save me."

Lucius looked doubtful. His gaze was piercing. "I have seen his soul, Enarius. Darkness shrouds him. Don't let it take you."

Enarius looked confused but grim.

"I must speak to the Ceori. Healer, begone. I've bled out, and you know it."

The little Herrene started to object.

"Leave him," Ciprion said curtly, and the healer stepped away. Ciprion took Enarius' arm and guided him over to his adopted father. Amelia went with them, her expression grave.

In stilted Volani the priest spoke formally, softly, to Hanuvar. "I shall ask the gods to aid you."

Hanuvar didn't think that would do him any good, but he was touched by the gesture, and answered quietly in Dervan. "May you find peace, and the warm embrace of lost family and friends." He reached out and gripped the man's arm. Lucius' return grasp was weak and cold.

Again, he addressed Hanuvar in his native tongue. "May you find your daughter in the living world."

Hanuvar nodded his appreciation, then called for Enarius to return. While the new emperor sat with the dying man, one almost as still and pale as the other, Hanuvar joined Ciprion. "I'm glad you found Enarius," he said. "I ran into some trouble."

"So I see. I found support faster than I expected and Enarius' quarters were close. I'd hoped we'd link back up. Are you all right?"

Hanuvar glanced down at his blood smeared uniform, then met his friend's eyes. "None of this is mine."

Ciprion nodded once. "Someone in the ranks is a traitor," he said tightly. "Someone high up. Antires sent a runner—one of the three restaurants serving goat meat in the first circle of our map was owned by a Cerdian, and tavern goers report that there were meetings taking place in the backroom. One of them believes he saw a praetorian go in and out a few times. They caught a glimpse of his armor. He was cloaked and hooded, though, so he couldn't be described."

Hanuvar sighed. He did not say what Ciprion would obviously agree with: it would have been nice to know that sooner.

Ciprion continued: "Only another day or two would have made all the difference. But that is ever the way. So far the only four I'm sure about are you, me, Enarius, and Metellus. I suspect Munius, the praetorian optio, because he can't be found. Heads will roll. Maybe mine should be with them."

"No. Not yours," Hanuvar said. "Don't be so sure of Metellus' innocence. He's the one who helped push this scheme. Suppose Metellus ordered a few more of the men to stay back than he had said. Suppose he was hoping all the advisors would die but himself and the new emperor."

Ciprion's frown deepened. "Those are alarming speculations."

"They're worth considering."

"He would have been a fool to take such risks," Ciprion mused, though he sounded unconvinced by his own doubt.

"We've known a lot of foolish men who wanted power," Hanuvar reminded him.

"He will bear watching." Ciprion met Hanuvar's eyes. "I'm glad it wasn't your daughter."

"Yes." Hanuvar managed to master his own feelings on the matter with a long eye blink. "We can all be pleased the false Eltyr is finished. They worked a little too hard to make it seem like the assassins were Volani. They were shouting slogans even when it didn't seem like anyone but dead men were nearby."

Ciprion smiled darkly. "Some were hailing you with Cerdian accents."

Hanuvar looked back to where the new emperor sat by the priest, now slumped and still. "Lucius is dead. I'm sorry for that. He was a good man."

"He was. And I'll be sorry to see the end of Sarnax, as well."

Enarius bowed his head over the dead man, ignoring the long line of onlookers.

The fire ate at the villa. They could hear its roar as it devoured its timbers. Wind carried the smoke westward and away.

"I'll leave you to the cleanup, and your new emperor. If I don't extricate myself now, I'll be even more exposed." He inclined his head toward Amelia, watching from a distance, and she bowed her own head in acknowledgment.

Ciprion offered his hand. The two men clasped arms tightly, and then Hanuvar retreated. The crowd eyed him as he pushed through, but most of their attention was devoted to the emperors before them, both motionless. Soon, from the flames, a new reign would begin, and they watched expectantly for history to unfold before them.

※ ※ ※

We retreated from the capital, and though we moved fast, news of the emperor's death moved faster. Violence sometimes follows in the wake of a leader's death, but in the empire of those days the majority of folk in the capital and beyond waited tensely, hopefully, for a peaceful turnover. Izivar convinced Hanuvar to retreat to Selanto until things were calmer, and men could be assured order would prevail.

As it happened, she had a surprise awaiting him. For the first two ships were finished at last and provisioned for their maiden voyages.

—Sosilos, Book Fourteen

Chapter 15:
Homeward

Hanuvar watched from the docks as the great ships glided out across the waters. Tiny white caps rustled at the sides of their hulls, slapping the close laid timber.

Two great masts towered above each of the decks, each billowing with a wide white sail. The vessels were deep bellied and high prowed, the result of generations of Volani expertise, designed to outrun and withstand and sustain. Each carried almost two hundred of Hanuvar's people, though only a few dozen sailors were visible upon the deck, manning lines and rudder.

Both vessels bore ample food and spare supplies, as well as the very future of his people. Each one of these lives seemed infinitely more precious than normal, for each should have been companioned by at least two hundred more.

The ocean was vast, and uncertain, and he worried for them.

Izivar squeezed his arm. "It's up to them now. You've done everything you could. No one could have done more."

And to her, and only her, he spoke his fears. Quietly, so Antires, waiting to their left and Julivar and Serliva on the right, would not hear. "But will they make it? Can they be safe?"

"They are in good hands. The ships are sturdy and well provisioned. We built them well."

The morning sun had lain a molten iron beam upon the waters

and the ships struck its glow. As they did, the sails caught the full force of the wind beyond the coast, and both ships surged forward like hounds catching the scent of prey. Hanuvar smiled in pride, and hope.

He clutched Izivar's hand, breathing in the scent of the salt air, and of freedom, and her floral perfume. He glanced at his friends and they smiled. Antires wiped away a tear. How like a poet, to cry even when happy.

Carthalo remained at the center of his web in Derva, always scheming to recover more of their people, but most of the living Hanuvar loved and trusted were here. He wished that his daughter could be as well. Somewhere she lived free, and he hoped he would find her soon.

He wished he might have shared the moment with Ciprion. His friend could not have attended, for fear of drawing more scrutiny to the Volani at this moment. He had written that rumors in the barracks were Metellus' assistant Munius was the one passing money around to a few bad apples, and Metellus blamed himself for not seeing through his underling's treachery. The centurion was throwing himself into the reorganization of the corps, no matter being plagued by terrible headaches. He had lost an eye and Ciprion thought his rage against traitors and Cerdians in particular was genuine.

The new emperor had asked what had happened to the Ceori who had borne the emperor from the burning flames.

Ciprion told him how he had answered in the next paragraph. *I said that you were so heartbroken by what you had seen that you had returned to your people. I think Enarius could profit by your counsel, too, my friend. You could shape the course of an empire if you wished to join me, though I understand why you will not.*

The position was too exposed, and risked his life, and Ciprion's, and the entire recovery effort. Much as he would have enjoyed working at Ciprion's side, the empire's future was important to him only as it might impact his people. There was much work to do still, for many of the Volani remained imprisoned in dire circumstances.

Well beyond the shore now, the ships dwindled into the distance.

Izivar leaned against him. "So, my brave one, we can celebrate at last. Are you hungry?"

He kissed the top of her head. "I am."

Her gaze was sharp as she looked up at him. "You look restless. Today, of all days, you must relax."

He bowed his head to her. "We will feast with our friends. But there's a trip to plan."

"You're thinking of the slaveholders in southern Tyvol. And the Volani children."

"Yes."

She nodded slowly. "That isn't a long journey by ship."

"No. And I had thought we might sail there together."

"You would want me there? I have a lot to keep track of here."

He smiled gently. "I would like you everywhere. But I suppose there are things that we both must do. Our people need us yet."

"What do you need?"

She looked as though she wished to be kissed, and he wished to kiss her anyway, for she was warm and clever and lovely. And so they briefly pressed lips to one another, and his heart soared as they broke apart, smiling at one another.

She took his hands. "Things ought to be a little simpler now. The emperor himself is our friend, and Ciprion is like your brother, and he's Enarius' top advisor. We are shielded."

He shook his head. "You know that winds can change, suddenly. The revenants are discredited, but they're not disbanded. Most Dervans distrust and hate us, and politicians are always looking for scapegoats. And then there's the small matter of my own identity. If Enarius should ever catch wind of that . . ." He let his thought trail off. "We must never be complacent. We can let down our guard when the goods are sold and the shop is closed and we are beyond the sunset."

She studied him seriously, then squeezed his waist. "Tomorrow we can take up our worrying once more. Today, we celebrate a victory. Even if you do not need to pause, your people do."

She spoke wisely. He turned with her and faced their friends. "Enough gawking," he said. "Who's for breakfast?"

They clapped and jested and cheered, then turned with him to walk for the harbor buildings and the waiting feast.

Afterword

Andronikos Sosilos

I approached this volume as I did its predecessor, retaining my great-great-great uncle's linking sections but removing the rest of his first-person narrative. I leaned once more upon the diligent research of Silenus to address certain gaps, and filled others with speculations of my own, though I think it likely they were well-founded ones.

It proved not terribly difficult to construct a preamble to this book from one of my ancestor's essays within the main body of *The Hanuvid*. I can only hope the preambles for further volumes will fall as easily into my hands as this did one morning, when I unrolled an old scroll from Antires' work and it stopped by chance at the ideal text segment.

In an earlier draft of this text, I attempted to incorporate some of the so-called "lost tales" of Hanuvar that Silenus accumulated during her research. It was not so difficult to recast her prose in a style similar to that I've presented thus far, but, of course, since these stories were acquired piecemeal there is no knowing precisely where they fit into my ancestor's narrative. And then there is the problem that there is none of Antires' text to link them in place. I have therefore decided to keep them separated. Perhaps, at the conclusion of the main narrative, I will present them in my best guess as to their chronological sequence.

As always, I have worked to present these adventures in a format more approachable than the original, in the hope that you will here find the same excitement enjoyed by previous generations. If you do not, I am afraid the failure is mine alone.

Acknowledgments

I am once again grateful to the fine folks at Baen for their support and encouragement, and to Joy Freeman and Scott Pearson for their final suggestions. Aiding behind the scenes was the usual band of advisors, among them the indefatigable Bob Mecoy, Chris Willrich, C.S.E. Cooney, Sydney Argenta, and Kelly McCullough. John Chris Hocking provided his customary sterling guidance. Darian Jones proved a fine sounding board and plot wrangler. Last, but never least, the inestimable Shannon Jones put in long hours helping shape the characters and text so that they shined as brightly on the page as they did in my imagination.

SHADOW OF THE SMOKING MOUNTAIN

The Chronicles of Hanuvar

Howard Andrew Jones

Available from Baen Books

October 2024

Hardcover

Chapter 1:
The Voices from the Mountain

As they followed the road around the piney mountain slopes that morning, they passed a rutted path Hanuvar had been expecting. It was distinguished by dozens of well-ordered tents partly screening impressive mounds of black soil excavated to reveal the blacker walls of an ancient ruin. Some of the slaves pushing wheelbarrows piled with dirt were Volani, but the reclusive scholar directing their efforts had so far been entirely disinterested in selling.

A lone sentinel observed their progress from beneath a shade tree. He might wonder at a two-horse carriage accompanied by a lone rider upon this old road, but rich landholders lived nearby, so surely such a conveyance was no true rarity. And probably the watchman's intense focus was centered upon Hanuvar because he was the obvious military escort, not because the man was suspicious of his true identity. Probably.

The stranger would be hard pressed to guess Hanuvar's age. Only last year his dark hair had been well-peppered with gray, but owing to a peculiar incident much of that gray had gone, along with his scars and the accumulated weathering of a warrior in his fifties. His arms were muscular and his shoulders strong beneath his off-white tunic, signaling a man in his prime, which pleased Hanuvar, for the Dervans sought an older enemy. His features were not dissimilar from the natives of this

502

peninsula, even though the long straight nose with a slight hook and small nostrils was characteristic of his Volani ancestors. And he deliberately cut his hair short with straight bangs and scrupulously shaved his face to emulate what Dervans considered proper—they rarely looked beyond these surface details.

Hanuvar acknowledged the sentinel by meeting his gaze and continued forward. Antires swore softly in the driver seat as his carriage rolled over a massive rut, and then they had passed out of sight.

The camp was a problem for another day. For now, he would steel himself for looking into the eyes of children who had witnessed the bloody end of their parents, siblings, and society. He couldn't be certain what it had done to them but dreaded what he might find.

And he tried not to expect his niece to be among them.

They soon turned through an open wooden gate and onto a dirt track half as wide as the carriage. They passed a field of barley, and then rectangular patches of other grains and long rows of half-grown cabbages. A variety of rakes and sheers lay along the edges of the plots, but the workers who had wielded them were absent.

The explanation became apparent soon after. The slight tremor they'd noted traveling here must have been more violently expressed in this vicinity. While the tidy red-roofed villa stood intact, one small stone outbuilding had collapsed entirely. Another was missing half its roof, the shingles of which had slid into a pile at its door. A small army of men, women, and children milled on the grounds outside the villa.

As Hanuvar and the wagon approached he perceived more organization than had been apparent from a distance. A number of adults cleared rubble and a few bent to inspect the villa's foundations. Others kept knots of children well-ordered in some open-air teaching or game arrangements. A dark-haired woman consulted a tall, gray-haired man, pointing to the villa's roof line before both turned to the clop of horses bearing their anticipated visitors. They exchanged brief glances of "they're here" and the taller motioned for someone nearer the children as the two of them strode for the rendezvous. His were plain but crisp work clothes. Her dress too was plain, but clearly of superior fabric, a white short-sleeved dress of summer length over a whiter under tunic, and her upswept hair was held with a spattering of tiny silver clips, which threw back the sun. Amelia, wife of Ciprion.

The track transformed into a bricked drive as it circled toward the villa's formal pillared entrance. A pair of sun browned attendants hurried to assist the carriage, and Antires brought it to a halt.

Hanuvar dismounted, passing the reins to a curious youth, then opened the carriage door. Izivar had no need of his aid, but took his hand as she stepped down, then brushed travel dust from her light clothing, a stola in two layers, the inner deeper blue than the outer. A trim woman with long, dark, curling hair, her sleeves were long, ornamented with clever oval gaps that showed her fine, clear brown skin. She favored Hanuvar with a dazzling smile she quickly abandoned, remembering her role as his employer, squeezed his fingertips as if in apology for her pretense, and stepped away. Hanuvar then offered his hand to assist Serliva, Izivar's gangly, sweet-faced maid. She stepped down with a bow of her head in thanks, and he relinquished her grip. A little taller than her mistress, she too wore a blue stola, though sleeveless, darker, and simpler. Serliva ran fingers through her own locks then fussed with the shoulders of Izivar's garment.

Antires, Hanuvar's trusted friend, patted at his green tunic. The handsome young man was one of those whose clothing always hung well, so he brushed only a few wrinkles out before abandoning the effort with disinterest. His dark, tightly coiled hair and his russet-brown skin instantly identified him as a Herrene. His chosen occupation as Hanuvar's chronicler was likely far less obvious, although Hanuvar saw him sizing up the grounds and the approach of Amelia and imagined him working out what words he'd use for his descriptions.

Amelia stopped before them with a pleasant hello.

The villa's mistress looked just as Hanuvar remembered; a stoutly handsome woman of middle years with a penetrating gaze and inborn aura of command. Apart from the pieces decorating her hair she wore minimal jewelry.

The tall, solemn steward waited at her left elbow. Coming up on her right was an aged Herrene with thin lips, a broad nose, and a gray beard cut straight across his chest as though he were ready to model as a scholar for an ancient sculptor. His long tunic was old fashioned and formally pleated, and his curling hair was worn long and pushed back so that he would closely resemble a Herrenic comic mask the moment he smiled.

Owing to the slaves and servants nearby Amelia pretended not to be familiar with Hanuvar, and bowed her head instead to Izivar. "Lady Izivar. Welcome to our summer home. I hope that the little quake wasn't too alarming for you." Her voice possessed a slight rasp. Her husband Ciprion had explained it had changed permanently over the course of a long illness two winters previous.

Izivar bowed her head. "The horses didn't care for it much, but we managed. Is everyone here alright?"

"The children are fine, only frightened or terribly curious, and my staff are all accounted for." Amelia gestured to the collapsed and damaged outbuildings with a sweep of her arm. "Fortunately those were just used for storage."

Antires had left the carriage in the hands of two old slaves who were driving the vehicle away. He cleared his throat and spoke from Hanuvar's left. "Forgive me, milady. Do these sorts of things happen often?"

Hanuvar was surprised by his bold address. Usually Antires was a stickler for remaining in character, and a cart driver would not ordinarily address a patrician out of turn.

Amelia replied easily enough. "Not at all, but still more often than I would prefer. Tremblors are the price one must pay for the lovely weather."

Izivar gestured to Antires. "This is my advisor, Stirses. I believe he may have assisted your husband upon one of his projects."

"I seem to recall the name," Amelia said with a polite nod. "And you look familiar as well," she said to Hanuvar.

"I just have one of those faces, milady."

His answer raised a sly smile from Amelia, quickly discarded.

"This is Decius, my steward and personal guard," Izivar explained, for the benefit of Amelia's staff. "He is fluent in both Dervan and Volani."

"A pleasure." Amelia gave the barest of nods to Hanuvar. She did not bother naming her steward, and gestured instead to the Herrene on her right, introducing him as the scholar Galinthias, hired as the chief instructor for the children. He exchanged greetings with Izivar, and Amelia resumed her address. "Normally I would invite you inside before we saw to the purpose of your visit, but I wish to make certain the roof won't fall in on us. Surely you would like refreshments, though." Amelia looked to her steward, who bowed his head and hurried away. She faced Izivar. "Or would you like to meet the children first?"

"The youngsters, please," Izivar said.

"Of course. Come with me." Amelia led them across the dense green sward, asking Galinthias to speak of his charges as they walked. In a slow, pleasant voice, he informed them those seven and younger were kept together with their caregivers. Boys and girls eight to fifteen were housed separately. Their numbers Hanuvar had long since committed to memory but the Herrene mentioned them as if to emphasize the breadth of his responsibility,

"We bought all that we could," Amelia explained. "We were worried for the young women of... marriageable age, but they were more expensive and we couldn't have purchased as many."

"If you had not protected the little children, who would have?" Izivar asked, voice rich with thanks. "I'm grateful to you."

Amelia bowed her head.

That the majority of surviving Volani children had been purchased by the kindly Ciprion and Amelia was one small mercy among innumerable horrors, and Hanuvar would be forever indebted to them for their generosity. They had gone so far as to buy Volani caretakers and tutors for the children as well, and to place a Herrene in charge, recognizing that the traditions of Dervan schools would be anathema to children used to Volani ways. The couple had even insisted that the girls were to continue to receive instruction in writing and mathematics and natural sciences, although as they walked Galinthias was describing additional training the young women were receiving in comportment and weaving, the better to acclimate to their new society.

Hanuvar kept his expression carefully bland, and Izivar nodded pleasantly. Serliva's expression was less guarded and betrayed her shock when she learned boys and girls were instructed separately. How were they to be comfortable with one another when not allowed to interact from a young age? Before they had walked very far some of Hanuvar's chief concerns had already been made manifest. If the children were left here for much longer, even the oldest children might be substantially different people from whom they'd have been if raised within Volanus, and the youngest might be indistinguishable from Dervans.

As they came nearer, the children's caretakers halted their games and separated them into groups by age to await review. The littlest were made to sit. Older ones were asked to stand in a line. Hanuvar already knew that there were more older girls than older boys, forty-four to twenty-one. The number of smaller children was fewer, and among those fourteen were three toddlers, minded by a young woman missing her left hand, another survivor.

Per their previous arrangement, Hanuvar held back. It was Izivar and

Serliva who would be spending the majority of time speaking with and assessing the children today. Both women had spent more time amongst younger people than he, and he meant to observe as unobtrusively as possible in case some sharp-eyed youngster recognized him even in disguise. His likeness had unfortunately been commonplace in numerous murals and sculptures throughout Volanus.

A tall graying tutor standing with the older girls watched Izivar with particular intensity, his expression shifting from caution to curiosity. When his attention travelled to Hanuvar his mouth gaped.

He had been recognized, and Hanuvar knew his observer. The man was Ahdanit, one of the leaders of the scientific faculty of Volanus. They had spoken many times during Hanuvar's years as one of the shofets of Volanus, for Ahdanit had been an advocate for his institution's research projects, which frequently seemed to run somewhat over budget—not owing to graft, but because of the tendency of the academy scholars to discover additional lines of inquiry during their investigation, most of which Ahdanit had supported. Hanuvar had usually agreed with him. The slim scholar's name hadn't been among the list of survivors, so he was clearly here under an assumed identity himself. Hanuvar shook his head ever so slightly. Ahdanit recovered with a tiny head bow and closed his mouth, confused but resolved to silence.

Knowing Hanuvar's hope for his niece Edonia, Izivar asked Amelia if they might meet the girls first, and Hanuvar readied himself for disappointment. He should be happy, he thought, that any of these young women had survived to be so well cared for. They and their clothes were clean, and they were well nourished. The youngest looked less curious about their visitors than bored or disappointed to have their activities interrupted, like any young people assembled before older ones.

Hanuvar had parlayed with more foreign leaders than he could quickly count, sometimes under very trying circumstances. And yet the thought of explaining to these children that they would have to be uprooted again seemed a far greater challenge. He had promised Izivar they would do this together, when the time was right. Amelia's letter had relayed that after many months most of the boys and girls were settled and content here, even happy. They had good meals and clean bedding, familiar company, and routine. How would they react when they were told they would be leaving this safe place for parts unknown, with strangers?

He was glad the topic would not be broached during this initial visit.

Izivar would try to get a sense for how best to group the children during transport. For now, he confined himself to searching the faces of the dark-eyed girls.

Four years was a third of a lifetime for his niece Edonia. At seven, when he'd last seen her, she had favored her mother, sharing honey-brown eyes and pointed chin, though her unruly dark hair had looked more like his brother Melgar's. Temperamentally she had resembled neither of her fiery parents, for she had been focused and deliberative. Hanuvar's duties in Volanus had left him too busy to frequently engage with his extended family, but he had known little Edonia because even at six she'd had the patience to sit down for games of draughts. In between contemplating her possible moves and twisting her hair around her fingers, she had talked about animals, her abiding interest, and also about the great winged serpents who had made Volanus their home since the city's founding. She had hoped to become one of the maidens at the temple of the asalda.

Hanuvar had enjoyed his moments with her, wondering if she was what his daughter Narisia had been like as a little girl.

Izivar bade the children good morning in their own language, introducing herself by her first name. The children looked surprised at hearing this elegant outsider speak their native tongue.

Edonia didn't seem to be here. But that short-haired girl there, or the one in back—no, she had a more prominent nose. But her, on the left . . . It was perhaps unfortunate that Hanuvar must remain in a disguise he could not set aside. Surely, if his hair were parted and he wore his beard, Edonia would have stepped forward with a glad cry.

If she were here.

He turned to Amelia and addressed her softly. "Milady, might I speak alone to this instructor?" He indicated Ahdanit. He wished to make it clear to the scholar that he spoke with Amelia's permission.

She inclined her head politely. "Of course."

Izivar was already chatting to the girls about their daily routines while the Herrenic instructor looked on with some bemusement. Her grace and easy manner had them warming to her.

Hanuvar motioned Ahdanit aside and they walked apart, the scholar's eyes drinking him in. Probably he wondered if this were some trick; even if the man hadn't seen Hanuvar's plummet into the sea he would have learned of it from his fellow prisoners or the Dervans themselves. He might also have heard wild rumors of Hanuvar's survival. But Ahdanit was an intellectual and a skeptic and would have judged those stories to be either fears or projected hopes.

Hanuvar halted at the side of a well-shaped myrtle twenty feet out from the children, and spoke to Ahdanit in Volani. He got straight to the point. "It is me, and you and the children will be freed. But the boys and girls and the rest of the staff cannot be trusted with my name or our intentions until they are away from here." He did not add that children might talk, and slaves overhear to spread gossip beyond the family holdings. Ahdanit was bright enough to understand.

The scholar struggled to sound normal as he replied. "Of course, Shofet. Freed? But how?"

Hanuvar dared not reveal specifics. "With few complications, and very soon. And do not bother with a title." Such honorifics were irrelevant here. He was glad he could offer further news. "Your wife lives. And your colleague Varahan."

Ahdanit blinked, and his eyes shown with moisture. He wiped at them. His voice was a hoarse whisper. "She lives?"

"Yes. I saw her myself only last week, and she was healthy. She is free now." He did not add that she had been one of those on board a ship for New Volanus. He had spoken with the great musician only briefly, but had been delighted by her beaming smile.

Ahdanit could not help laughing in pleasure. "I thank you...this news is hard to take in. And so are you. Is Varahan alright? How are you doing this? How did you survive?"

"He's in good health. As for me...these are stories for another time. Now, tell me. Surely you're not the only one under an assumed name here. Are any of these young ladies Edonia Cabera?"

Ahdanit's expression fell. "I don't believe so. Not that they've told me. And we've talked a lot over the months." He took in Hanuvar's troubled look. "If you will permit me?"

Hanuvar didn't know what he was permitting but acquiesced with a head nod.

Ahdanit turned and called a girl's name, Esherah. One of the older girls asked approval of Galinthias, and then Amelia and, given it, stepped clear of the others, her expression tentative. Ahdanit waved her forward. She started toward them.

Ahdanit looked back to Hanuvar as she neared. "What do I call you?"

"Decius."

The young lady stopped in front of them and sought reassurance from Ahdanit's gaze. Her thick hair was combed forward, likely in an attempt to hide the long white scar visible upon her forehead. In her girl's stola and sandals she looked a proper young Dervan maiden, but as her eyes searched Hanuvar's own he was reminded of an entirely different young lady of about the same age who had assessed him with a skeptical look much like this. He did not outwardly reveal the pang he experienced in recalling Takava, long since buried in the sands of a distant isle.

"Do not worry, Esherah," Ahdanit said in Volani. "Decius is a friend. Decius, Esherah is the clever young woman who warned children of the famous or those in training with coveted institutions to lie about their names. She's one of my best students."

Hanuvar supposed Ahdanit was teaching them mathematics. As far as the information he had shared about Esherah, Hanuvar understood Ahdanit meant it as a kindness to him to thoroughly investigate the whereabouts of his niece, though he had little hope it would lead to anything useful. The scholar couldn't know how diligently Carthalo's people had already acquired the few other Volani children from slave holders less trustworthy than Ciprion. Still, Hanuvar nodded his head politely to the girl. "Were there any such children among you?"

Her expression brightened in surprise to be addressed by a Dervan in such flawless Volani. She pursed her lips and gathered her thoughts. Hanuvar liked that she checked with Ahdanit a final time. The scholar nodded his approval.

"I don't know, sir," Esherah responded respectfully. She glanced again at Ahdanit, as if asking for permission to provide more sensitive information.

"Speak the whole truth to him," he insisted.

"I know that some of them were maidens at the temple of the asalda. One of them is here."

The temple where Edonia had hoped to become a hand maiden, and where her mother had once served as one. Hanuvar kept rising interest from his expression.

"Why don't you ask her over?" Ahdanit suggested. Esherah turned and called another girl's name, waving her toward them, and that young girl sought approval from her minders, who then received permission from Amelia. Izivar and Serliva, meanwhile, talked animatedly with a now larger group of girls of mixed ages. The boys had been led aside, the younger playing fox and geese while the older were seated before an instructor. Antires, standing with the ladies, looked longingly toward Hanuvar, but he had not been invited into the conversation and did not presume to intrude.

Soon a grave young girl with short curling brown hair was standing closely to Esherah, her soft brown eyes searching. Hanuvar guessed her for nine or ten. She was introduced as Teonia.

Hanuvar took a knee and offered a smile. "Hello."

She would not meet his eyes. One of her arms was streaked with burn scars.

"Were you a hand maiden at the Hall of the Asalda?" Hanuvar asked.

"I was in training, sir," she answered after a long silence. Her voice was thin and remote.

"Do you know Edonia Cabera?"

She nodded; her expression revealed nothing more but she moved a bit further behind Esherah.

Hanuvar pretended calm. "Is she here?"

She shook her head, no. Esherah took her hand, and the young girl clung tightly to her fingers.

That flare of hope had been foolish. It would be painful, but another question was necessary. "Do you know if she survived?"

Teonia's eyes were grave as she finally looked at him. He could not read her meaning beyond shyness, or perhaps fear.

And then she nodded. Yes.

Hanuvar managed to keep intensity from his voice. He did not want to frighten the girl. "You saw her? You are certain?"

Teonia nodded vigorously. "She was in the pens."

"The slave pens in Derva," Ahdanit explained.

Suddenly Teonia was talking quickly, although her voice was soft. "They let her in back at the holding area in Volanus. But they wouldn't let my cousin in even though he wasn't too badly wounded. He could still walk a little. The Dervans took him away and I never saw him again."

Some Dervan overseer must have decided there was little enough value to be had from a child, let alone one that would have to be nursed back to health. Young Teonia was fortunate that her cousin hadn't been killed in front of her.

Hanuvar fell silent in shared remorse for the lost child, and bit back his anger. That another had survived only to be culled by a Dervan like a sickly lamb all but shattered his composure.

He mastered his ire with a breath and turned his attention to the more positive aspects of Teonia's information: Edonia had survived to reach Derva, which meant she had to have been sold on. Hanuvar knew every name on the Dervan slave list, as well as those names upon the supplemental lists of Volani purchased by the government and foreign nationals, and Edonia's name had not been among them. It might be that she had already been recovered by one of his agents, and he had been completely unaware of her identity because of her assumed name. "Do you know what she was calling herself?"

"She said to tell everyone she was Betsara."

Her grandmother's name on her mother's side. And a name among those that Hanuvar had seen, listed as sold with two other young women to a foreign dignitary. His nostrils flared as he inhaled in frustration. He mentioned their names as well. "Did you know them?"

"They were all my friends," Teonia said. "The robed men took them. They led them away. They looked like wizards but weren't really, or they would have known that my brother and I had the touch and Edonia and the others didn't."

Hanuvar wanted to make sure he understood what she meant. "What touch do you have?"

She looked down at her sandaled feet.

"It's alright," Ahdanit said. "Decius won't be afraid."

She hesitated. "But he's a Dervan. We're not supposed to talk to them about magic things."

Ahdanit addressed Hanuvar. "The Dervans don't usually care for magic except in the hands of the authorities."

"It's wise of you to be careful what you say," Hanuvar told her. "But you can talk to me about this. Some of my friends have the kind of touch I think you mean, and pretending you don't have it is like pretending you can't hear. Who would want to do that?"

Teonia looked into his eyes then for the first time. She didn't exactly smile, but her expression cleared, and he recognized a spark of excitement in her eyes. "That's exactly how it is," she said.

She had just confirmed she was one of the rare few who were tuned to senses beyond the normal five; such were prized by the asalda because they found them easier to communicate with. The girl grew more comfortable as she continued. "I can feel things from far away. Like the power of the man in the mountain. I can sense him from here. So can my brother."

"Teonia's brother is here as well," Ahdanit explained.

Hanuvar nodded his thanks and returned his attention to Teonia. "The man in the mountain?"

"He has many Volani voices with him, and he's using the voices to talk to the mountain and its old stones."

Hanuvar's interest quickened. Could she mean the scholar working in the ruins with the Volani slaves? "How do you know they're Volani?"

"I can hear them talking."

"What are they saying?"

"They are crying to be let out. They're lonely and scared, and he won't let them go. But he's lonely, too."

"Do you know this man's name?"

She shook her head. "He came to speak to the Lady this week."

"She means Calenius," Ahdanit explained, confirming Hanuvar's suspicion, for that was the name of the scholar digging in the ruins. "He was there, at the siege. I remember seeing him wandering around the enclosures, and I heard his name called."

Hanuvar had heard that as well. "And he's a wizard?"

"That I do not know," Ahdanit said. "He's excavating some ruins south of here, near the base of Mount Esuvia. I'm not sure what he spoke with Lady Amelia about."

Hanuvar smiled reassuringly to the girl and put his hand out, palm up. Hesitantly, she extended her own, and then he gently squeezed her fingers. "Thank you, Teonia. I am sorry about your cousin. And I'm sorry you have to hide."

Her expression was blank. Sorrow and sympathy were poor currency, so he continued. "But you have given me good news, and I'm grateful. Now I can try to find Edonia."

"Why?"

"So I can help her."

"Are you going to take us away?" Esherah asked. The older girl's eyes were suddenly piercing.

He could not tell her he would take her away, yet he could not lie to her. "Do you want to stay here?"

"I want to stay with my friends."

"You and your friends will not be separated," Hanuvar pledged. He debated asking which of the girls were her favorites, the better to know which ones should be kept together during the wagon transport to the coast, but he didn't want to imply that any of them would be parted.

"Are you really a Dervan?" Esherah asked. From Teonia's searching look it was clear she wondered the same thing.

"Does it matter? The important thing is that I am a friend to Lady Izivar, and she's Volani. I will help her all I can."

They mulled that over.

Hanuvar climbed to his feet and nodded at them. "Thank you. Why don't you rejoin the others?"

They nodded politely to their elders, and then Esherah led the younger girl off by the hand.

"Your niece lives," Ahdanit said softly.

"So it seems." While Hanuvar struggled to adjust to this welcome news, he was already considering the challenges lying in front of Edonia's recovery. "The men in robes who took her are Ilodoneans. They might have purchased the girls because they have experience with asalda." Some said that a previous Ildonean emperor had even enslaved asalda, though Hanuvar had never credited the stories. The reclusive and arrogant Ilodoneans claimed many unlikely things.

"Ilodonea is a long way off."

"It is." And the Ilodoneans were famously difficult to interact with—in many ways, more difficult than the Dervans. But Edonia lived, and she was among girls from her own people. If her owners thought her some kind of specialized worker, all the better, because that virtually guaranteed her better treatment.

Hanuvar tried not to think about all the dangers she faced, and to find joy in the simple truth that Edonia had survived. For now there was nothing he could do for her.

After a moment, Ahdanit spoke with quiet restraint. "My wife, she is well? She suffered no . . . hardship?"

Hanuvar understood Ahdanit's reluctance to mention terrible fates by name, as if doing so might give them the power to be real. And he realized he'd allowed himself to become too fixated upon his own worries, while this man had quietly waited for further word about the woman he loved.

"Forgive me, Ahdanit. I should have told you more. She looked well, and she hadn't been treated harshly. She'd been fortunate, and was working as a musical tutor. Her previous owners had even gifted her with a high quality flute."

"My darling," he said softly. "She is such a talent."

"She is. And she will ensure our musical heritage survives as she will, I'm sure, be welcomed at the academy in New Volanus." Ahdanit's eyes widened at mention of the colony, but Hanuvar gently shifted topics before the scholar could ask for more details. "Tell me. How well are you and the children truly being cared for here?"

He answered after only a moment of reflection. "The rest of the instructors and I have been very lucky. The children... well, I suppose they've been lucky, too, overall. When I think of all those who didn't make it, it's hard to complain, but—"

"Your honest assessment," Hanuvar said, striving not to sound overly curt.

"Plenty of food, the company of their own people, even an education probably better than a lot of Dervans receive is nothing to object to. But Galinthias' lectures are wandering and unfocused, like the worst stereotype of a Herrenic philosopher, and the children have learned how to get him off on tangents so that he often isn't teaching them much. He could certainly be far worse, of course. He's never abusive or impatient."

Hanuvar nodded encouragement, and Ahdanit continued. "The Dervan language instructor is actually quite sweet, but completely oblivious about why any of these children would be disinterested in the finer points of Dervan society. The woman in charge of teaching the young ladies comportment is rigid and disliked, but the worst thing is that there aren't any real apprenticeship programs. Some of the older boys and girls were already apprenticed in Volanus and there aren't even a third of the possible crafting positions being offered here. Unless you're a young woman, in which case the only skills you're allowed to practice are the household arts. Young Esherah could be a world class mathematician, and she seems to enjoy the academic pursuits immensely, but I think they intend her to be a ladies maid."

Hanuvar knew this to be a profession Dervans considered desirable for unmarried women from non-patrician families. He happened to think a skilled assistant was invaluable to most any enterprise, but he'd hate to see someone gifted in one profession forced into another because of factors outside of merit and preference. "That's not what's going to happen now," he vowed.

Ahdanit searched his eyes as if assuring himself that Hanuvar's confidence was warranted.

Hanuvar hadn't paid particular note to the bright chirping of orioles until they suddenly went silent. He knew another tremor was on its way a breath before the ground rolled. The rumbling came this time with the shrill screams of young children. Adults called for calm, though some of them cried out in fear as well.

Hanuvar looked for Izivar, saw her seated on the ground near the girls, far from danger, caught sight of Serliva and Amelia and Antires, then turned to scan Esuvia, as he had during the earlier tremor. The mountain's gray cone rose above its green girt slopes just to the southeast. If it were to erupt, the chances for everyone's survival were rather slim.

But there came no smoke, nor even an avalanche, much less roiling ash plumes, and the cones of the old volcano's two distant sisters to the south were quiescent as well.

The shaking grew more violent. Behind him a louder rumble of stone sounded, and he turned as a corner of the villa gave way. The red shingles slid down in a clatter.

And then, only a few yards from himself, the earth was rent asunder. The grass parted and a gap of darkness yawned. Dirt and chaff mushroomed. Hanuvar struggled to keep his feet, and threw out a hand to steady Ahdanit.

The quaking ceased just as suddenly as it had begun. Silence persisted for long moments, and then a few cautious orioles took up their chirping, joined quickly by the shrill whisper of starlings, angry about the disturbance.

Hanuvar again checked the children, and the volcano, and his lover and friends. None seemed harmed. He then strode for the gap that had opened, for he thought he'd glimpsed dark bricks within.

He had not imagined it. The earth had revealed a subterranean structure. Only ten feet down the crumbling slope lay a floor of shining black pavers, half hidden by mounded dirt, collapsed walls, and broken stone that was almost certainly a fallen ceiling.

Ahdanit came to stand at his side, peering with him. "What is that?"

Hanuvar didn't know. "A hallway, I think." Some fifteen feet of passage had been exposed. A few spans of floor were cracked or pushed diagonally upright, but the majority remained flat and even as a Dervan highway, stretching into lost darkness beneath the earth.

After a moment, someone smelling of clover and scented bath oils drew beside him. Amelia stepped fearlessly to the edge. Hanuvar kept at her side, ready to grab her should the ground give way. Divining his intent, she frowned irritably at him, as if to assert that she was perfectly capable of watching out for herself.

Antires and Izivar arrived a moment later, though neither ventured as close to the side.

"What do you suppose this is?" Amelia asked him.

"Something Calenius will be interested in," Hanuvar said. "I'm told he came to see you."

Amelia responded with a single nod. "He did. He wished to dig on our ground, even if he could not buy it. He said he expected there were ruins beneath."

"Looks like he was right," Antires said dryly.

Amelia ignored him and spoke to Hanuvar. "Why does that interest you?"

"He holds Volani slaves that he will not sell. What did you tell him?"

"That our land was not for sale, nor was it currently for rent. He countered with the offer of large sums merely to explore, and I told him I would consider it. Now, I believe you've something in mind."

He did. There was little more he would be useful for here. He had satisfied his own curiosity as to the children's general health and the quality of their education, and learned more than he'd hoped in that his niece was likely still alive, though very far away. Izivar had already planned out her strategy for evaluating the rest of the situation, and his part in it was very small. An opportunity like this couldn't be ignored. "Let me act as your negotiator. He's likely to offer more now that there's proof these ruins exist."

"And you will ask for the Volani slaves as part of the fee."

"If you would permit me."

Amelia hesitated. "It was my thought his excavators should not have close proximity to pretty girls just this side of puberty."

"A wise precaution. What will you do with the land once the children are gone?"

She considered him gravely. "How soon are you planning to leave with them?"

"In a matter of weeks. Perhaps sooner, for their own safety."

"Safety?" Her expression darkened, and then she understood his meaning was not a rebuke for her standards of care. "Oh, this is nothing. The quakes happen from time to time. Esuvia just turns in her sleep. You do realize that the younger children have already grown attached to this place? And many are showing affinity for the skills they're learning. Wouldn't they be happier, here, settled and with a more certain future?"

Hanuvar kept his voice level. "The colony is settled. And they will be among their own people."

"I expected you would say that."

"Just as you would, if our roles were reversed."

No matter her intelligence, Amelia's blank stare suggested a mental block in conceiving a mirrored version of their fates. She recovered, returning to her central concern. "As someone who has many more years of direct experience with childcare, I ask for you to think not of the prior wrongs done to these children, but the benefits to them having a stable situation. Rather than displacing them. Again."

Hanuvar might have pointed out that they were slaves here, but that would be unfair, for they were hardly being treated as slaves, and Amelia and her husband had outlaid a great deal of money into their upkeep and obviously planned to continue to do so. Then too, there was great practical sense in what Amelia said. Thus he answered diplomatically. "I will certainly consider your experienced counsel in this matter. But as to the matter of Calenius, I suggest you offer to have him inspect this tunnel. I can accompany his every move after you relocate the children far from of his view."

Amelia considered her reply only briefly. "Very well. Tell him the price of looking over the tunnels is the freeing of your slaves. If he wishes to do more, then he and I will have to come to an agreement. Size him up. Tell me what you think of his aims and the character of his men."

"I will."